TEGAN AND SARA

JUNIOR HIGH

Words by **Tegan Quin** & **Sara Quin**
Pictures by **Tillie Walden**

Farrar Straus Giroux
New York

I'm Tegan.

Got it?

I'm Sara.

They don't got it.

Ok, ok, let us explain.

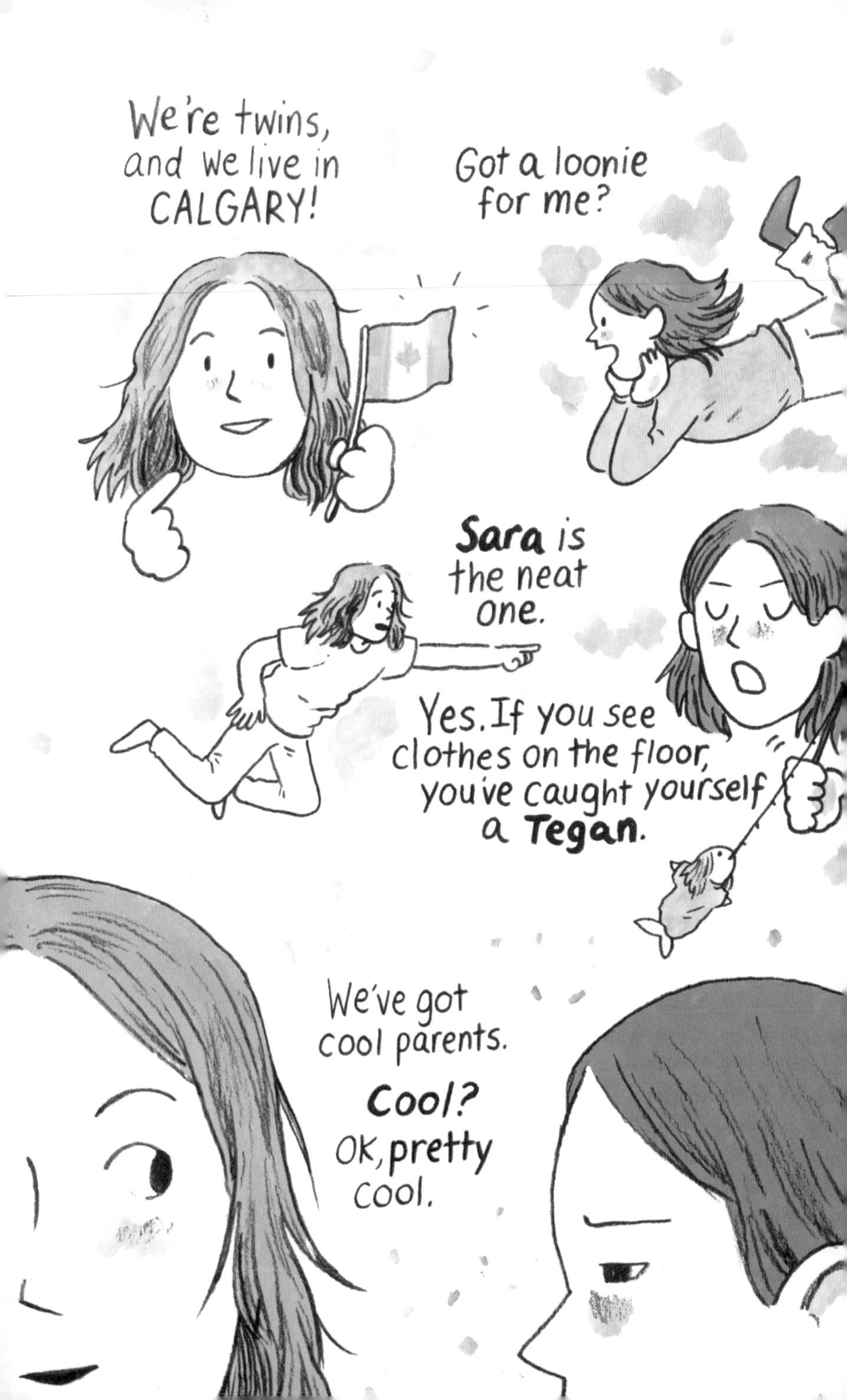
We're twins, and we live in CALGARY!
Got a loonie for me?
Sara is the neat one.
Yes. If you see clothes on the floor, you've caught yourself a **Tegan**.
We've got cool parents.
Cool?
OK, **pretty** cool.

We've got Mom— She's got a real name, though. **Sonia**. She dresses fancy and knows when we lie about cleaning the cat's litter box. She's a therapist, so she's pretty on the nose with **feelings** stuff.

Mom dates **BRUCE**. We call him Batman because he's tall and has muscles from all the construction work he does. But deep down he's a real softy.

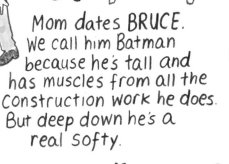

And then there's **Dad**.

His name is Steve, short for Stephen.

We love him. But also...

He wears the DORKIEST T-SHIRTS!

Anyways, I think we're about to wake up.

See you on the other side.

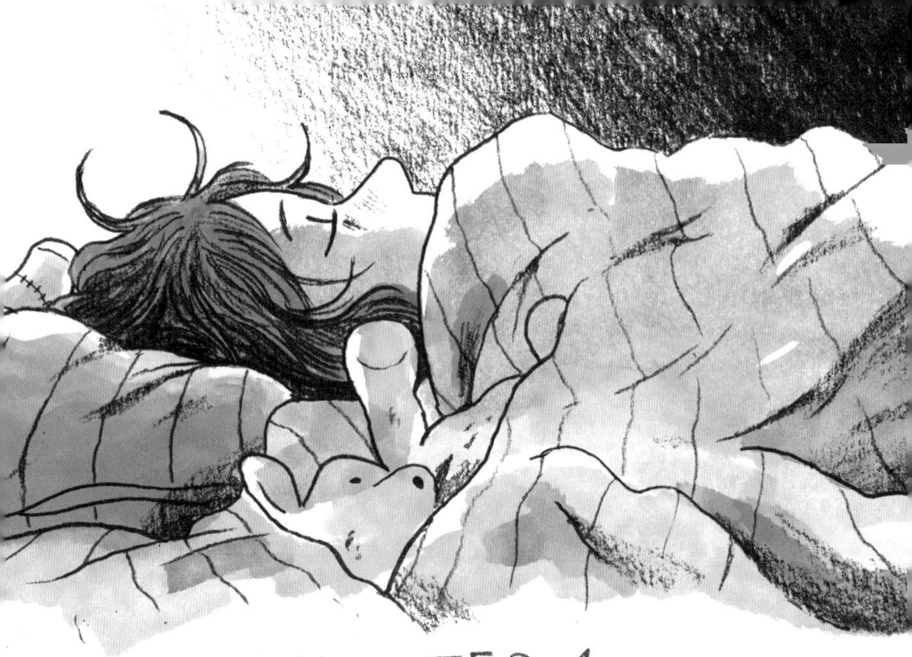

CHAPTER 1
Teenage Babies

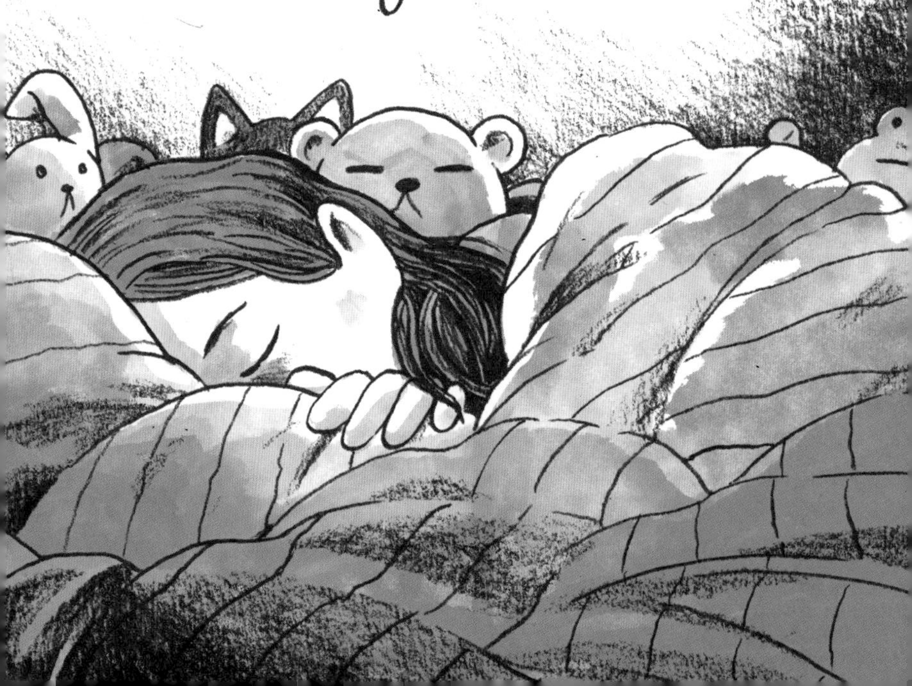

We spent all summer driving by
Bob Edmunds Junior High. It looked
so huge.

Why do we have to go to a new school?

You KNOW why. Mom and Bruce
moved, and now we're closer to Dad.

Can you believe we'll be in separate
classes? DIFFERENT HOMEROOMS?

I'm going to pass out.

Don't freak out! Just answer me
this.

What?

WHAT DO WE WEAR?

Now I'm really freaking out.

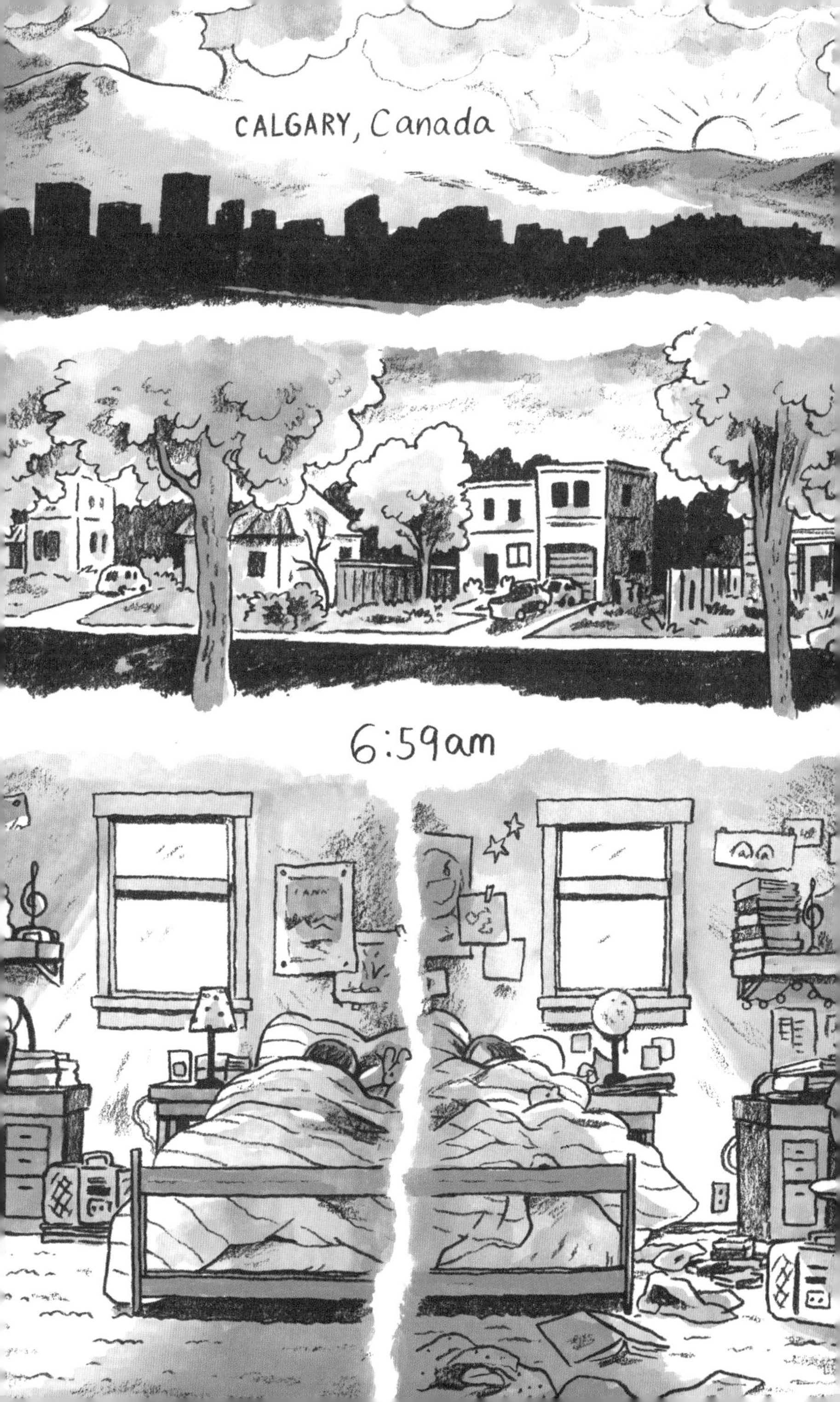
CALGARY, Canada
6:59am

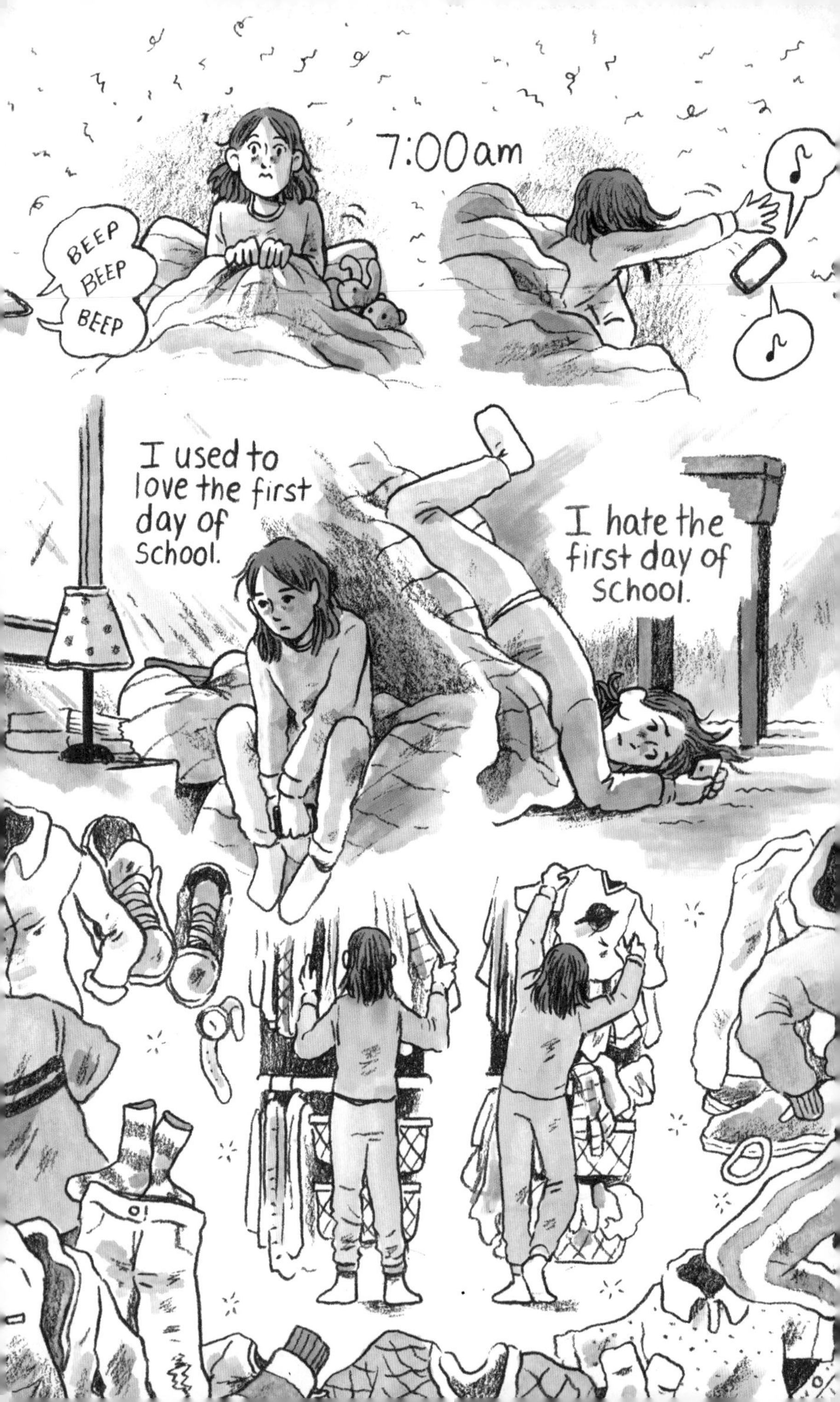
7:00am
BEEP BEEP BEEP
I used to love the first day of school.
I hate the first day of school.

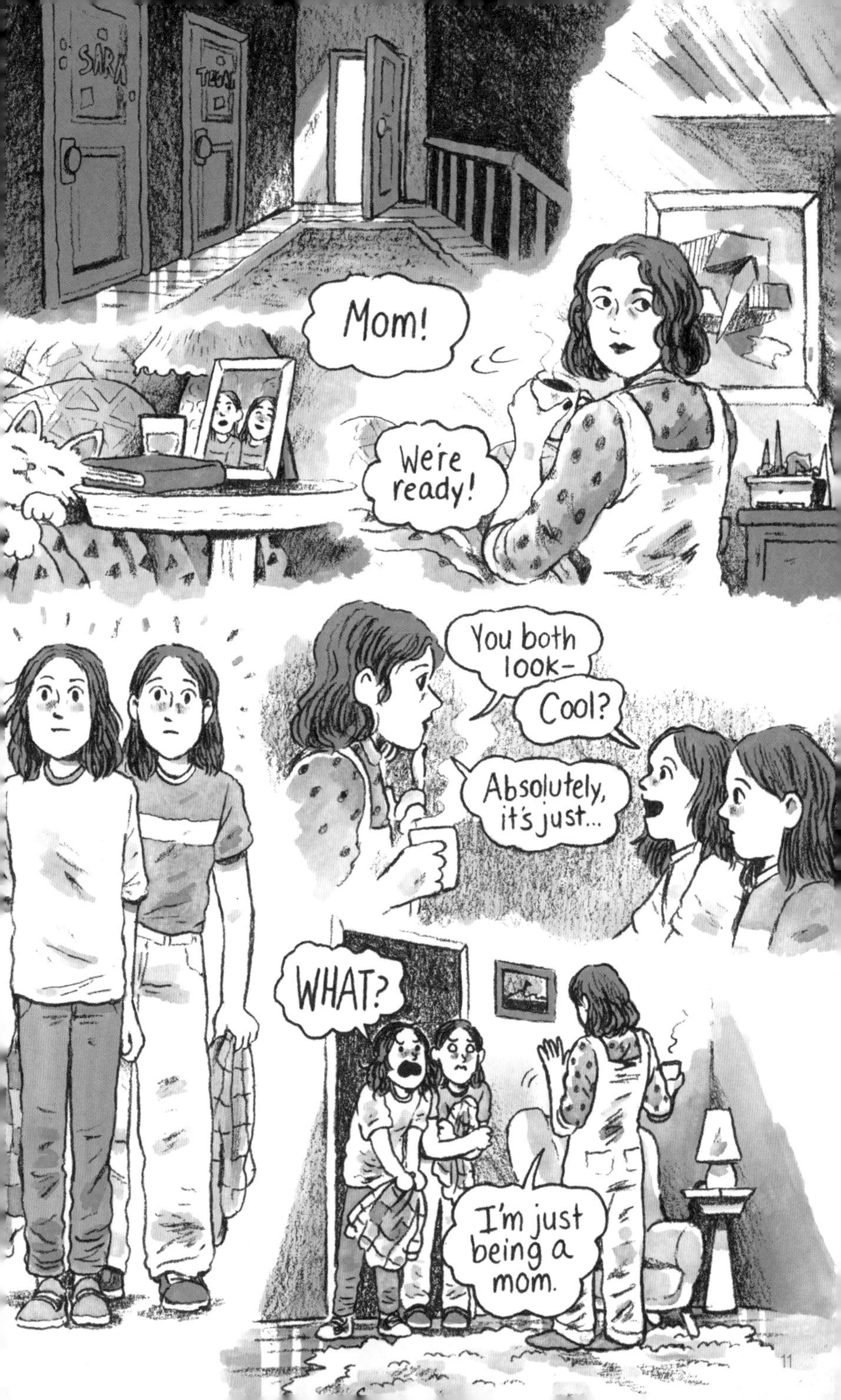
SARA
TEGAN
Mom!
We're ready!
You both look–
Cool?
Absolutely, it's just...
WHAT?
I'm just being a mom.

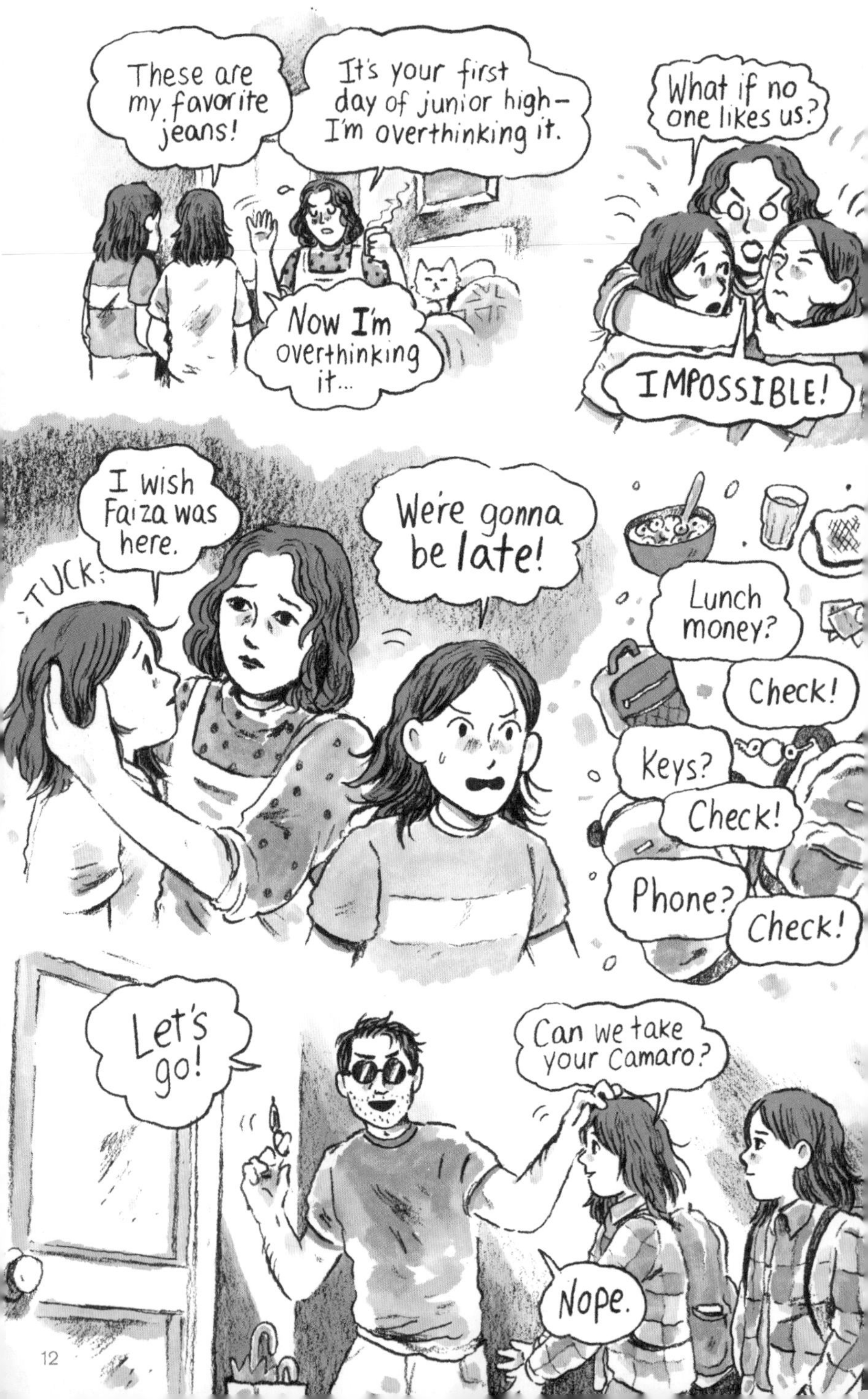
These are my favorite jeans!
It's your first day of junior high— I'm overthinking it.
Now I'm overthinking it...
What if no one likes us?
IMPOSSIBLE!
I wish Faiza was here.
TUCK
We're gonna be late!
Lunch money?
Check!
Keys?
Check!
Phone?
Check!
Let's go!
Can we take your Camaro?
Nope.

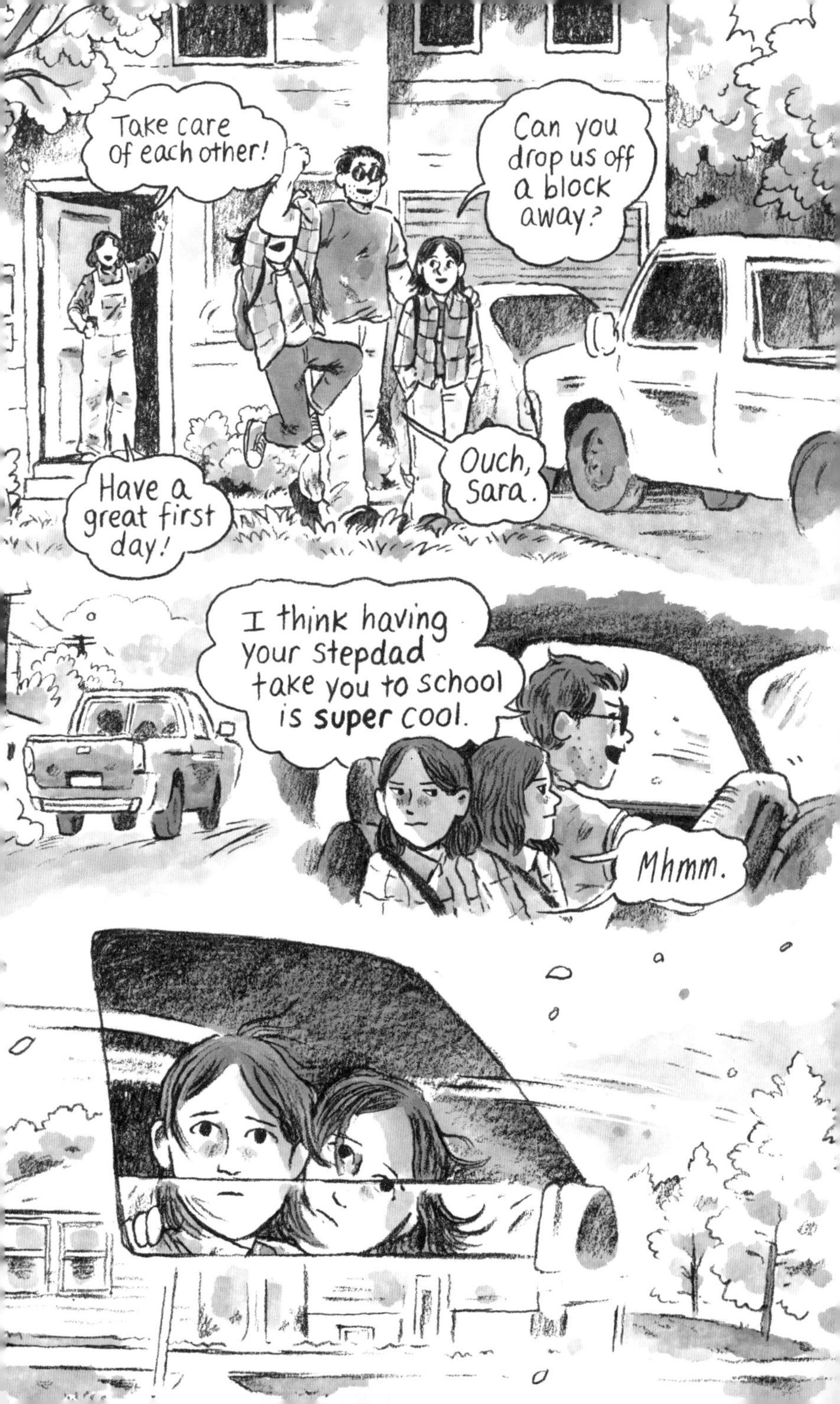
Take care of each other!
Can you drop us off a block away?
Have a great first day!
Ouch, Sara.
I think having your stepdad take you to school is **super** cool.
Mhmm.

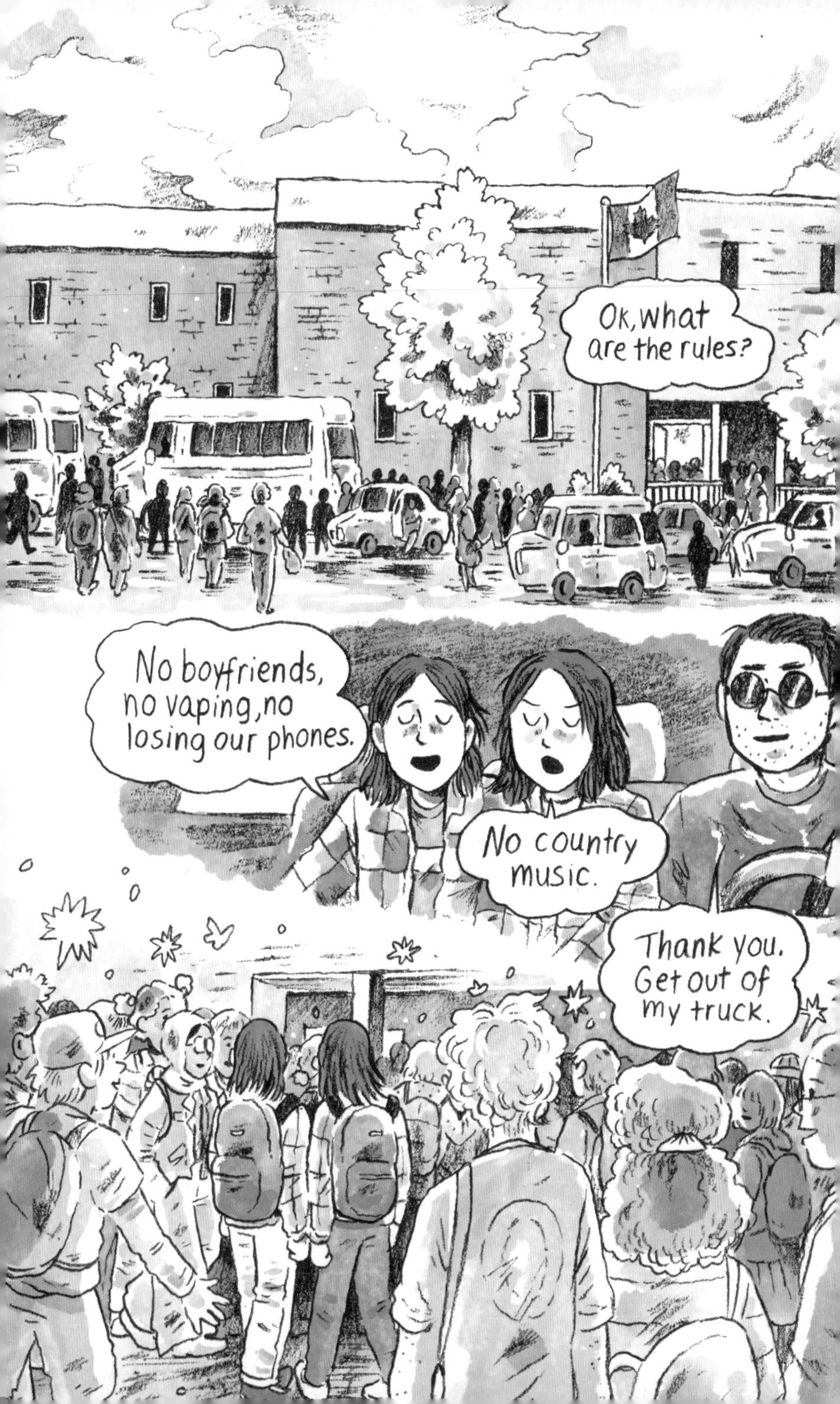
Ok, what are the rules?
No boyfriends, no vaping, no losing our phones.
No country music.
Thank you. Get out of my truck.

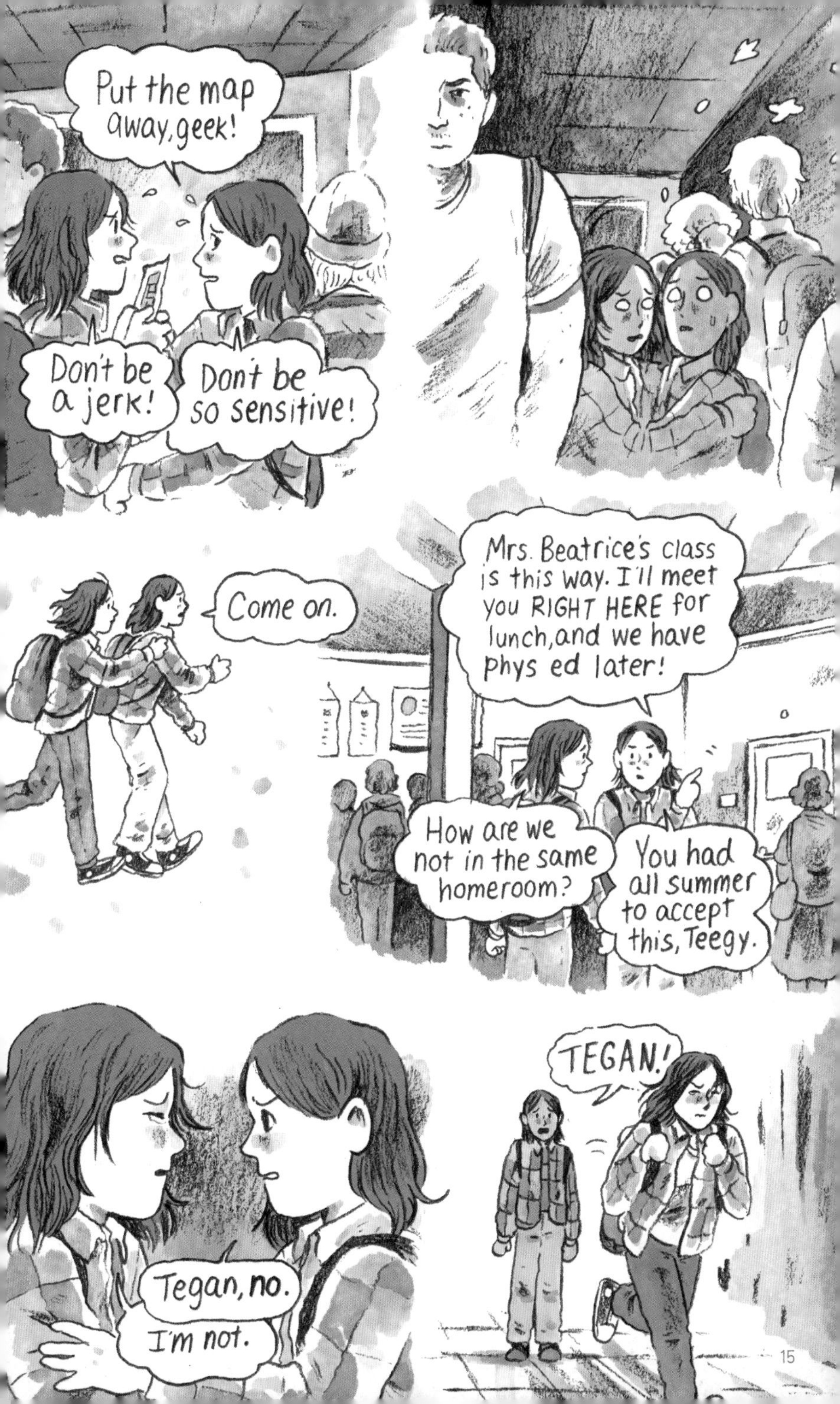

Put the map away, geek!
Don't be a jerk!
Don't be so sensitive!
Come on.
Mrs. Beatrice's class is this way. I'll meet you RIGHT HERE for lunch, and we have phys ed later!
How are we not in the same homeroom?
You had all summer to accept this, Teegy.
Tegan, no.
I'm not.
TEGAN!

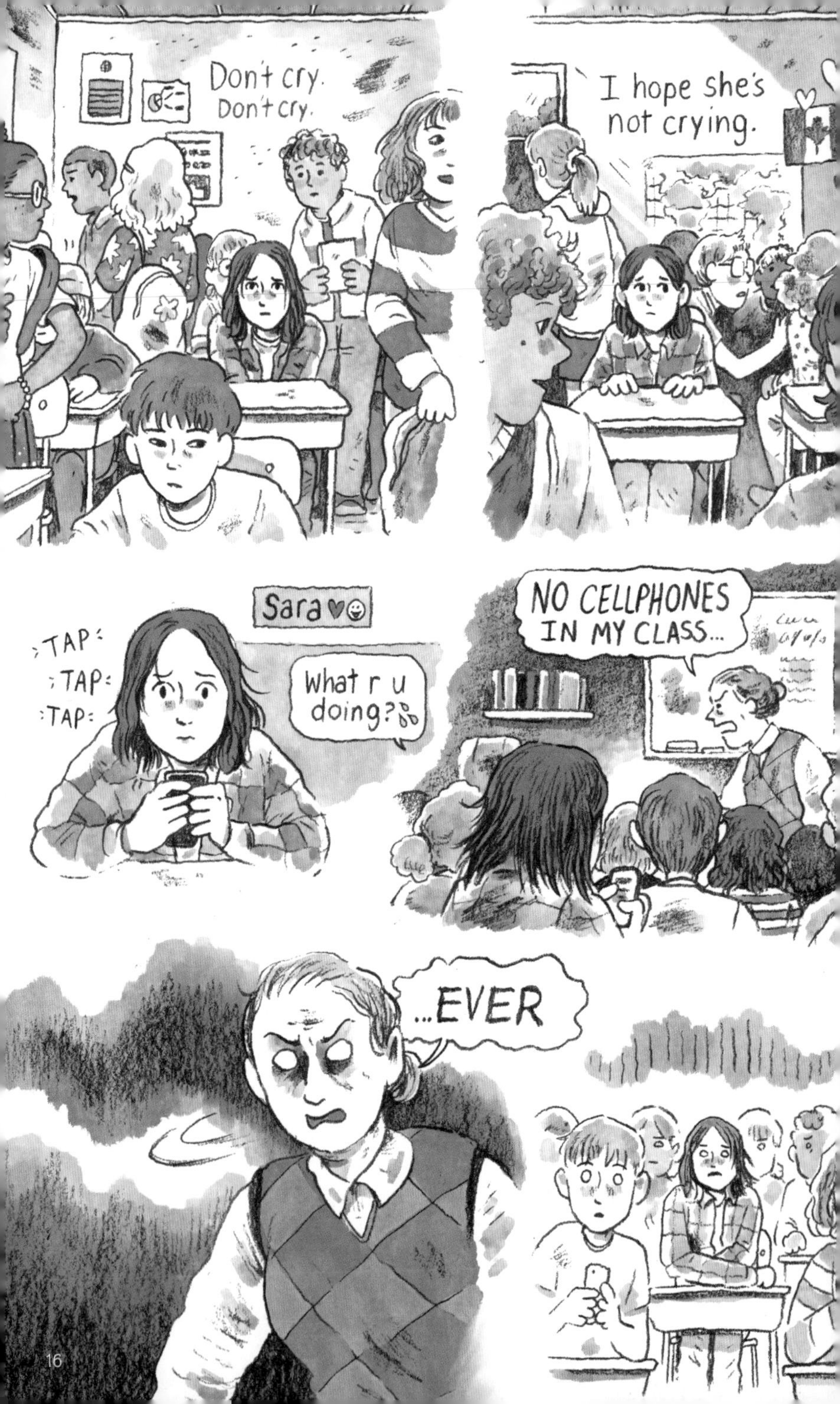
Don't cry.
Don't cry.
I hope she's not crying.
Sara
TAP
TAP
TAP
What r u doing?
NO CELLPHONES IN MY CLASS...
...EVER

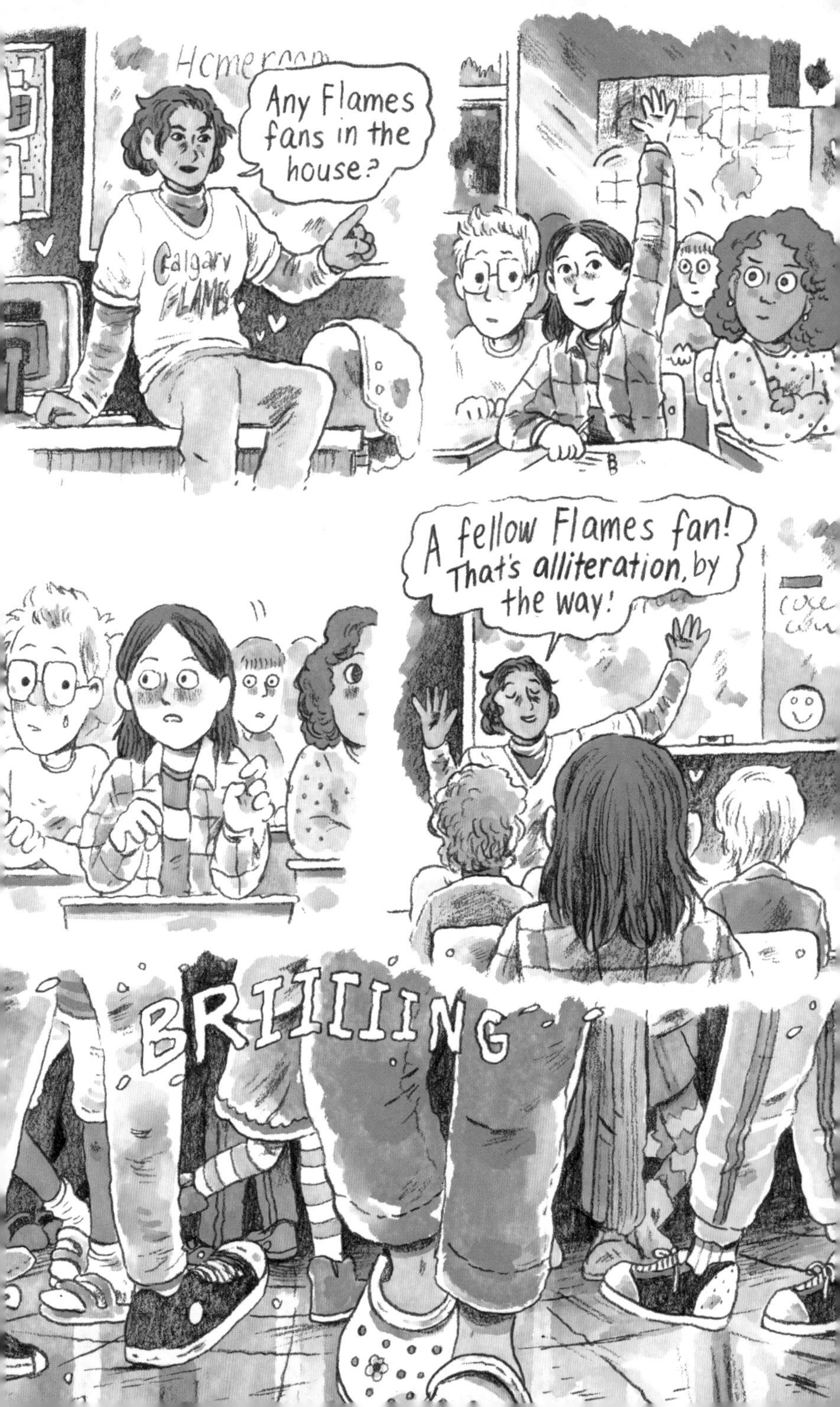
Homeroom
Any Flames fans in the house?
Calgary Flames
A fellow Flames fan! That's alliteration, by the way!
BRIIIING

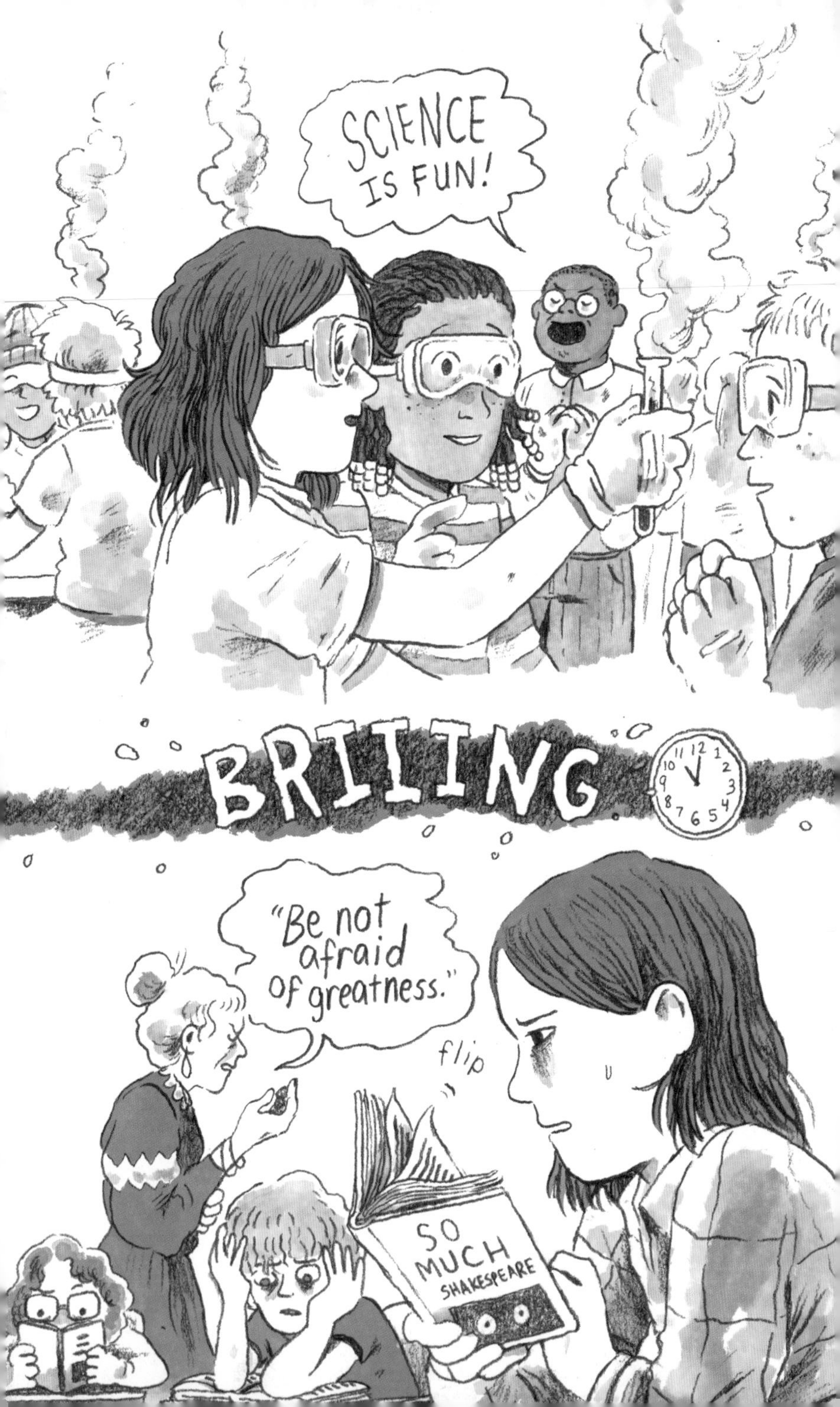
SCIENCE IS FUN!
BRIIING
"Be not afraid of greatness."
flip
SO MUCH SHAKESPEARE

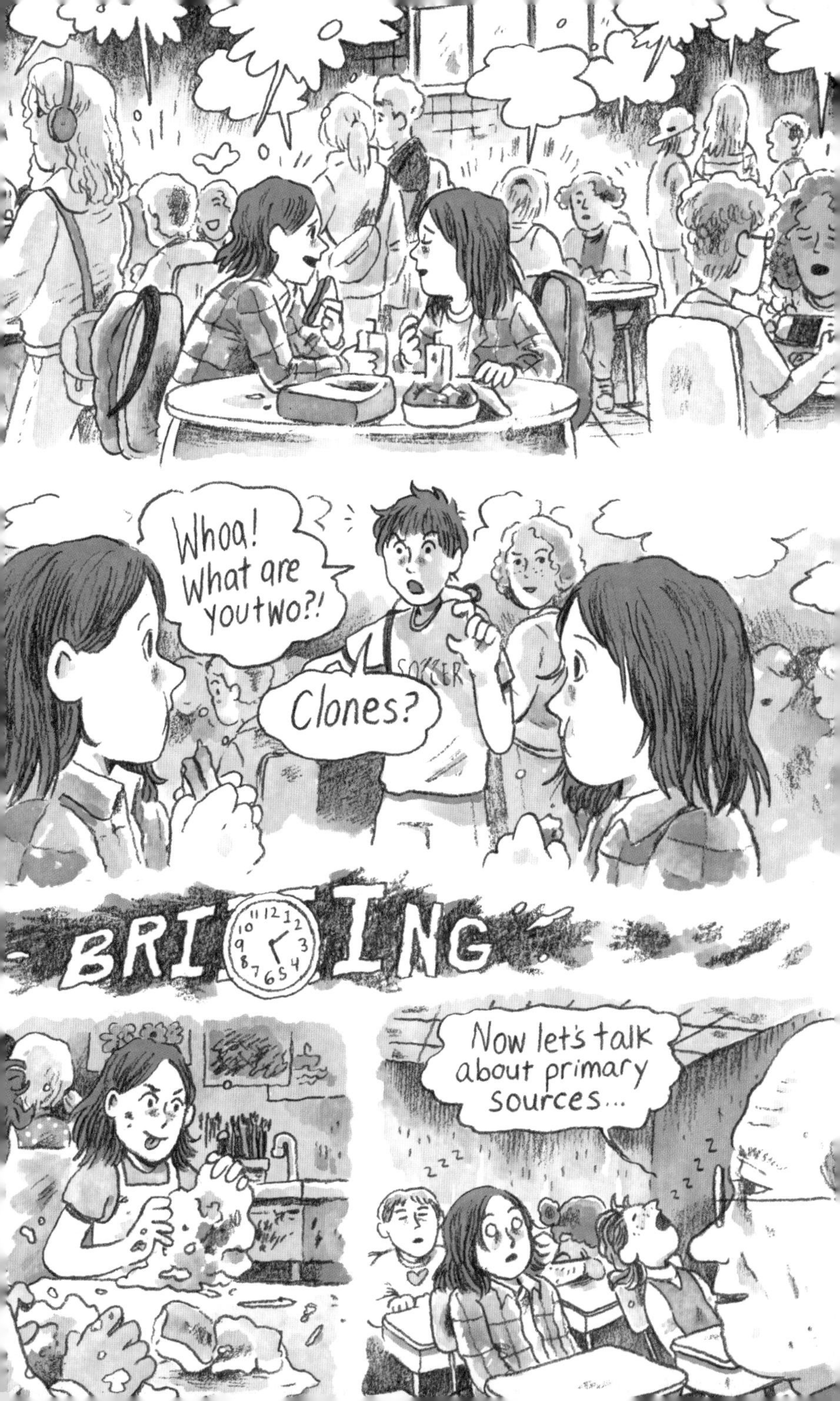
Whoa! What are you two?!
Clones?
BRI[clock]NG
Now let's talk about primary sources...

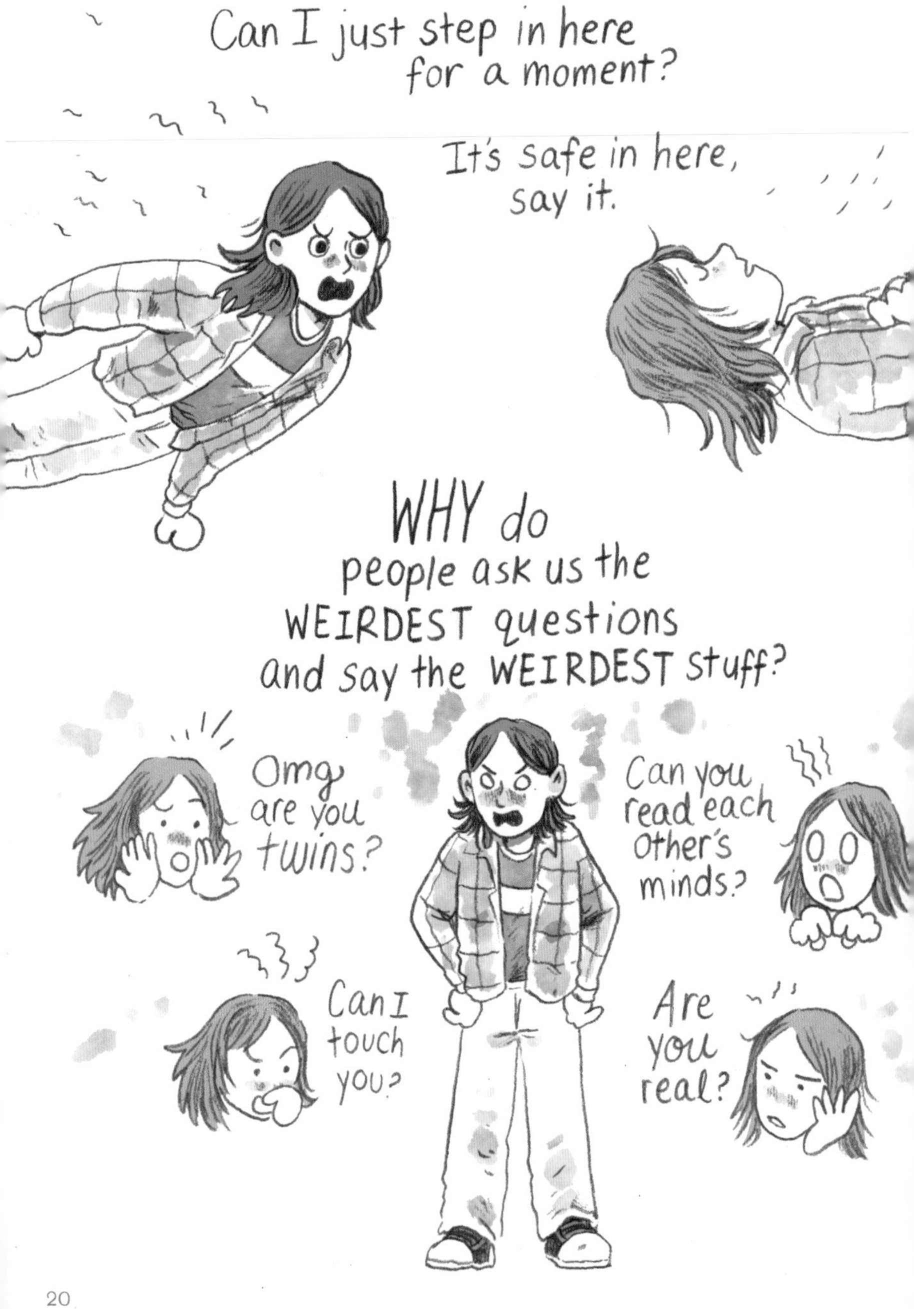

Can I just step in here for a moment?
It's safe in here, say it.
WHY do people ask us the WEIRDEST questions and say the WEIRDEST stuff?
Omg are you twins?
Can you read each other's minds?
Can I touch you?
Are you real?

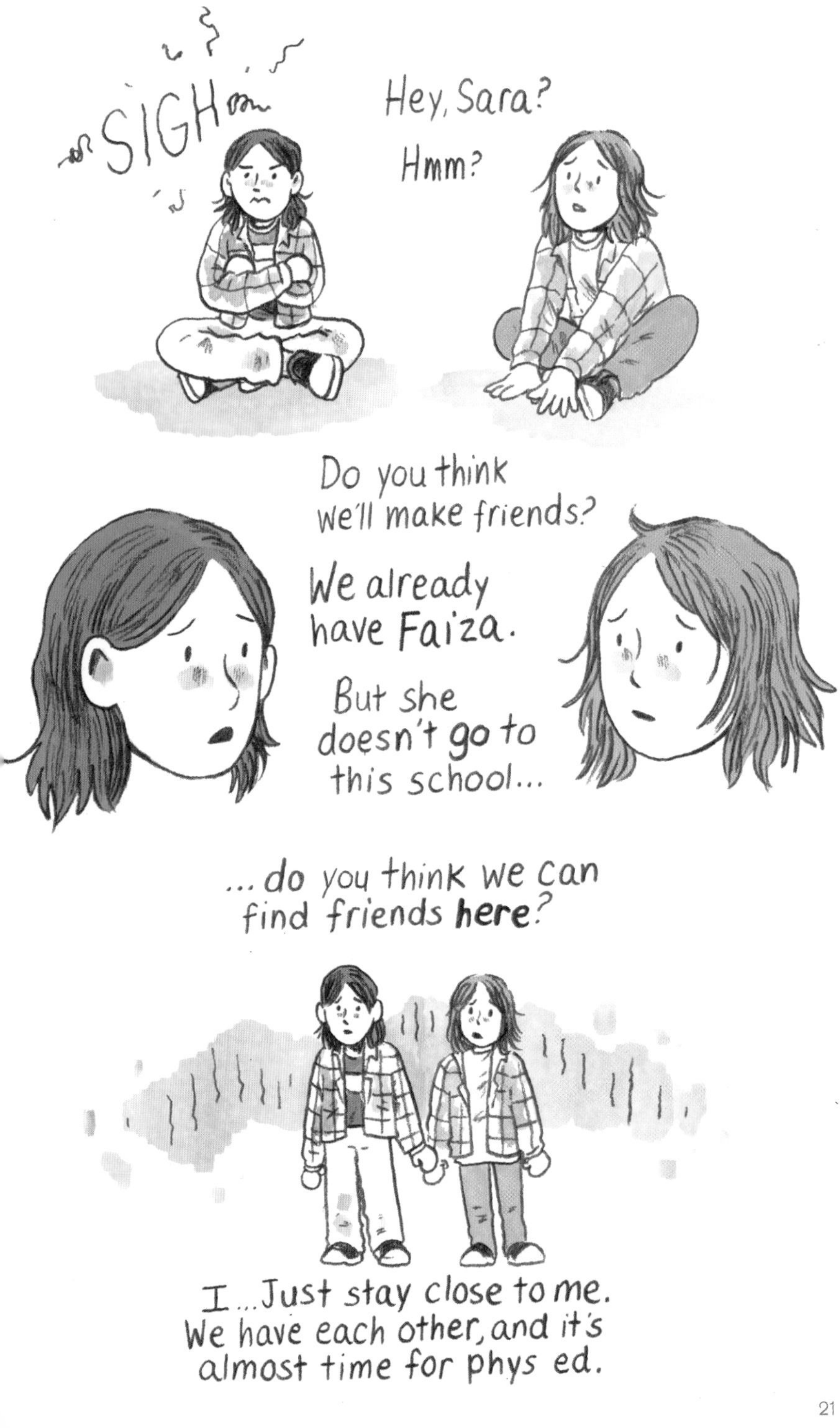
SIGH
Hey, Sara?
Hmm?
Do you think we'll make friends?
We already have Faiza.
But she doesn't go to this school...
...do you think we can find friends here?
I...Just stay close to me. We have each other, and it's almost time for phys ed.

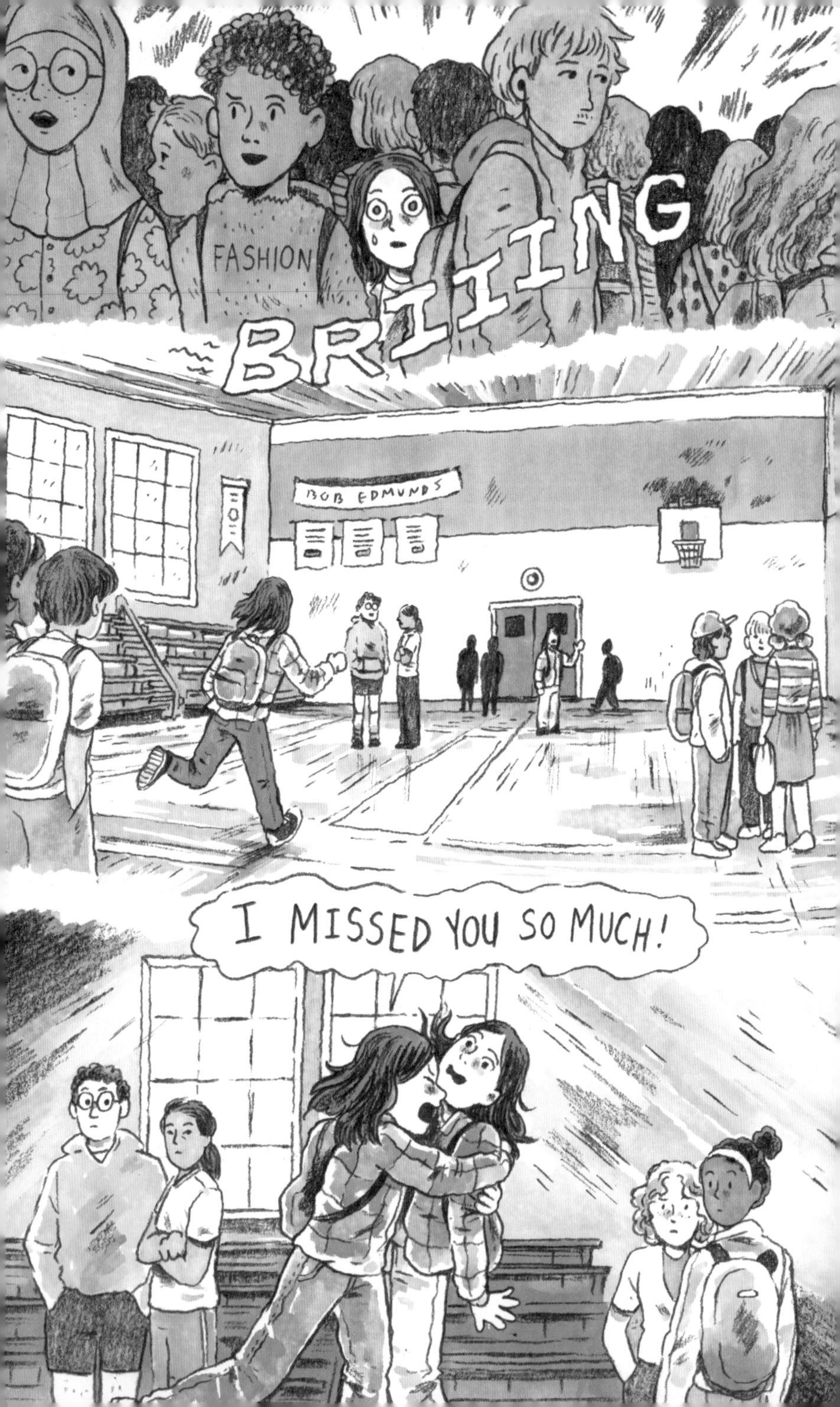
FASHION
BRIIING
BOB EDMUNDS
I MISSED YOU SO MUCH!

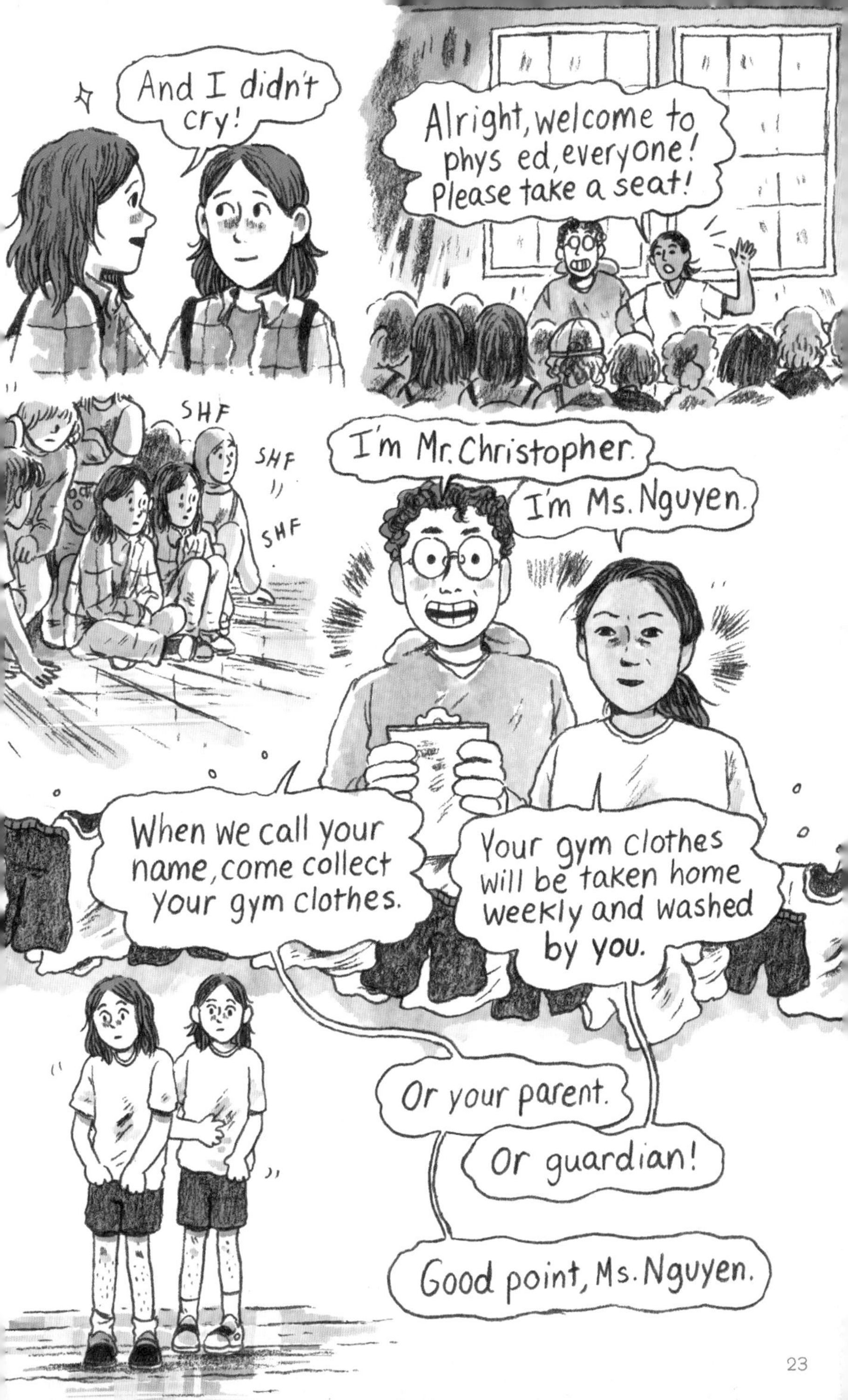
And I didn't cry!
Alright, welcome to phys ed, everyone! Please take a seat!
SHF
SHF
SHF
I'm Mr. Christopher.
I'm Ms. Nguyen.
When we call your name, come collect your gym clothes.
Your gym clothes will be taken home weekly and washed by you.
Or your parent.
Or guardian!
Good point, Ms. Nguyen.

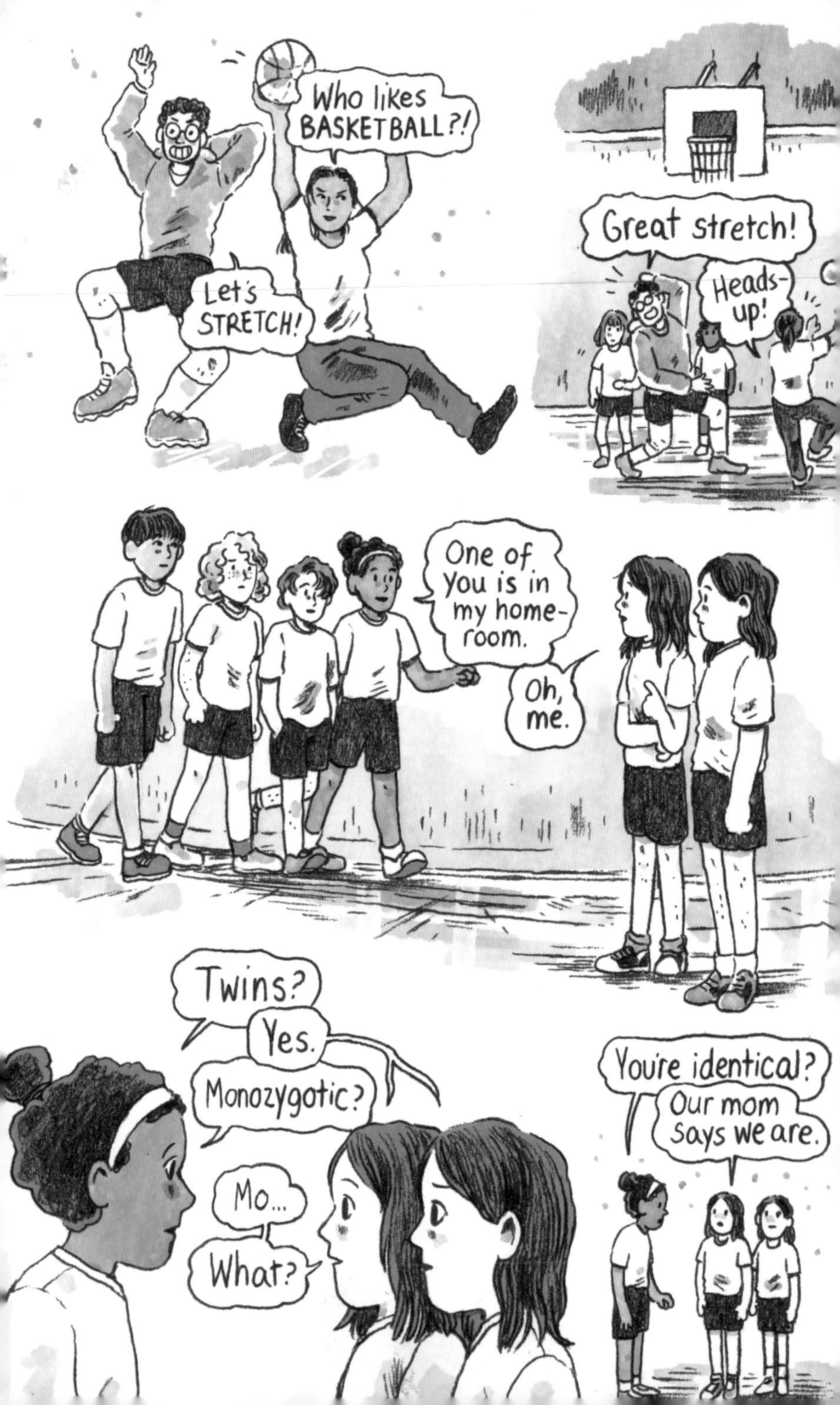
Who likes BASKETBALL?!
Let's STRETCH!
Great stretch!
Heads-up!
One of you is in my home-room.
Oh, me.
Twins?
Yes.
Monozygotic?
Mo...
What?
You're identical?
Our mom says we are.

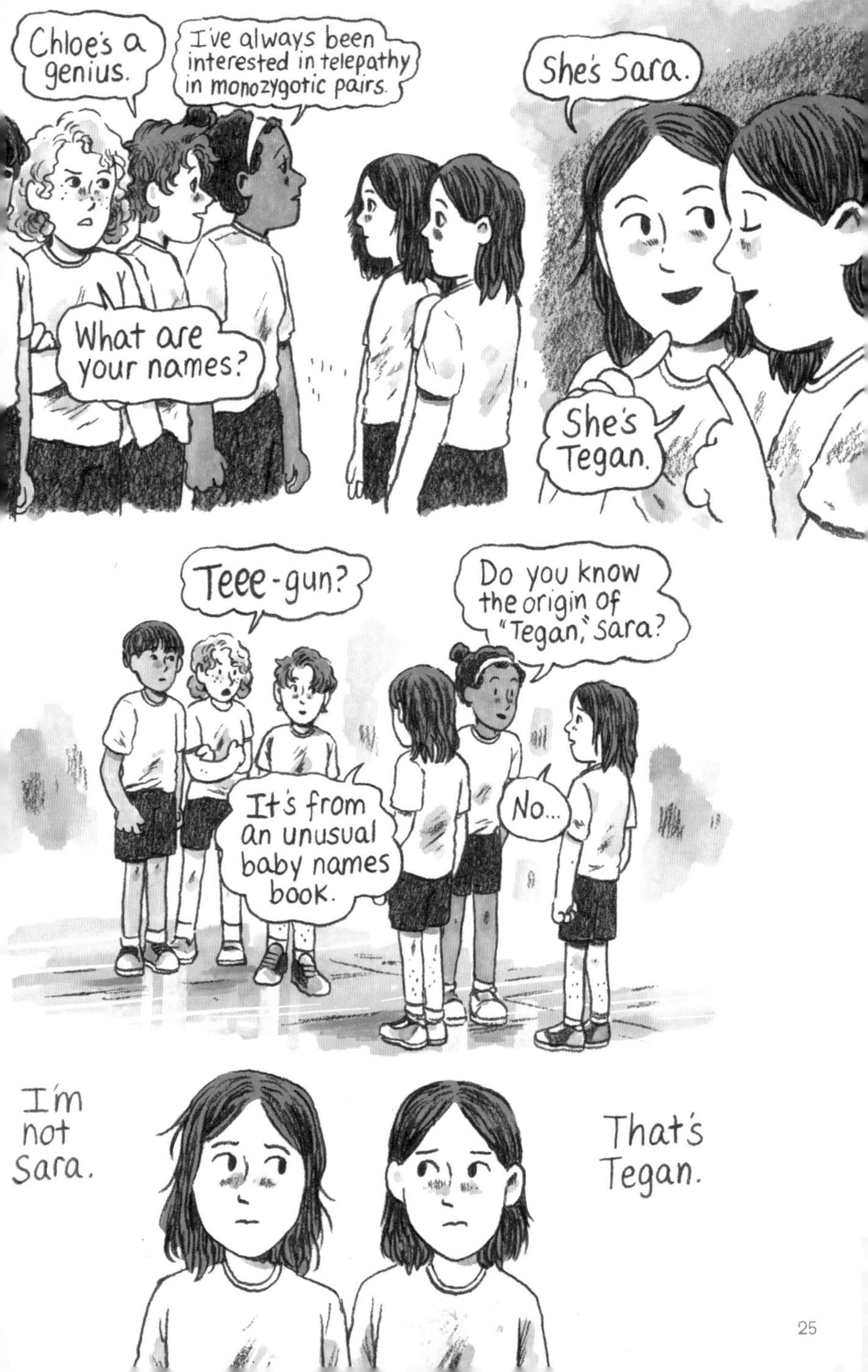

Chloe's a genius.
I've always been interested in telepathy in monozygotic pairs.
What are your names?
She's Sara.
She's Tegan.
Teee-gun?
Do you know the origin of "Tegan," Sara?
It's from an unusual baby names book.
No...
I'm not Sara.
That's Tegan.

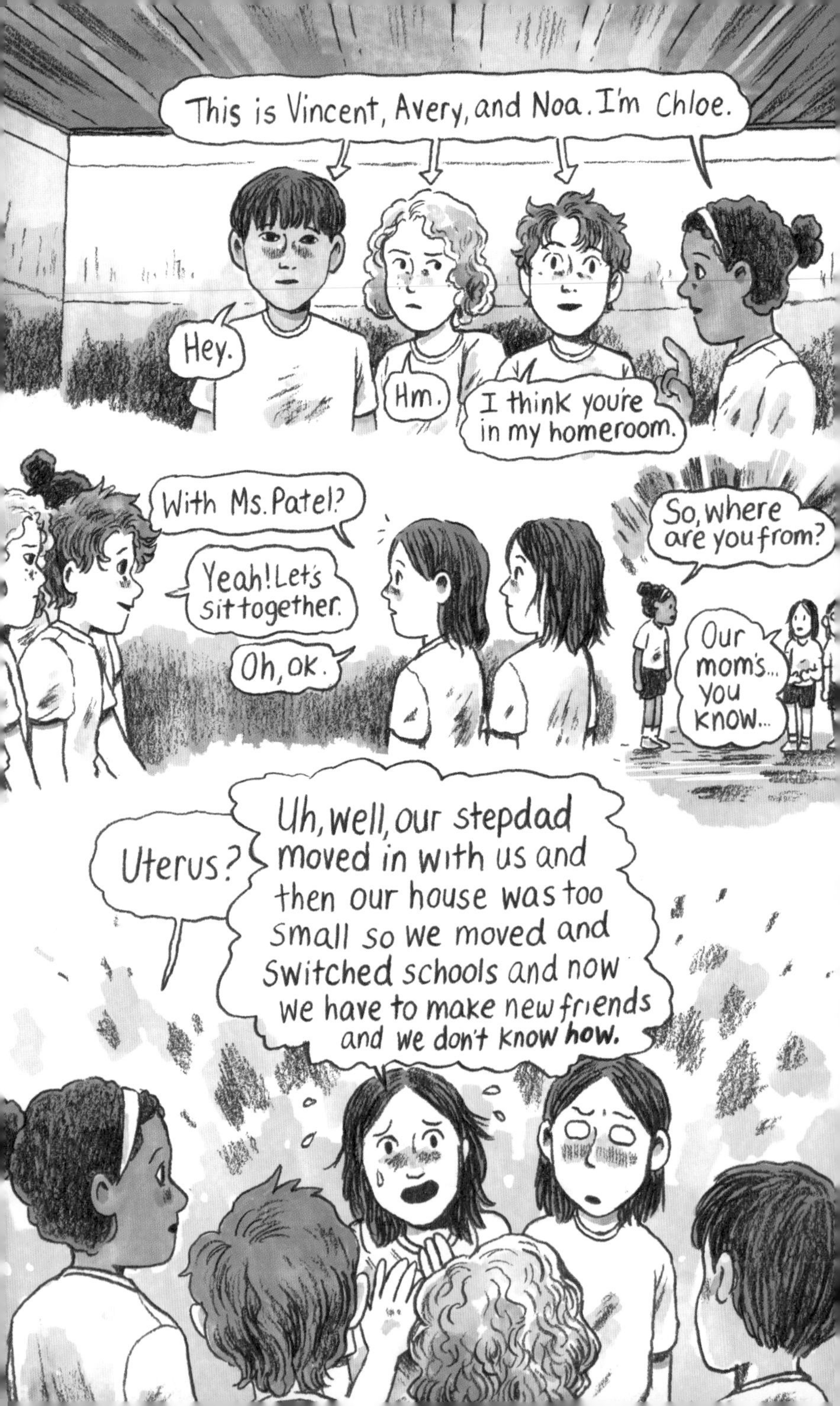
This is Vincent, Avery, and Noa. I'm Chloe.
Hey.
Hm.
I think you're in my homeroom.
With Ms. Patel?
Yeah! Let's sit together.
Oh, ok.
So, where are you from?
Our mom's... you know...
Uterus?
Uh, well, our stepdad moved in with us and then our house was too small so we moved and switched schools and now we have to make new friends and we don't know **how.**

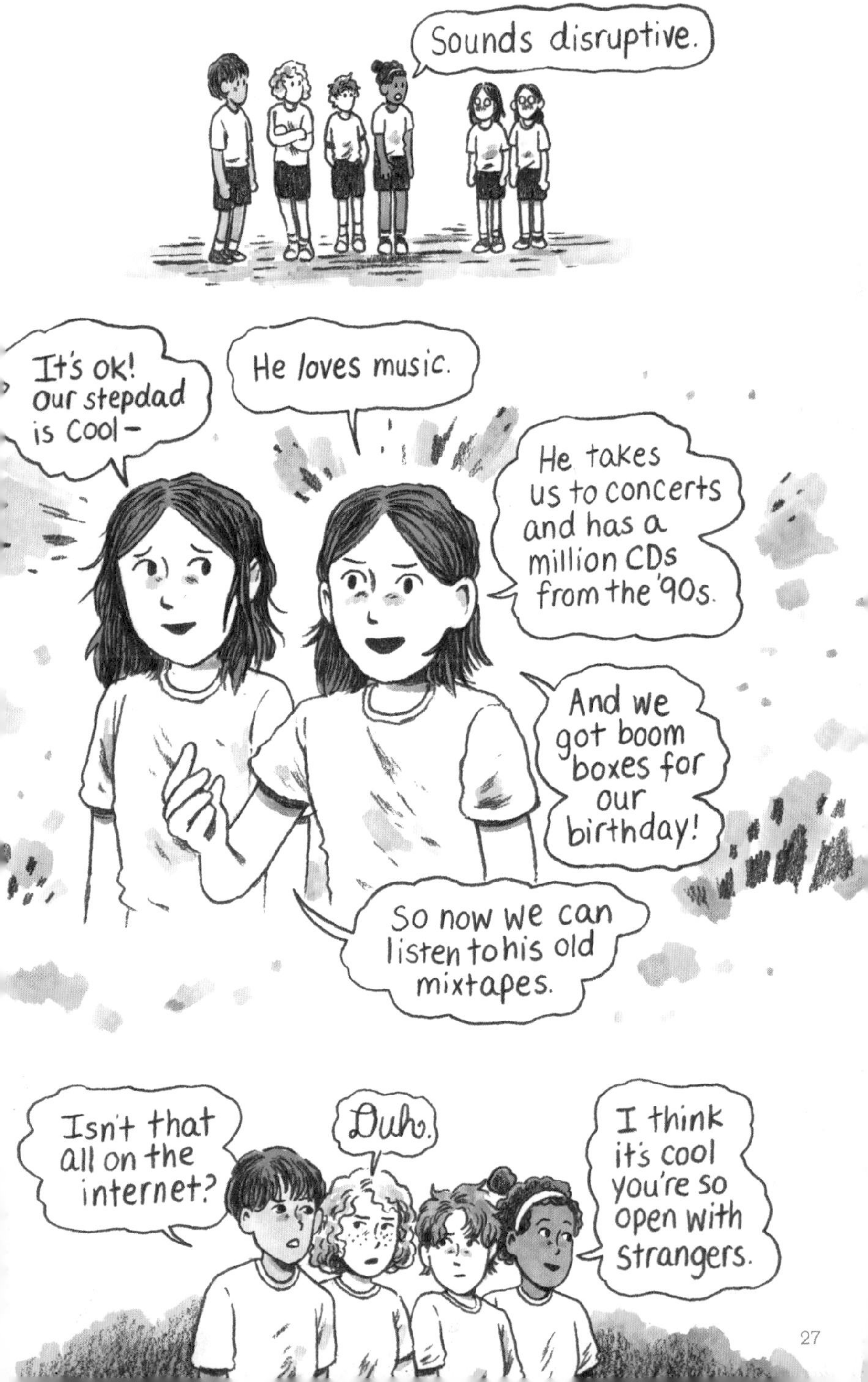
Sounds disruptive.
It's ok! our stepdad is cool–
He loves music.
He takes us to concerts and has a million CDs from the '90s.
And we got boom boxes for our birthday!
So now we can listen to his old mixtapes.
Isn't that all on the internet?
Duh.
I think it's cool you're so open with strangers.

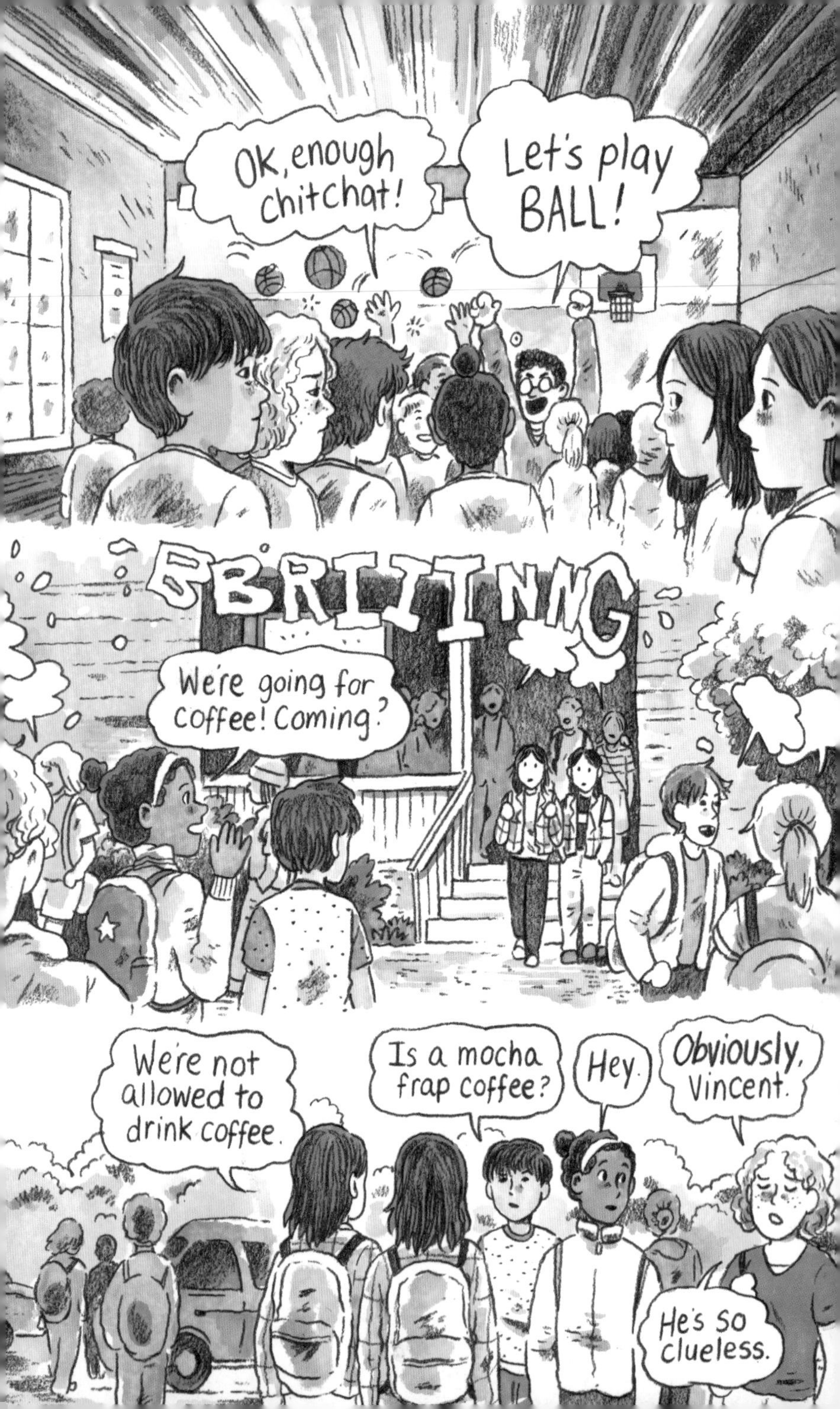
Ok, enough chitchat!
Let's play BALL!
BRIIINNG
We're going for coffee! Coming?
We're not allowed to drink coffee.
Is a mocha frap coffee?
Hey.
Obviously, Vincent.
He's so clueless.

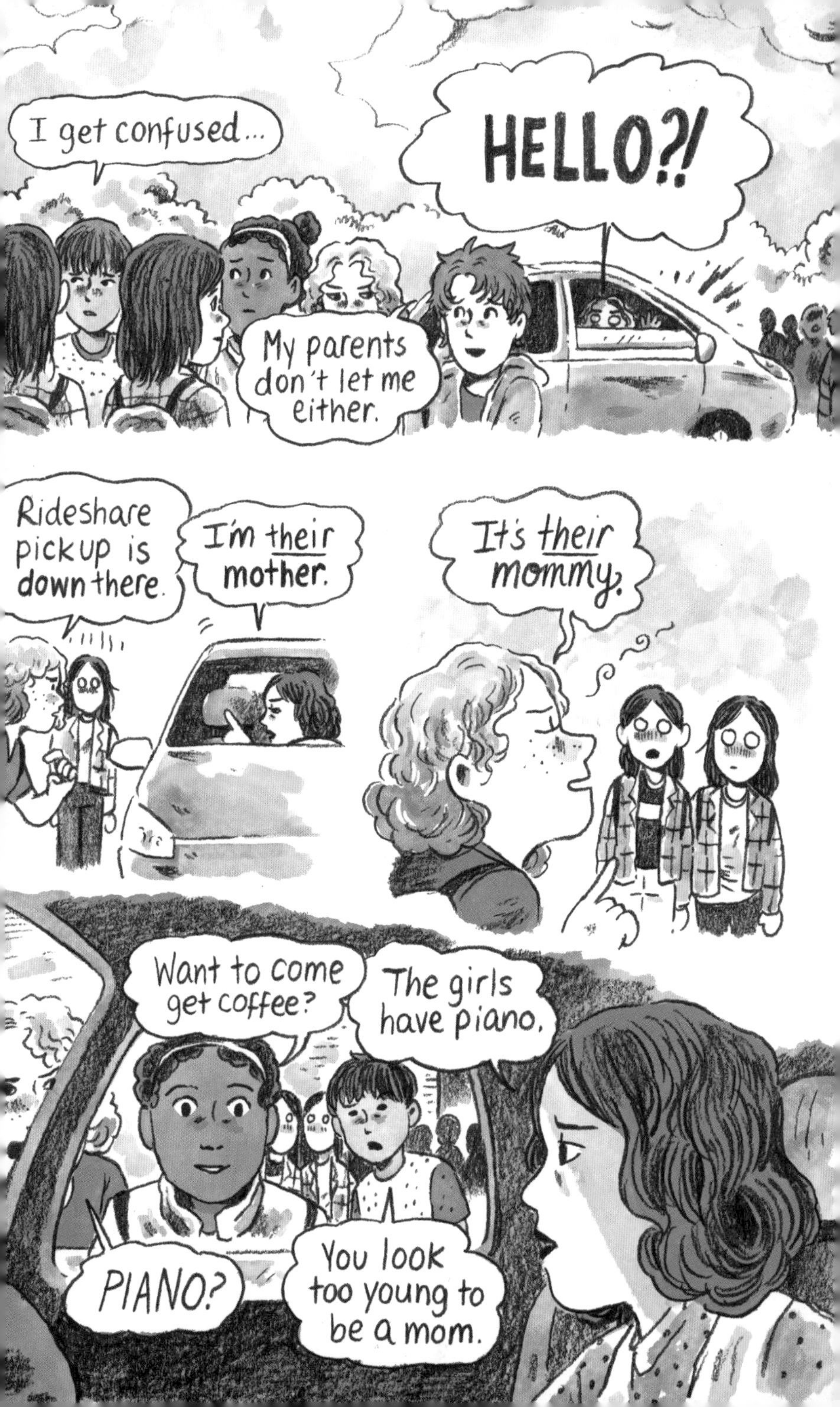

I get confused...
HELLO?!
My parents don't let me either.
Rideshare pickup is down there.
I'm their mother.
It's their mommy.
Want to come get coffee?
The girls have piano.
PIANO?
You look too young to be a mom.

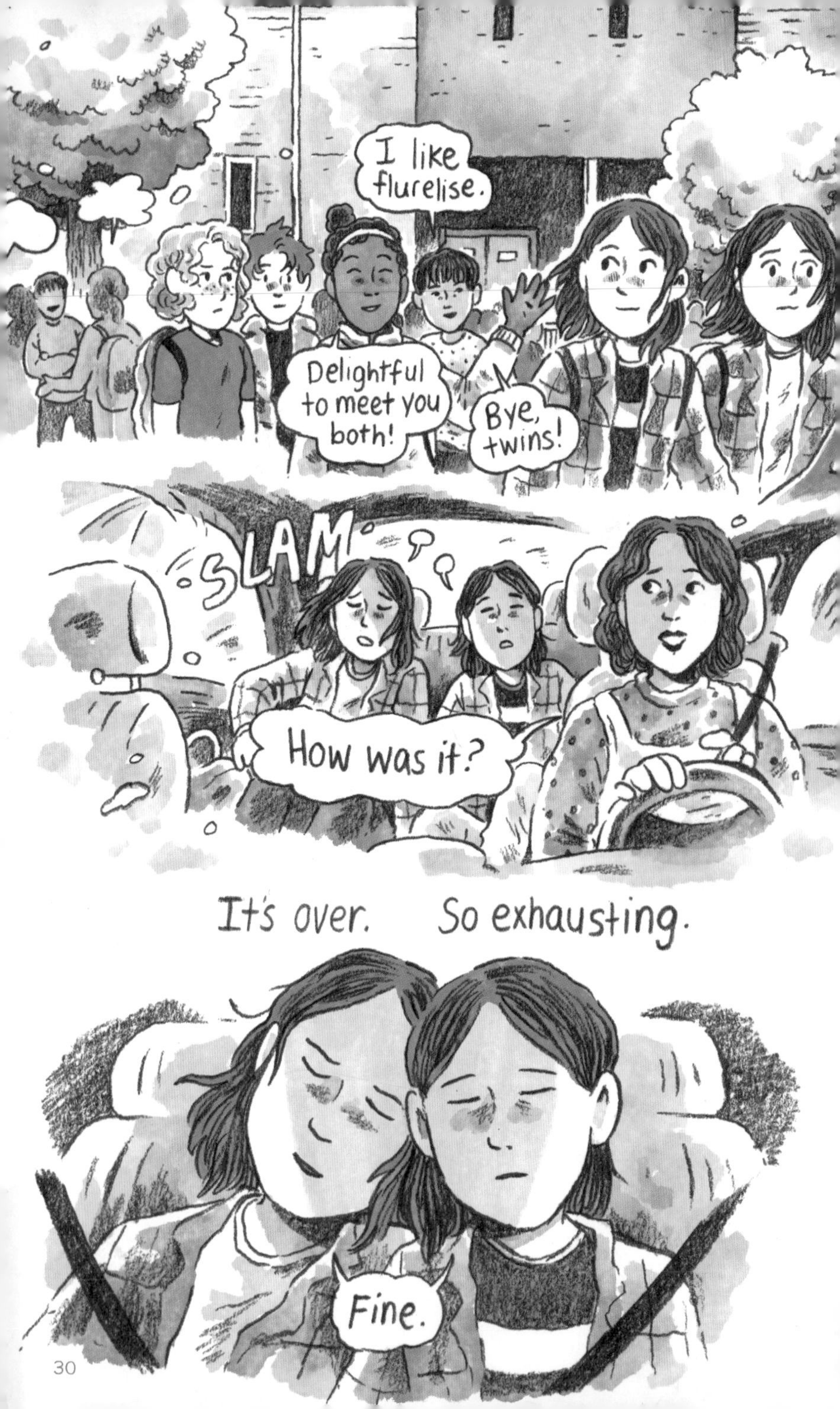
I like flurelise.
Delightful to meet you both!
Bye, twins!
SLAM
How was it?
It's over. So exhausting.
Fine.

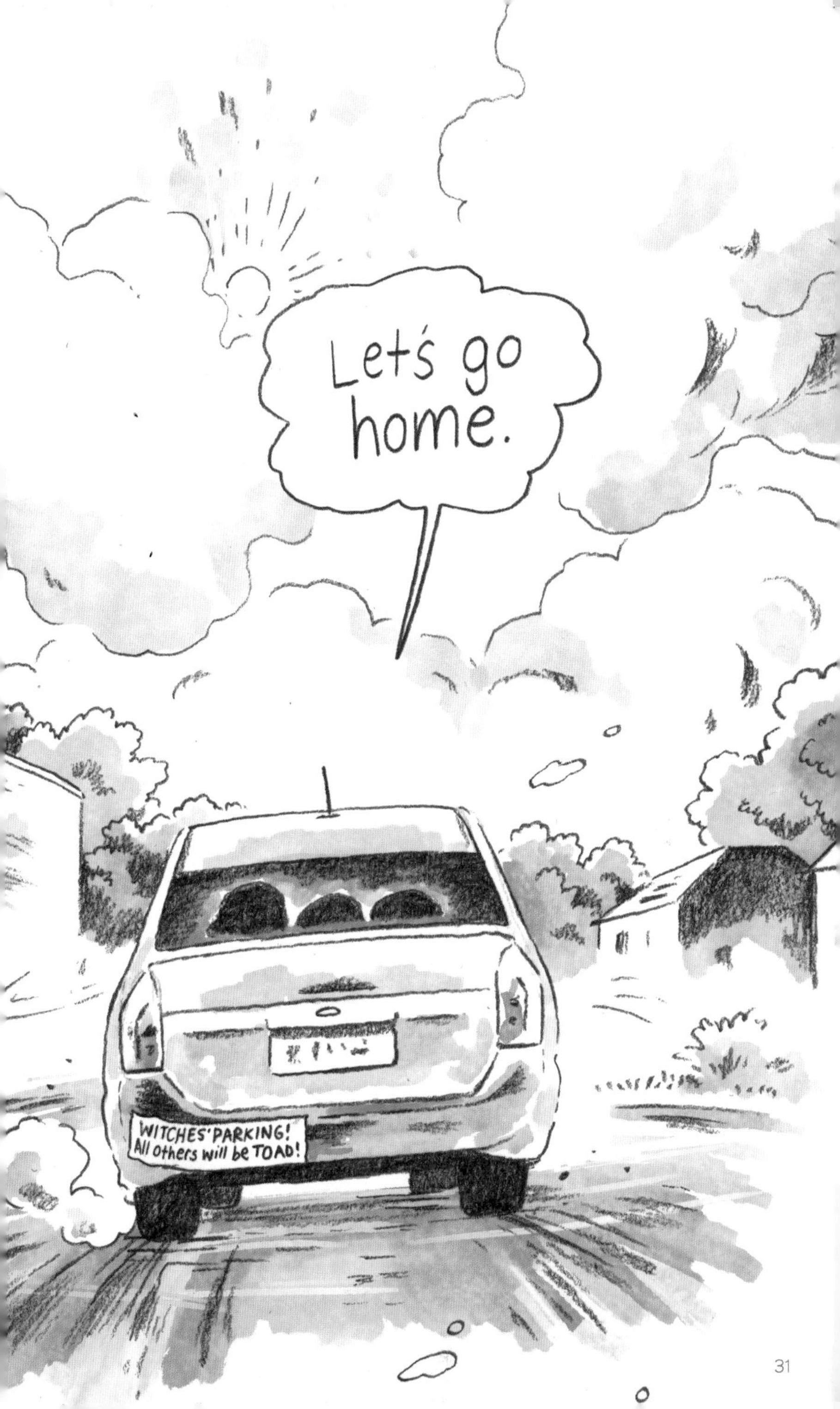
Let's go home.
WITCHES' PARKING! All others will be TOAD!

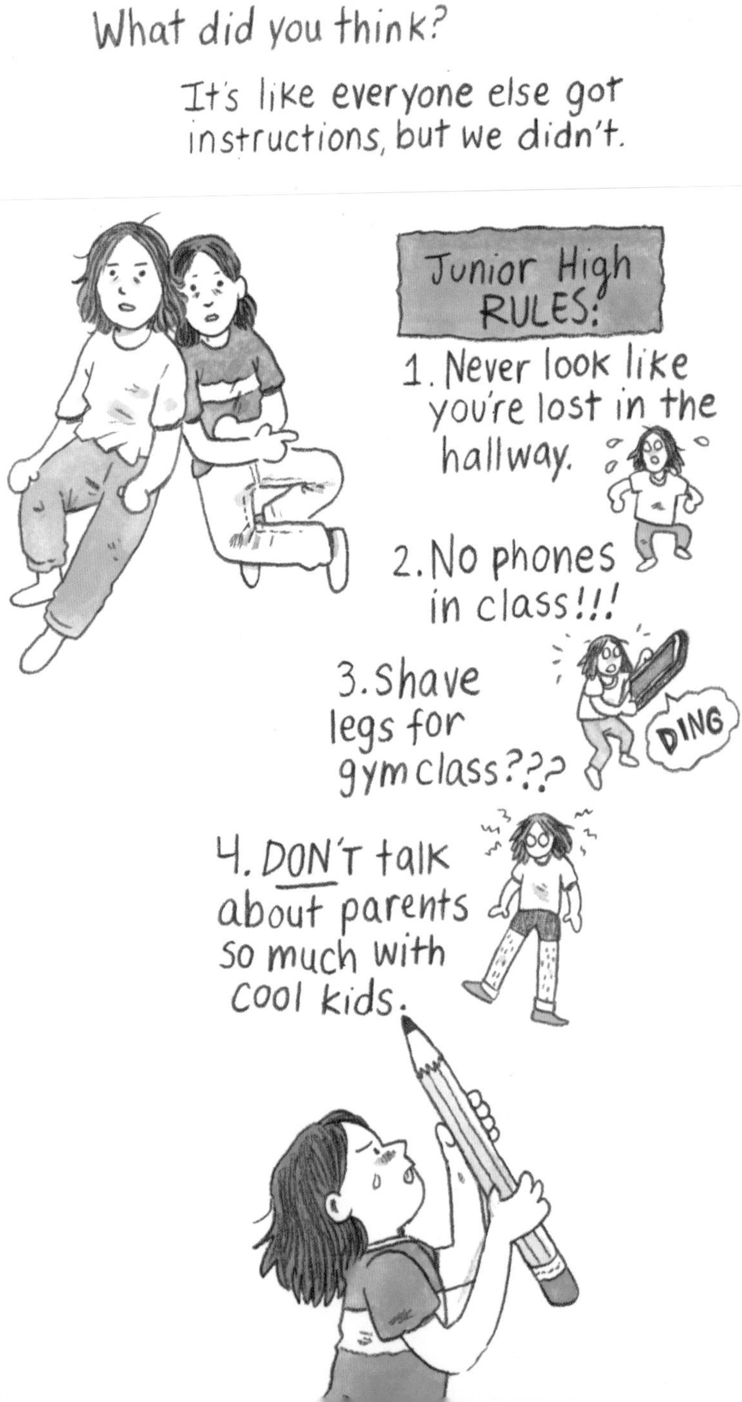
What did you think?
It's like everyone else got instructions, but we didn't.
Junior High RULES:
1. Never look like you're lost in the hallway.
2. No phones in class!!!
3. Shave legs for gym class???
DING
4. DON'T talk about parents so much with cool kids.

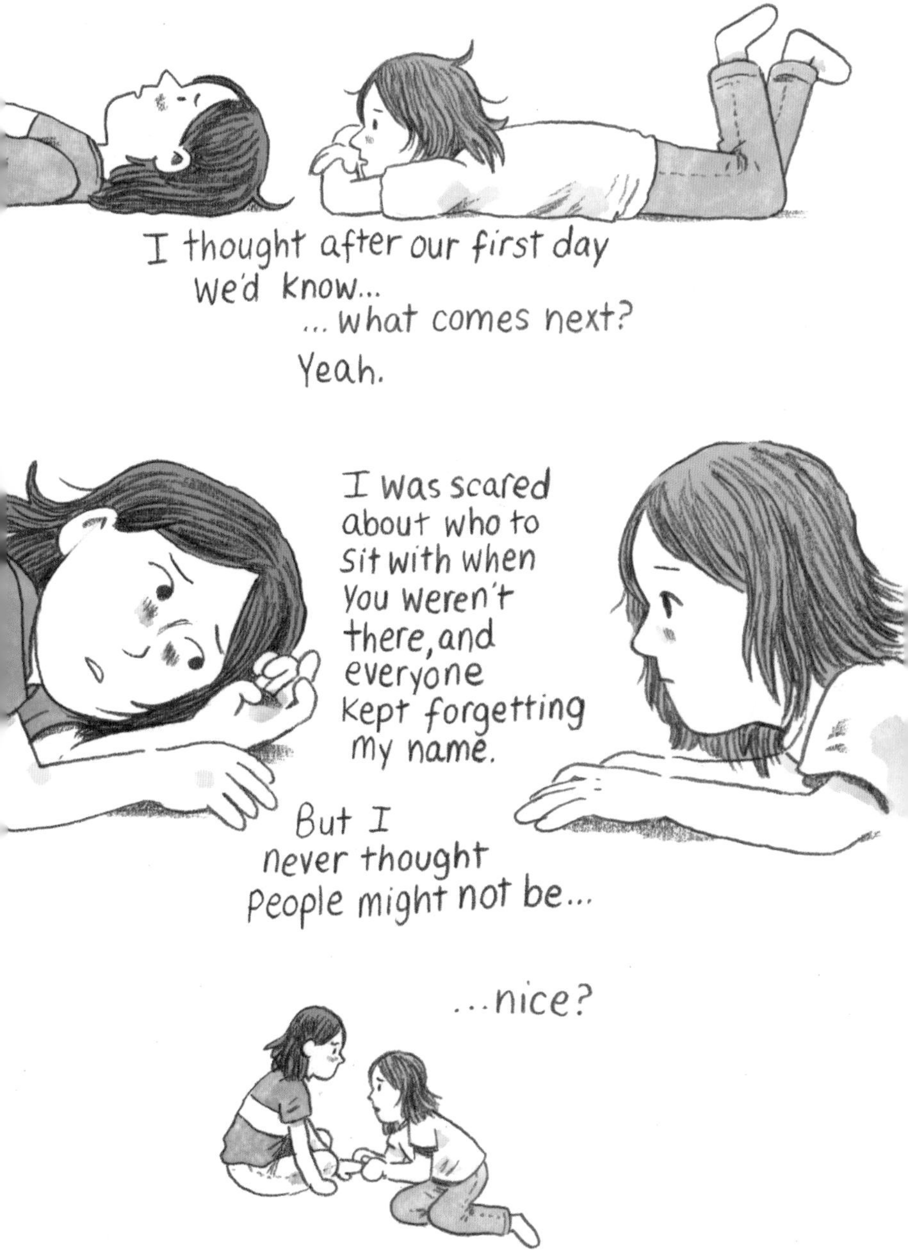
I thought after our first day we'd know...
...what comes next?
Yeah.
I was scared about who to sit with when you weren't there, and everyone kept forgetting my name.
But I never thought people might not be...
...nice?

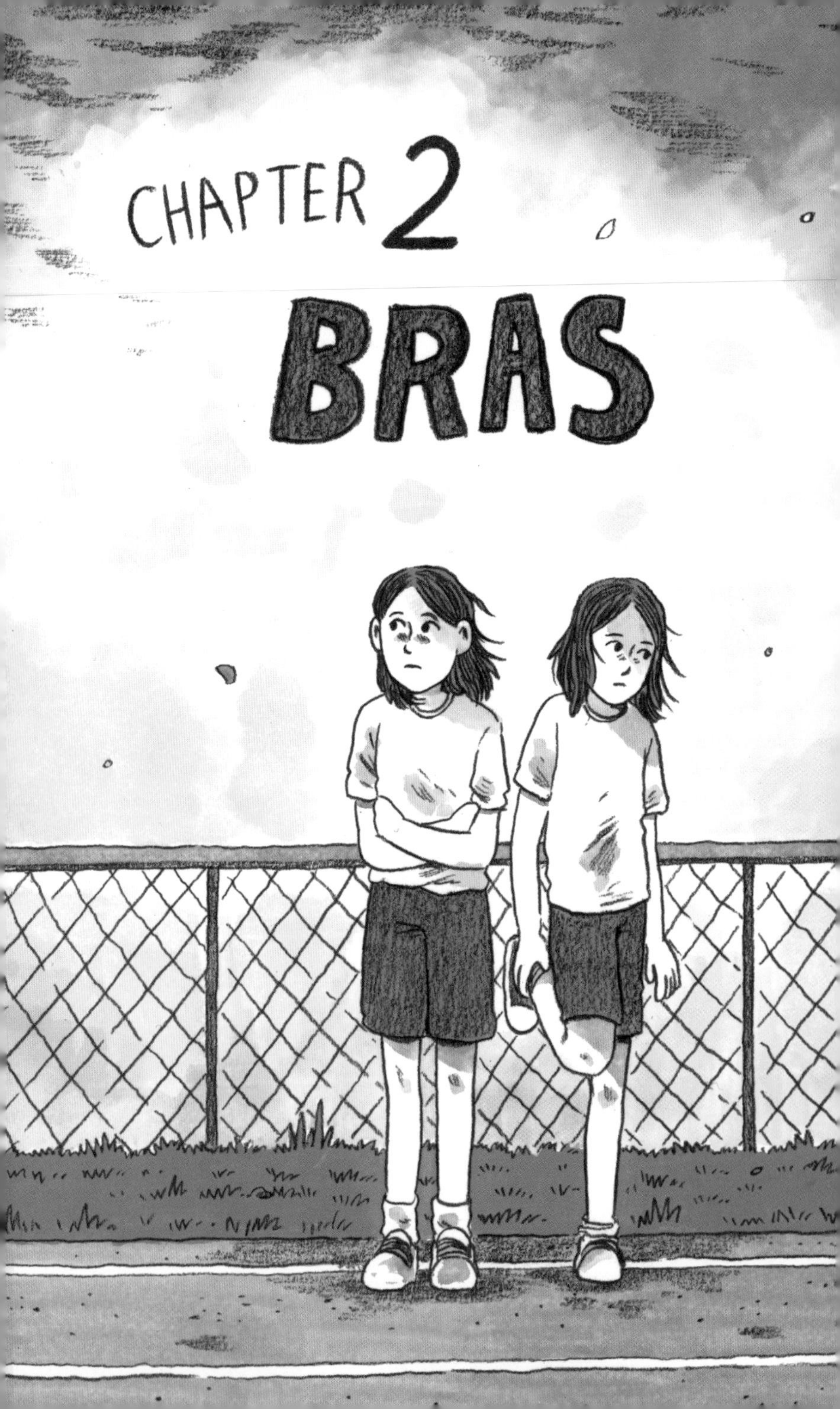
CHAPTER 2
BRAS

You think there's a way to
stop growing?

Let me google it.

Well?

It's not looking good.
But, hey, at least we have
gym tomorrow, so we can
be together! I think Noa
will be there too.

So will that Avery girl...

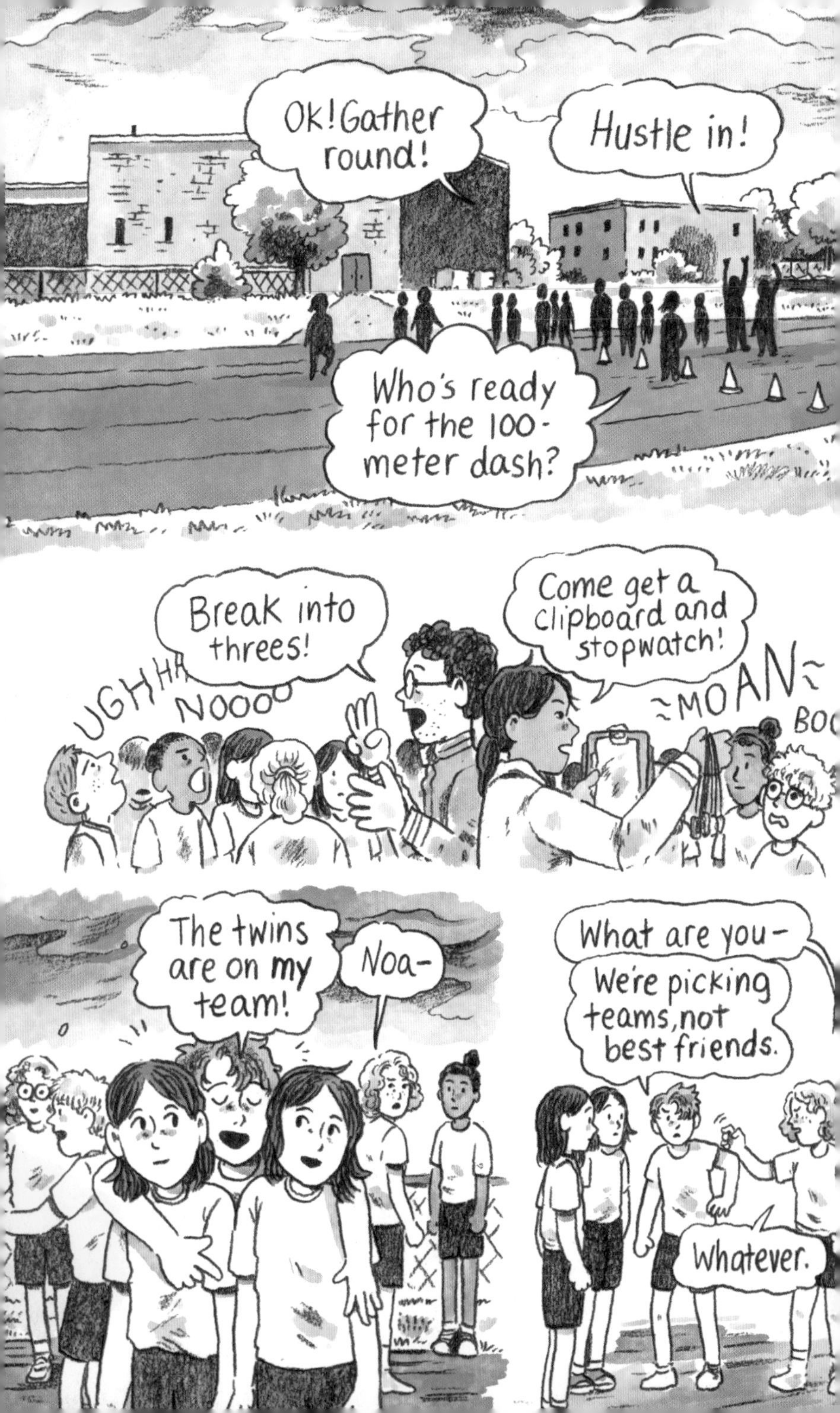
Ok! Gather round!
Hustle in!
Who's ready for the 100-meter dash?
Break into threes!
Come get a clipboard and stopwatch!
UGHH
NOOOO
MOAN
The twins are on my team!
Noa-
What are you-
We're picking teams, not best friends.
Whatever.

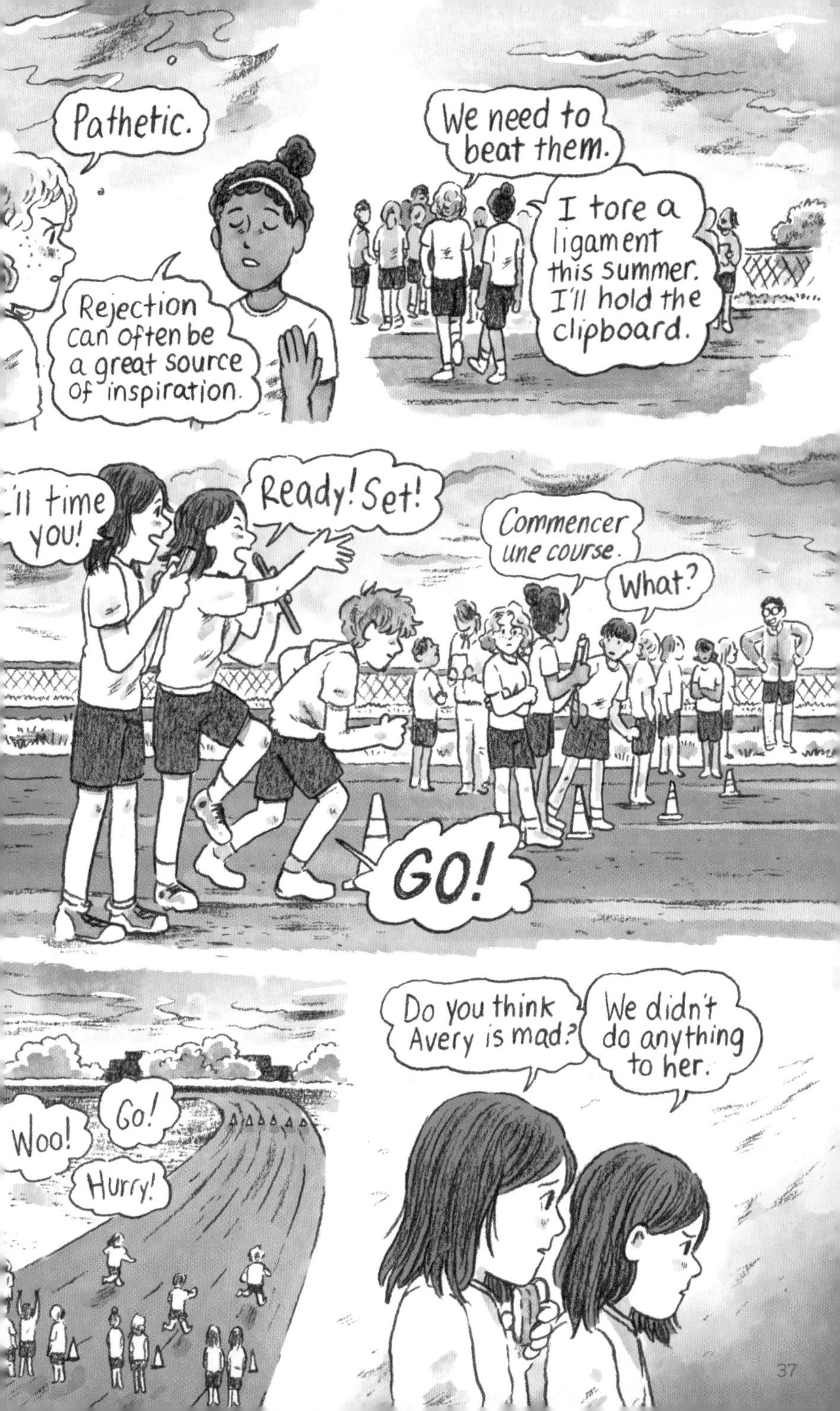

Pathetic.
Rejection can often be a great source of inspiration.
We need to beat them.
I tore a ligament this summer. I'll hold the clipboard.
I'll time you!
Ready! Set!
Commencer une course.
What?
GO!
Woo!
Go!
Hurry!
Do you think Avery is mad?
We didn't do anything to her.

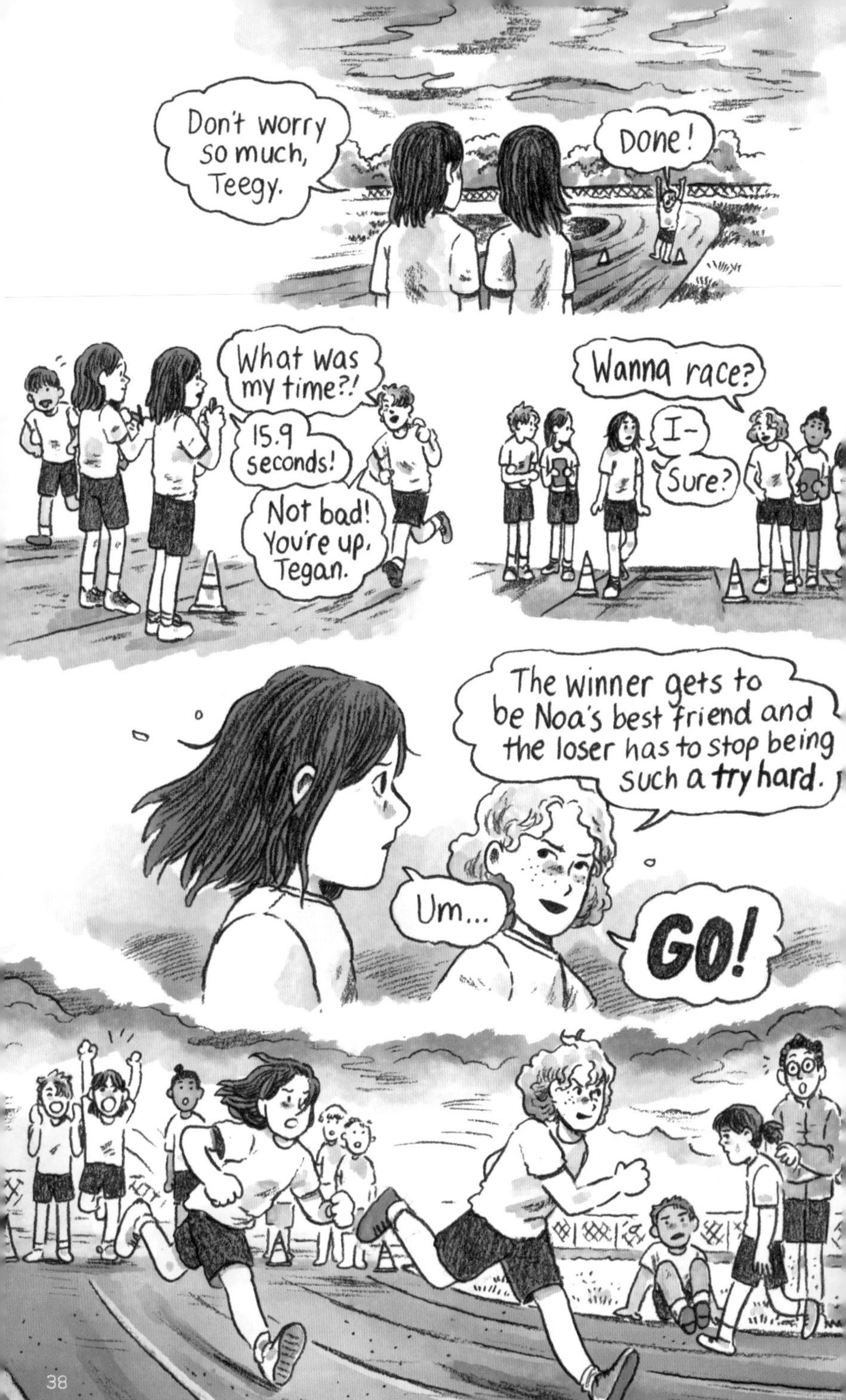
Don't worry so much, Teegy.
Done!
What was my time?!
15.9 seconds!
Not bad! You're up, Tegan.
Wanna race?
I-
Sure?
The winner gets to be Noa's best friend and the loser has to stop being such a **try hard**.
Um...
GO!

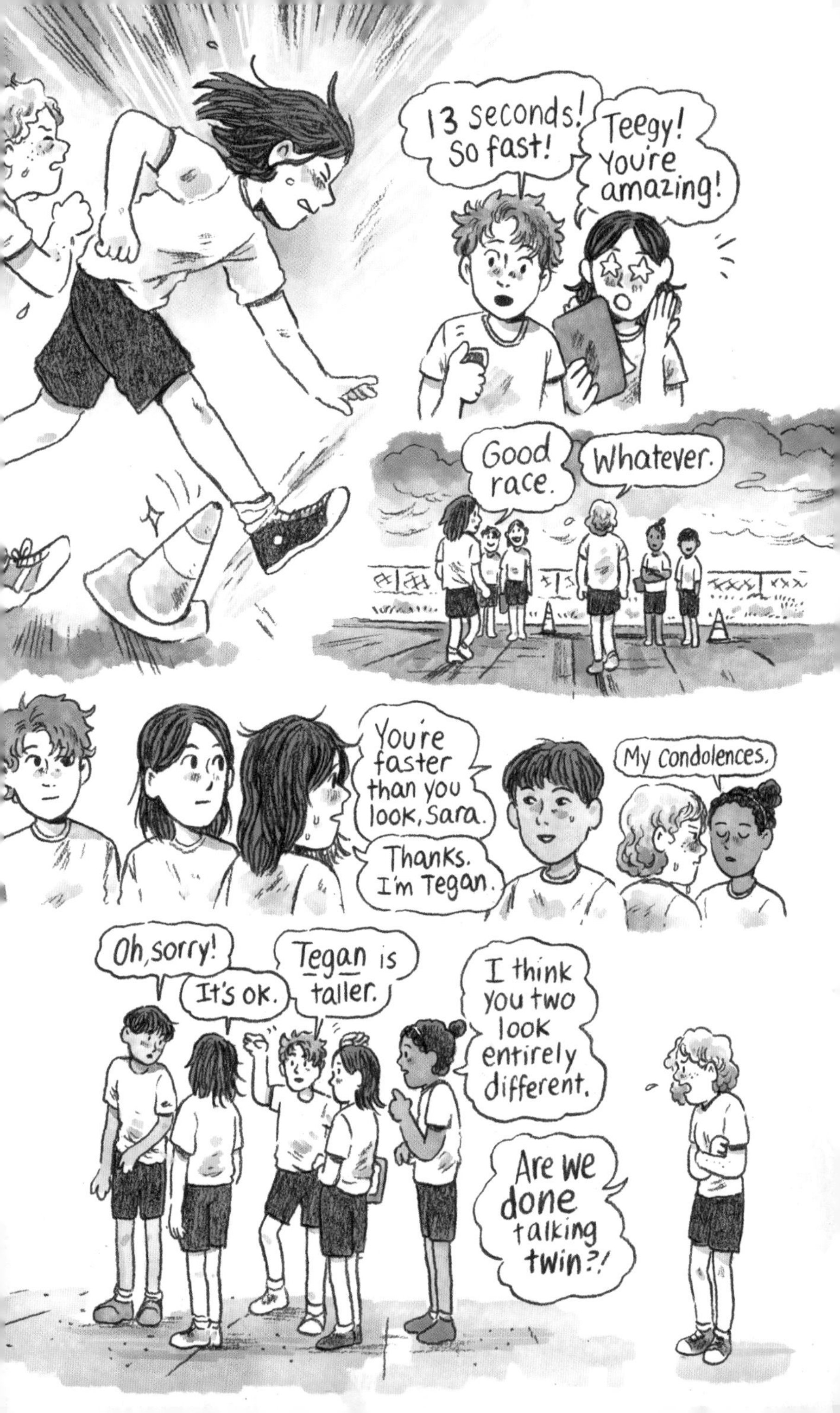
13 seconds! So fast!
Teegy! You're amazing!
Good race.
Whatever.
You're faster than you look, Sara.
Thanks. I'm Tegan.
My condolences.
Oh, sorry!
It's OK.
Tegan is taller.
I think you two look entirely different.
Are we done talking twin?!

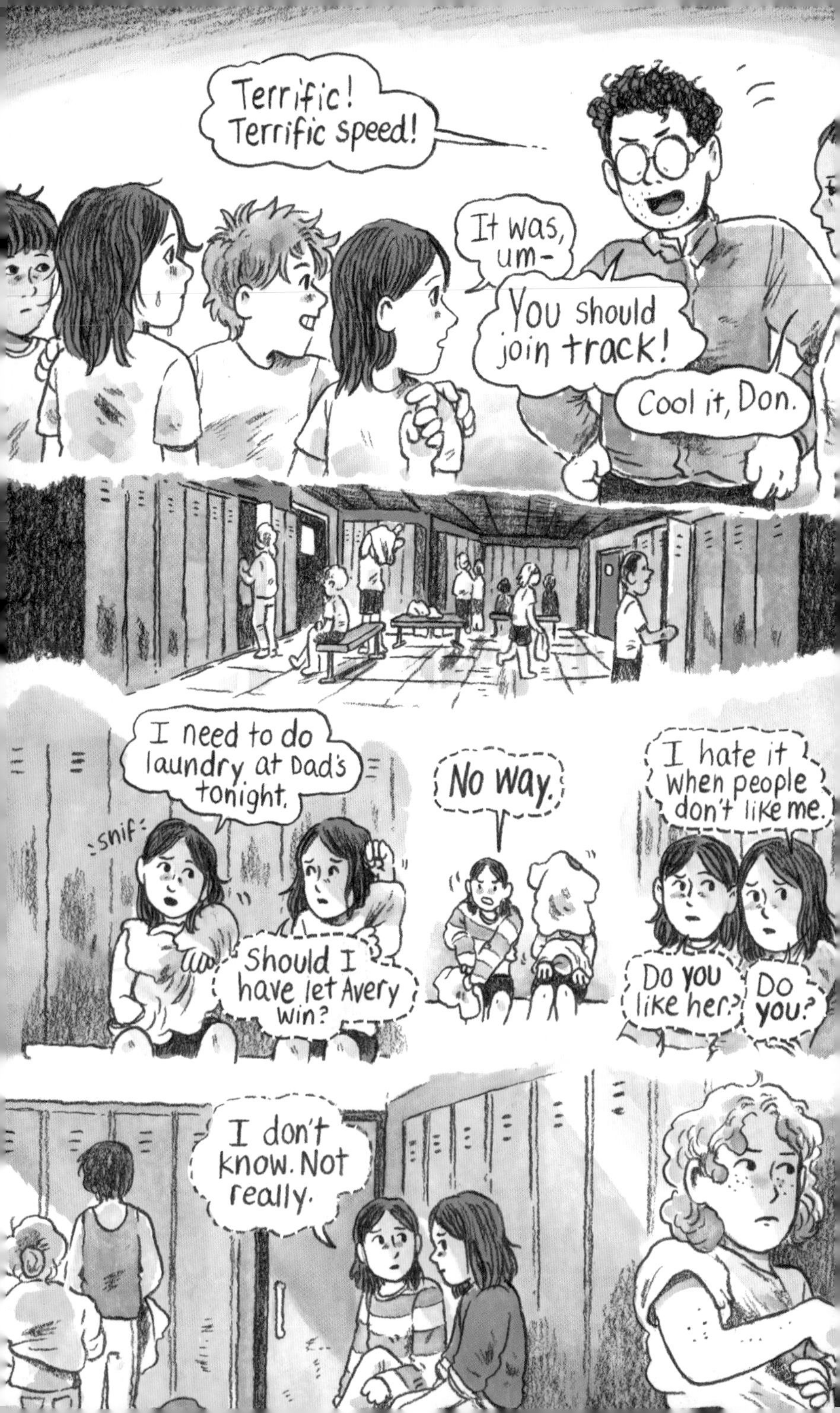
Terrific! Terrific speed!
It was, um-
You should join track!
Cool it, Don.
I need to do laundry at Dad's tonight.
snif
Should I have let Avery win?
No way.
I hate it when people don't like me.
Do you like her?
Do you?
I don't know. Not really.

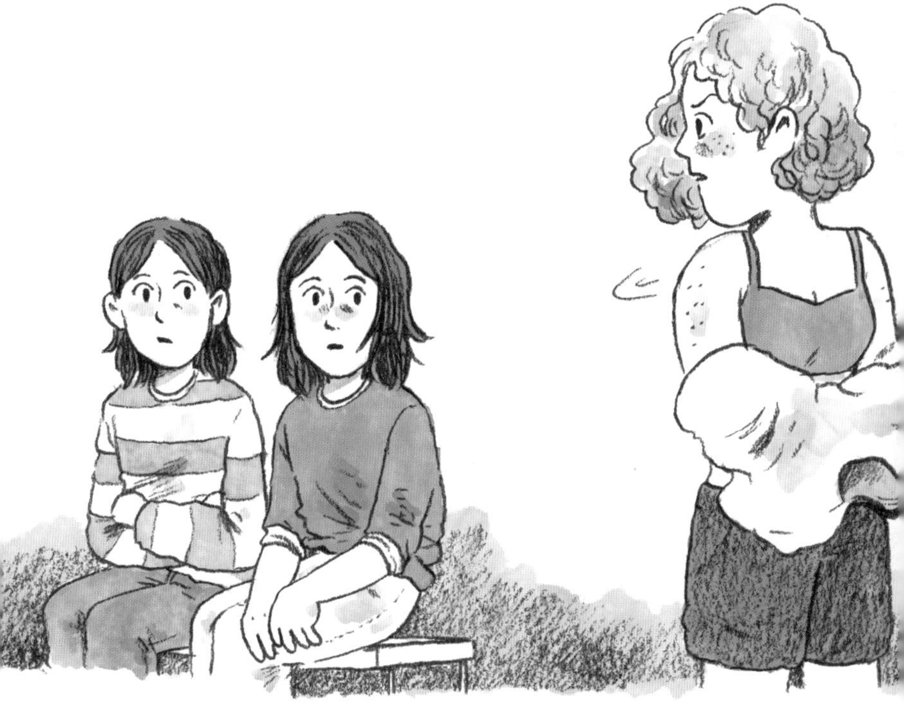

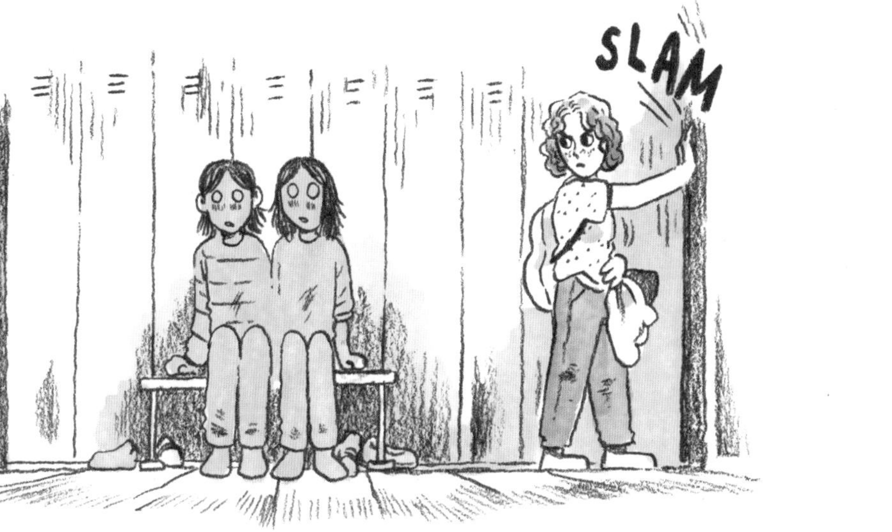
SLAM
Oh my god Ohmygod Oh no Ohnonononononon

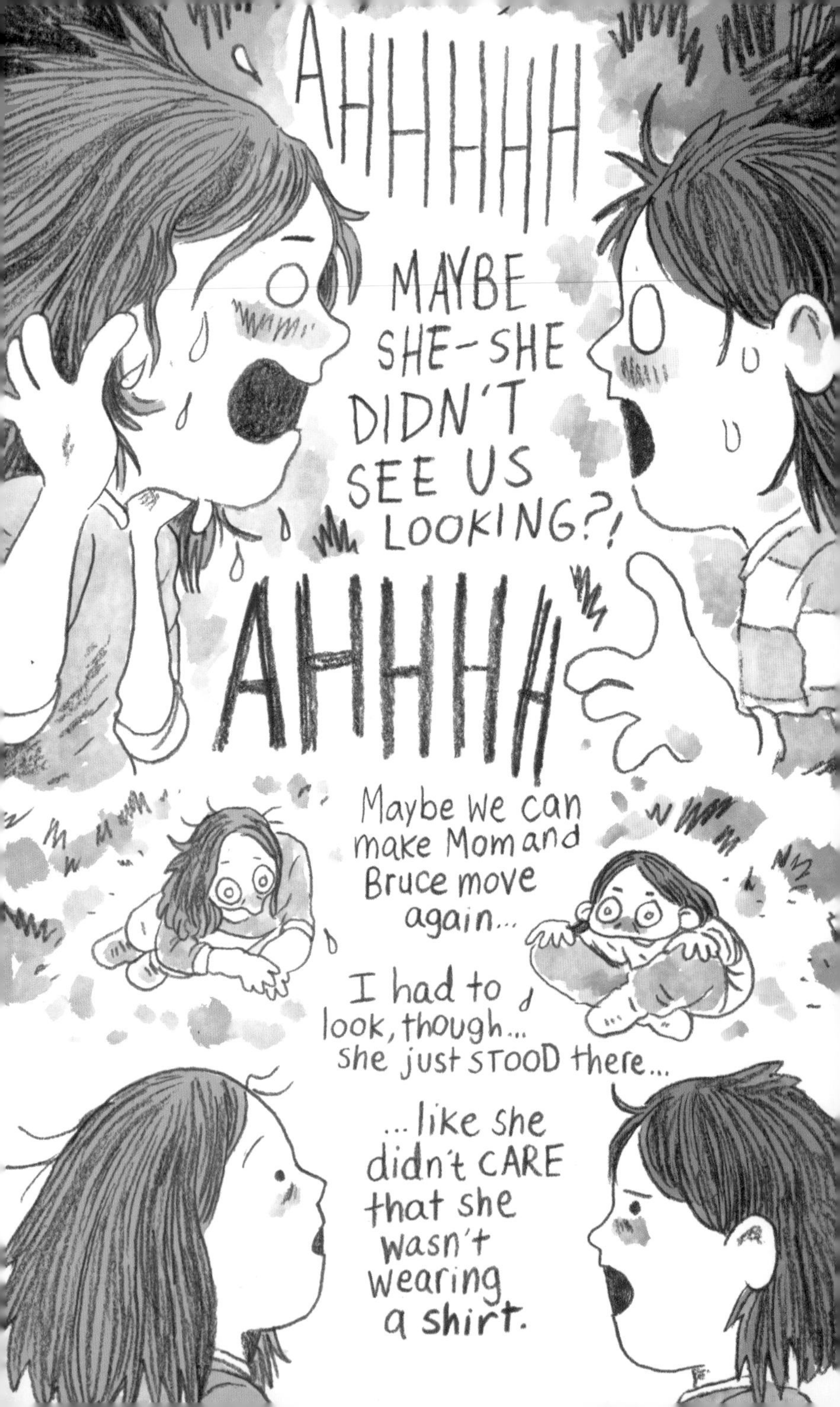
AHHHHHH
MAYBE SHE-SHE DIDN'T SEE US LOOKING?!
AHHHA
Maybe we can make Mom and Bruce move again...
I had to look, though... she just STOOD there...
...like she didn't CARE that she wasn't wearing a shirt.

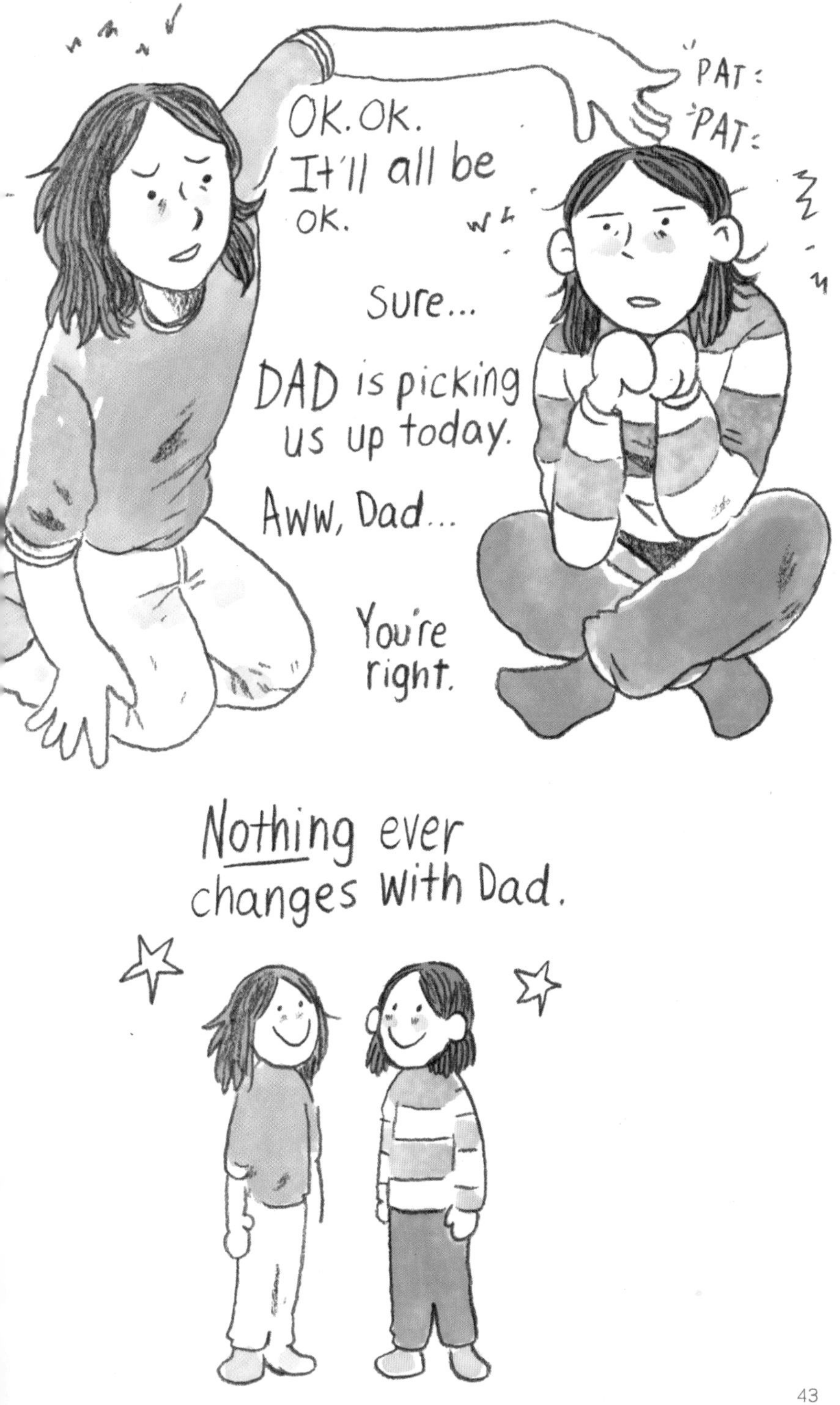
PAT
PAT
OK. OK. It'll all be OK.
Sure...
DAD is picking us up today.
Aww, Dad...
You're right.
Nothing ever changes with Dad.

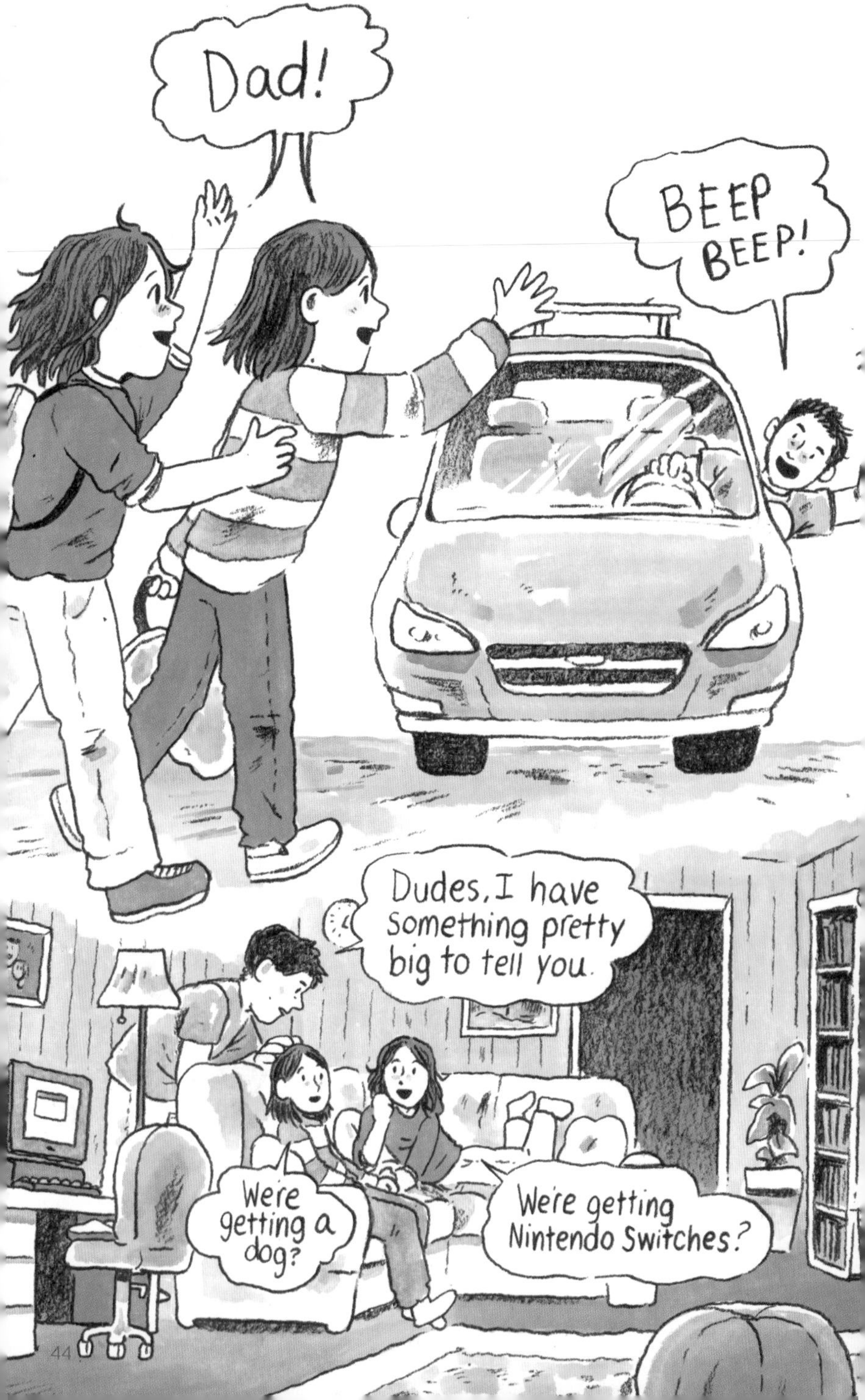
Dad!
BEEP BEEP!
Dudes, I have something pretty big to tell you.
We're getting a dog?
We're getting Nintendo Switches?

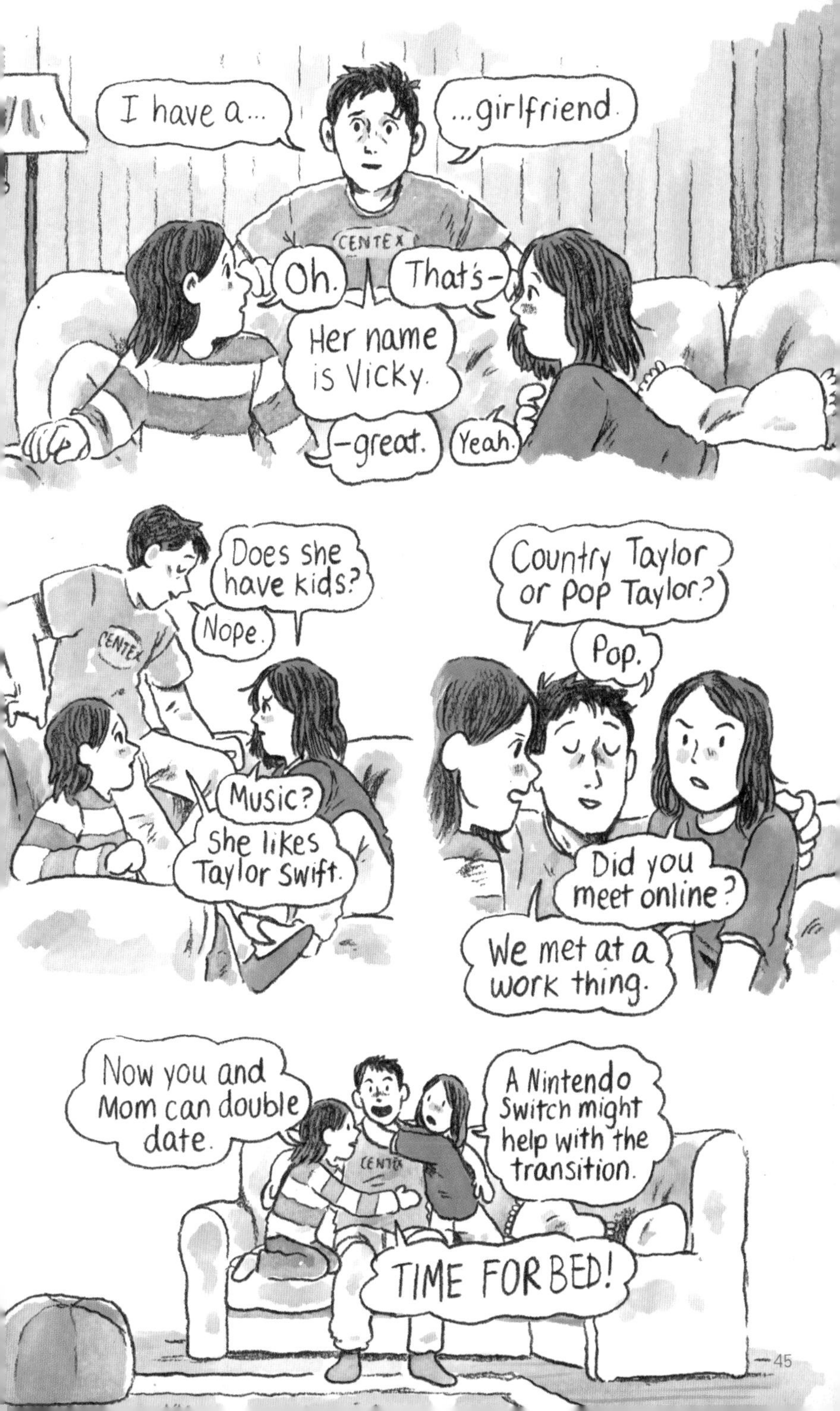
I have a...
...girlfriend.
Oh.
That's–
Her name is Vicky.
–great.
Yeah.
Does she have kids?
Nope.
Music?
She likes Taylor Swift.
Country Taylor or pop Taylor?
Pop.
Did you meet online?
We met at a work thing.
Now you and Mom can double date.
A Nintendo Switch might help with the transition.
TIME FOR BED!

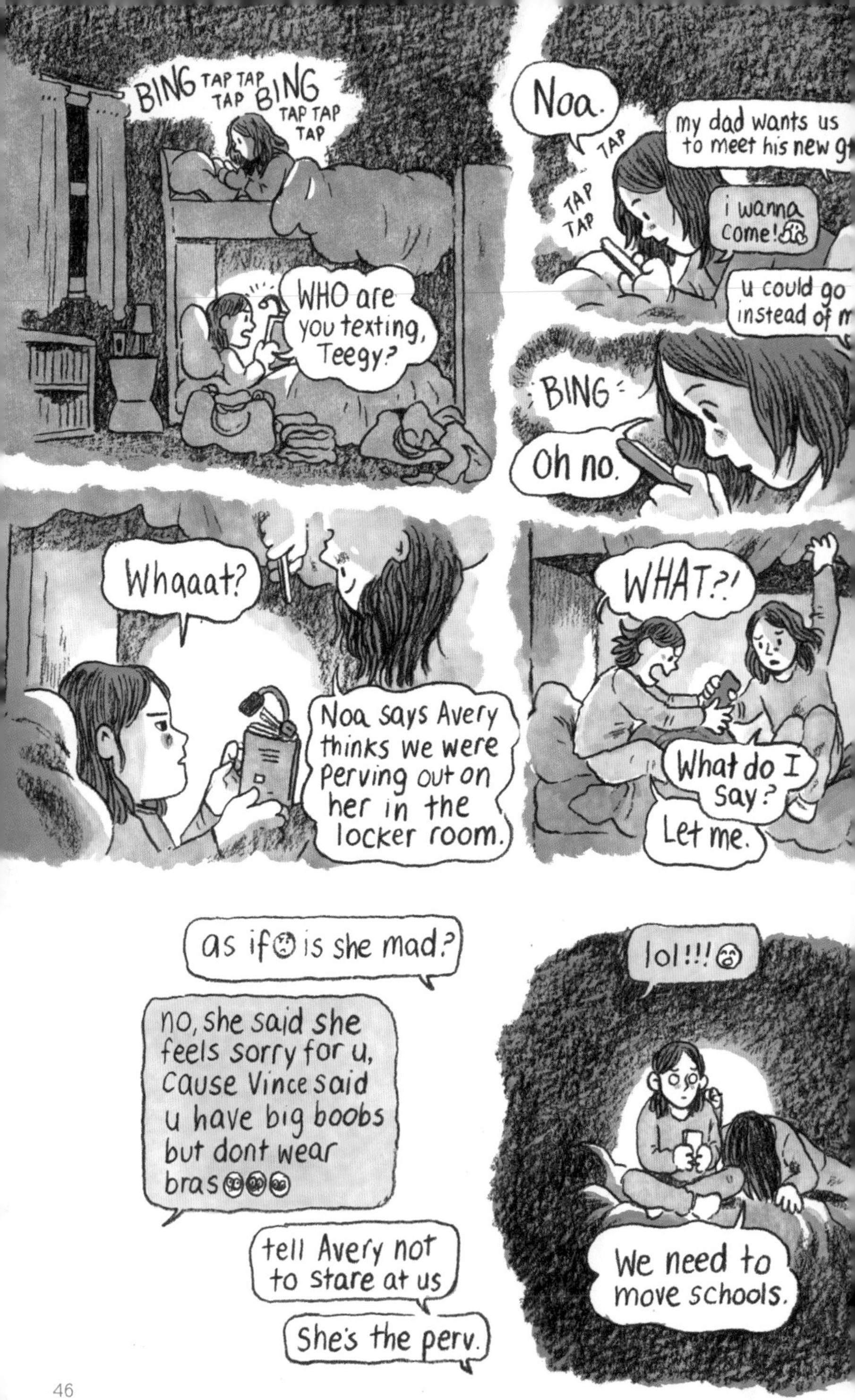
BING TAP TAP TAP BING TAP TAP TAP
WHO are you texting, Teegy?
Noa.
TAP TAP TAP
Whaaat?
Noa says Avery thinks we were perving out on her in the locker room.
WHAT?!
What do I say?
Let me.
as if is she mad?
no, she said she feels sorry for u, cause Vince said u have big boobs but dont wear bras
tell Avery not to stare at us
She's the perv.
lol!!!
We need to move schools.

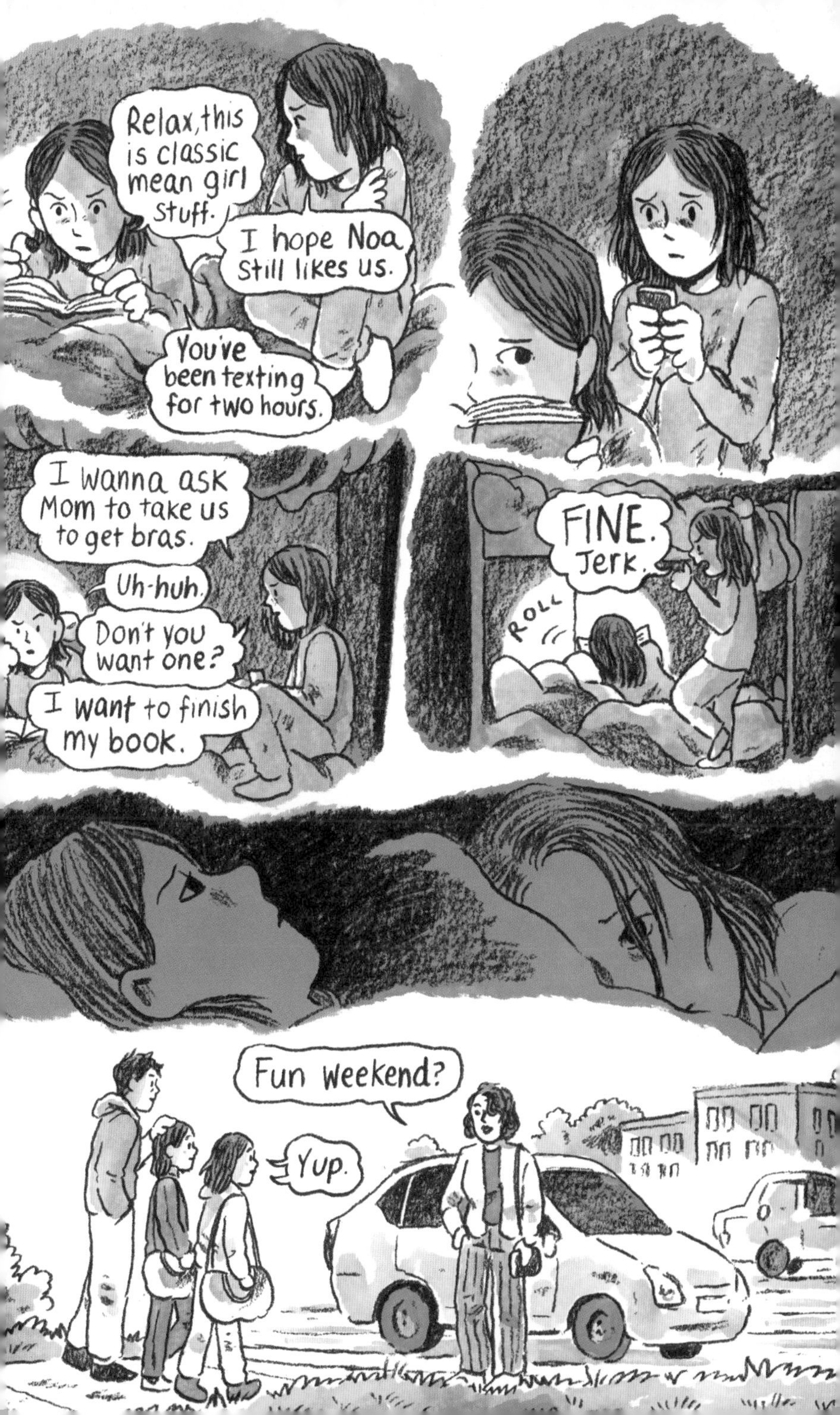
Relax, this is classic mean girl stuff.
I hope Noa still likes us.
You've been texting for two hours.
I wanna ask Mom to take us to get bras.
Uh-huh.
Don't you want one?
I want to finish my book.
FINE. Jerk.
ROLL
Fun weekend?
Yup.

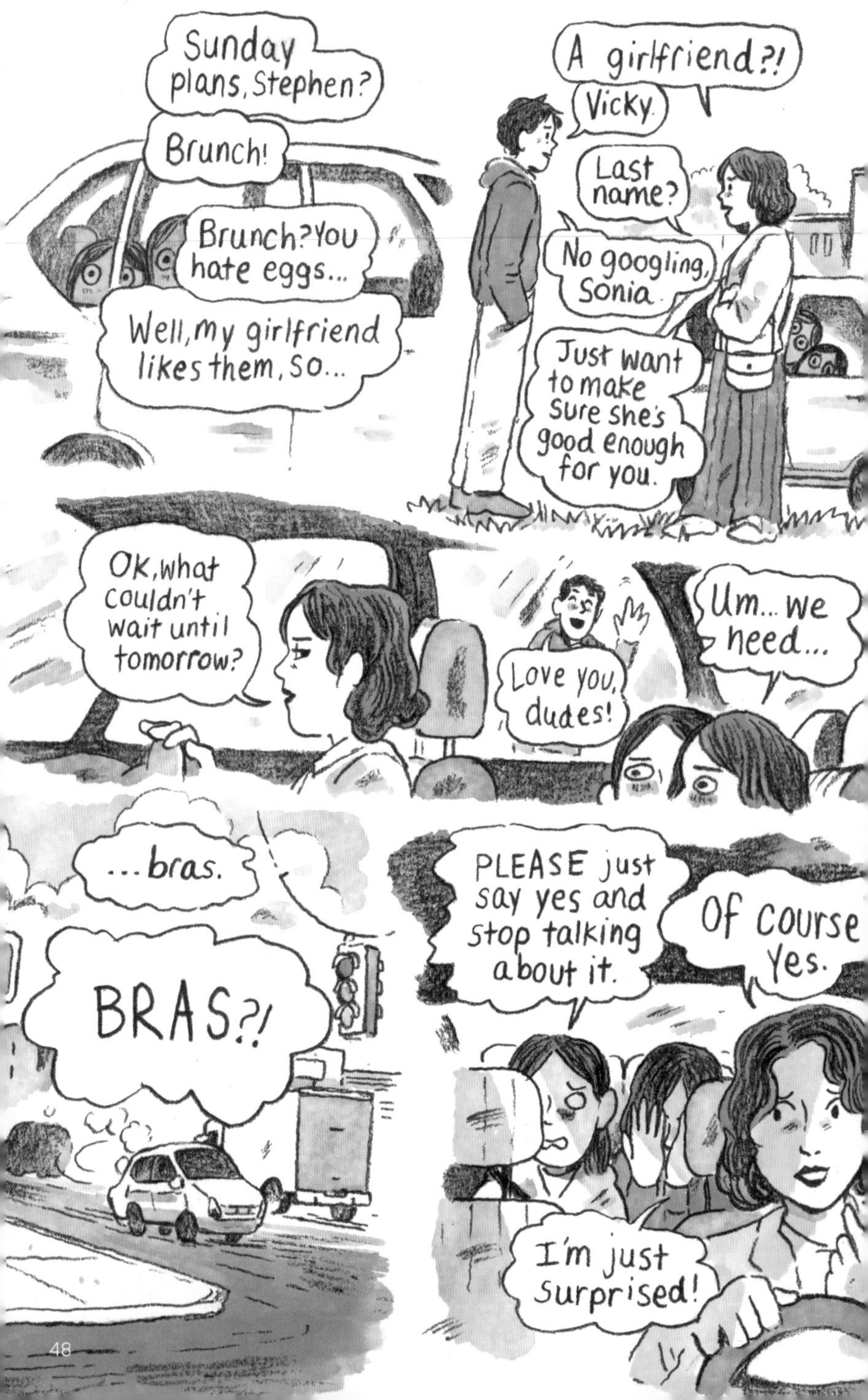
Sunday plans, Stephen?
Brunch!
Brunch? You hate eggs...
Well, my girlfriend likes them, so...
A girlfriend?!
Vicky.
Last name?
No googling, Sonia.
Just want to make sure she's good enough for you.
Ok, what couldn't wait until tomorrow?
Love you, dudes!
Um... we need...
...bras.
BRAS?!
PLEASE just say yes and stop talking about it.
Of course yes.
I'm just surprised!

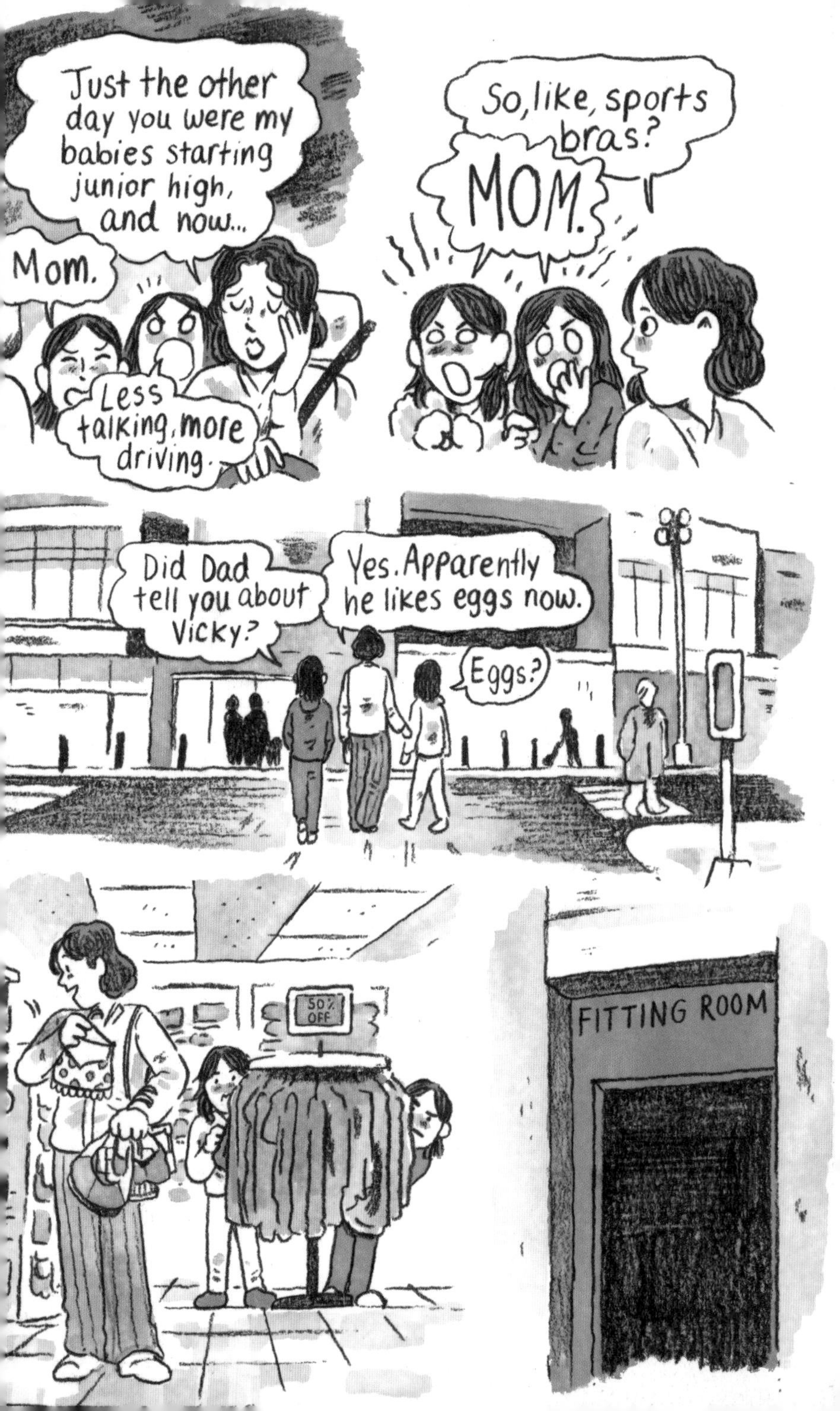
Just the other day you were my babies starting junior high, and now...
Mom.
Less talking, more driving.
So, like, sports bras?
MOM.
Did Dad tell you about Vicky?
Yes. Apparently he likes eggs now.
Eggs?
50% OFF
FITTING ROOM

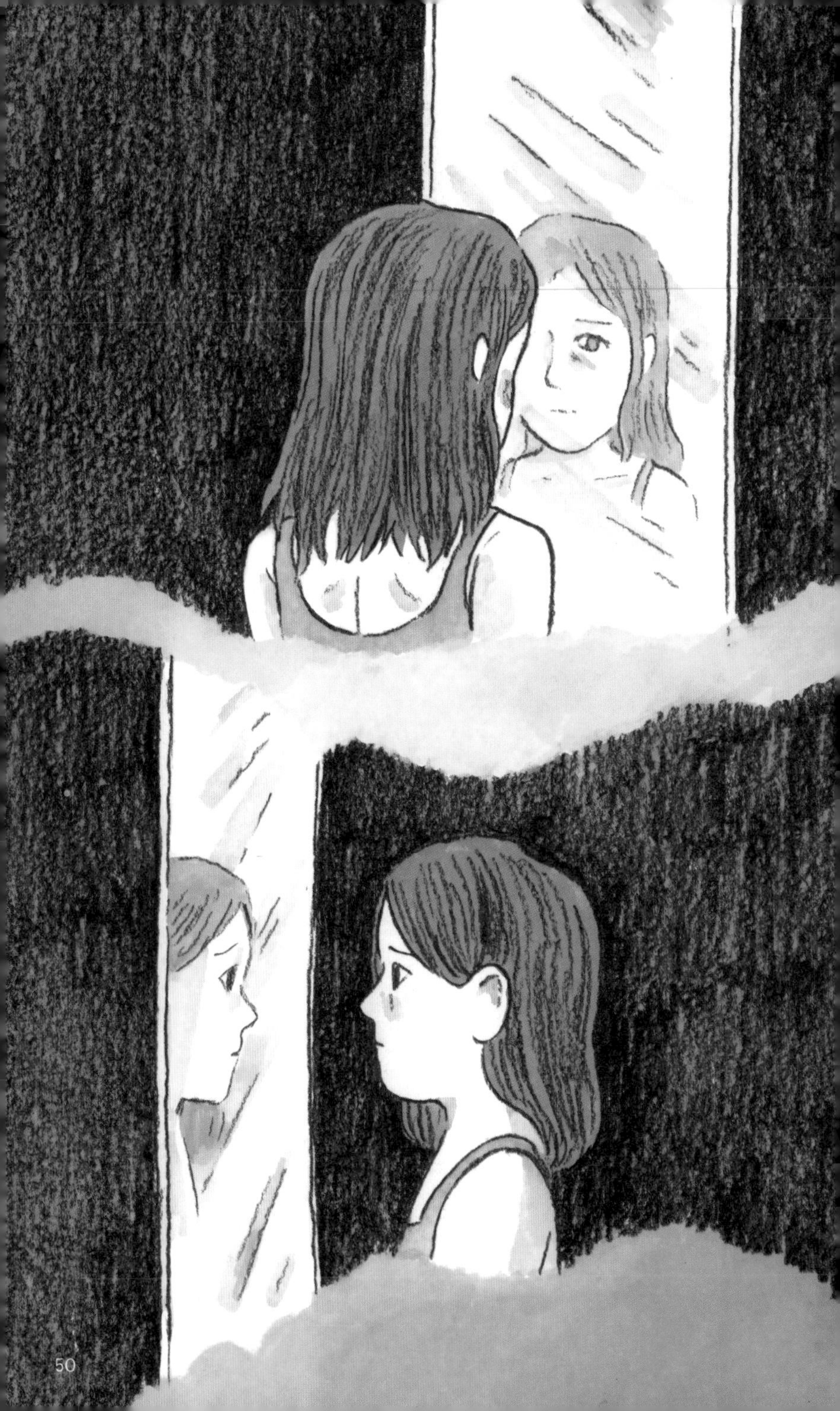

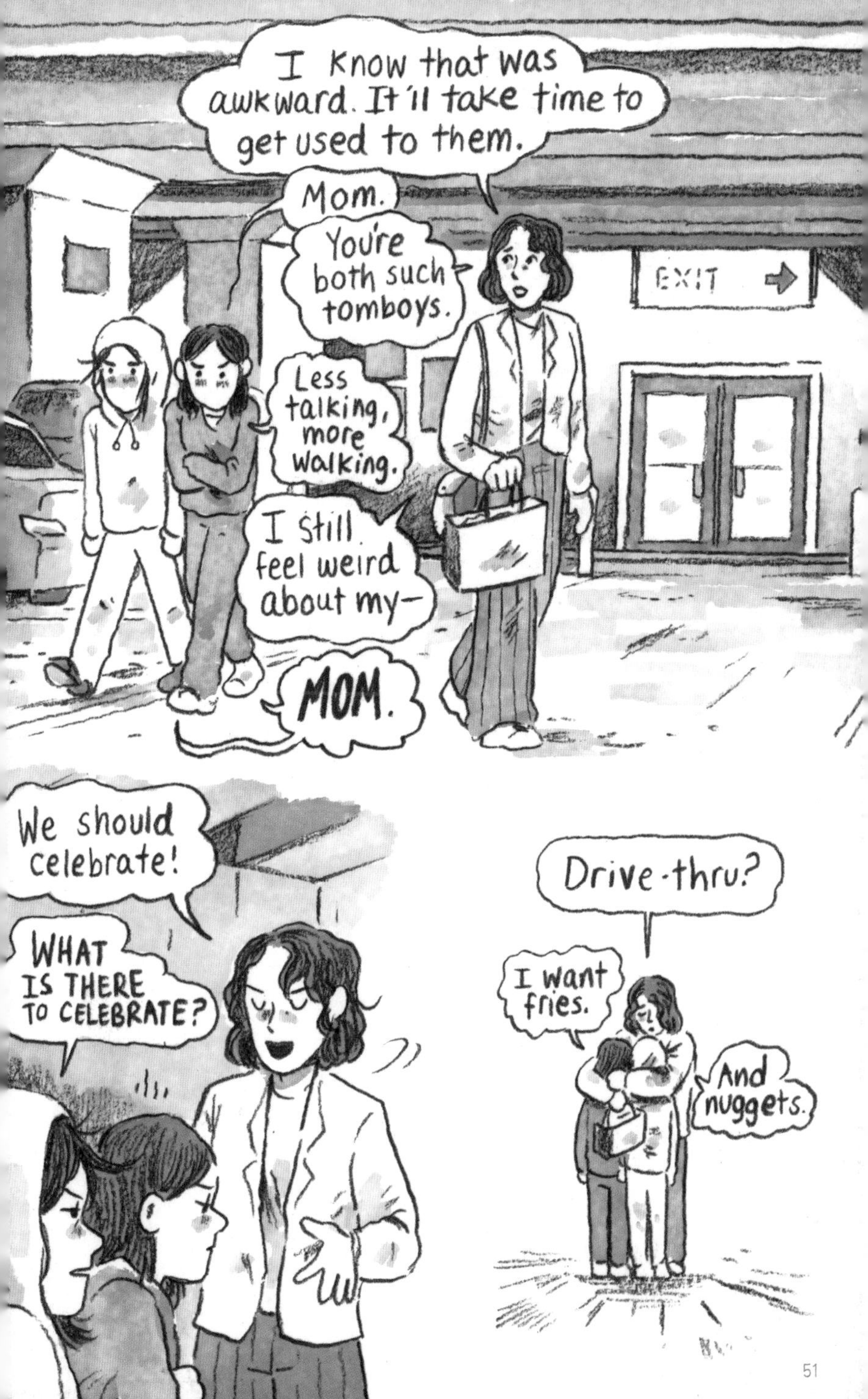
I know that was awkward. It'll take time to get used to them.
Mom.
You're both such tomboys.
Less talking, more walking.
I still feel weird about my—
MOM.
EXIT
We should celebrate!
WHAT IS THERE TO CELEBRATE?
Drive-thru?
I want fries.
And nuggets.

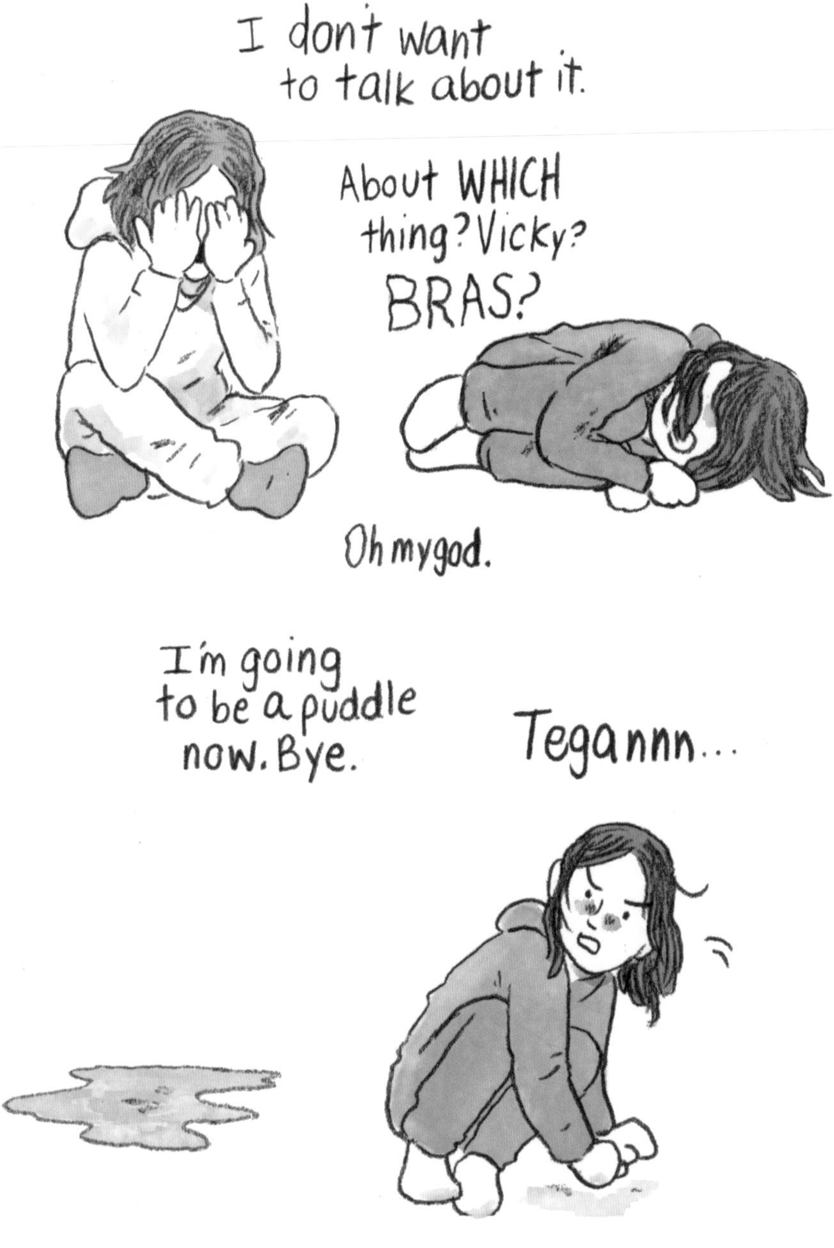
I don't want to talk about it.
About WHICH thing? Vicky? BRAS?
Ohmygod.
I'm going to be a puddle now. Bye.
Tegannn...

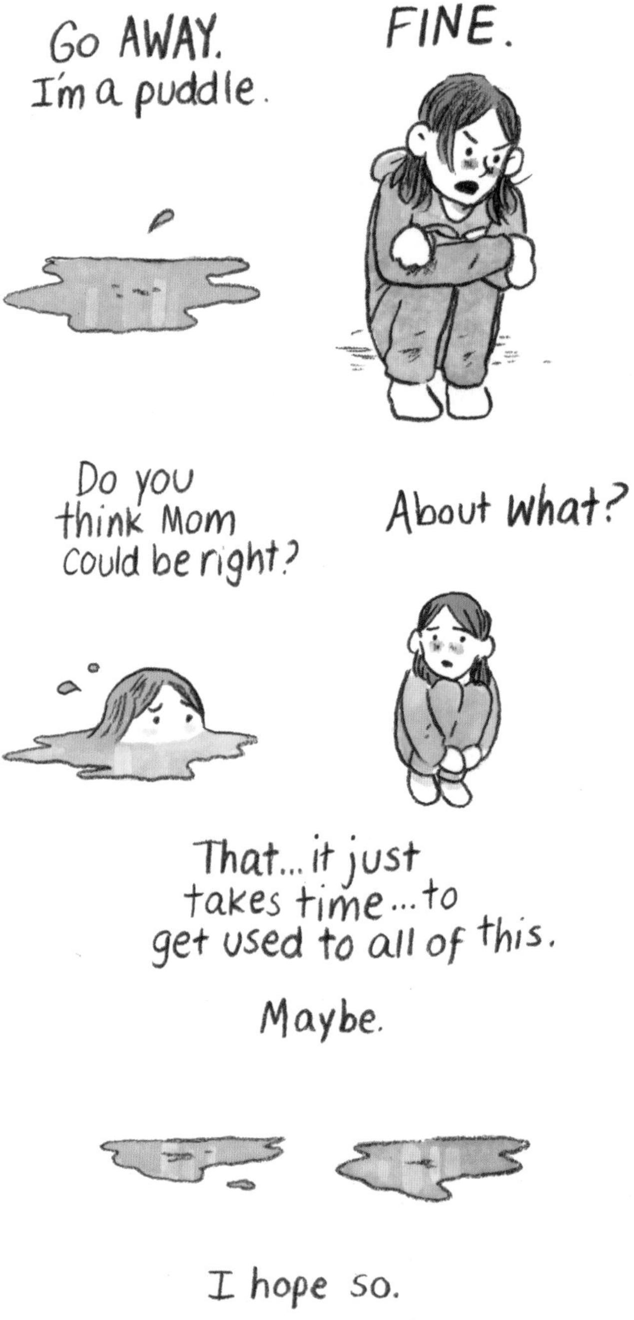
Go AWAY.
I'm a puddle.
FINE.
Do you think Mom could be right?
About what?
That... it just takes time... to get used to all of this.
Maybe.
I hope so.

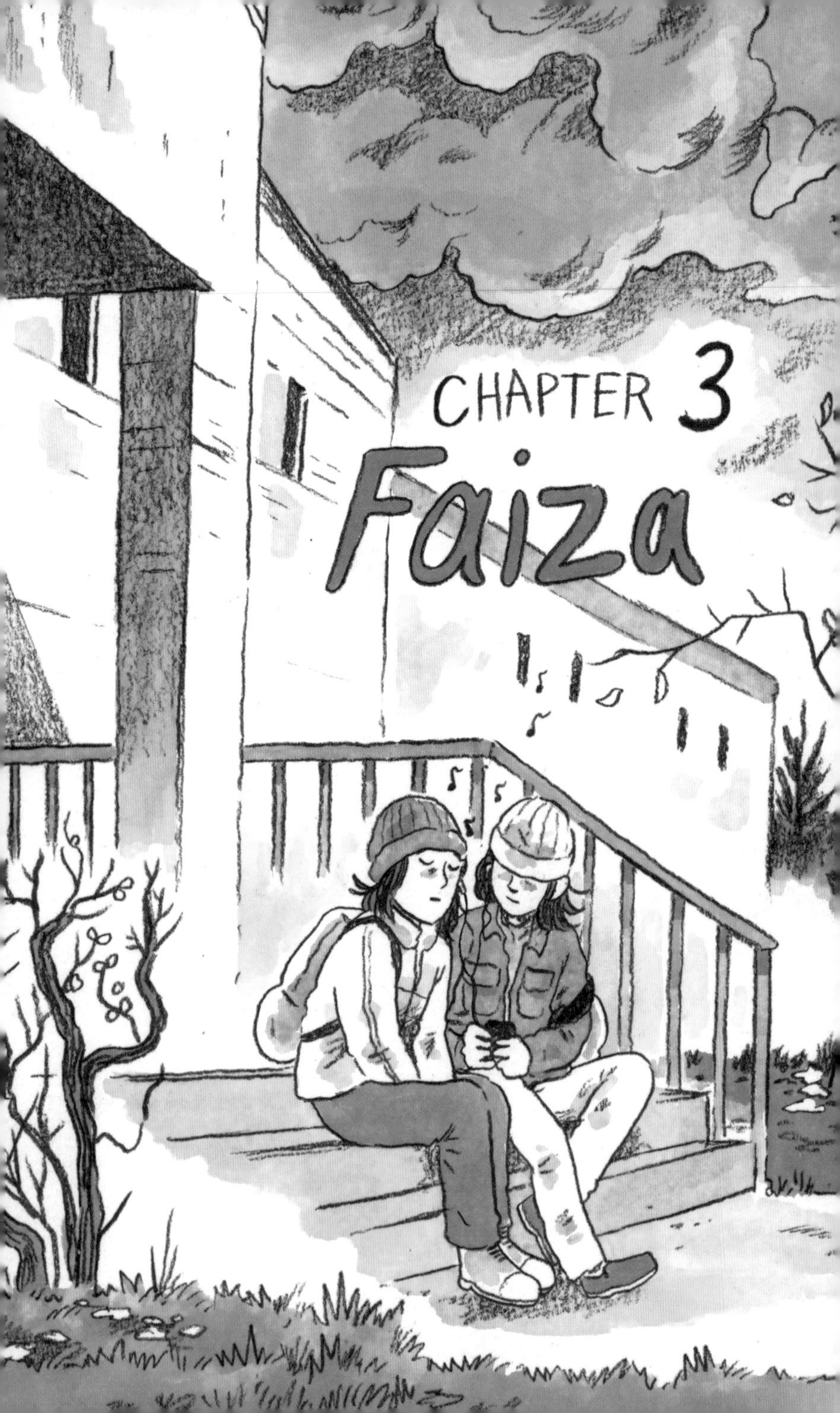
CHAPTER 3
Faiza

Well?

Mom may have had a point...

Time is going so fast, the snow
is almost here.

I don't even have to try anymore
to remember everyone's names,
and they know mine!

The school doesn't even seem
that big now, and our grades
are good...

It feels like a weird time
to see Faiza...

Why? She's our best friend!

I know... but doesn't it feel like...
she's friends with some other
version of us?

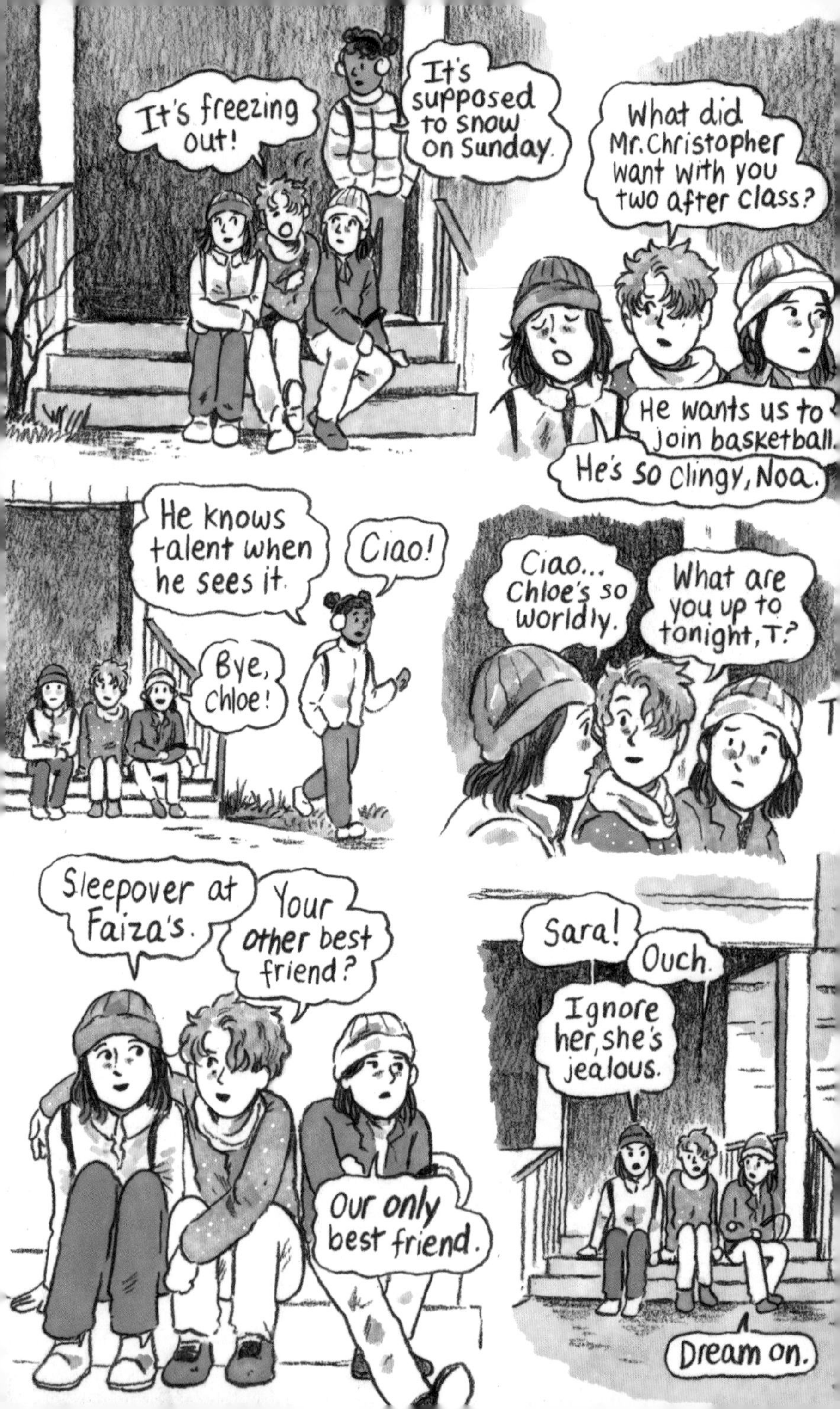
It's freezing out!
It's supposed to snow on Sunday.
What did Mr. Christopher want with you two after class?
He wants us to join basketball.
He's so clingy, Noa.
He knows talent when he sees it.
Ciao!
Bye, Chloe!
Ciao... Chloe's so worldly.
What are you up to tonight, T?
Sleepover at Faiza's.
Your other best friend?
Our only best friend.
Sara!
Ouch.
Ignore her, she's jealous.
Dream on.

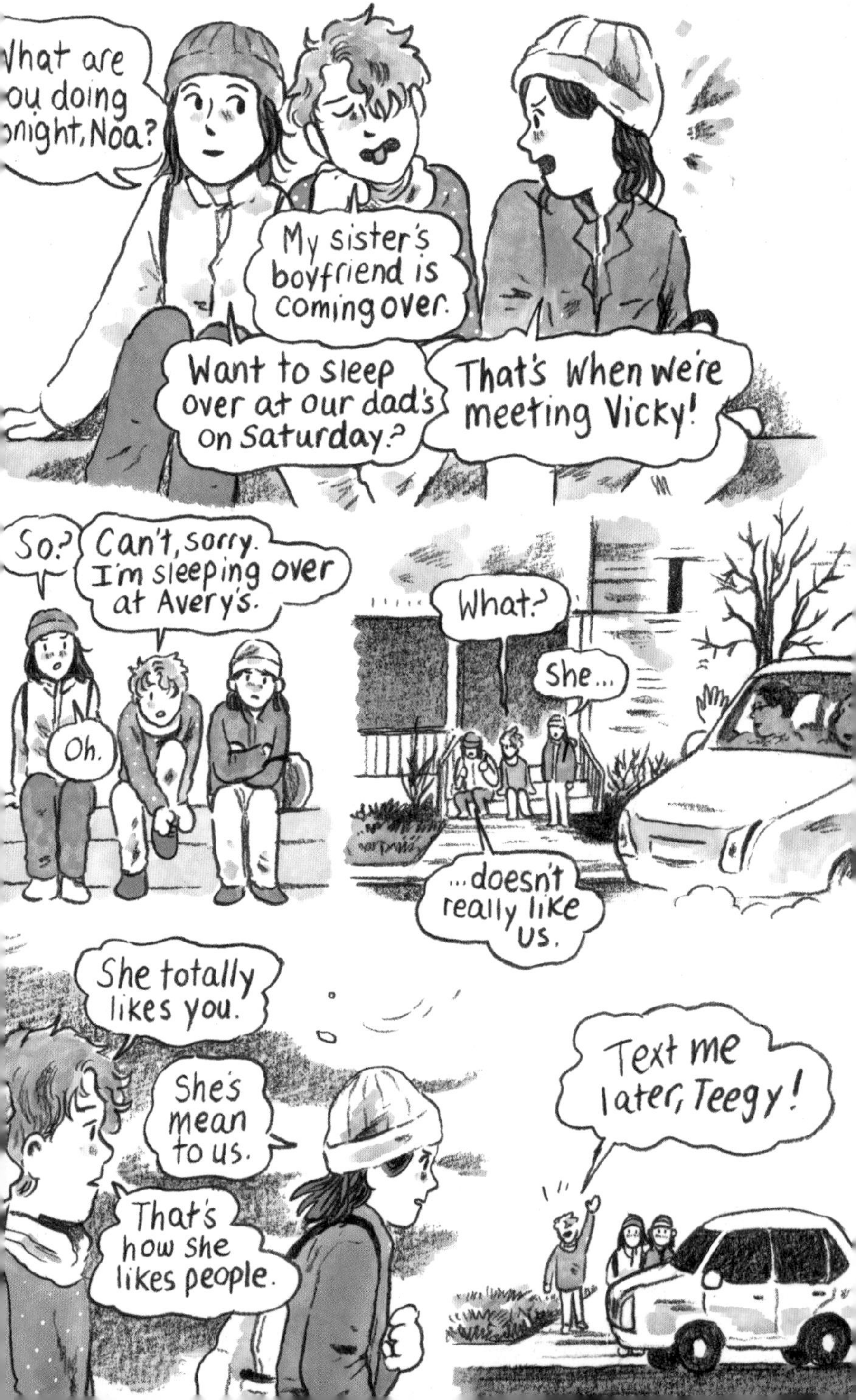
What are you doing tonight, Noa?
My sister's boyfriend is coming over.
Want to sleep over at our dad's on Saturday?
That's when we're meeting Vicky!
So?
Can't, sorry. I'm sleeping over at Avery's.
Oh.
What?
She...
...doesn't really like us.
She totally likes you.
She's mean to us.
That's how she likes people.
Text me later, Teegy!

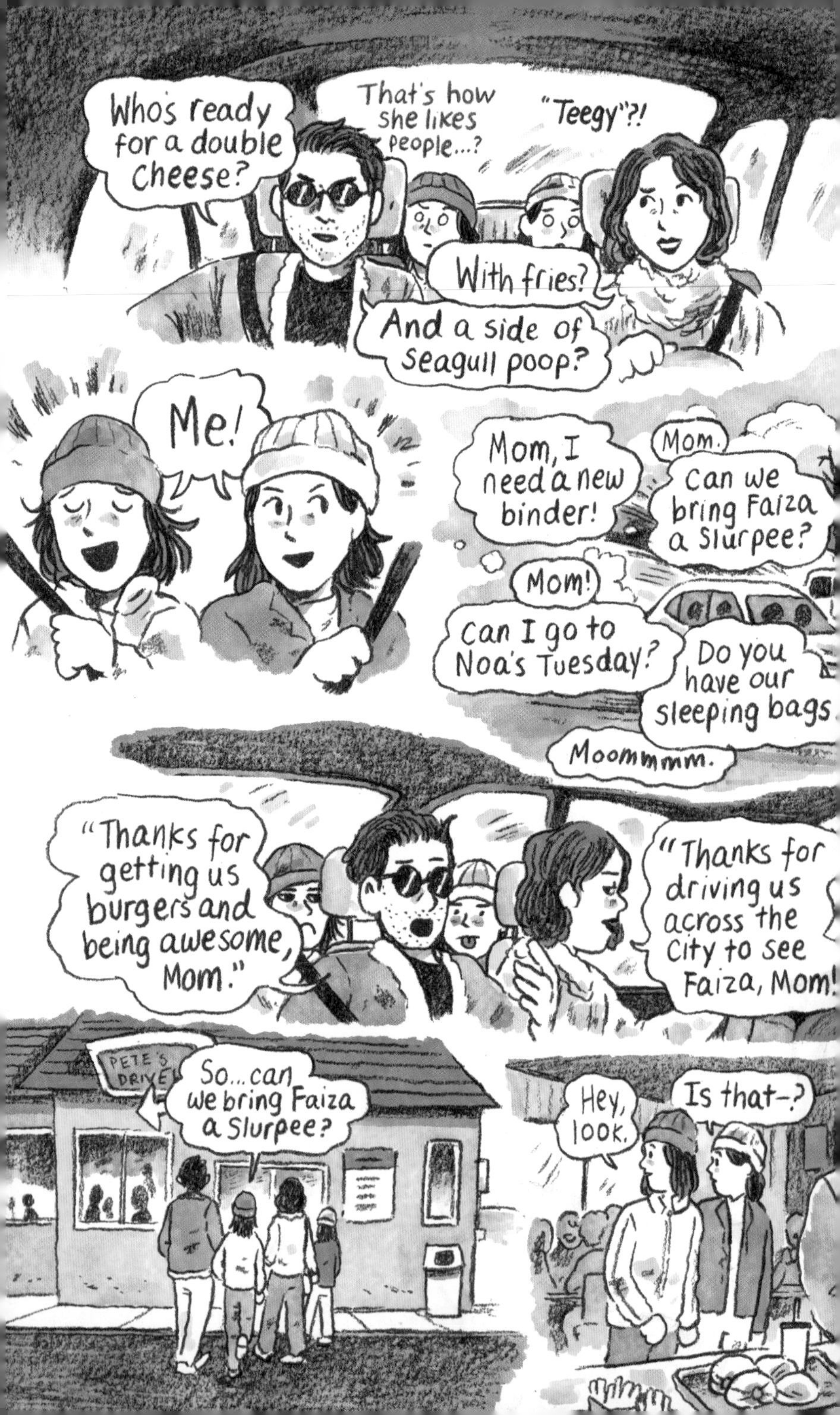
Who's ready for a double cheese?
That's how she likes people...?
"Teegy"?!
With fries?
And a side of seagull poop?
Me!
Mom, I need a new binder!
Mom.
Can we bring Faiza a Slurpee?
Mom!
Can I go to Noa's Tuesday?
Do you have our sleeping bags
Moommmm.
"Thanks for getting us burgers and being awesome, Mom."
"Thanks for driving us across the city to see Faiza, Mom!
PETE'S DRIVE
So...can we bring Faiza a Slurpee?
Hey, look.
Is that-?

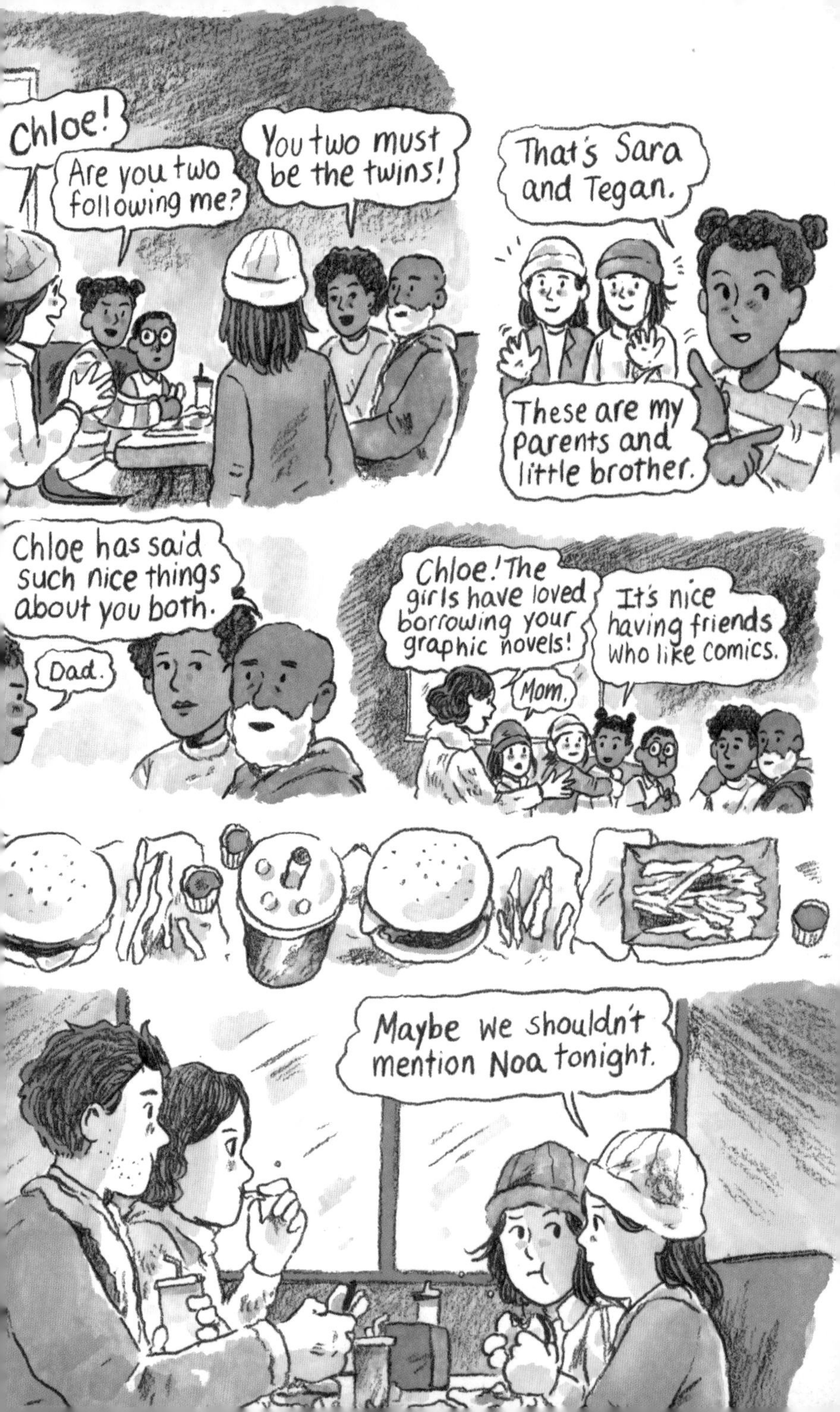
Chloe!
Are you two following me?
You two must be the twins!
That's Sara and Tegan.
These are my parents and little brother.
Chloe has said such nice things about you both.
Dad.
Chloe! The girls have loved borrowing your graphic novels!
Mom.
It's nice having friends who like comics.
Maybe we shouldn't mention Noa tonight.

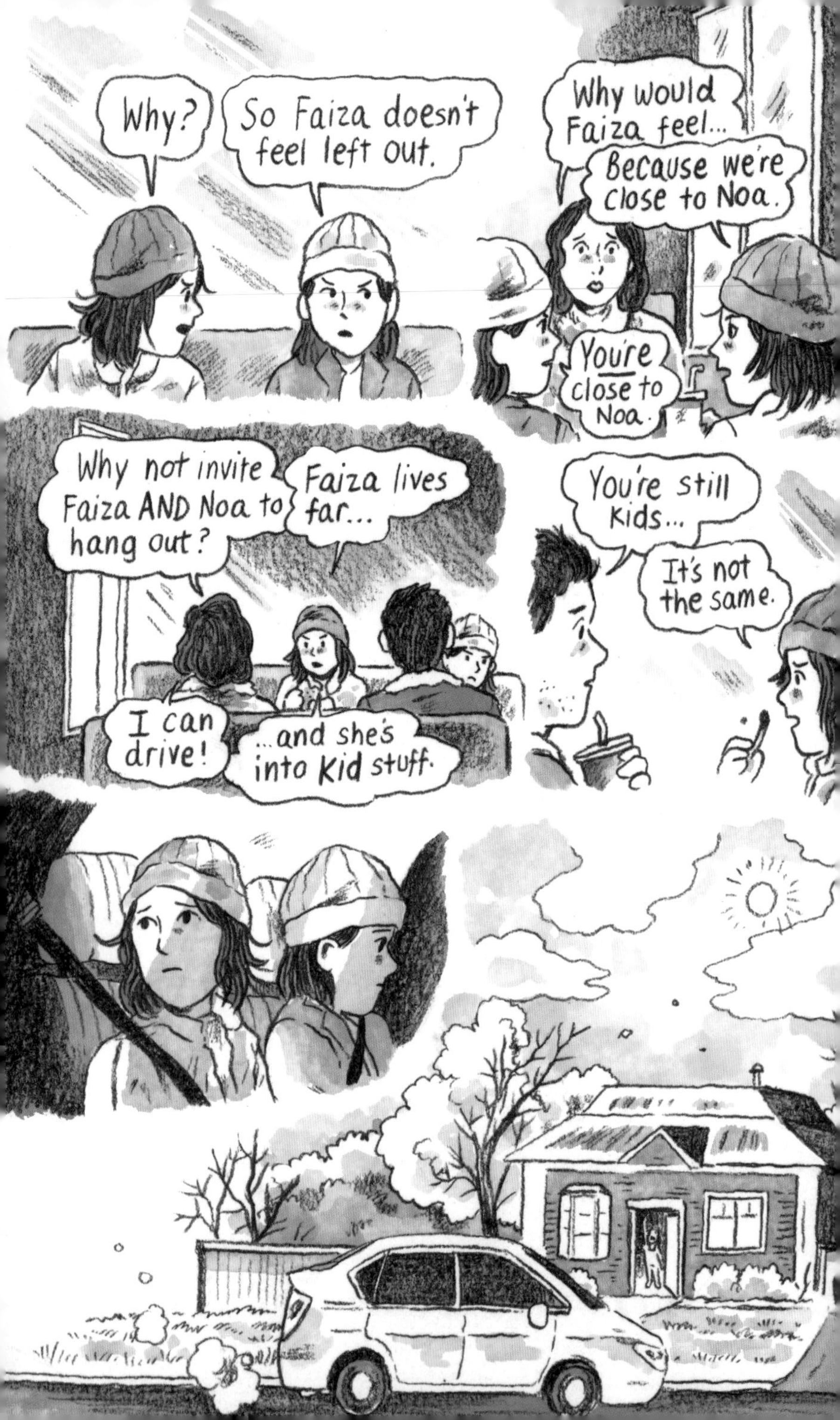
Why?
So Faiza doesn't feel left out.
Why would Faiza feel...
Because we're close to Noa.
You're close to Noa.
Why not invite Faiza AND Noa to hang out?
Faiza lives far...
I can drive!
...and she's into kid stuff.
You're still kids...
It's not the same.

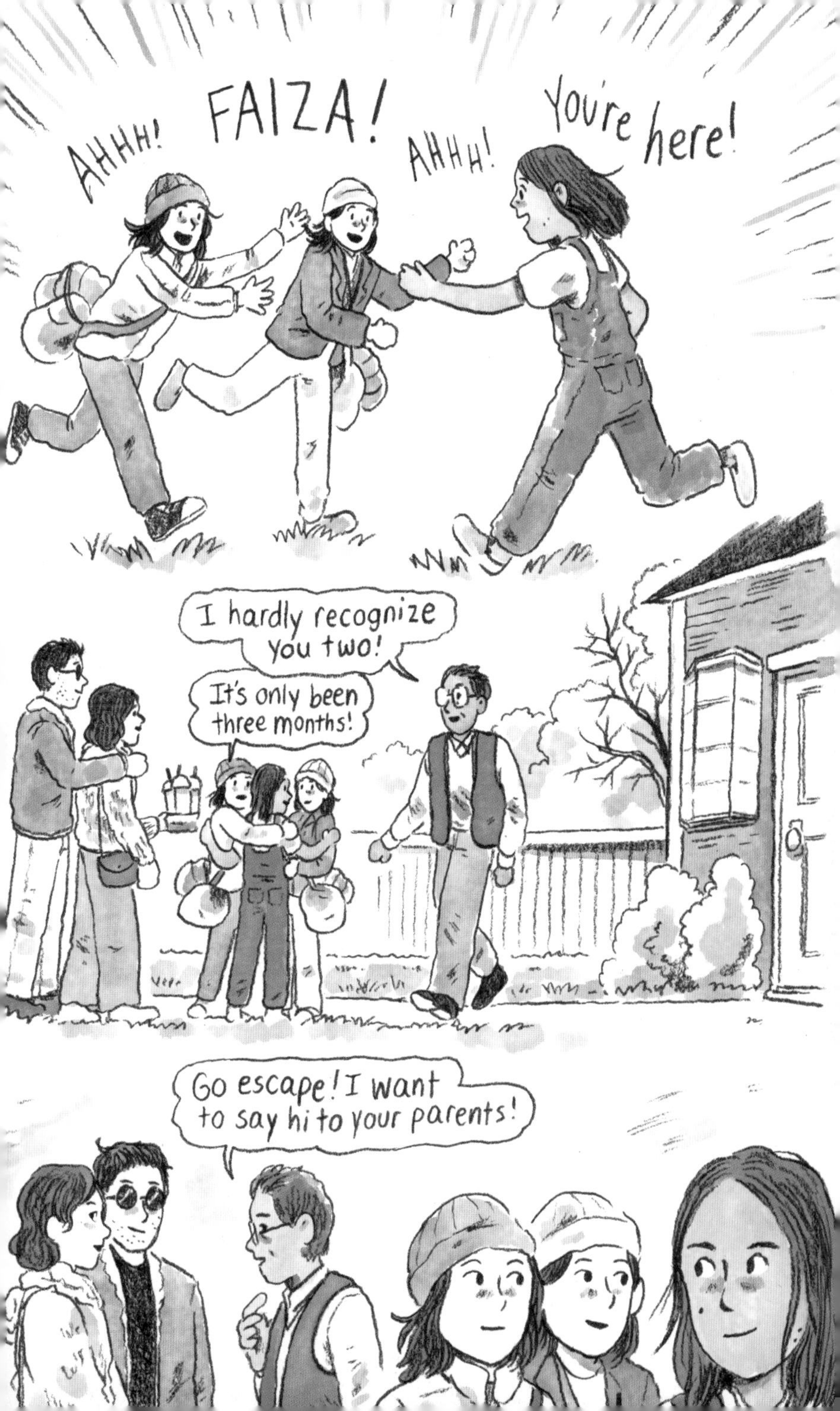
AHHH!
FAIZA!
AHHH!
You're here!
I hardly recognize you two!
It's only been three months!
Go escape! I want to say hi to your parents!

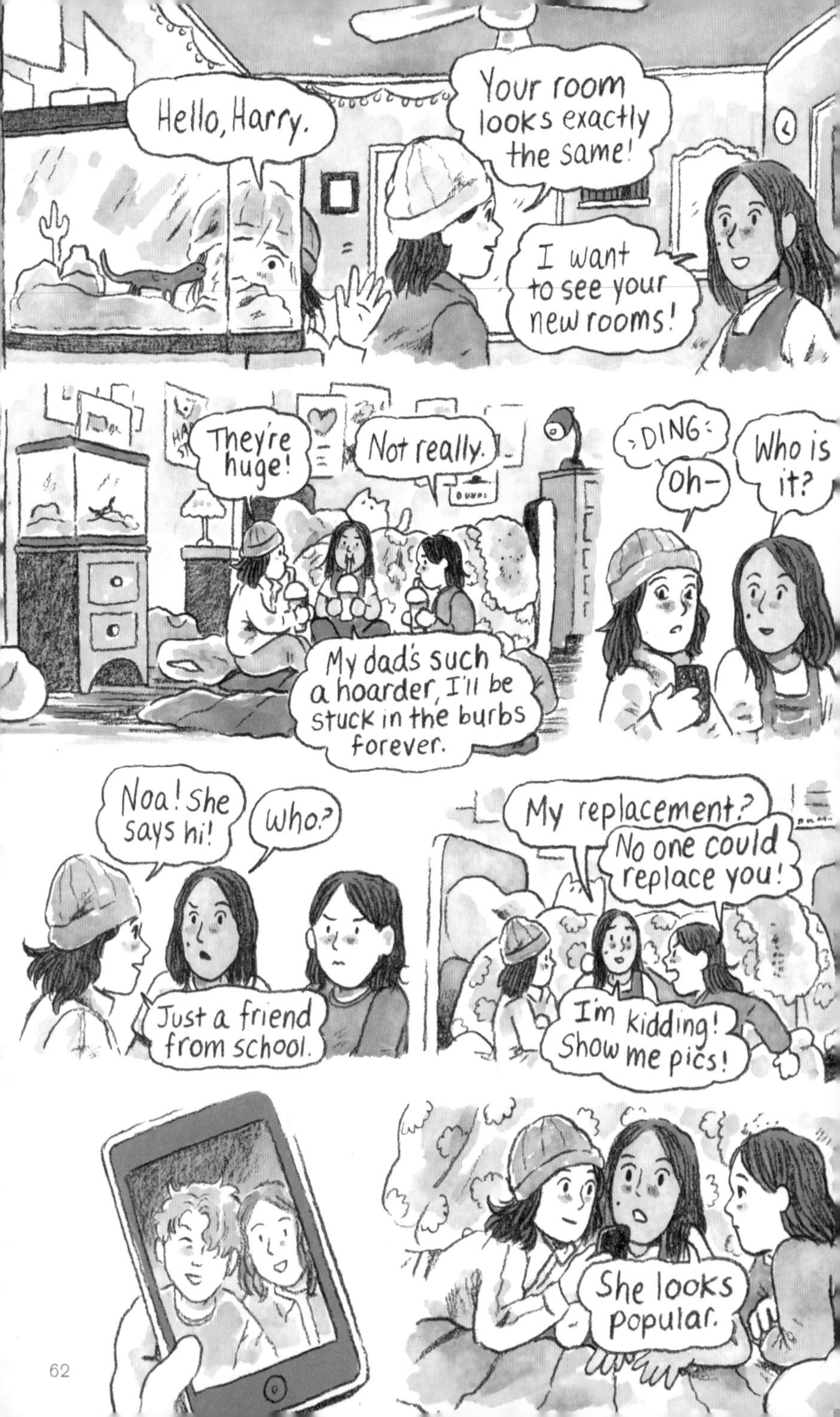

Hello, Harry.
Your room looks exactly the same!
I want to see your new rooms!
They're huge!
Not really.
My dad's such a hoarder, I'll be stuck in the burbs forever.
DING
Oh-
Who is it?
Noa! She says hi!
Who?
Just a friend from school.
My replacement?
No one could replace you!
I'm kidding! Show me pics!
She looks popular.

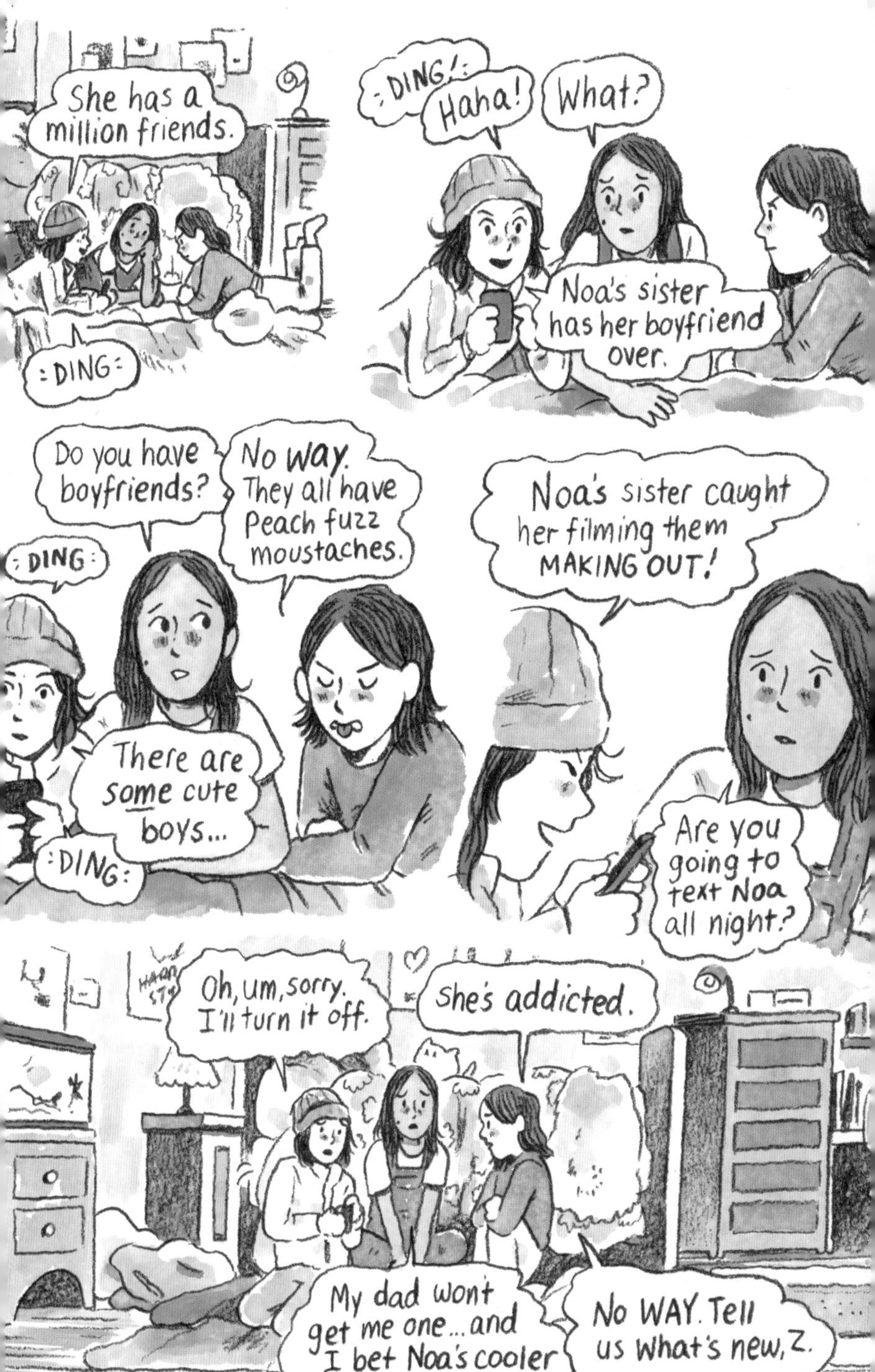
She has a million friends.
DING
DING!
Haha!
What?
Noa's sister has her boyfriend over.
Do you have boyfriends?
No way. They all have peach fuzz moustaches.
DING
There are some cute boys...
DING
Noa's sister caught her filming them MAKING OUT!
Are you going to text Noa all night?
Oh, um, sorry. I'll turn it off.
She's addicted.
My dad won't get me one... and I bet Noa's cooler than me...
No WAY. Tell us what's new, Z.

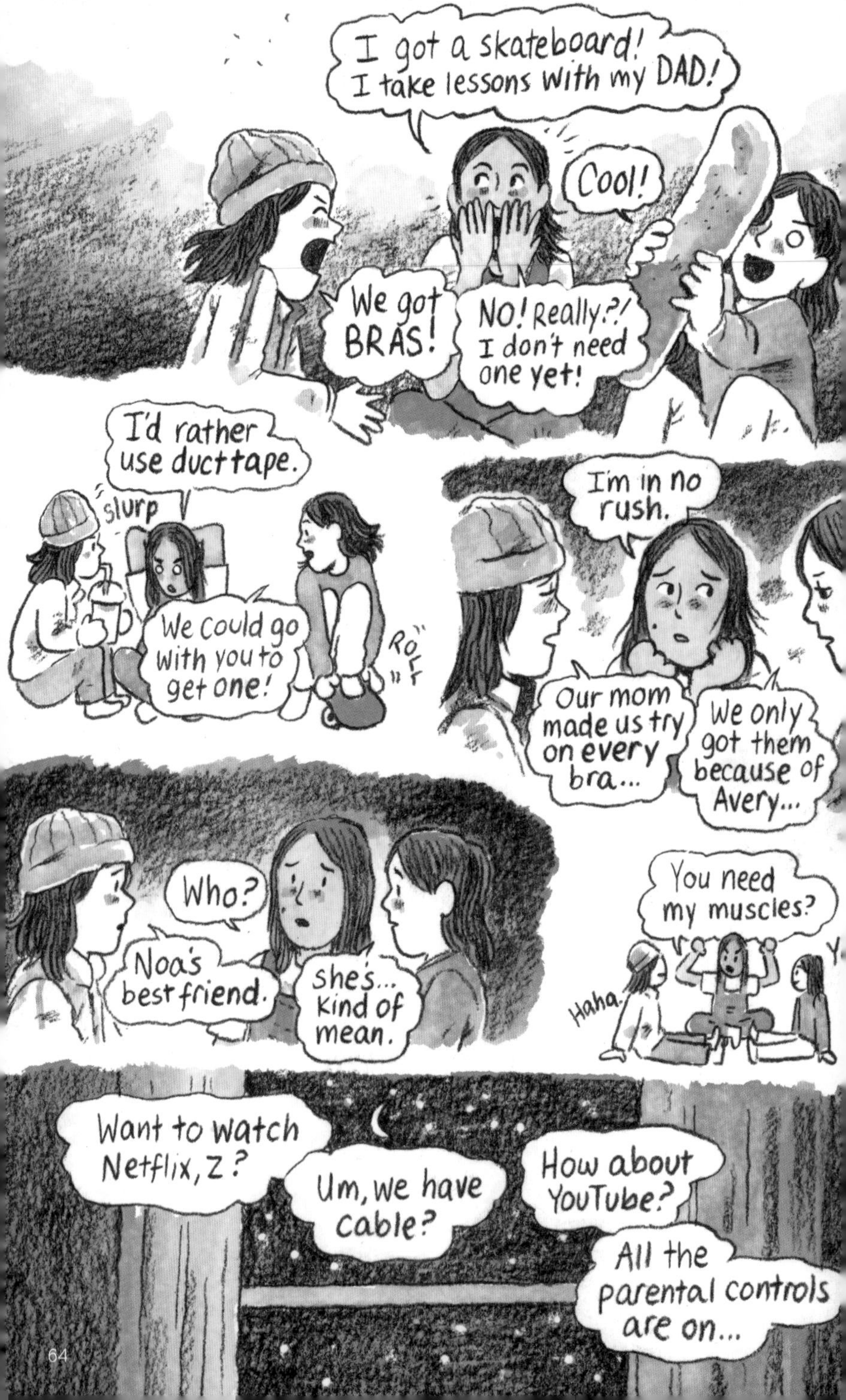
I got a skateboard! I take lessons with my DAD!
Cool!
We got BRAS!
NO! Really?! I don't need one yet!
I'd rather use duct tape.
slurp
We could go with you to get one!
Roll
I'm in no rush.
Our mom made us try on every bra...
We only got them because of Avery...
Who?
Noa's best friend.
She's... kind of mean.
You need my muscles?
Haha.
Want to watch Netflix, Z?
Um, we have cable?
How about YouTube?
All the parental controls are on...

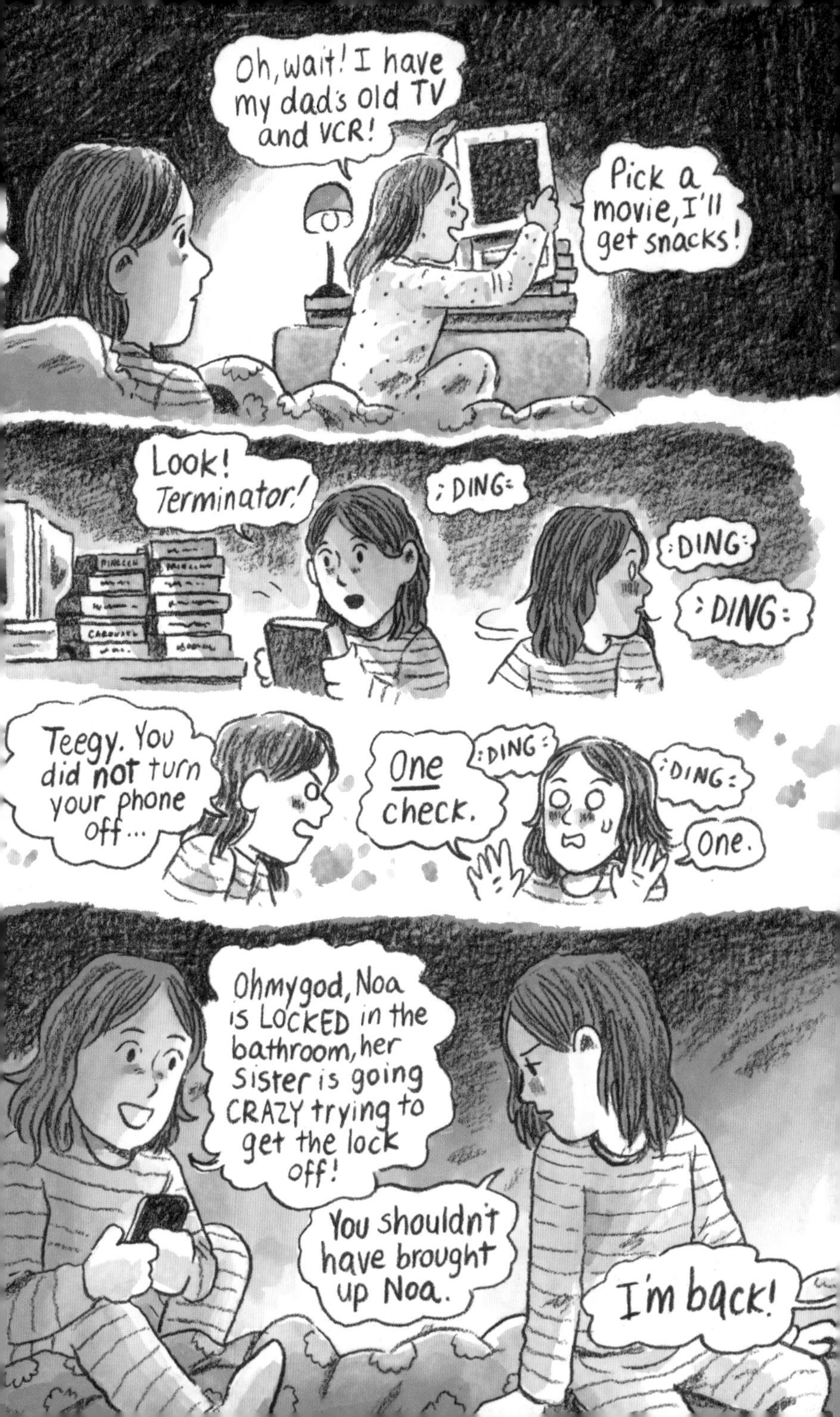
Oh, wait! I have my dad's old TV and VCR!
Pick a movie, I'll get snacks!
Look! Terminator!
DING
DING
DING
Teegy. You did **not** turn your phone off...
One check.
DING
DING
One.
Ohmygod, Noa is LOCKED in the bathroom, her sister is going CRAZY trying to get the lock off!
You shouldn't have brought up Noa.
I'm back!

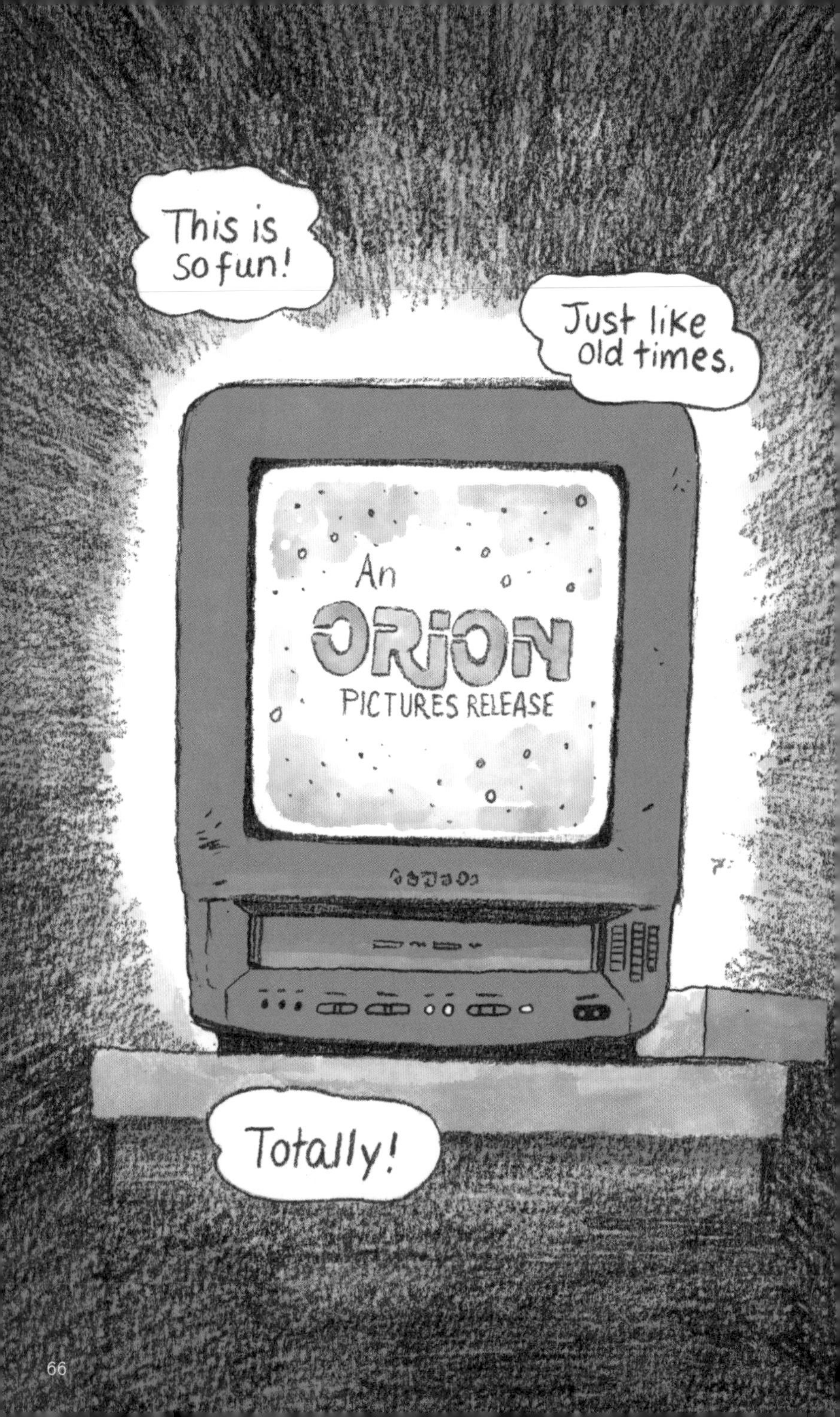
This is so fun!
Just like old times.
An
ORION
PICTURES RELEASE
Totally!

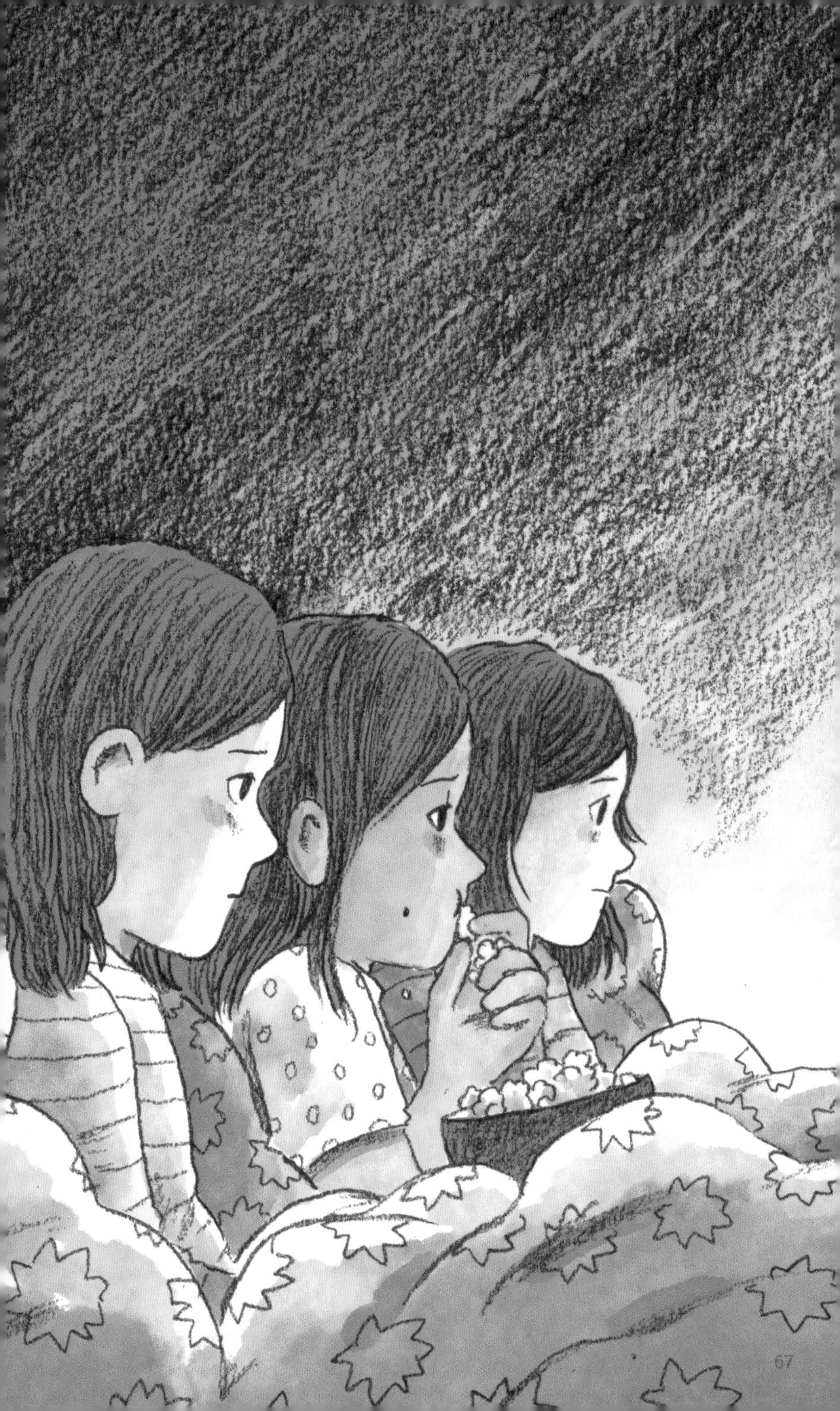

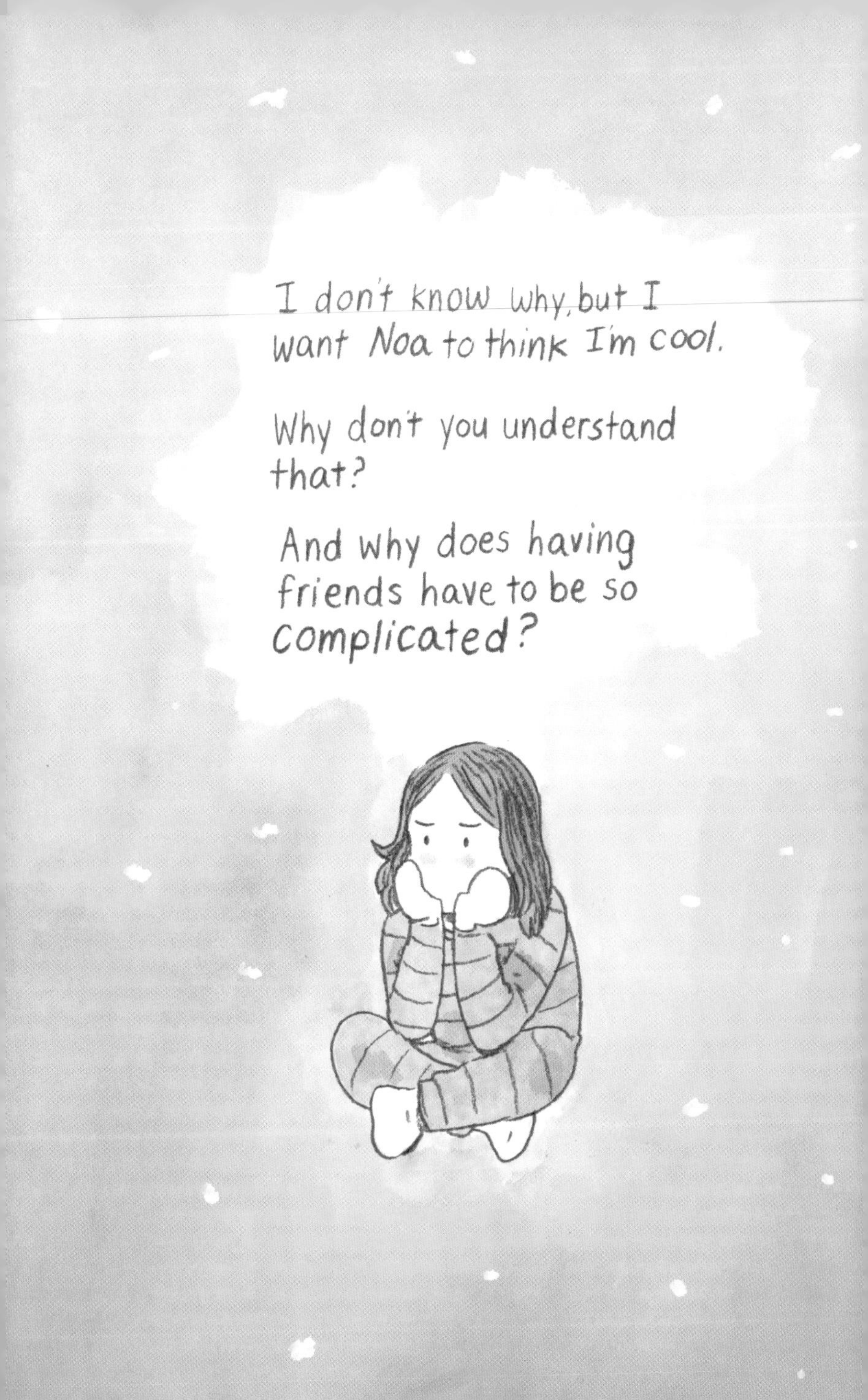
I don't know why, but I want Noa to think I'm cool.
Why don't you understand that?
And why does having friends have to be so complicated?

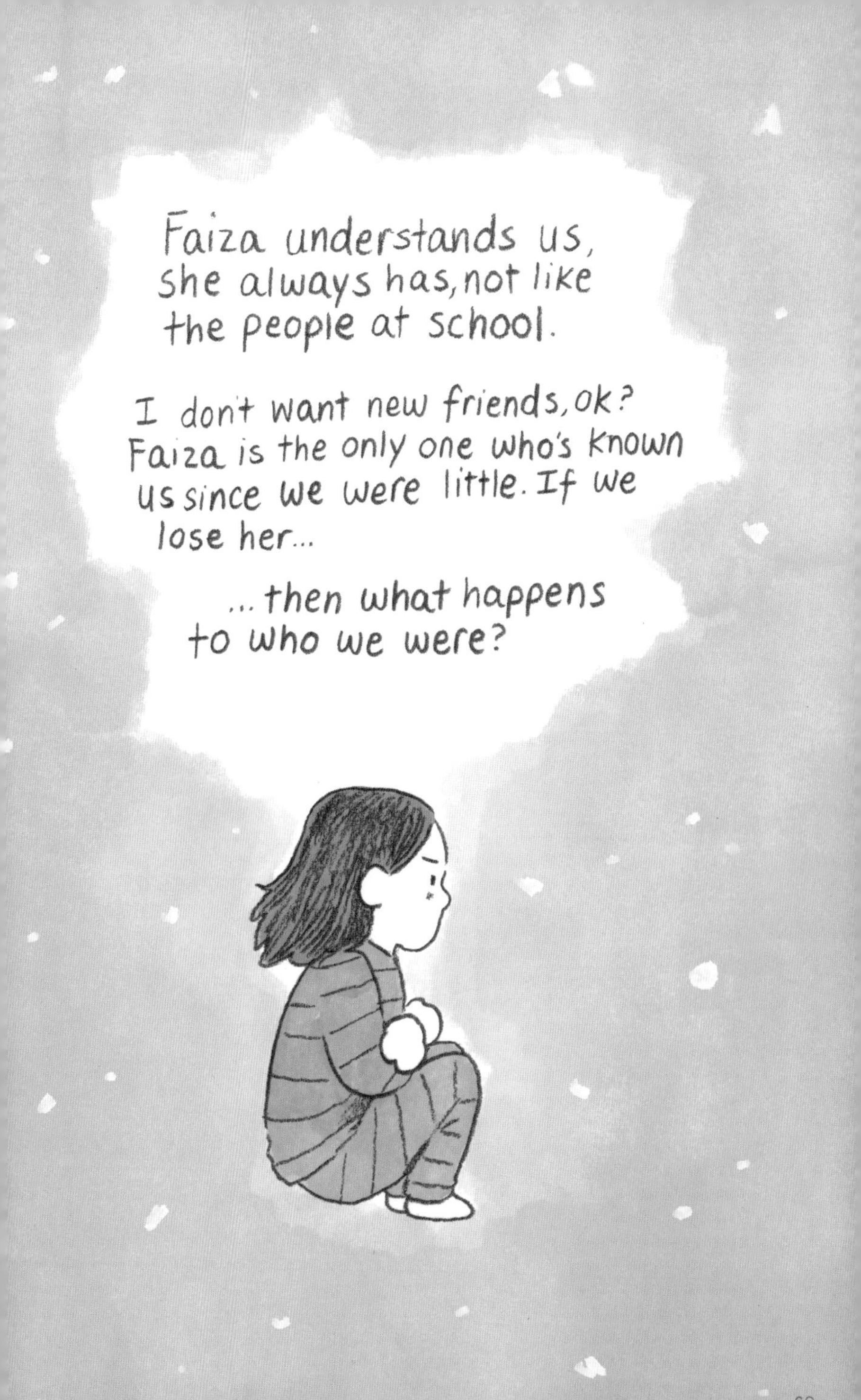
Faiza understands us, she always has, not like the people at school.
I don't want new friends, ok? Faiza is the only one who's known us since we were little. If we lose her...
...then what happens to who we were?

CHAPTER 4
PARTY

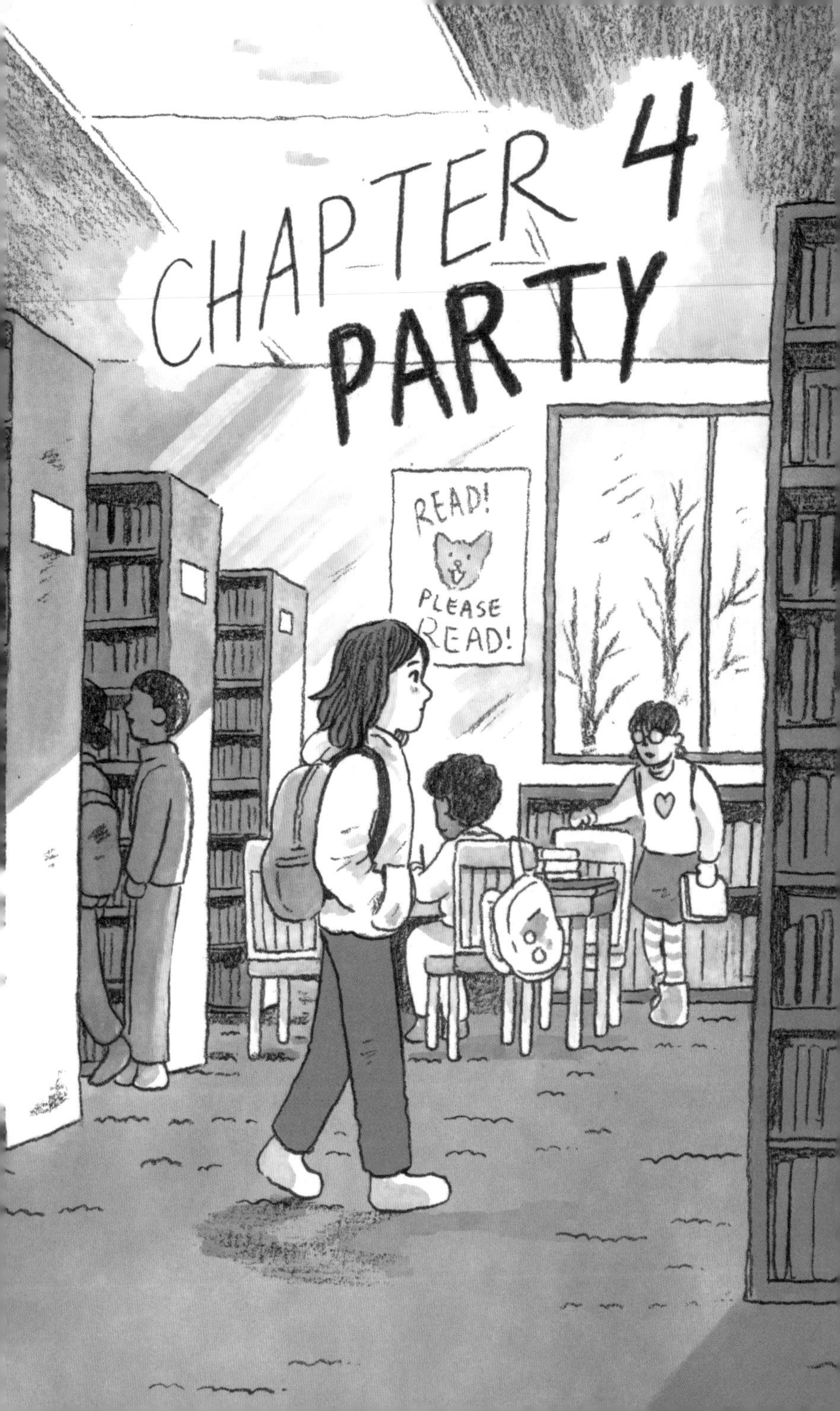

READ!
PLEASE
READ!

I have this
feeling, like...

... something
big is on its way.

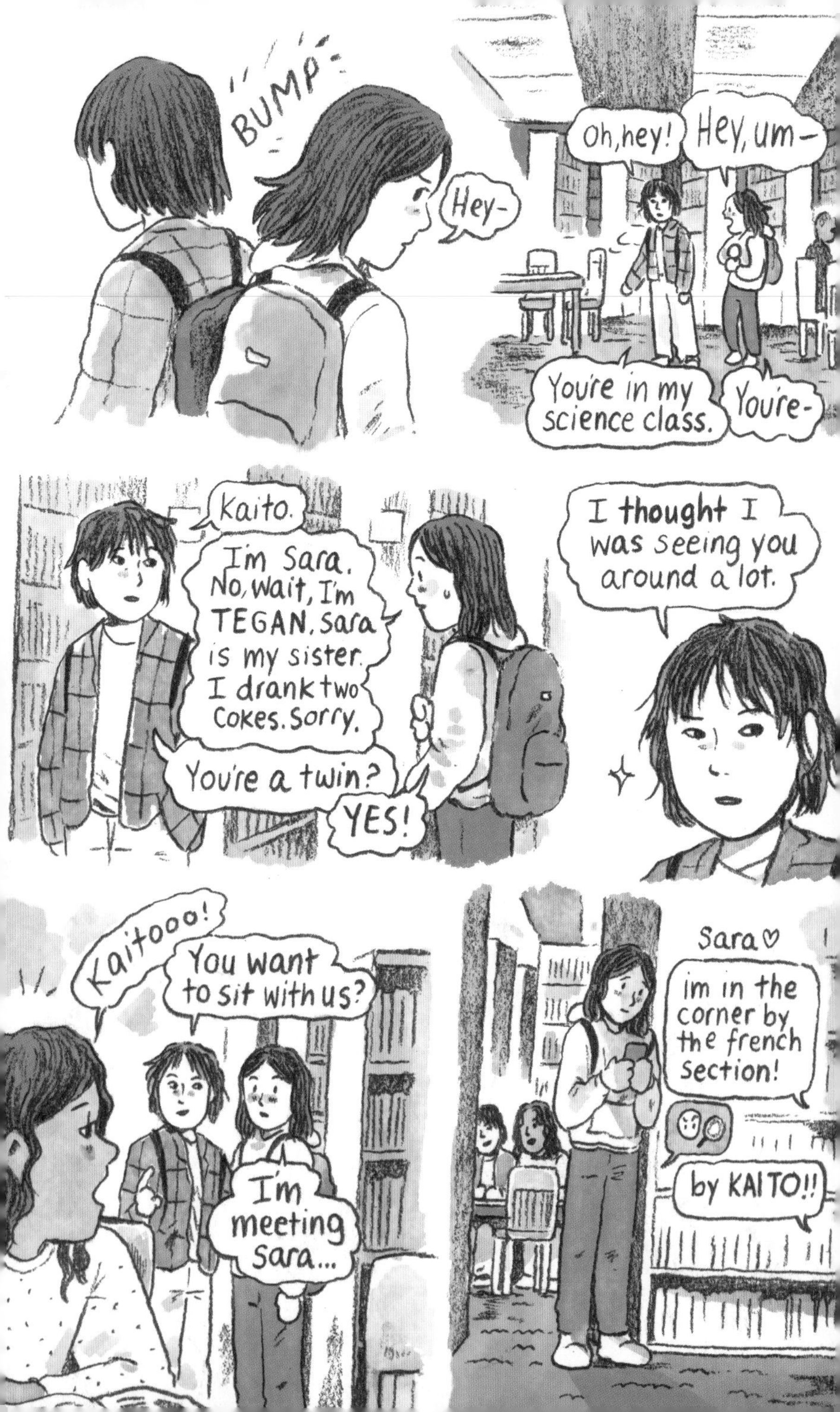
BUMP
Hey-
Oh, hey!
Hey, um-
You're in my science class.
You're-
Kaito.
I'm Sara. No, wait, I'm TEGAN. Sara is my sister. I drank two Cokes. Sorry.
You're a twin?
YES!
I thought I was seeing you around a lot.
Kaitooo!
You want to sit with us?
I'm meeting Sara...
Sara ♡
im in the corner by the french section!
by KAITO!!

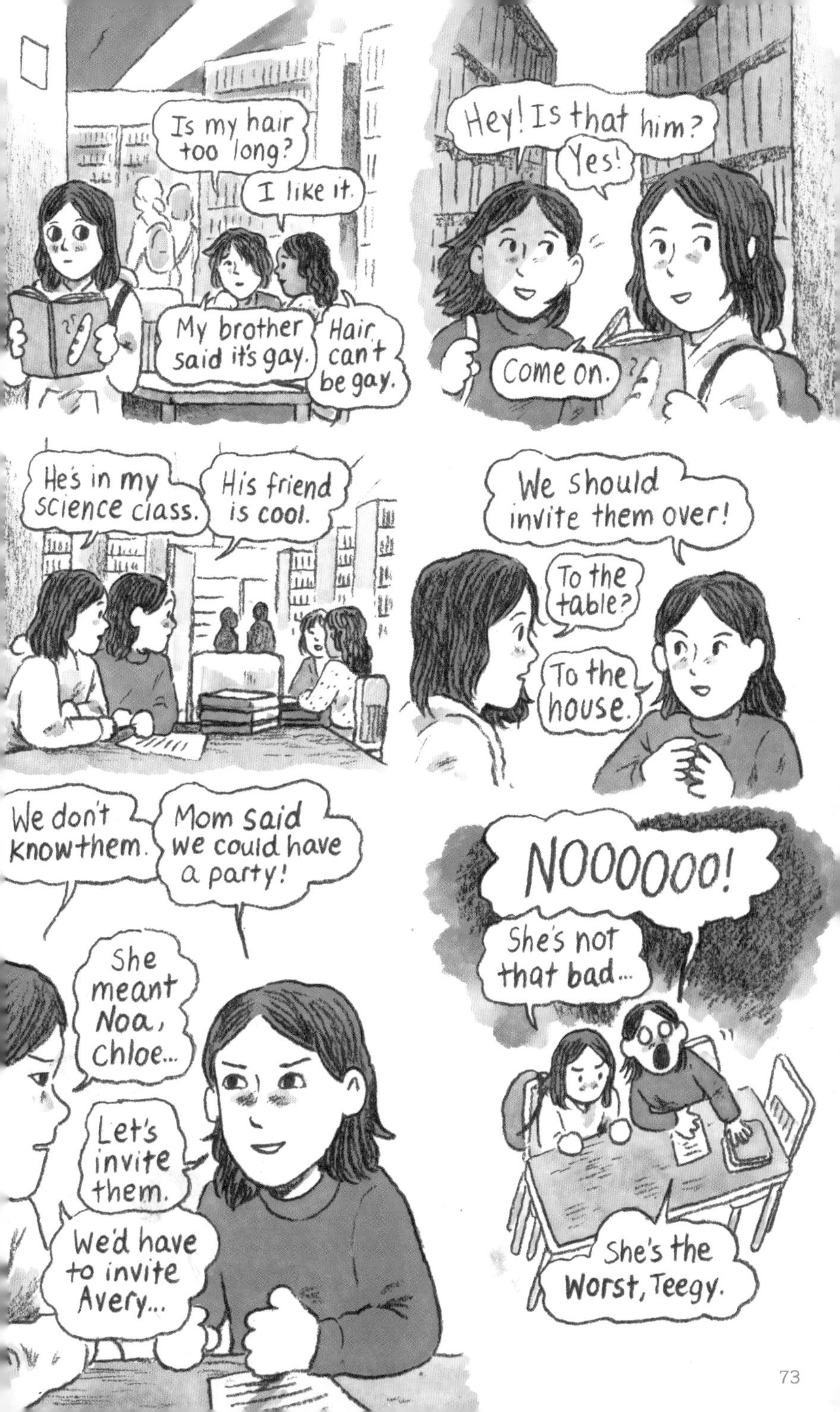
Is my hair too long?
I like it.
My brother said it's gay.
Hair can't be gay.
Hey! Is that him?
Yes!
Come on.
He's in my science class.
His friend is cool.
We should invite them over!
To the table?
To the house.
We don't know them.
Mom said we could have a party!
She meant Noa, Chloe...
Let's invite them.
We'd have to invite Avery...
NOOOOOO!
She's not that bad...
She's the Worst, Teegy.

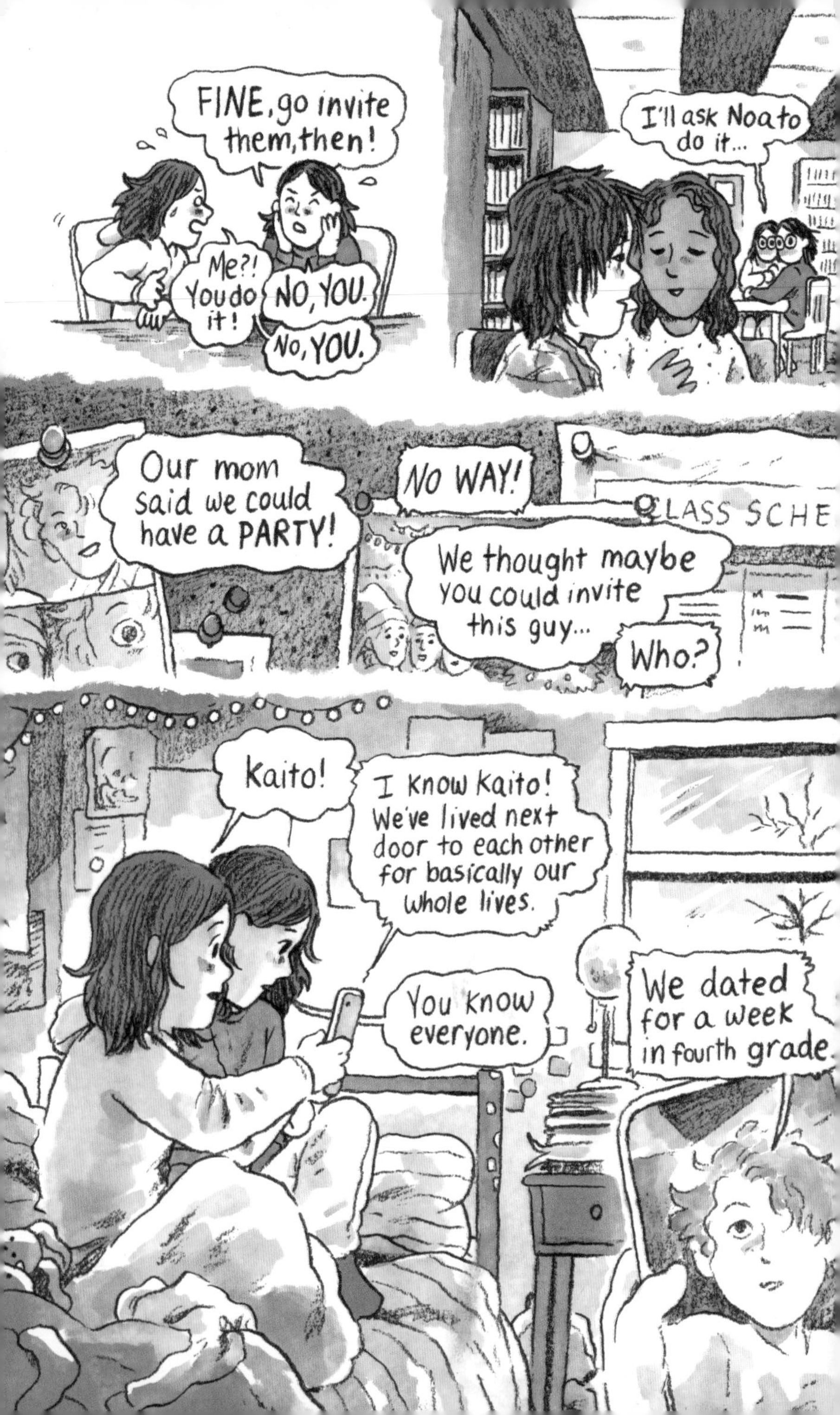
FINE, go invite them, then!
Me?! You do it!
NO, YOU.
No, YOU.
I'll ask Noa to do it...
Our mom said we could have a PARTY!
NO WAY!
CLASS SCHE
We thought maybe you could invite this guy...
Who?
Kaito!
I know Kaito! We've lived next door to each other for basically our whole lives.
You know everyone.
We dated for a week in fourth grade.

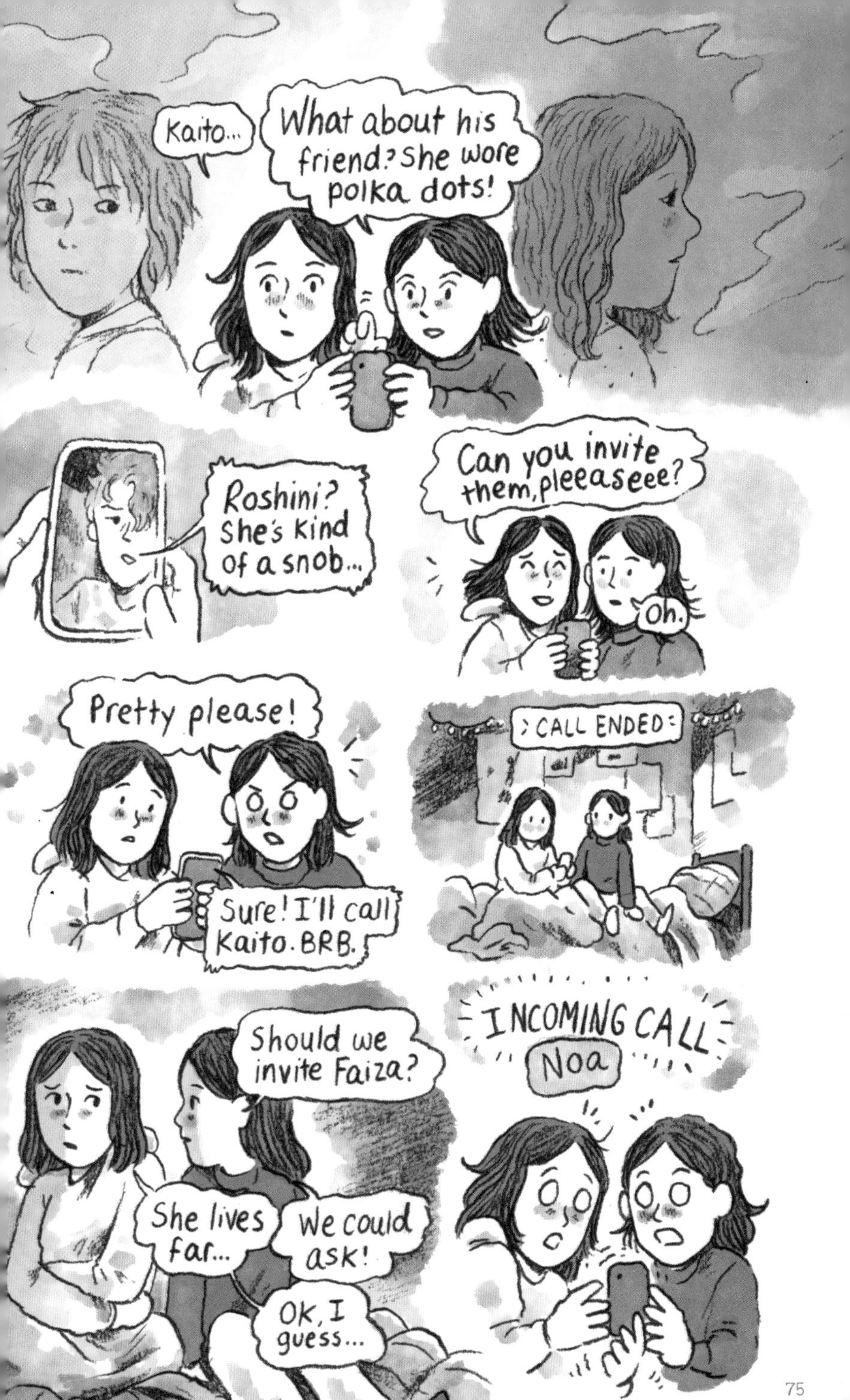
Kaito...
What about his friend? She wore polka dots!
Roshini? She's kind of a snob...
Can you invite them, pleeaseee?
Oh.
Pretty please!
Sure! I'll call Kaito. BRB.
CALL ENDED
Should we invite Faiza?
She lives far...
We could ask!
Ok, I guess...
INCOMING CALL
Noa

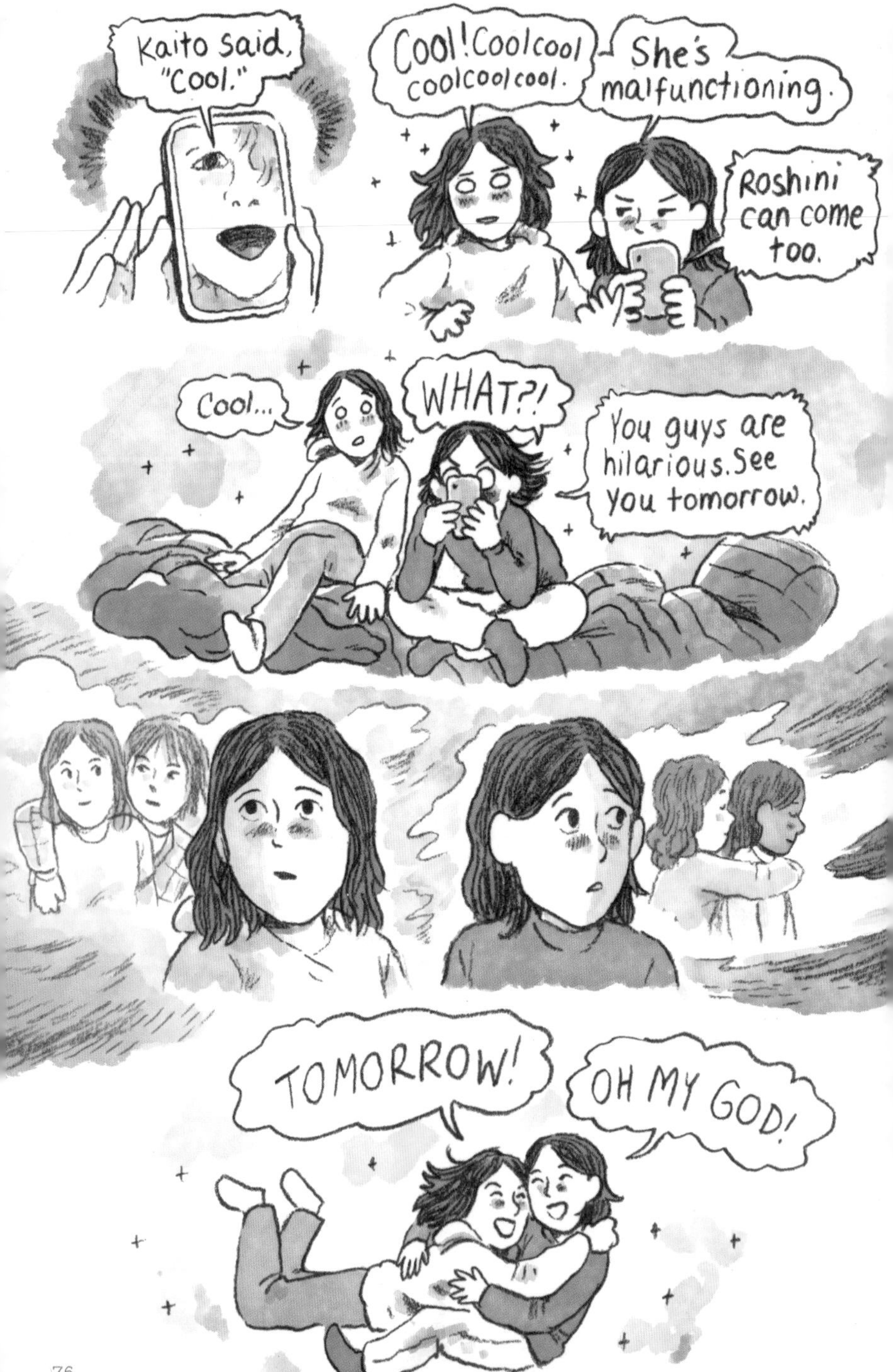
Kaito said, "Cool."
Cool! Coolcool coolcoolcool.
She's malfunctioning.
Roshini can come too.
Cool...
WHAT?!
You guys are hilarious. See you tomorrow.
TOMORROW!
OH MY GOD!

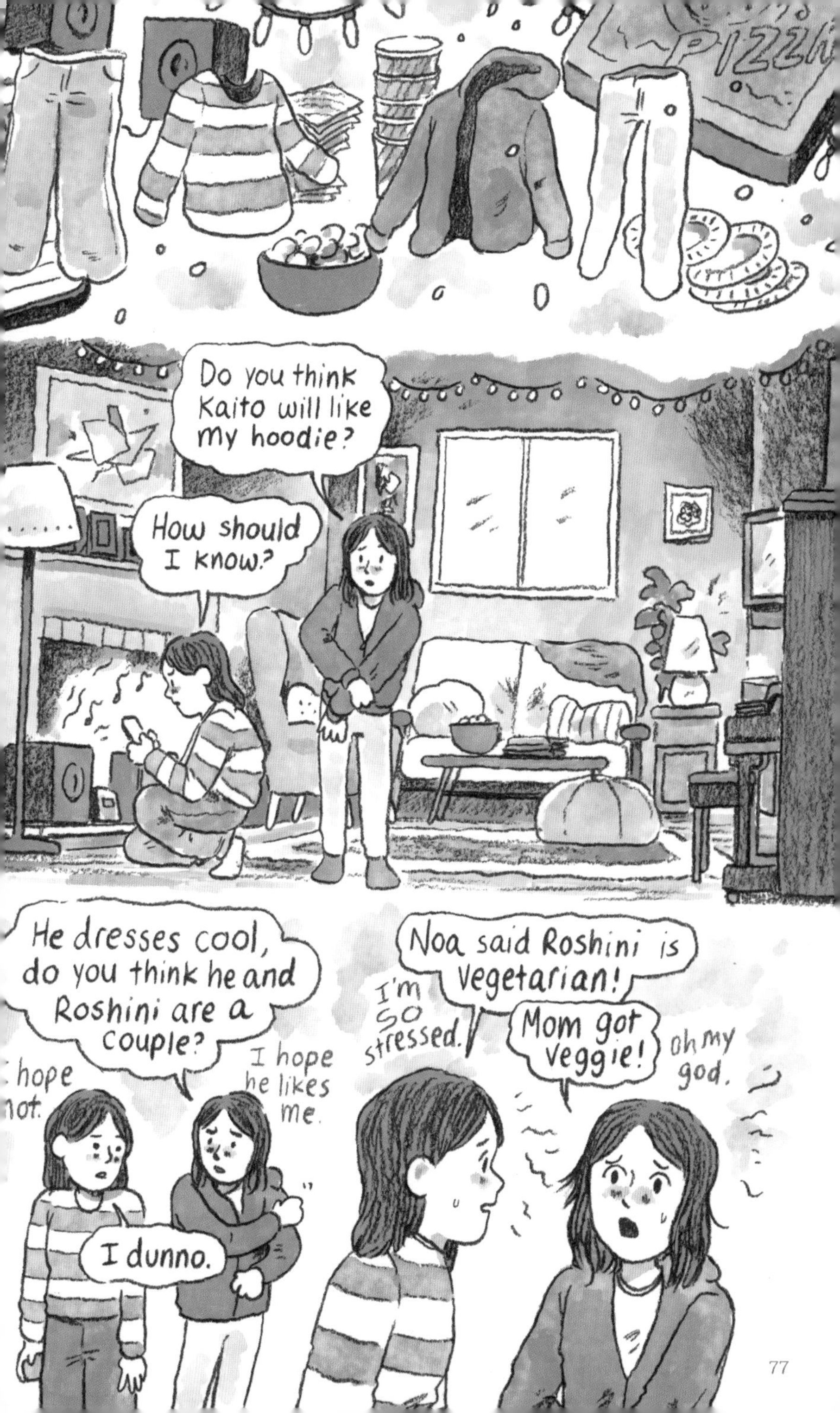

Do you think Kaito will like my hoodie?
How should I know?
He dresses cool, do you think he and Roshini are a couple?
I hope not.
I hope he likes me.
I dunno.
Noa said Roshini is vegetarian!
I'm so stressed.
Mom got veggie!
oh my god.

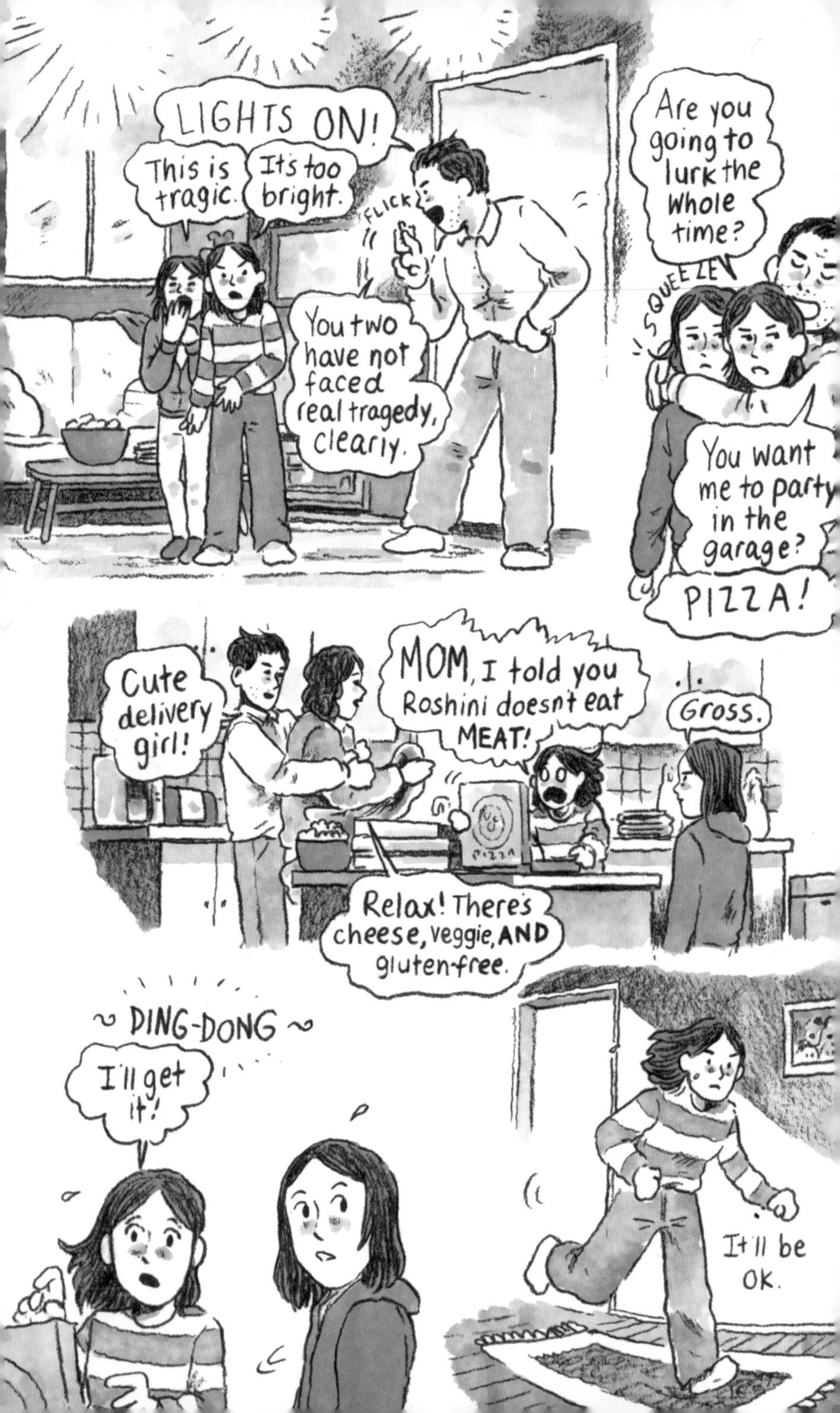
LIGHTS ON!
This is tragic.
It's too bright.
FLICK
You two have not faced real tragedy, clearly.
Are you going to lurk the whole time?
SQUEEZE
You want me to party in the garage?
PIZZA!
Cute delivery girl!
MOM, I told you Roshini doesn't eat MEAT!
Gross.
PIZZA
Relax! There's cheese, veggie, AND gluten-free.
~ DING-DONG ~
I'll get it!
It'll be OK.

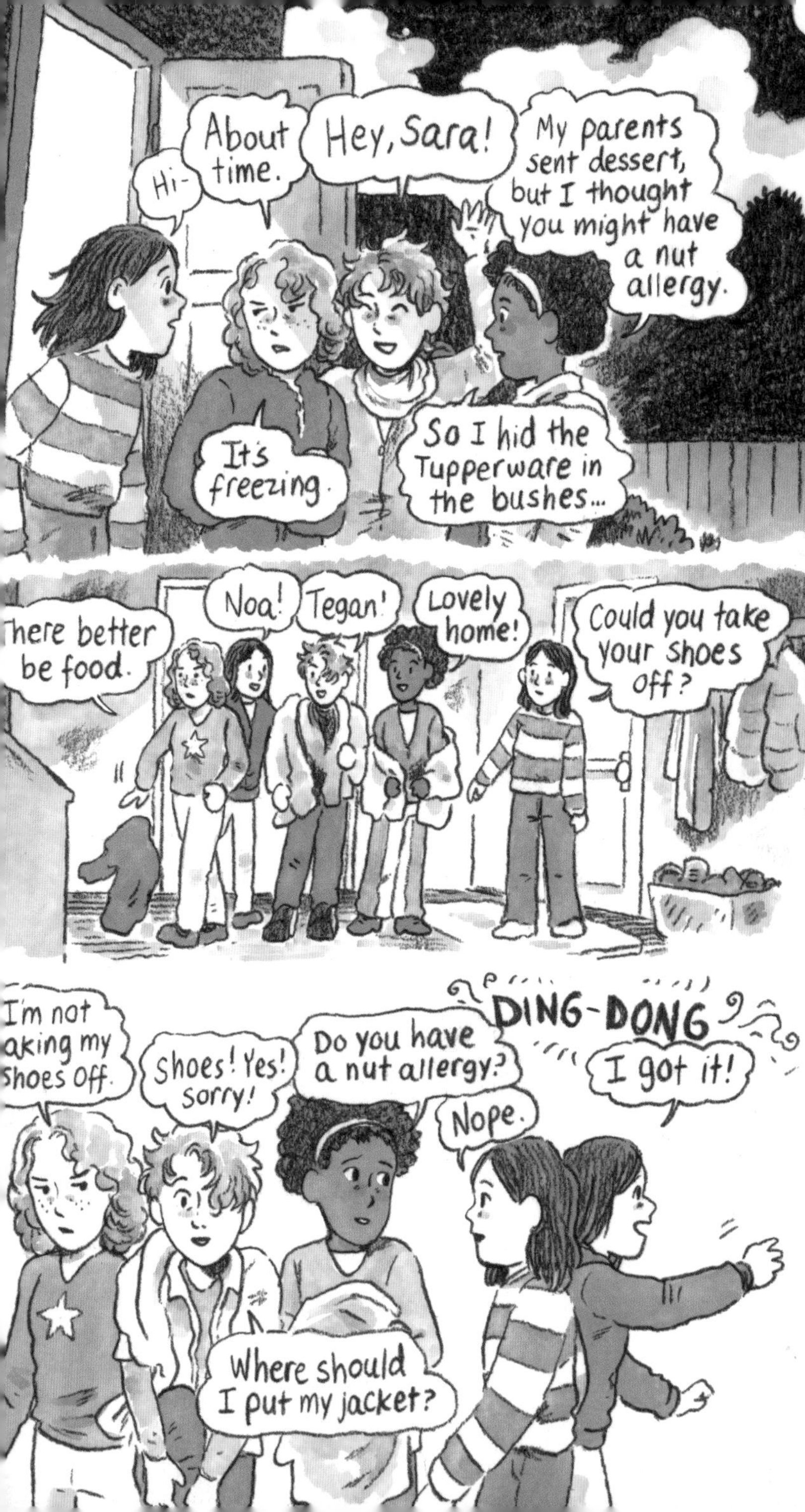
Hi-
About time.
Hey, Sara!
My parents sent dessert, but I thought you might have a nut allergy.
It's freezing.
So I hid the Tupperware in the bushes...
here better be food.
Noa!
Tegan!
Lovely home!
Could you take your shoes off?
I'm not aking my shoes off.
Shoes! Yes! sorry!
Do you have a nut allergy?
Nope.
DING-DONG
I got it!
Where should I put my jacket?

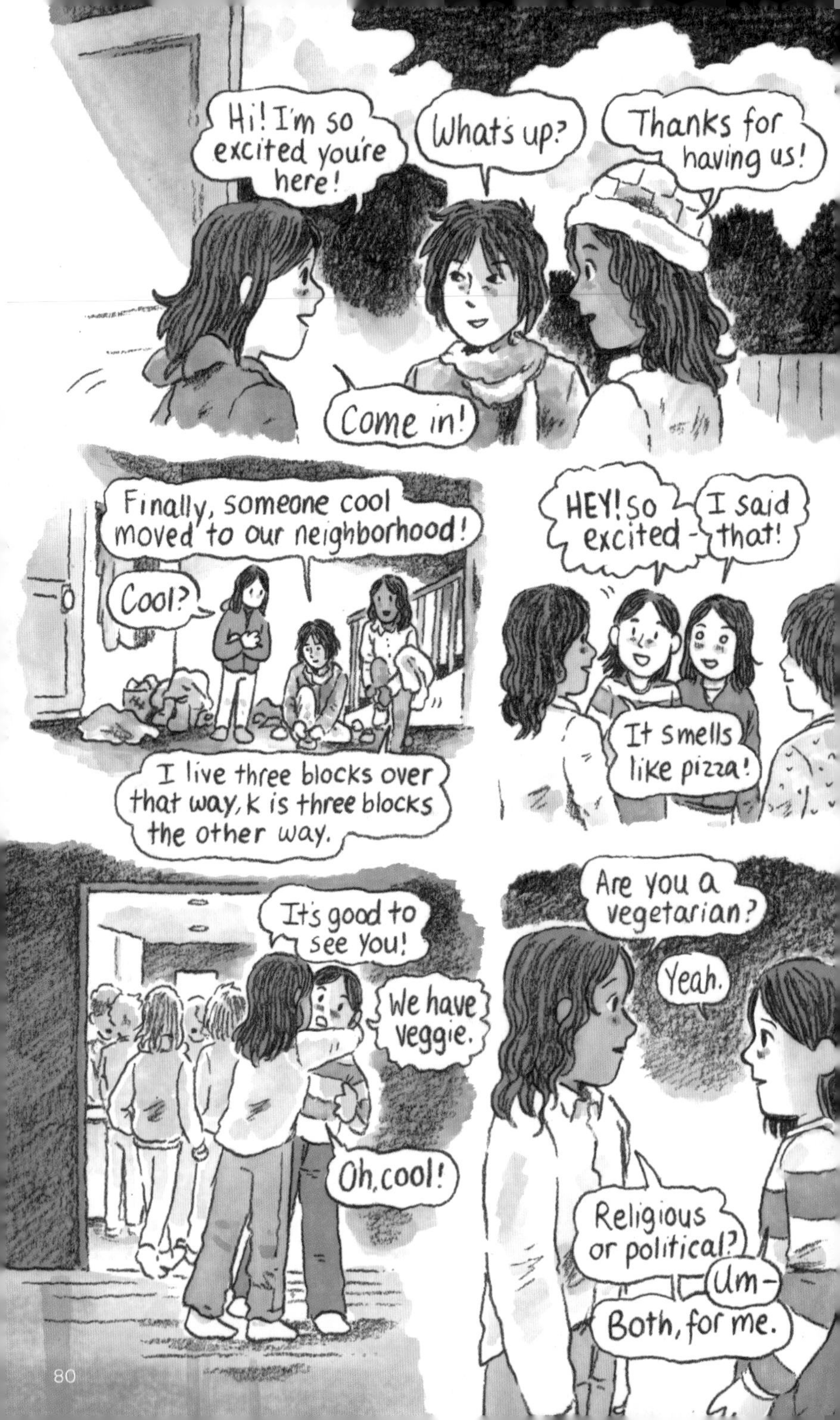
Hi! I'm so excited you're here!
What's up?
Thanks for having us!
Come in!
Finally, someone cool moved to our neighborhood!
Cool?
I live three blocks over that way, K is three blocks the other way.
HEY! SO excited -
I said that!
It smells like pizza!
It's good to see you!
We have veggie.
Oh, cool!
Are you a vegetarian?
Yeah.
Religious or political?
Um-
Both, for me.

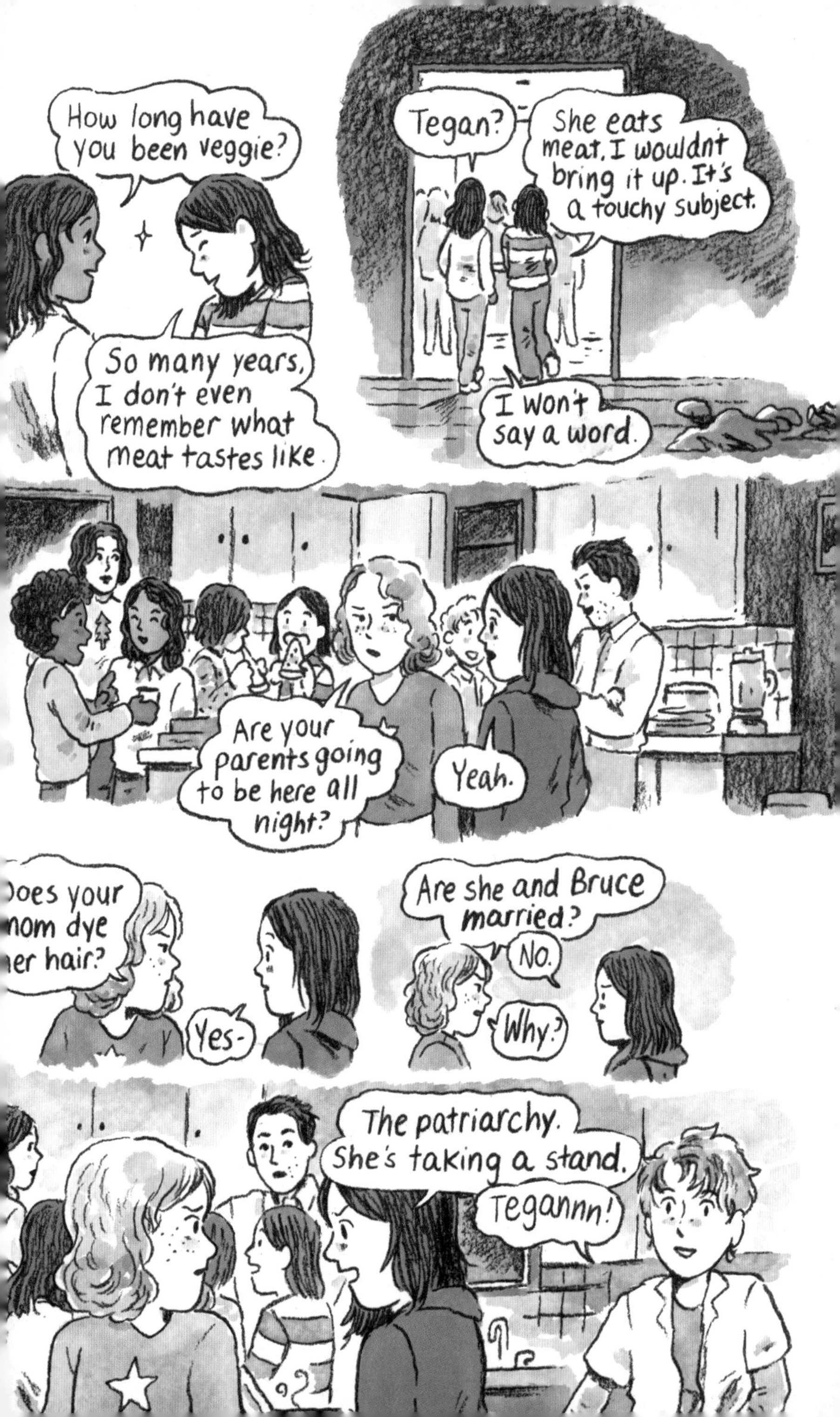
How long have you been veggie?
So many years, I don't even remember what meat tastes like.
Tegan?
She eats meat. I wouldn't bring it up. It's a touchy subject.
I won't say a word.
Are your parents going to be here all night?
Yeah.
oes your om dye er hair?
Yes-
Are she and Bruce married?
No.
Why?
The patriarchy. She's taking a stand.
Tegannn!

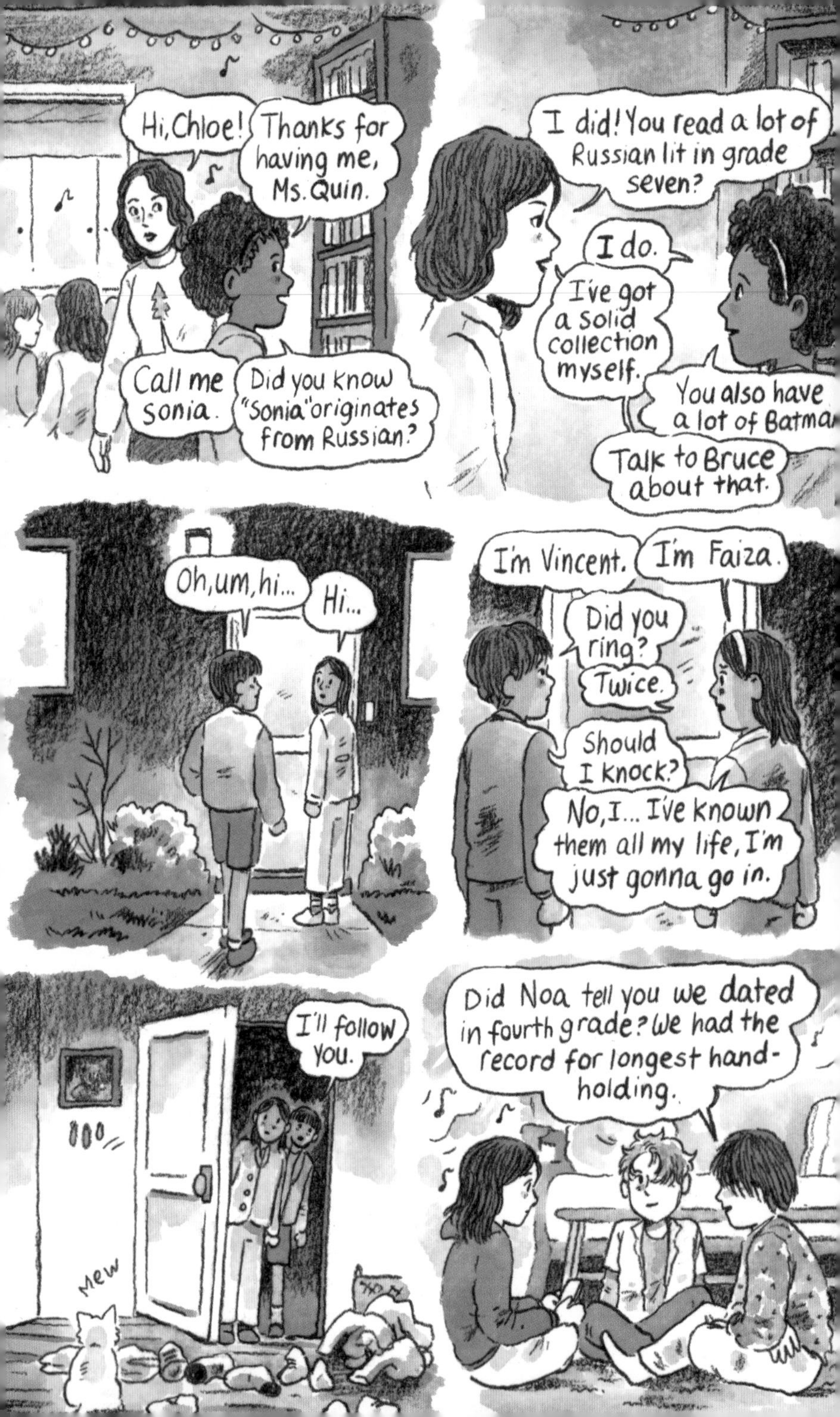
Hi, Chloe!
Thanks for having me, Ms. Quin.
Call me Sonia.
Did you know "Sonia" originates from Russian?
I did! You read a lot of Russian lit in grade seven?
I do.
I've got a solid collection myself.
You also have a lot of Batma
Talk to Bruce about that.
Oh, um, hi...
Hi...
I'm Vincent.
I'm Faiza.
Did you ring?
Twice.
Should I knock?
No, I... I've known them all my life, I'm just gonna go in.
I'll follow you.
MEW
Did Noa tell you we dated in fourth grade? We had the record for longest hand-holding.

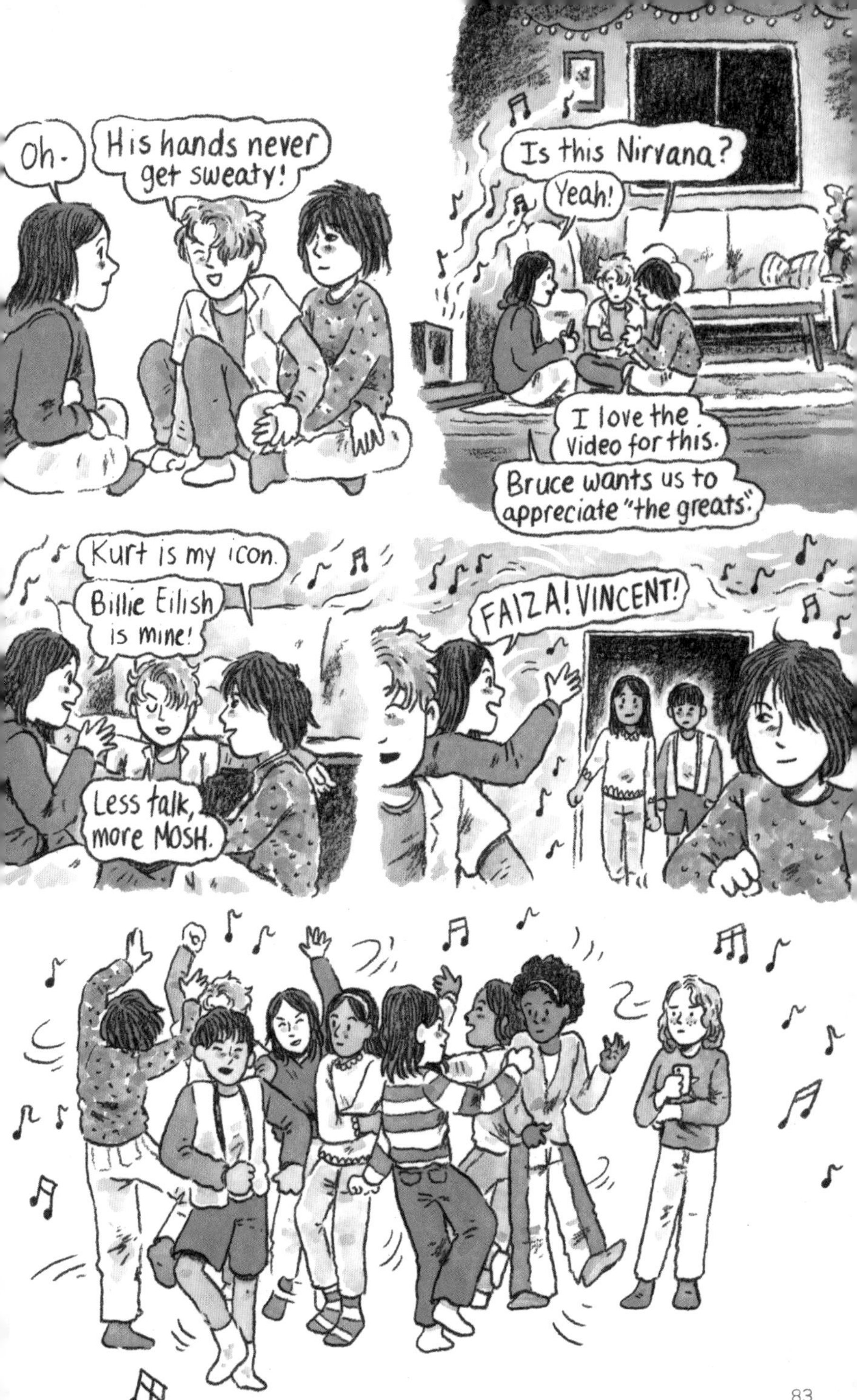
Oh.
His hands never get sweaty!
Is this Nirvana?
Yeah!
I love the video for this.
Bruce wants us to appreciate "the greats."
Kurt is my icon.
Billie Eilish is mine!
Less talk, more MOSH.
FAIZA! VINCENT!

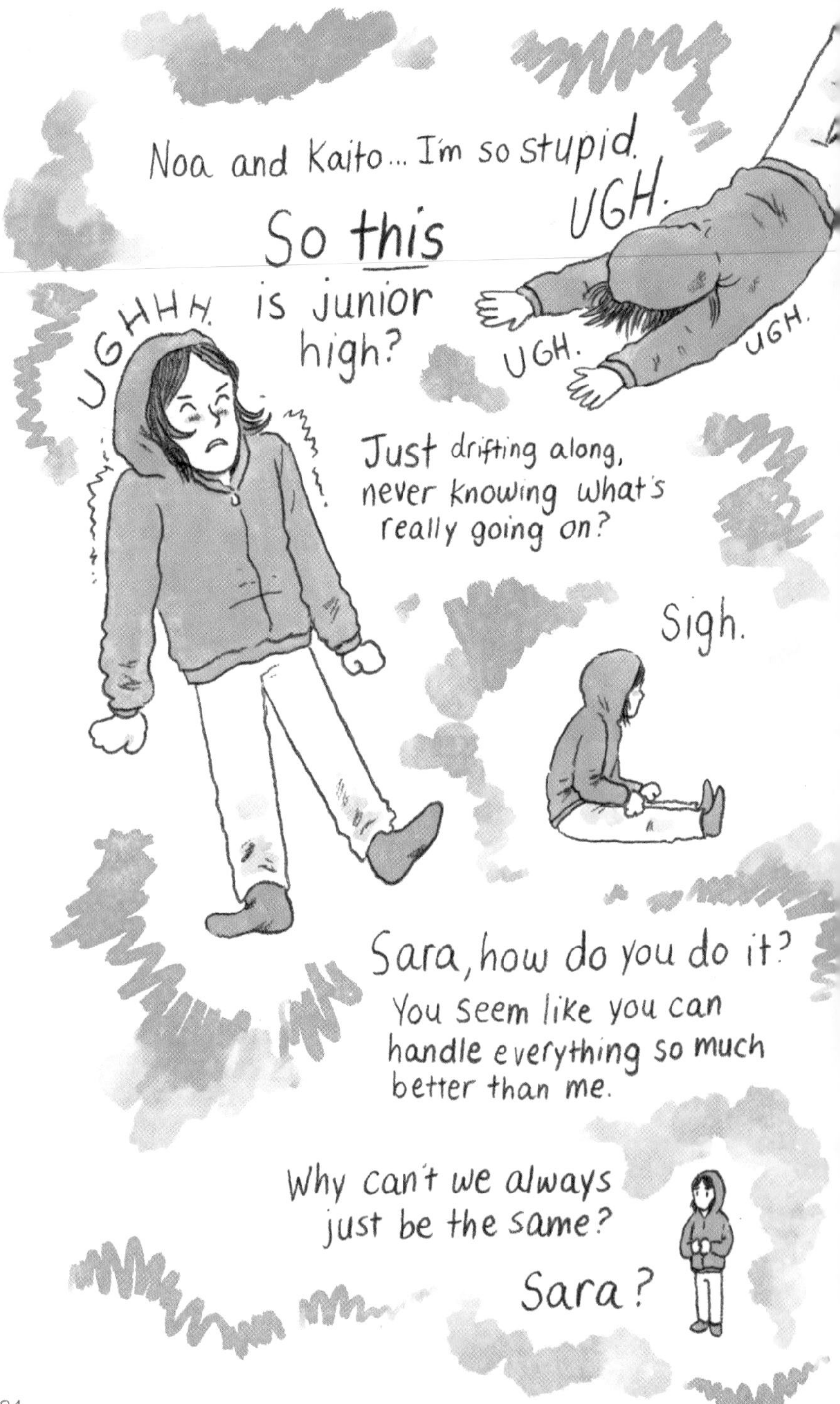
Noa and Kaito... I'm so stupid.
UGH.
So this is junior high?
UGHHH.
UGH.
UGH.
Just drifting along, never knowing what's really going on?
Sigh.
Sara, how do you do it?
You seem like you can handle everything so much better than me.
Why can't we always just be the same?
Sara?

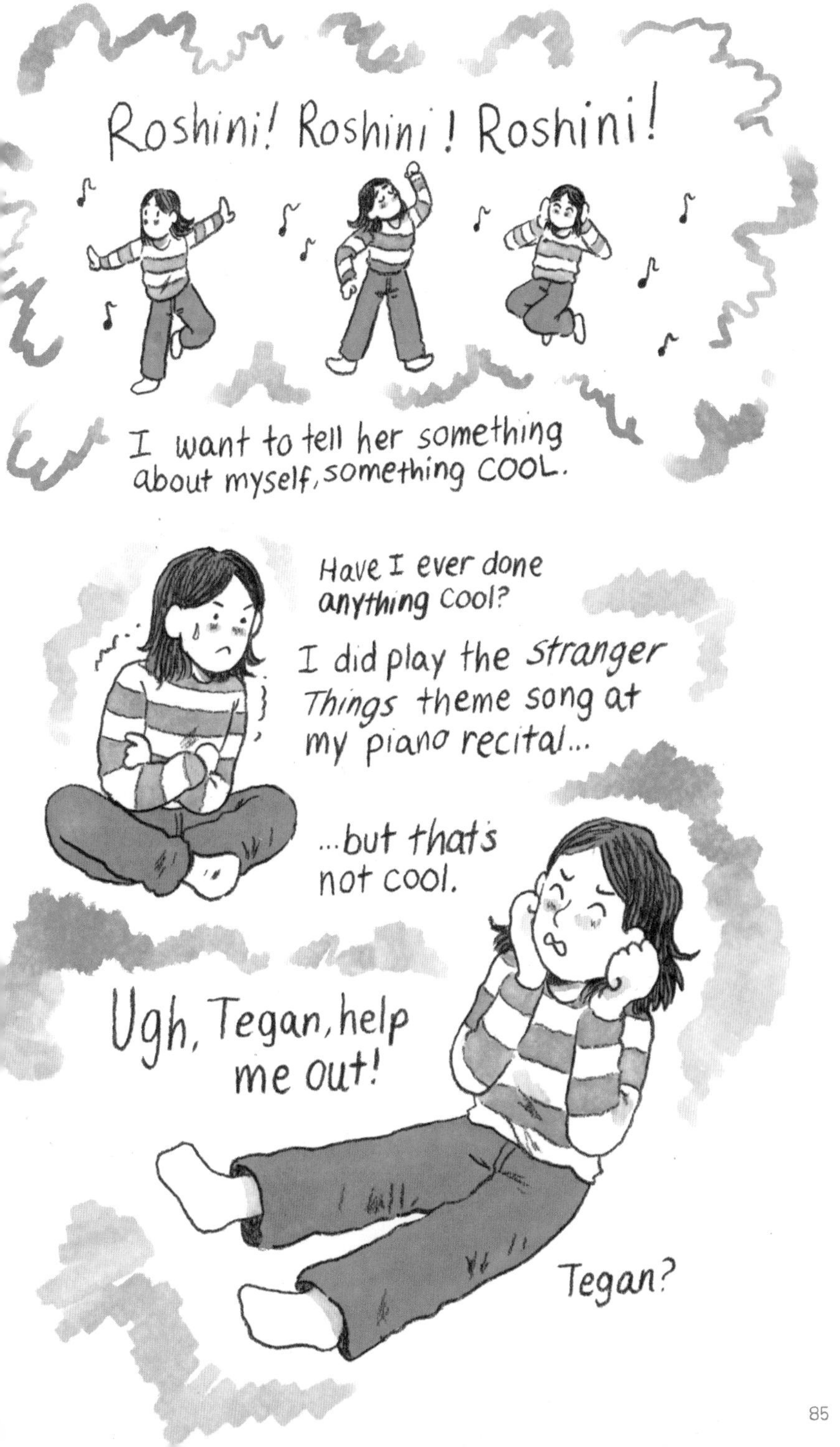
Roshini! Roshini! Roshini!
I want to tell her something about myself, something COOL.
Have I ever done anything cool?
I did play the *Stranger Things* theme song at my piano recital...
...but that's not cool.
Ugh, Tegan, help me out!
Tegan?

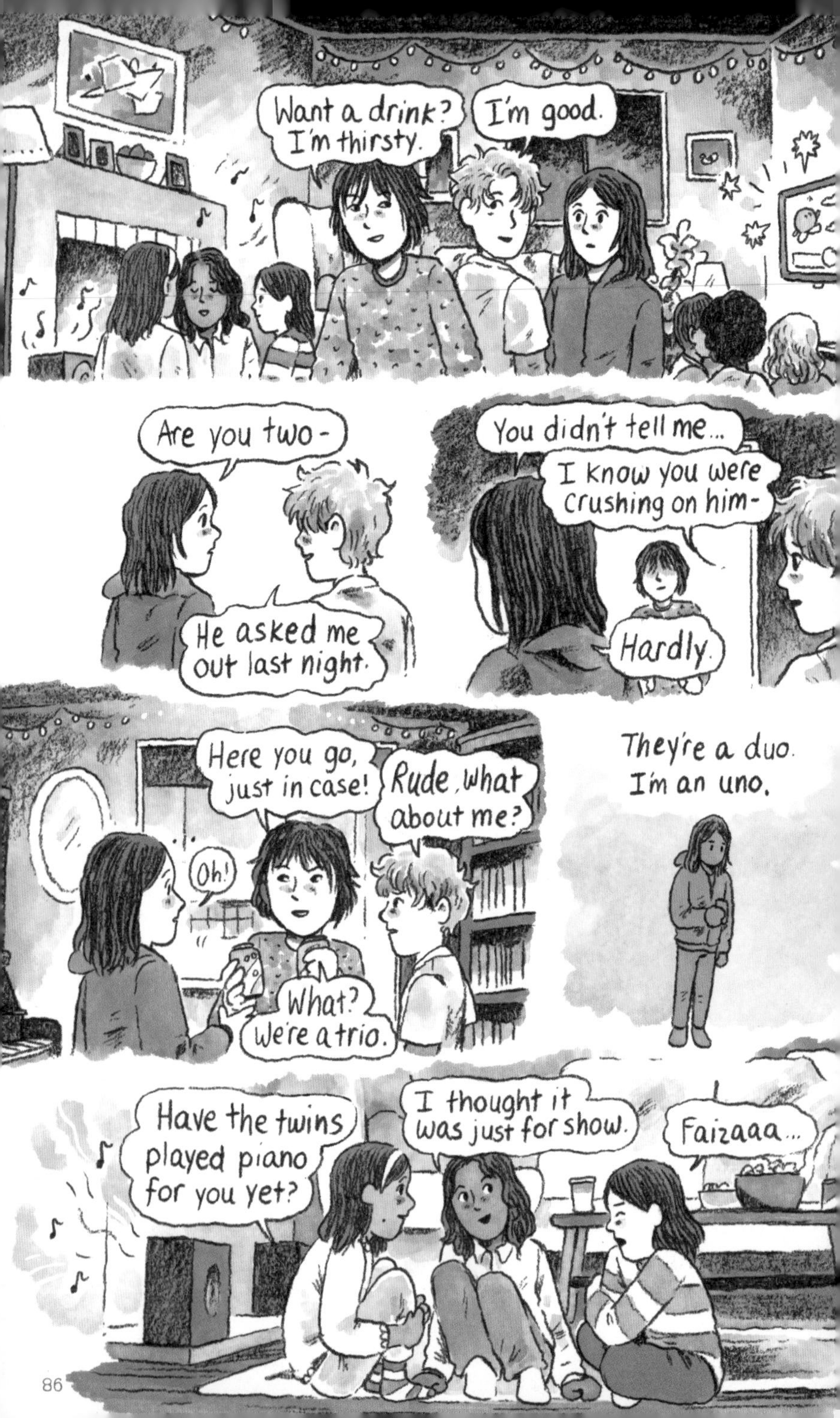
Want a drink? I'm thirsty.
I'm good.
Are you two-
He asked me out last night.
You didn't tell me...
I know you were crushing on him-
Hardly.
Here you go, just in case!
Rude, what about me?
Oh!
What? We're a trio.
They're a duo. I'm an uno.
Have the twins played piano for you yet?
I thought it was just for show.
Faizaaa...

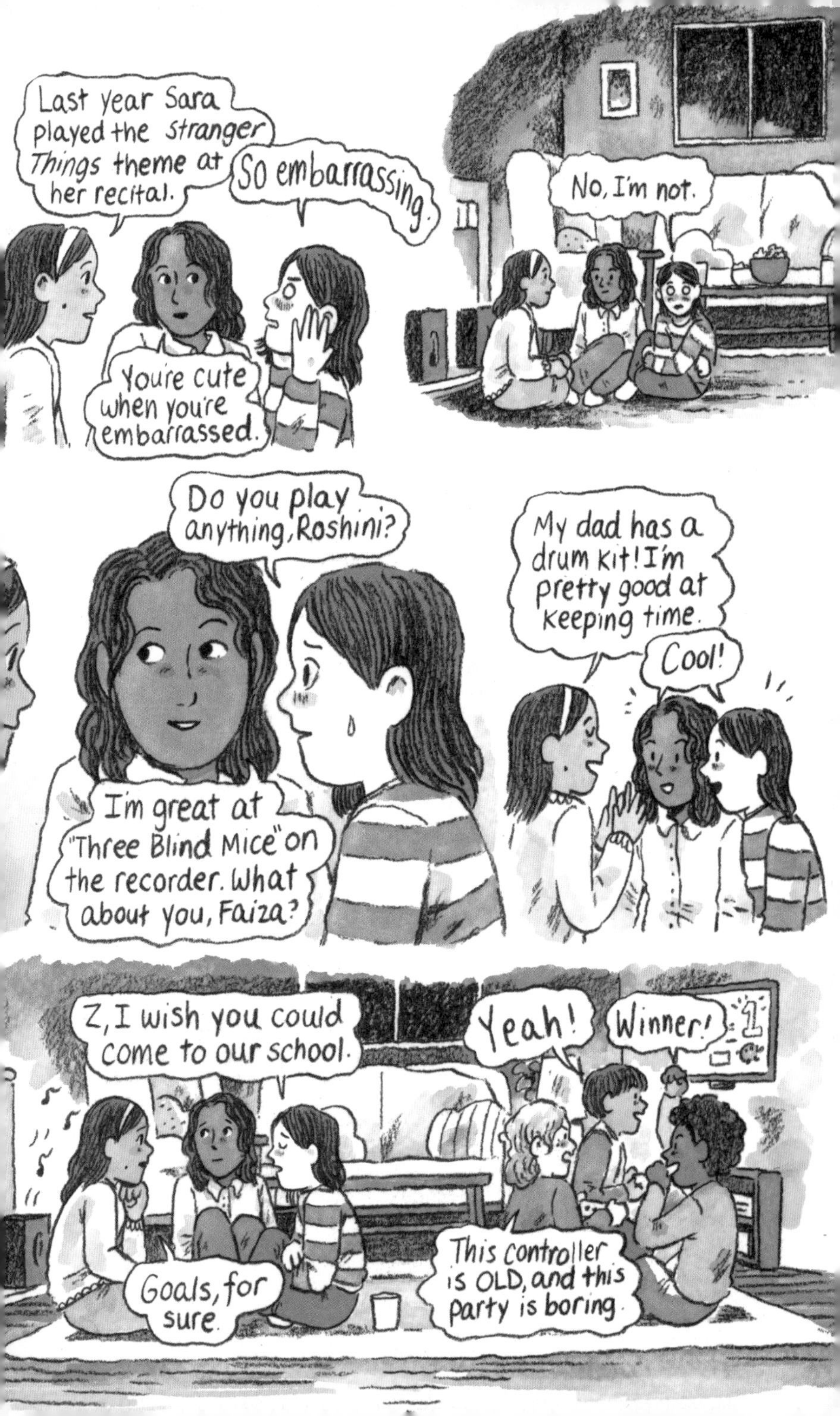
Last year Sara played the *Stranger Things* theme at her recital.
So embarrassing.
You're cute when you're embarrassed.
No, I'm not.
Do you play anything, Roshini?
I'm great at "Three Blind Mice" on the recorder. What about you, Faiza?
My dad has a drum kit! I'm pretty good at keeping time.
Cool!
Z, I wish you could come to our school.
Goals, for sure.
Yeah!
Winner!
This controller is OLD, and this party is boring.

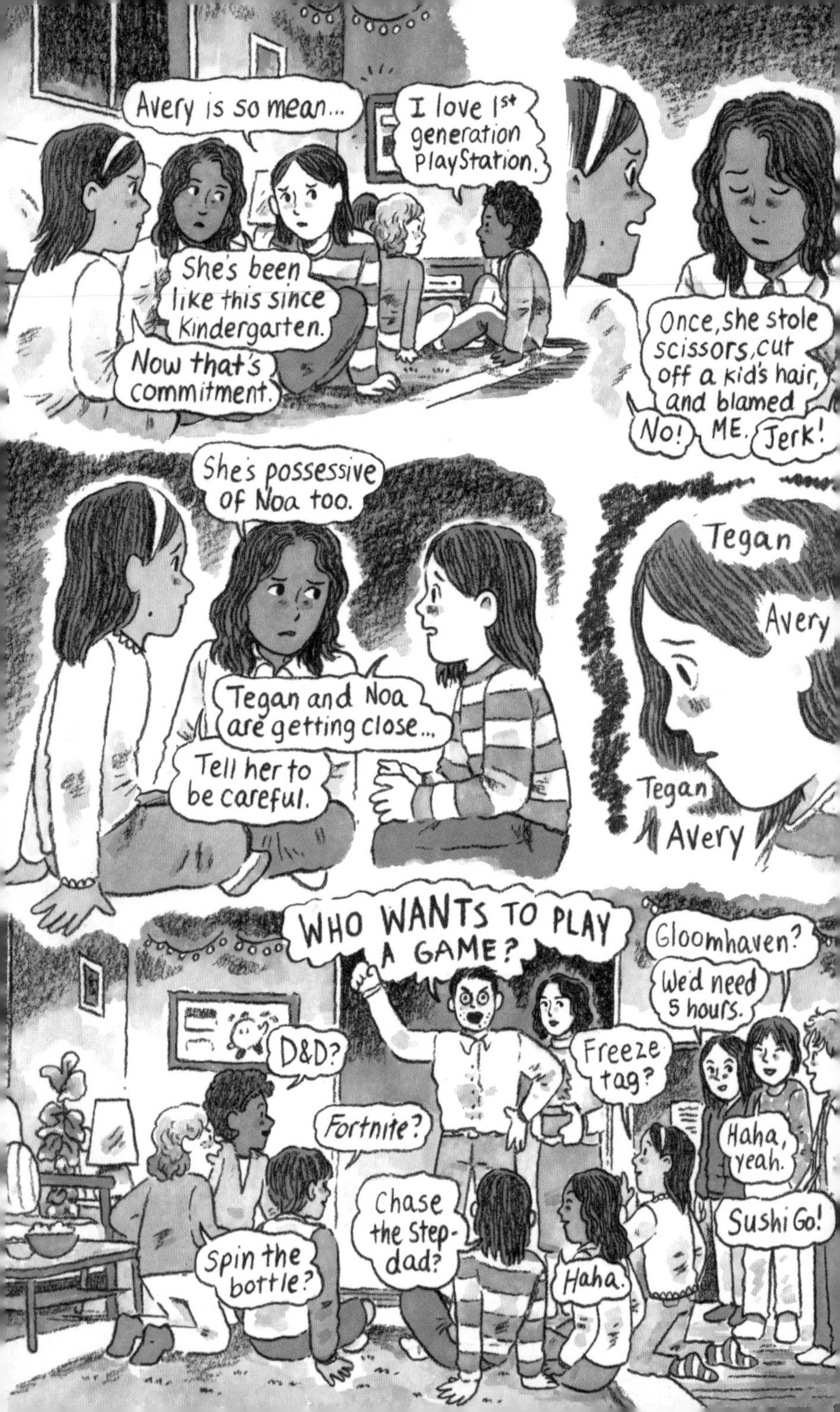
Avery is so mean...
I love 1st generation PlayStation.
She's been like this since Kindergarten.
Now that's commitment.
Once, she stole scissors, cut off a kid's hair, and blamed ME.
No!
Jerk!
She's possessive of Noa too.
Tegan and Noa are getting close...
Tell her to be careful.
Tegan
Avery
Tegan
Avery
WHO WANTS TO PLAY A GAME?
Gloomhaven?
We'd need 5 hours.
D&D?
Freeze tag?
Fortnite?
Haha, yeah.
Chase the Step-dad?
Sushi Go!
Spin the bottle?
Haha.

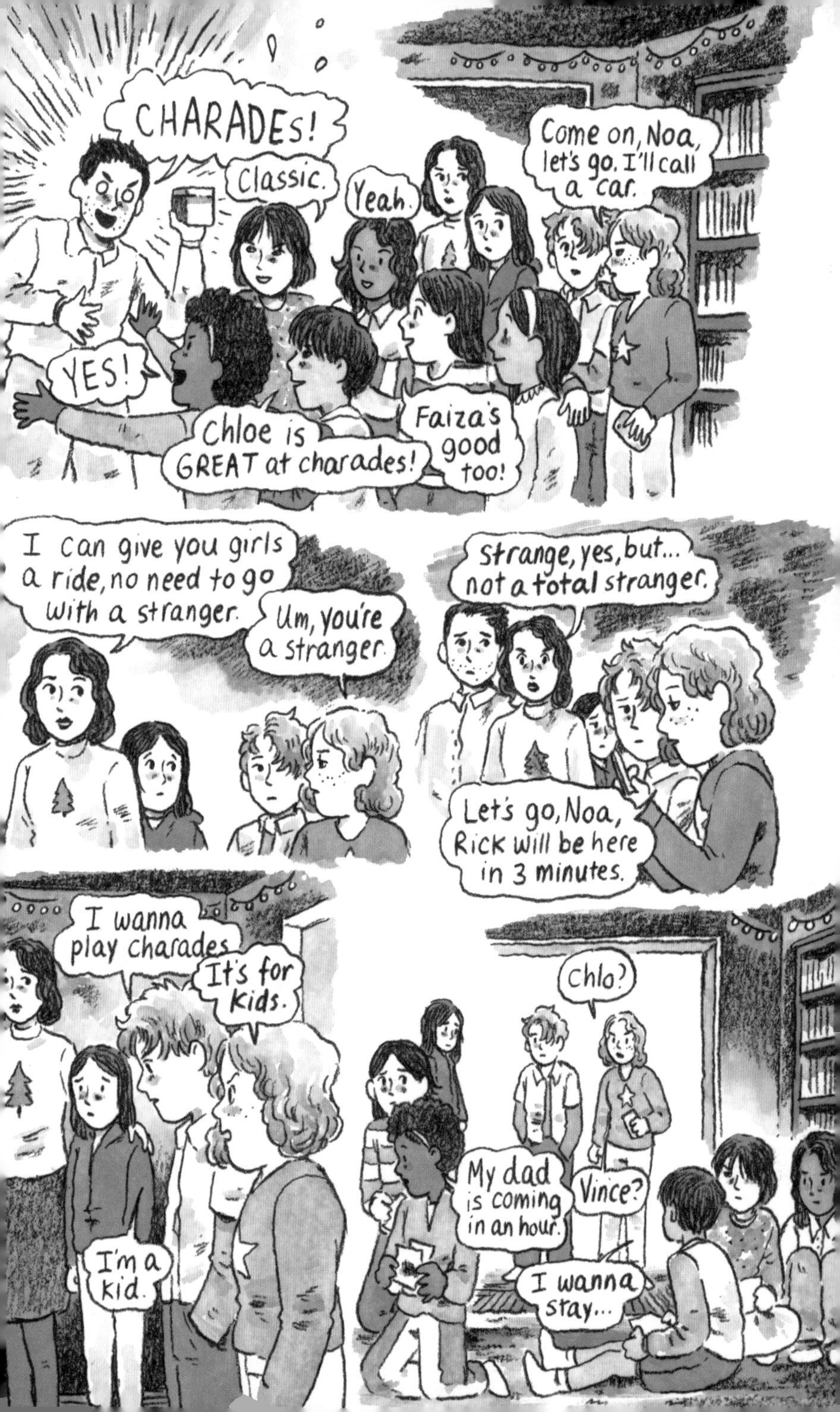
CHARADES!
Classic.
Yeah.
Come on, Noa, let's go. I'll call a car.
YES!
Chloe is GREAT at charades!
Faiza's good too!
I can give you girls a ride, no need to go with a stranger.
Um, you're a stranger.
Strange, yes, but... not a total stranger.
Let's go, Noa, Rick will be here in 3 minutes.
I wanna play charades.
It's for kids.
I'm a kid.
Chlo?
My dad is coming in an hour.
Vince?
I wanna stay...

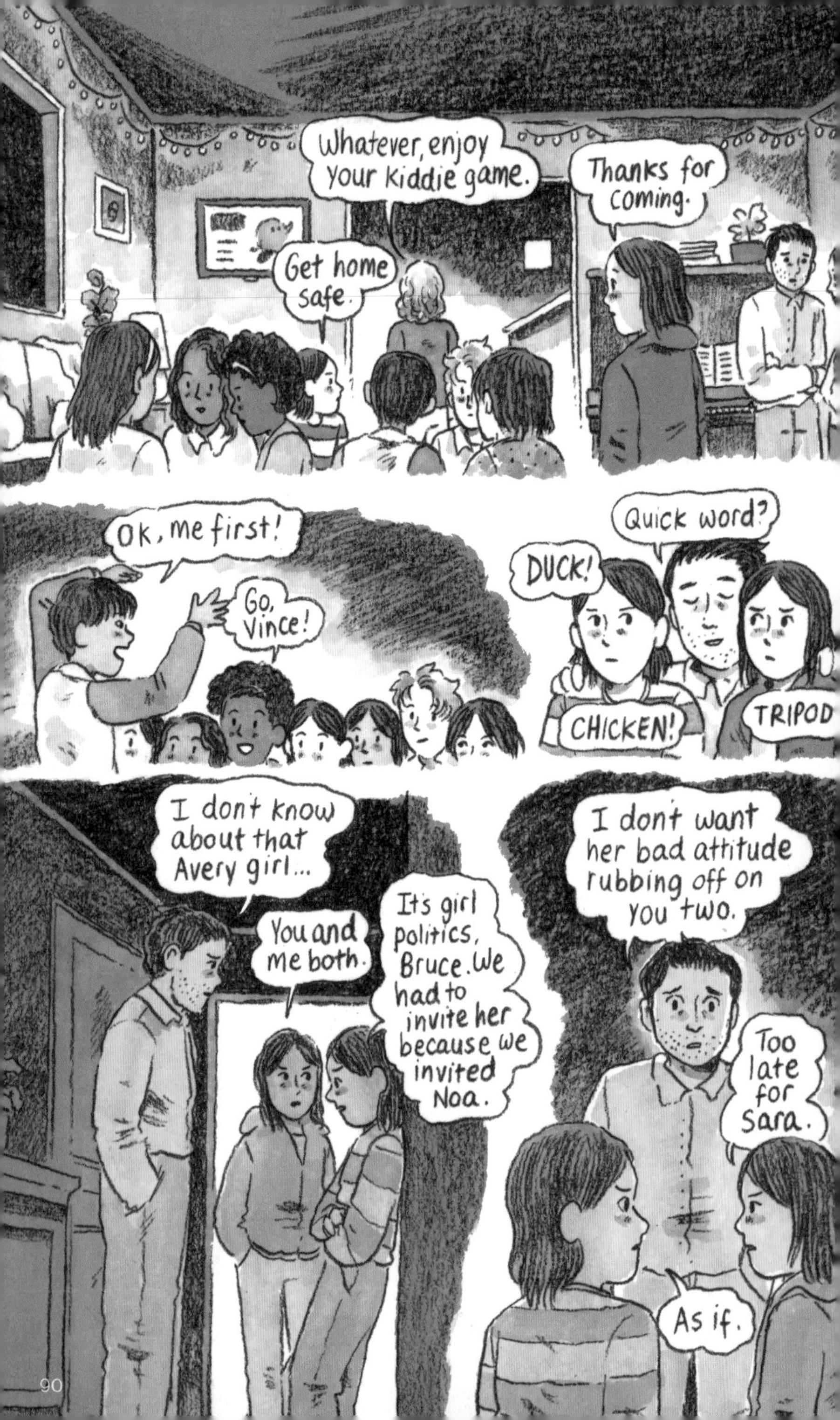
Whatever, enjoy your kiddie game.
Thanks for coming.
Get home safe.
Ok, me first!
Go, Vince!
Quick word?
DUCK!
CHICKEN!
TRIPOD
I don't know about that Avery girl...
You and me both.
It's girl politics, Bruce. We had to invite her because we invited Noa.
I don't want her bad attitude rubbing off on you two.
Too late for Sara.
As if.

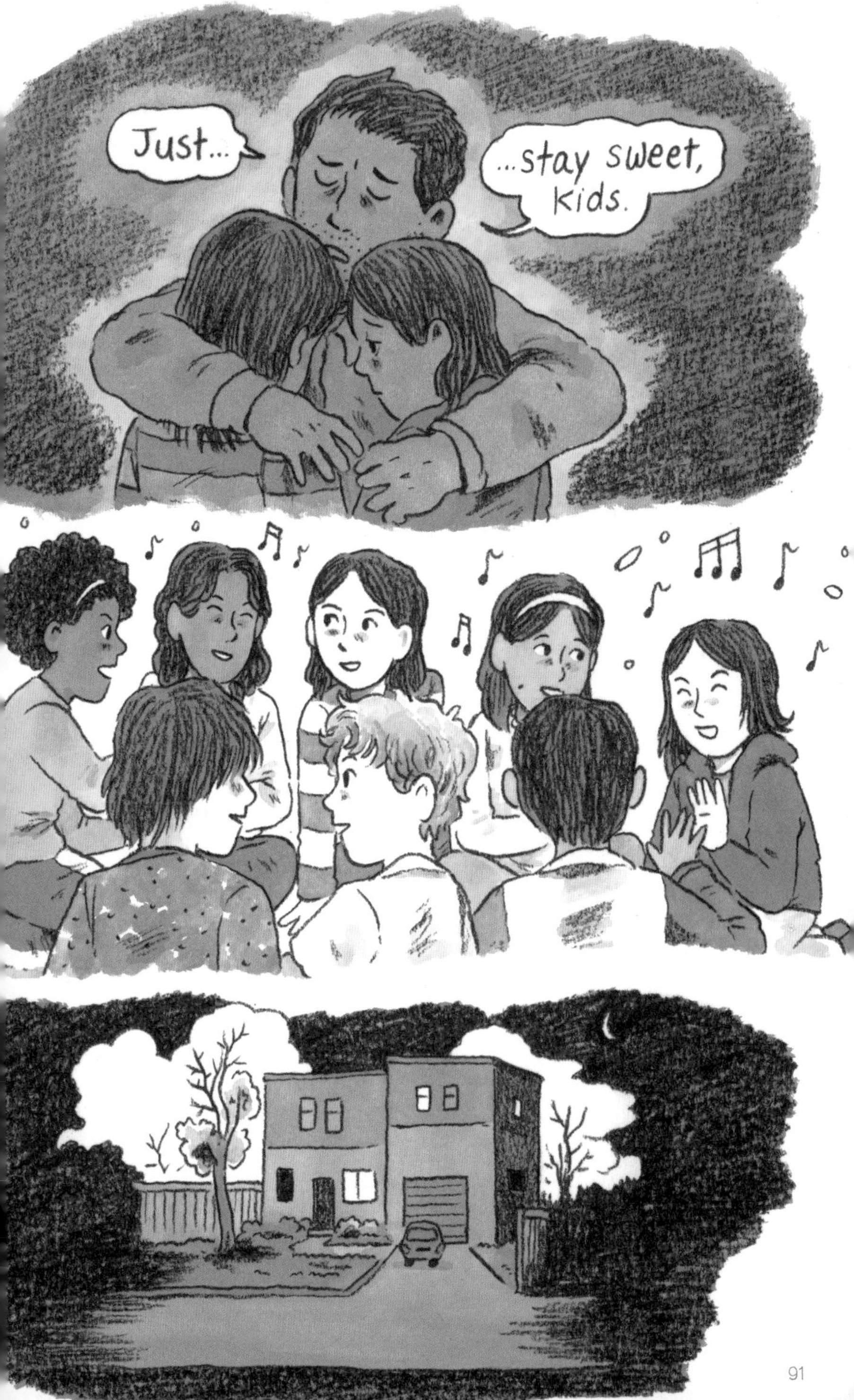
Just...
...stay sweet, kids.

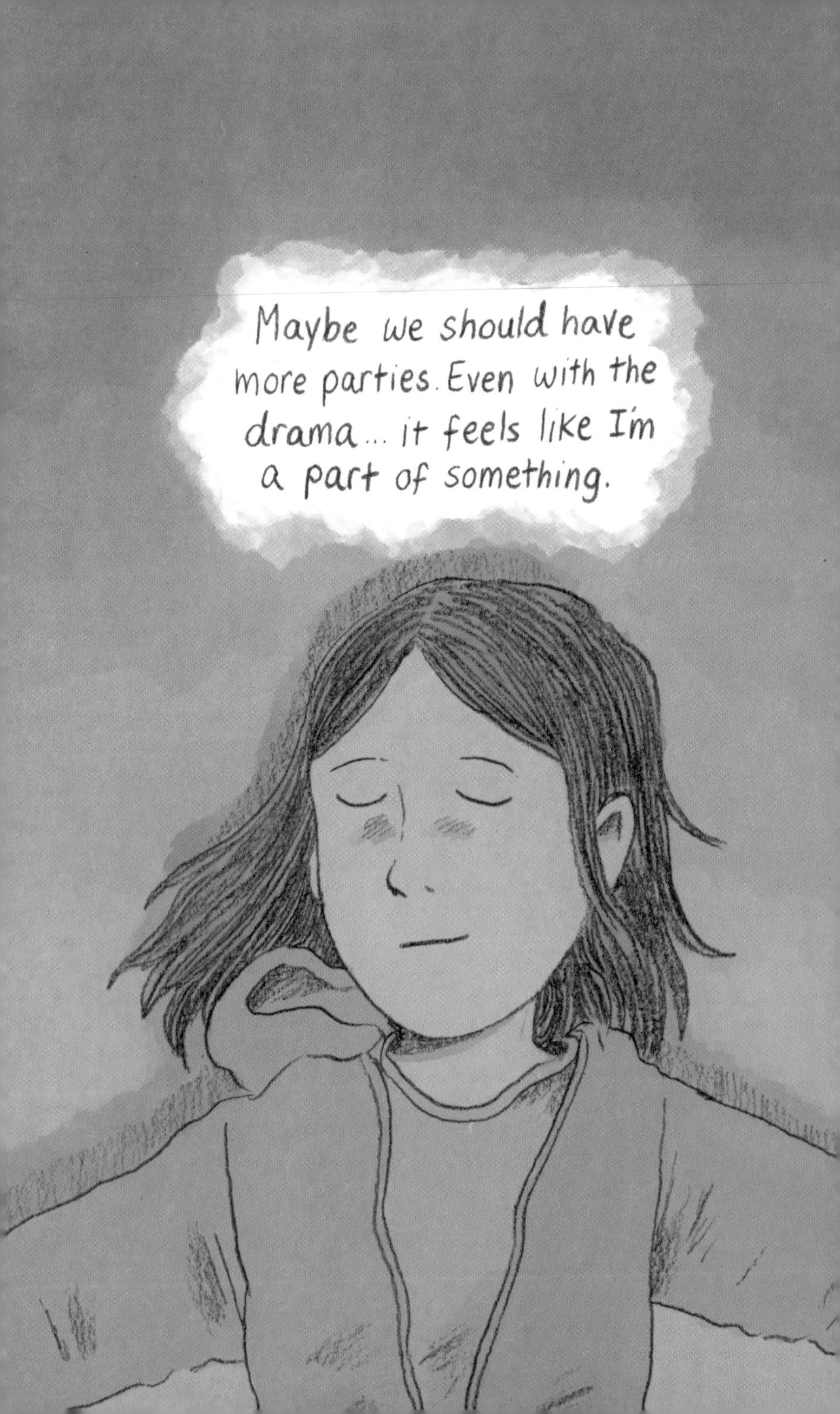
Maybe we should have more parties. Even with the drama... it feels like I'm a part of something.

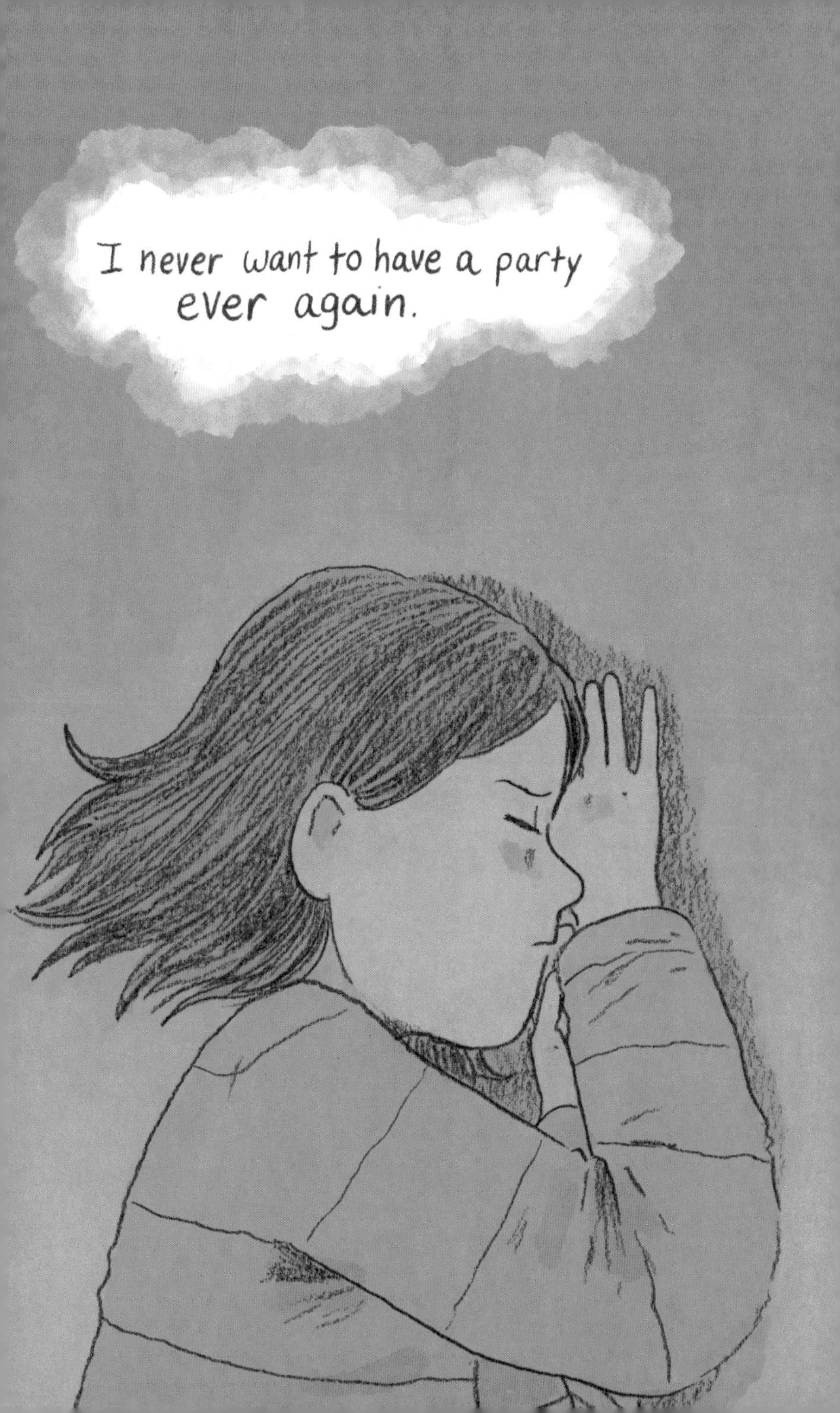
I never want to have a party ever again.

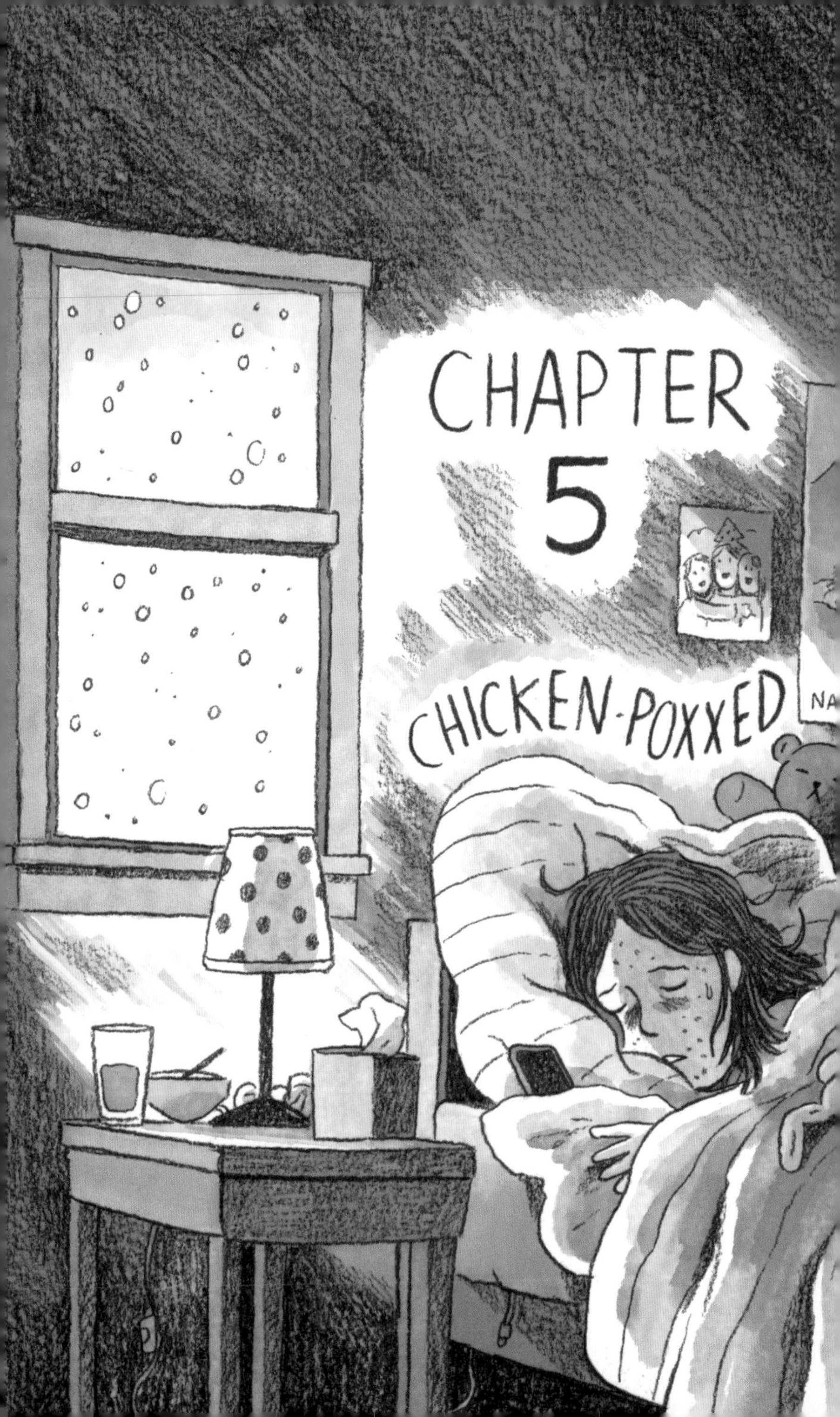
CHAPTER
5
CHICKEN-POXXED

When I was little, being sick
was kind of fun. Staying home,
eating Popsicles, watching TV.

But being sick in junior high,
even with Mom and Bruce
staying home to take care of
me, really stinks.

Tegan and all the kids at
school are doing things
without me...

... what if I miss something?

What if no one even
notices I'm gone?

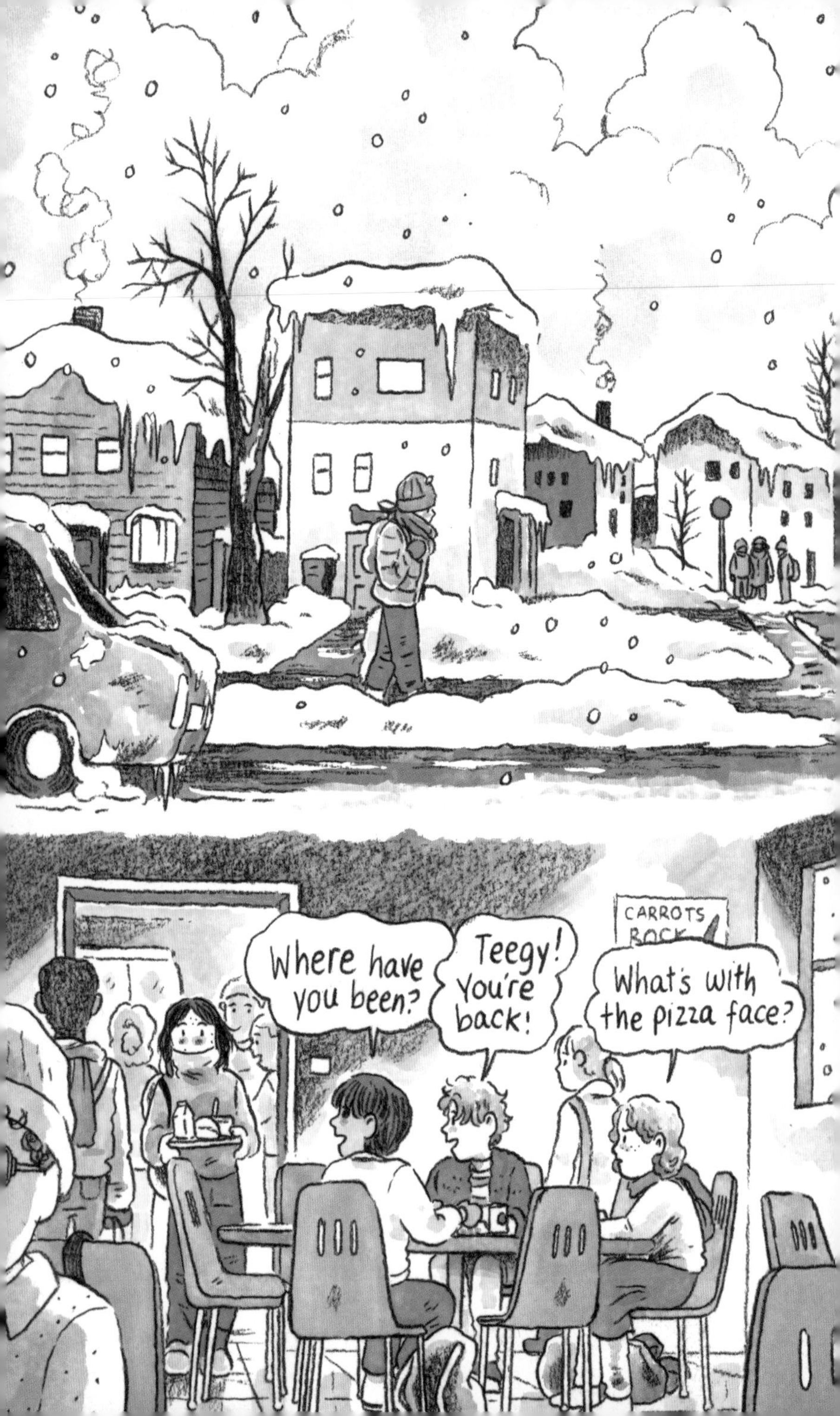
CARROTS ROCK
Where have you been?
Teegy! You're back!
What's with the pizza face?

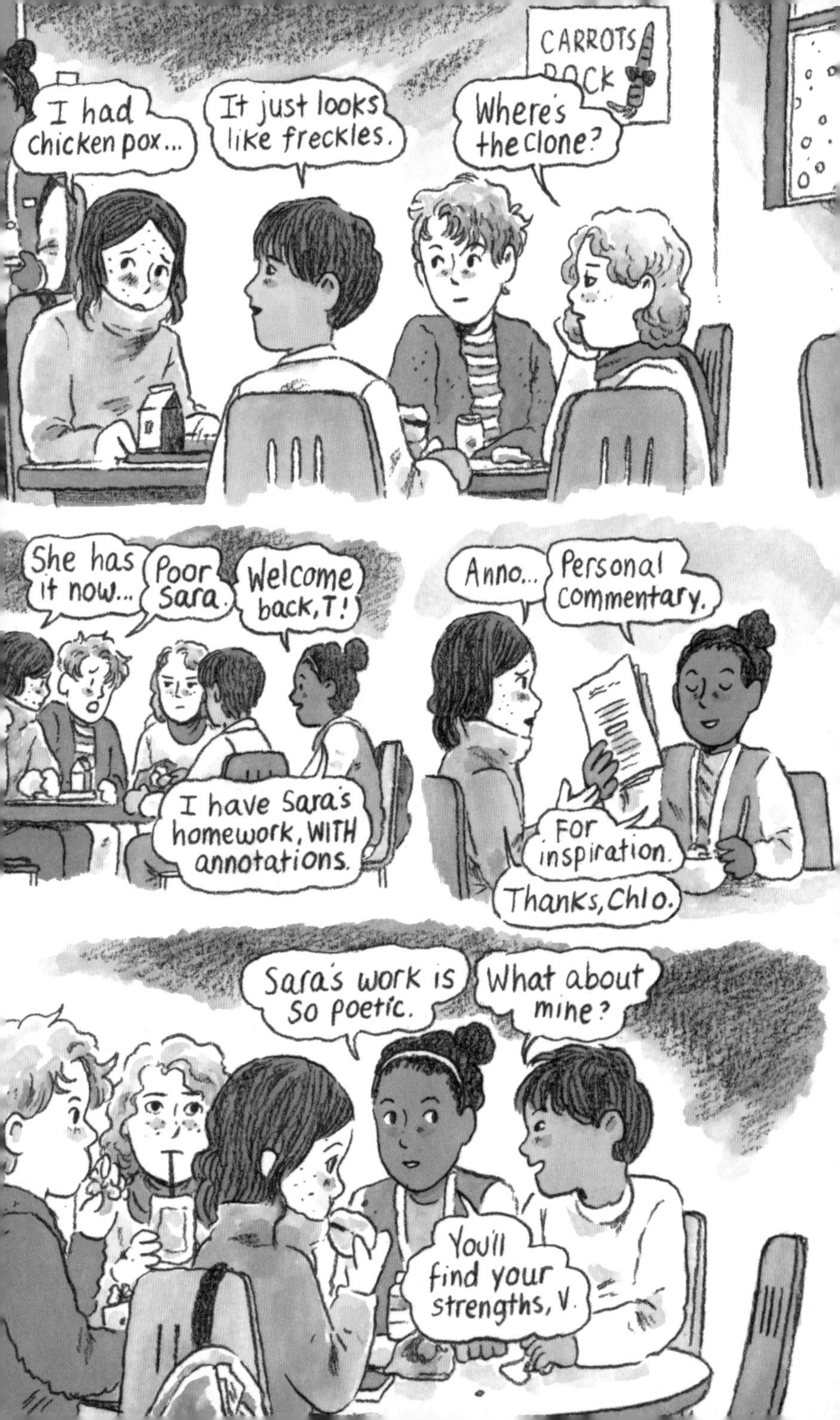
CARROTS ROCK
I had chicken pox...
It just looks like freckles.
Where's the clone?
She has it now...
Poor Sara.
Welcome back, T!
I have Sara's homework, WITH annotations.
Anno...
Personal commentary.
For inspiration.
Thanks, Chlo.
Sara's work is so poetic.
What about mine?
You'll find your strengths, V.

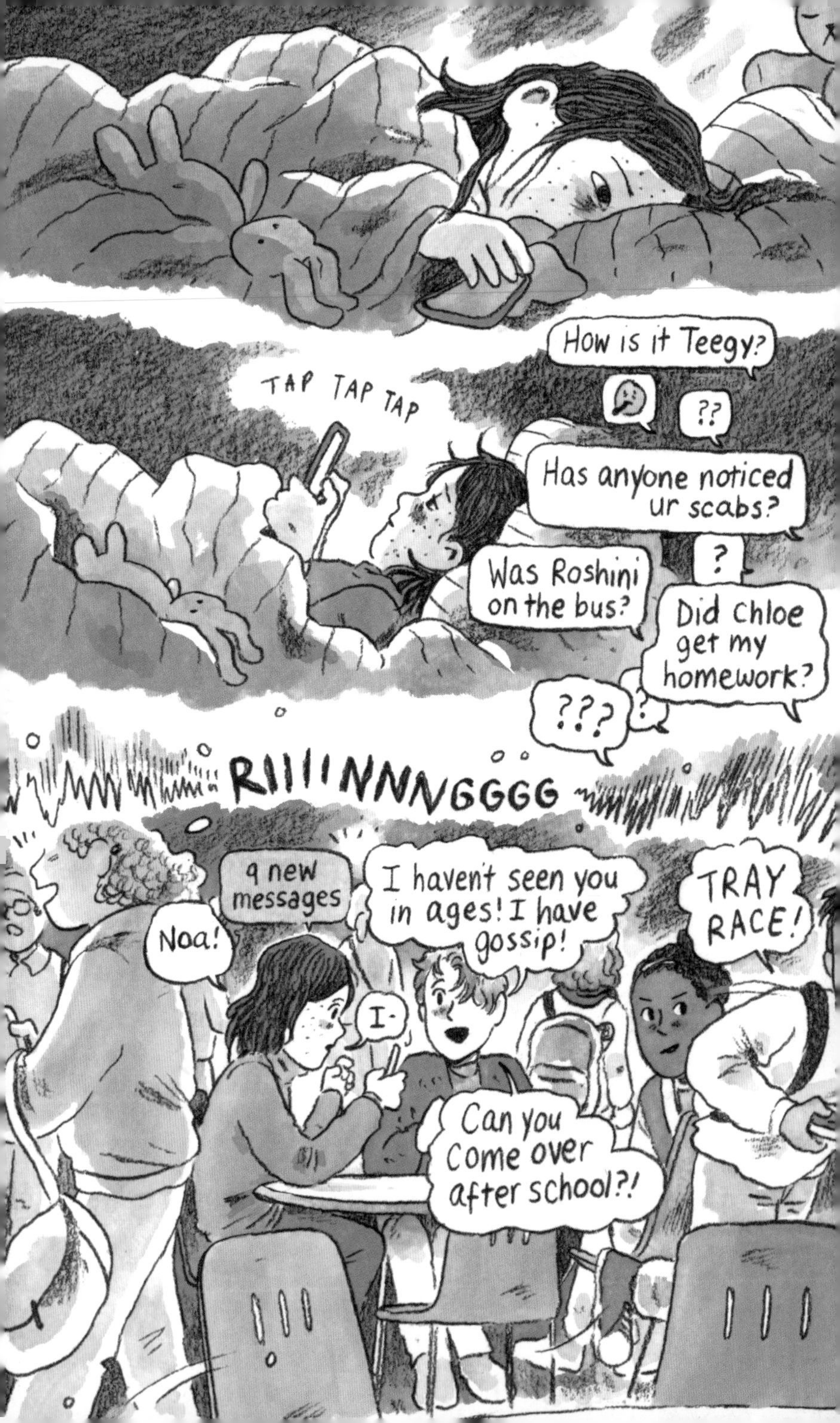
TAP TAP TAP
How is it Teegy?
??
Has anyone noticed ur scabs?
?
Was Roshini on the bus?
Did Chloe get my homework?
???
?
RIIIINNNGGGG
9 new messages
Noa!
I haven't seen you in ages! I have gossip!
TRAY RACE!
I-
Can you come over after school?!

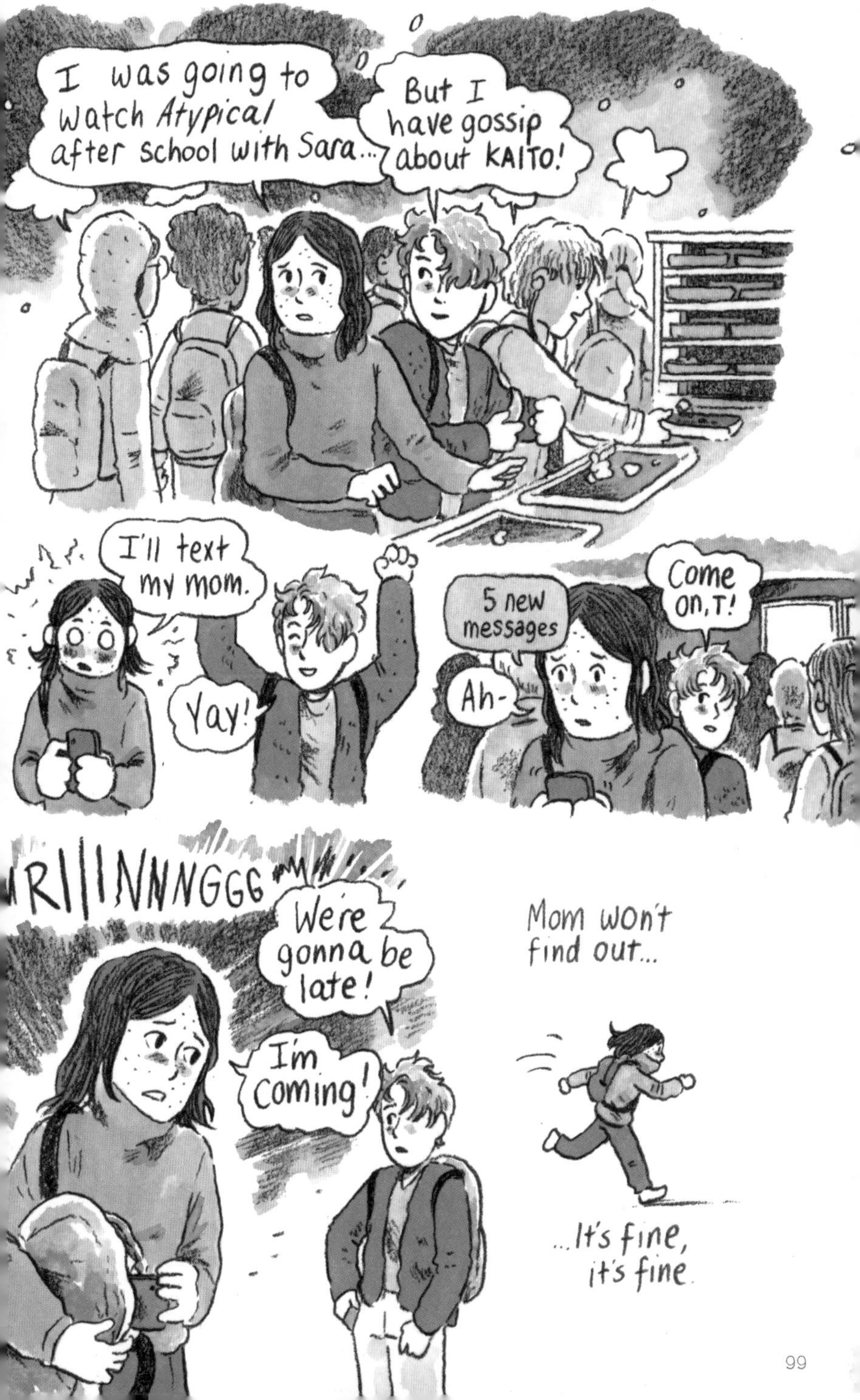
I was going to watch *Atypical* after school with Sara...
But I have gossip about KAITO!
I'll text my mom.
Yay!
5 new messages
Ah-
Come on, T!
RIIINNNGGG
We're gonna be late!
I'm coming!
Mom won't find out...
...It's fine, it's fine

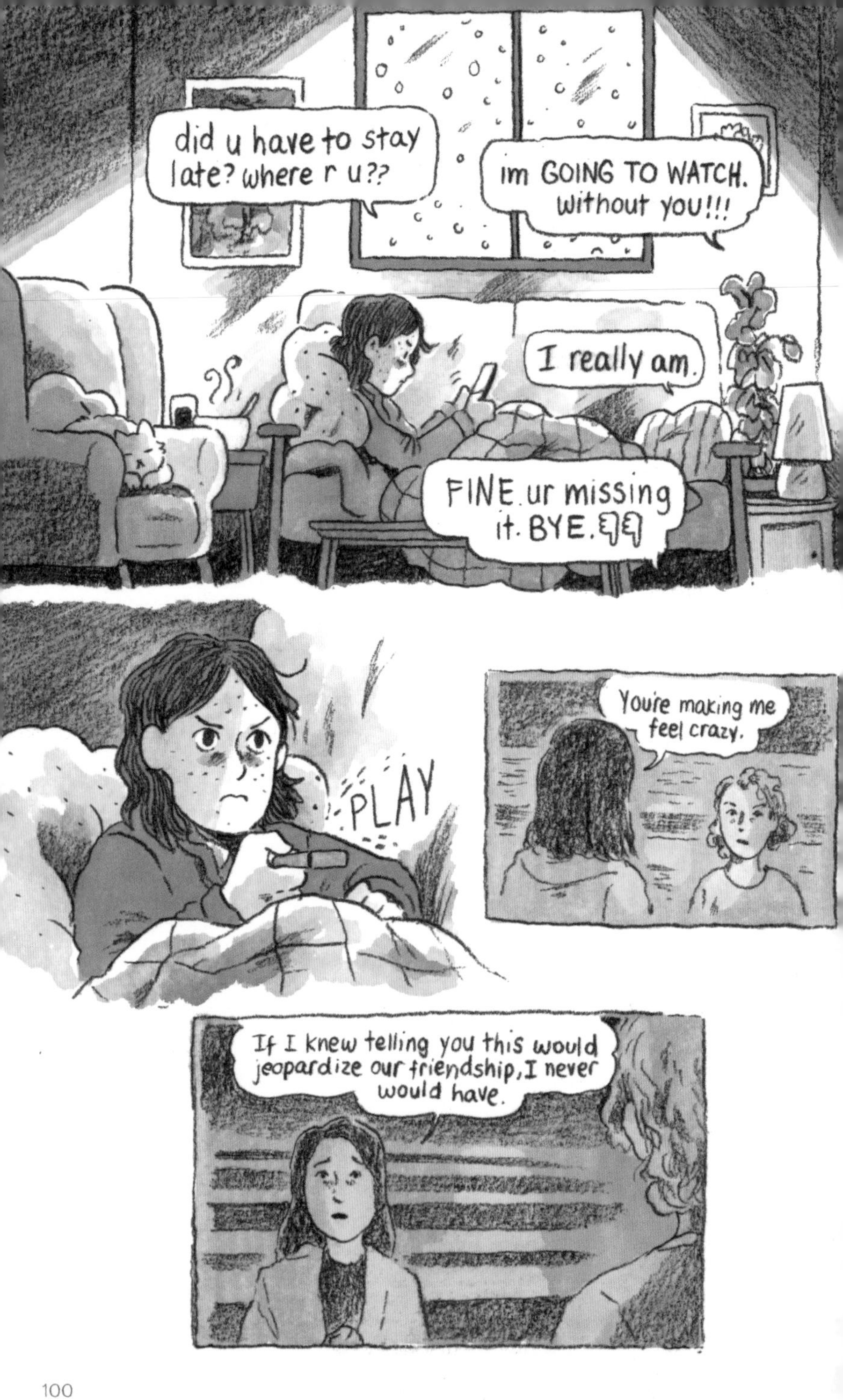
did u have to stay late? where r u??
im GOING TO WATCH. without you!!!
I really am.
FINE. ur missing it. BYE.
PLAY
You're making me feel crazy.
If I knew telling you this would jeopardize our friendship, I never would have.

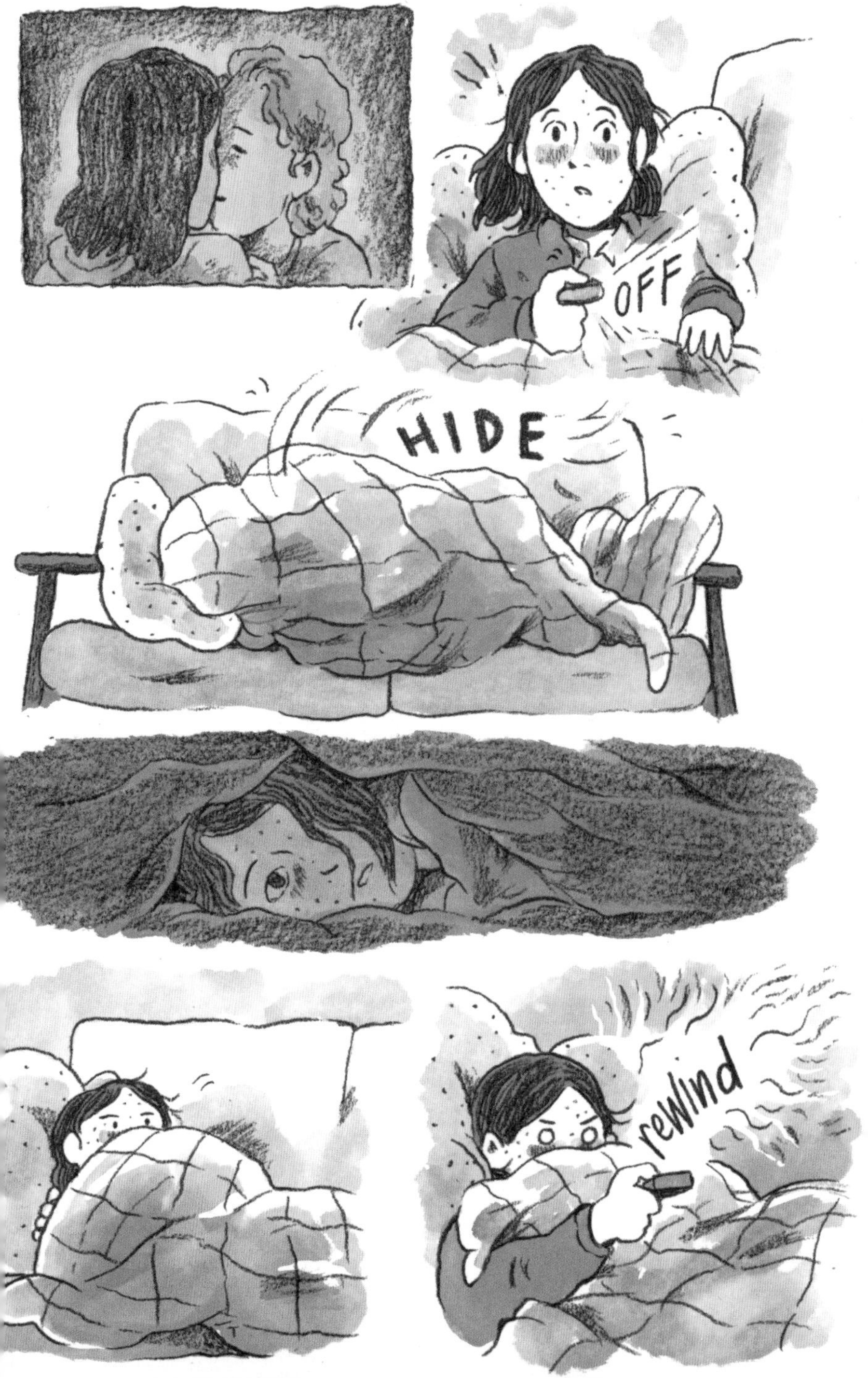
OFF
HIDE
rewind

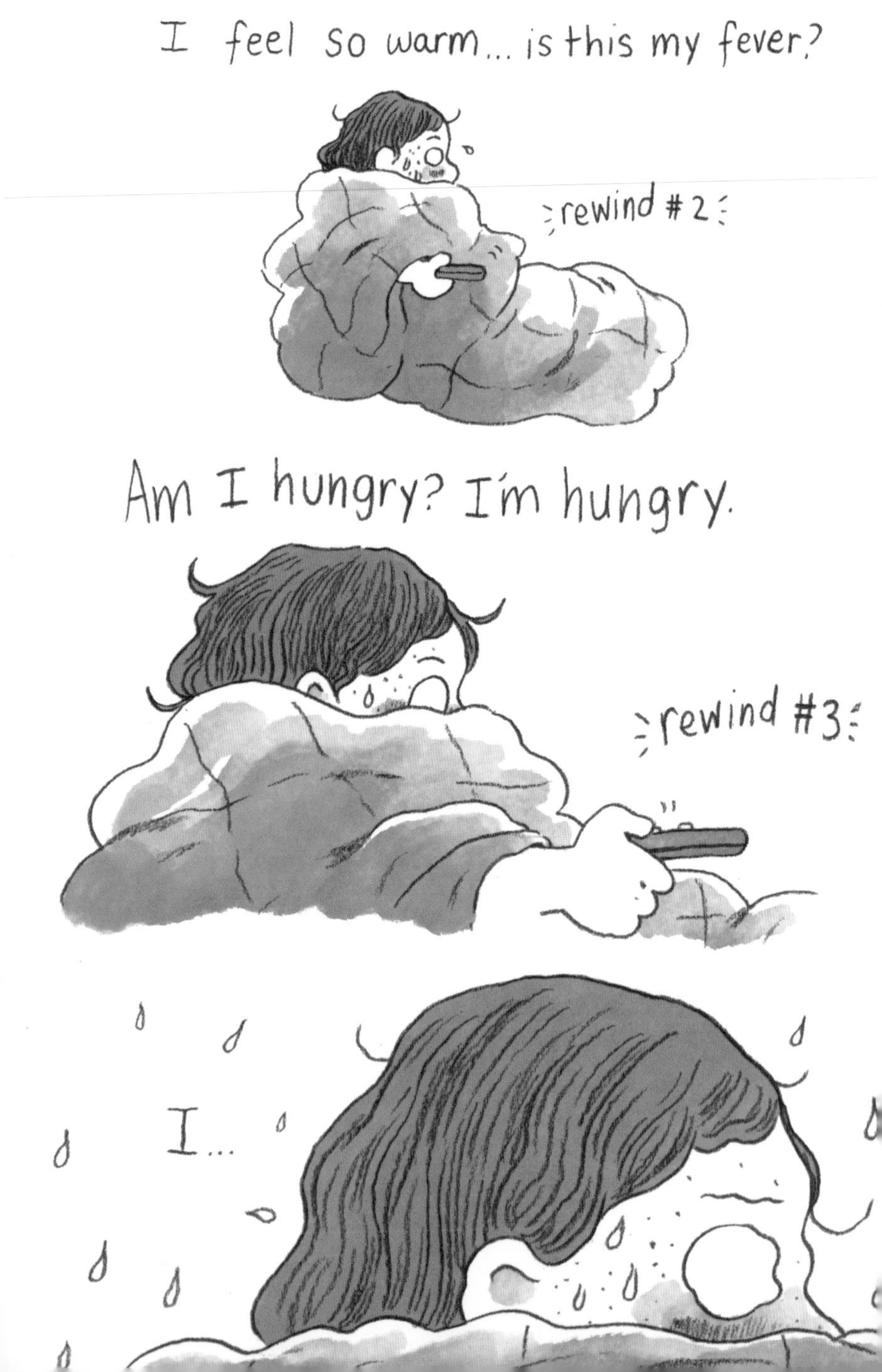
I feel so warm... is this my fever?
rewind #2
Am I hungry? I'm hungry.
rewind #3
I...

Does the TV keep track of how many times I watched this one part?

I'll just watch it one more time. Just one.

rewind #7

I... I don't think I'll tell Tegan about this.

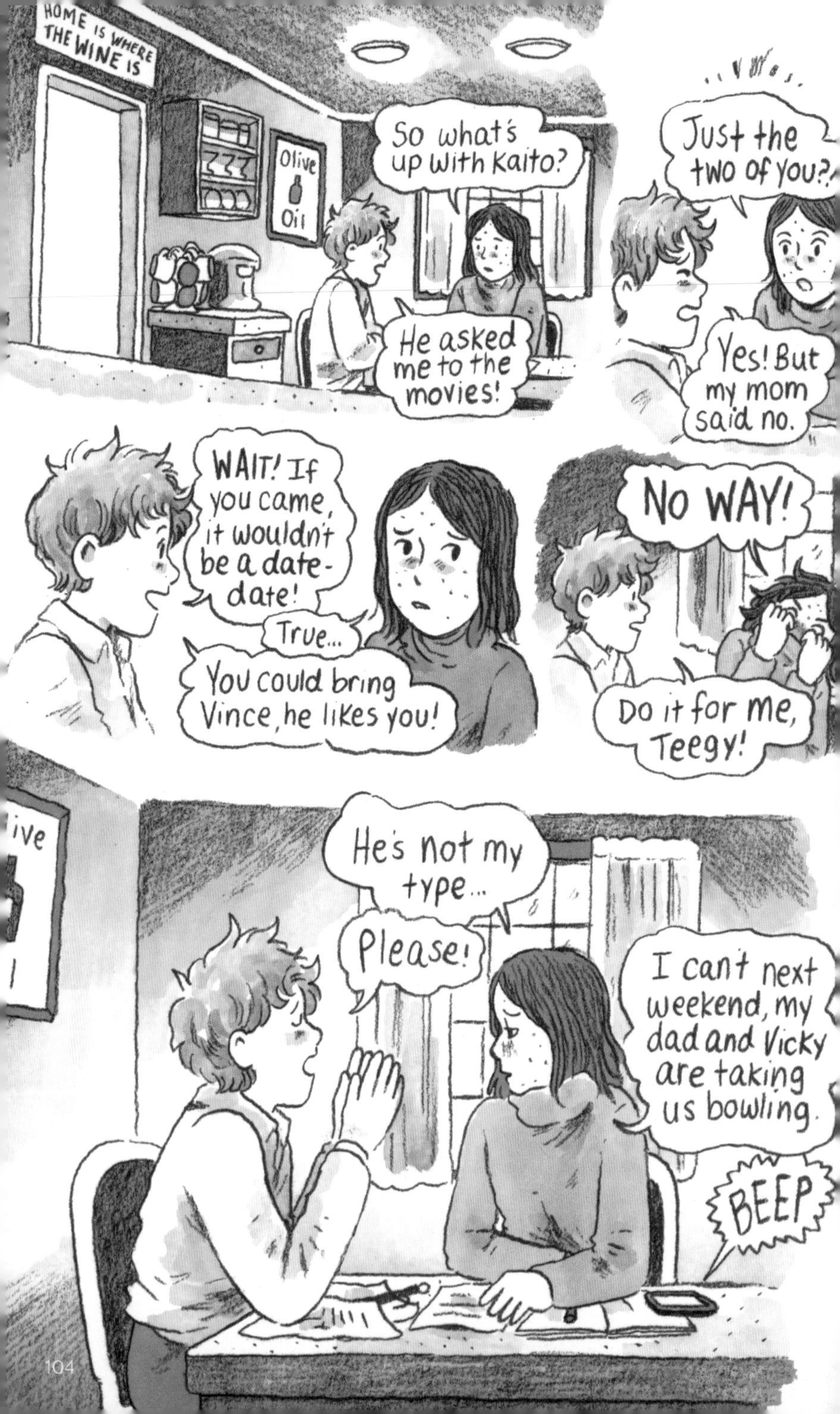
HOME IS WHERE THE WINE IS
Olive Oil
So what's up with Kaito?
He asked me to the movies!
Just the two of you?!
Yes! But my mom said no.
WAIT! If you came, it wouldn't be a date-date!
True...
You could bring Vince, he likes you!
NO WAY!
Do it for me, Teegy!
He's not my type...
Please!
I can't next weekend, my dad and Vicky are taking us bowling.
BEEP

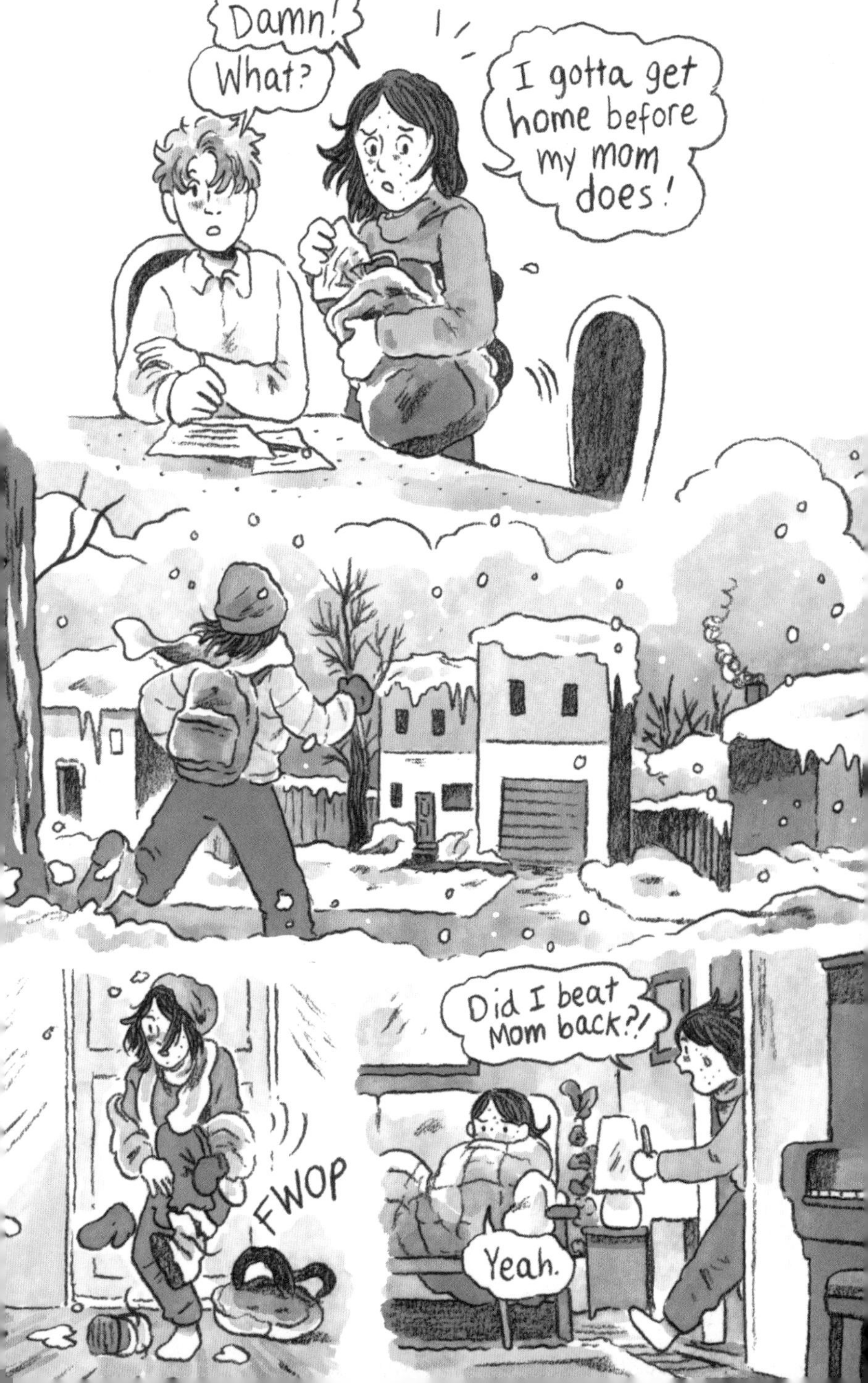
Damn!
What?
I gotta get home before my mom does!
FWOP
Did I beat Mom back?!
Yeah.

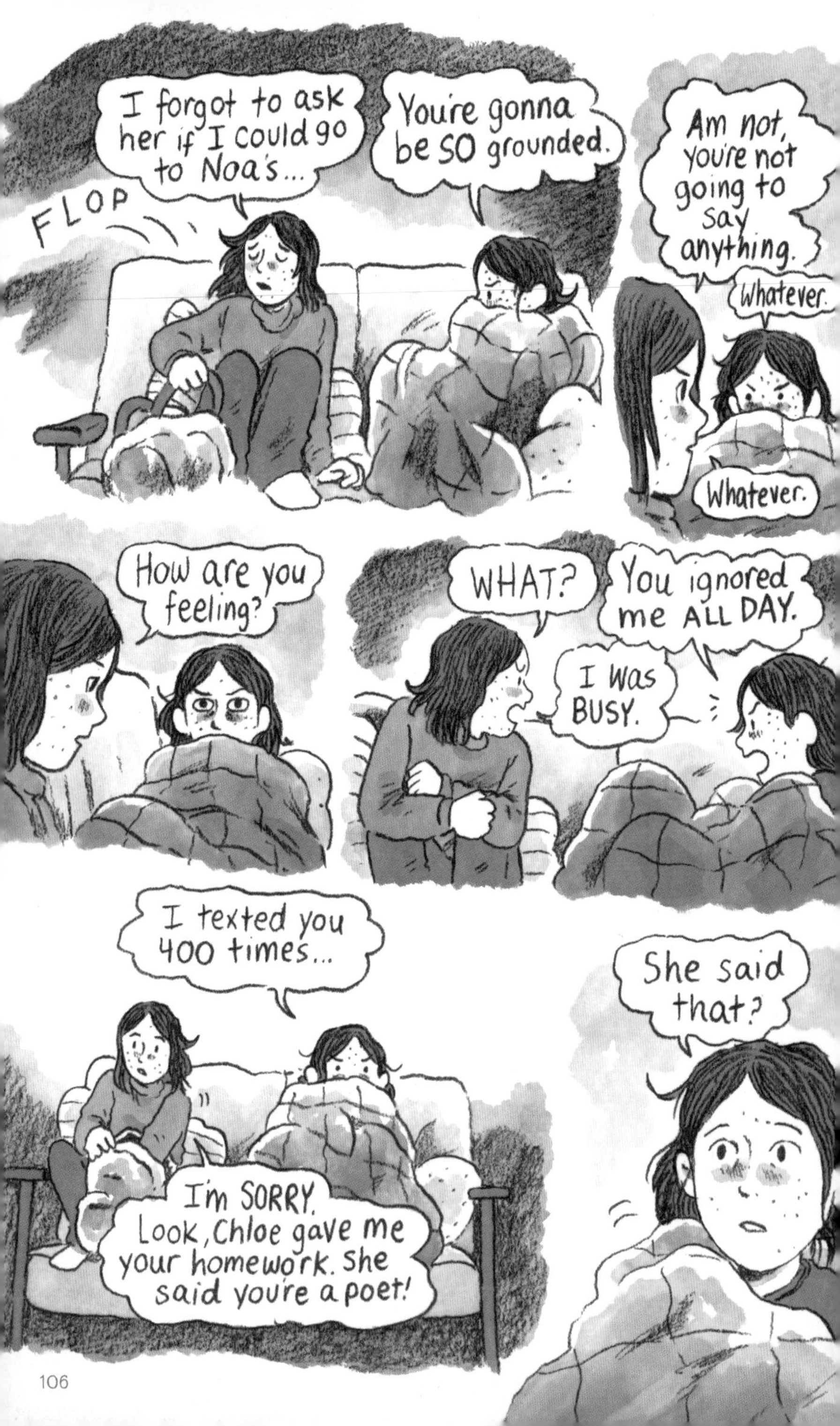
I forgot to ask her if I could go to Noa's...
FLOP
You're gonna be SO grounded.
Am not, you're not going to say anything.
Whatever.
Whatever.
How are you feeling?
WHAT?
You ignored me ALL DAY.
I was BUSY.
I texted you 400 times...
I'm SORRY. Look, Chloe gave me your homework. She said you're a poet!
She said that?

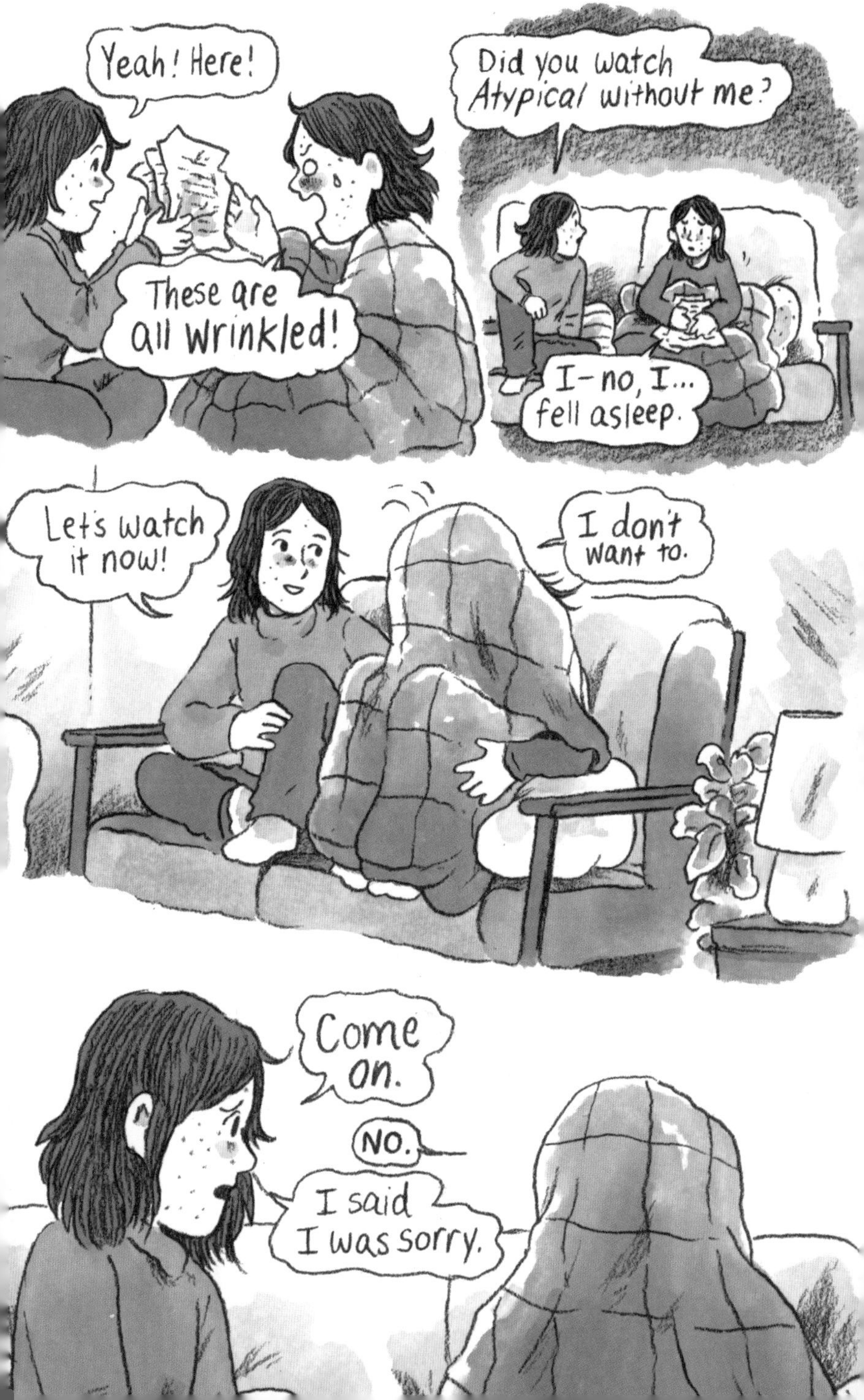
Yeah! Here!
These are all wrinkled!
Did you watch Atypical without me?
I–no, I... fell asleep.
Let's watch it now!
I don't want to.
Come on.
NO.
I said I was sorry.

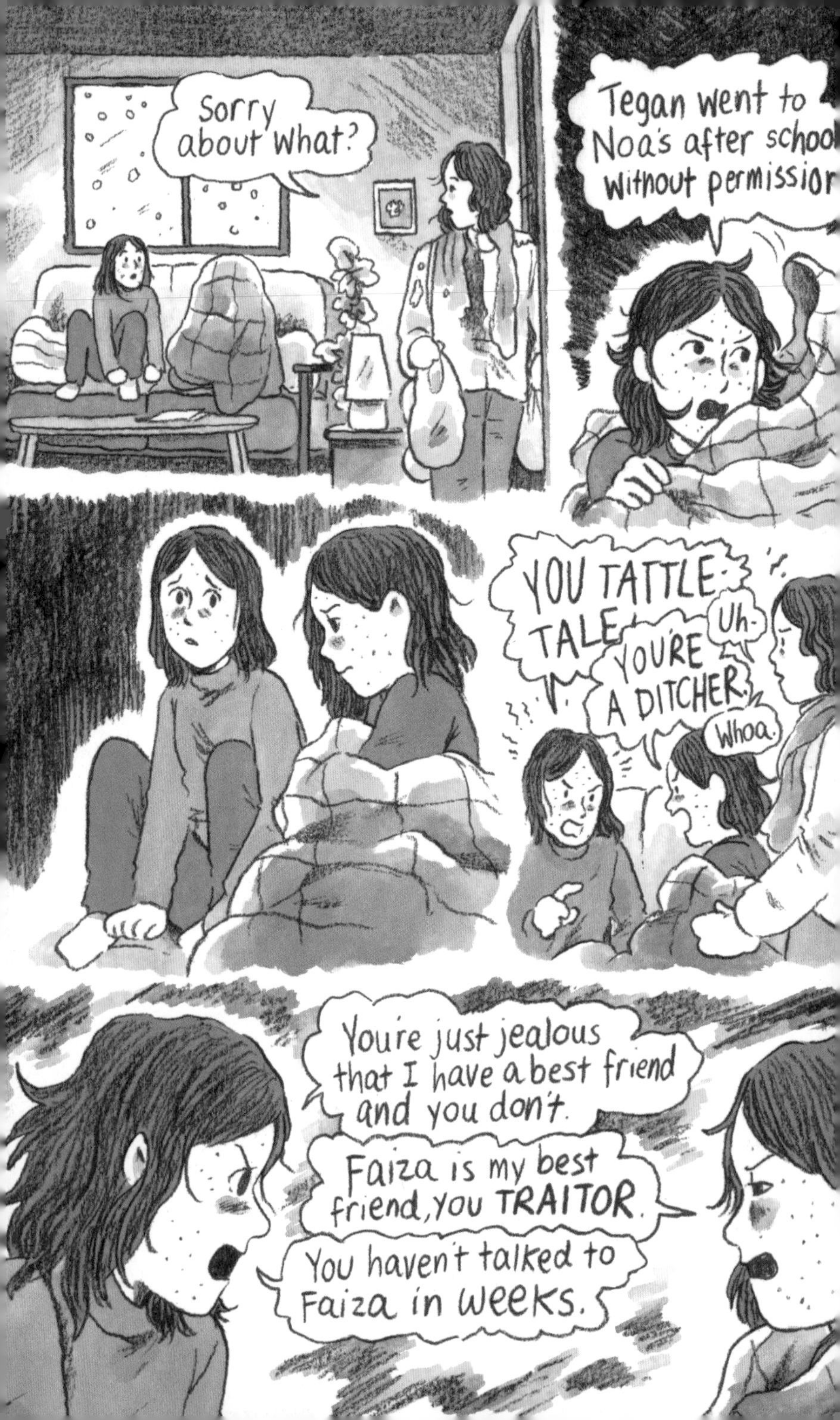
Sorry about what?
Tegan went to Noa's after school without permission
YOU TATTLE-TALE!
Uh-
YOU'RE A DITCHER.
Whoa.
You're just jealous that I have a best friend and you don't.
Faiza is my best friend, you TRAITOR.
You haven't talked to Faiza in weeks.

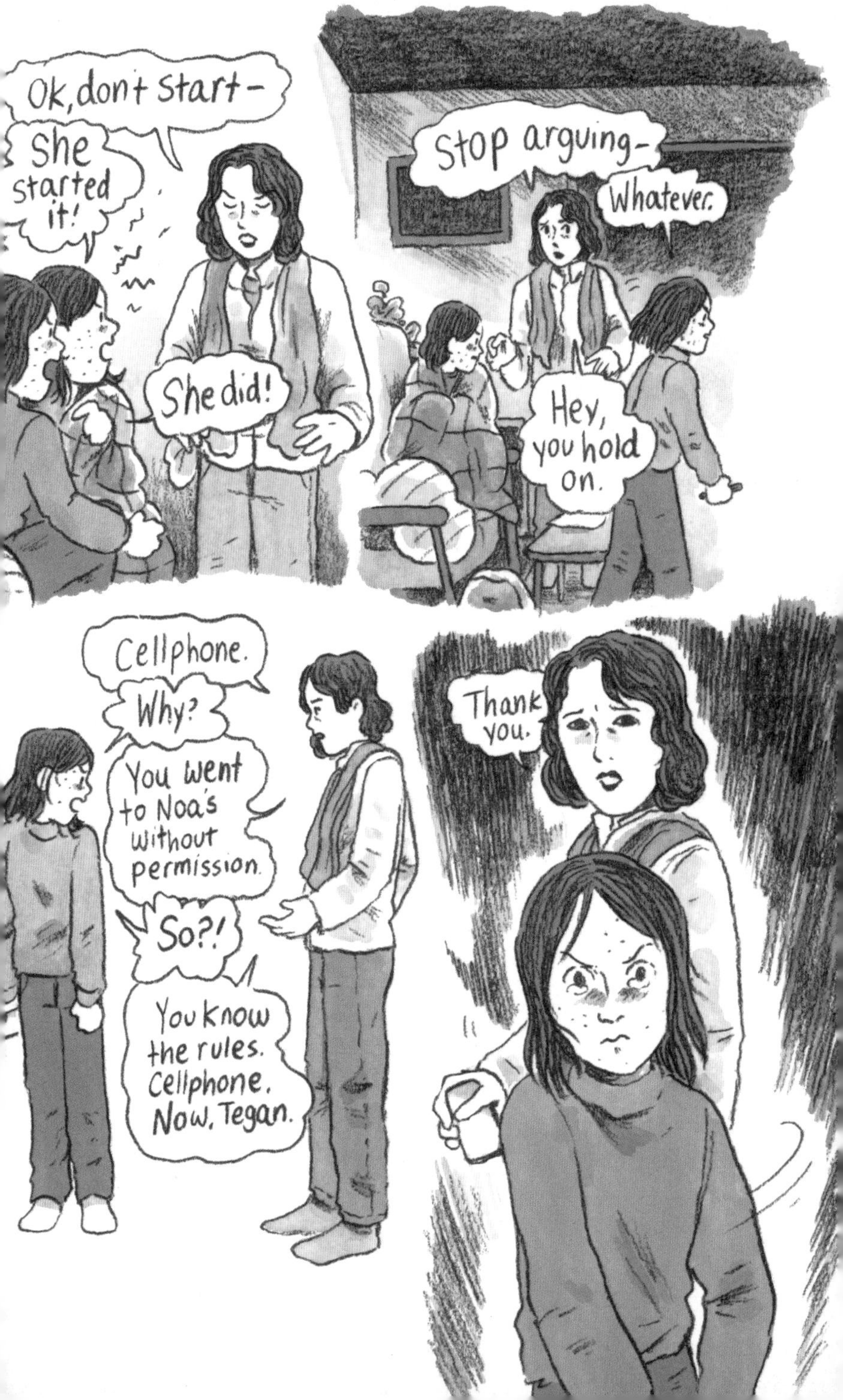
Ok, don't start-
She started it!
She did!
Stop arguing-
Whatever.
Hey, you hold on.
Cellphone.
Why?
You went to Noa's without permission.
So?!
You know the rules. Cellphone. Now, Tegan.
Thank you.

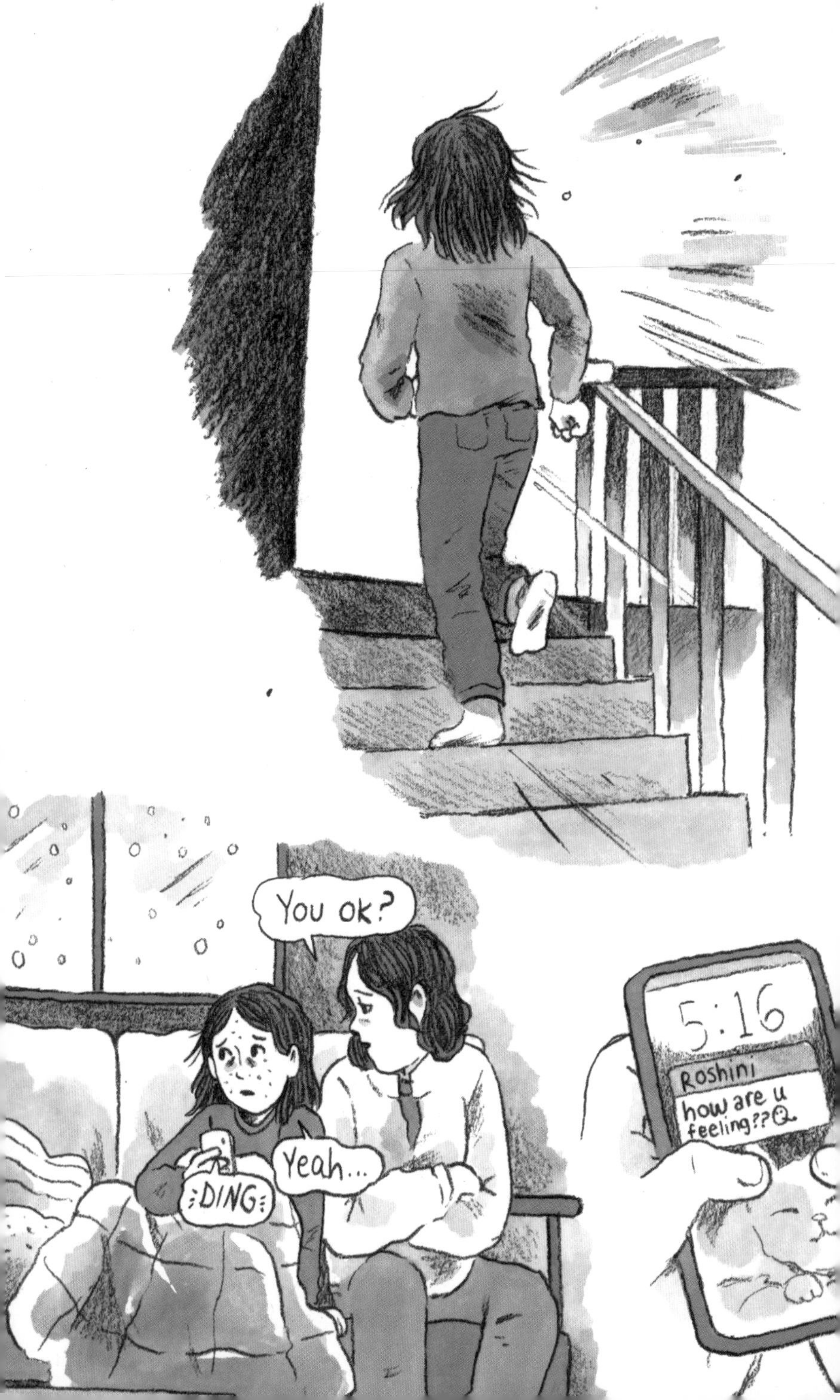
You ok?
DING
Yeah...
5:16
Roshini
how are u feeling??

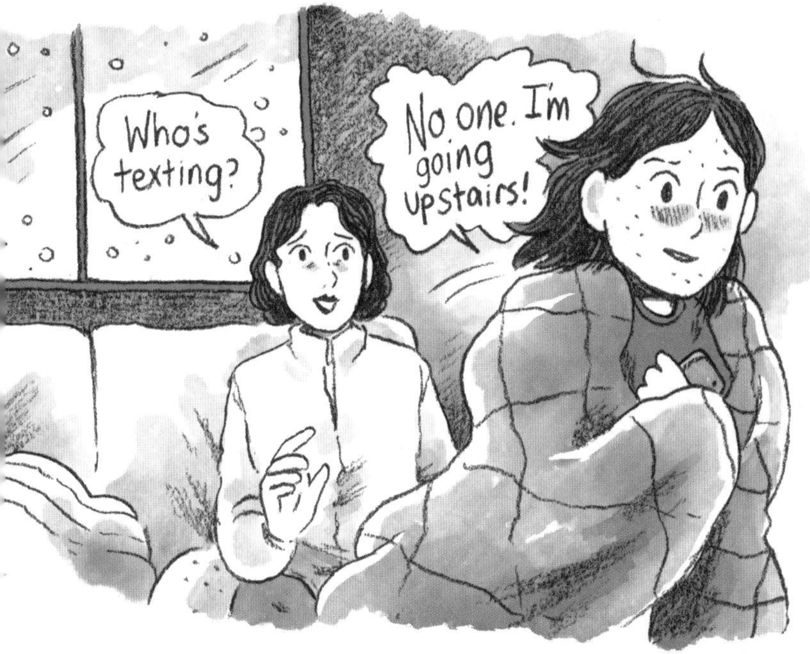
Who's texting?
No one. I'm going upstairs!

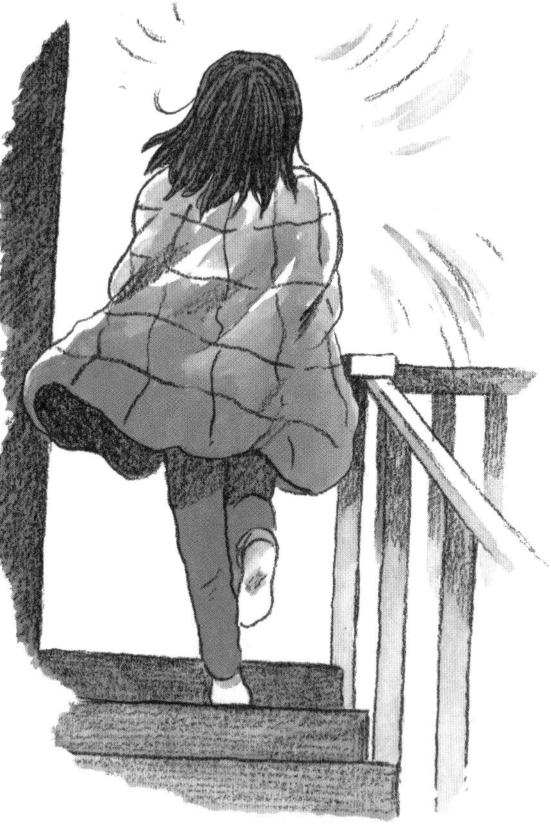

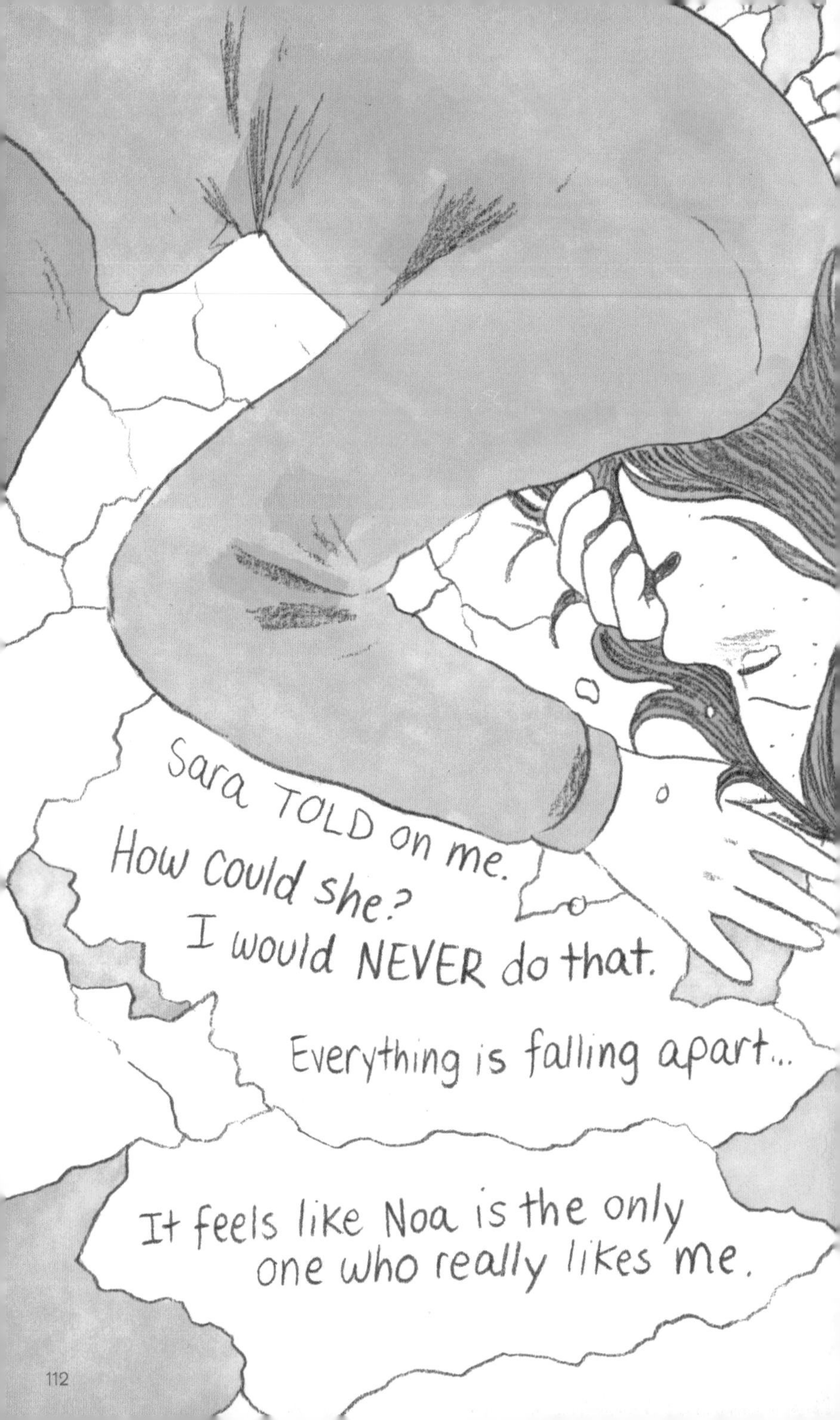
Sara TOLD on me.
How could she?
I would NEVER do that.
Everything is falling apart...
It feels like Noa is the only one who really likes me.

But even Noa... what does she really think of me?
Whatever. I don't care.
I don't care what anyone says.
I just want to cry.

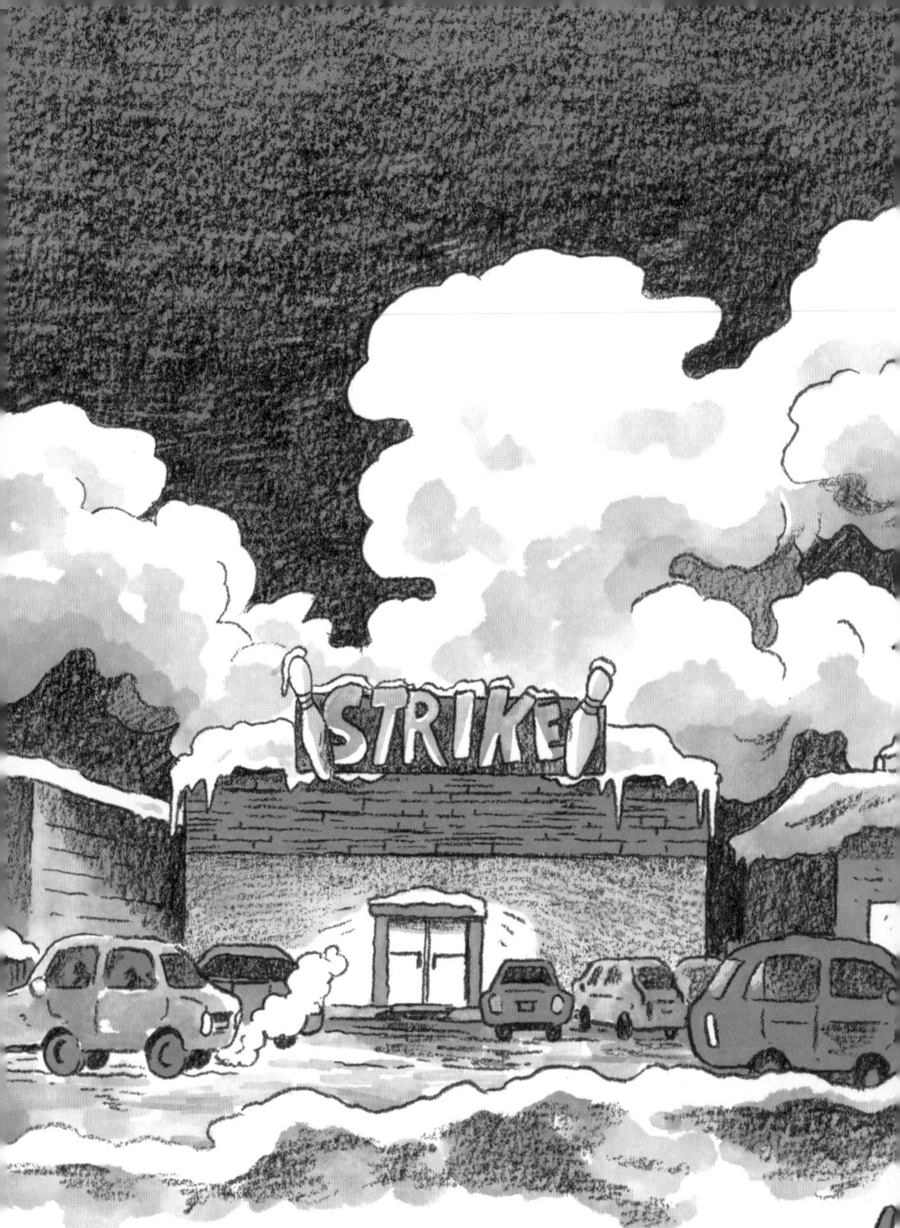
STRIKE

CHAPTER 6
STRIKE!

Sara feels so far away
lately...

I'm still kinda mad at her,
but I still wish she'd talk
to me.

It used to be that
everything happened to
us at the same time,
and we could deal
with it together.

Now, things aren't so simple.

There's so much to deal with.
Like Dad's new girlfriend...

... Vicky.

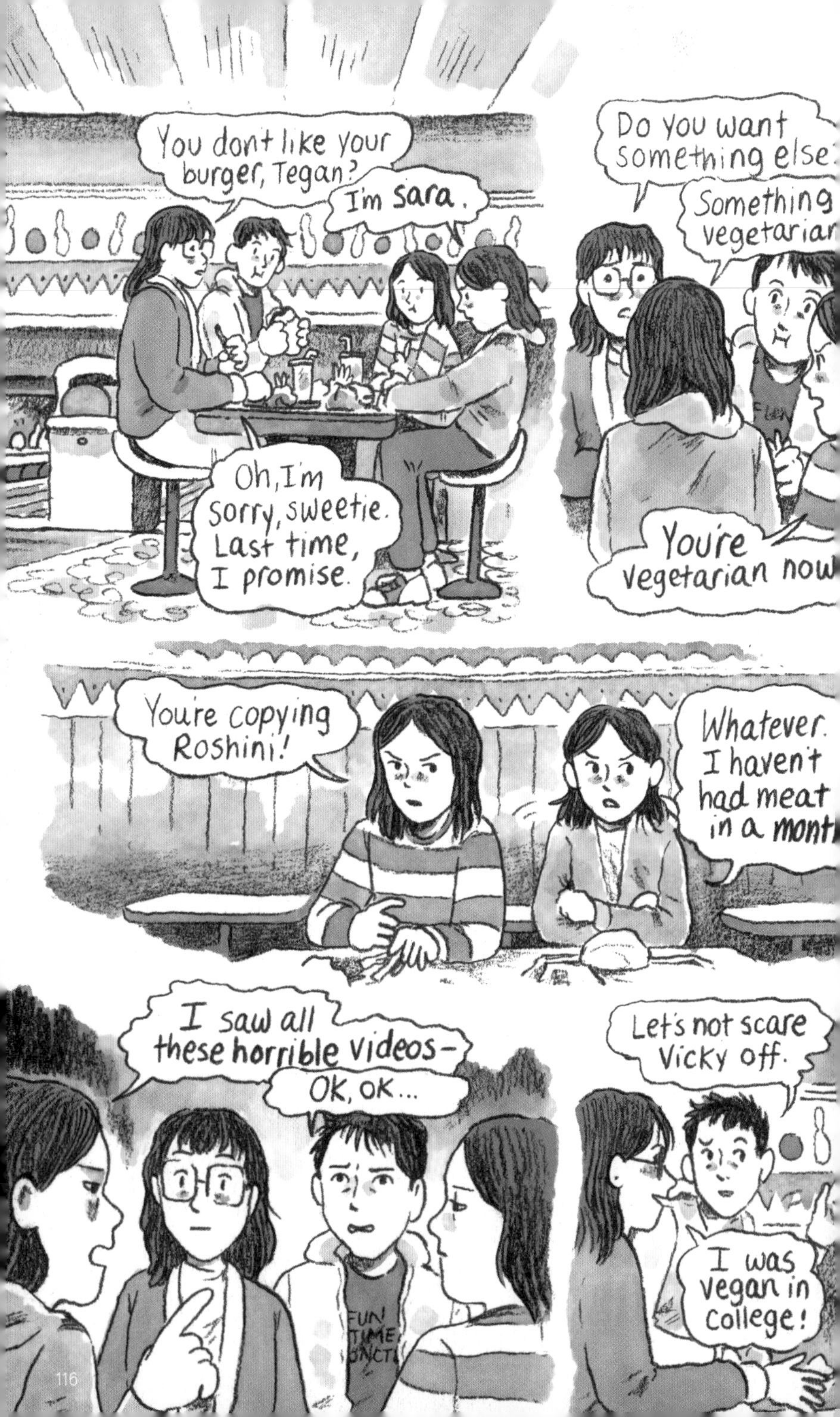
You don't like your burger, Tegan?
I'm Sara.
Oh, I'm sorry, sweetie. Last time, I promise.
Do you want something else?
Something vegetarian
You're vegetarian now
You're copying Roshini!
Whatever. I haven't had meat in a mont
I saw all these horrible videos–
OK, OK...
FUN TIME
Let's not scare Vicky off.
I was vegan in college!

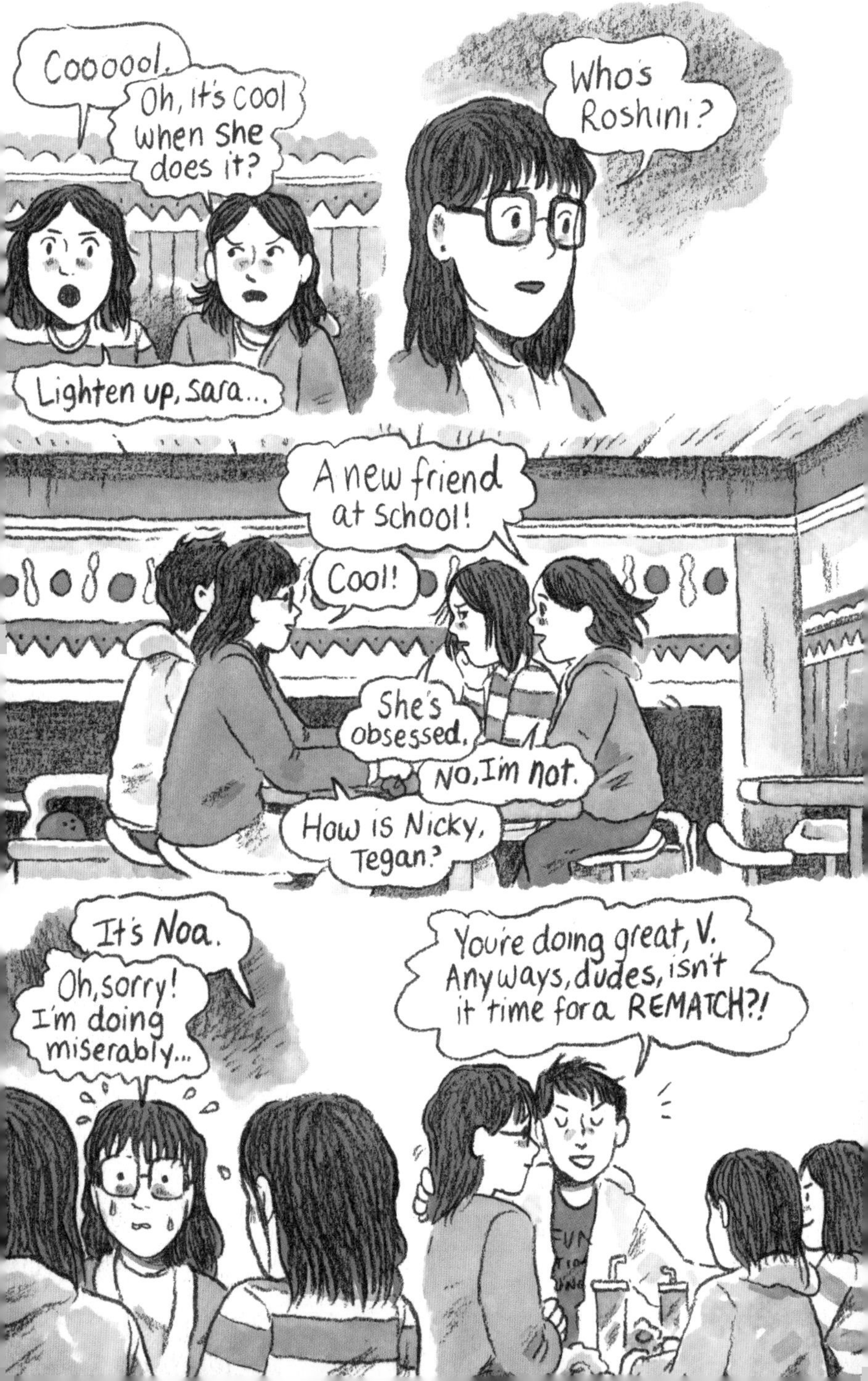
Coooool.
Oh, it's cool when she does it?
Lighten up, Sara...
Who's Roshini?
A new friend at school!
Cool!
She's obsessed.
No, I'm not.
How is Nicky, Tegan?
It's Noa.
Oh, sorry! I'm doing miserably...
You're doing great, V. Anyways, dudes, isn't it time for a REMATCH?!

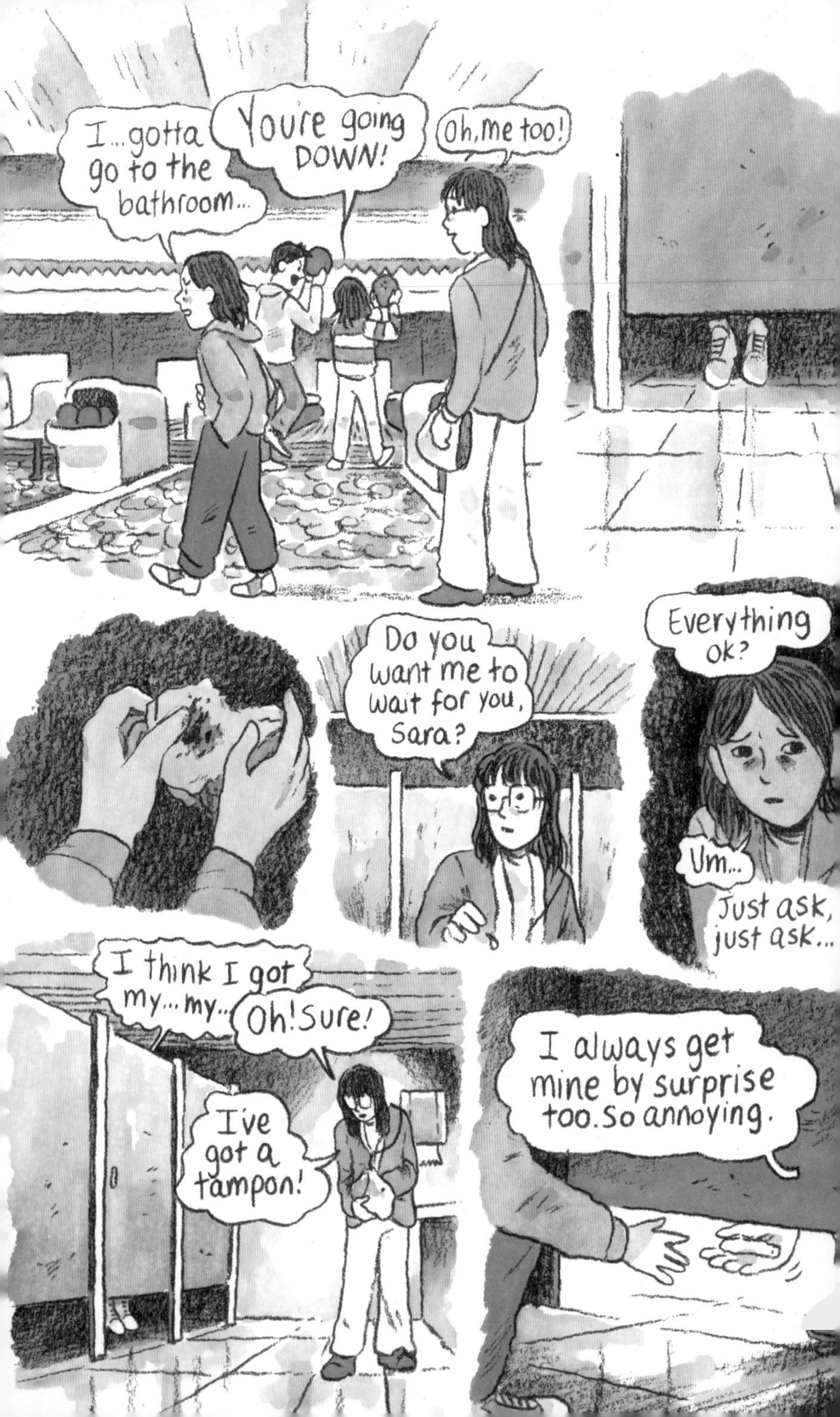
I...gotta go to the bathroom...
You're going DOWN!
Oh, me too!
Do you want me to wait for you, Sara?
Everything ok?
Um...
Just ask, just ask...
I think I got my...my...
Oh! Sure!
I've got a tampon!
I always get mine by surprise too. So annoying.

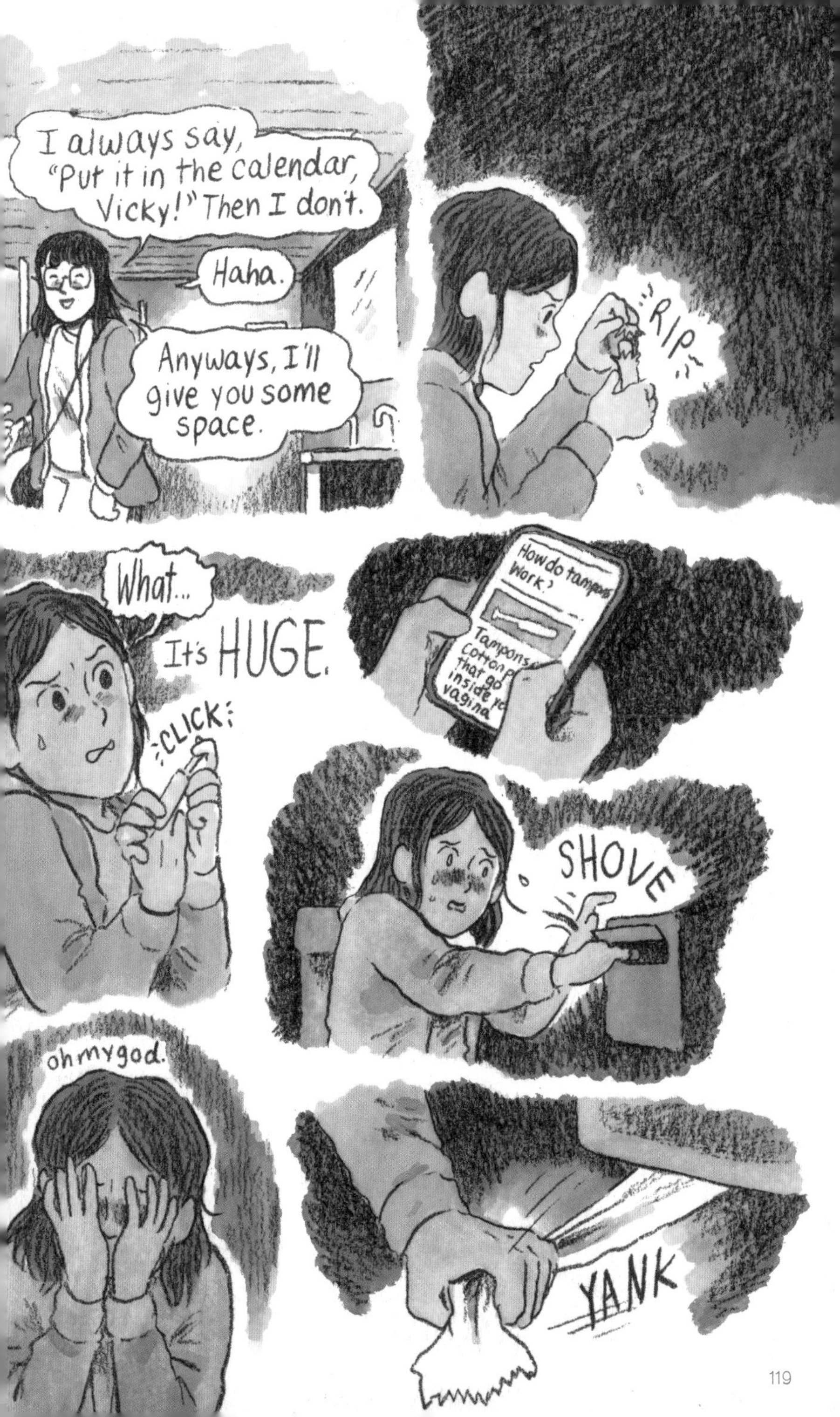
I always say, "Put it in the calendar, Vicky!" Then I don't.
Haha.
Anyways, I'll give you some space.
RIP
What...
It's HUGE.
CLICK
How do tampons work?
Tampons
SHOVE
ohmygod.
YANK

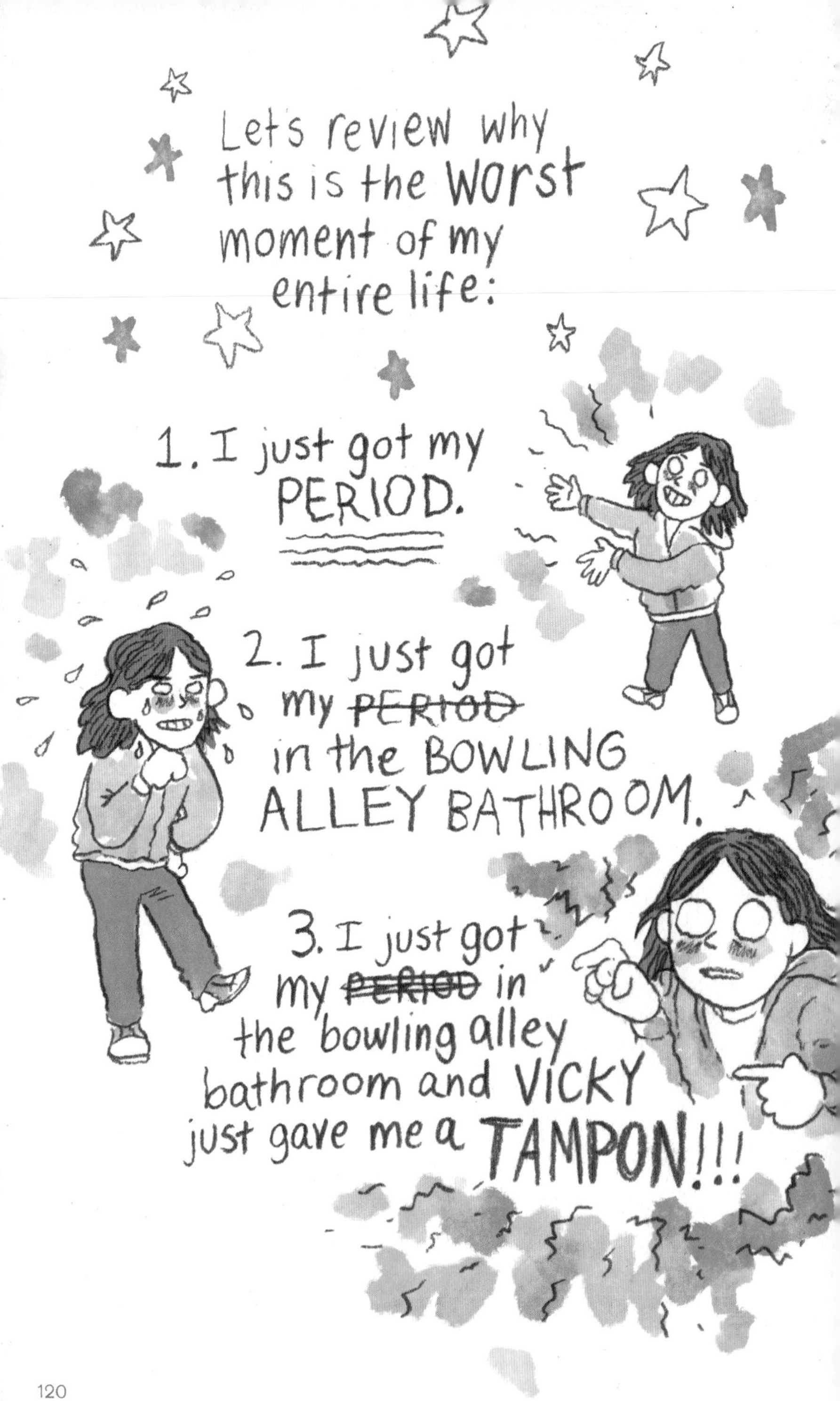
Let's review why this is the WORST moment of my entire life:
1. I just got my PERIOD.
2. I just got my ~~PERIOD~~ in the BOWLING ALLEY BATHROOM.
3. I just got my ~~PERIOD~~ in the bowling alley bathroom and VICKY just gave me a TAMPON!!!

4. I just got my PERIOD in the bowling alley bathroom and VICKY just gave me a TAMPON and I don't know how to use it because I'm scared and what if it gets stuck and I can't get it out and who will I call for help and this whole time I've been wearing STINKY BOWLING SHOES!!!

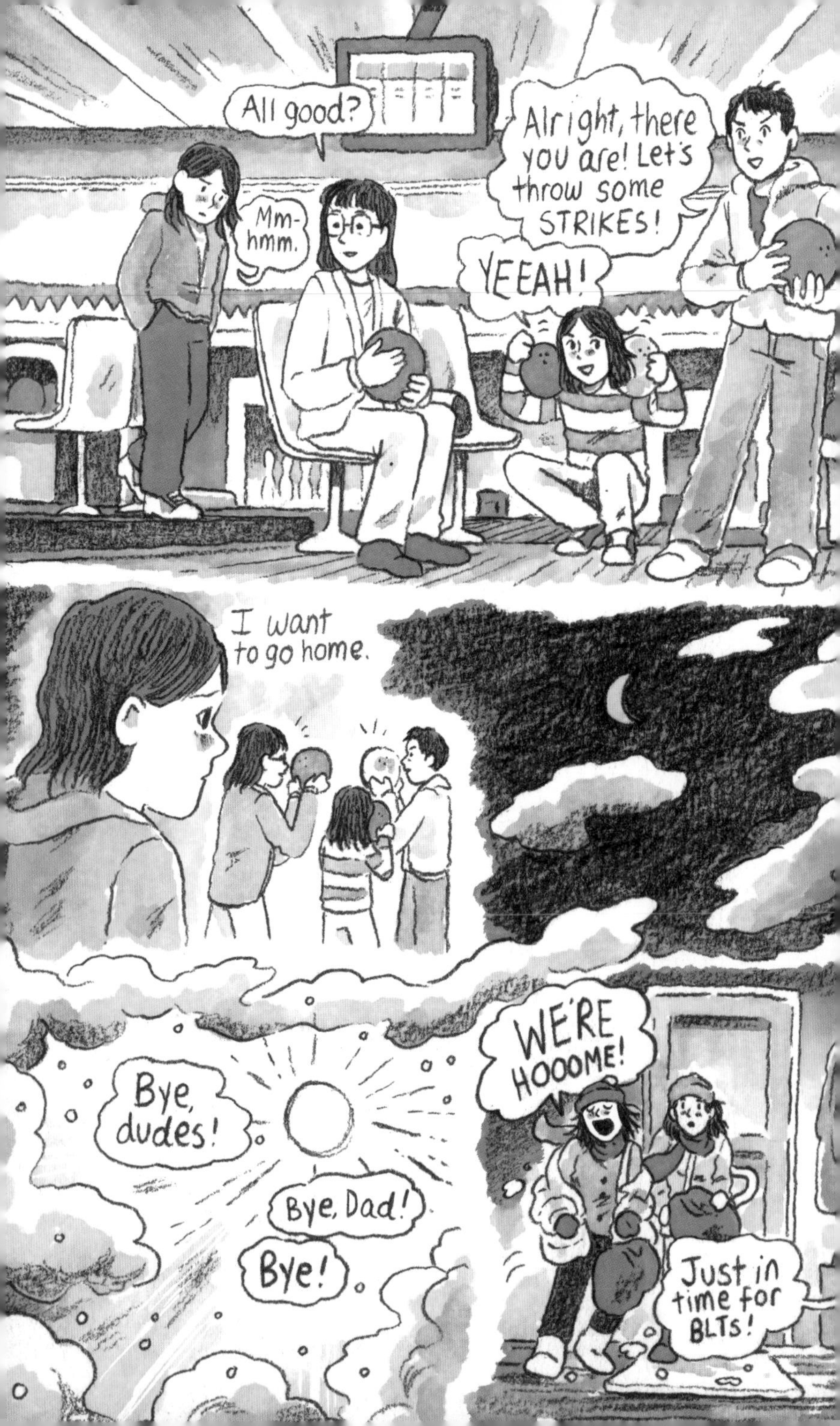
All good?
Mm-hmm.
Alright, there you are! Let's throw some STRIKES!
YEEAH!
I want to go home.
Bye, dudes!
Bye, Dad!
Bye!
WE'RE HOOOME!
Just in time for BLTS!

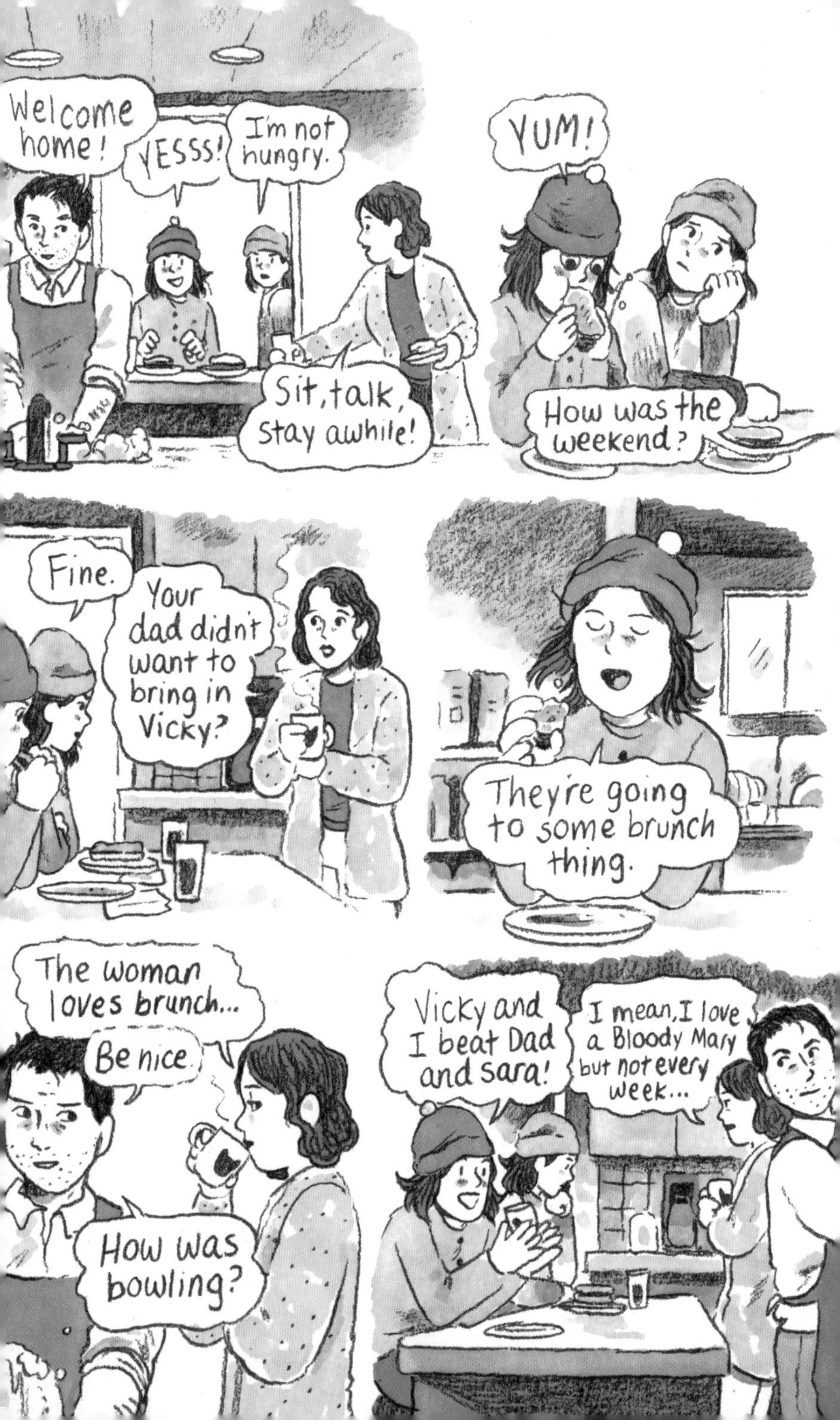

Welcome home!
YESSS!
I'm not hungry.
Sit, talk, stay awhile!
YUM!
How was the weekend?
Fine.
Your dad didn't want to bring in Vicky?
They're going to some brunch thing.
The woman loves brunch...
Be nice.
How was bowling?
Vicky and I beat Dad and sara!
I mean, I love a Bloody Mary but not every week...

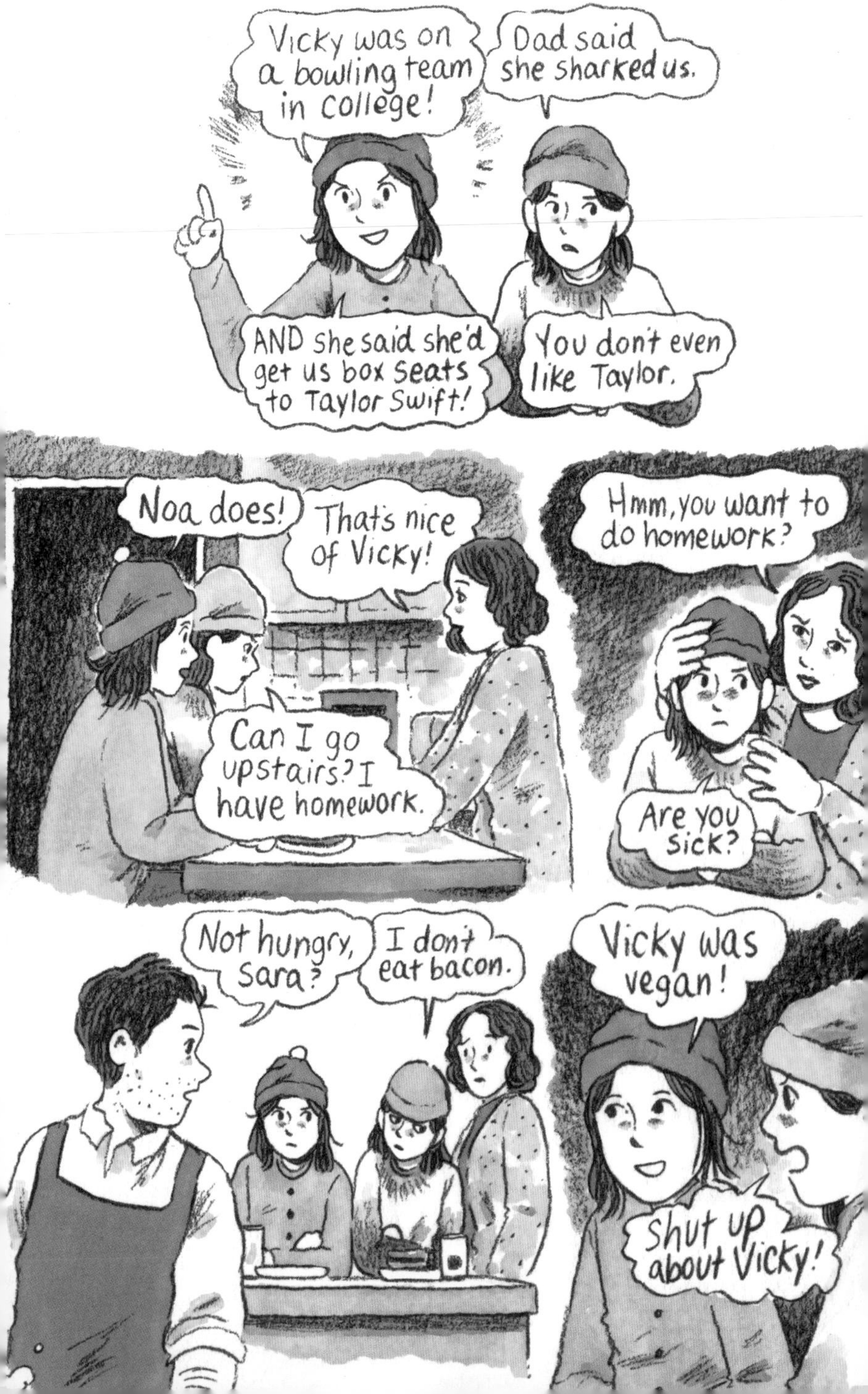
Vicky was on a bowling team in college!
Dad said she sharked us.
AND she said she'd get us box seats to Taylor Swift!
You don't even like Taylor.
Noa does!
That's nice of Vicky!
Can I go upstairs? I have homework.
Hmm, you want to do homework?
Are you sick?
Not hungry, Sara?
I don't eat bacon.
Vicky was vegan!
Shut up about Vicky!

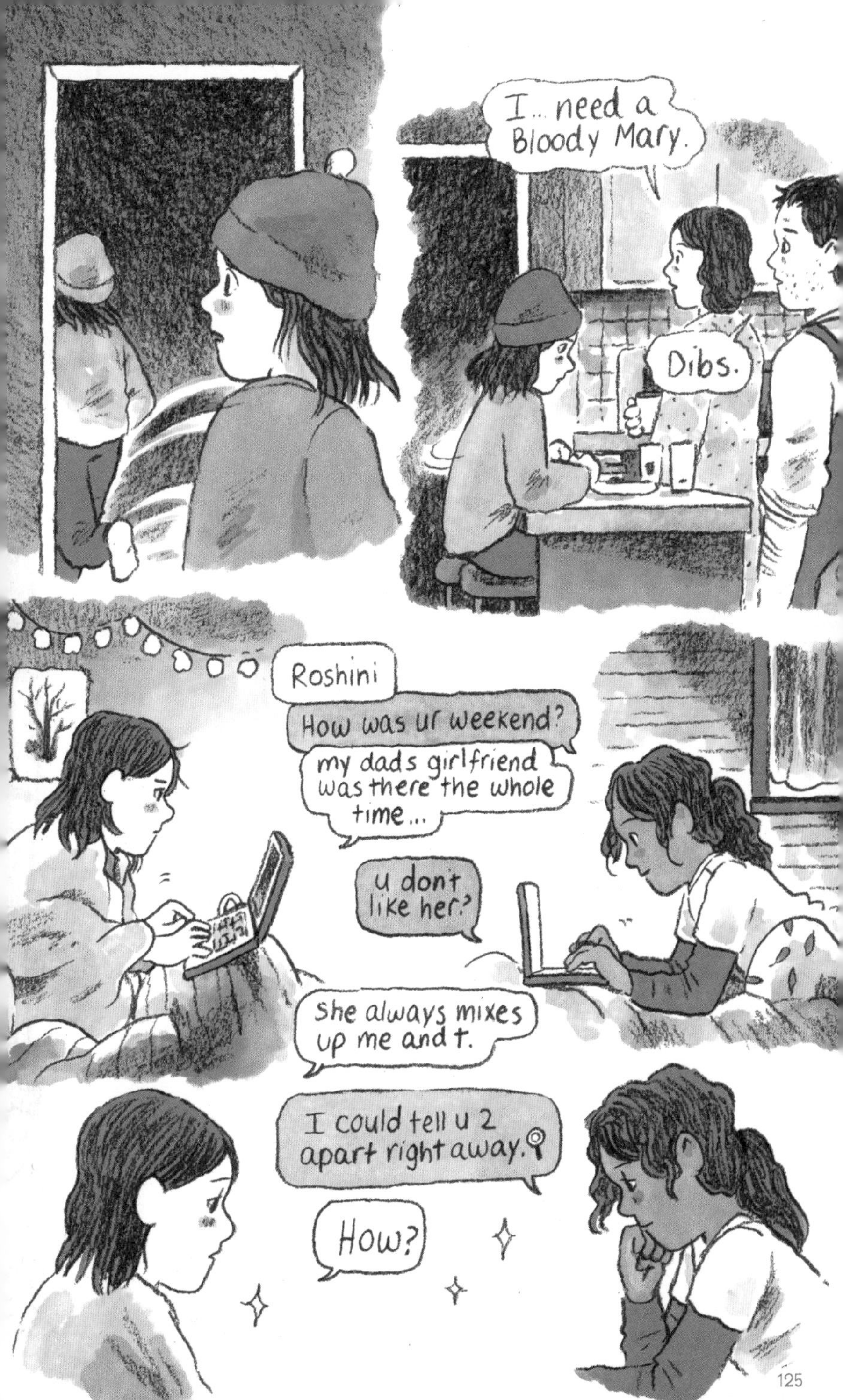
I... need a Bloody Mary.
Dibs.
Roshini
How was ur weekend?
my dads girlfriend was there the whole time...
u don't like her?
she always mixes up me and t.
I could tell u 2 apart right away.
How?

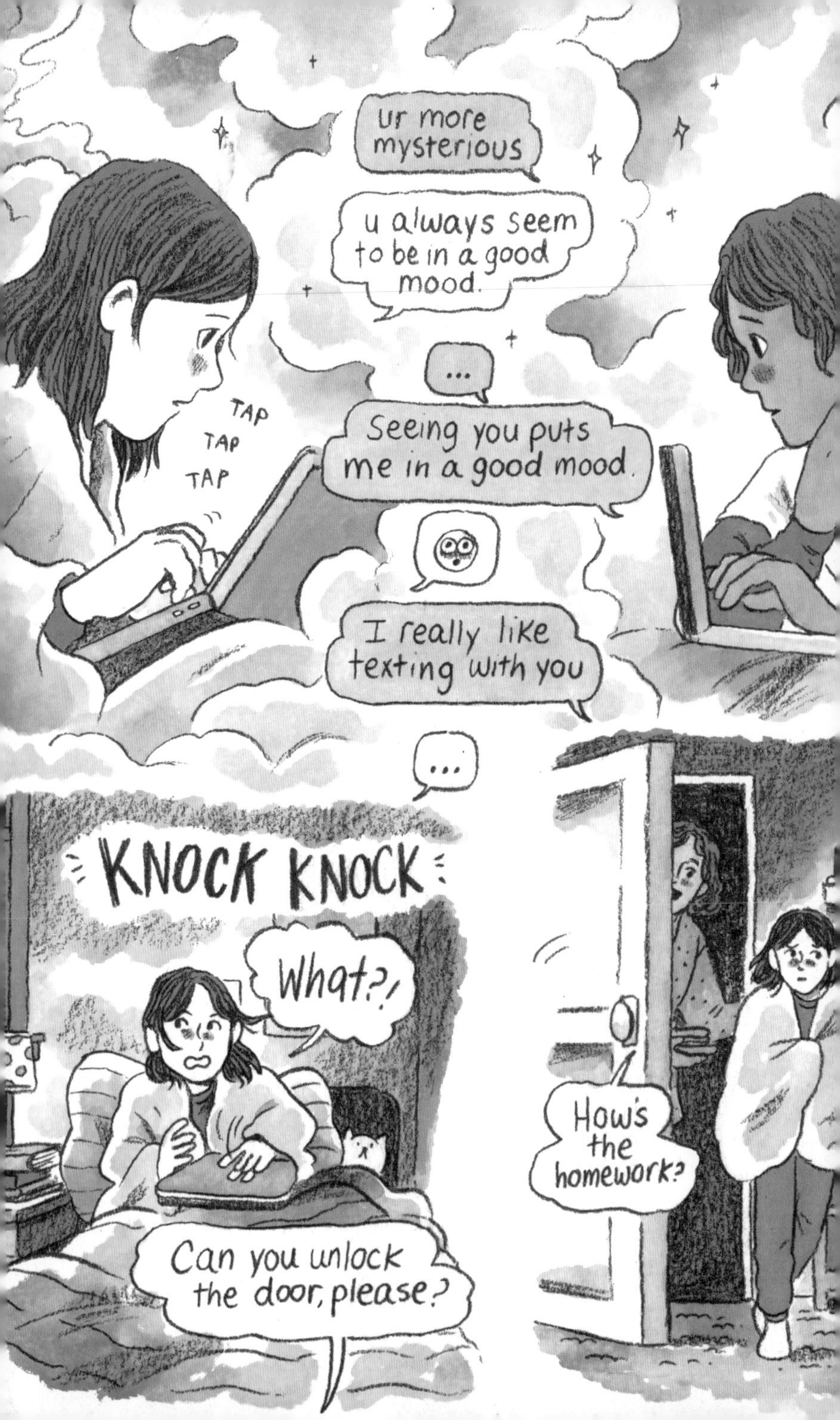

ur more mysterious
u always seem to be in a good mood.
...
Seeing you puts me in a good mood.
I really like texting with you
TAP TAP TAP
...
KNOCK KNOCK
What?!
Can you unlock the door, please?
How's the homework?

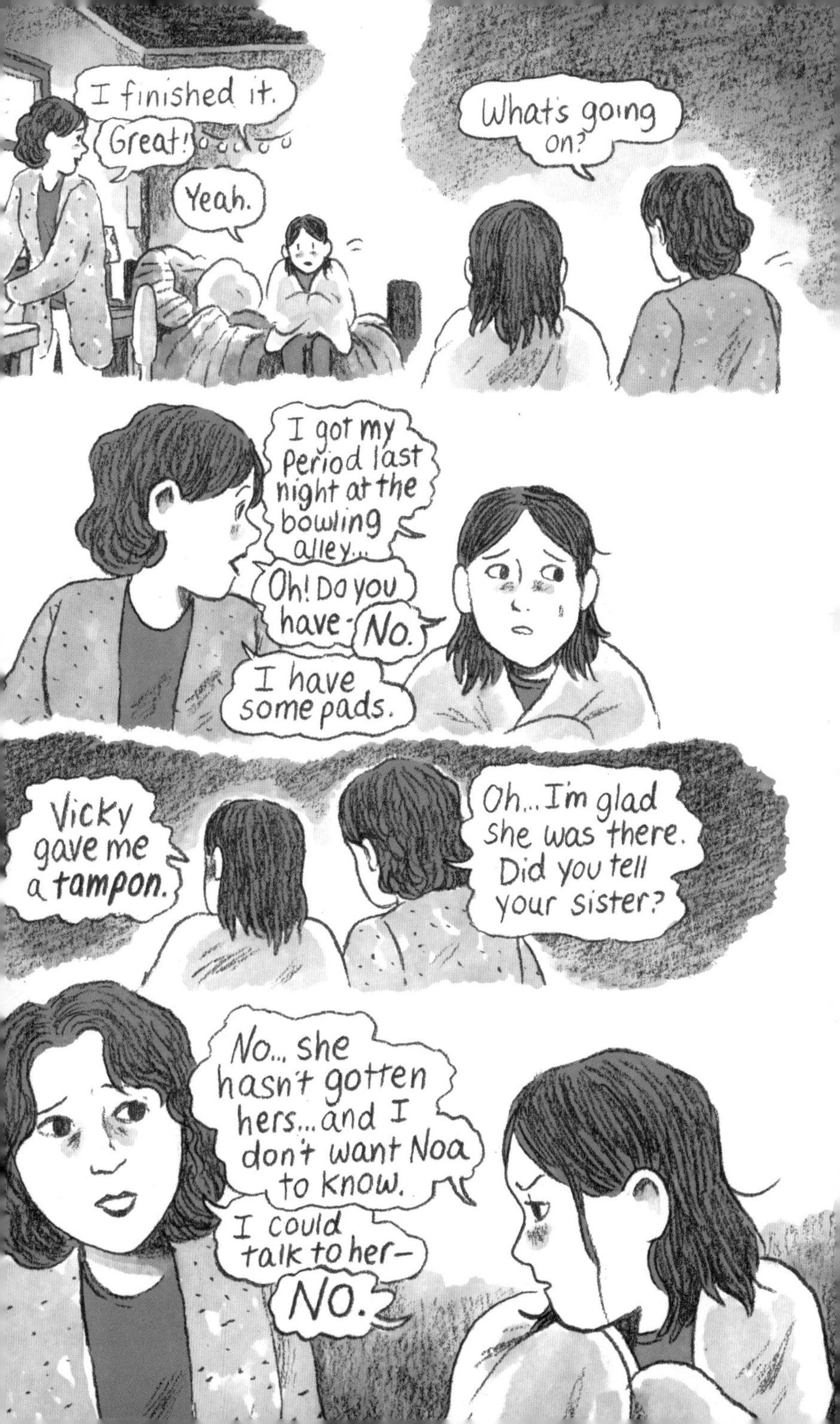
I finished it.
Great!
Yeah.
What's going on?
I got my period last night at the bowling alley...
Oh! Do you have-
No.
I have some pads.
Vicky gave me a **tampon**.
Oh... I'm glad she was there. Did you tell your sister?
No... she hasn't gotten hers... and I don't want Noa to know.
I could talk to her-
NO.

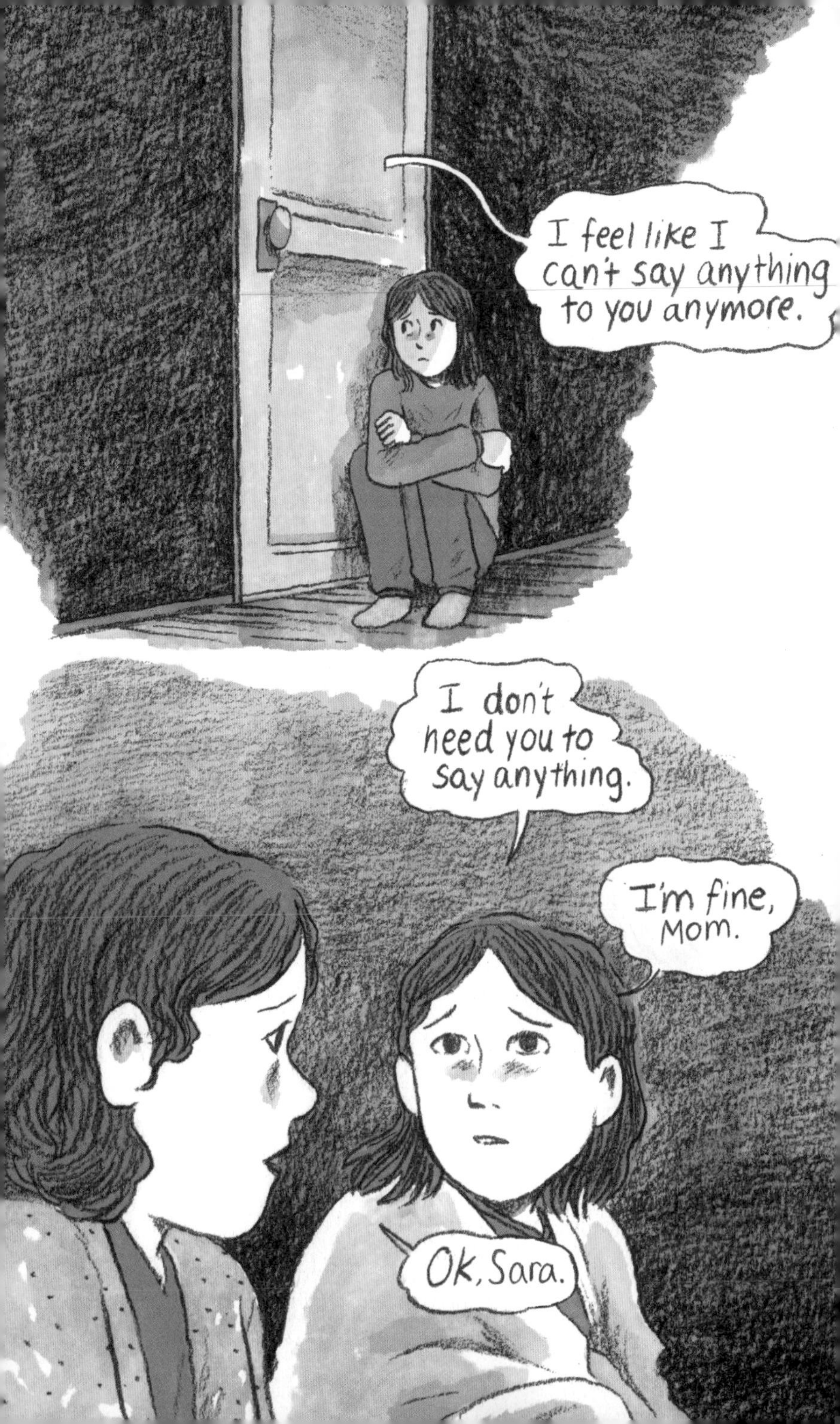
I feel like I can't say anything to you anymore.
I don't need you to say anything.
I'm fine, Mom.
Ok, Sara.

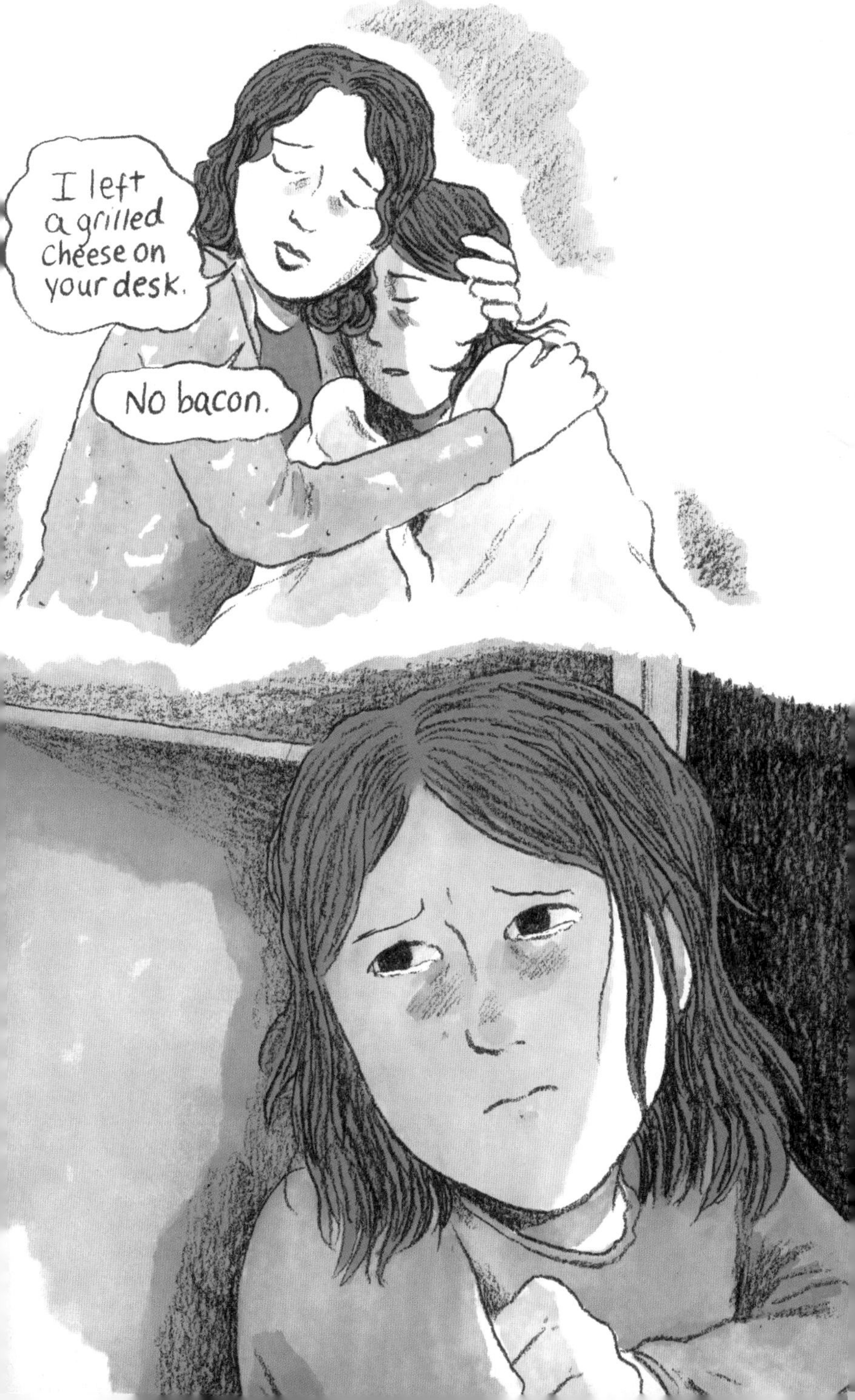
I left a grilled cheese on your desk.
No bacon.

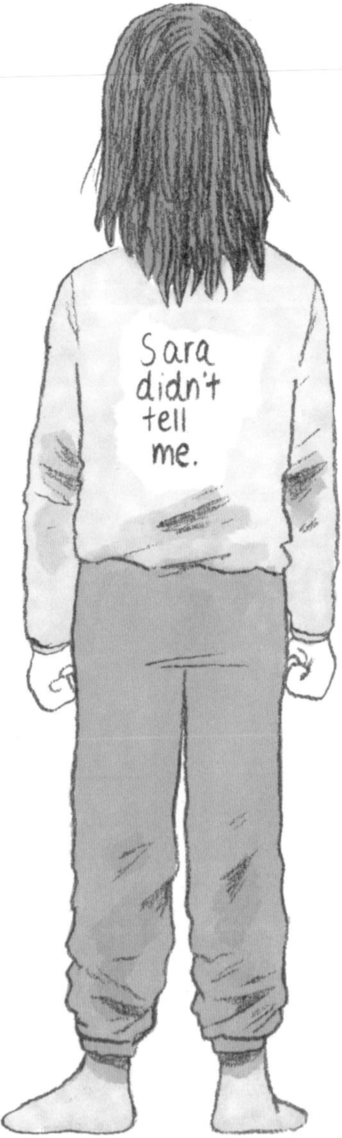
Sara didn't tell me.

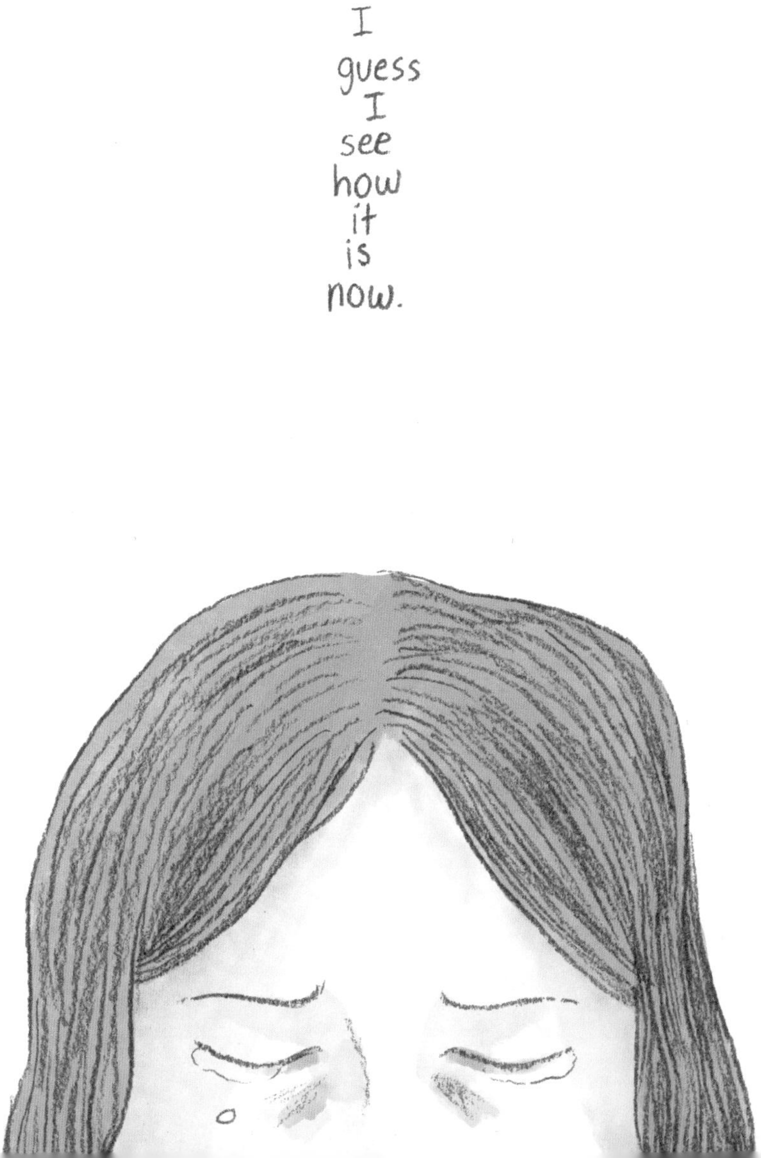
I guess I see how it is now.

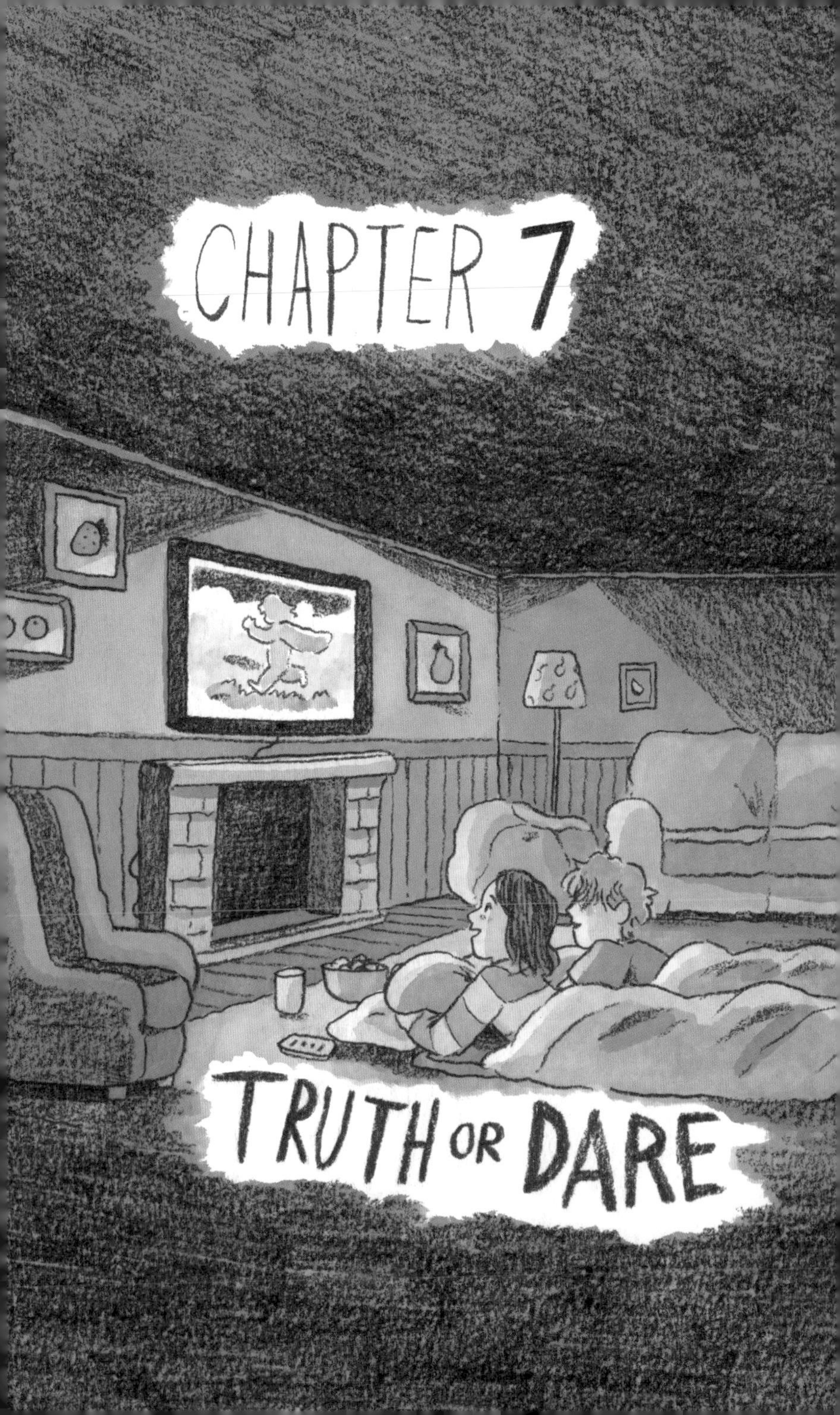
CHAPTER 7
TRUTH OR DARE

Sleepovers are a
big deal now.

No silly pajamas.
No big groups.
NO living rooms
where parents are
lurking.

We're in JUNIOR HIGH...
now it's the big leagues.

We hang out in basements.
We watch SCARY movies.

We tell secrets.

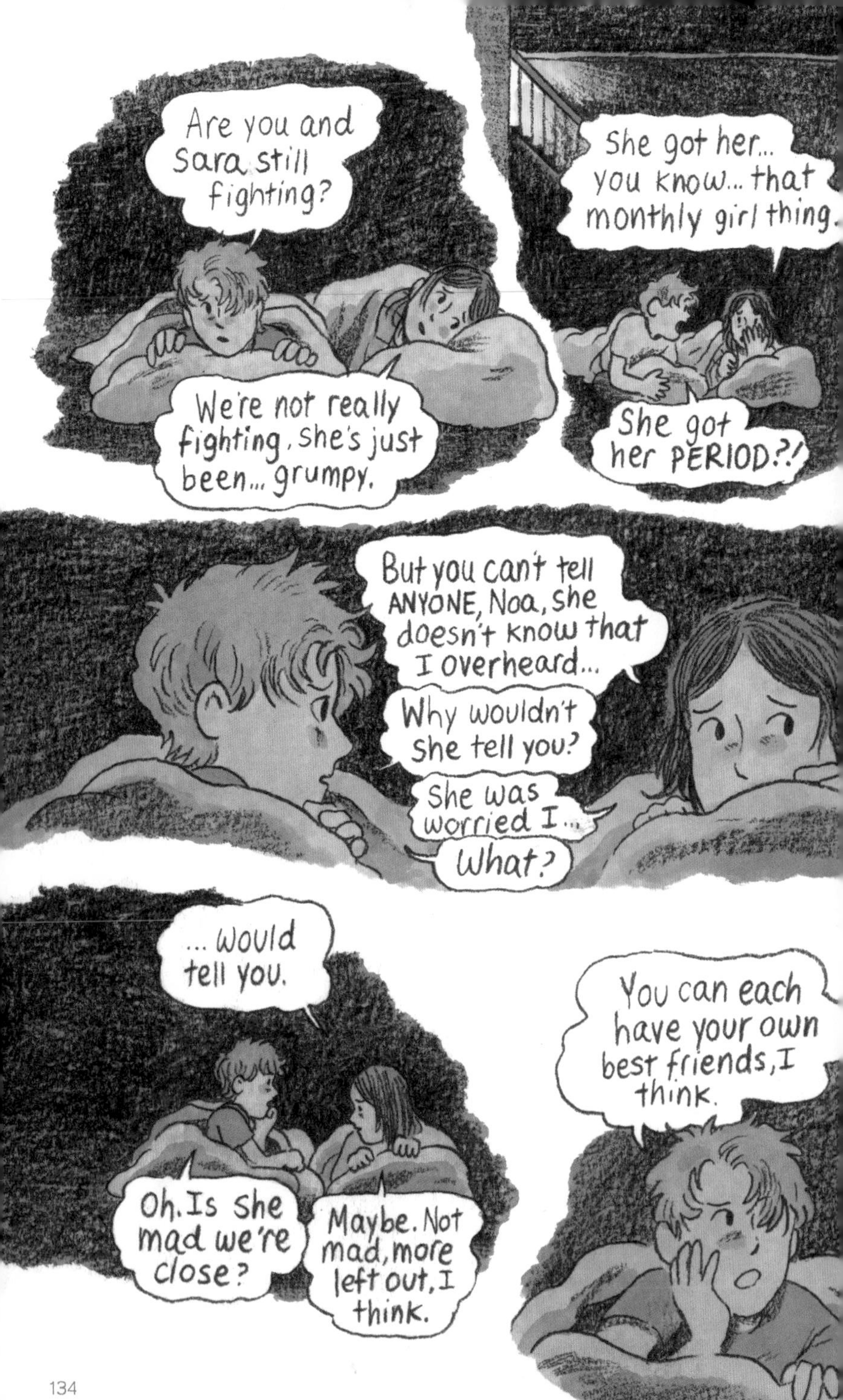
Are you and Sara still fighting?
We're not really fighting, she's just been... grumpy.
She got her... you know... that monthly girl thing.
She got her PERIOD?!
But you can't tell ANYONE, Noa, she doesn't know that I overheard...
Why wouldn't she tell you?
She was worried I...
What?
...would tell you.
Oh. Is she mad we're close?
Maybe. Not mad, more left out, I think.
You can each have your own best friends, I think.

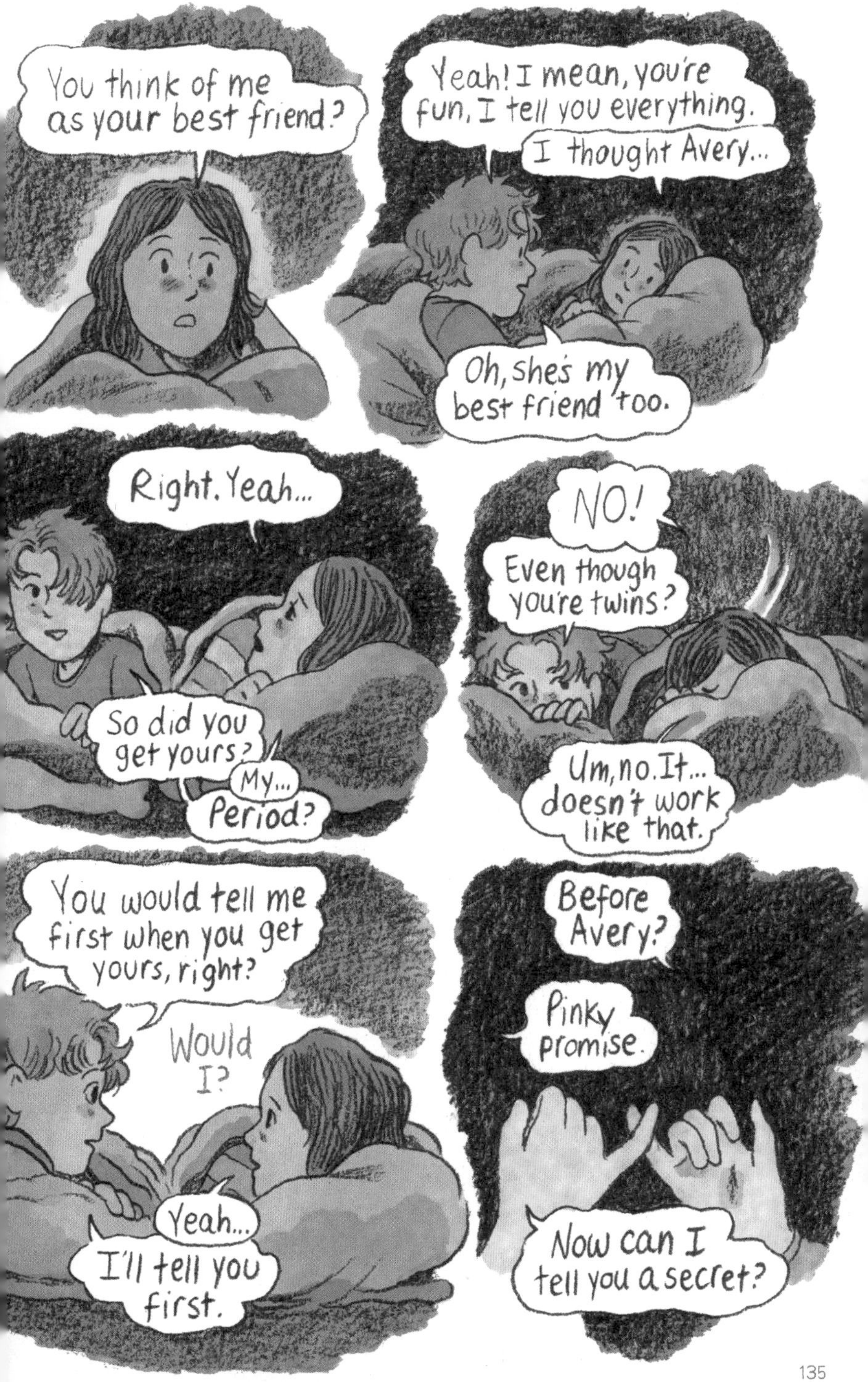
You think of me as your best friend?
Yeah! I mean, you're fun, I tell you everything.
I thought Avery...
Oh, she's my best friend too.
Right. Yeah...
So did you get yours?
My...
Period?
NO!
Even though you're twins?
Um, no. It... doesn't work like that.
You would tell me first when you get yours, right?
Would I?
Yeah...
I'll tell you first.
Before Avery?
Pinky promise.
Now can I tell you a secret?

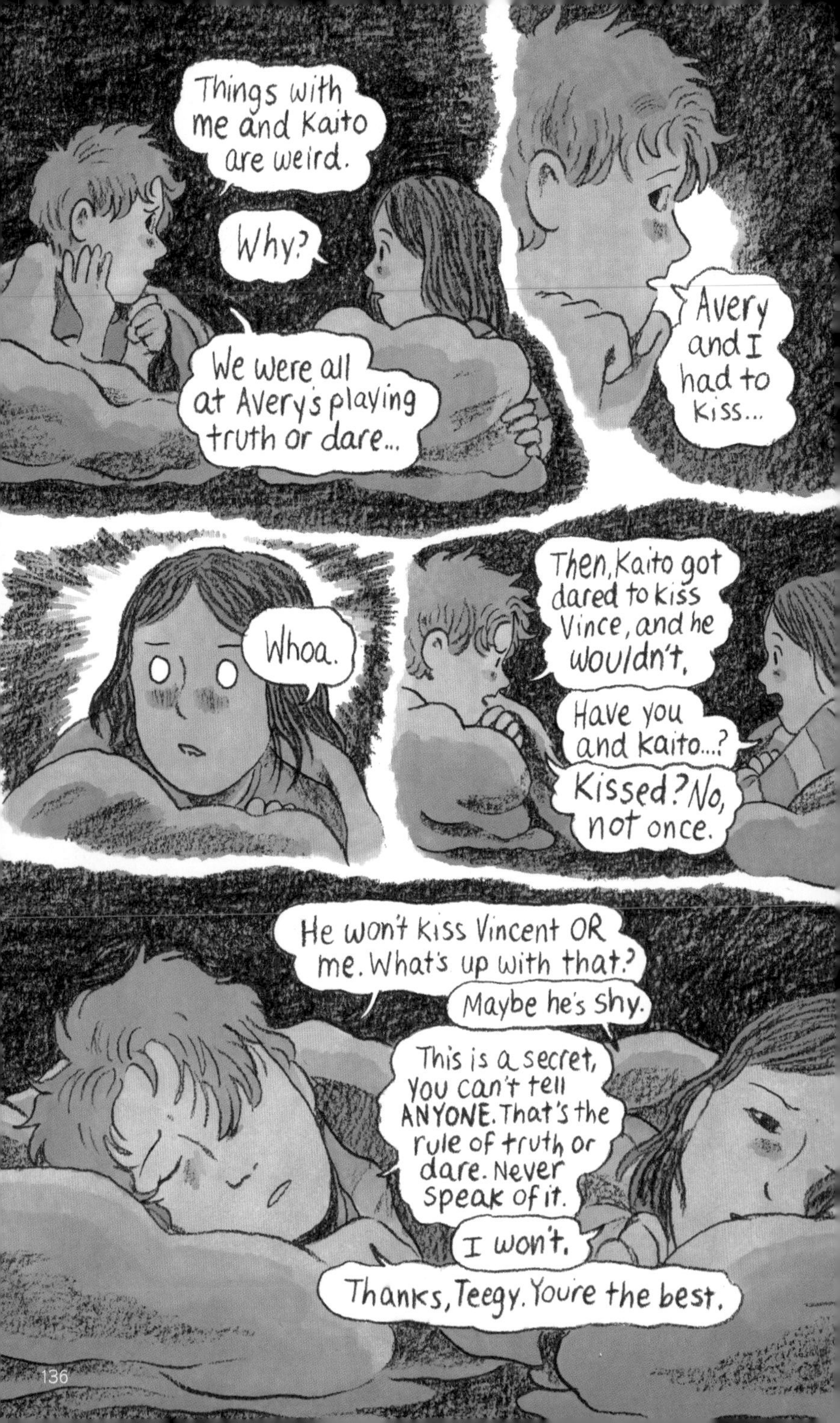
Things with me and Kaito are weird.
Why?
We were all at Avery's playing truth or dare...
Avery and I had to kiss...
Whoa.
Then, Kaito got dared to kiss Vince, and he wouldn't.
Have you and Kaito...?
Kissed? No, not once.
He won't kiss Vincent OR me. What's up with that?
Maybe he's shy.
This is a secret, you can't tell ANYONE. That's the rule of truth or dare. Never speak of it.
I won't.
Thanks, Teegy. You're the best.

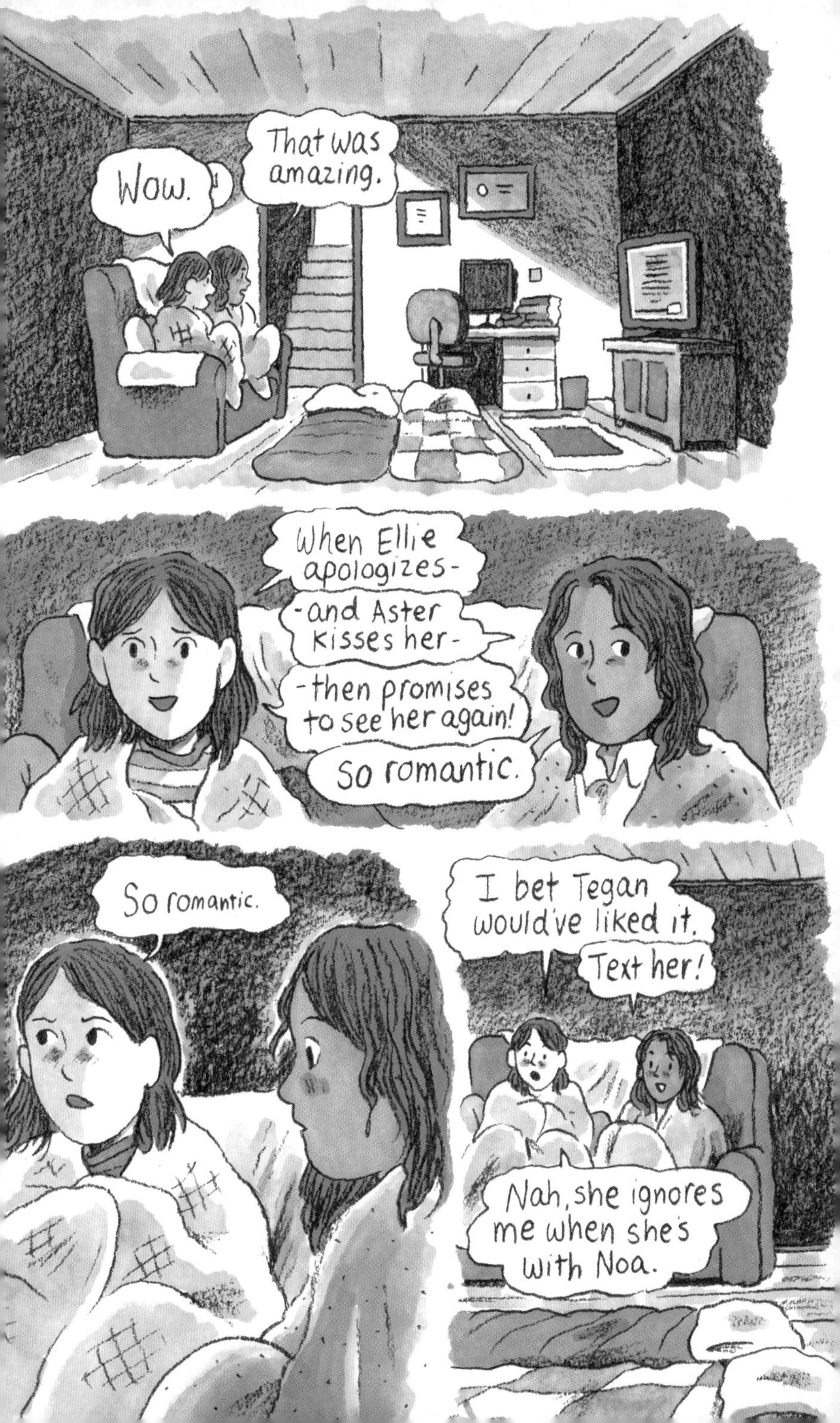
Wow.
That was amazing.
When Ellie apologizes-
-and Aster kisses her-
-then promises to see her again!
So romantic.
So romantic.
I bet Tegan would've liked it.
Text her!
Nah, she ignores me when she's with Noa.

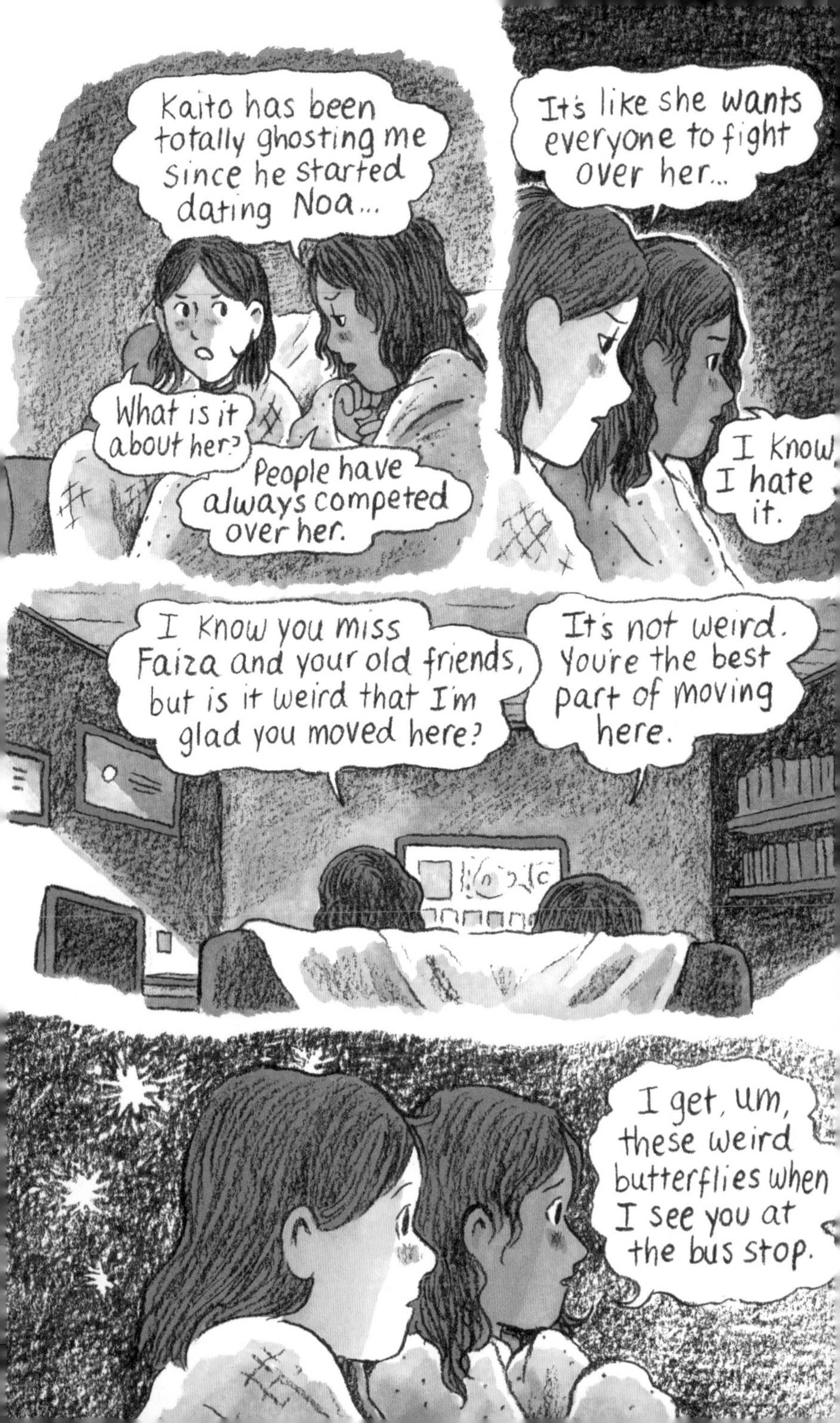
Kaito has been totally ghosting me since he started dating Noa...
What is it about her?
People have always competed over her.
It's like she wants everyone to fight over her...
I know. I hate it.
I know you miss Faiza and your old friends, but is it weird that I'm glad you moved here?
It's not weird. You're the best part of moving here.
I get, um, these weird butterflies when I see you at the bus stop.

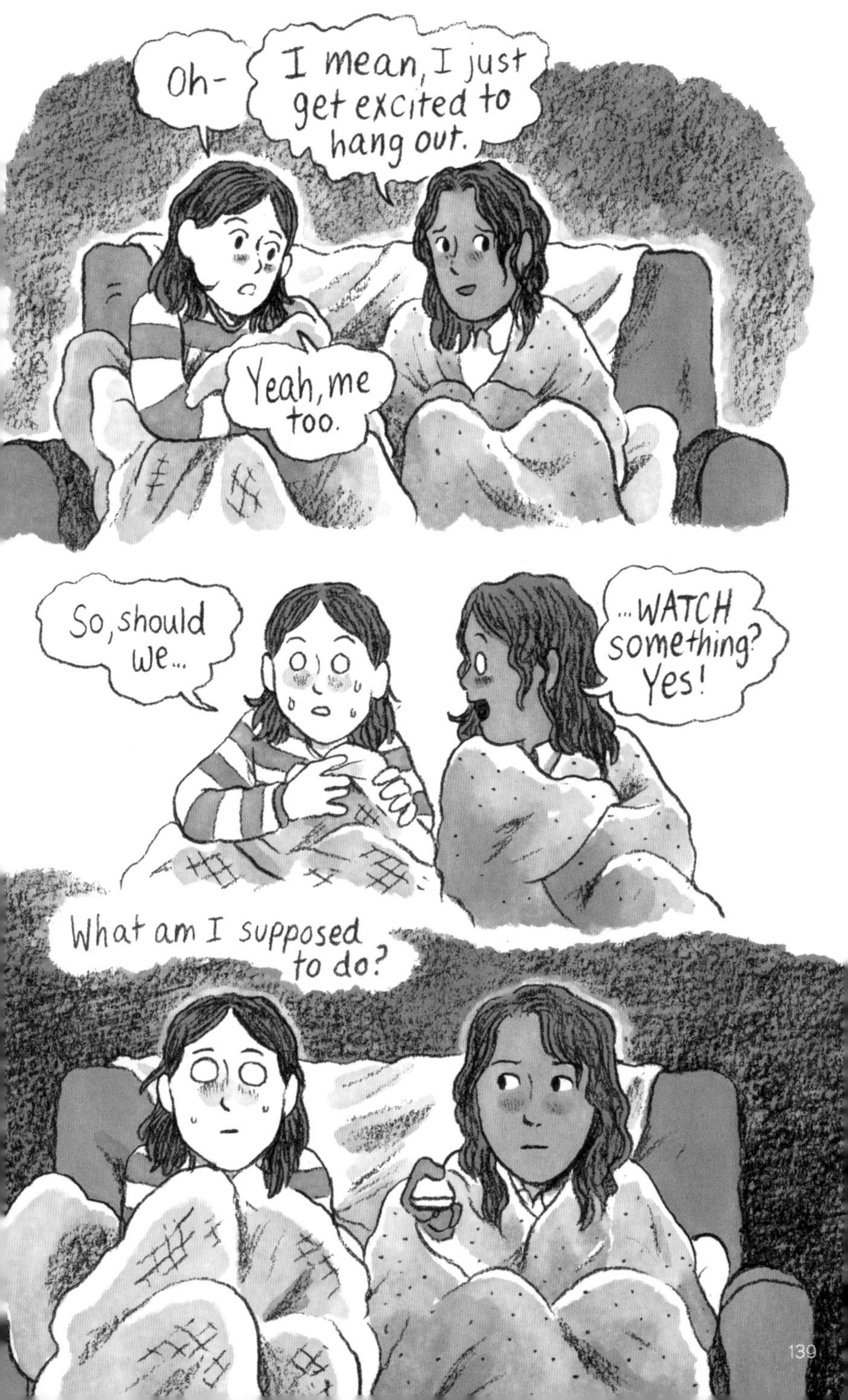
Oh-
I mean, I just get excited to hang out.
Yeah, me too.
So, should we...
...WATCH something? Yes!
What am I supposed to do?

Noa will keep the secret for sure.

I know I shouldn't have told her about Sara's period... but it felt good to talk about it.

I think it's ok to tell secrets to best friends.

I'm happy she trusted me with hers.

This is totally normal.
Roshini is asleep next to me.

TOTALLY NORMAL.

She said she's glad
we moved.

She said she gets butterflies when...

Why didn't I say that
I do too?

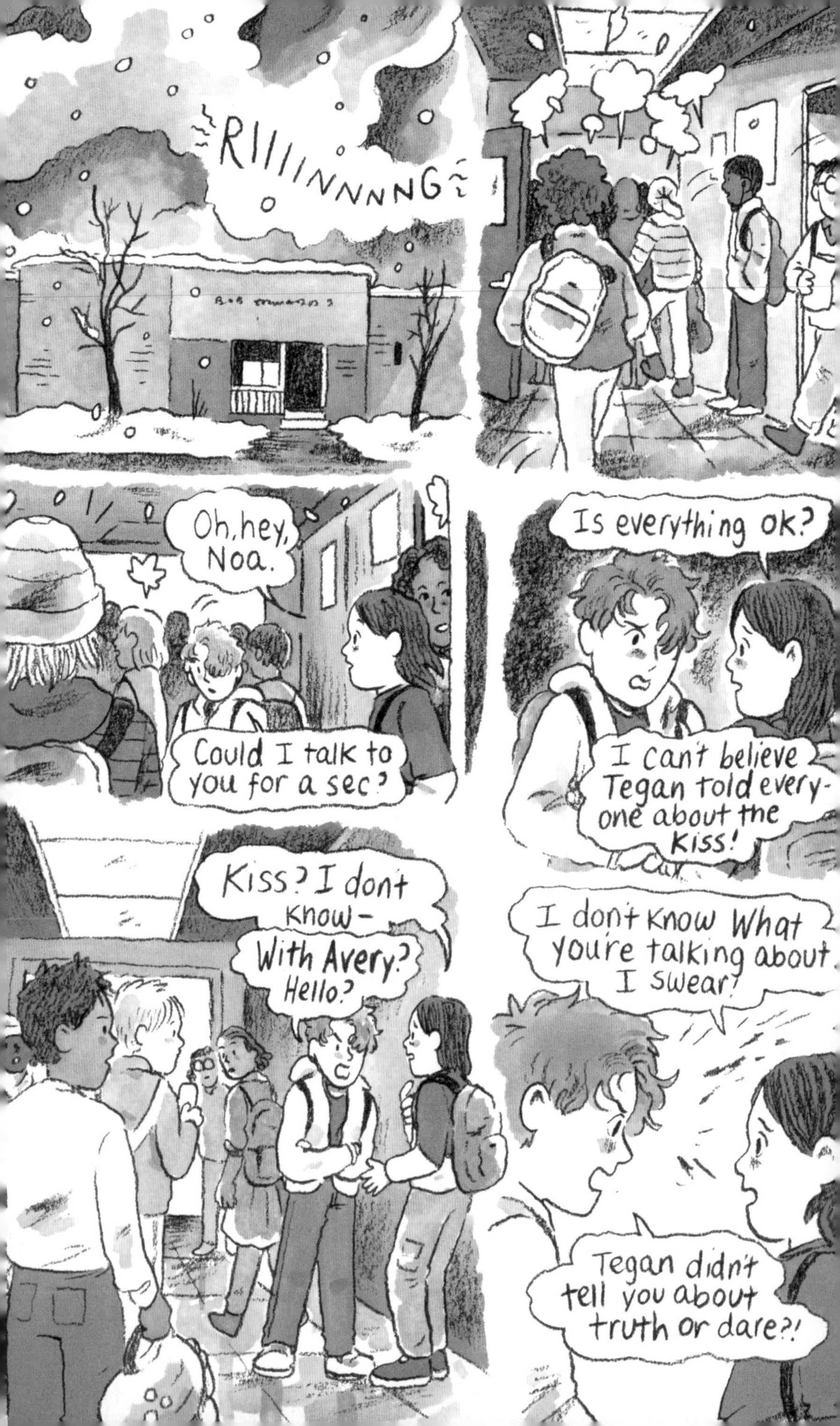
RIIIINNNNNG
Oh, hey, Noa.
Could I talk to you for a sec?
Is everything ok?
I can't believe Tegan told every-one about the kiss!
Kiss? I don't know—
With Avery? Hello?
I don't know what you're talking about. I swear!
Tegan didn't tell you about truth or dare?!

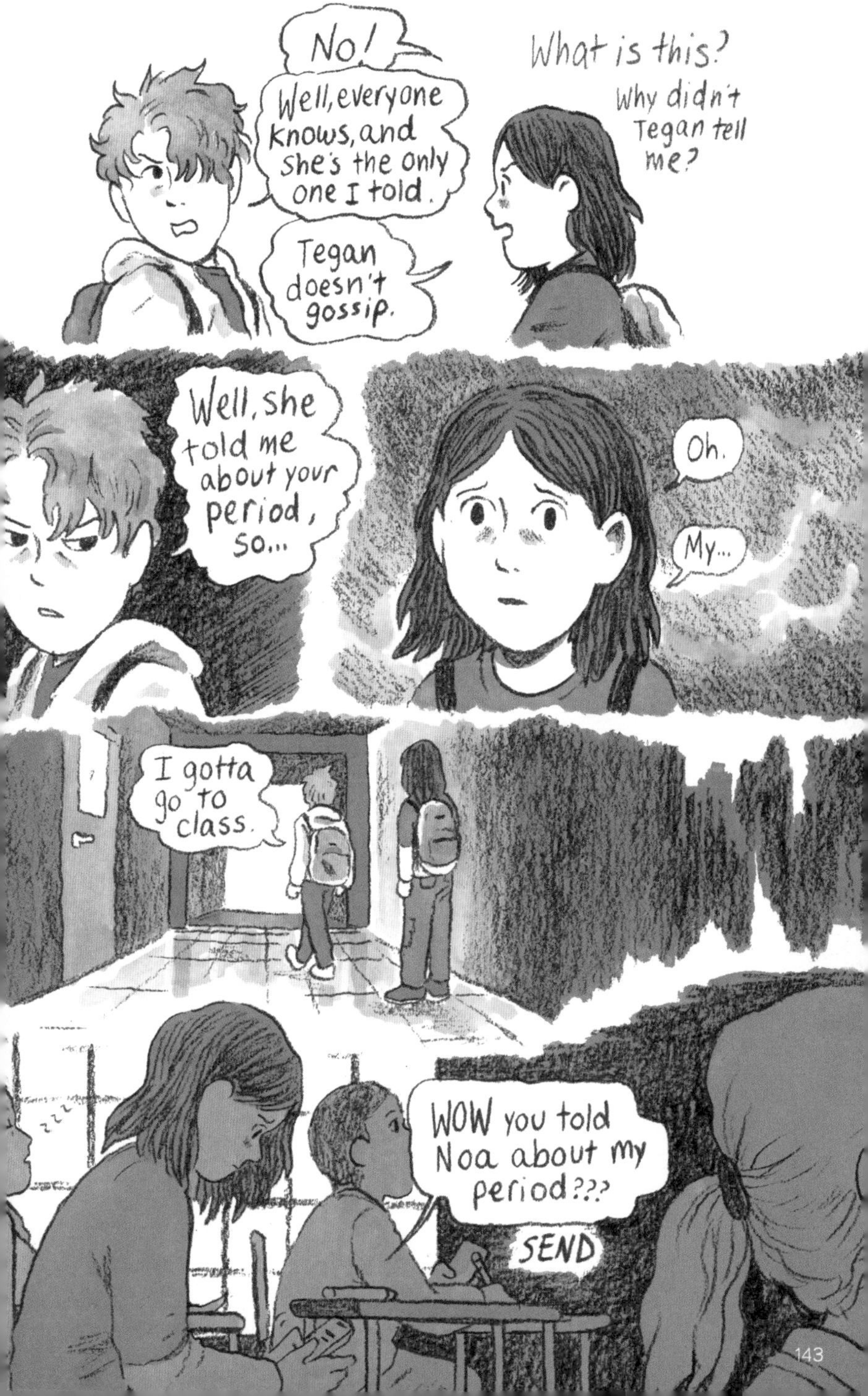
No!
Well, everyone knows, and she's the only one I told.
Tegan doesn't gossip.
What is this?
Why didn't Tegan tell me?
Well, she told me about your period, so...
Oh.
My...
I gotta go to class.
WOW you told Noa about my period???
SEND

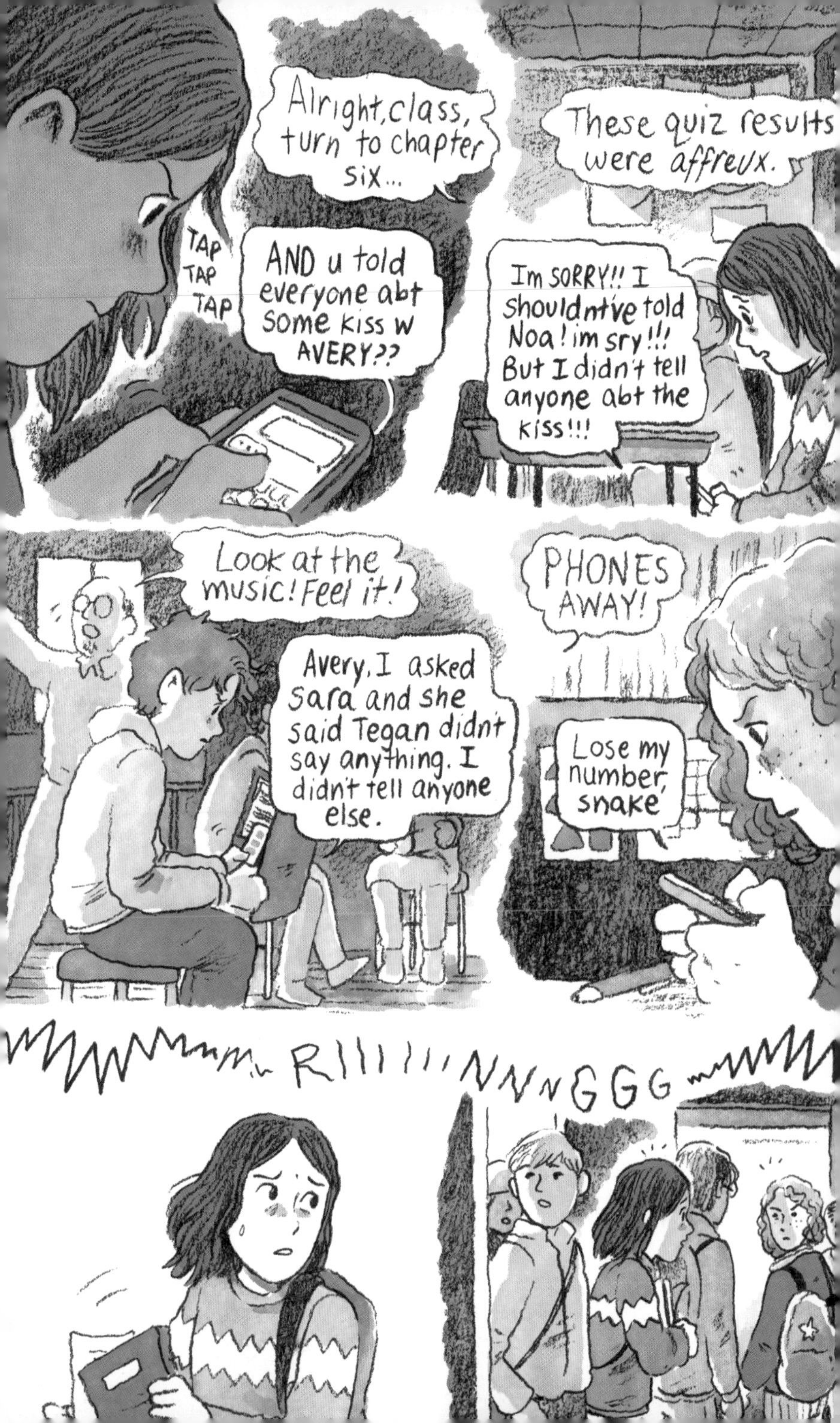
Alright, class, turn to chapter six...
TAP TAP TAP
AND u told everyone abt some kiss w AVERY??
These quiz results were affreux.
Im SORRY!! I shouldntve told Noa! im sry!!! But I didn't tell anyone abt the kiss!!!
Look at the music! Feel it!
Avery, I asked Sara and she said Tegan didn't say anything. I didn't tell anyone else.
PHONES AWAY!
Lose my number, snake
MMMMMmm RIIIIIIINNNGGG

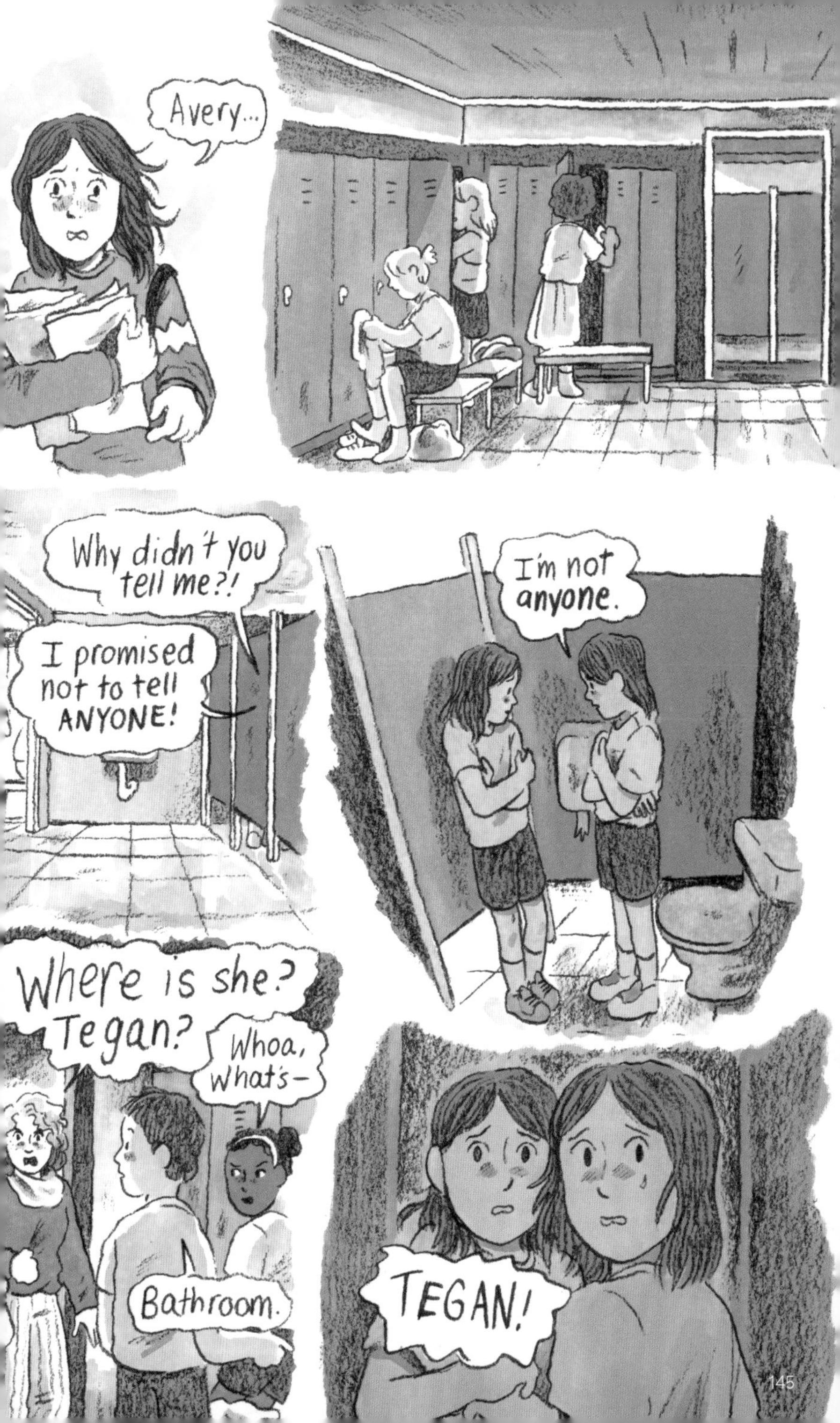
Avery...
Why didn't you tell me?!
I promised not to tell ANYONE!
I'm not anyone.
Where is she? Tegan?
Whoa, What's–
Bathroom.
TEGAN!

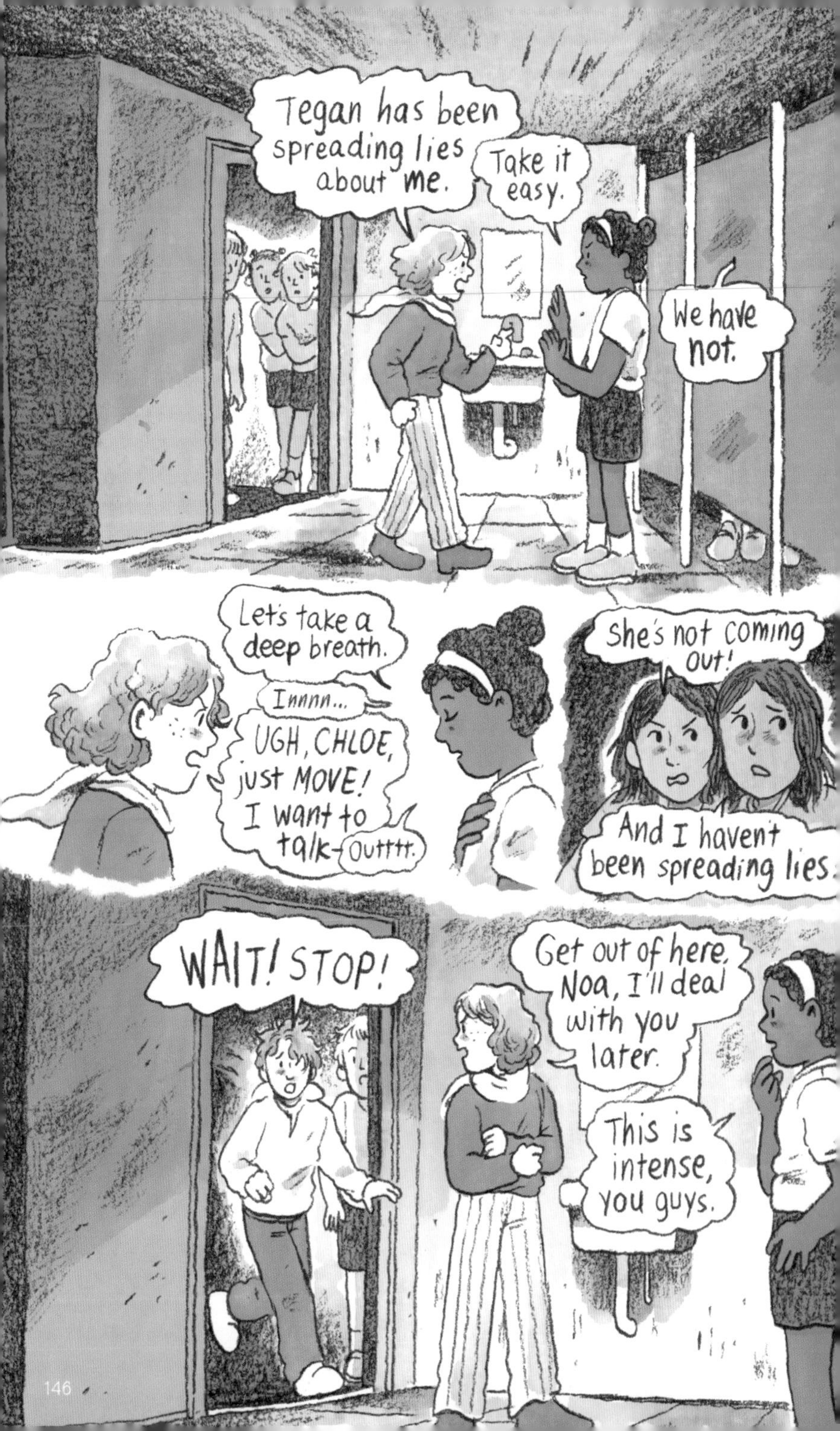
Tegan has been spreading lies about me.
Take it easy.
We have not.
Let's take a deep breath.
Innnn...
UGH, CHLOE, just MOVE! I want to talk-
Outtttt.
She's not coming out!
And I haven't been spreading lies.
WAIT! STOP!
Get out of here, Noa, I'll deal with you later.
This is intense, you guys.

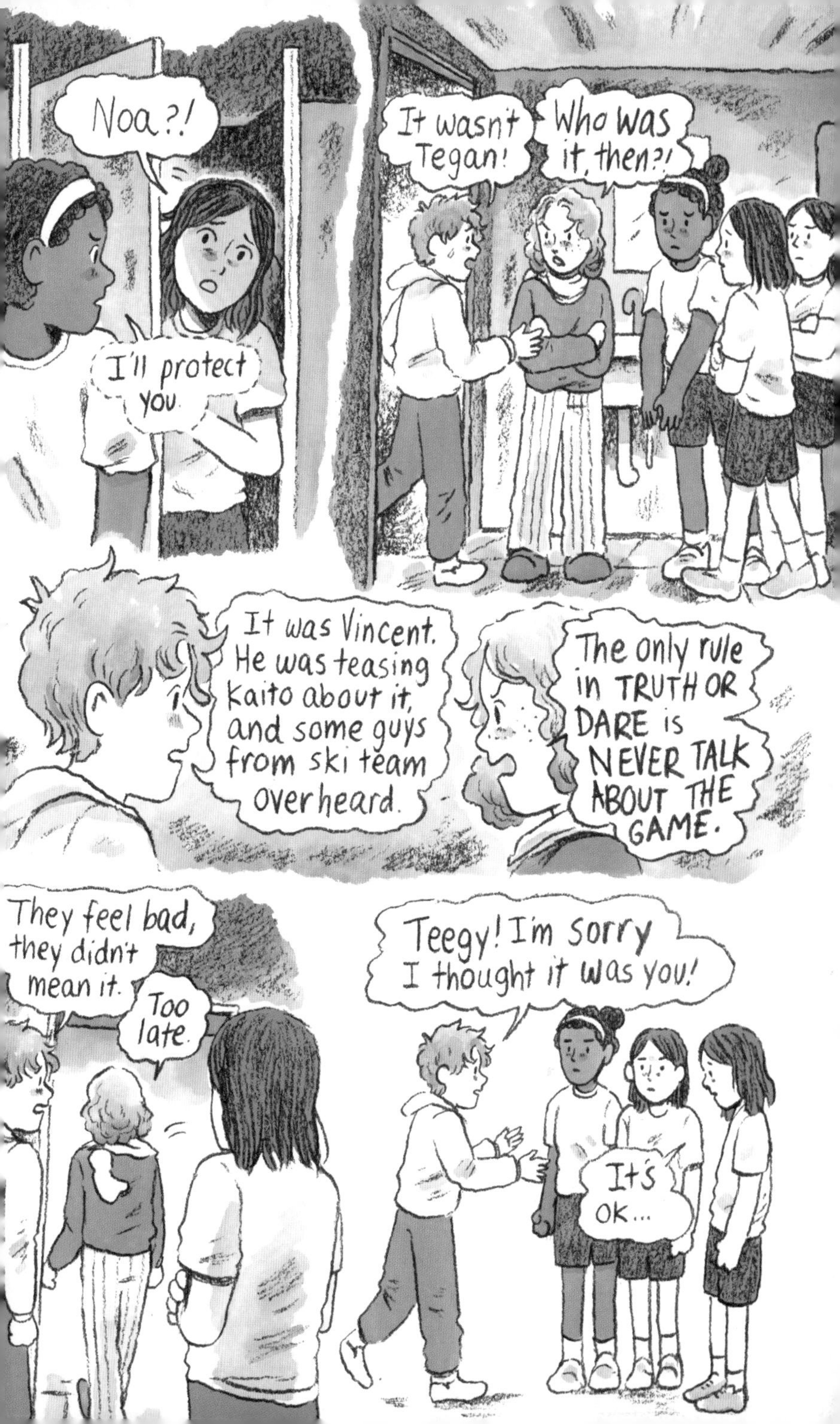

Noa?!
I'll protect you.
It wasn't Tegan!
Who was it, then?!
It was Vincent. He was teasing Kaito about it, and some guys from ski team overheard.
The only rule in TRUTH OR DARE is NEVER TALK ABOUT THE GAME.
They feel bad, they didn't mean it.
Too late.
Teegy! I'm sorry I thought it was you!
It's ok...

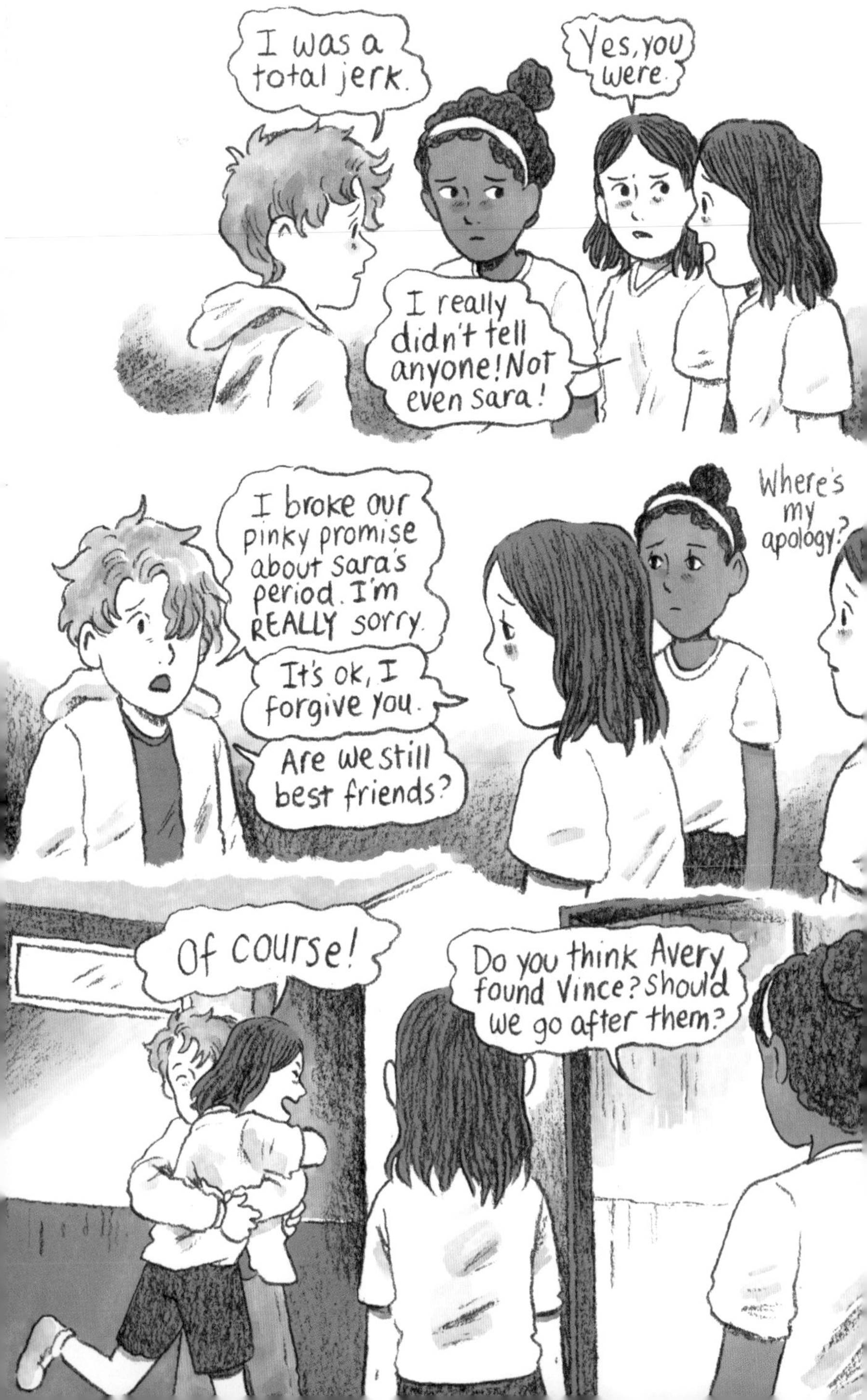
I was a total jerk.
Yes, you were.
I really didn't tell anyone! Not even Sara!
I broke our pinky promise about Sara's period. I'm REALLY sorry.
It's ok, I forgive you.
Are we still best friends?
Where's my apology?
Of course!
Do you think Avery found Vince? Should we go after them?

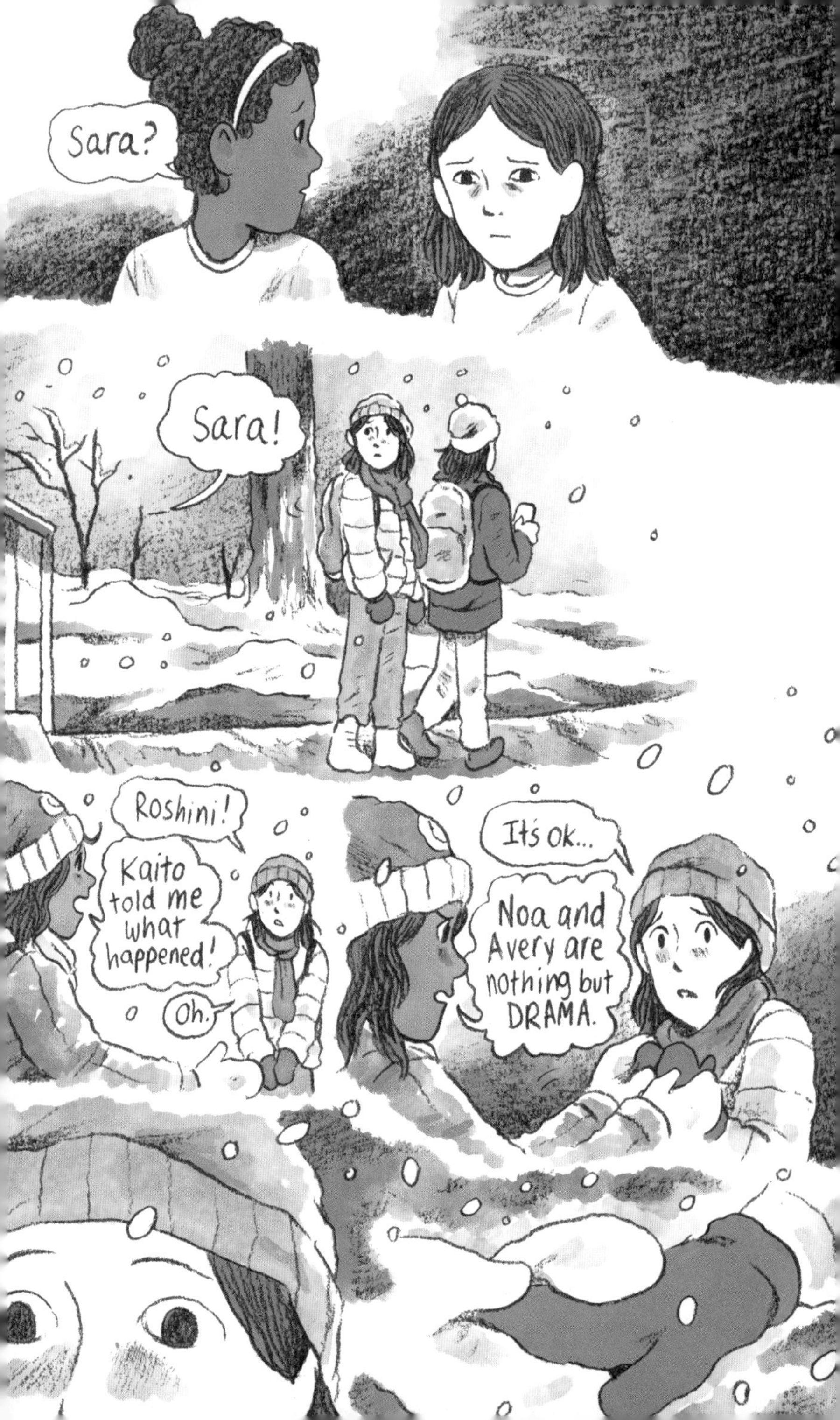
Sara?
Sara!
Roshini!
Kaito told me what happened!
Oh.
It's ok...
Noa and Avery are nothing but DRAMA.

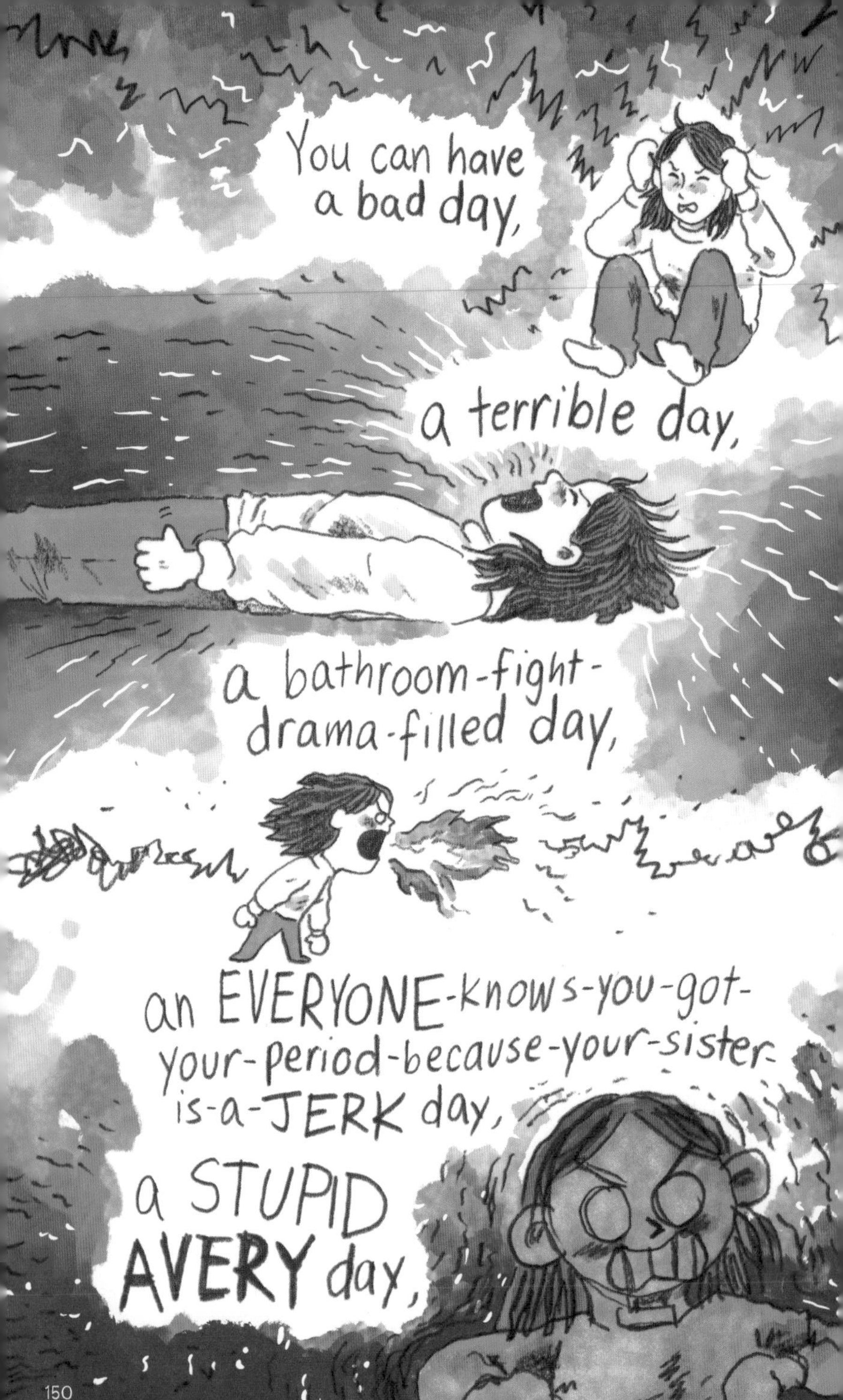

You can have a bad day,
a terrible day,
a bathroom-fight-drama-filled day,
an EVERYONE-knows-you-got-your-period-because-your-sister-is-a-JERK day,
a STUPID AVERY day,

but holding
Roshini's hand

makes it all

disappear.

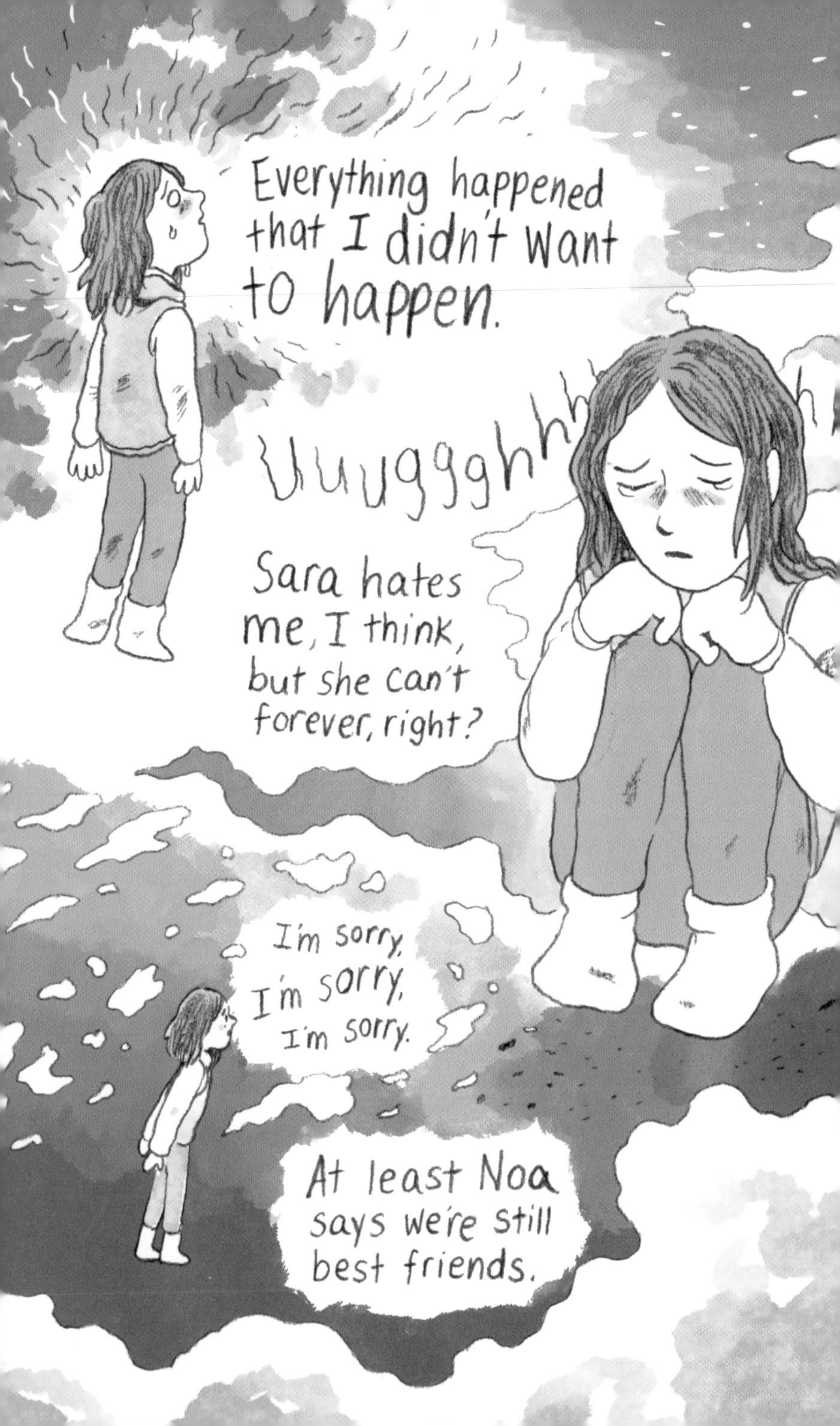
Everything happened that I didn't want to happen.
Uuuggghhhh
Sara hates me, I think, but she can't forever, right?
I'm sorry, I'm sorry, I'm sorry.
At least Noa says we're still best friends.

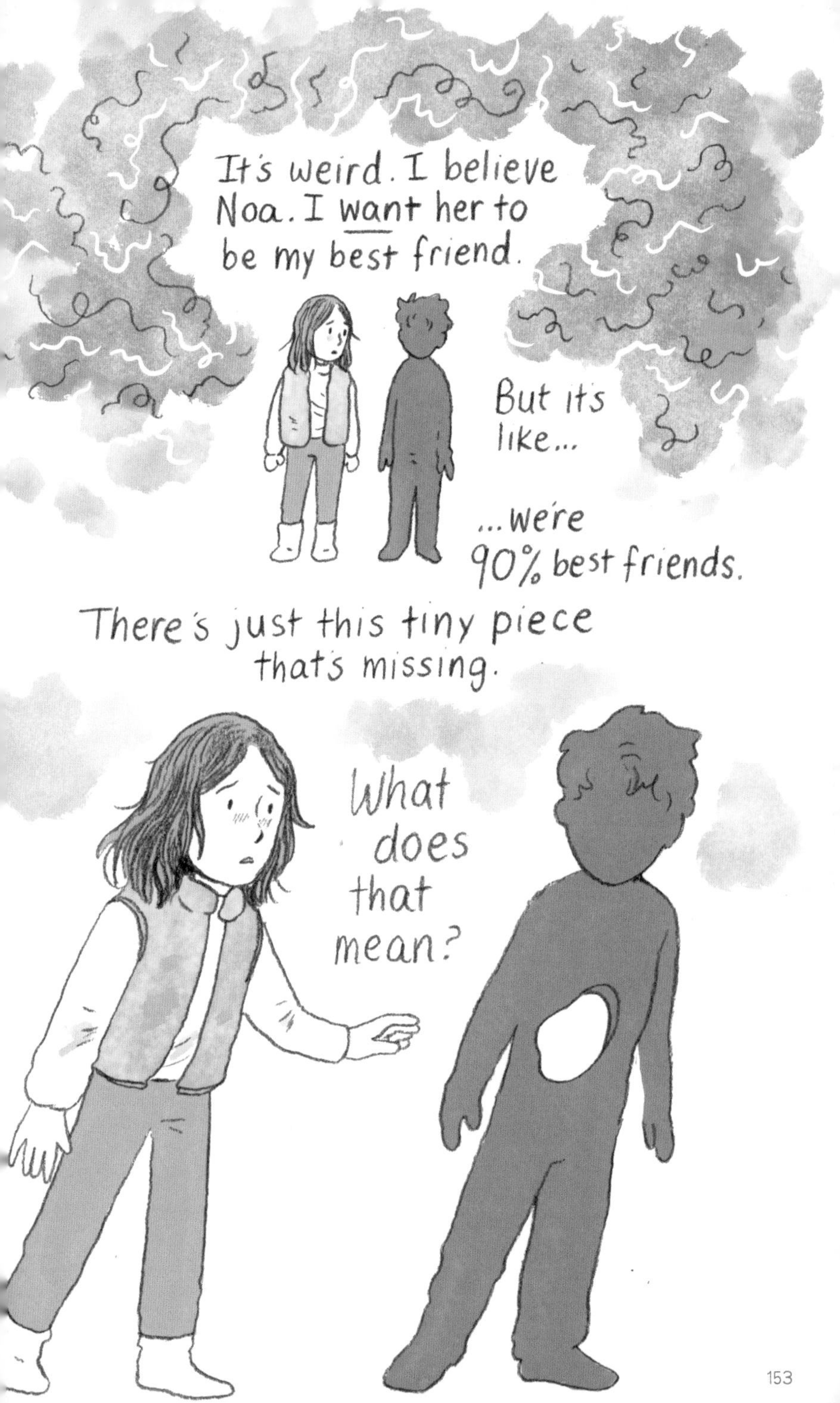

It's weird. I believe Noa. I want her to be my best friend.
But it's like...
...we're 90% best friends.
There's just this tiny piece that's missing.
What does that mean?

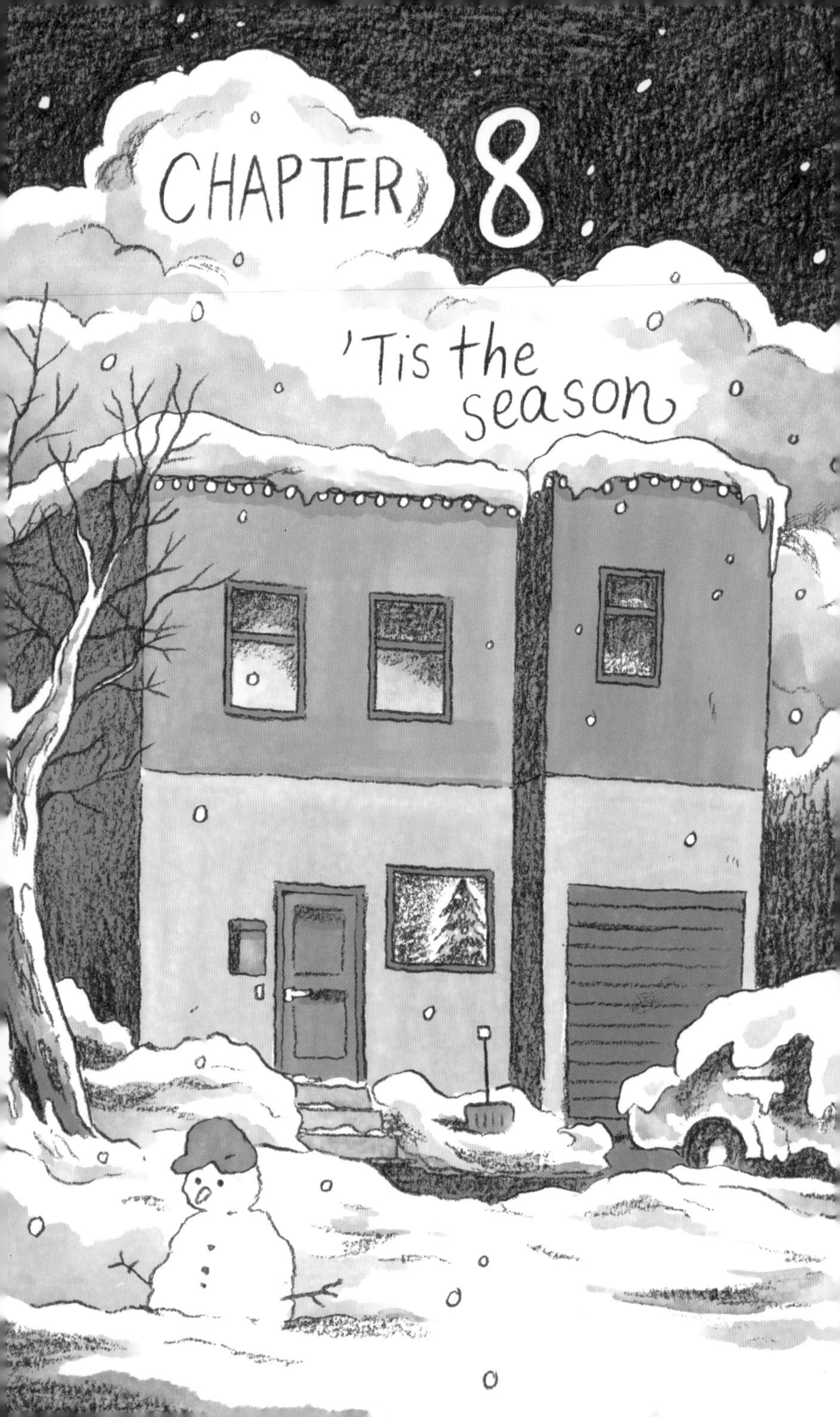
CHAPTER 8
'Tis the season

Things I didn't know
about junior high
#6,709,253:

Turns out tons of homework,
friends, tests, lunches, and
texts makes you
TIRED.

Its winter break, and all
I want to do is

SLEEP.

(And get presents.)

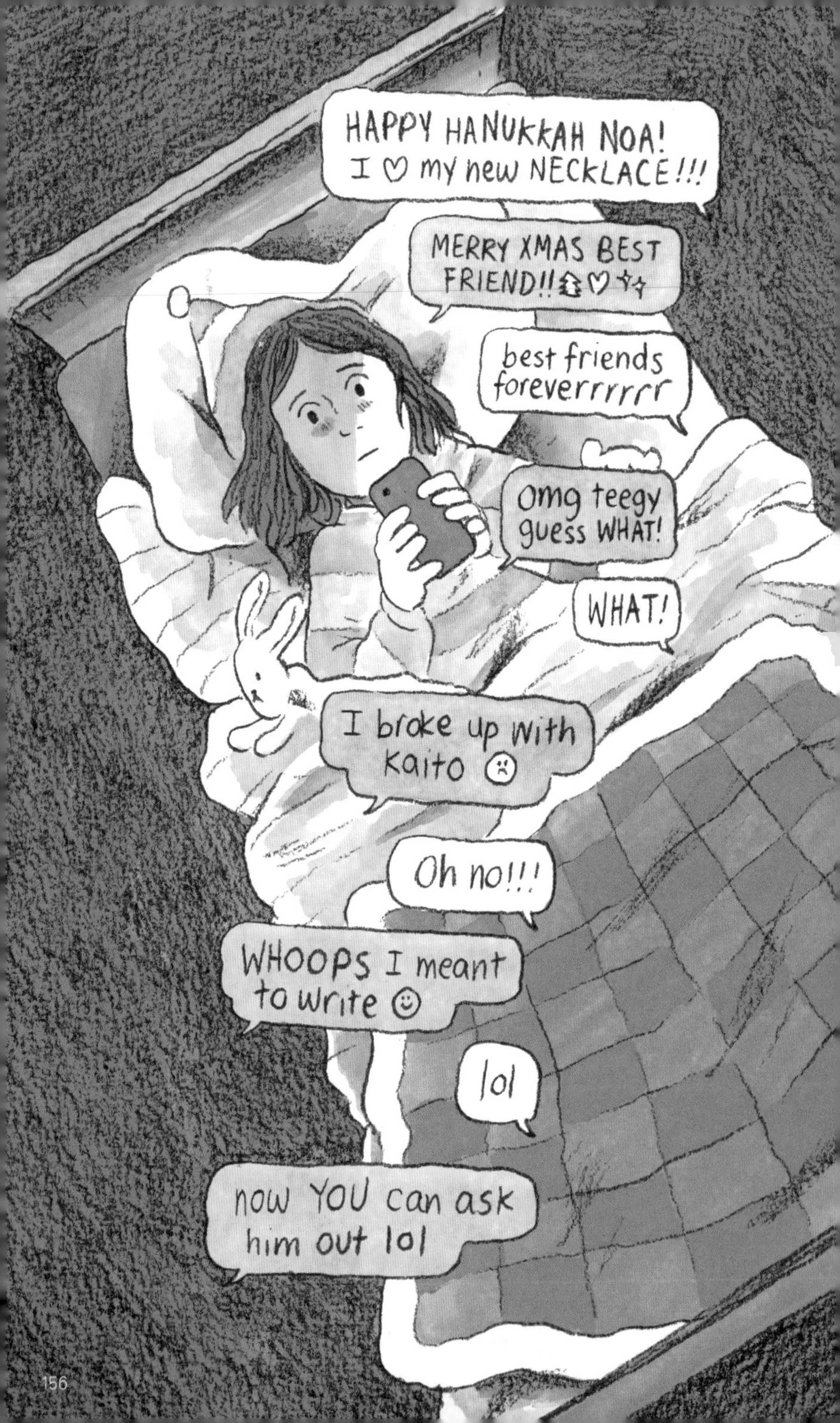
HAPPY HANUKKAH NOA! I ♡ my new NECKLACE!!!
MERRY XMAS BEST FRIEND!!
best friends foreverrrrrr
omg teegy guess WHAT!
WHAT!
I broke up with kaito ☹
Oh no!!!
WHOOPS I meant to write ☺
lol
now YOU can ask him out lol

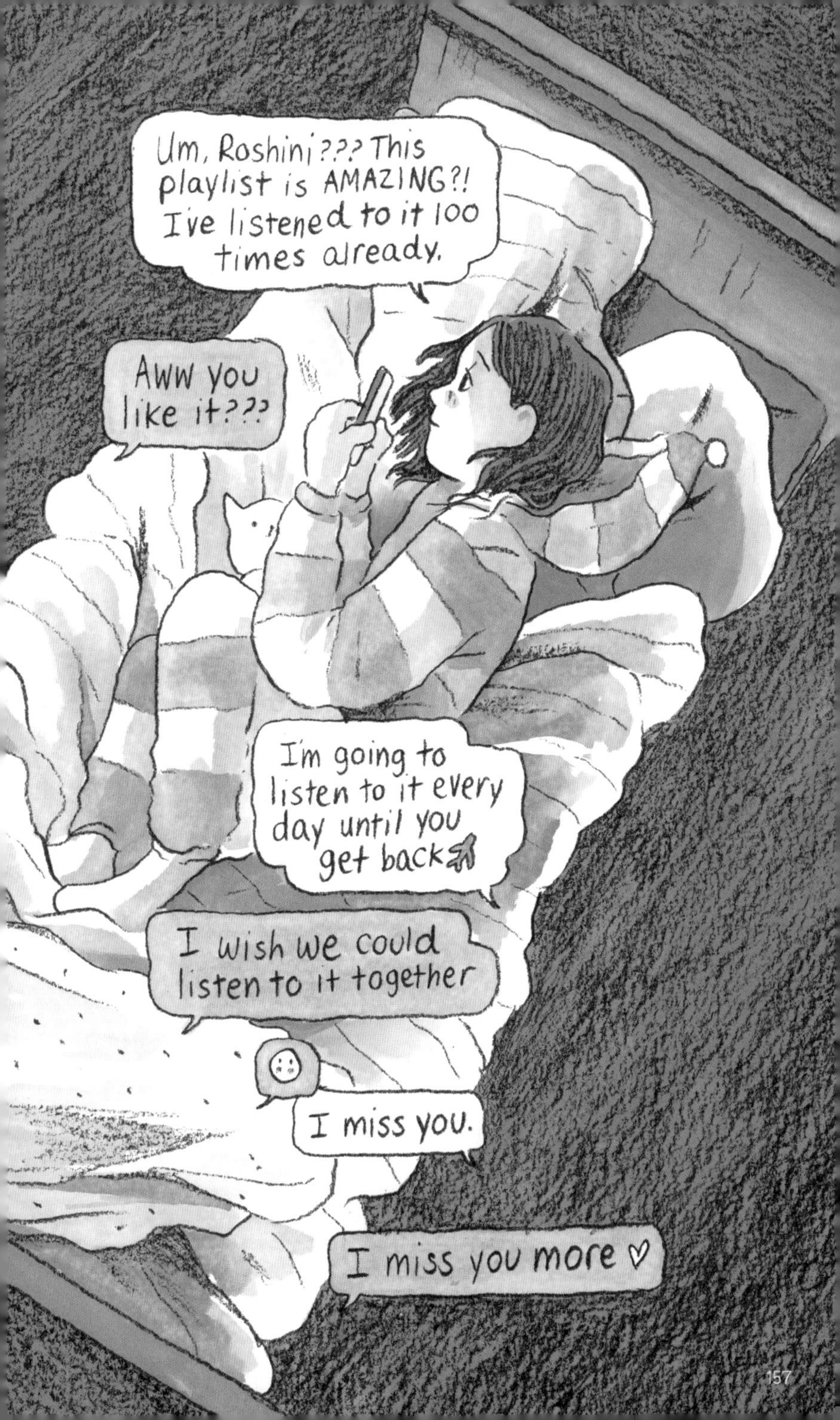

Um, Roshini??? This playlist is AMAZING?! I've listened to it 100 times already.
Aww you like it???
I'm going to listen to it every day until you get back
I wish we could listen to it together
I miss you.
I miss you more ♡

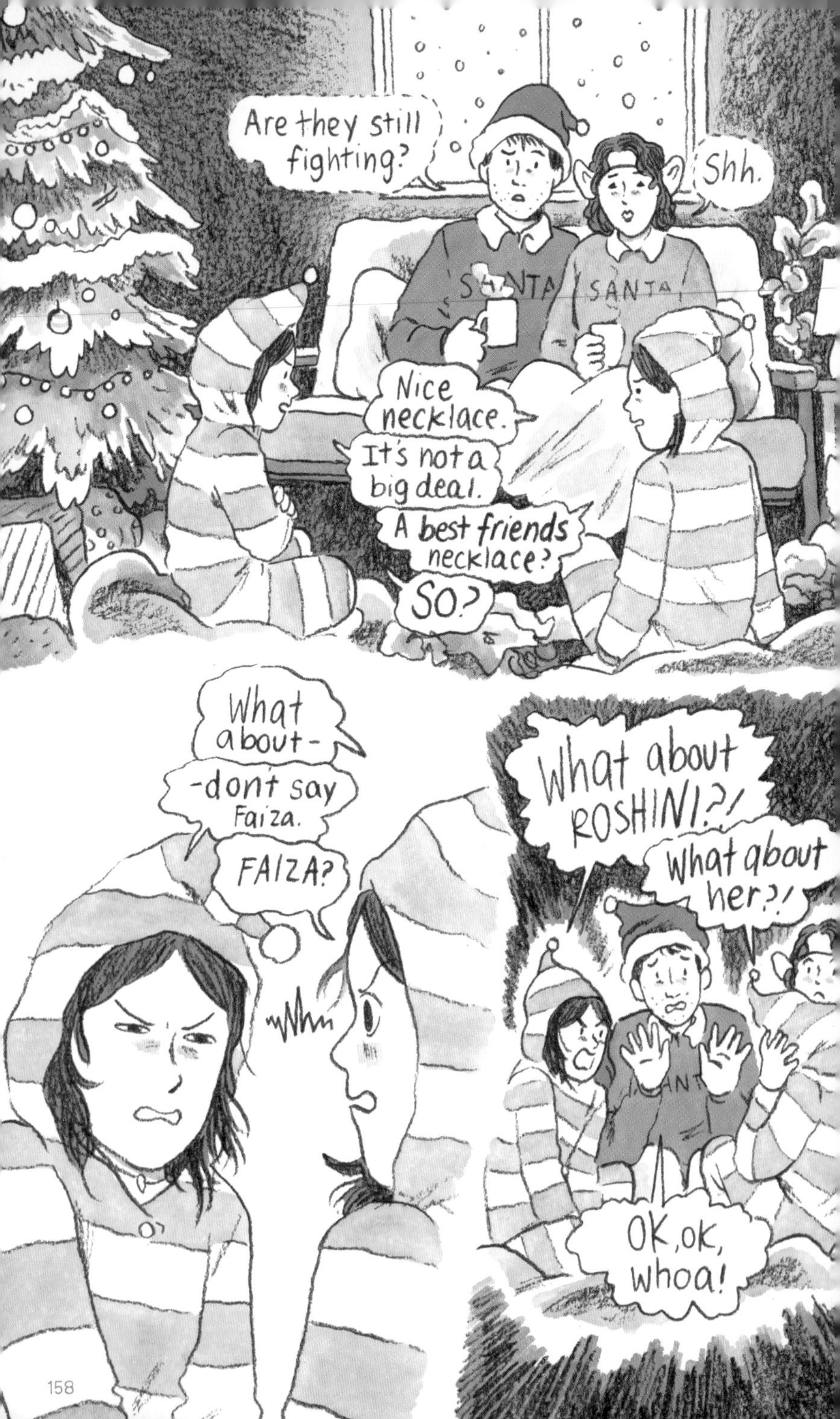

Are they still fighting?
Shh.
SANTA
SANTA
Nice necklace.
It's not a big deal.
A best friends necklace?
So?
What about-
-don't say Faiza.
FAIZA?
What about ROSHINI?!
What about her?!
OK, ok, whoa!

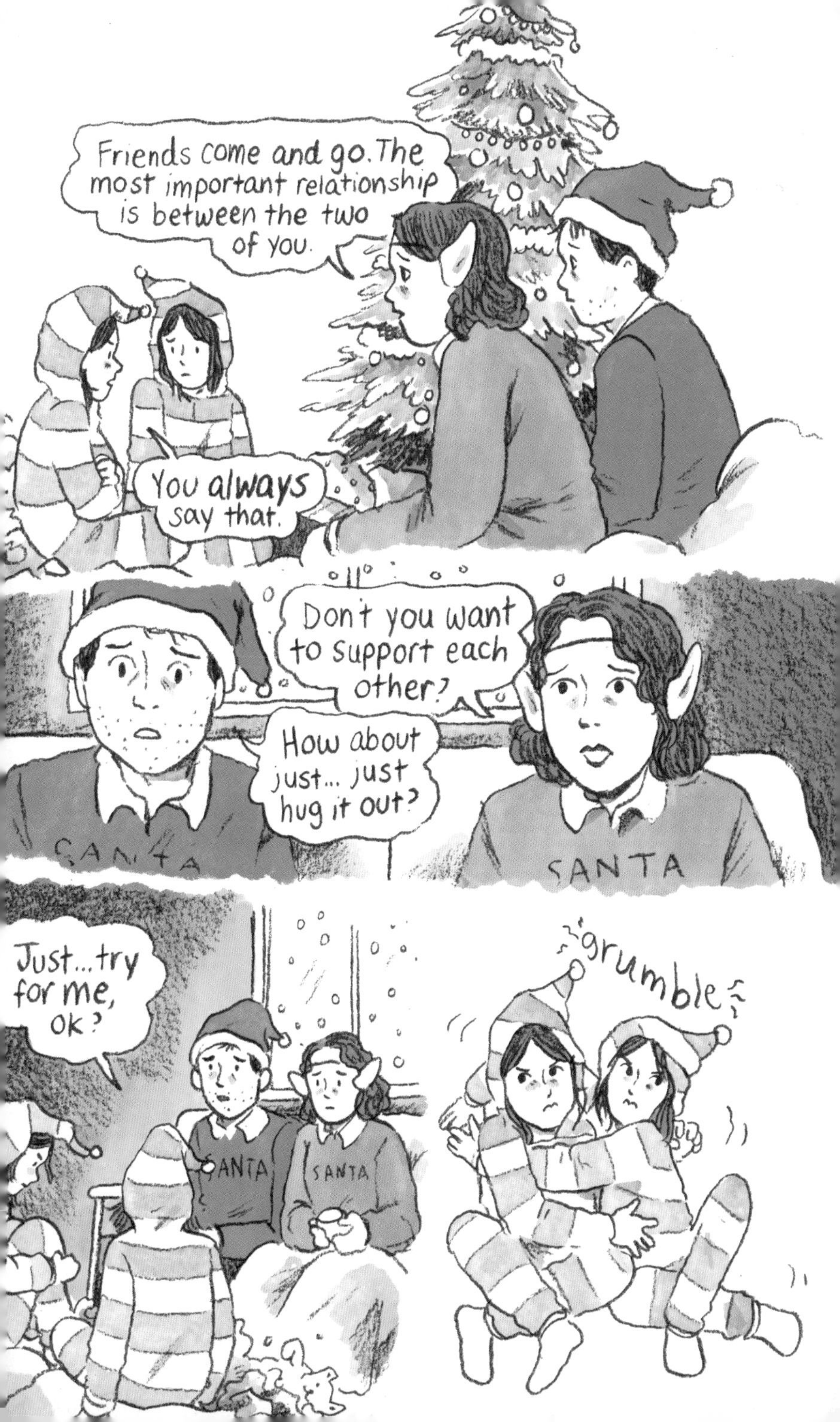
Friends come and go. The most important relationship is between the two of you.
You always say that.
Don't you want to support each other?
How about just... just hug it out?
SANTA
SANTA
Just... try for me, ok?
SANTA
SANTA
grumble

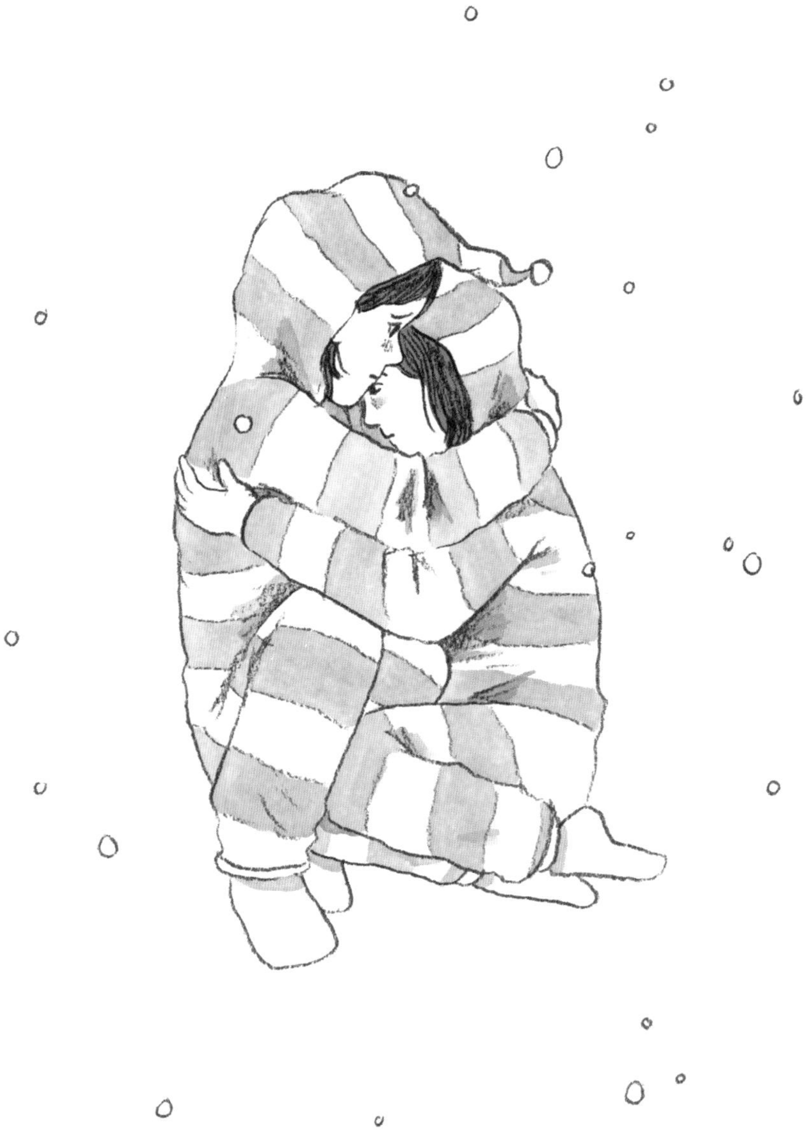

Well?
What?
There's so much to say...
...so much to tell you.
We've already done half a year of school.
I know, it went by so fast.

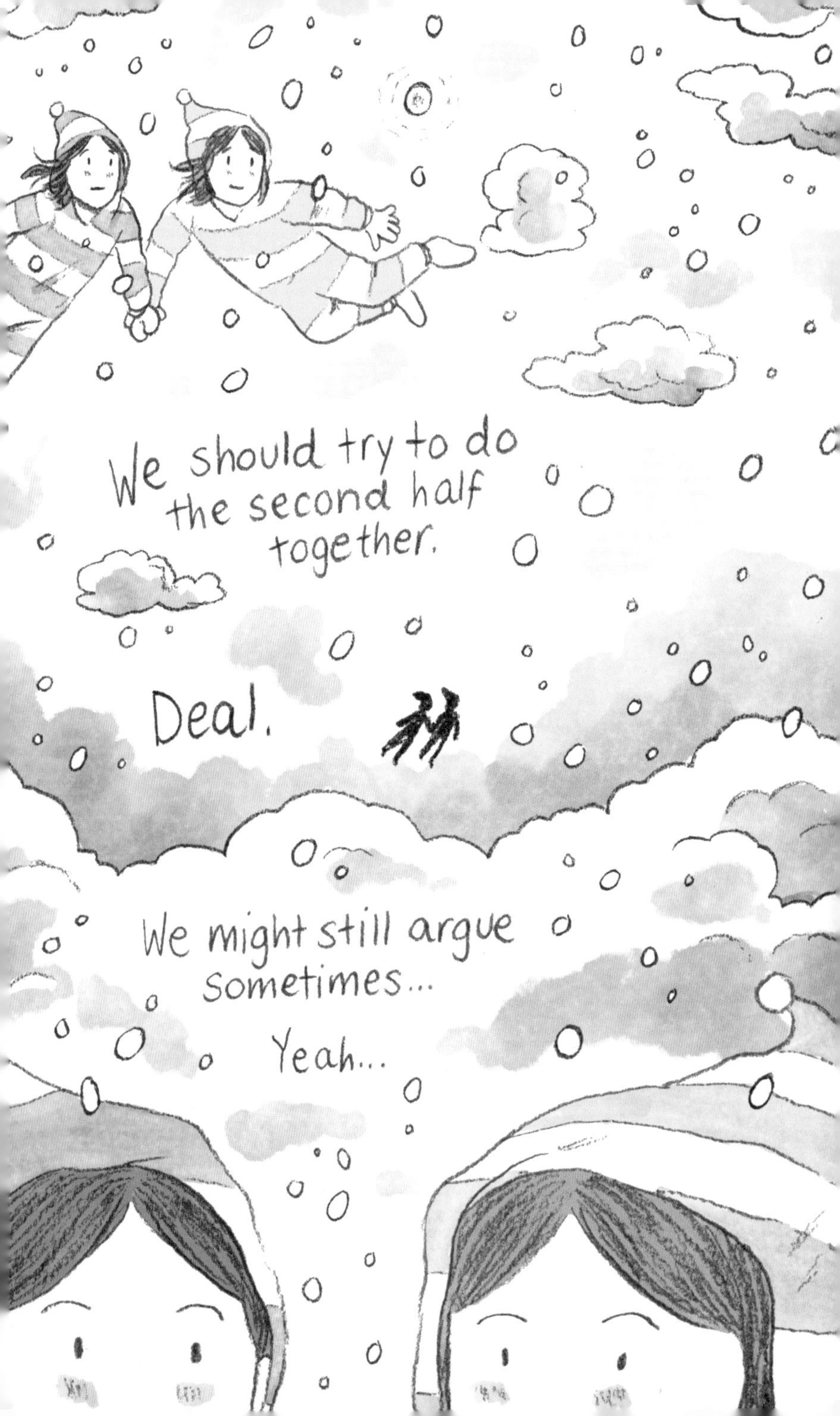
We should try to do the second half together.
Deal.
We might still argue sometimes...
Yeah...

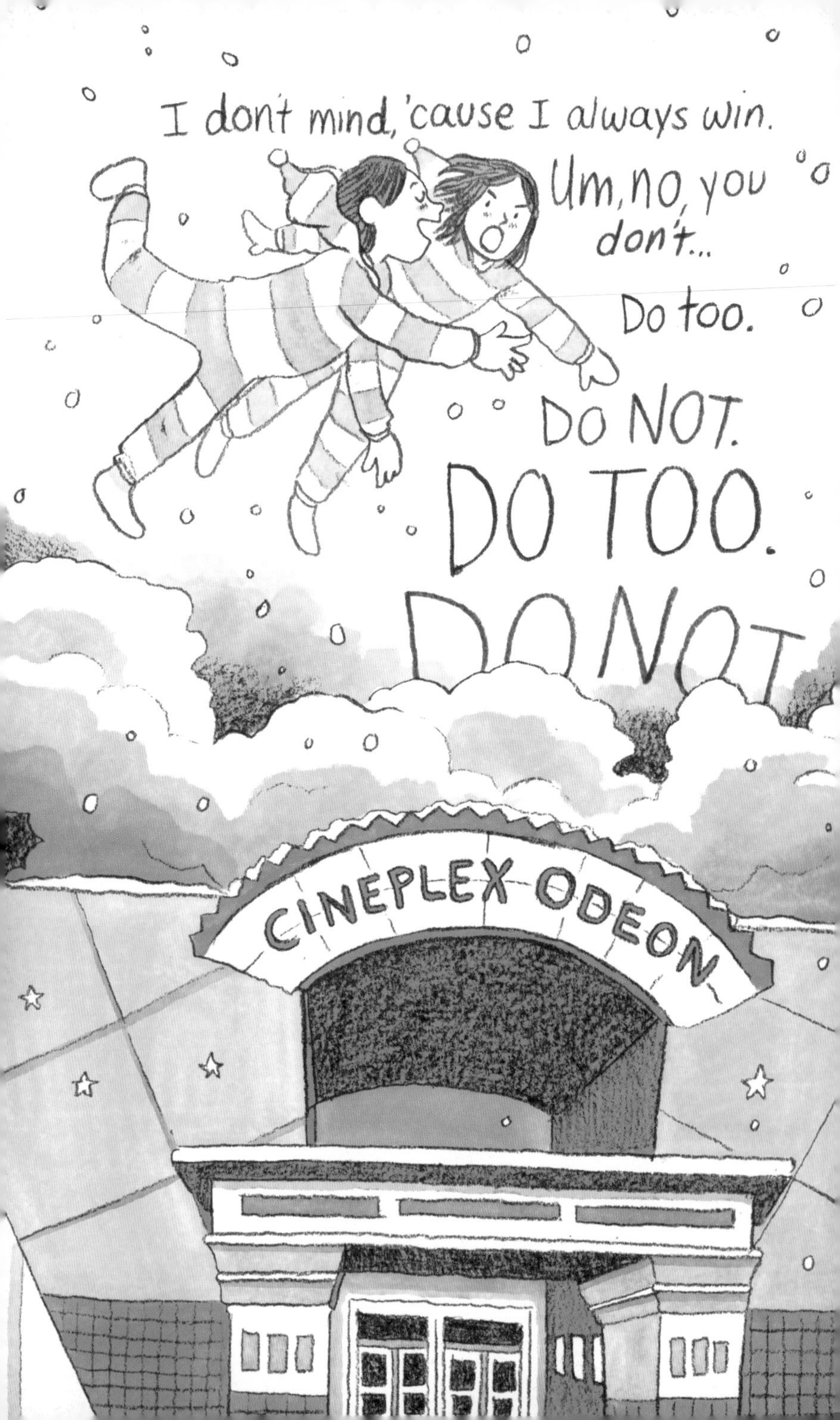
I don't mind, 'cause I always win.
Um, no, you don't...
Do too.
Do NOT.
DO TOO.
DO NOT
CINEPLEX ODEON

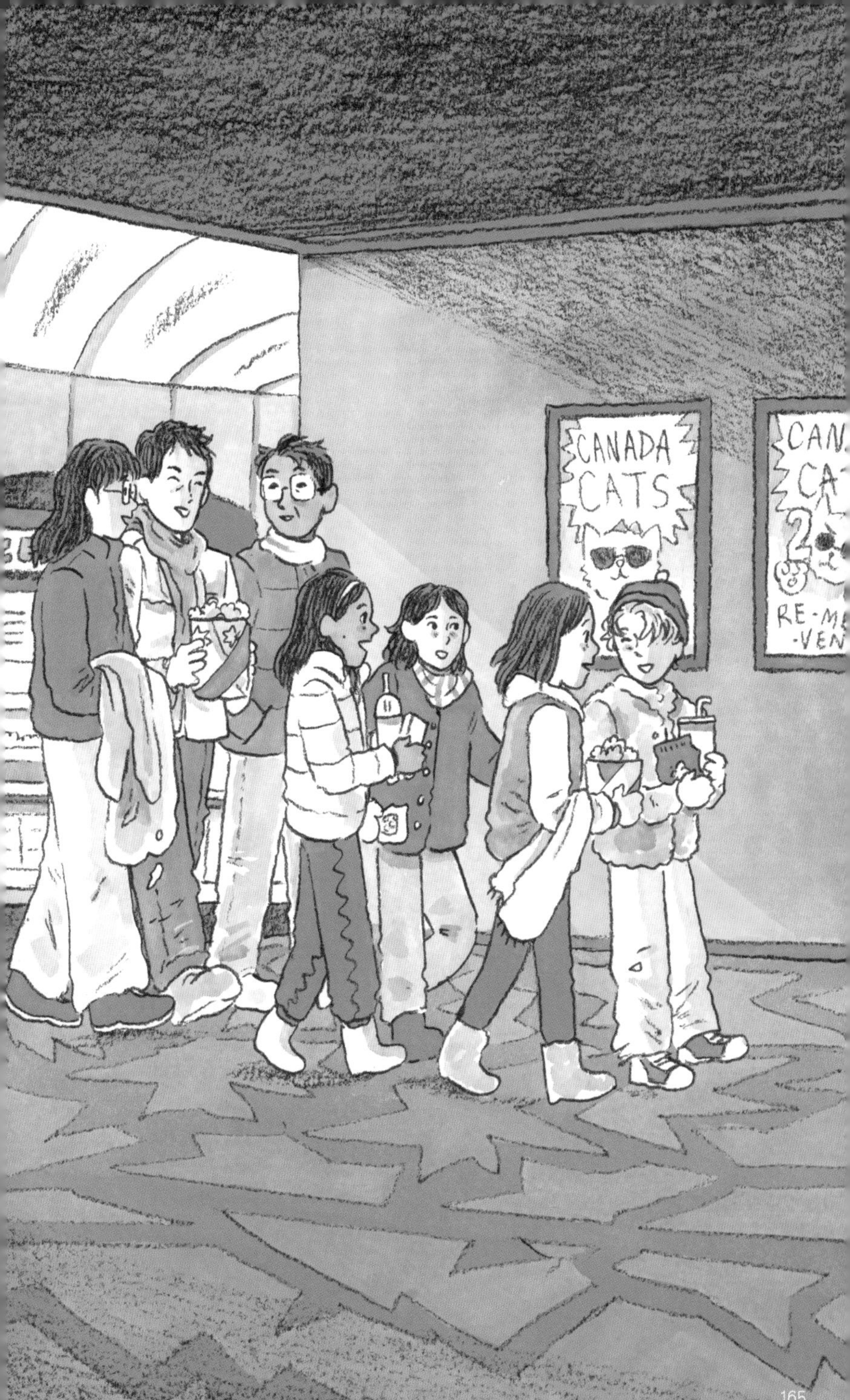
CANADA
CATS

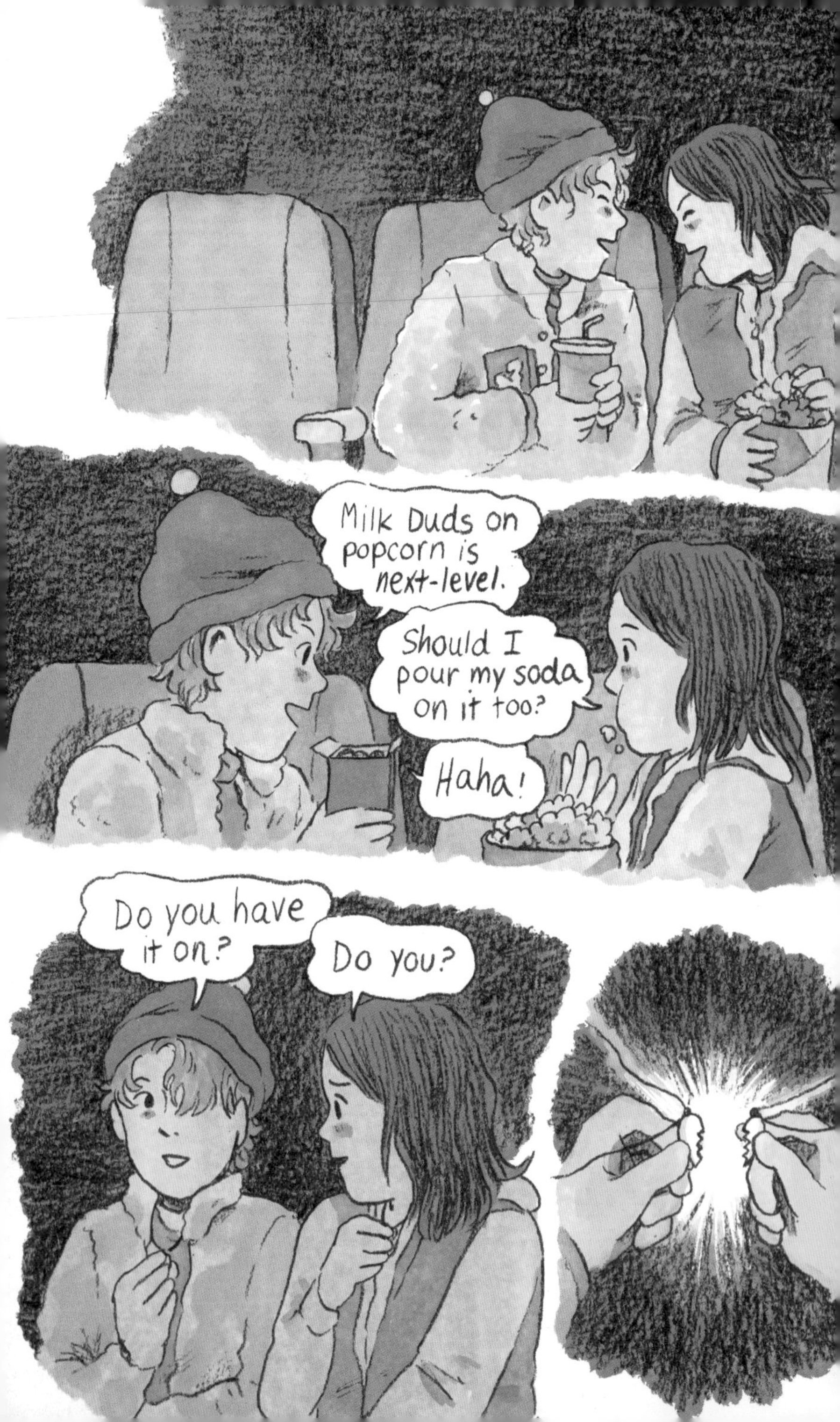
Milk Duds on popcorn is next-level.
Should I pour my soda on it too?
Haha!
Do you have it on?
Do you?

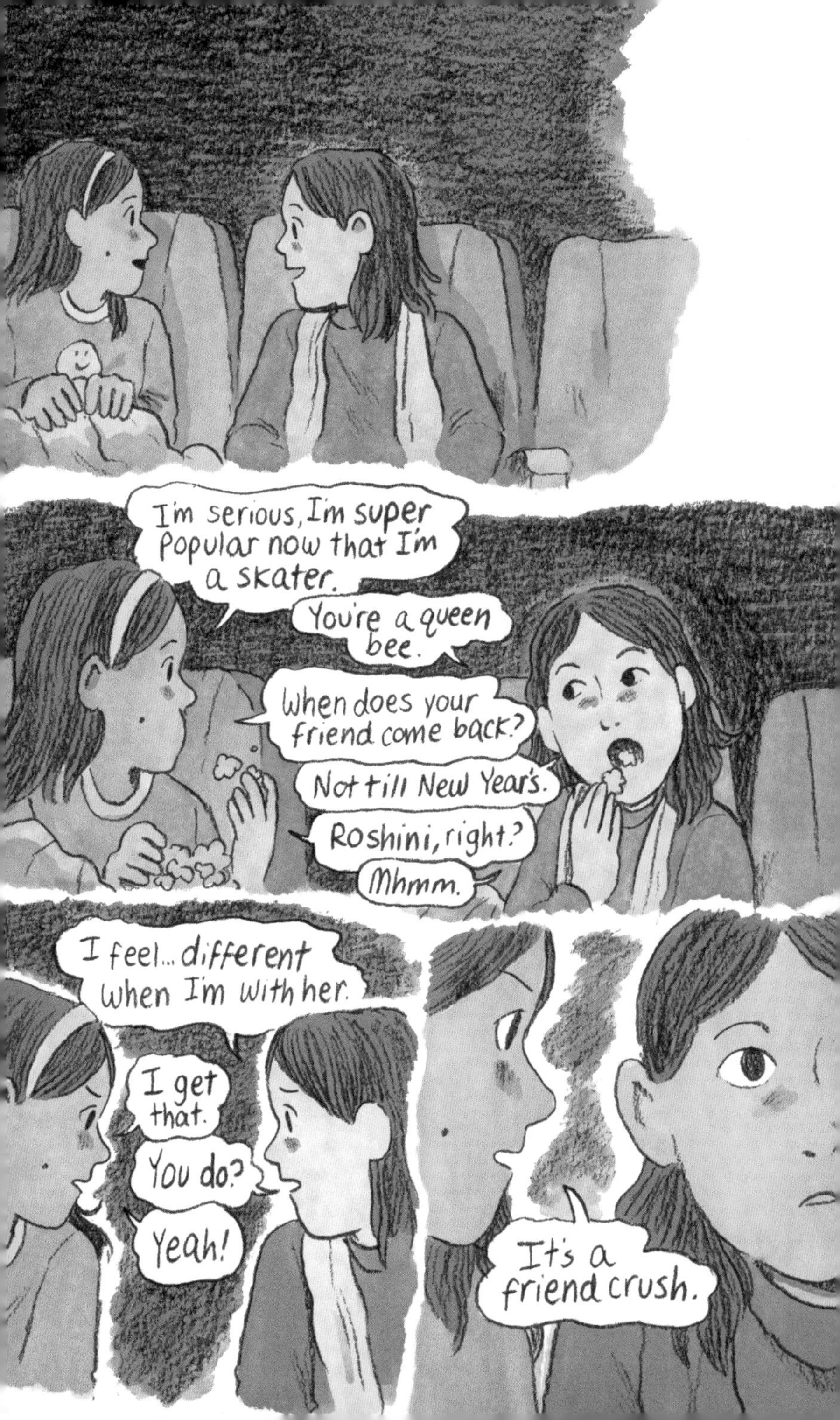
I'm serious, I'm super popular now that I'm a skater.
You're a queen bee.
When does your friend come back?
Not till New Year's.
Roshini, right?
Mhmm.
I feel... different when I'm with her.
I get that.
You do?
Yeah!
It's a friend crush.

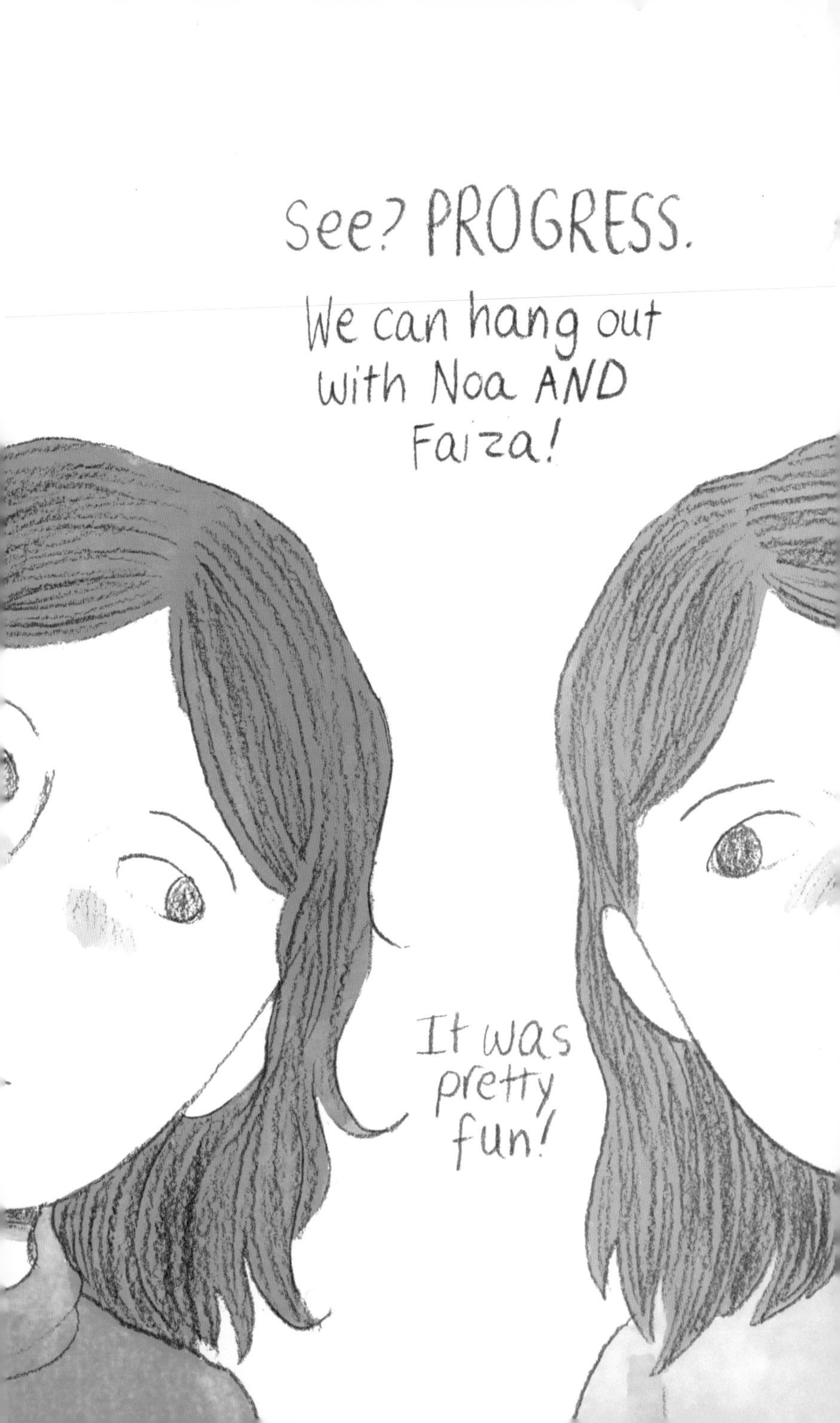
See? PROGRESS.
We can hang out with Noa AND Faiza!
It was pretty fun!

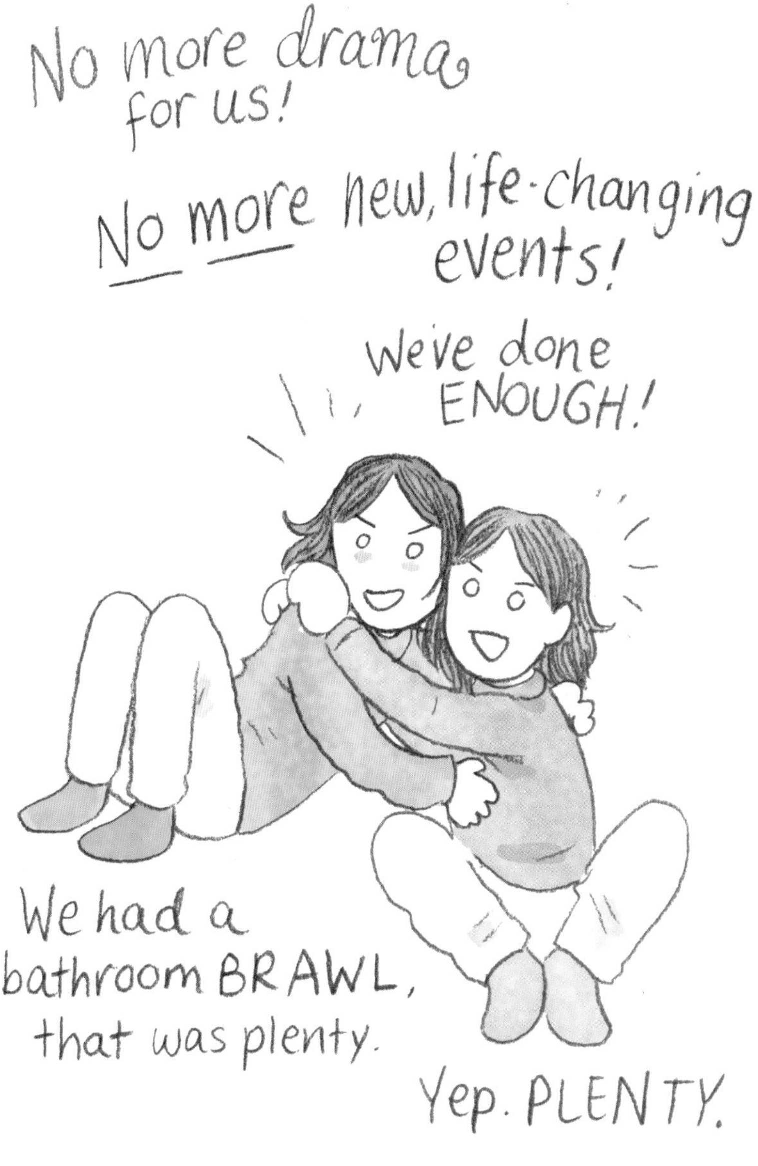
No more drama for us!
No more new, life-changing events!
We've done ENOUGH!
We had a bathroom BRAWL, that was plenty.
Yep. PLENTY.

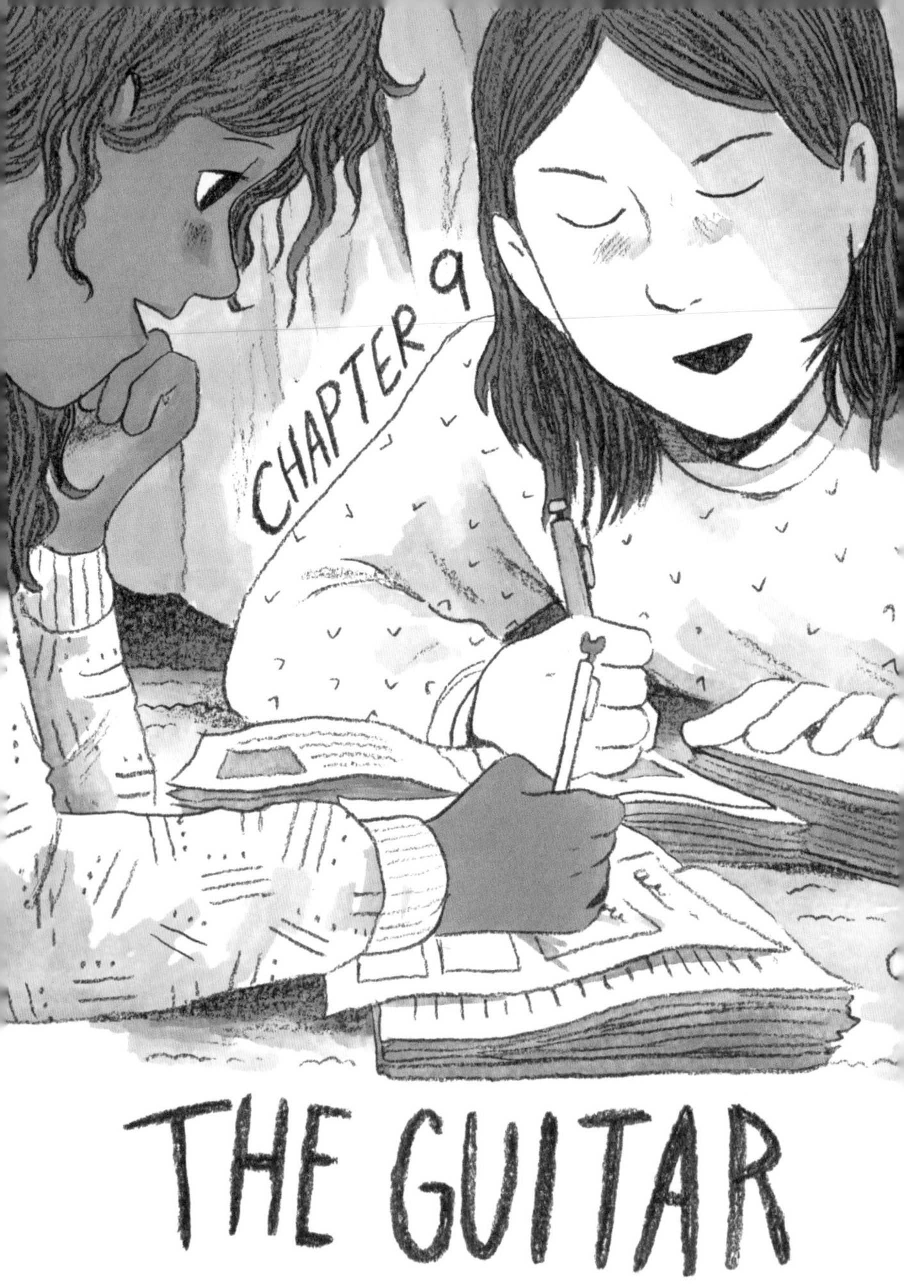
CHAPTER 9

THE GUITAR

We jinxed ourselves,
didn't we?

I don't think so.

You're right.
That was when
we found it.

Yeah.

Yeah.

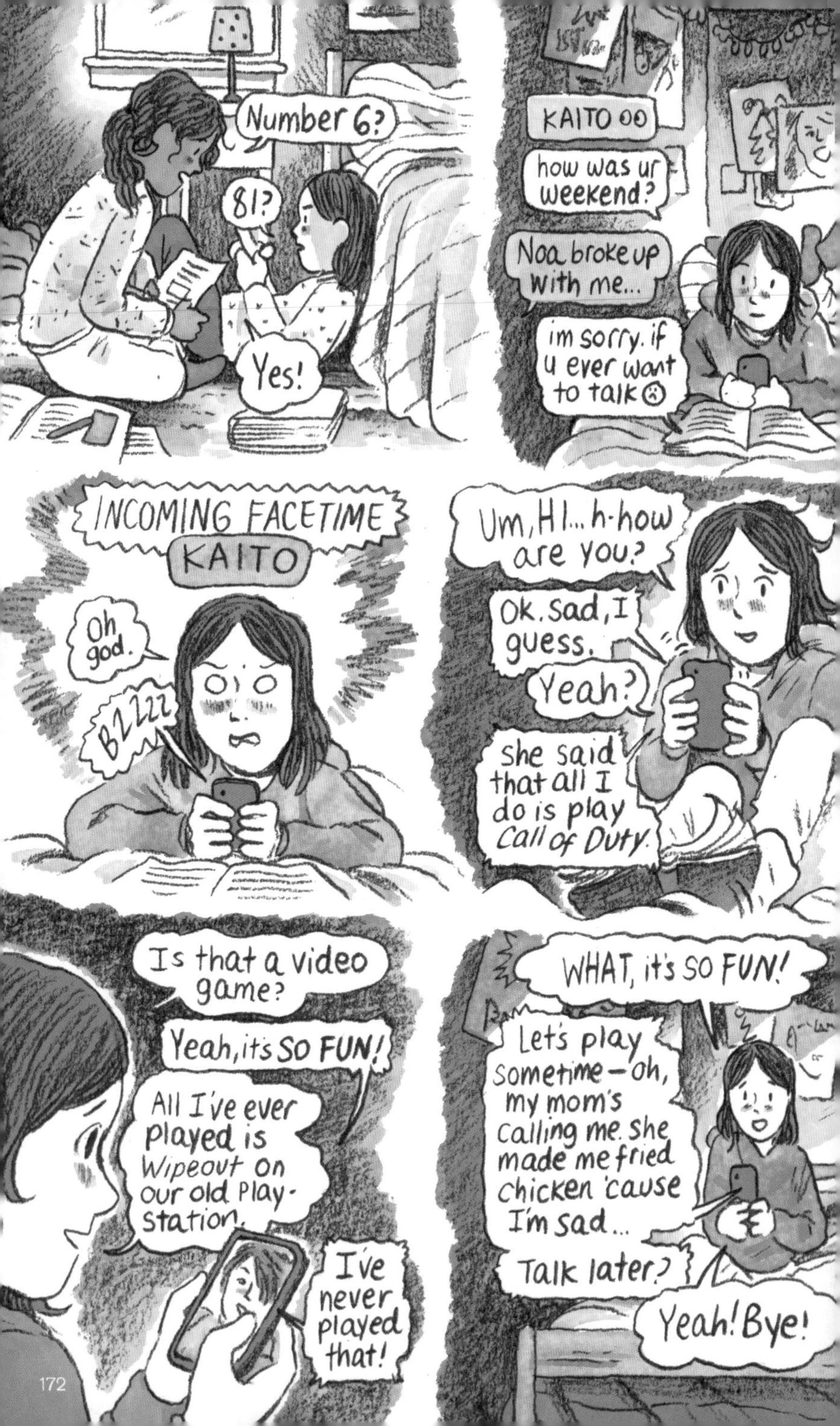
Number 6?
81?
Yes!
KAITO
how was ur weekend?
Noa broke up with me...
im sorry. if u ever want to talk ☹
INCOMING FACETIME
KAITO
Oh god.
BZZZZ
Um, HI... h-how are you?
Ok. Sad, I guess.
Yeah?
She said that all I do is play *Call of Duty*.
Is that a video game?
Yeah, it's SO FUN!
All I've ever played is *Wipeout* on our old Play-Station.
I've never played that!
WHAT, it's SO FUN!
Let's play sometime—oh, my mom's calling me. She made me fried chicken 'cause I'm sad...
Talk later?
Yeah! Bye!

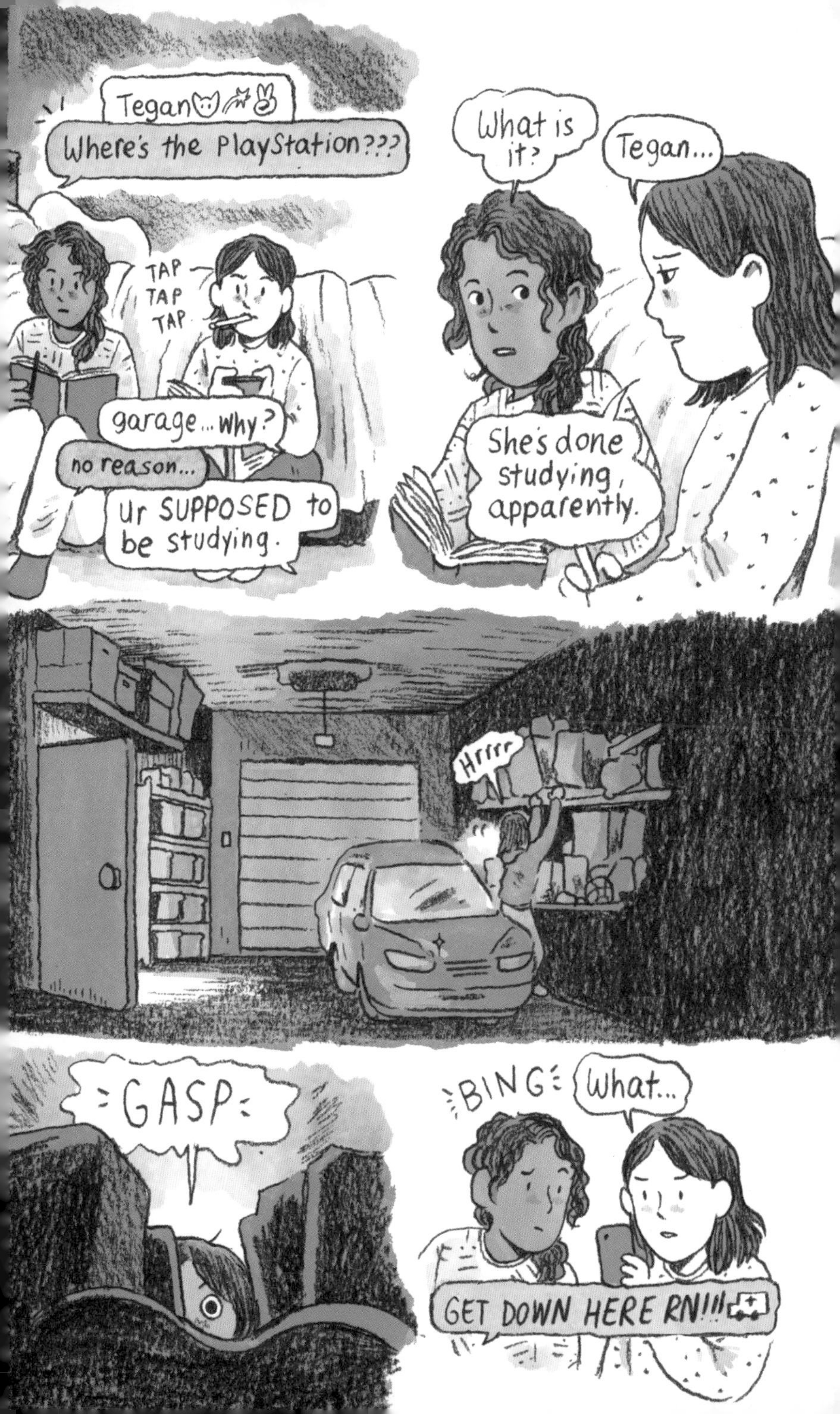
Tegan
Where's the PlayStation???
TAP TAP TAP
garage...why?
no reason...
Ur SUPPOSED to be studying.
What is it?
Tegan...
She's done studying, apparently.
Hrrrr
GASP
BING
What...
GET DOWN HERE RN!!!

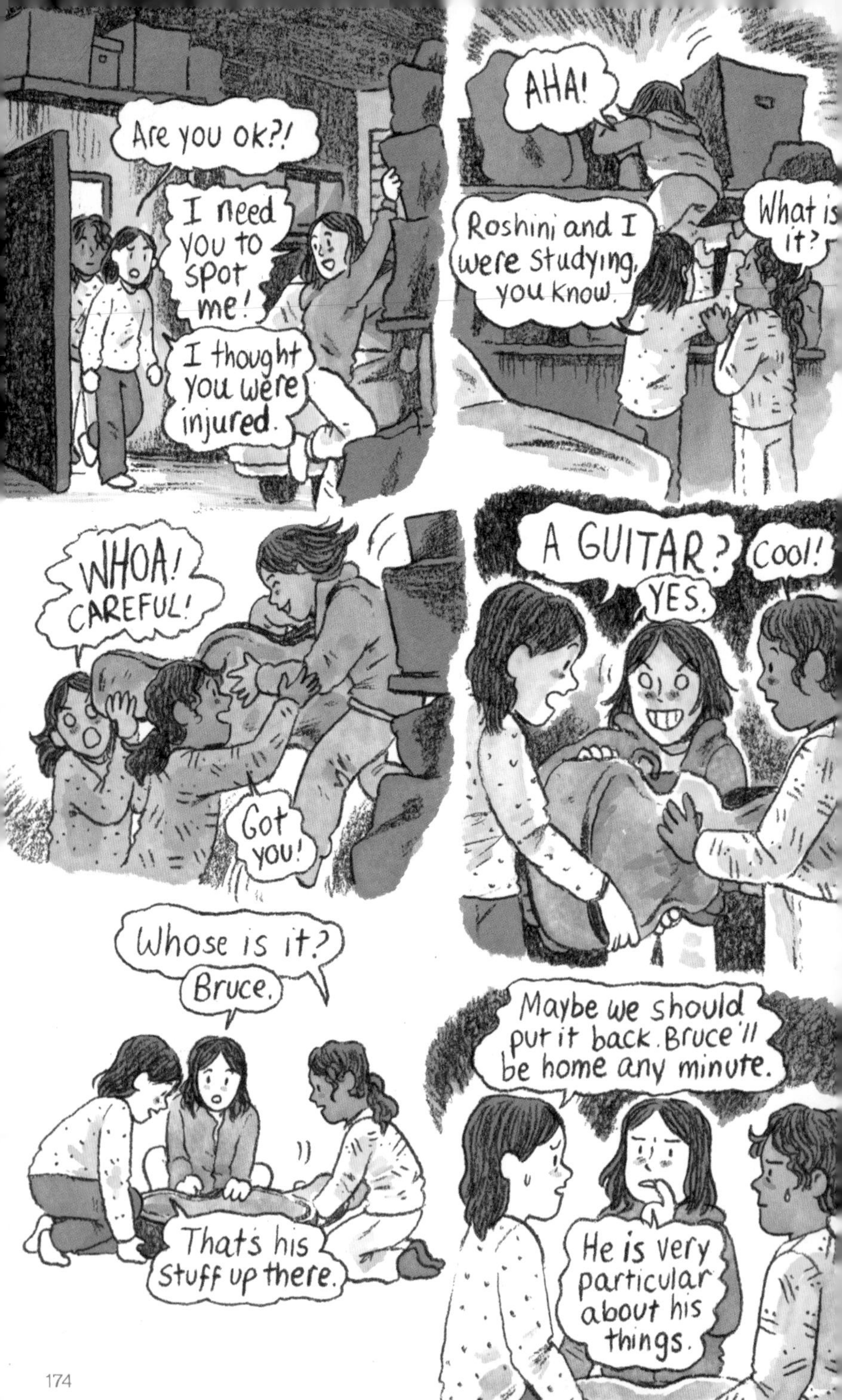
Are you OK?!
I need you to spot me!
I thought you were injured.
AHA!
Roshini and I were studying, you know.
What is it?
WHOA! CAREFUL!
Got you!
A GUITAR?
YES.
Cool!
Whose is it?
Bruce.
That's his stuff up there.
Maybe we should put it back. Bruce'll be home any minute.
He is very particular about his things.

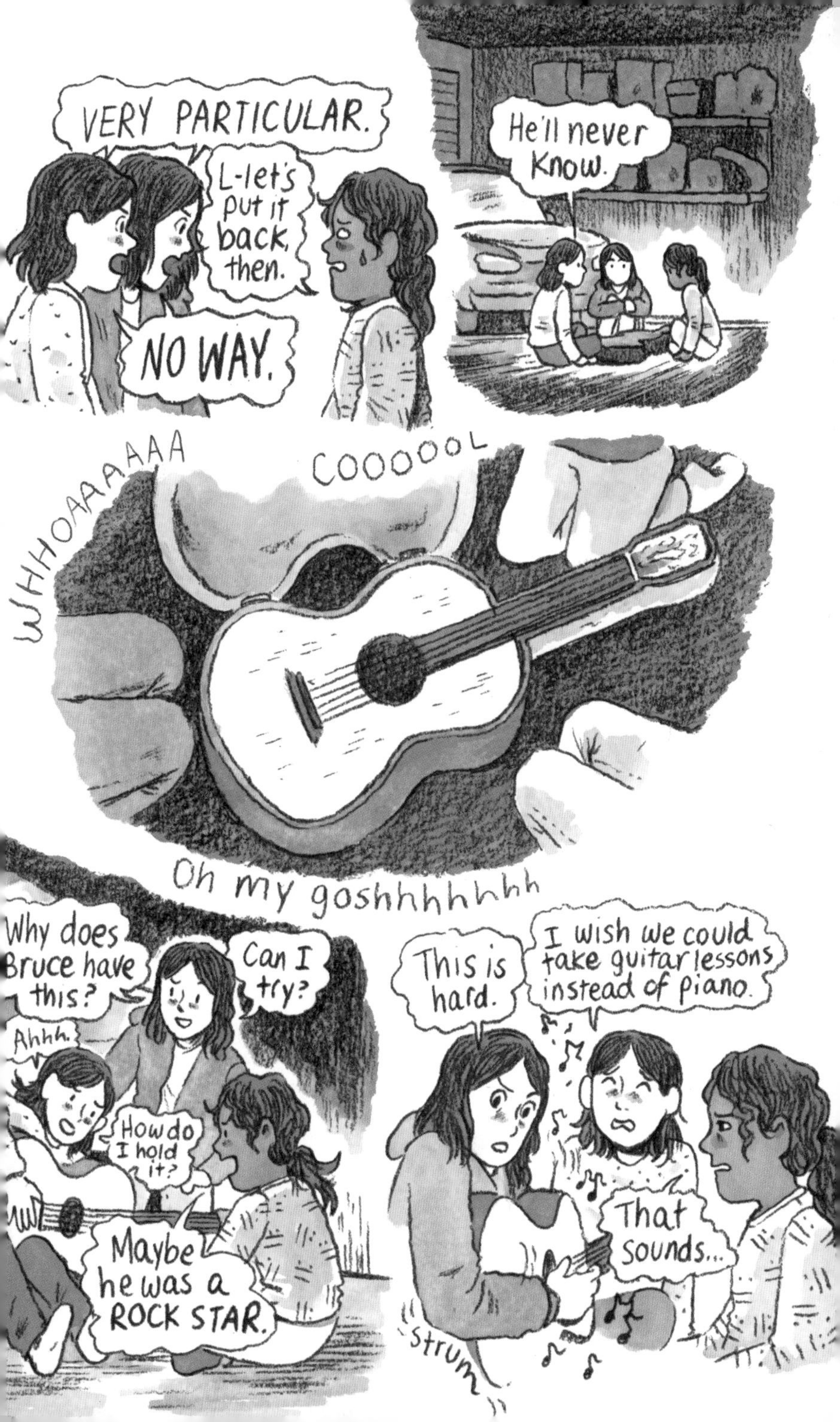
VERY PARTICULAR.
L-let's put it back, then.
NO WAY.
He'll never know.
WHHOAAAAAAA
COOOOOL
Oh my goshhhhhhh
Why does Bruce have this?
Can I try?
Ahhh.
How do I hold it?
Maybe he was a ROCK STAR.
This is hard.
I wish we could take guitar lessons instead of piano.
That sounds...
STRUM

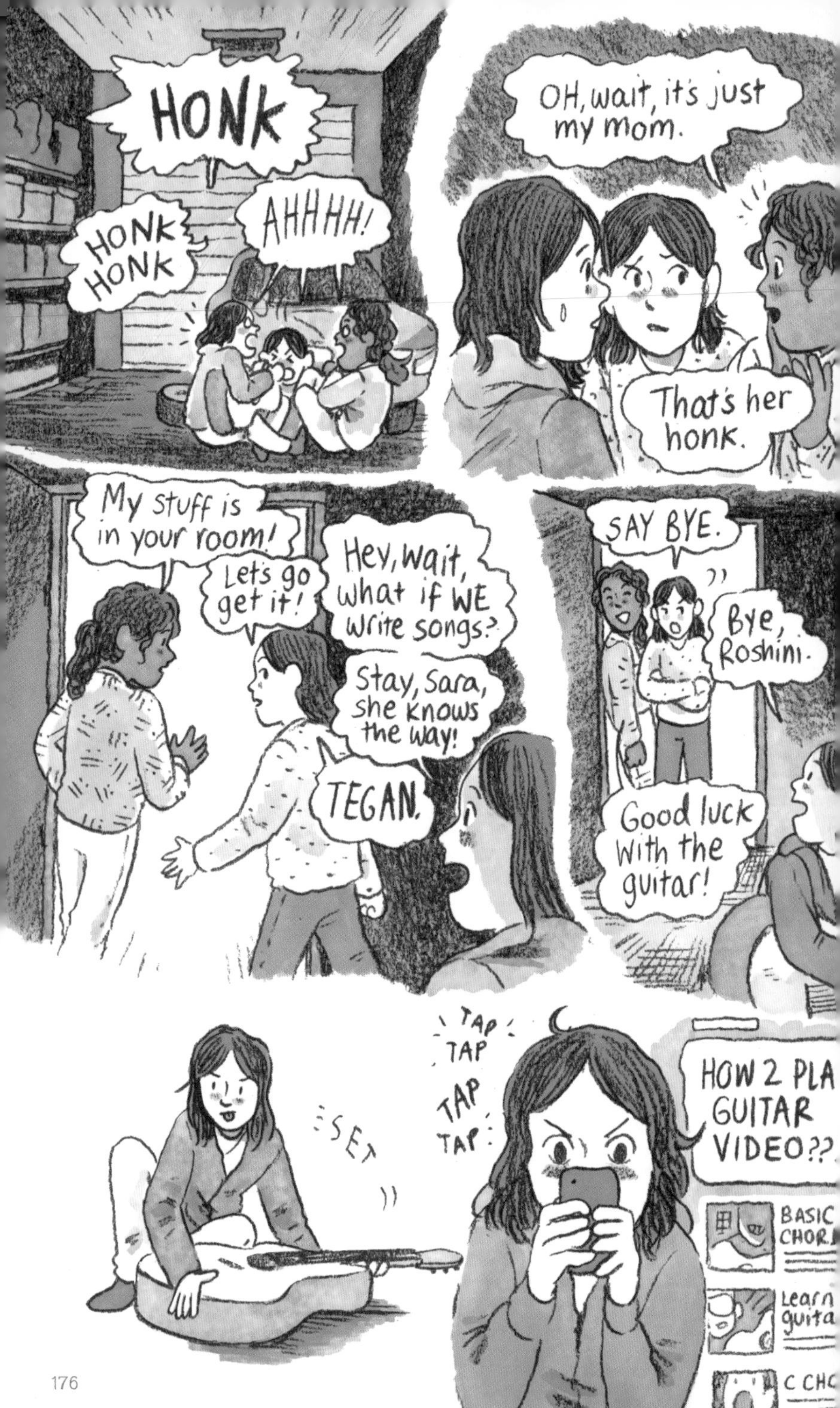
HONK
HONK HONK
AHHHH!
OH, wait, it's just my mom.
That's her honk.
My stuff is in your room!
Let's go get it!
Hey, wait, what if WE write songs?
Stay, Sara, she knows the way!
TEGAN.
SAY BYE.
Bye, Roshini.
Good luck with the guitar!
SET
TAP TAP
TAP TAP
HOW 2 PLA
GUITAR
VIDEO??
BASIC
CHOR
Learn
guita
C CHO

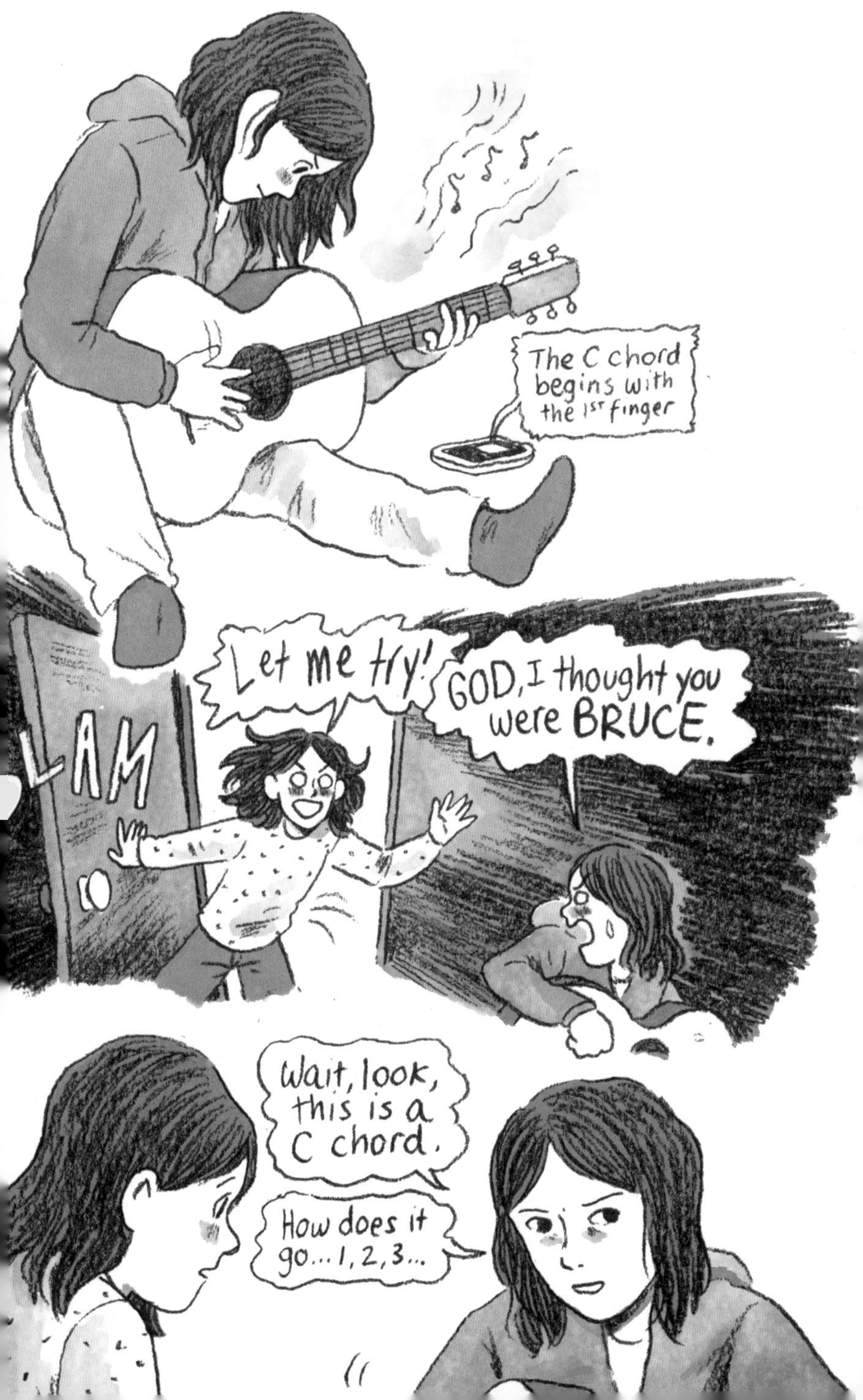
The C chord begins with the 1st finger
SLAM
Let me try!
GOD, I thought you were BRUCE.
Wait, look, this is a C chord.
How does it go... 1, 2, 3...

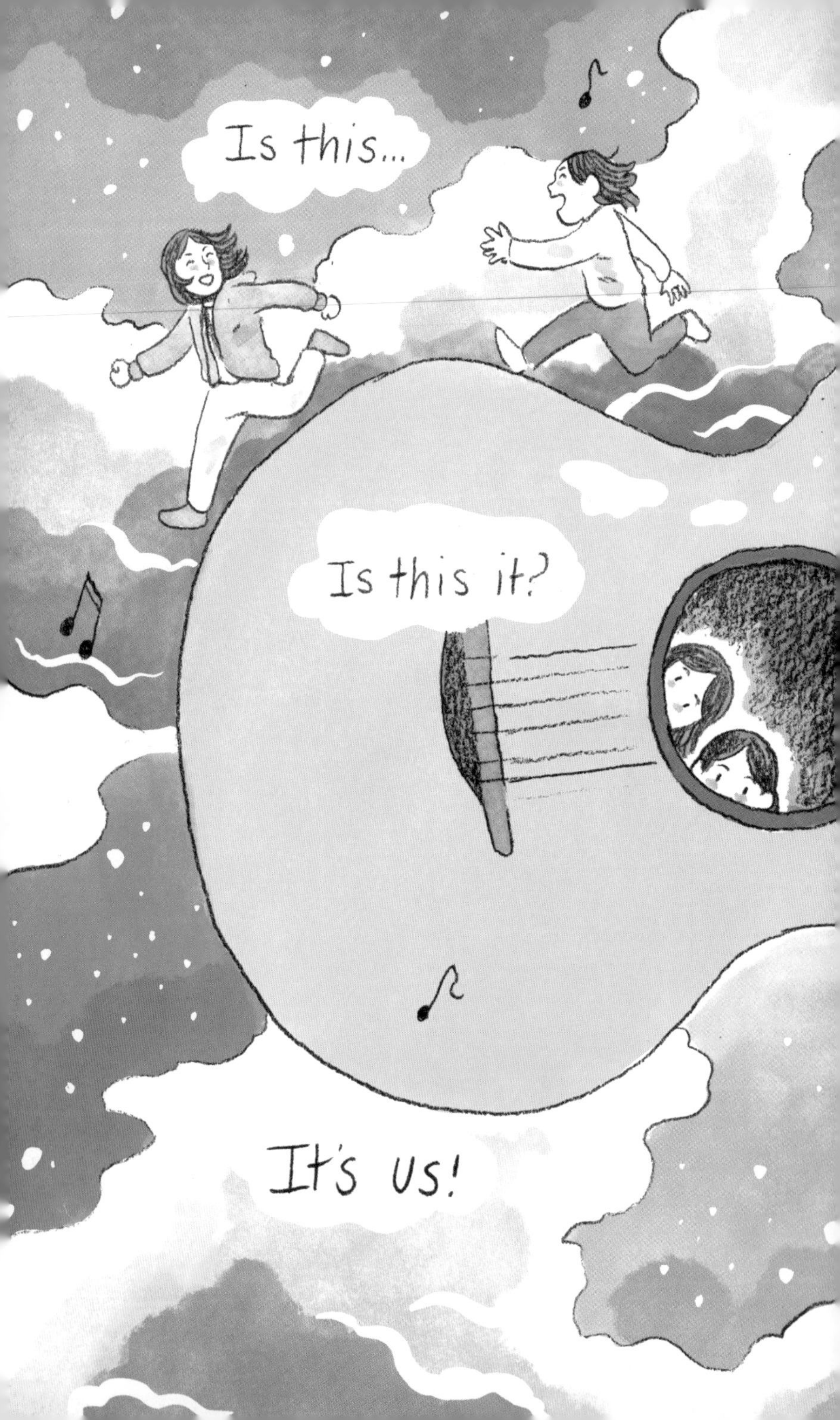
Is this...
Is this it?
It's us!

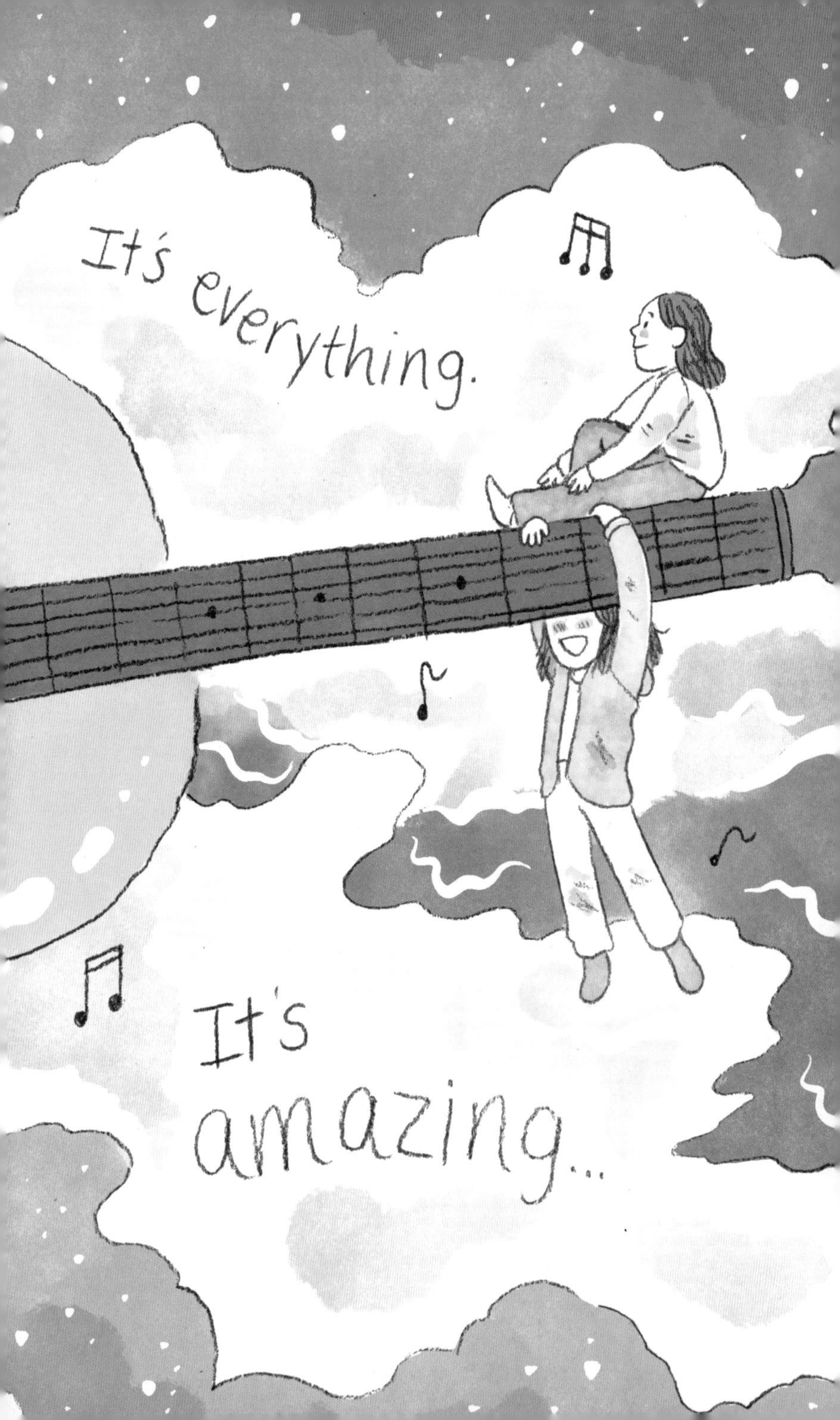
It's everything.
It's amazing...

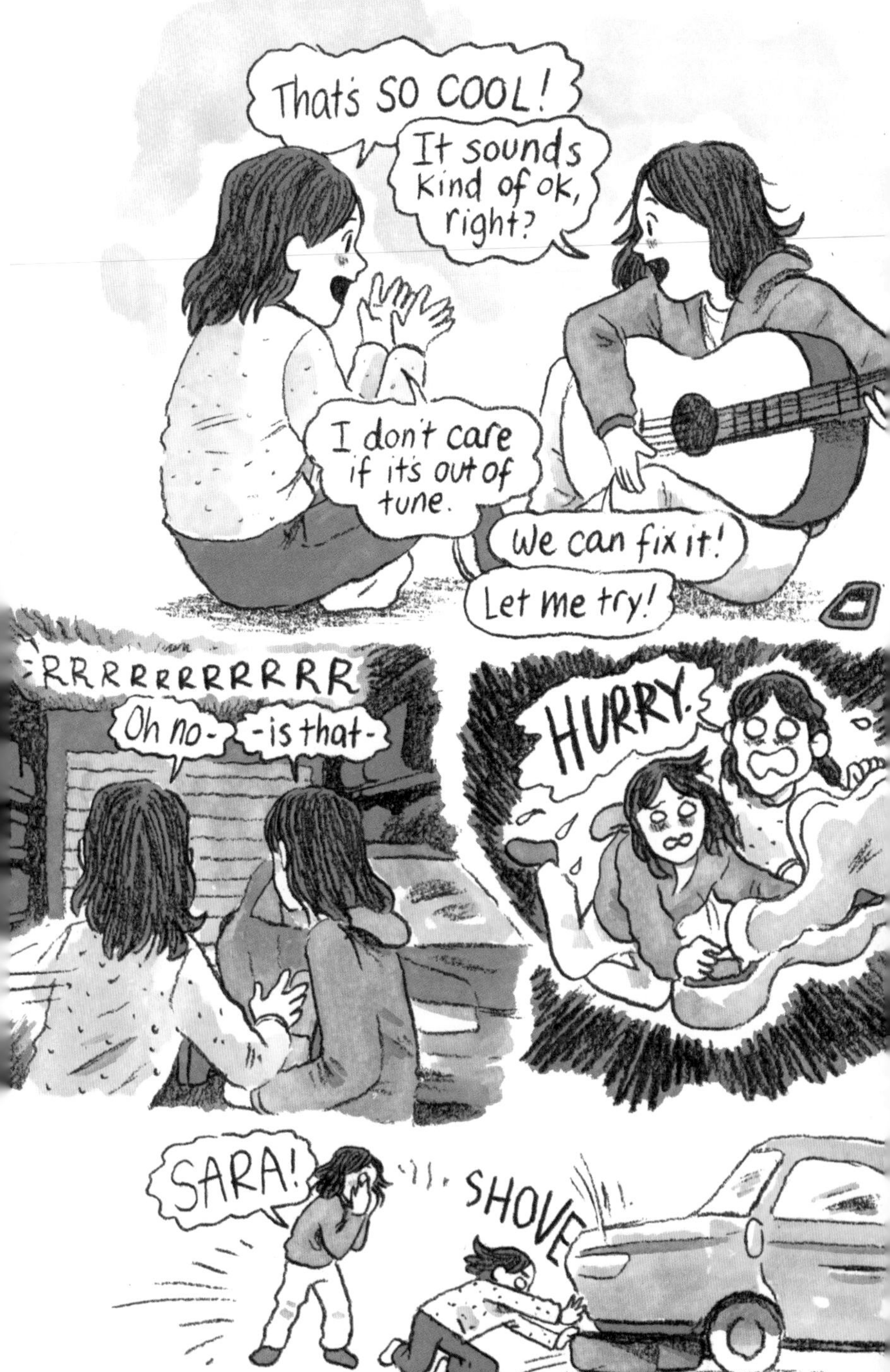
That's SO COOL!
It sounds kind of ok, right?
I don't care if it's out of tune.
We can fix it!
Let me try!
RRRRRRRRRRRR
Oh no-
-is that-
HURRY.
SARA!
SHOVE

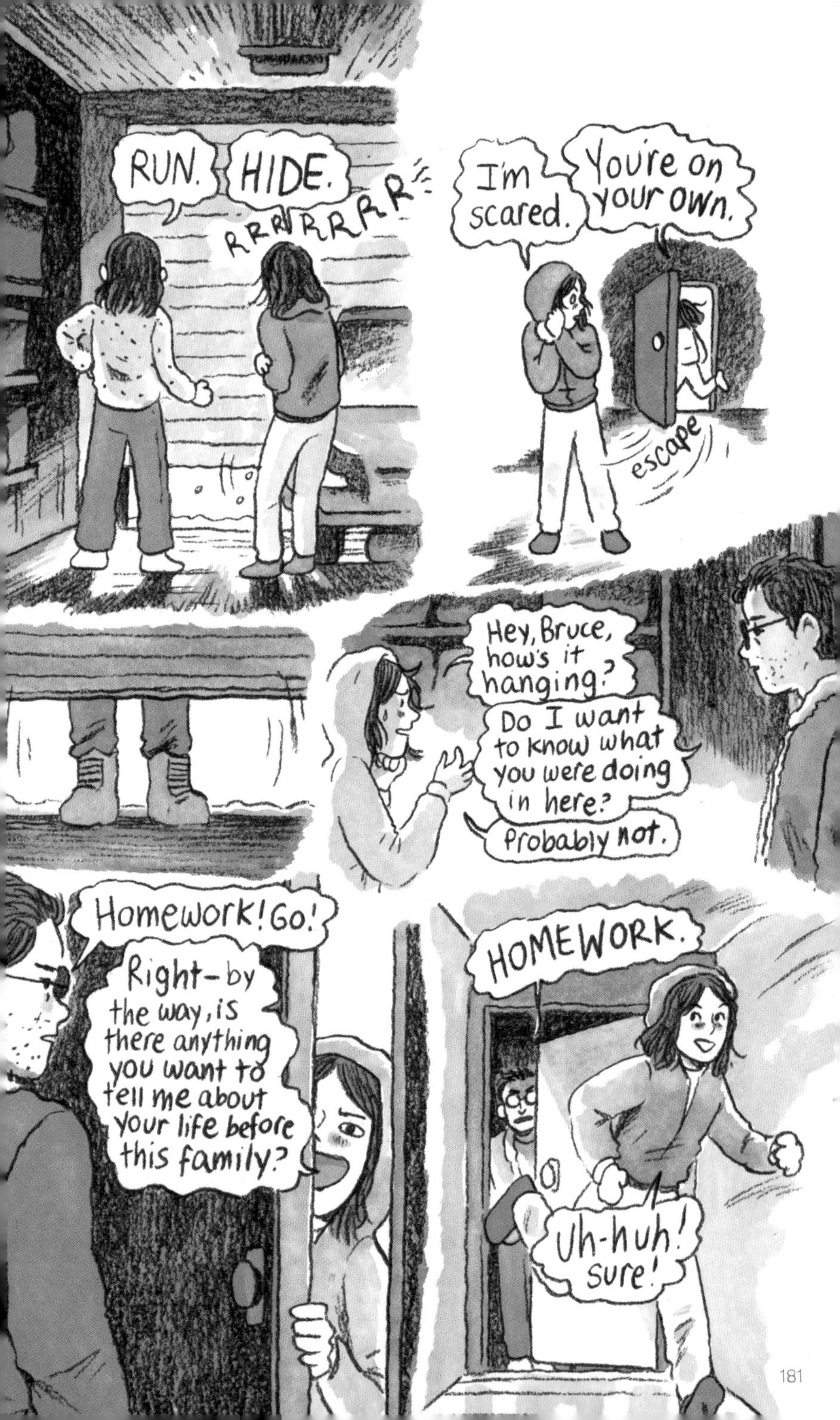
RUN.
HIDE.
RRRRRRRRR
I'm scared.
You're on your own.
escape
Hey, Bruce, how's it hanging?
Do I want to know what you were doing in here?
Probably not.
Homework! Go!
Right—by the way, is there anything you want to tell me about your life before this family?
HOMEWORK.
Uh-huh! sure!

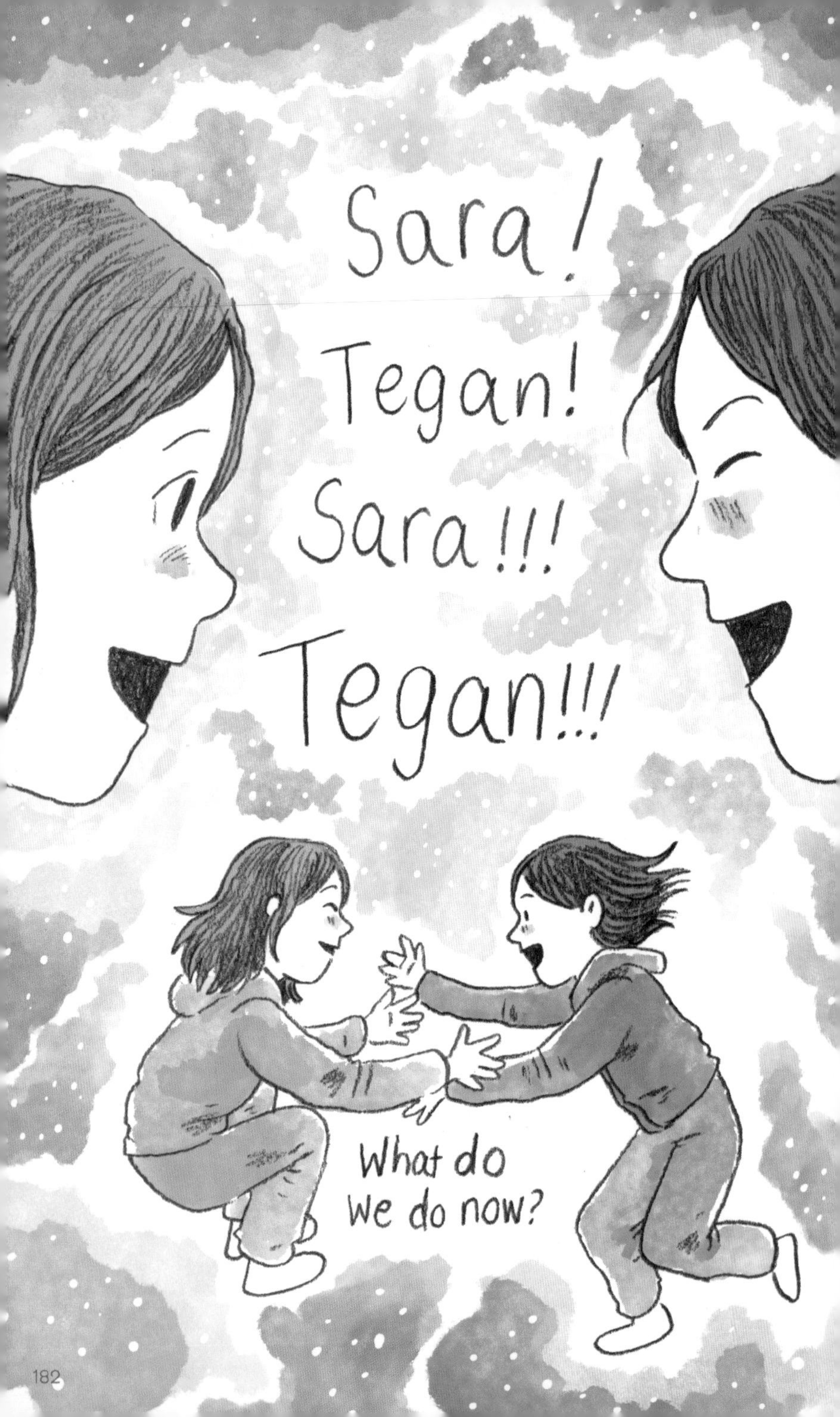
Sara!
Tegan!
Sara!!!
Tegan!!!
What do we do now?

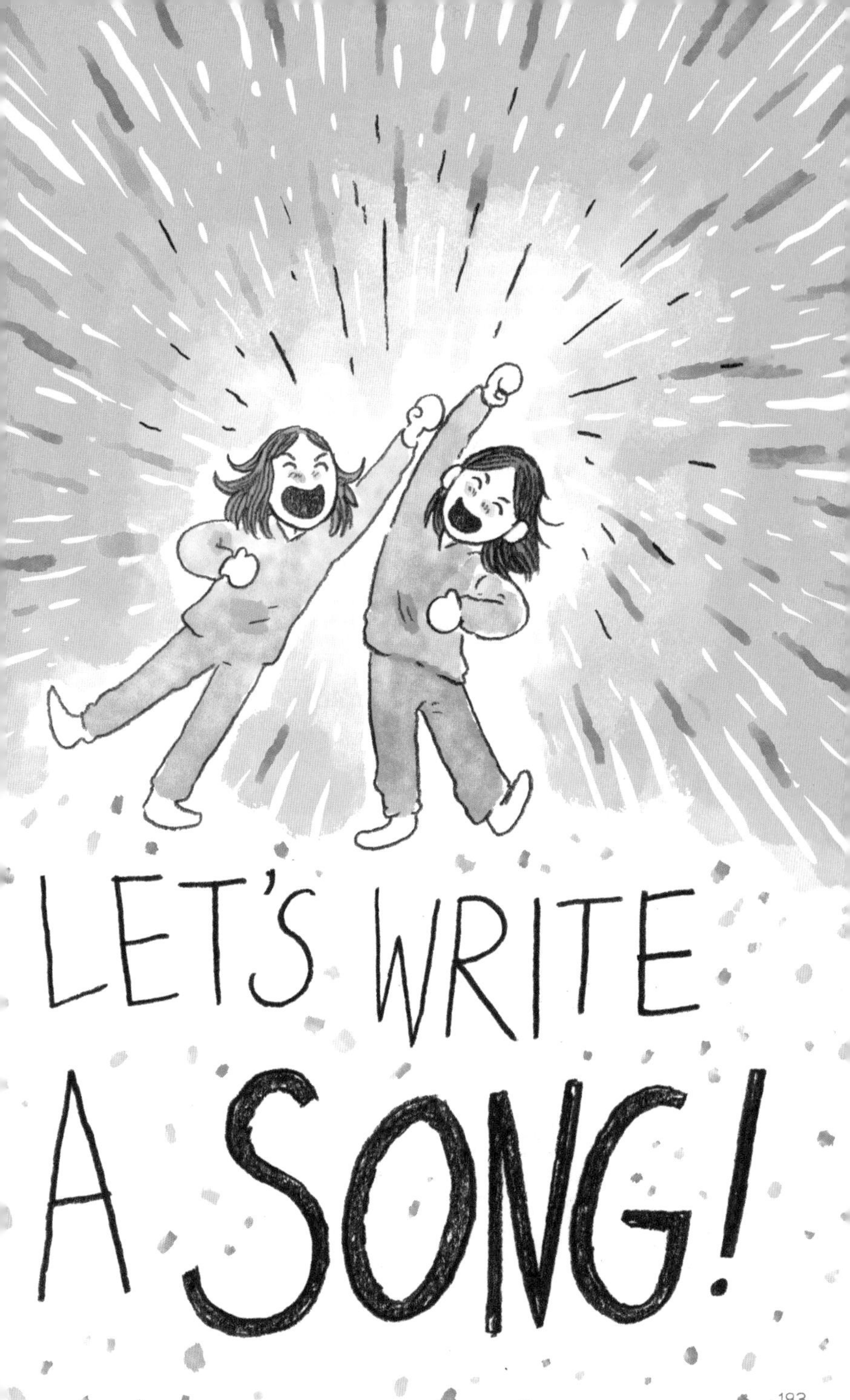
LET'S WRITE
A SONG!

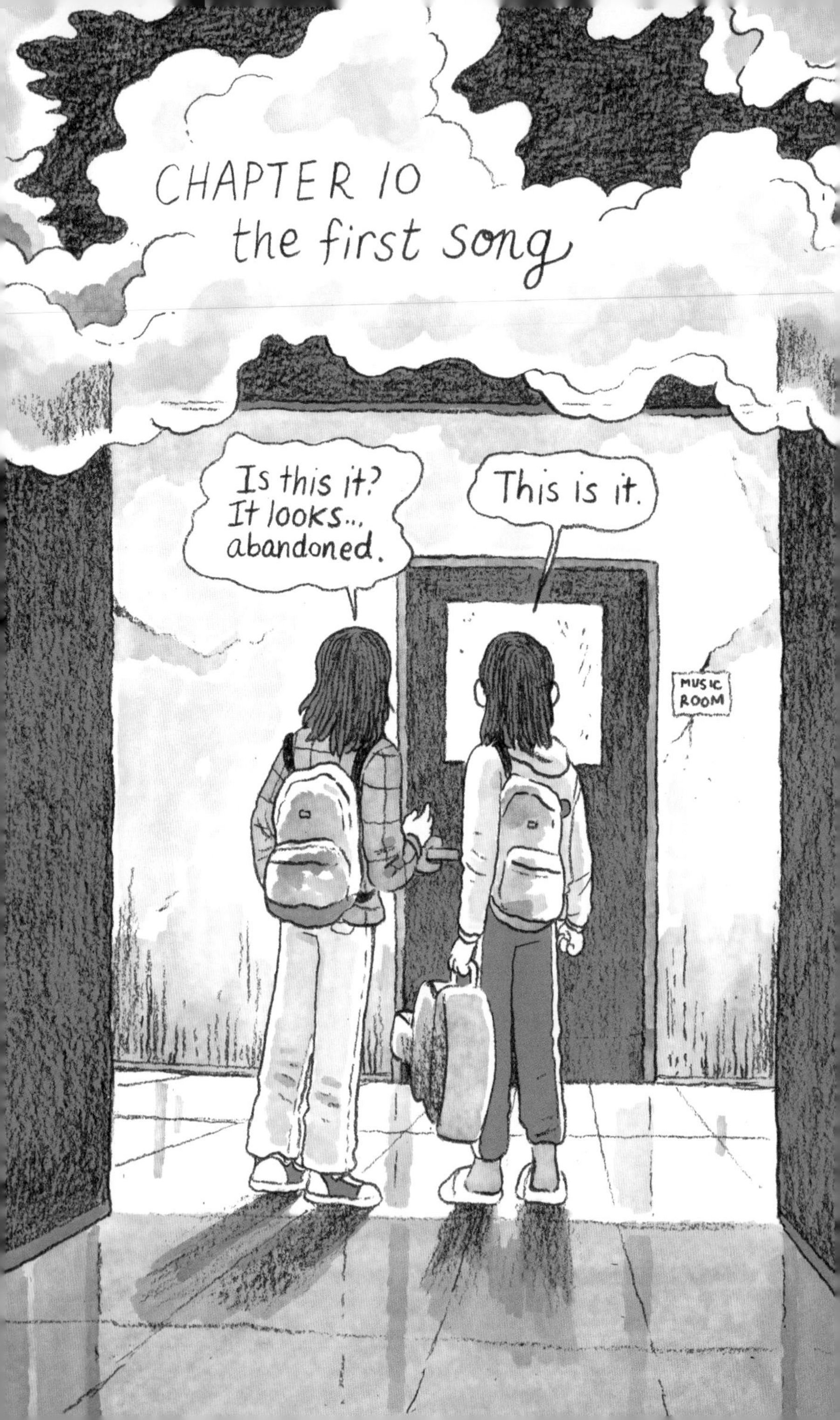
CHAPTER 10
the first song
Is this it? It looks..., abandoned.
This is it.
MUSIC ROOM

Sooo... how **do** you write
a song?

Well, it's just, like, words
and music, right?

I guess I could write
some words.

YEAH! Write something
DEEP, Sara!

Deep...? Can you do
the chords?

Oh, yeah. I know *three!*

Maybe you should learn
a few more...

Don't rush my
genius.

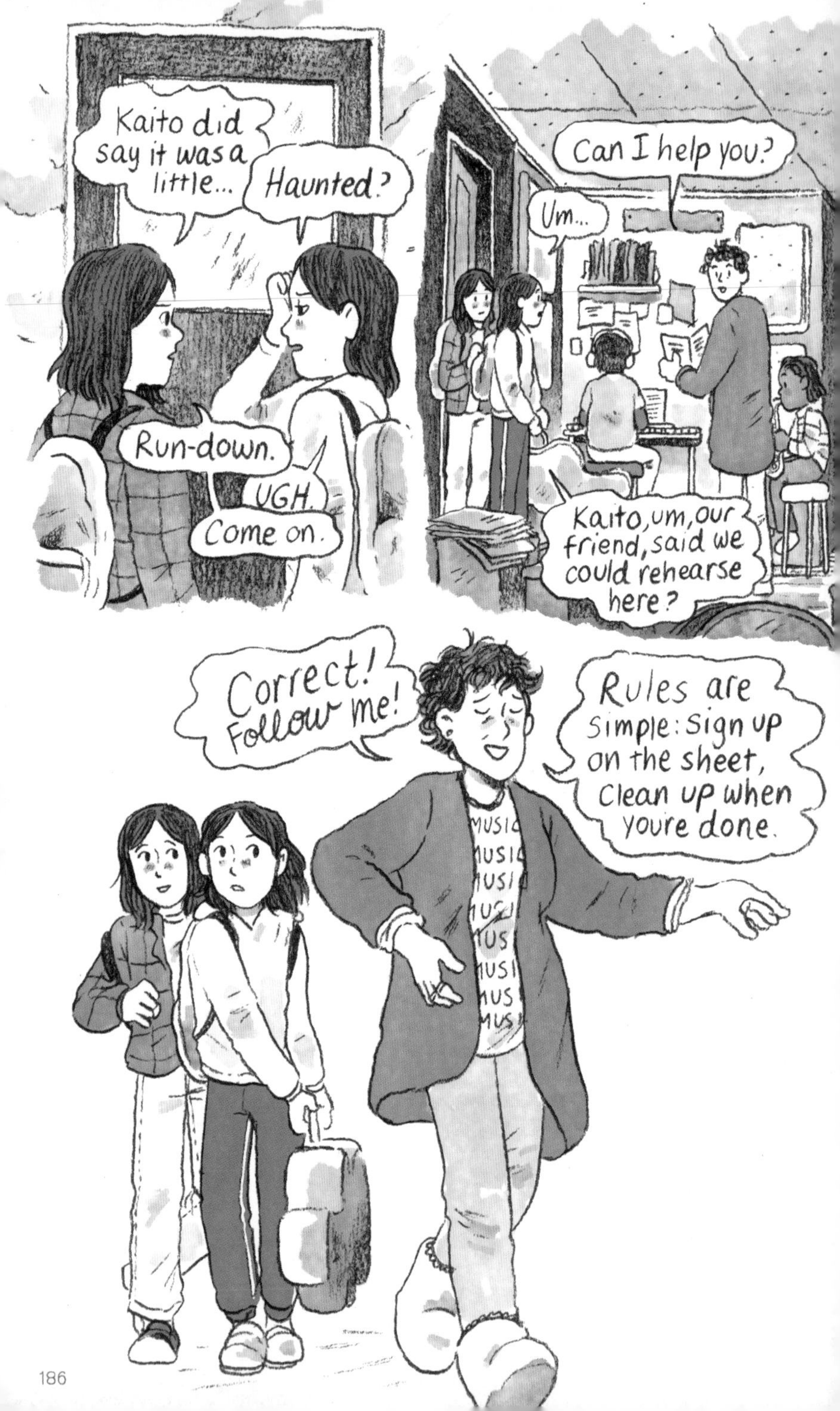
Kaito did say it was a little...
Haunted?
Run-down.
UGH.
Come on.
Can I help you?
Um...
Kaito, um, our friend, said we could rehearse here?
Correct! Follow me!
Rules are simple: sign up on the sheet, clean up when you're done.
MUSIC

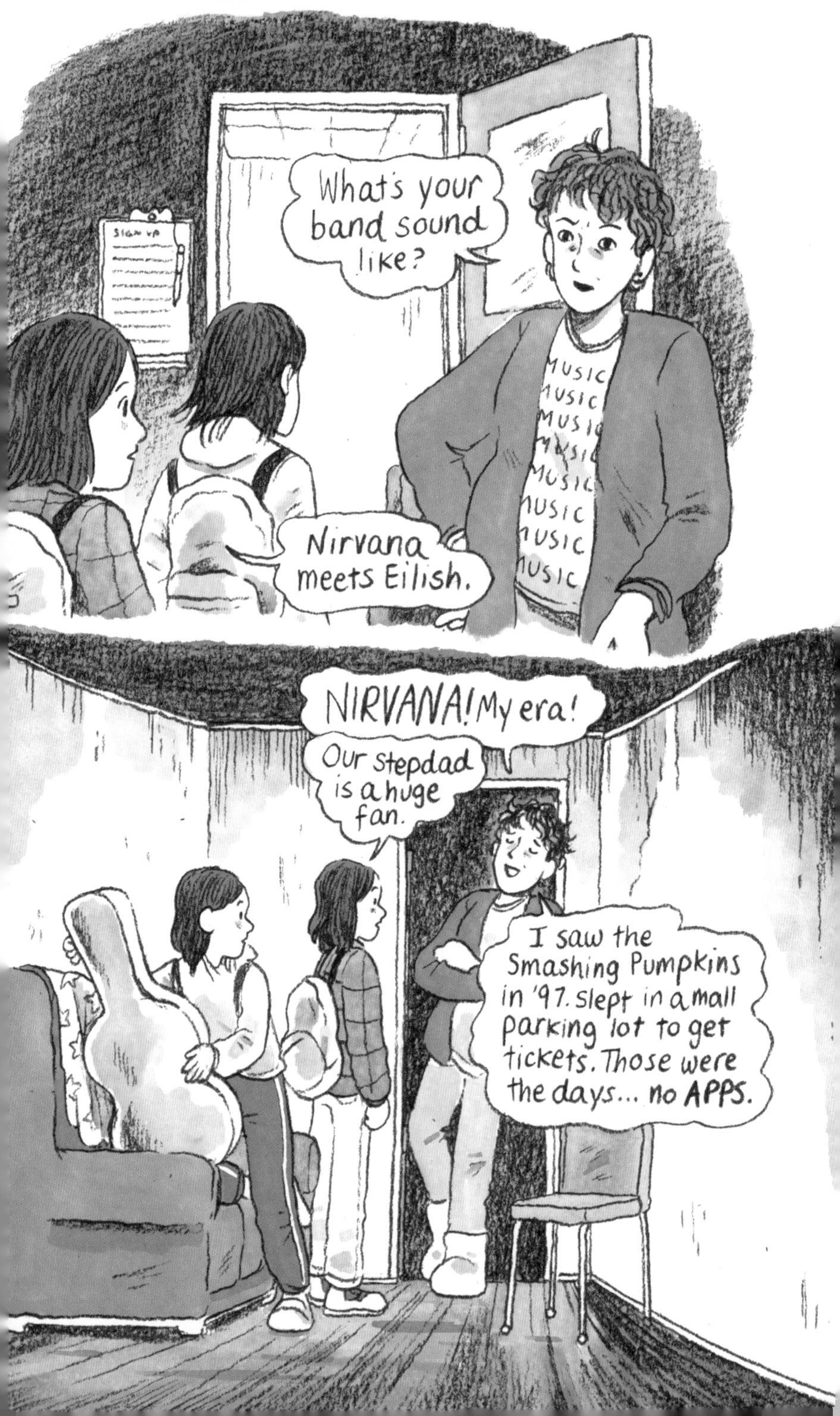
What's your band sound like?
Nirvana meets Eilish.
NIRVANA! My era!
Our stepdad is a huge fan.
I saw the Smashing Pumpkins in '97. Slept in a mall parking lot to get tickets. Those were the days... no APPS.

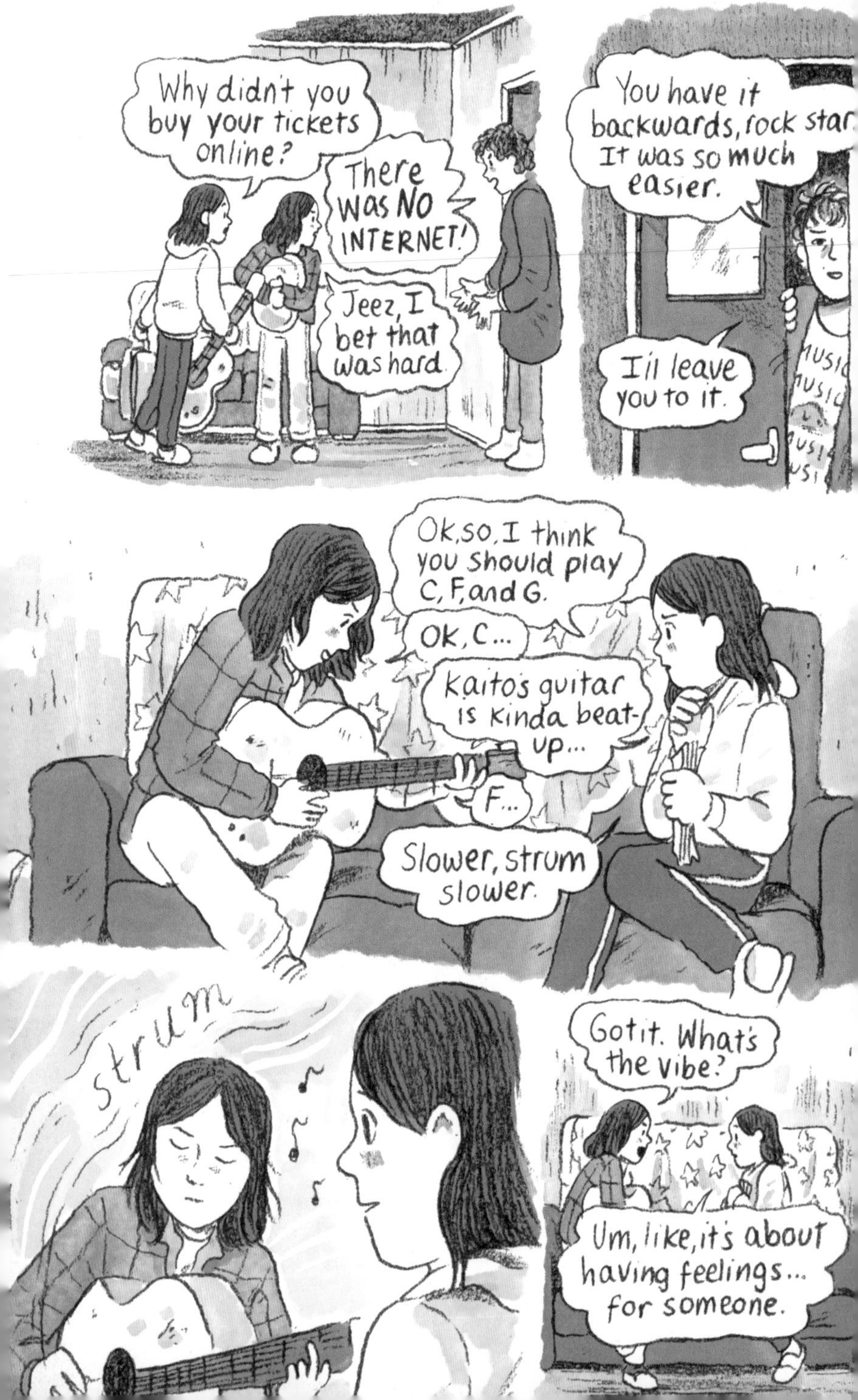
Why didn't you buy your tickets online?
There was NO INTERNET!
Jeez, I bet that was hard.
You have it backwards, rock star. It was so much easier.
I'll leave you to it.
MUSIC
Ok, so, I think you should play C, F, and G.
Ok, C...
Kaito's guitar is kinda beat-up...
F...
Slower, strum slower.
strum
Got it. What's the vibe?
Um, like, it's about having feelings... for someone.

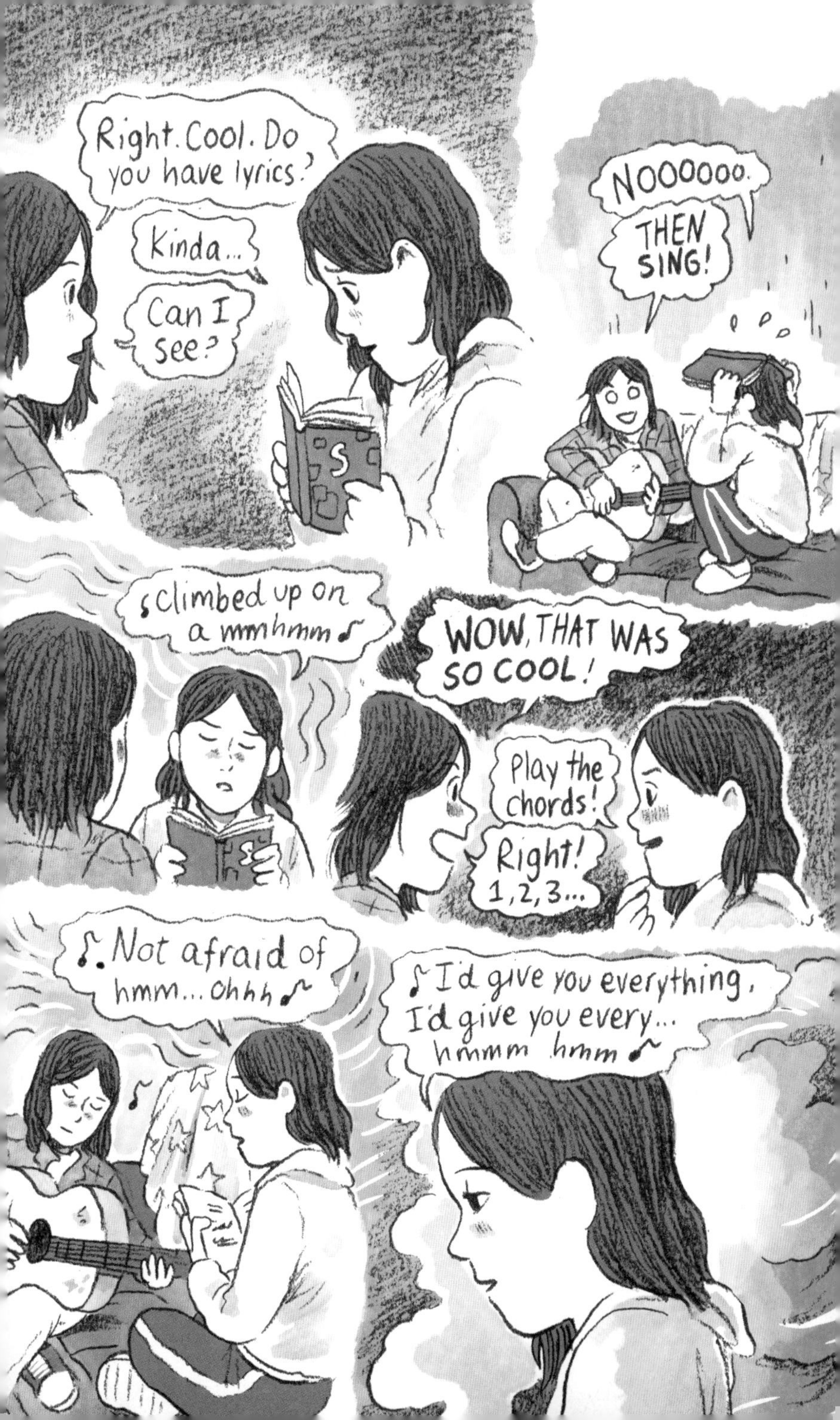
Right. Cool. Do you have lyrics?
Kinda...
Can I see?
NOOOOOO.
THEN SING!
Climbed up on a mmhmm
WOW, THAT WAS SO COOL!
Play the chords!
Right! 1, 2, 3...
Not afraid of hmm... ohhh
I'd give you everything, I'd give you every... hmmm hmm

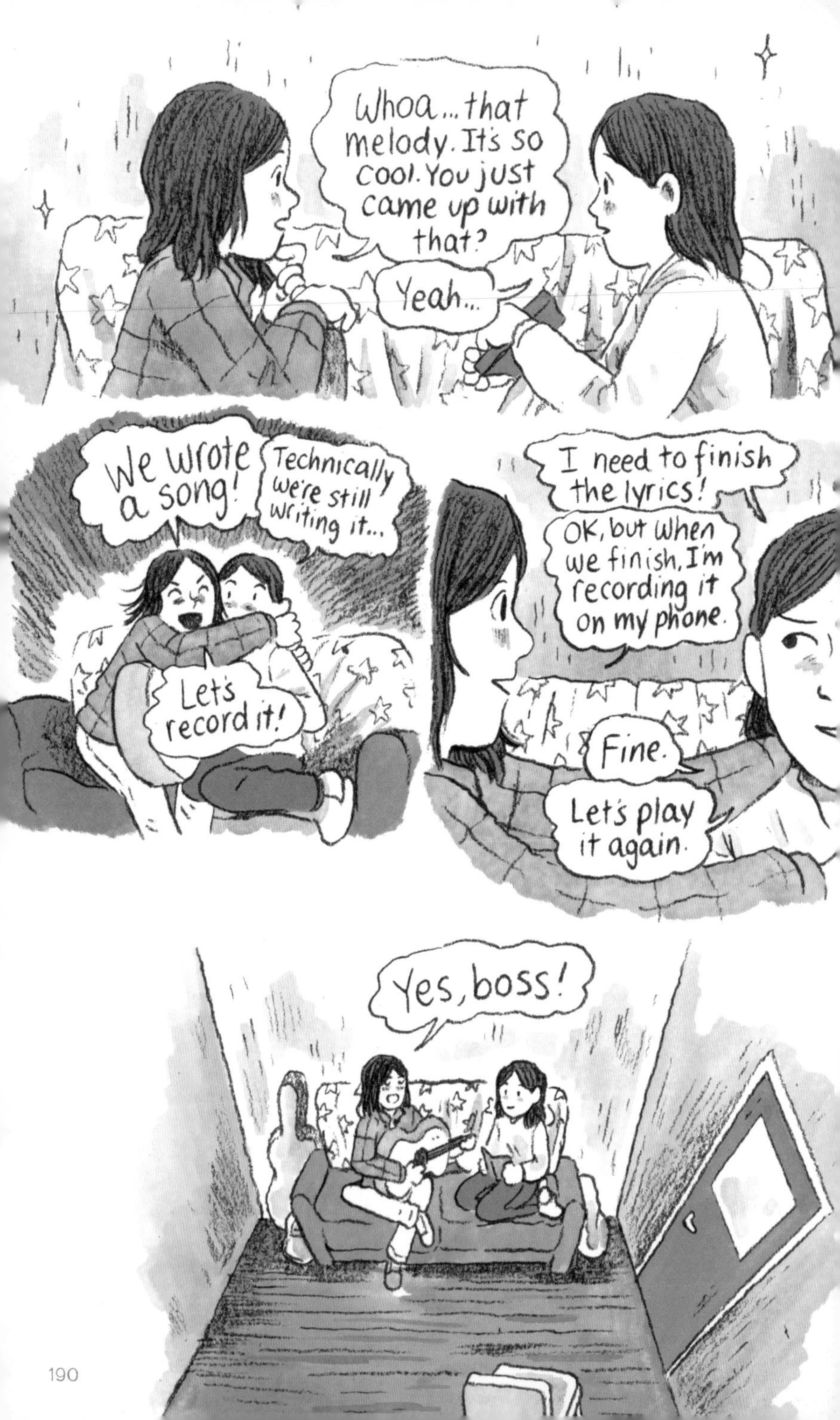
Whoa... that melody. It's so cool. You just came up with that?
Yeah...
We wrote a song!
Technically we're still writing it...
Let's record it!
I need to finish the lyrics!
OK, but when we finish, I'm recording it on my phone.
Fine.
Let's play it again.
Yes, boss!

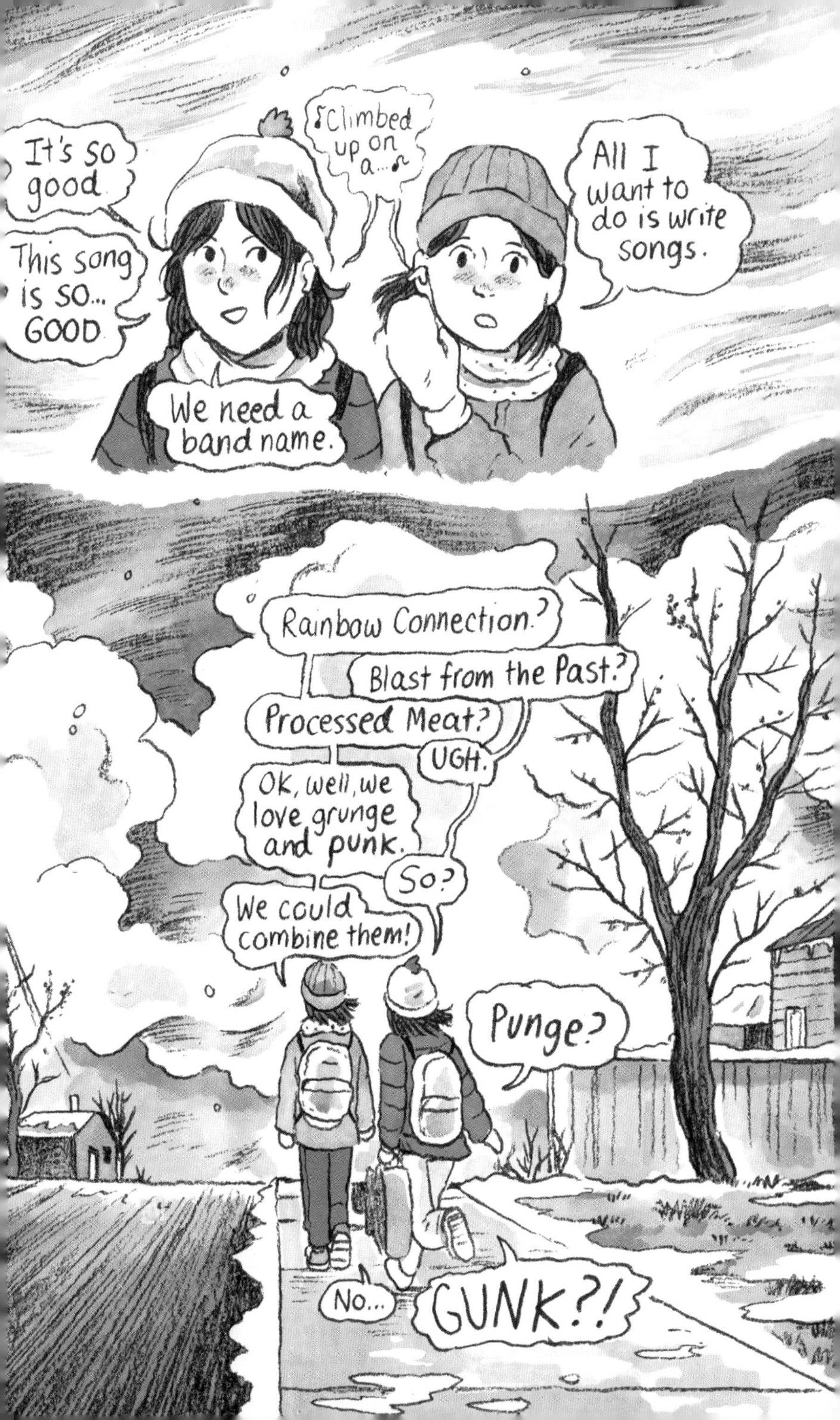
It's so good.
This song is so... GOOD.
♪Climbed up on a...♪
All I want to do is write songs.
We need a band name.
Rainbow Connection?
Blast from the Past?
Processed Meat?
UGH.
Ok, well, we love grunge and punk.
So?
We could combine them!
Punge?
No...
GUNK?!

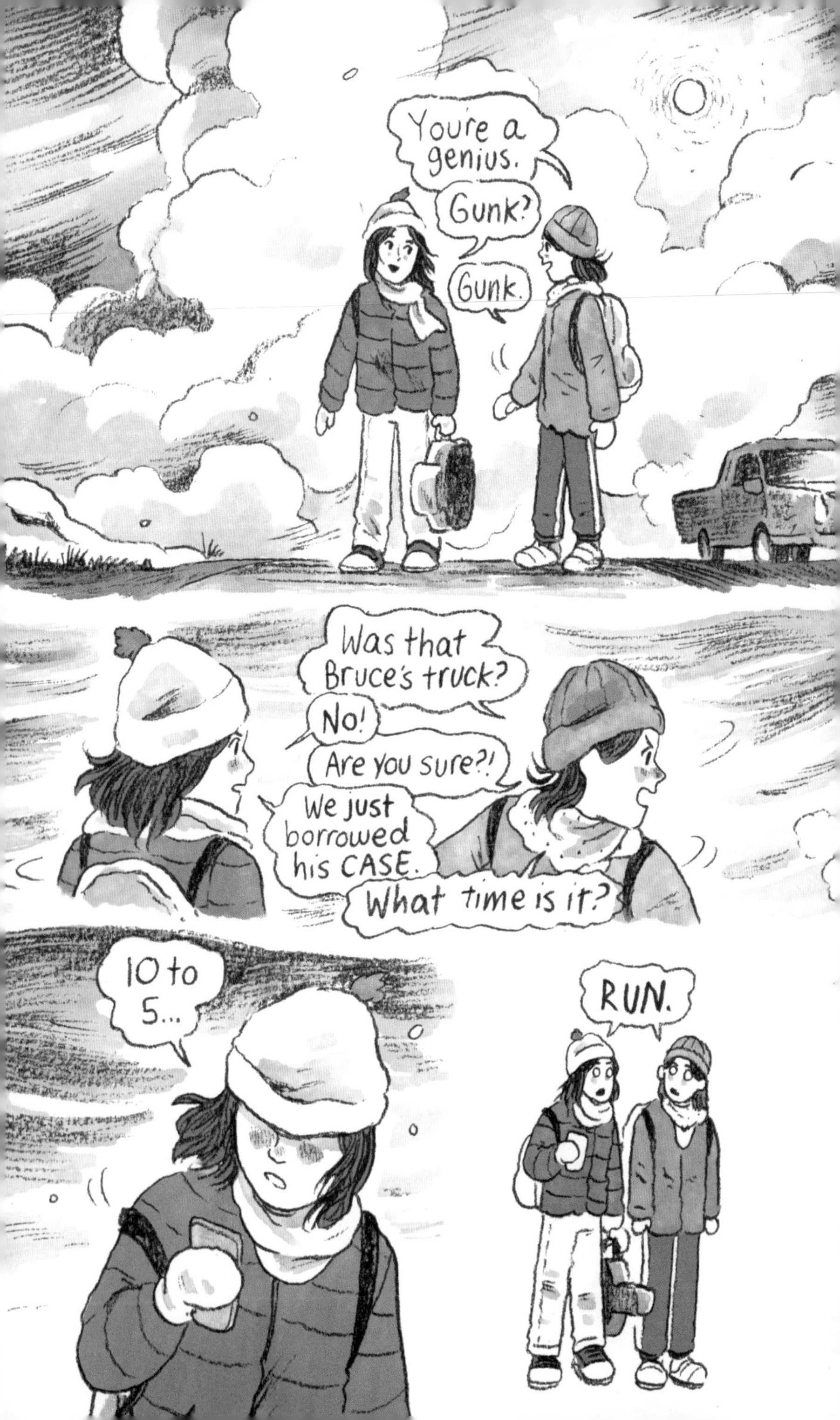
You're a genius.
Gunk?
Gunk.
Was that Bruce's truck?
No!
Are you sure?!
We just borrowed his CASE.
What time is it?
10 to 5...
RUN.

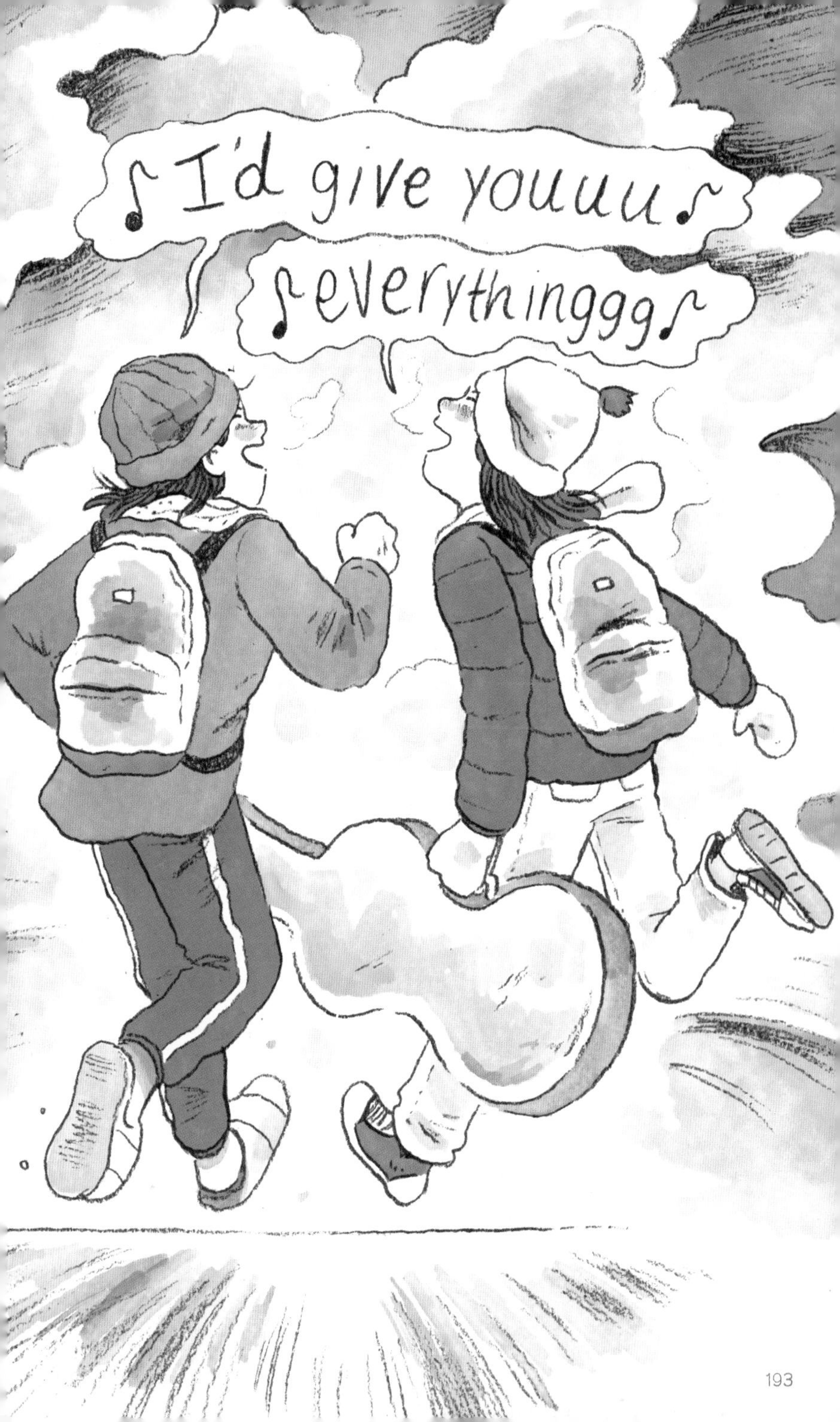
♪ I'd give youuu ♪
♪ everythinggg ♪

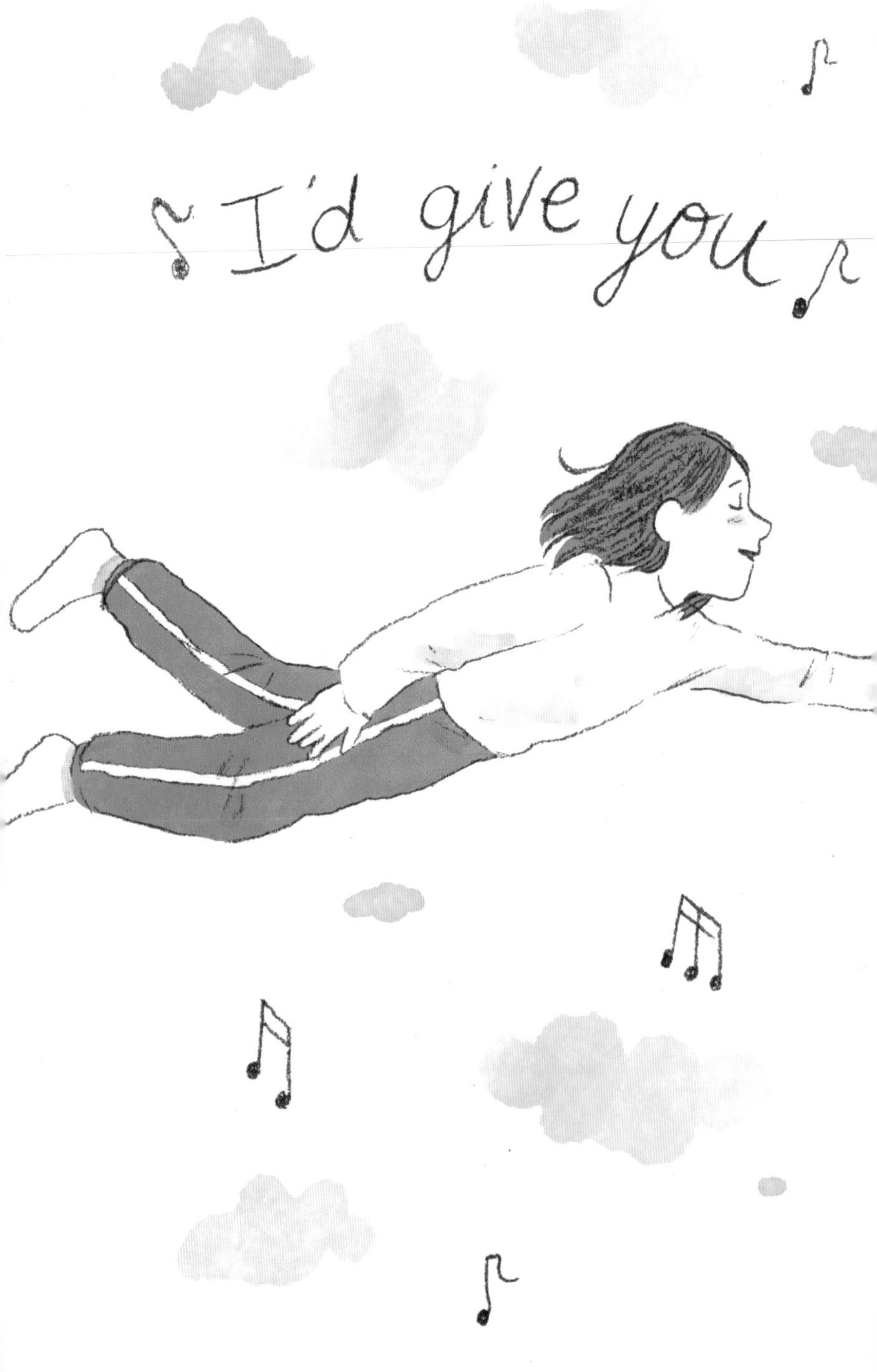
I'd give you

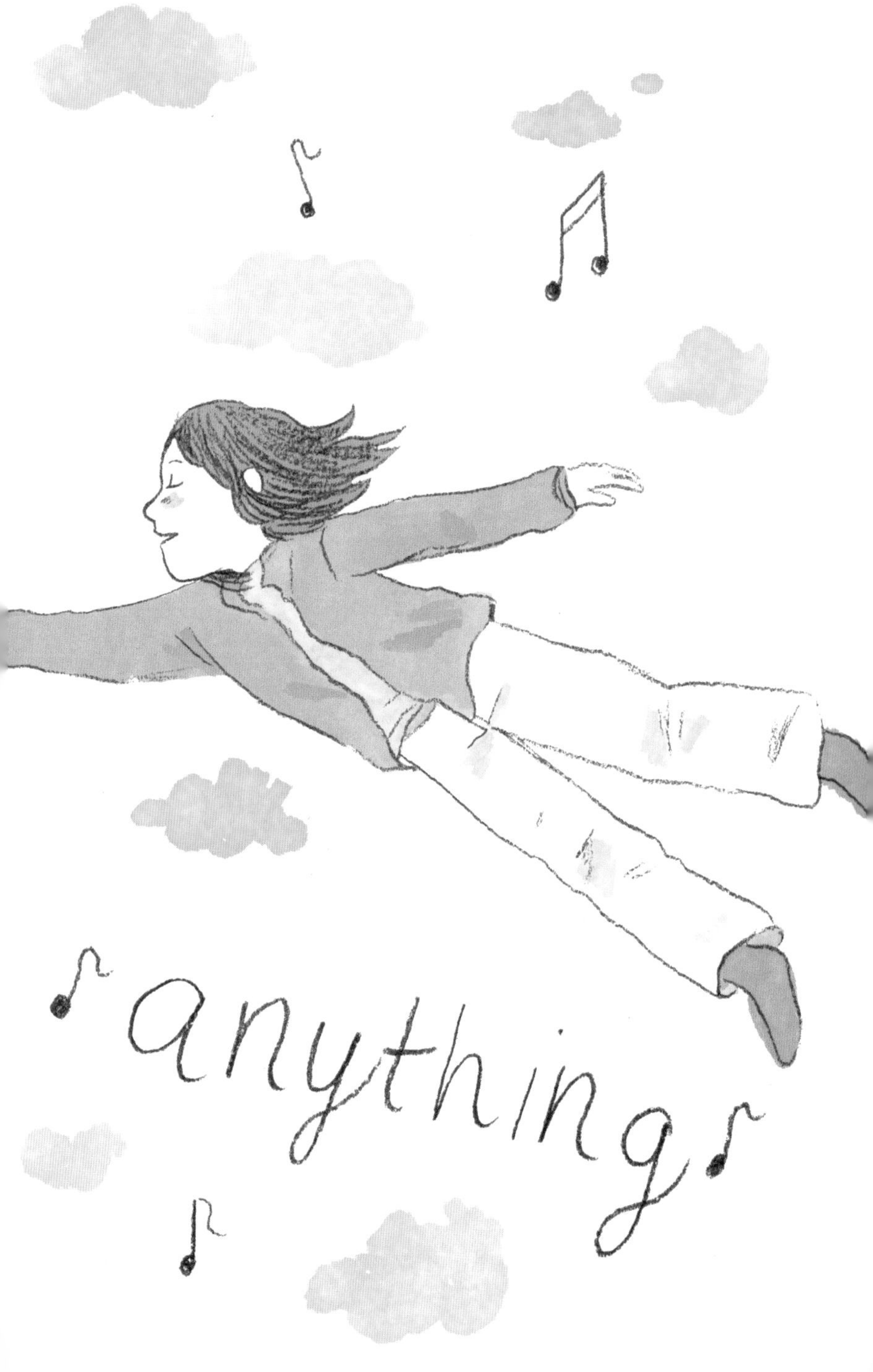
anything

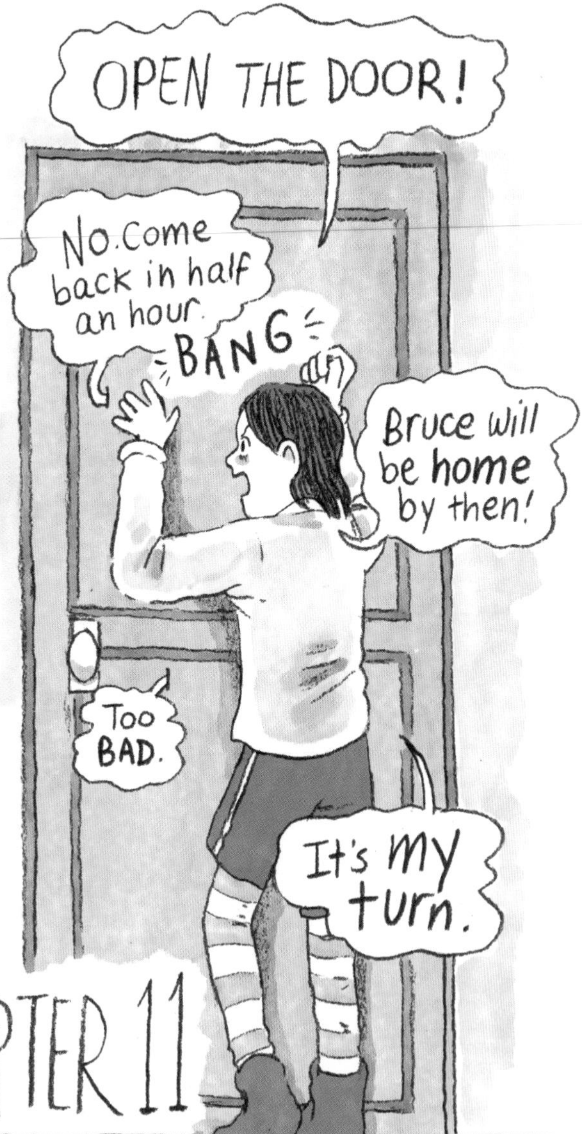
OPEN THE DOOR!
No. Come back in half an hour.
BANG
Bruce will be **home** by then!
Too BAD.
It's my turn.

CHAPTER 11

THE TEST

♪ I'm not afraid ♪

Tegan.

♪ I'd give youuuu ♪

TEGAN.

WHAT?!

You know we still have
SCHOOL, right? Maybe you
should stop HOGGING the
guitar and STUDY?!

♪ I'm not
afraid ♪

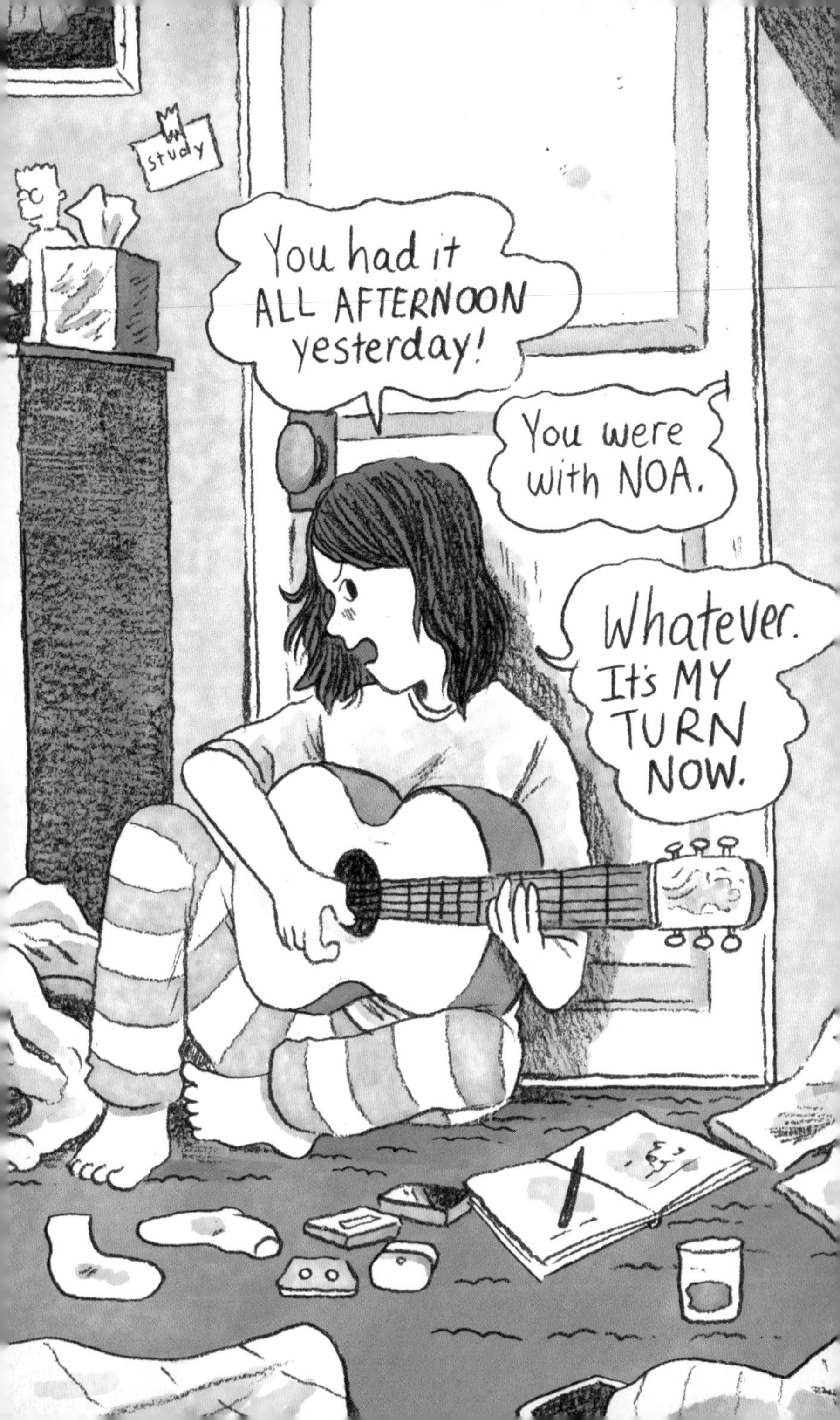
study
You had it ALL AFTERNOON yesterday!
You were with NOA.
Whatever. It's MY TURN NOW.

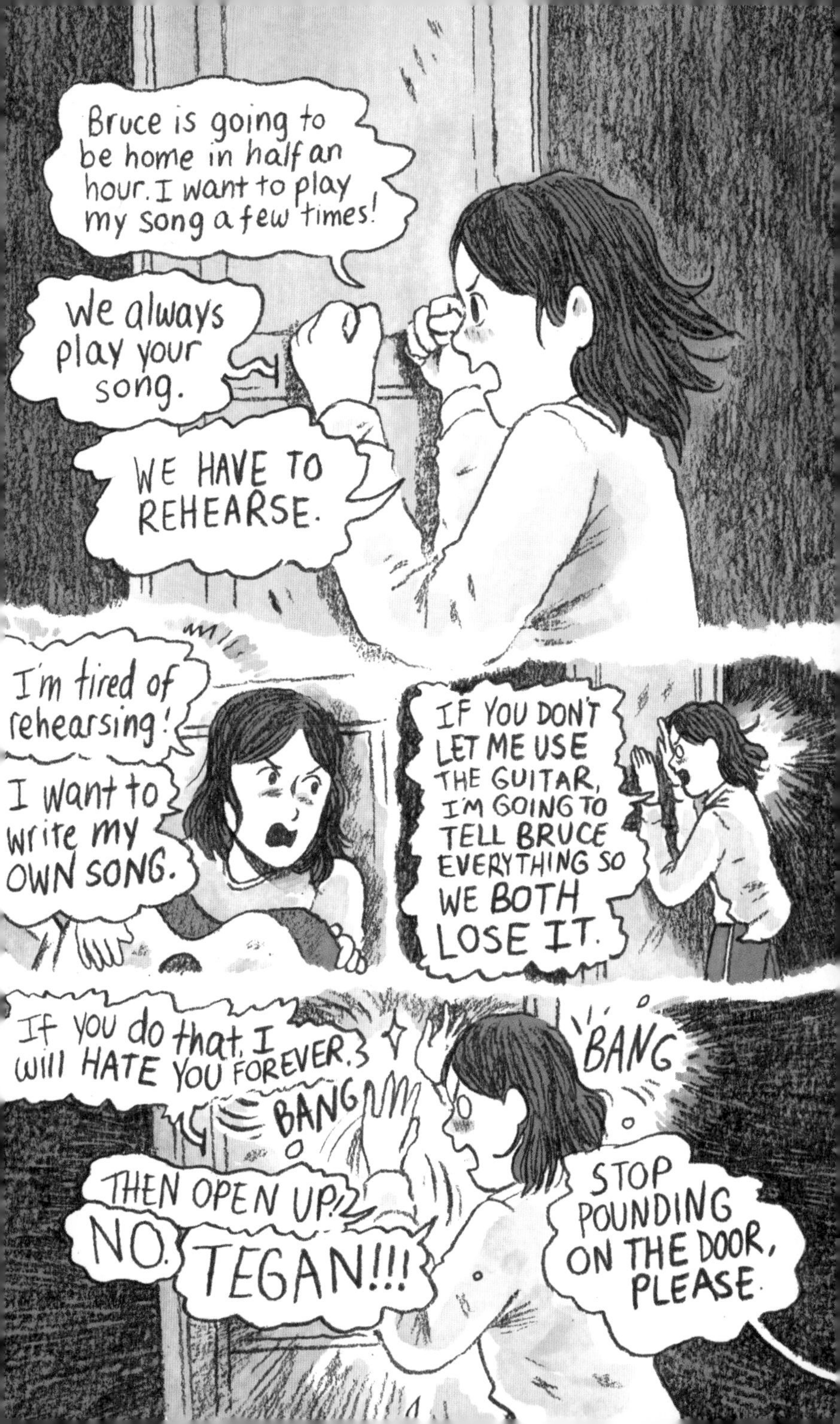
Bruce is going to be home in half an hour. I want to play my song a few times!
We always play your song.
WE HAVE TO REHEARSE.
I'm tired of rehearsing!
I want to write my OWN SONG.
IF YOU DON'T LET ME USE THE GUITAR, I'M GOING TO TELL BRUCE EVERYTHING SO WE BOTH LOSE IT.
If you do that, I will HATE YOU FOREVER.
BANG
BANG
THEN OPEN UP!
NO.
TEGAN!!!
STOP POUNDING ON THE DOOR, PLEASE.

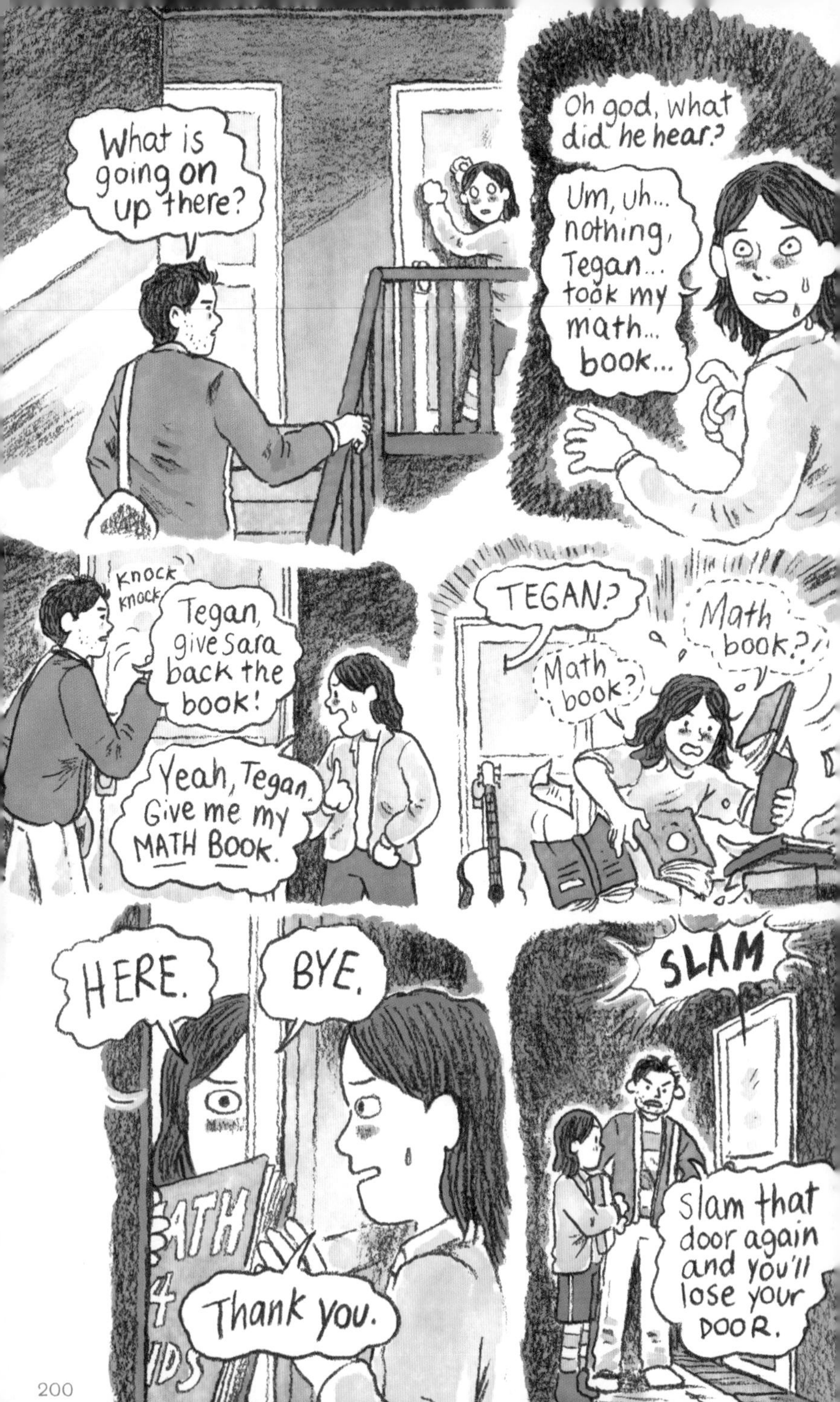
What is going on up there?
Oh god, what did he hear?
Um, uh... nothing, Tegan... took my math... book...
KNOCK KNOCK
Tegan, give Sara back the book!
Yeah, Tegan. Give me my MATH BOOK.
TEGAN?
Math book?
Math book?
HERE.
BYE.
ATH 4 IDS
Thank you.
SLAM
Slam that door again and you'll lose your DOOR.

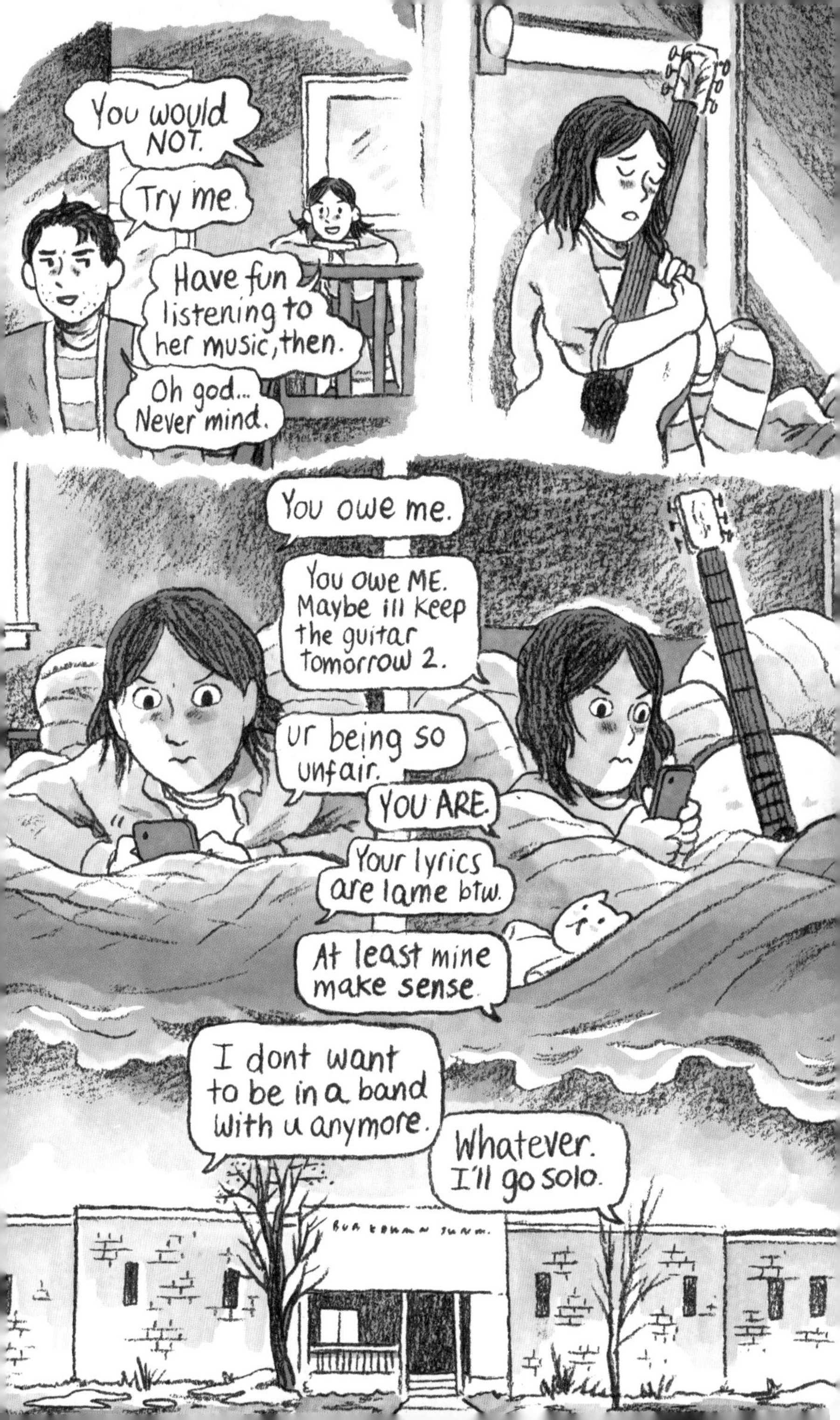
You would NOT.
Try me.
Have fun listening to her music, then.
Oh god... Never mind.
You owe me.
You owe ME. Maybe ill keep the guitar tomorrow 2.
Ur being so unfair.
YOU ARE.
Your lyrics are lame btw.
At least mine make sense.
I dont want to be in a band with u anymore.
Whatever. I'll go solo.

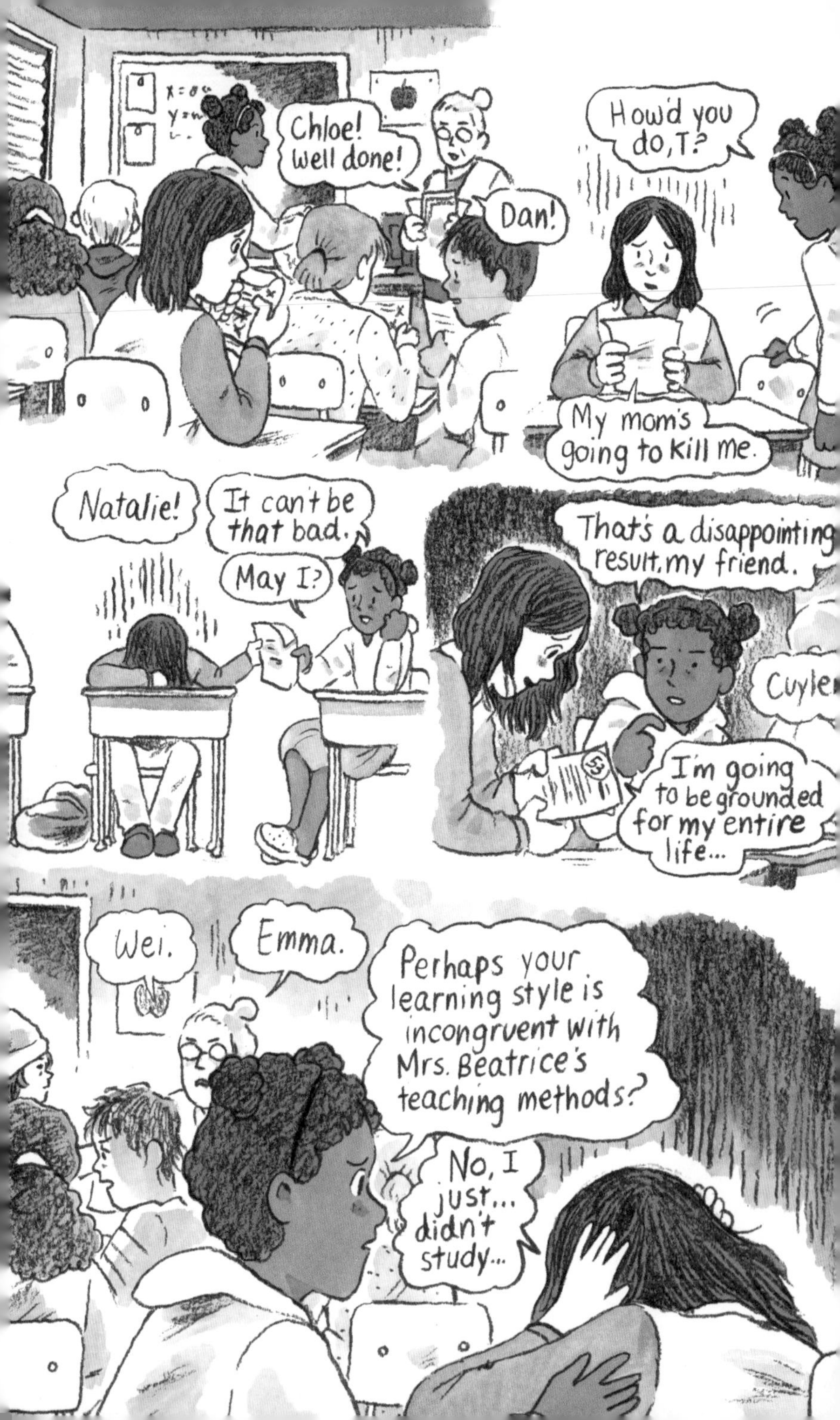
Chloe! Well done!
Dan!
How'd you do, T?
My mom's going to kill me.
Natalie!
It can't be that bad.
May I?
That's a disappointing result, my friend.
I'm going to be grounded for my entire life...
Wei.
Emma.
Perhaps your learning style is incongruent with Mrs. Beatrice's teaching methods?
No, I just... didn't study...

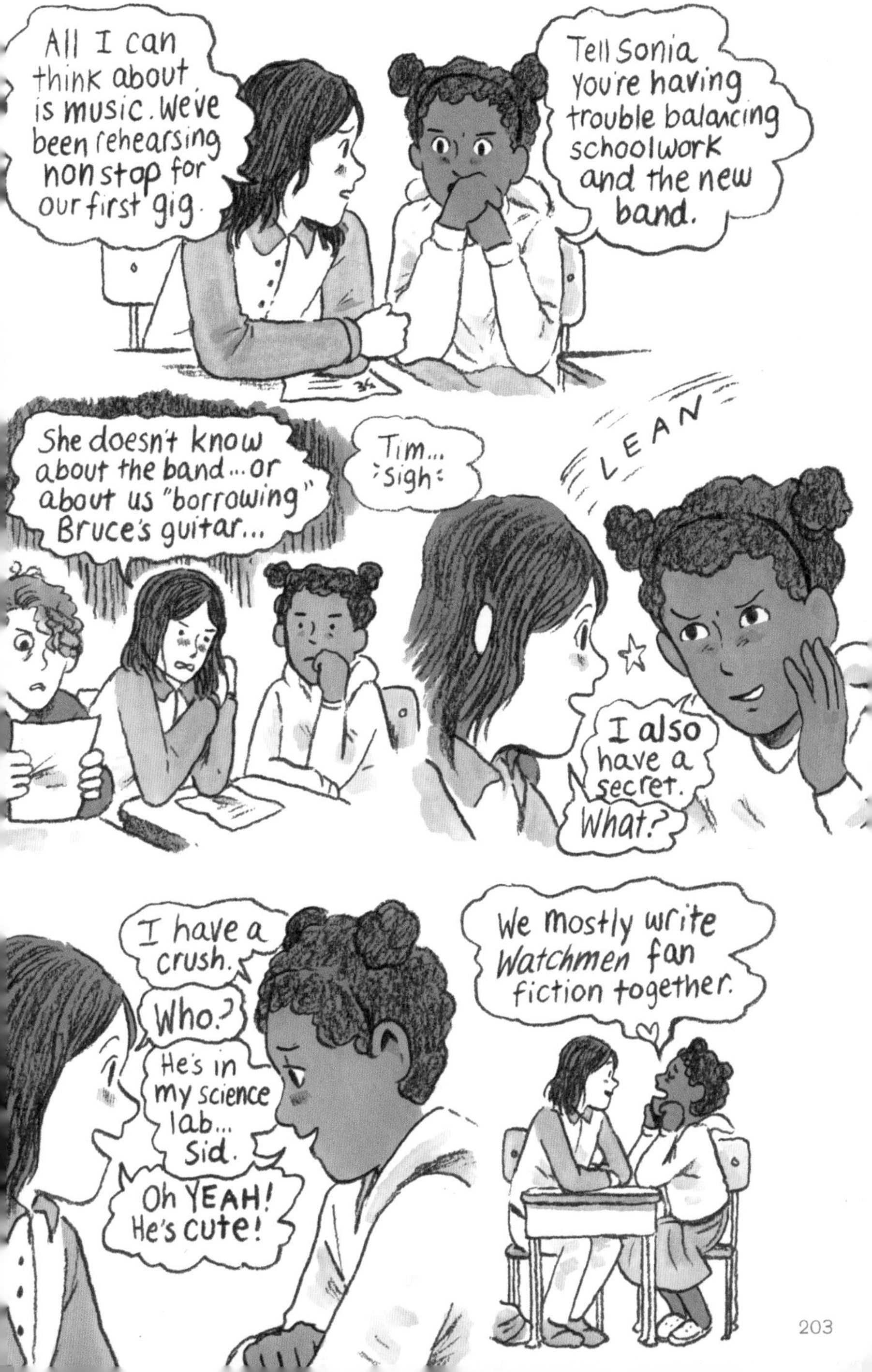

All I can think about is music. We've been rehearsing nonstop for our first gig.
Tell Sonia you're having trouble balancing schoolwork and the new band.
She doesn't know about the band... or about us "borrowing" Bruce's guitar...
Tim... :sigh:
LEAN
I also have a secret.
What?
I have a crush.
Who?
He's in my science lab... Sid.
Oh YEAH! He's cute!
We mostly write Watchmen fan fiction together.

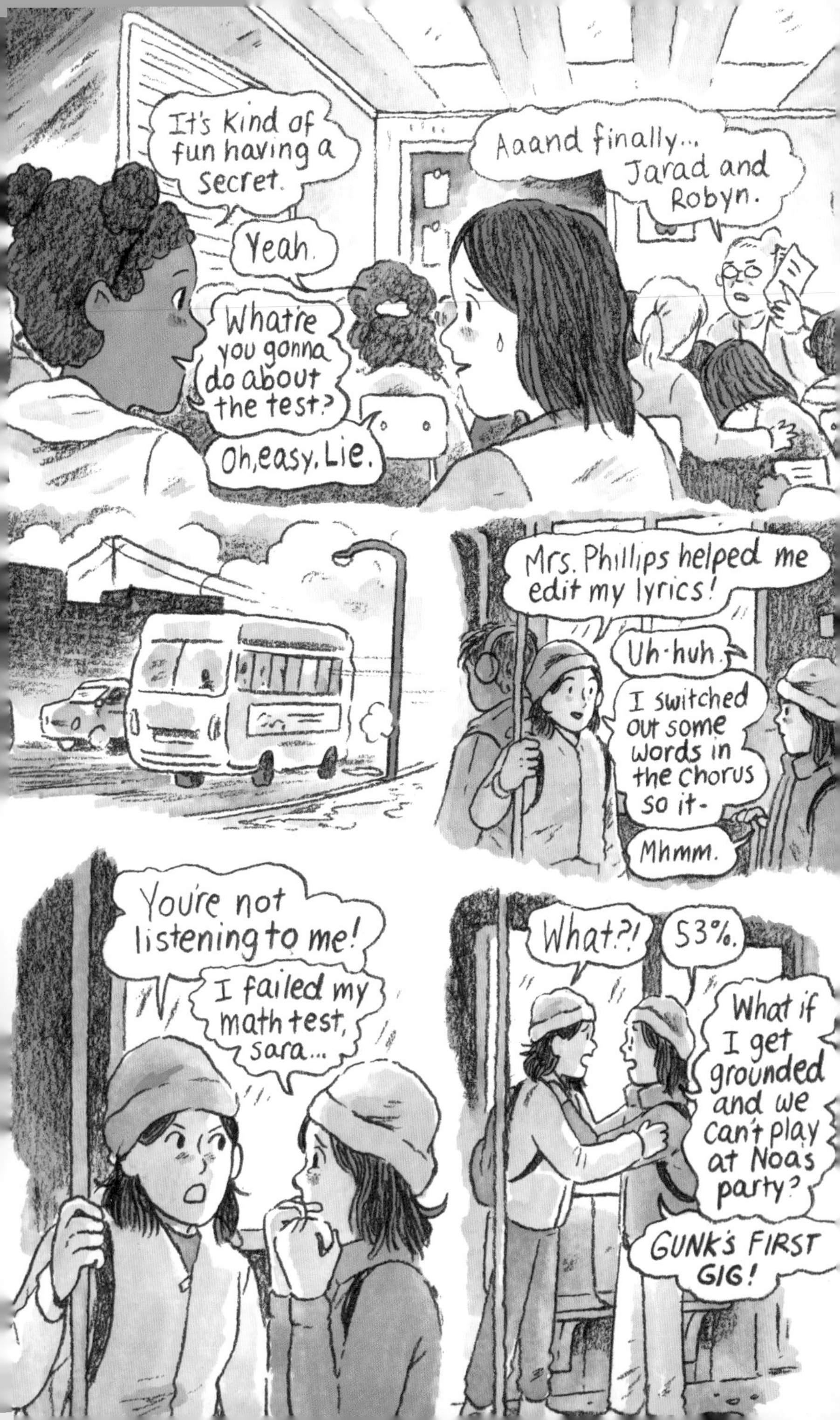
It's kind of fun having a secret.
Aaand finally... Jarad and Robyn.
Yeah.
Whatre you gonna do about the test?
Oh, easy. Lie.
Mrs. Phillips helped me edit my lyrics!
Uh-huh.
I switched out some words in the chorus so it-
Mhmm.
You're not listening to me!
I failed my math test, Sara...
What?!
53%.
What if I get grounded and we can't play at Noa's party?
GUNK's FIRST GIG!

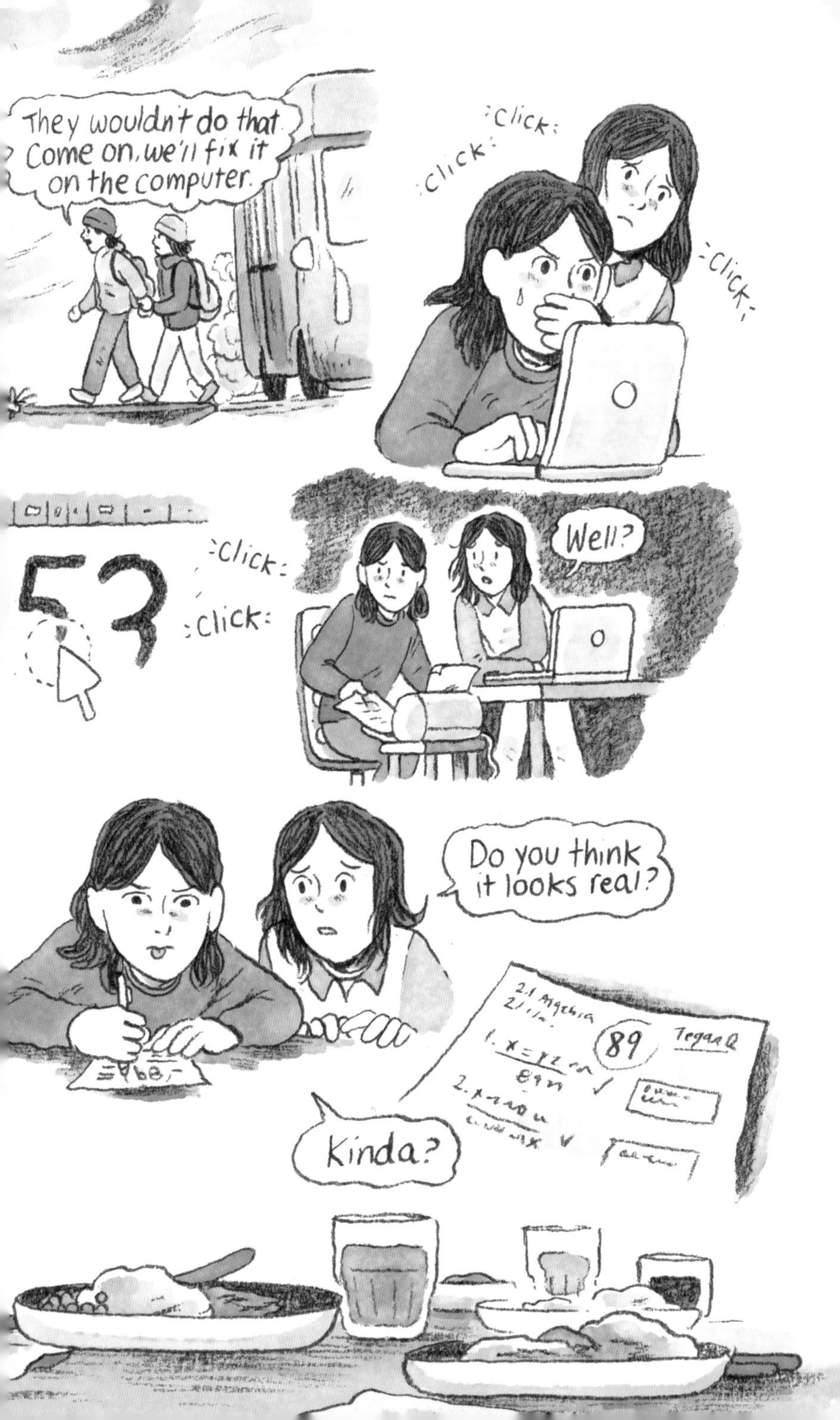

They wouldn't do that. Come on, we'll fix it on the computer.
Click
Click
Click
53
Click
Click
Well?
Do you think it looks real?
89
Kinda?

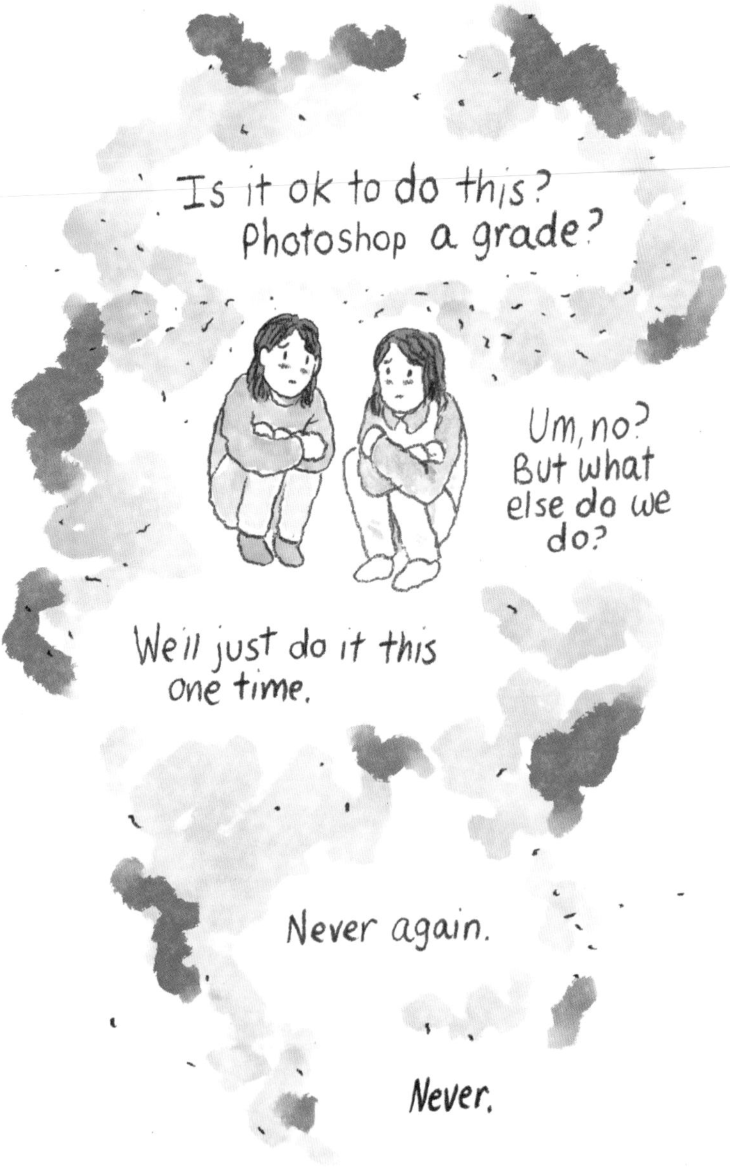
Is it ok to do this?
Photoshop a grade?
Um, no? But what else do we do?
We'll just do it this one time.
Never again.
Never.

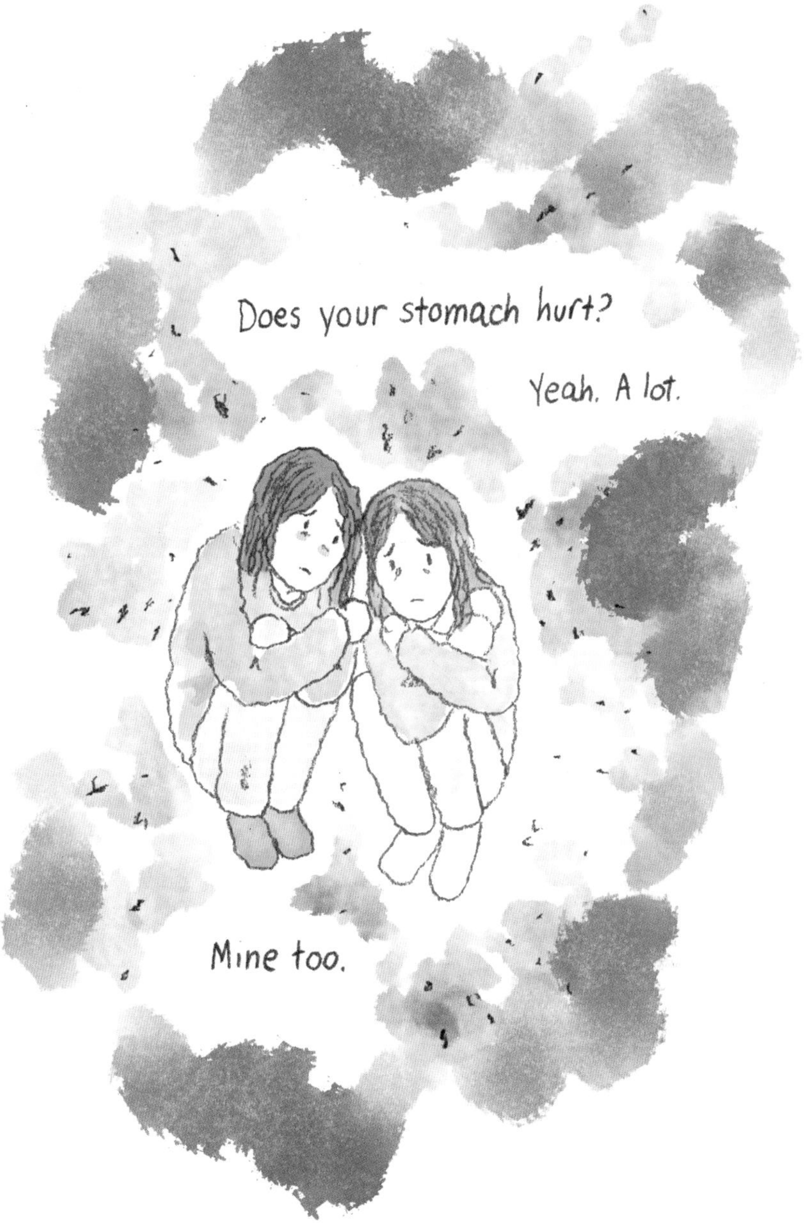
Does your stomach hurt?
Yeah. A lot.
Mine too.

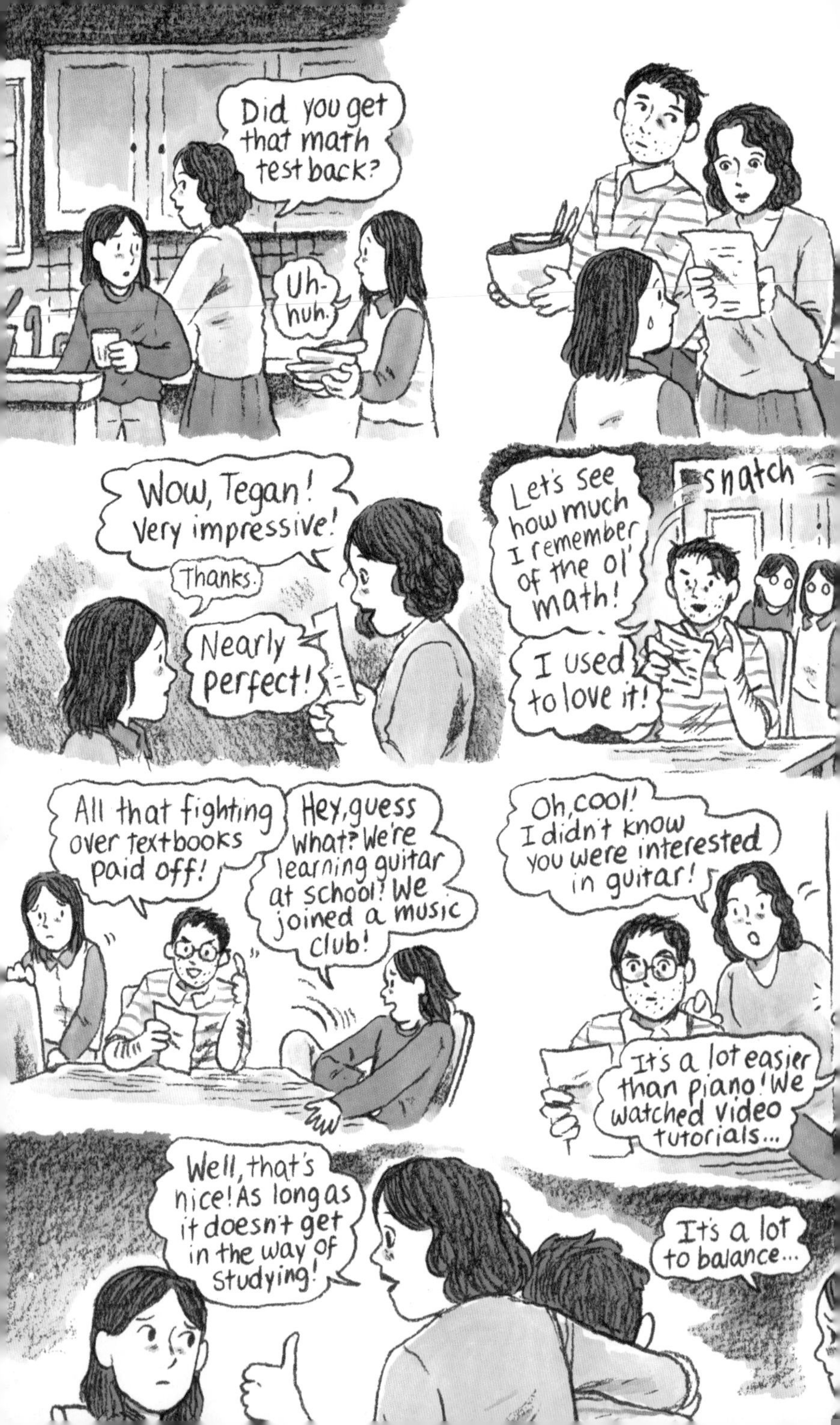
Did you get that math test back?
Uh-huh.
Wow, Tegan! Very impressive!
Thanks.
Nearly perfect!
Let's see how much I remember of the ol' math!
snatch
I used to love it!
All that fighting over textbooks paid off!
Hey, guess what? We're learning guitar at school! We joined a music club!
Oh, cool! I didn't know you were interested in guitar!
It's a lot easier than piano! We watched video tutorials...
Well, that's nice! As long as it doesn't get in the way of studying!
It's a lot to balance...

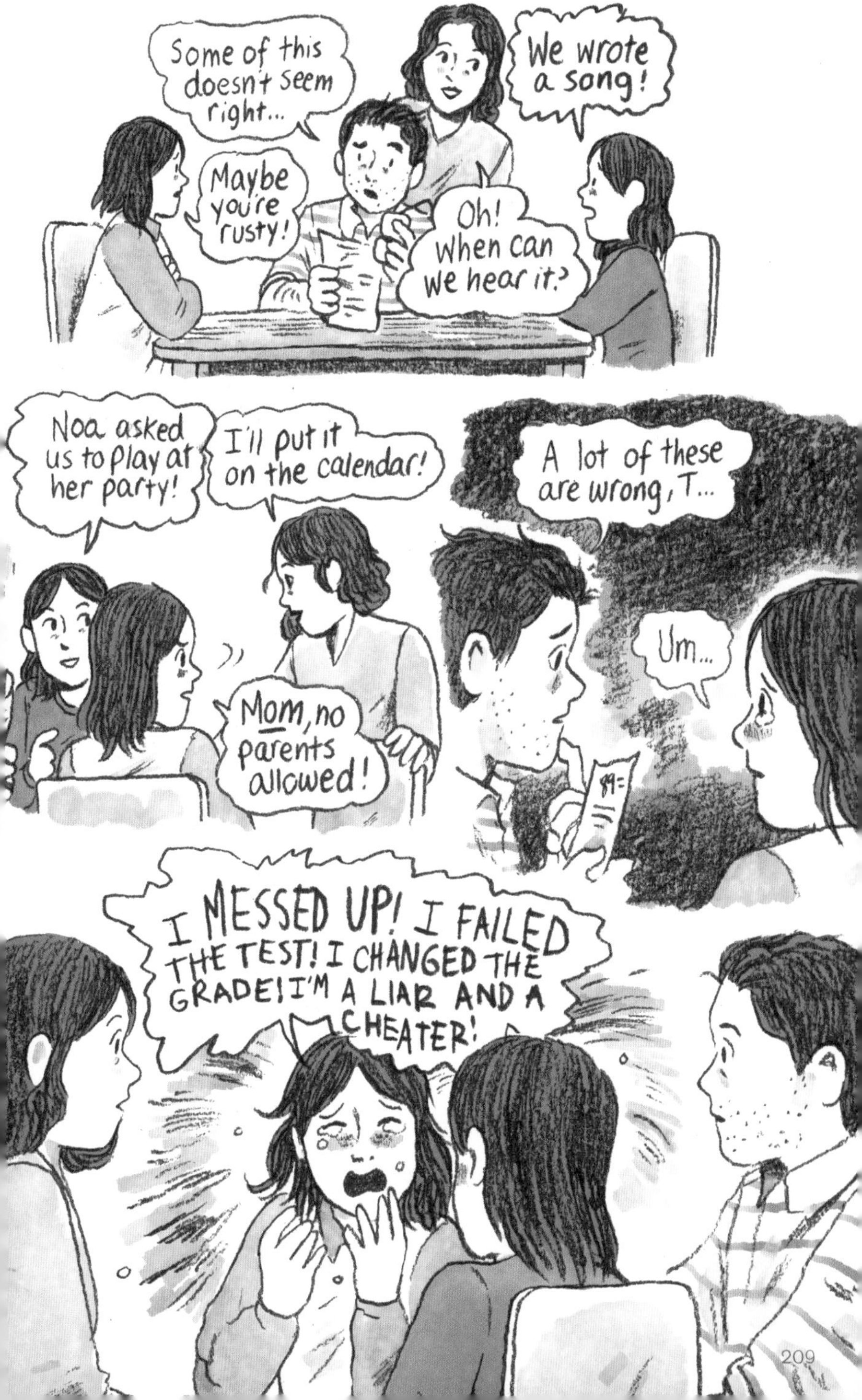

Some of this doesn't seem right...
We wrote a song!
Maybe you're rusty!
Oh! When can we hear it?
Noa asked us to play at her party!
I'll put it on the calendar!
Mom, no parents allowed!
A lot of these are wrong, T...
Um...
I MESSED UP! I FAILED THE TEST! I CHANGED THE GRADE! I'M A LIAR AND A CHEATER!

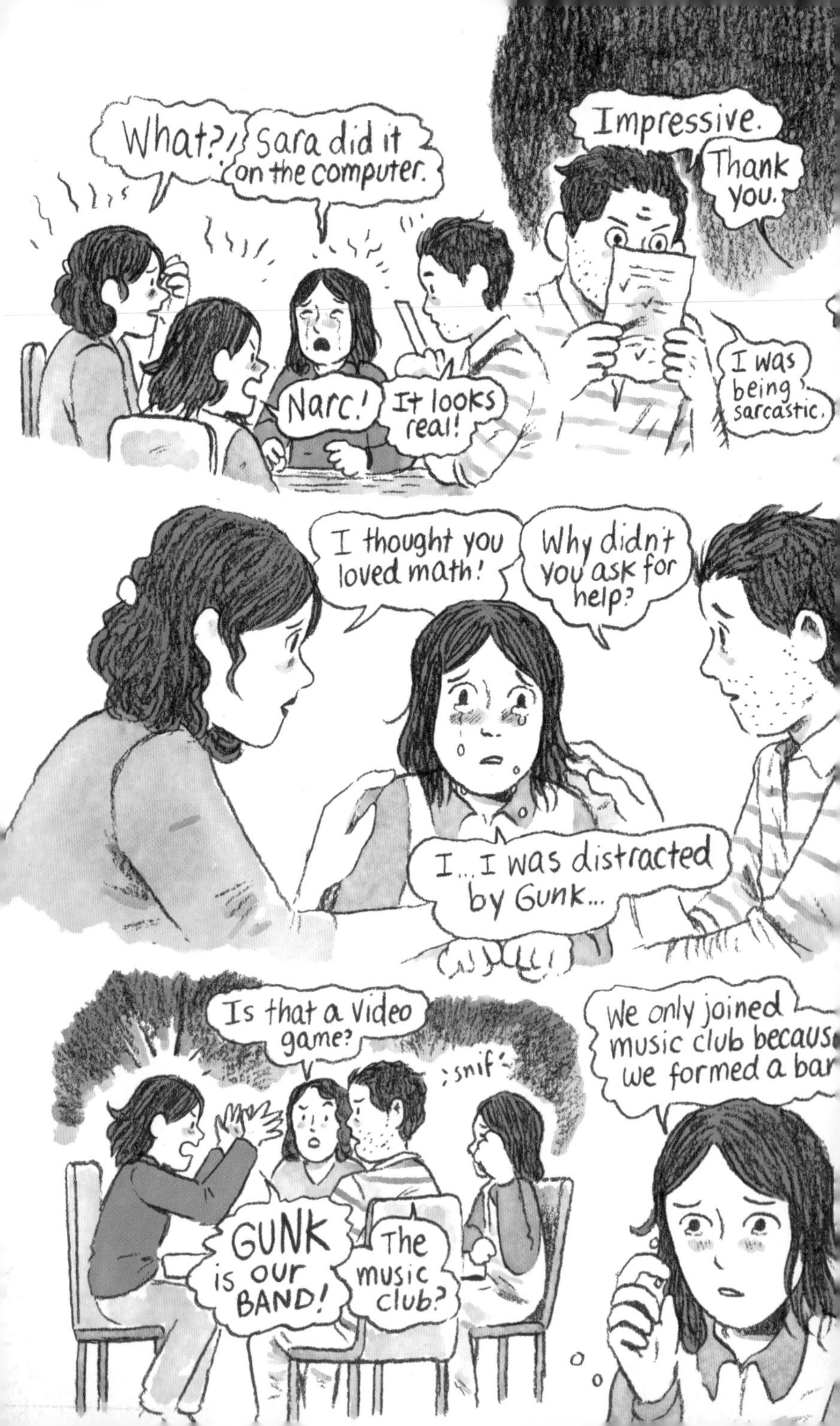
What?!
Sara did it on the computer.
Narc!
It looks real!
Impressive.
Thank you.
I was being sarcastic.
I thought you loved math!
Why didn't you ask for help?
I... I was distracted by Gunk...
Is that a video game?
snif
GUNK is our BAND!
The music club?
We only joined music club becaus we formed a bar

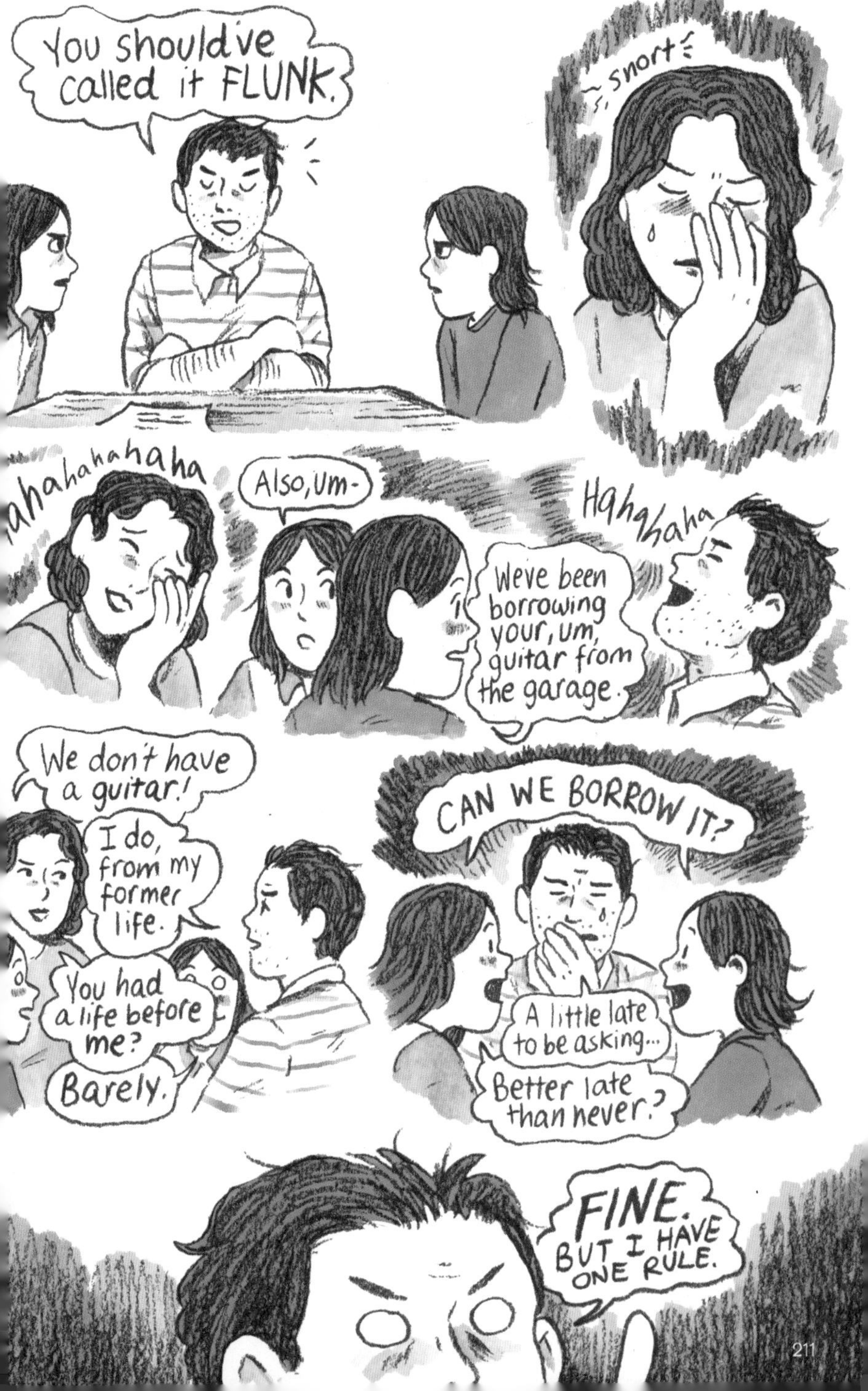
You should've called it FLUNK.
snort
ahahahahahaha
Also, um-
Hahahaha
We've been borrowing your, um, guitar from the garage.
We don't have a guitar!
I do, from my former life.
You had a life before me?
Barely.
CAN WE BORROW IT?
A little late to be asking...
Better late than never?
FINE. BUT I HAVE ONE RULE.

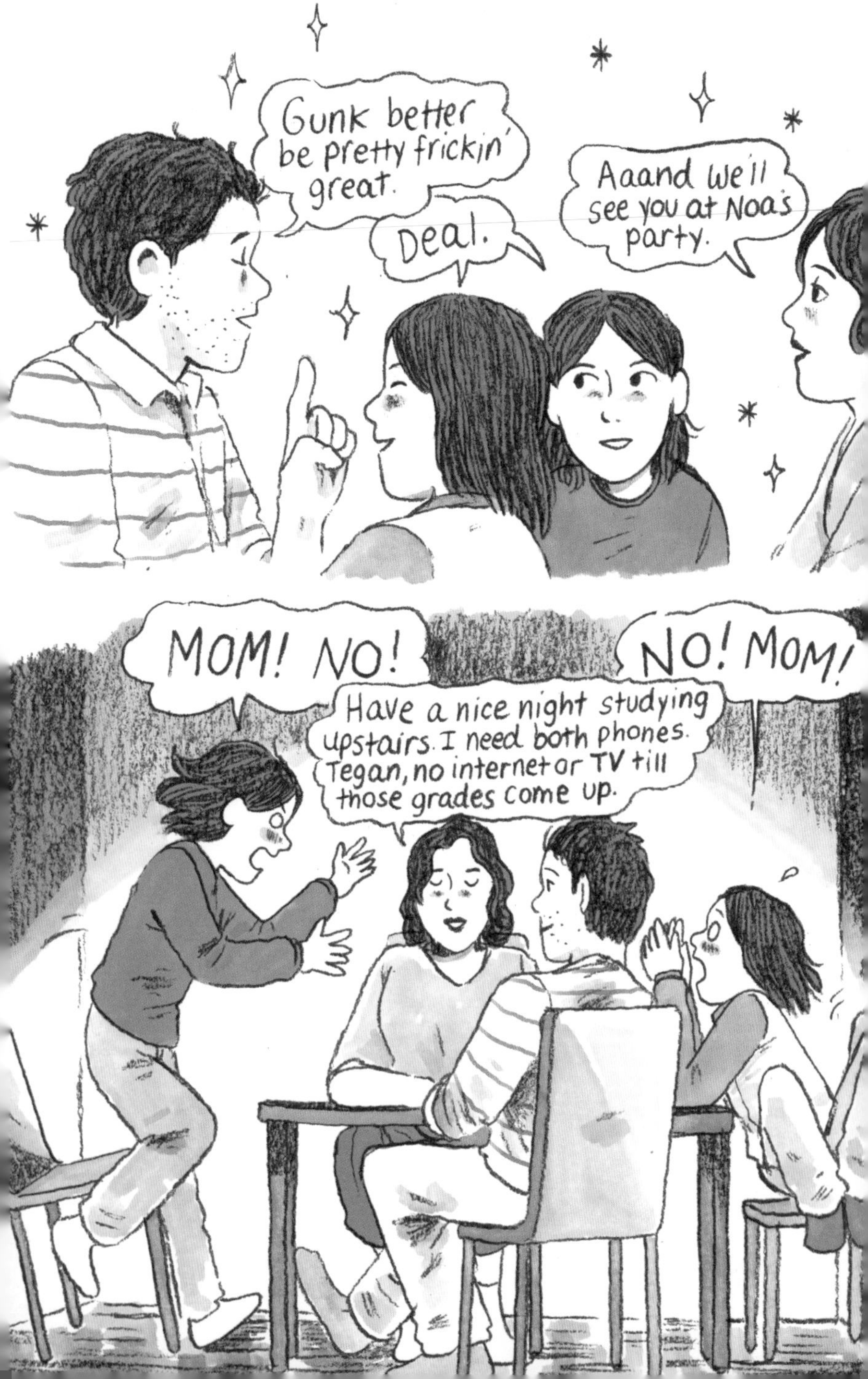
Gunk better be pretty frickin' great.
Deal.
Aaand we'll see you at Noa's party.
MOM! NO!
NO! MOM!
Have a nice night studying upstairs. I need both phones. Tegan, no internet or TV till those grades come up.

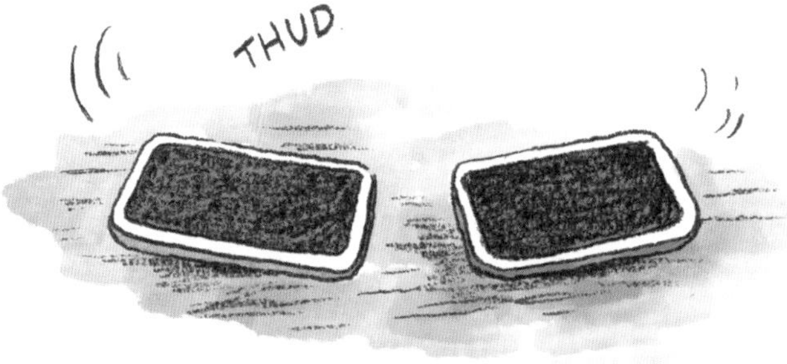
THUD

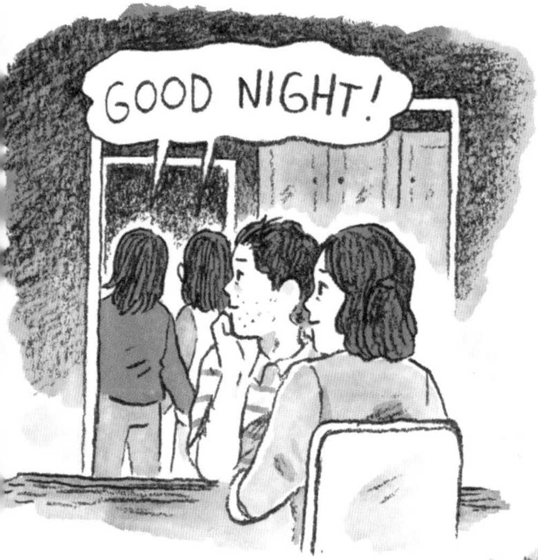
GOOD NIGHT!

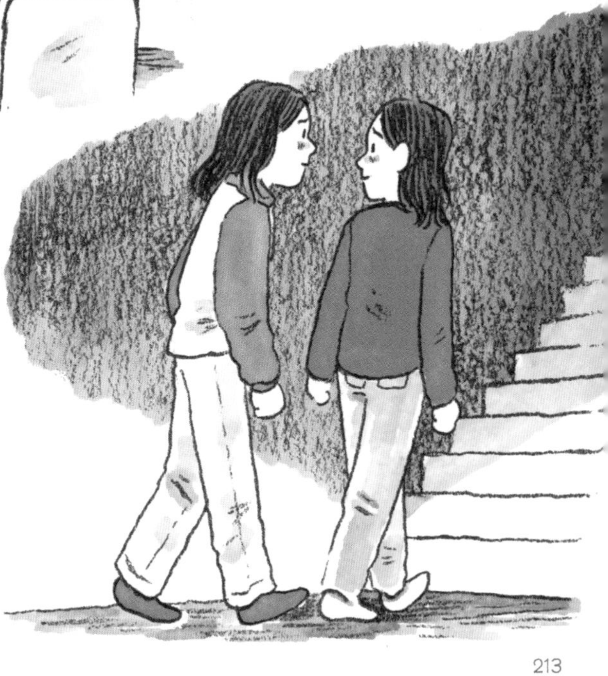

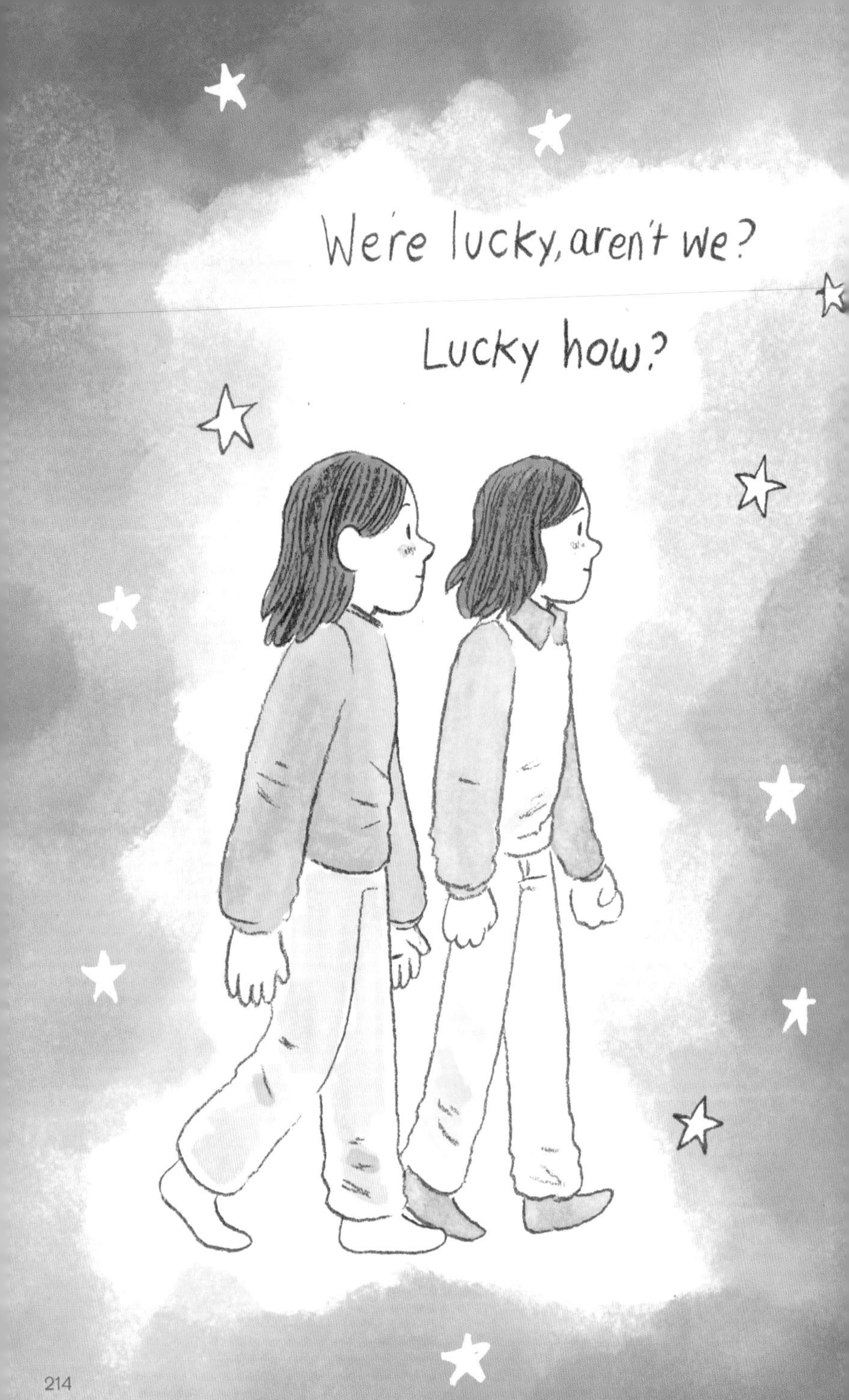
We're lucky, aren't we?
Lucky how?

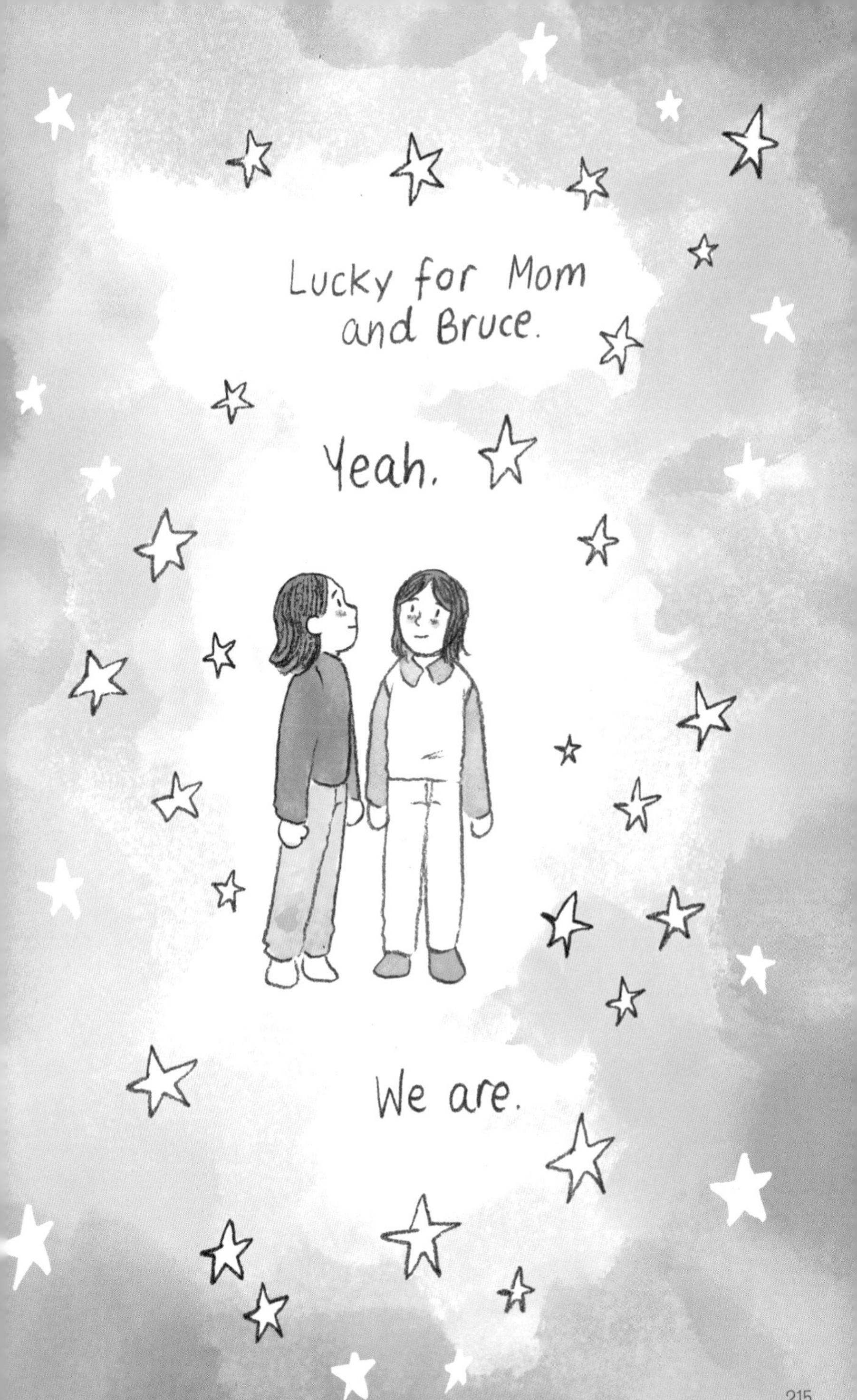
Lucky for Mom and Bruce.
Yeah.
We are.

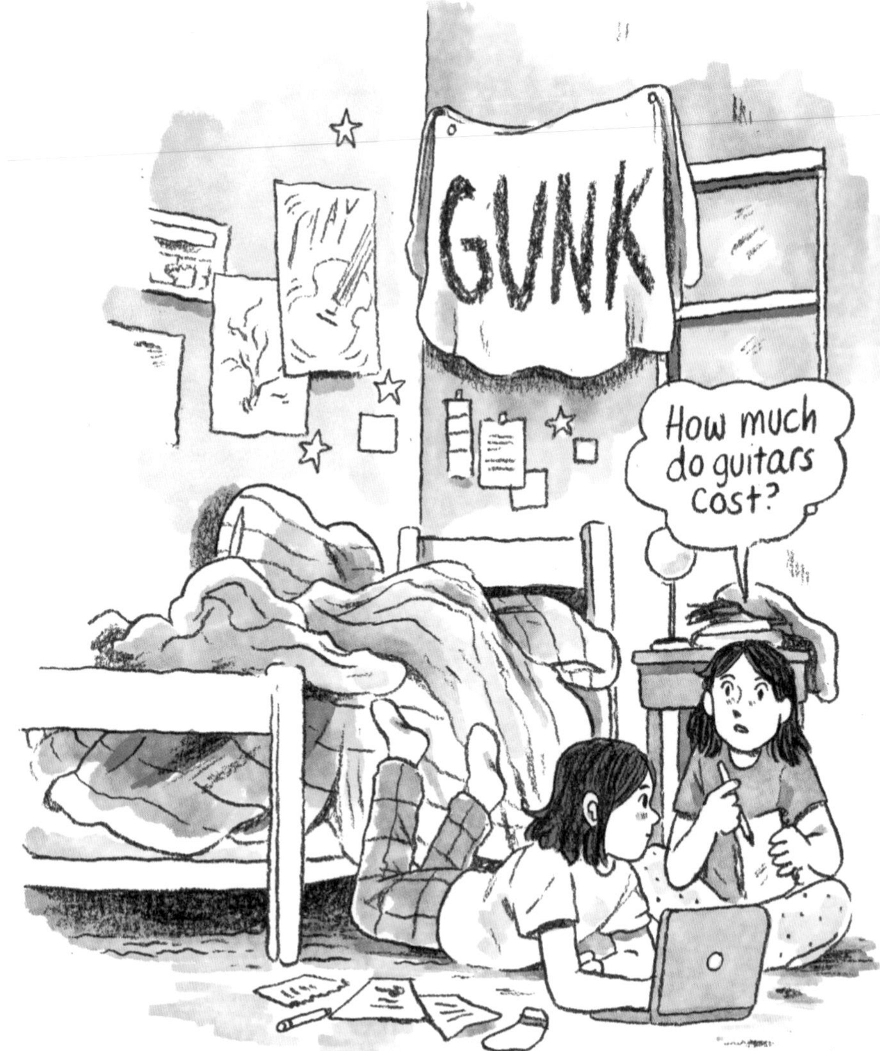
GUNK
How much do guitars cost?

CHAPTER 12
dreams

Remember how at the beginning of the year, everything moved so slow?

Yeah. It's different now.

There's so much going on —

— it's hard to keep up.

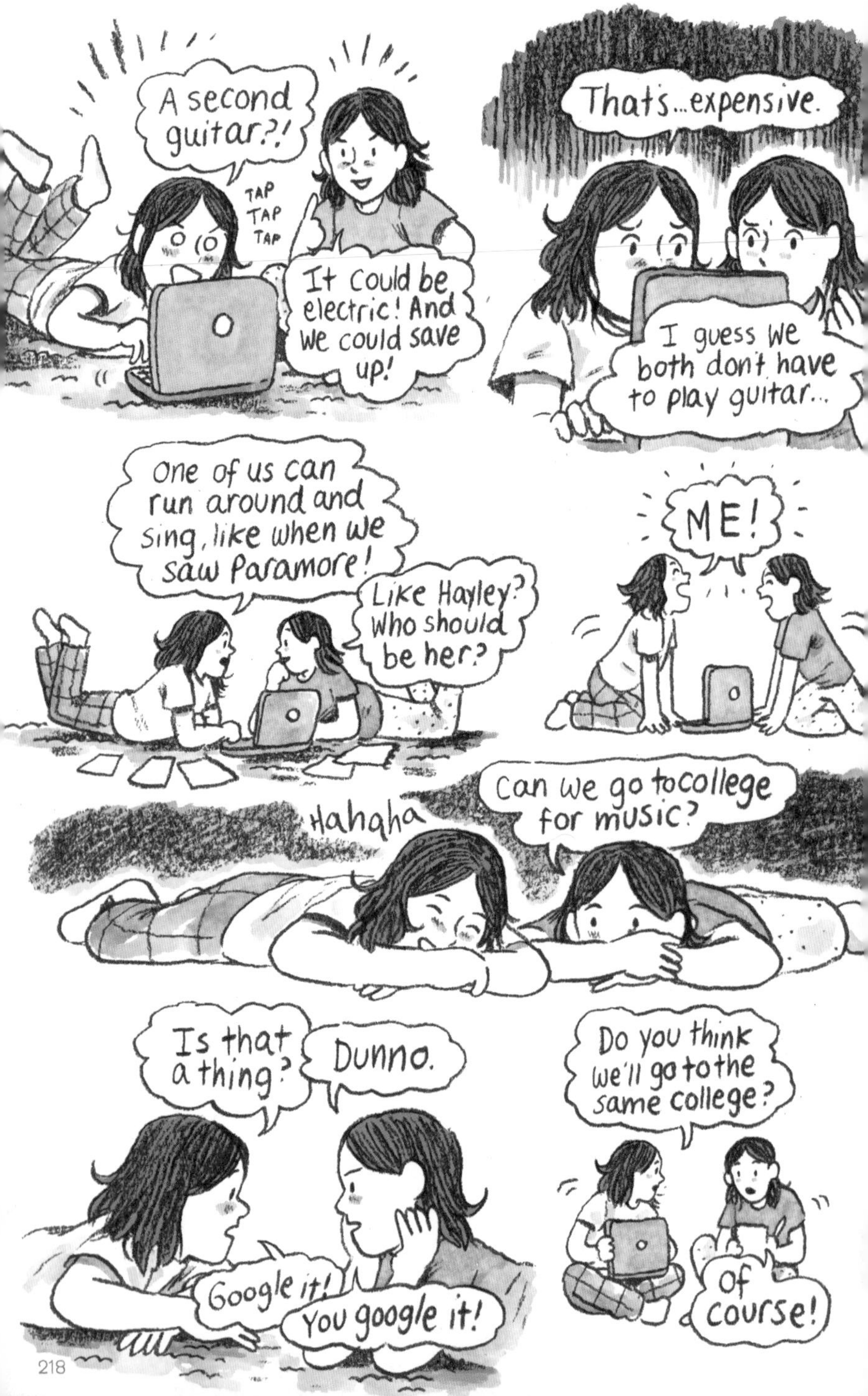
A second guitar?!
TAP TAP TAP
It could be electric! And we could save up!
That's...expensive.
I guess we both don't have to play guitar...
One of us can run around and sing, like when we saw Paramore!
Like Hayley? Who should be her?
ME!
Hahaha
Can we go to college for music?
Is that a thing?
Dunno.
Google it!
You google it!
Do you think we'll go to the same college?
Of course!

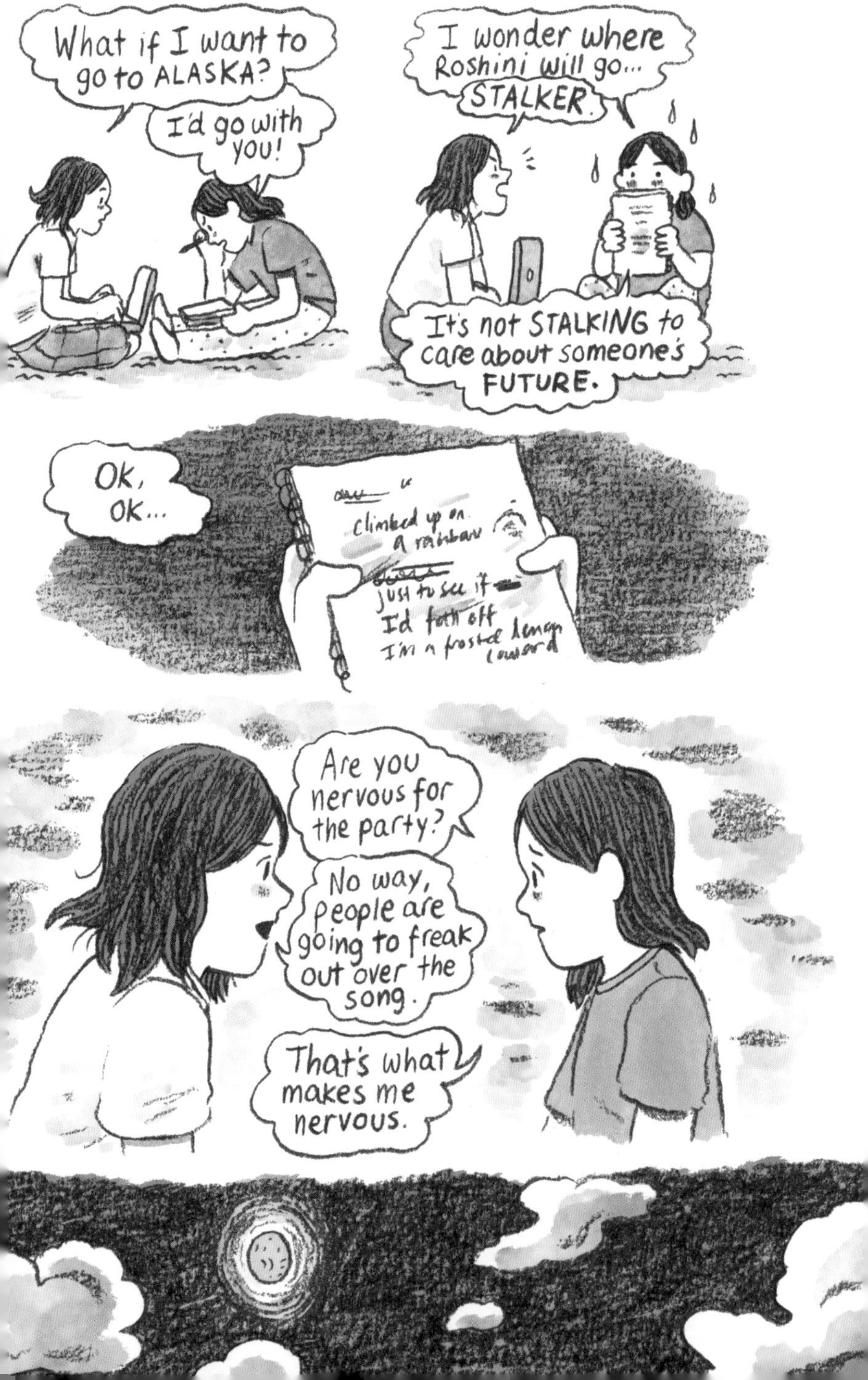
What if I want to go to ALASKA?
I'd go with you!
I wonder where Roshini will go...
STALKER.
It's not STALKING to care about someone's FUTURE.
Ok, ok...
Climbed up on
just to see if
Are you nervous for the party?
No way, people are going to freak out over the song.
That's what makes me nervous.

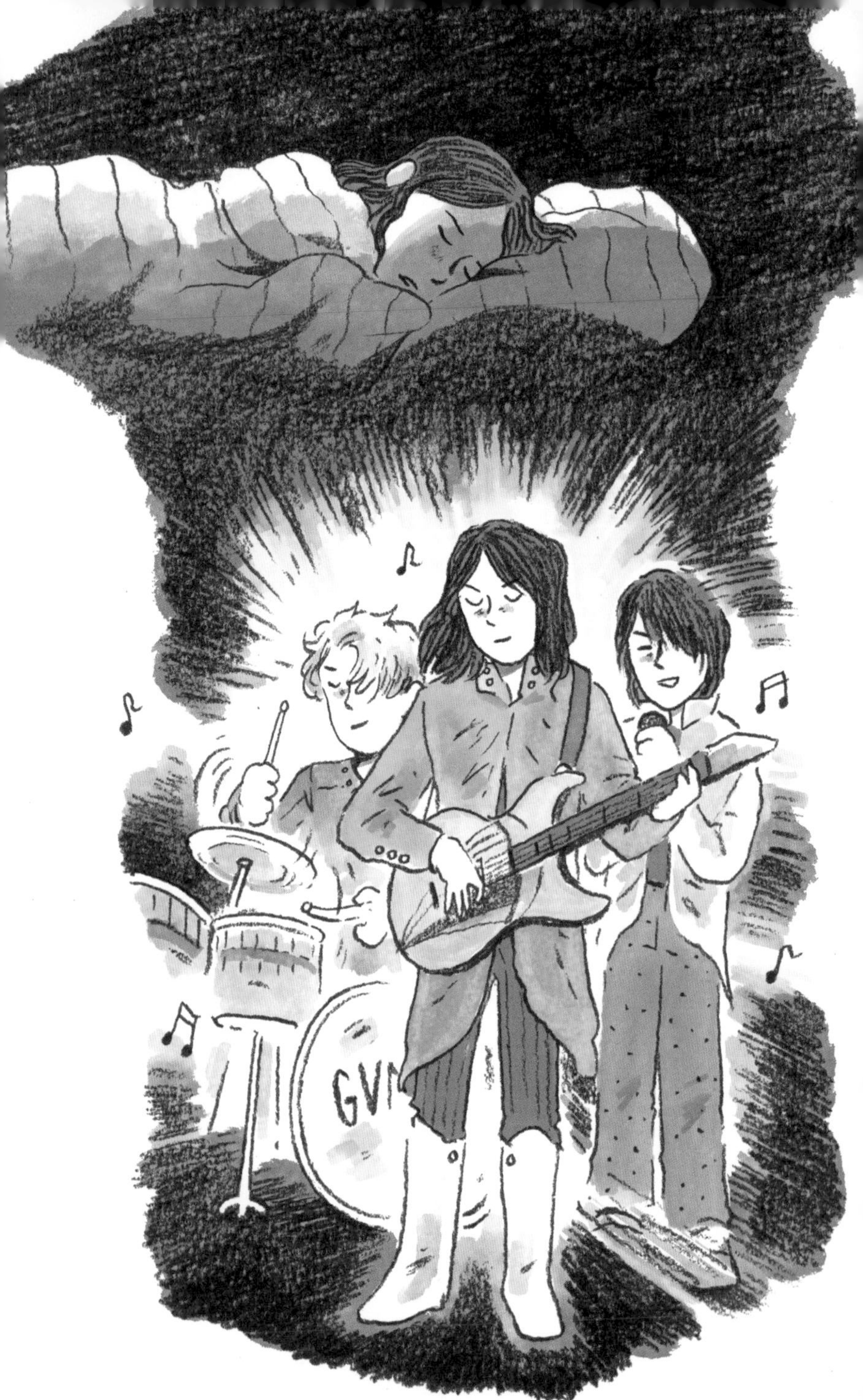

Our band will be
amazing,
everyone will want to
hear us play...

Noa and Kaito will join
GUNK, We'll tour ALL of Canada,
make millions, release a
thousand albums, and
we'll be friends
FOREVER.

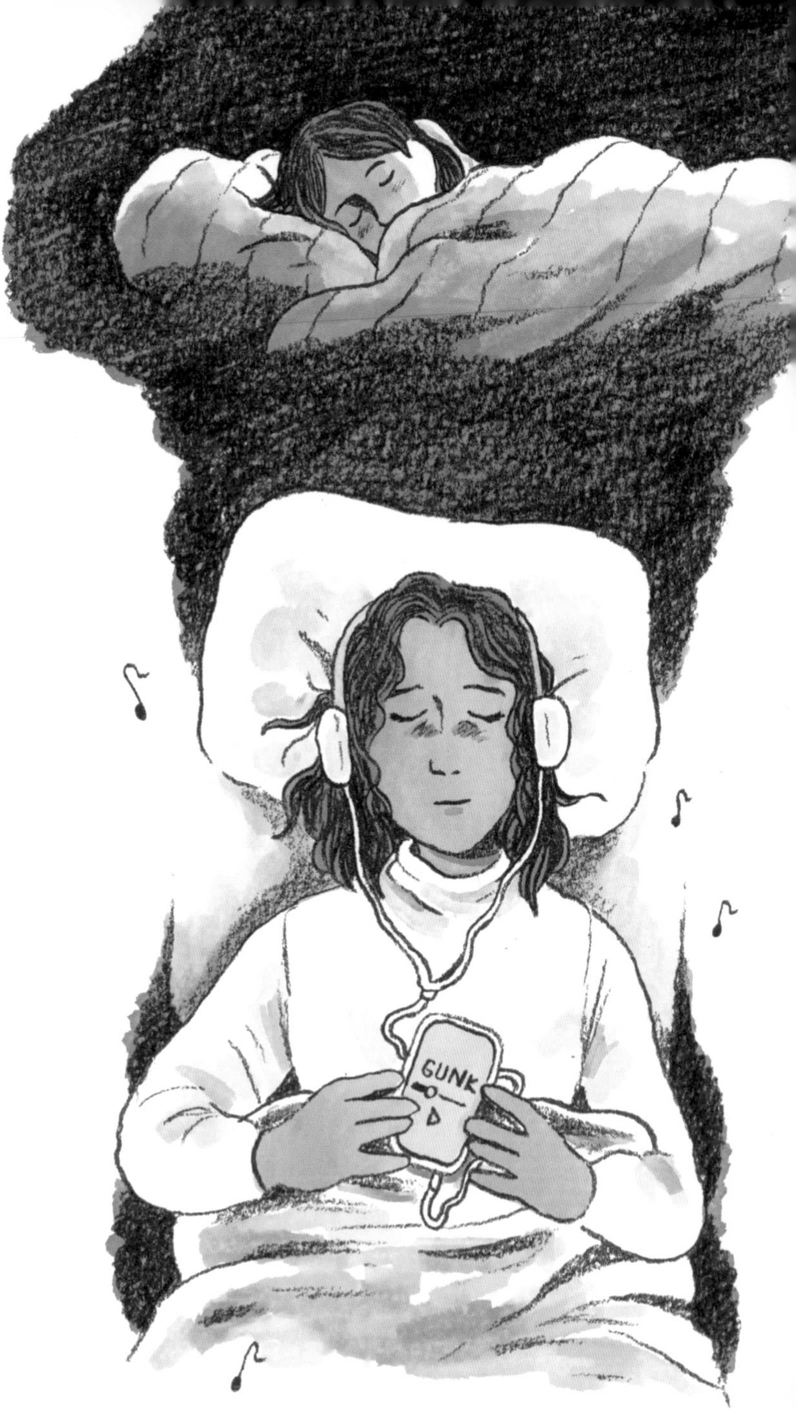
GUNK

Roshini is trying to
fall asleep, but can't.

So she opens her phone
and puts on our song.

And it makes
her feel so
          safe...

    so far away...

        that she
            finally...
                drifts...

                    off.

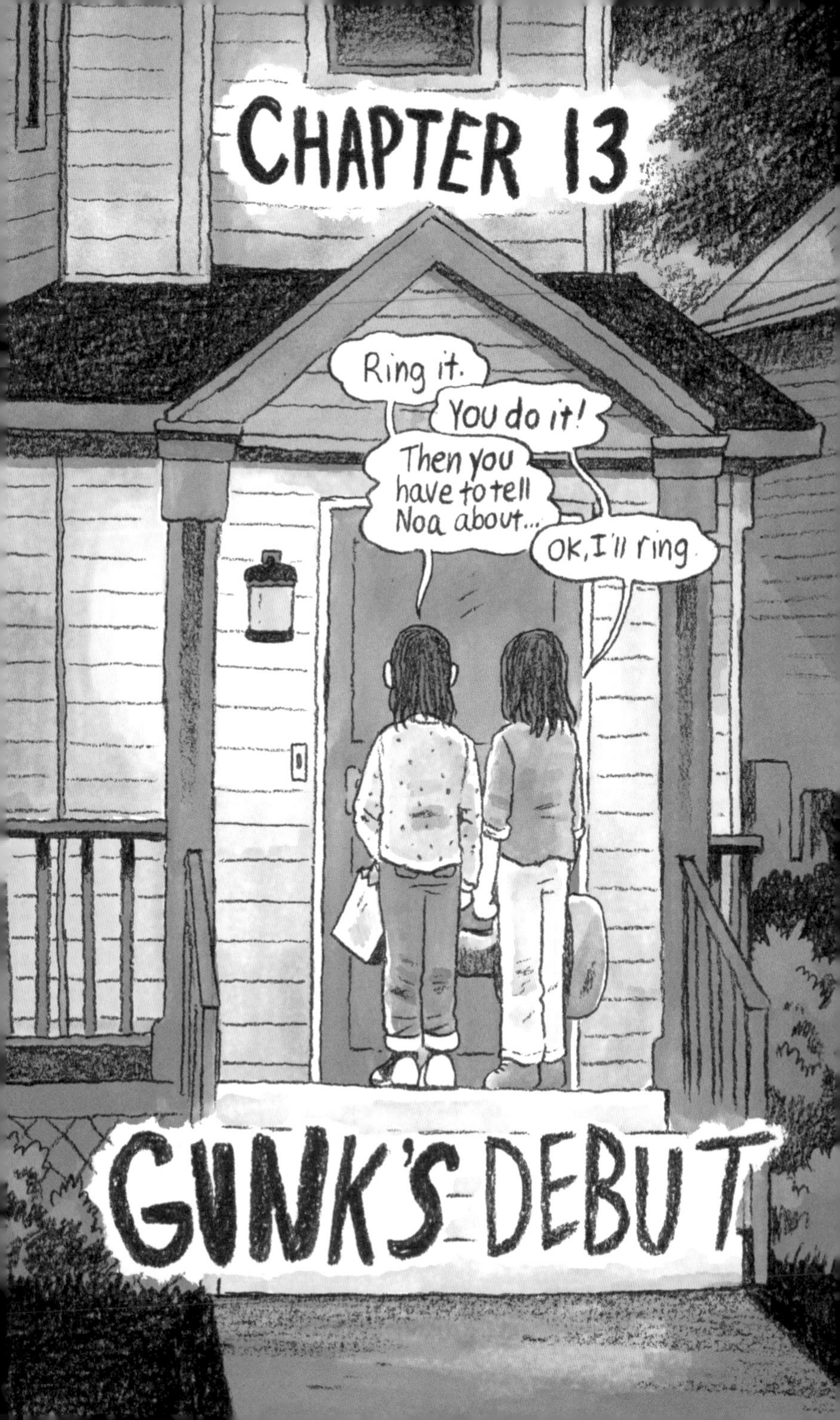
CHAPTER 13
Ring it.
You do it!
Then you have to tell Noa about...
Ok, I'll ring.
GUNK'S DEBUT

THIS IS HUGE!
THIS IS BIG!
WE'RE GOING TO PLAY IN
FRONT OF ALL OUR FRIENDS!

AND ALSO OUR PARENTS.

ARE YOU READY?!

I DON'T KNOW.
ARE YOU READY?!?

I ALSO
DON'T
KNOW!!!

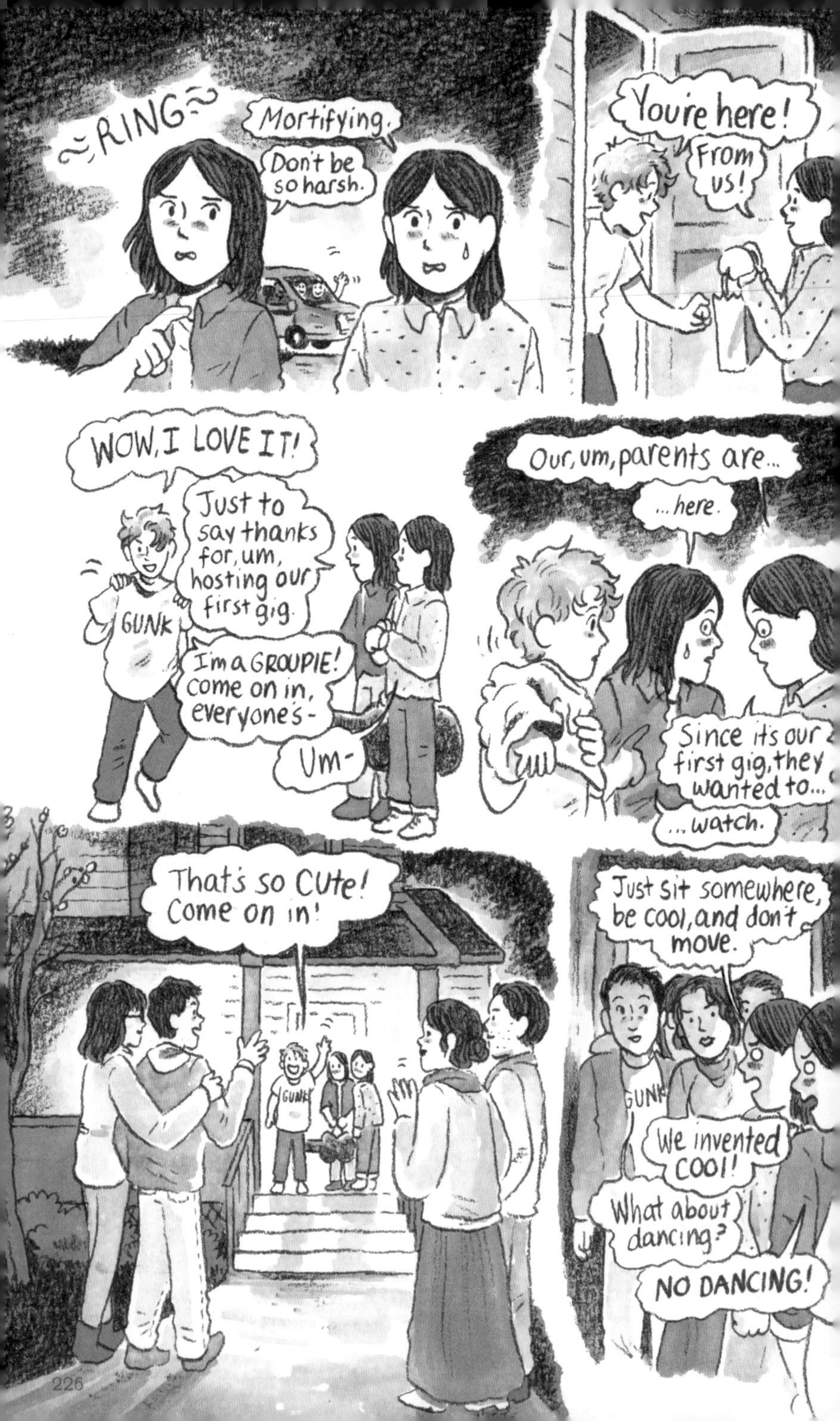
RING
Mortifying.
Don't be so harsh.
You're here!
From us!
WOW, I LOVE IT!
Just to say thanks for, um, hosting our first gig.
I'm a GROUPIE! come on in, everyone's-
Um-
Our, um, parents are...
...here.
Since it's our first gig, they wanted to...
...watch.
GUNK
That's so CUte! Come on in!
Just sit somewhere, be cool, and don't move.
We invented cool!
What about dancing?
NO DANCING!

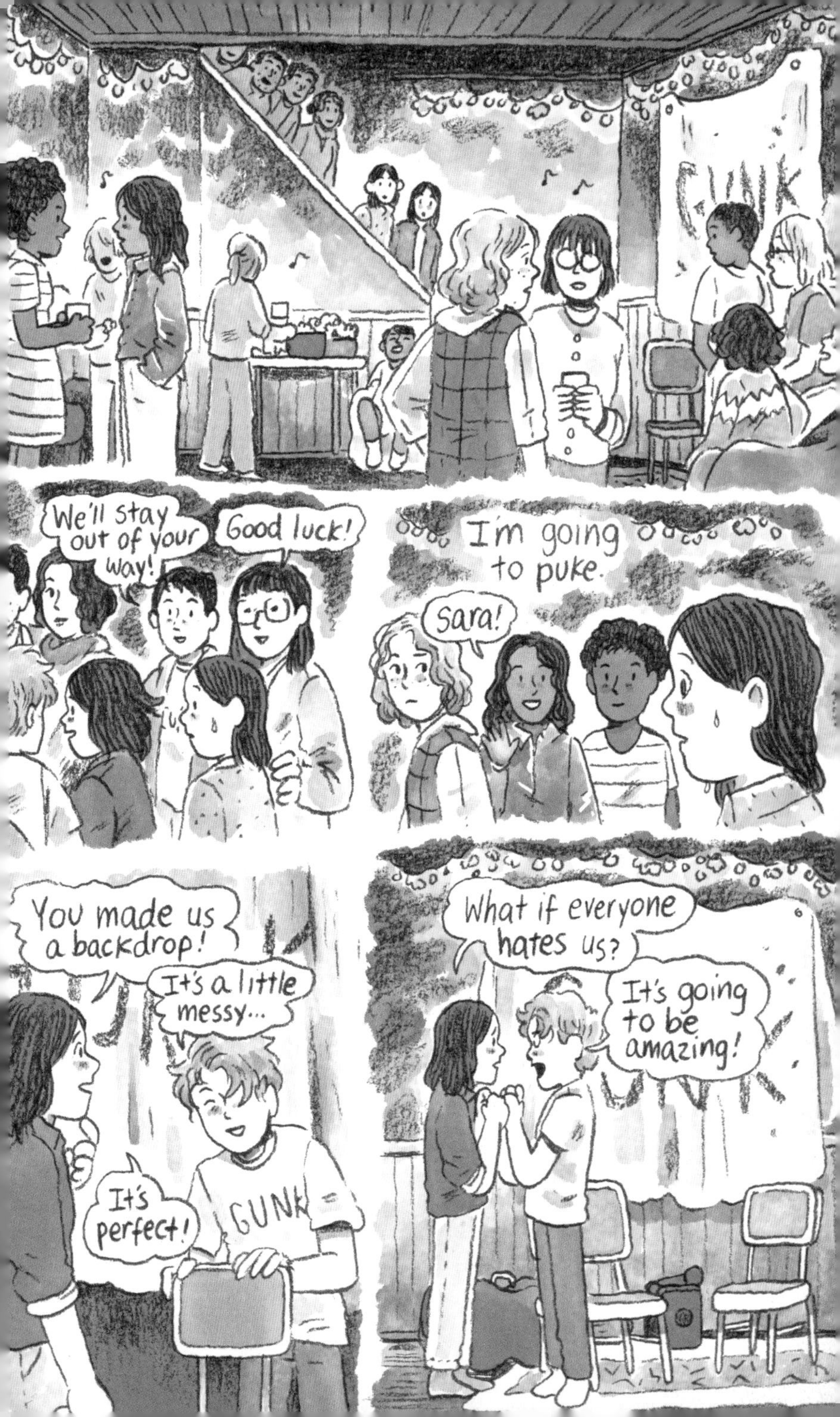
GUNK
We'll stay out of your way!
Good luck!
I'm going to puke.
Sara!
You made us a backdrop!
It's a little messy...
It's perfect!
GUNK
What if everyone hates us?
It's going to be amazing!

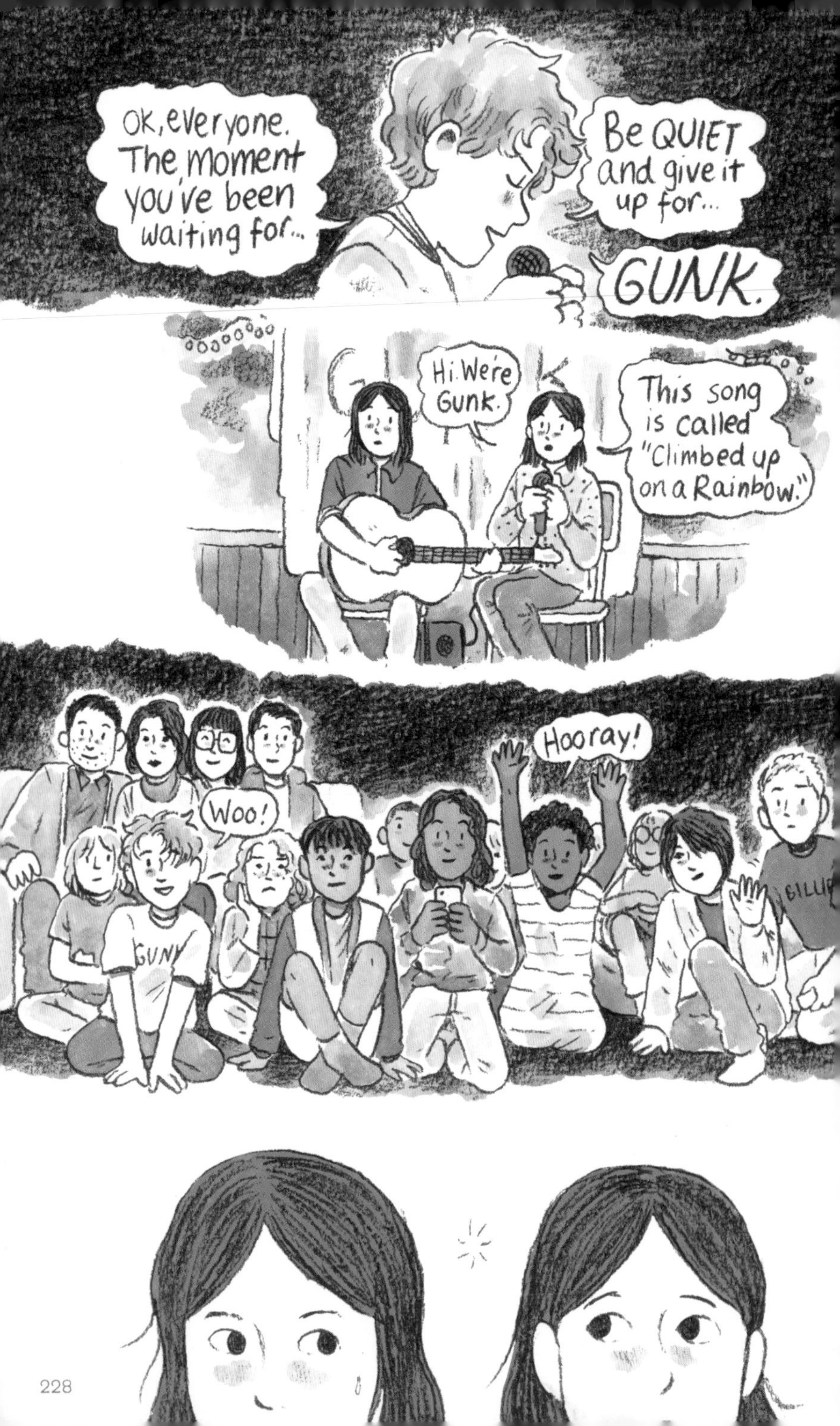

Ok, everyone. The moment you've been waiting for...
Be QUIET and give it up for...
GUNK.
Hi. We're Gunk.
This song is called "Climbed up on a Rainbow."
Hooray!
Woo!
GUNK
BILLIE

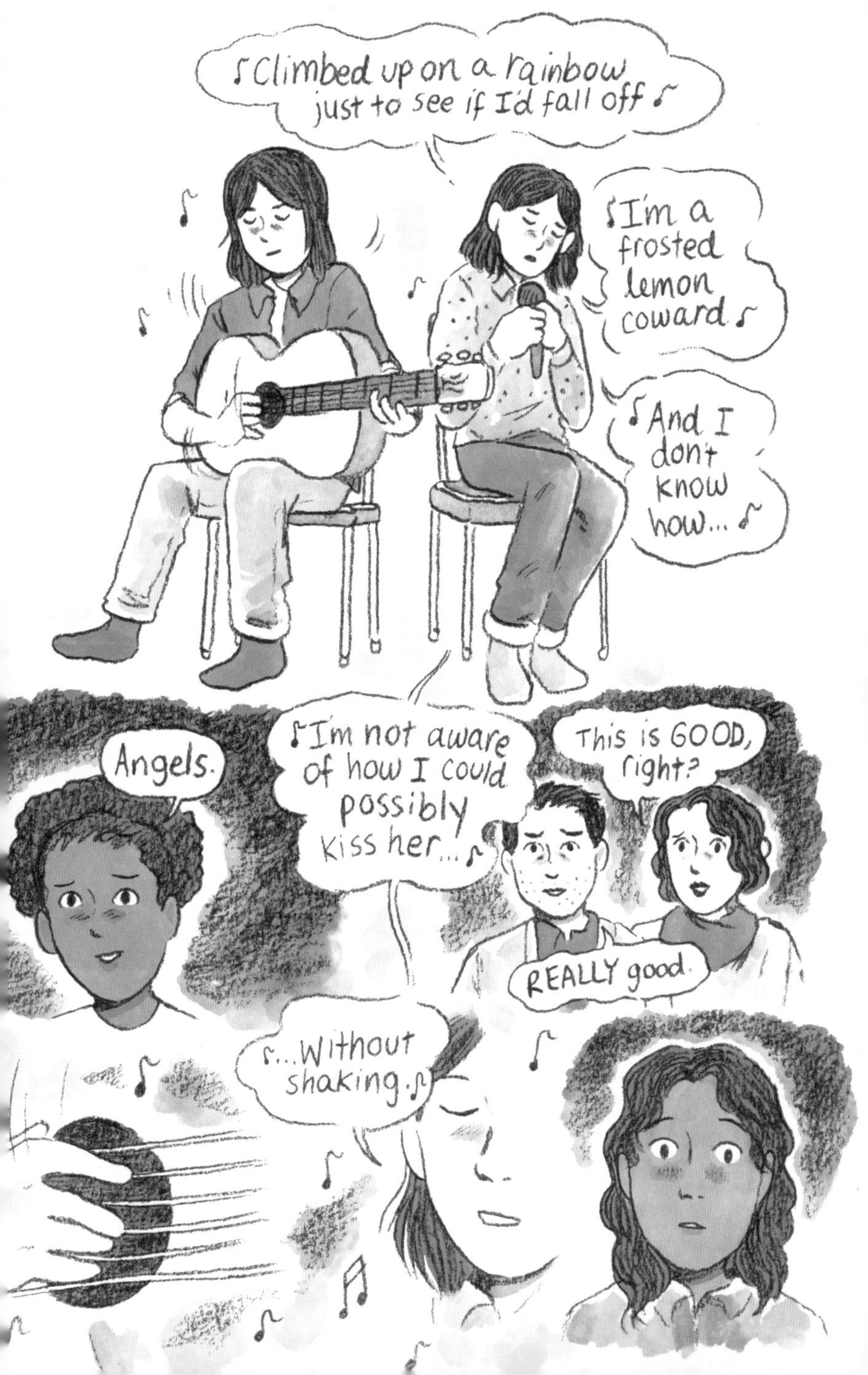
Climbed up on a rainbow just to see if I'd fall off
I'm a frosted lemon coward.
And I don't know how...
Angels.
I'm not aware of how I could possibly kiss her...
This is GOOD, right?
REALLY good.
...without shaking.

Playing guitar makes me feel
weightless
high up in the sky
the sound of the strings is like the sound of my thoughts.

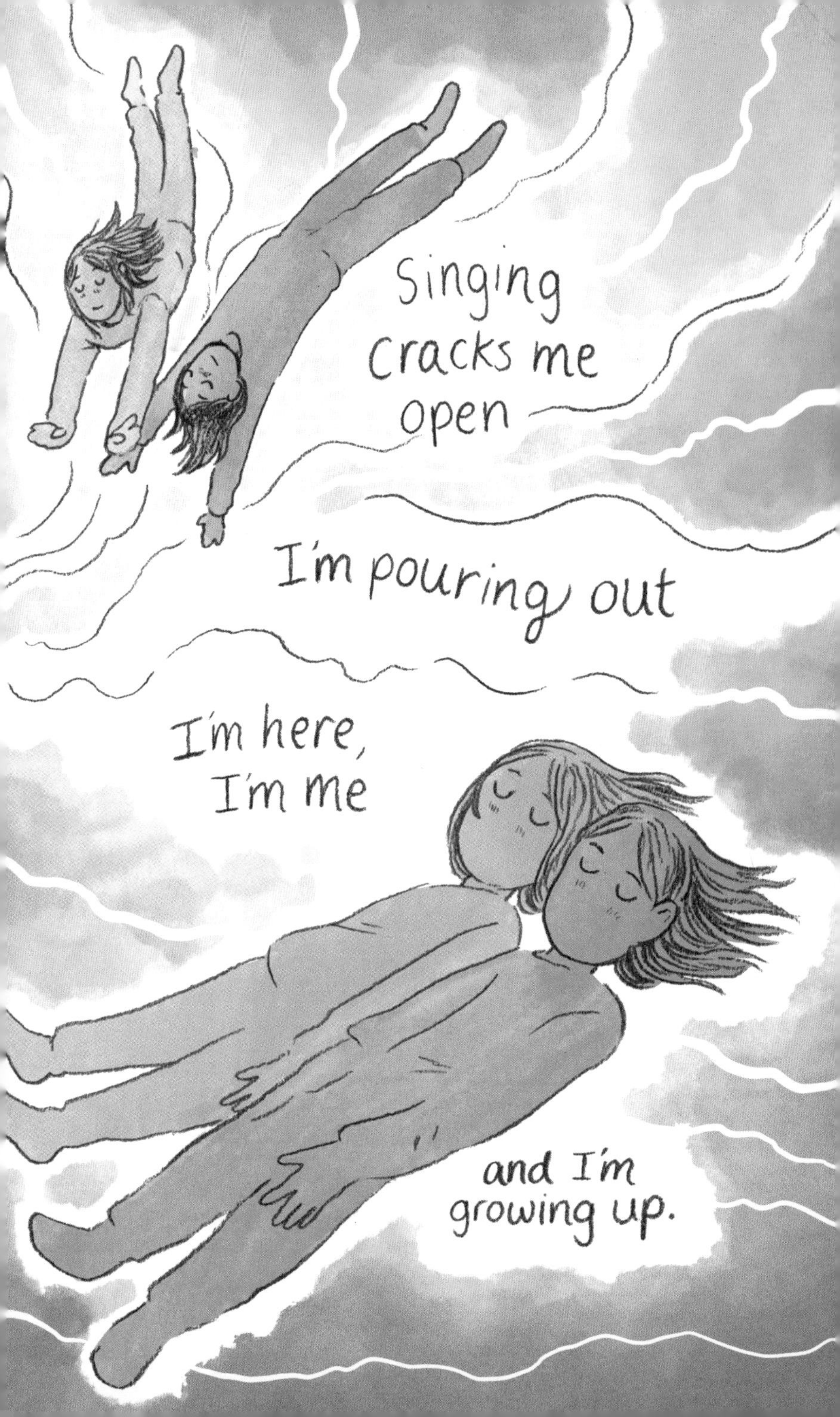
Singing cracks me open
I'm pouring out
I'm here, I'm me
and I'm growing up.

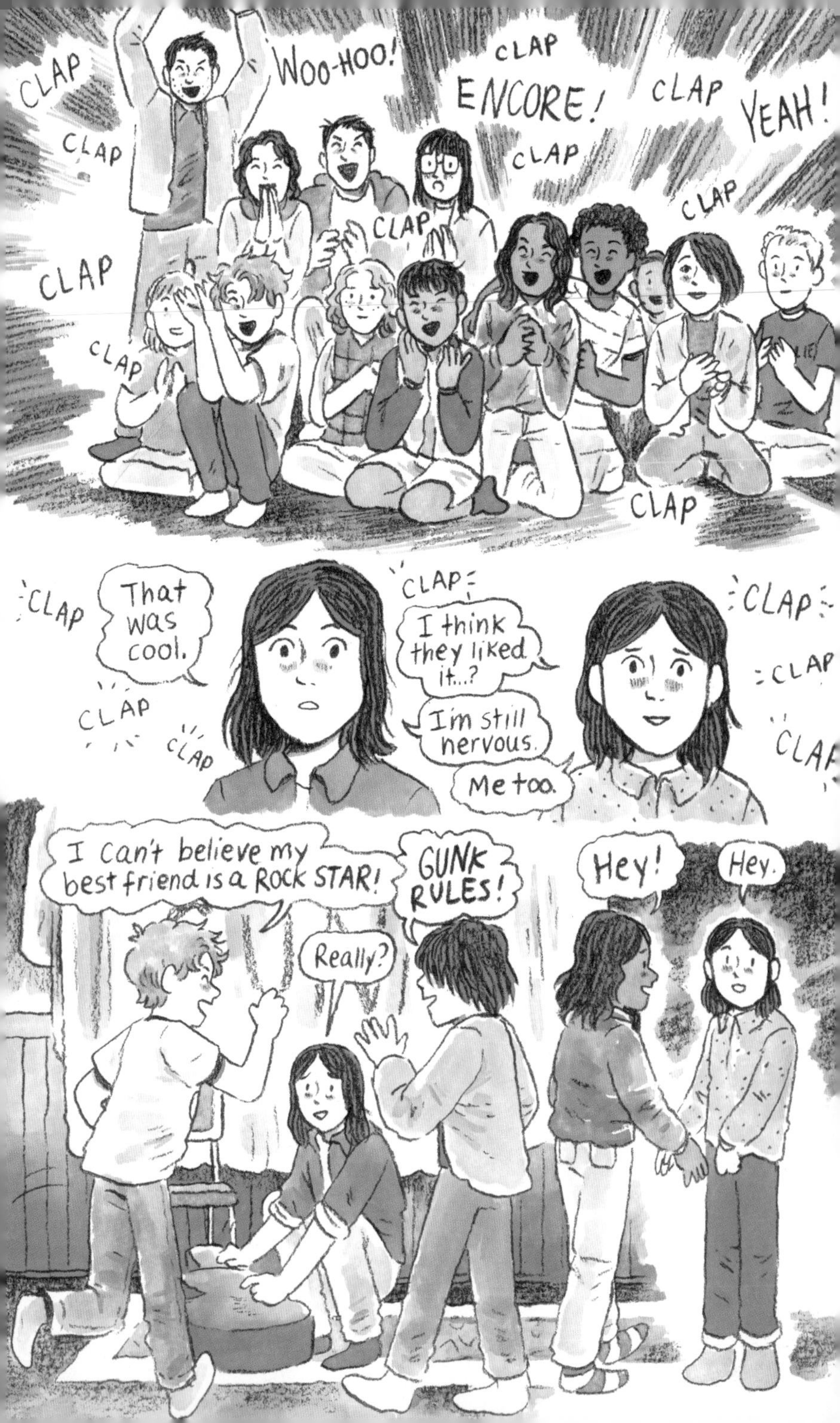
CLAP
WOO-HOO!
CLAP
ENCORE!
CLAP
YEAH!
CLAP
CLAP
CLAP
CLAP
CLAP
CLAP
CLAP
CLAP
That was cool.
CLAP
I think they liked it...?
CLAP
I'm still nervous.
CLAP
CLAP
Me too.
CLAP
CLAP
I can't believe my best friend is a ROCK STAR!
Really?
GUNK RULES!
Hey!
Hey.

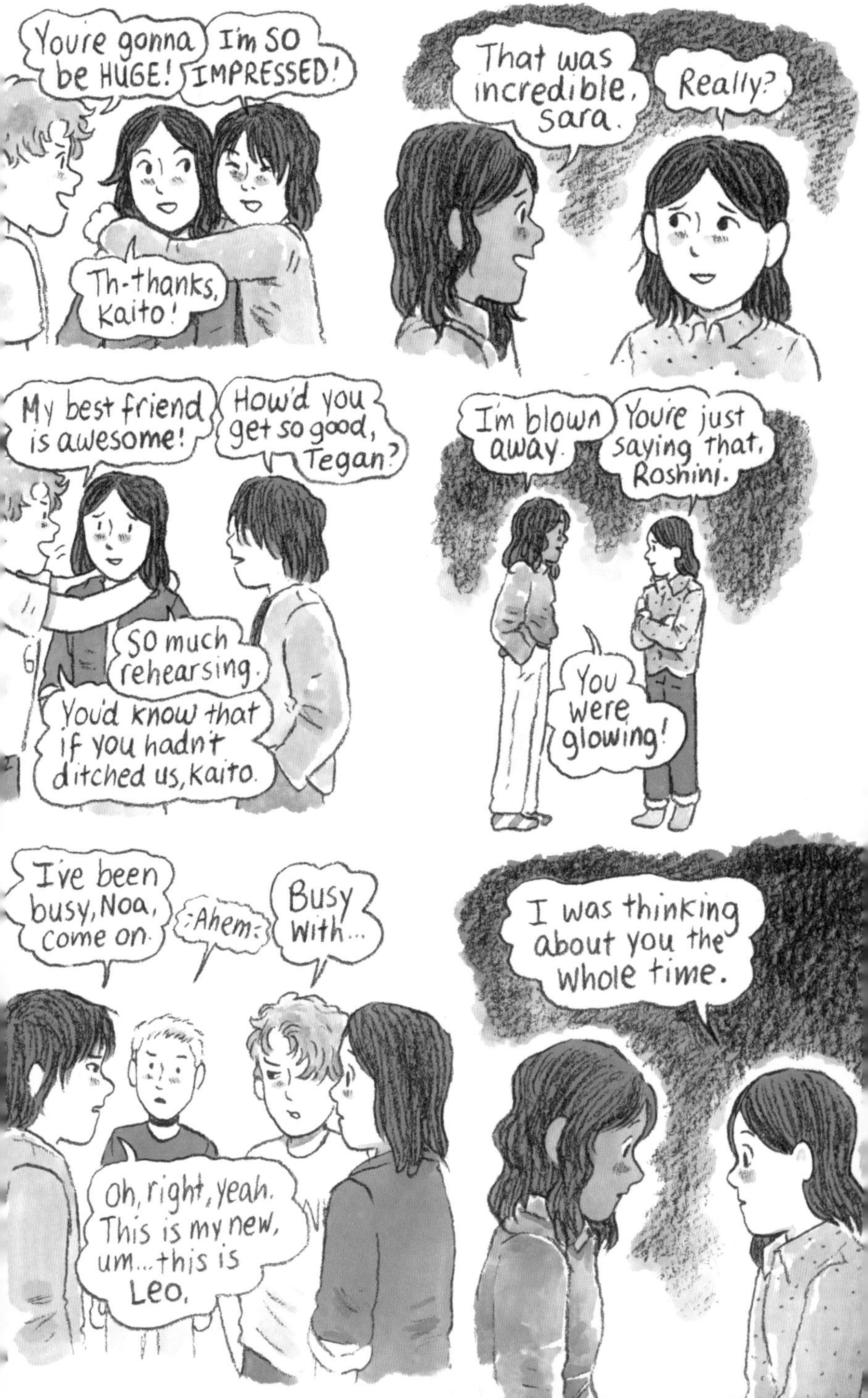
You're gonna be HUGE!
I'm SO IMPRESSED!
Th-thanks, Kaito!
That was incredible, Sara.
Really?
My best friend is awesome!
How'd you get so good, Tegan?
So much rehearsing.
You'd know that if you hadn't ditched us, Kaito.
I'm blown away.
You're just saying that, Roshini.
You were glowing!
I've been busy, Noa, come on.
:Ahem:
Busy with...
Oh, right, yeah. This is my new, um... this is Leo.
I was thinking about you the whole time.

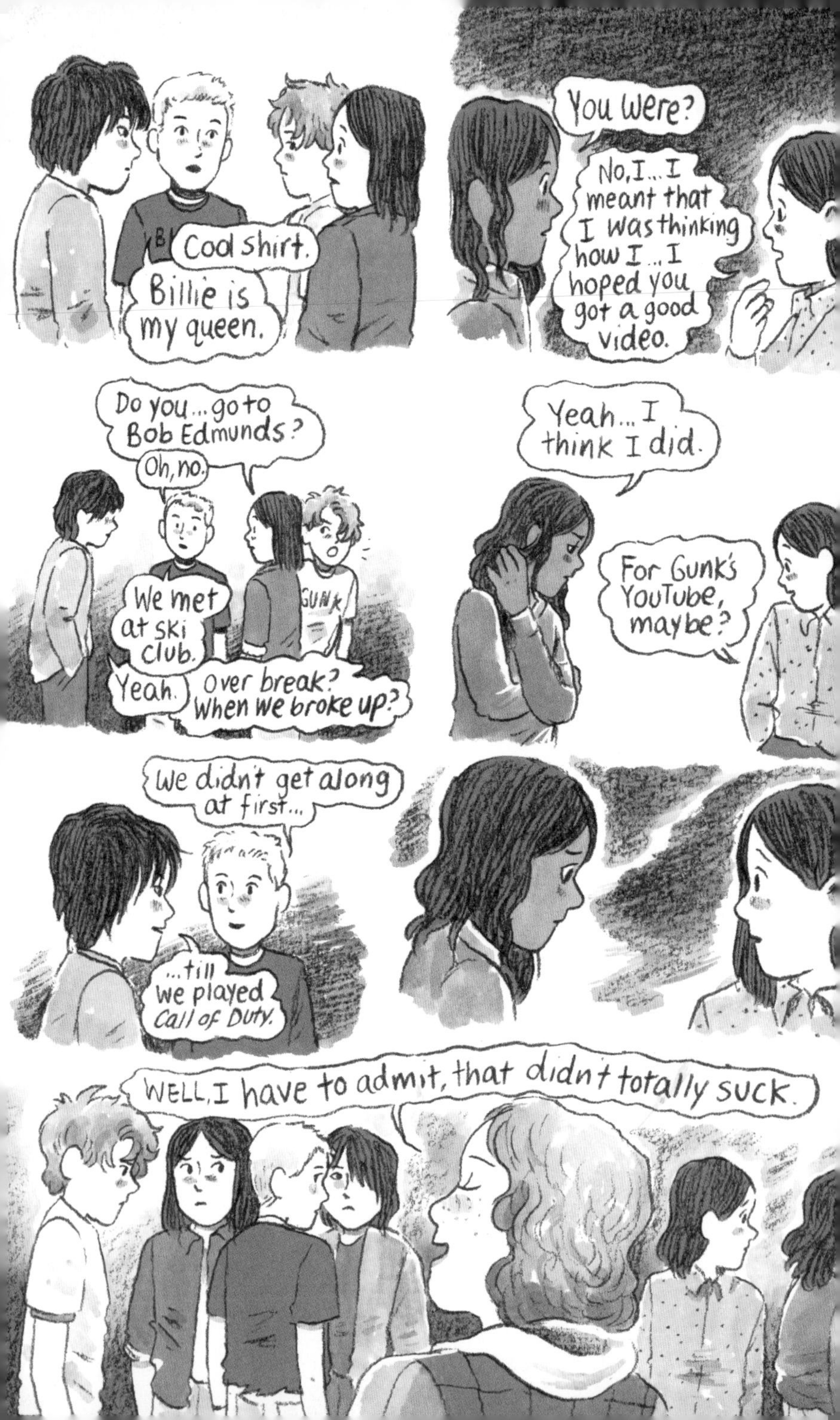

Cool shirt.
Billie is my queen.
You were?
No, I... I meant that I was thinking how I... I hoped you got a good video.
Do you... go to Bob Edmunds?
Oh, no.
We met at ski club.
Yeah.
Over break? When we broke up?
Yeah... I think I did.
For Gunk's YouTube, maybe?
We didn't get along at first...
...till we played *Call of Duty.*
WELL, I have to admit, that didn't totally suck.

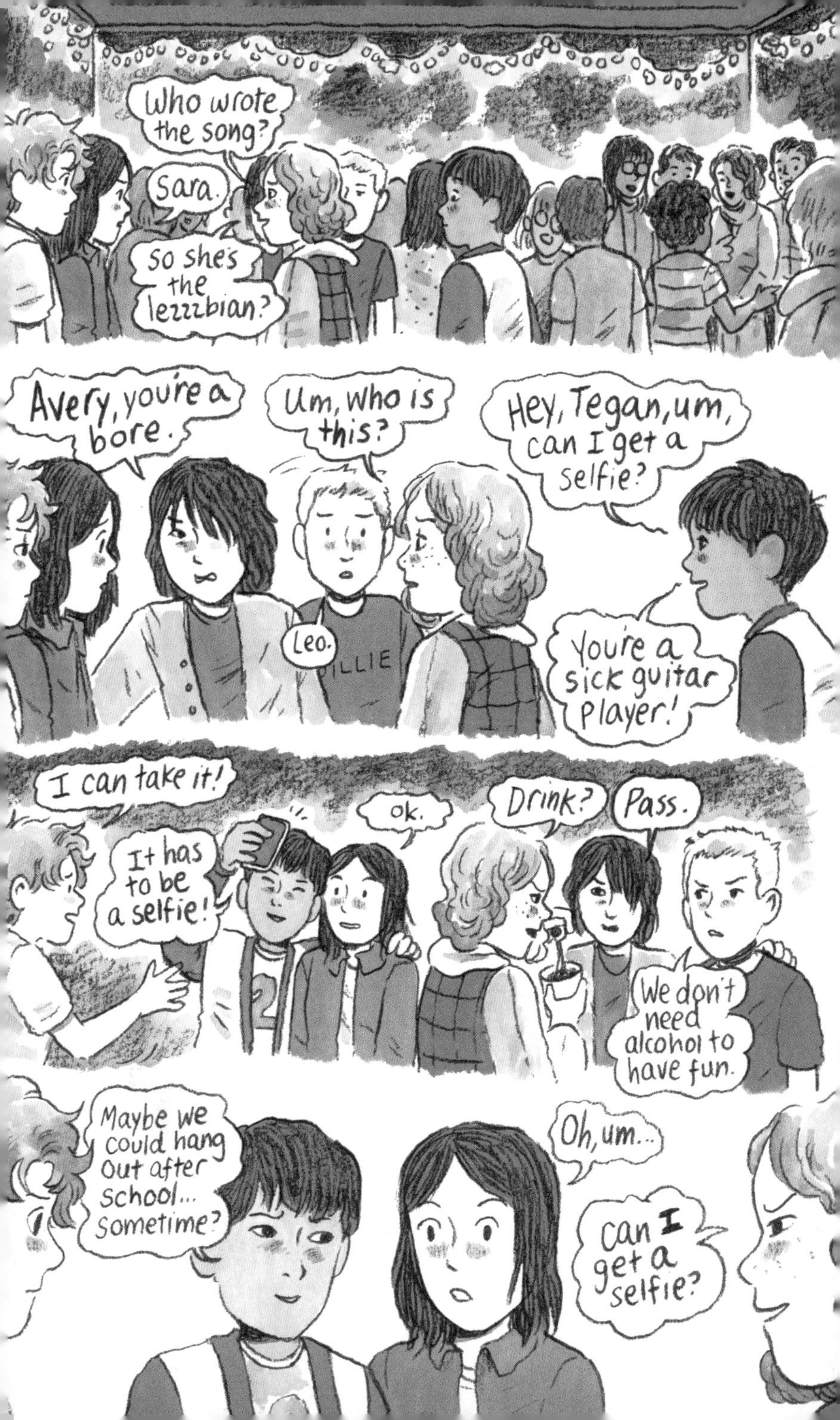
Who wrote the song?
Sara.
So she's the lezzzbian?
Avery, you're a bore.
Um, who is this?
Leo.
ILLIE
Hey, Tegan, um, can I get a selfie?
You're a sick guitar player!
I can take it!
It has to be a selfie!
ok.
Drink?
Pass.
We don't need alcohol to have fun.
Maybe we could hang out after school... sometime?
Oh, um...
Can I get a selfie?

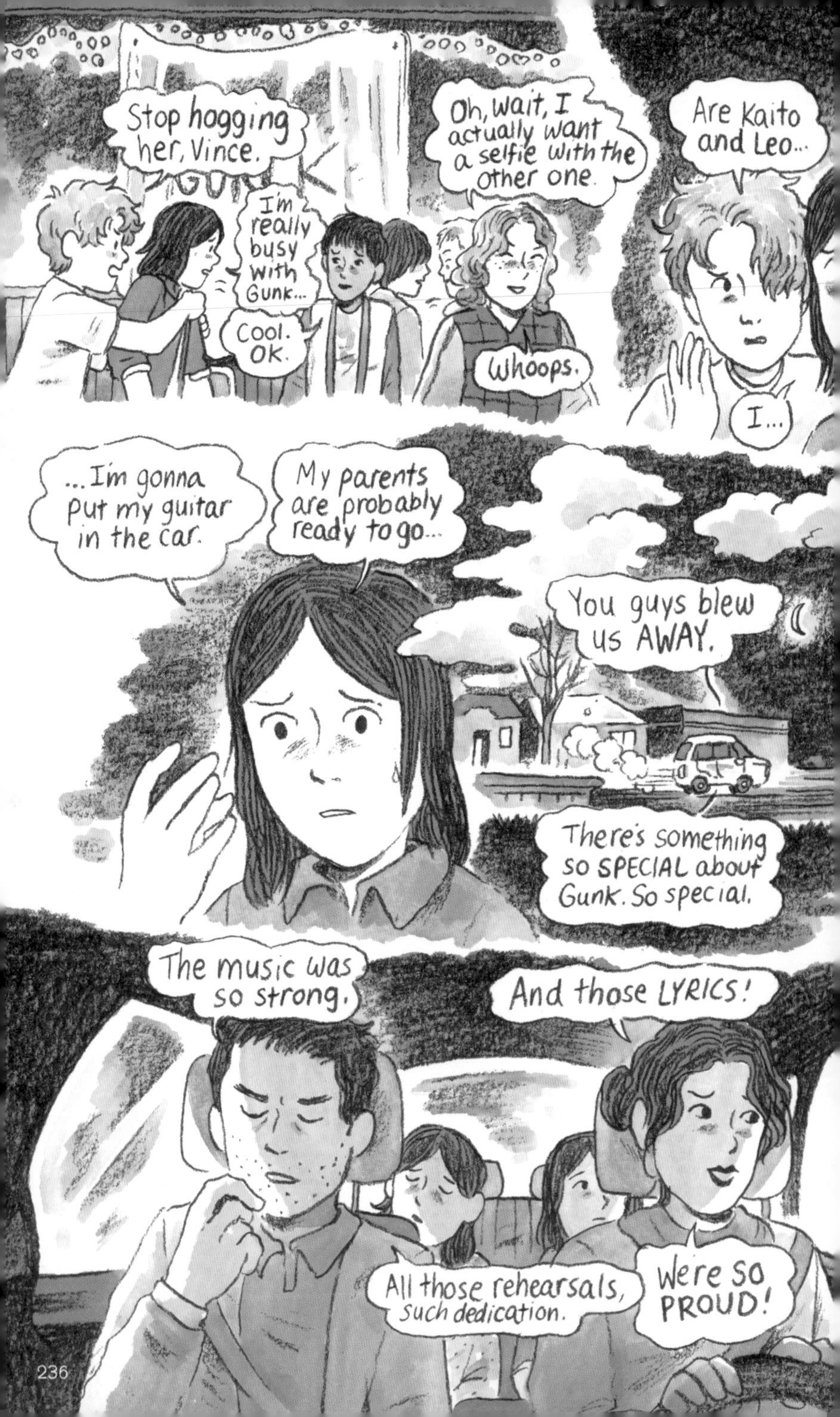
Stop hogging her, Vince.
I'm really busy with Gunk...
Cool. OK.
Oh, wait, I actually want a selfie with the other one.
Whoops.
Are Kaito and Leo...
I...
...I'm gonna put my guitar in the car.
My parents are probably ready to go...
You guys blew us AWAY.
There's something so SPECIAL about Gunk. So special.
The music was so strong.
And those LYRICS!
All those rehearsals, such dedication.
We're so PROUD!

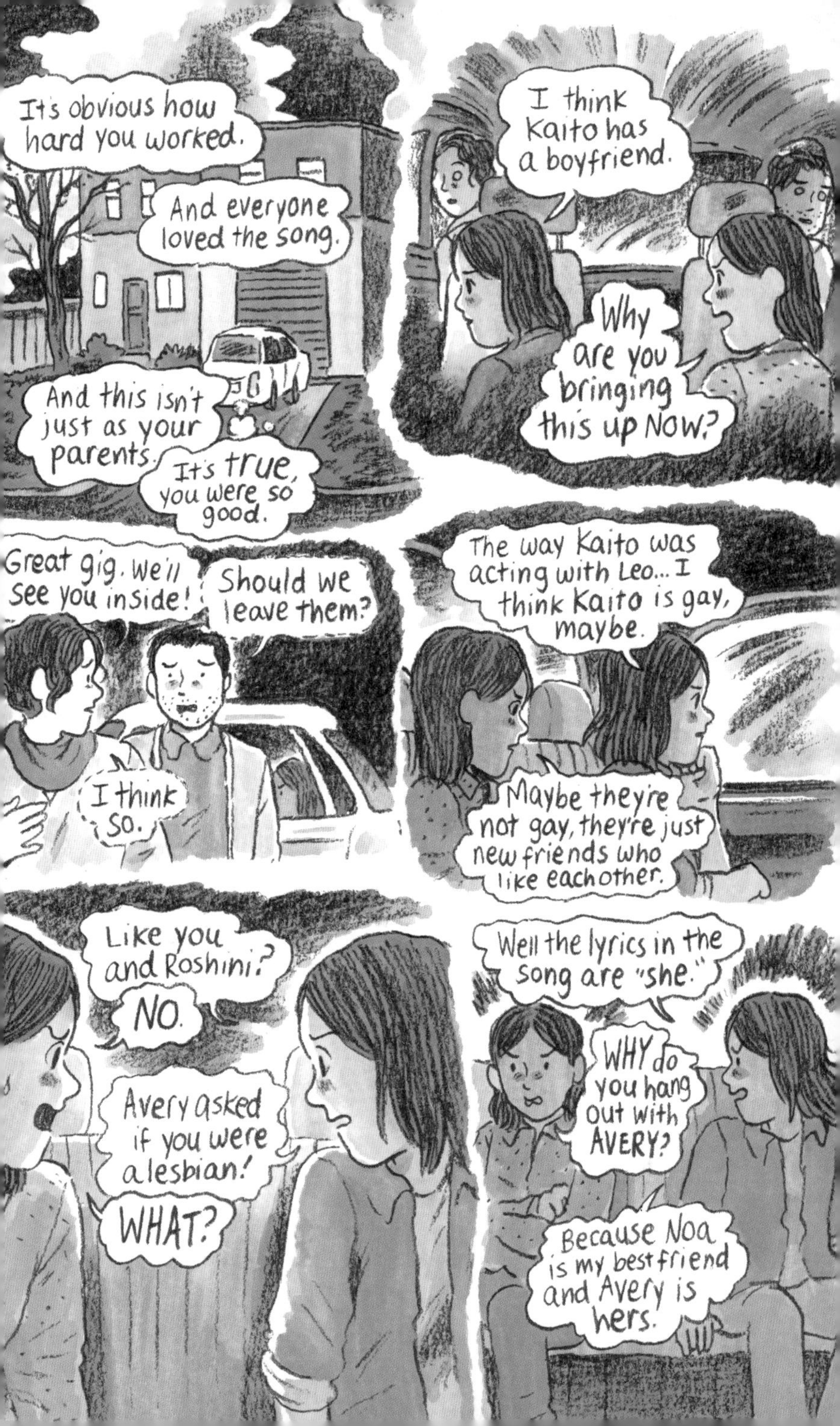
It's obvious how hard you worked.
And everyone loved the song.
And this isn't just as your parents.
It's true, you were so good.
I think Kaito has a boyfriend.
Why are you bringing this up NOW?
Great gig. We'll see you inside!
Should we leave them?
I think so.
The way Kaito was acting with Leo... I think Kaito is gay, maybe.
Maybe they're not gay, they're just new friends who like eachother.
Like you and Roshini?
NO.
Avery asked if you were a lesbian!
WHAT?
Well the lyrics in the song are "she."
WHY do you hang out with AVERY?
Because Noa is my best friend and Avery is hers.

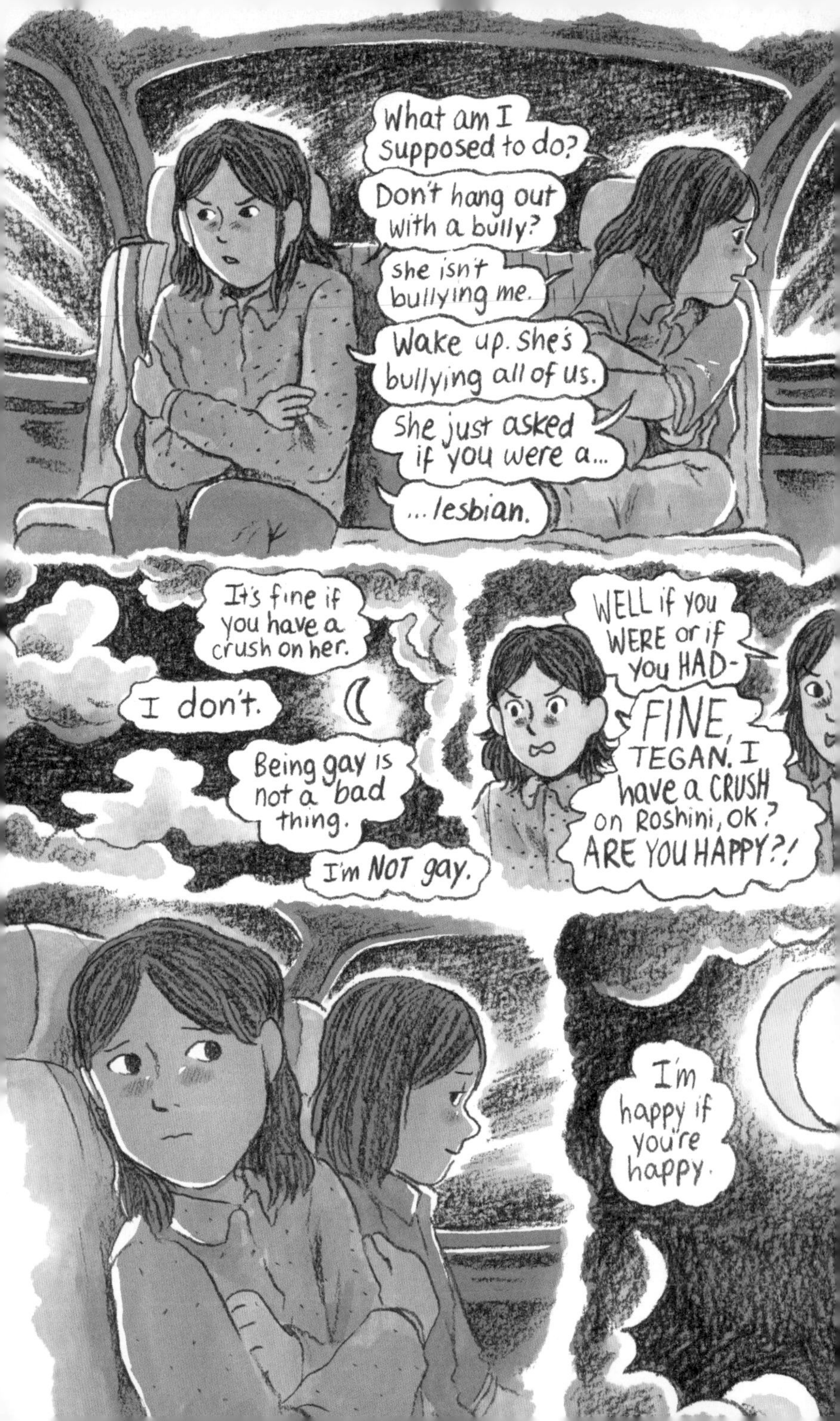
What am I supposed to do?
Don't hang out with a bully?
She isn't bullying me.
Wake up. She's bullying all of us.
She just asked if you were a...
...lesbian.
It's fine if you have a crush on her.
I don't.
Being gay is not a bad thing.
I'm NOT gay.
WELL if you WERE or if you HAD-
FINE, TEGAN. I have a CRUSH on Roshini, OK? ARE YOU HAPPY?!
I'm happy if you're happy.

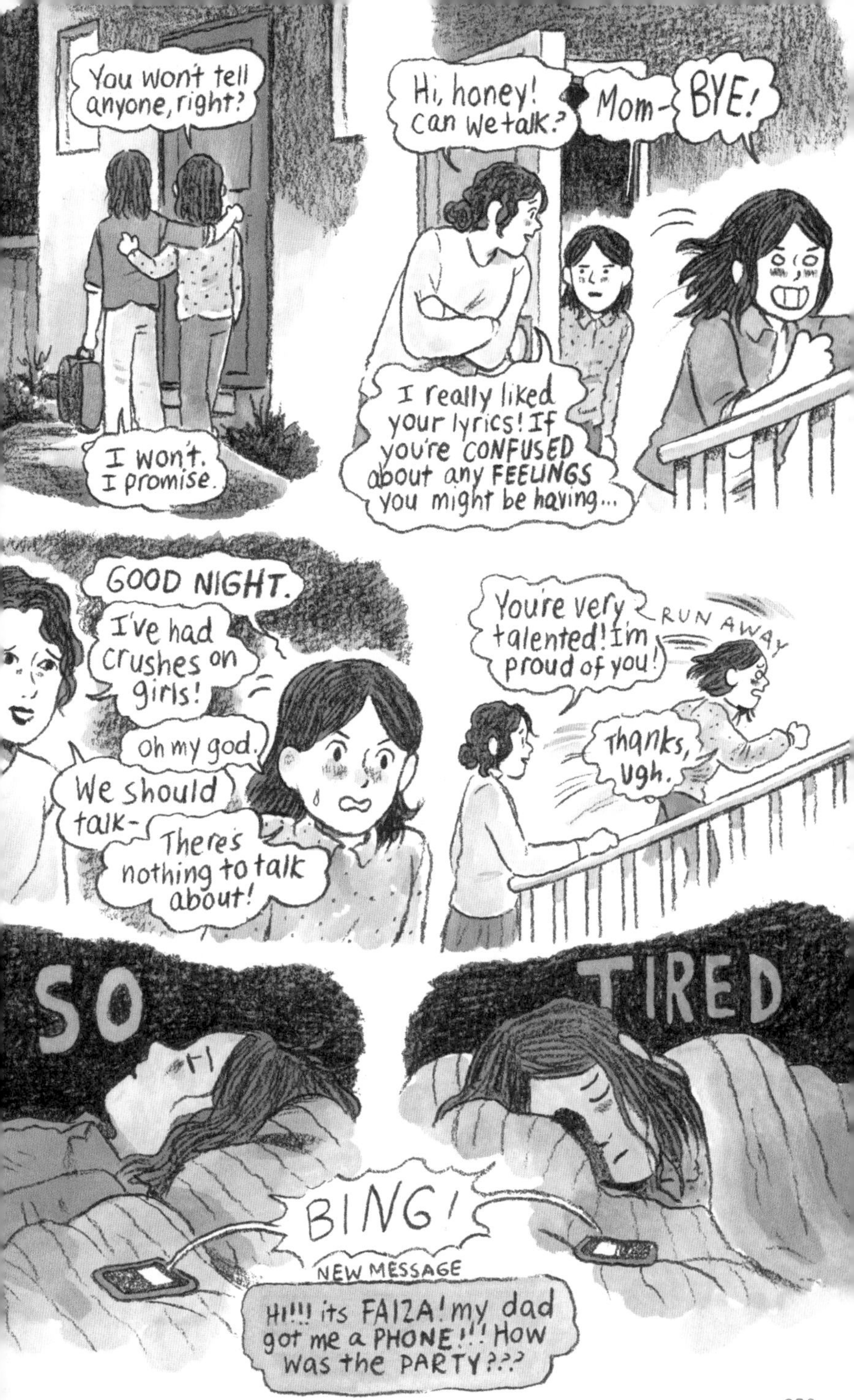

You won't tell anyone, right?
I won't. I promise.
Hi, honey! can we talk?
Mom-
BYE!
I really liked your lyrics! If you're CONFUSED about any FEELINGS you might be having...
GOOD NIGHT.
I've had crushes on girls!
oh my god.
We should talk-
There's nothing to talk about!
You're very talented! I'm proud of you!
RUN AWAY
Thanks, ugh.
SO
TIRED
BING!
NEW MESSAGE
HI!!! its FAIZA! my dad got me a PHONE!!! How was the PARTY???

I never realized that there would be people you could meet

and sometimes when you're with them

you act in ways you don't expect

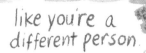

like you're a different person.

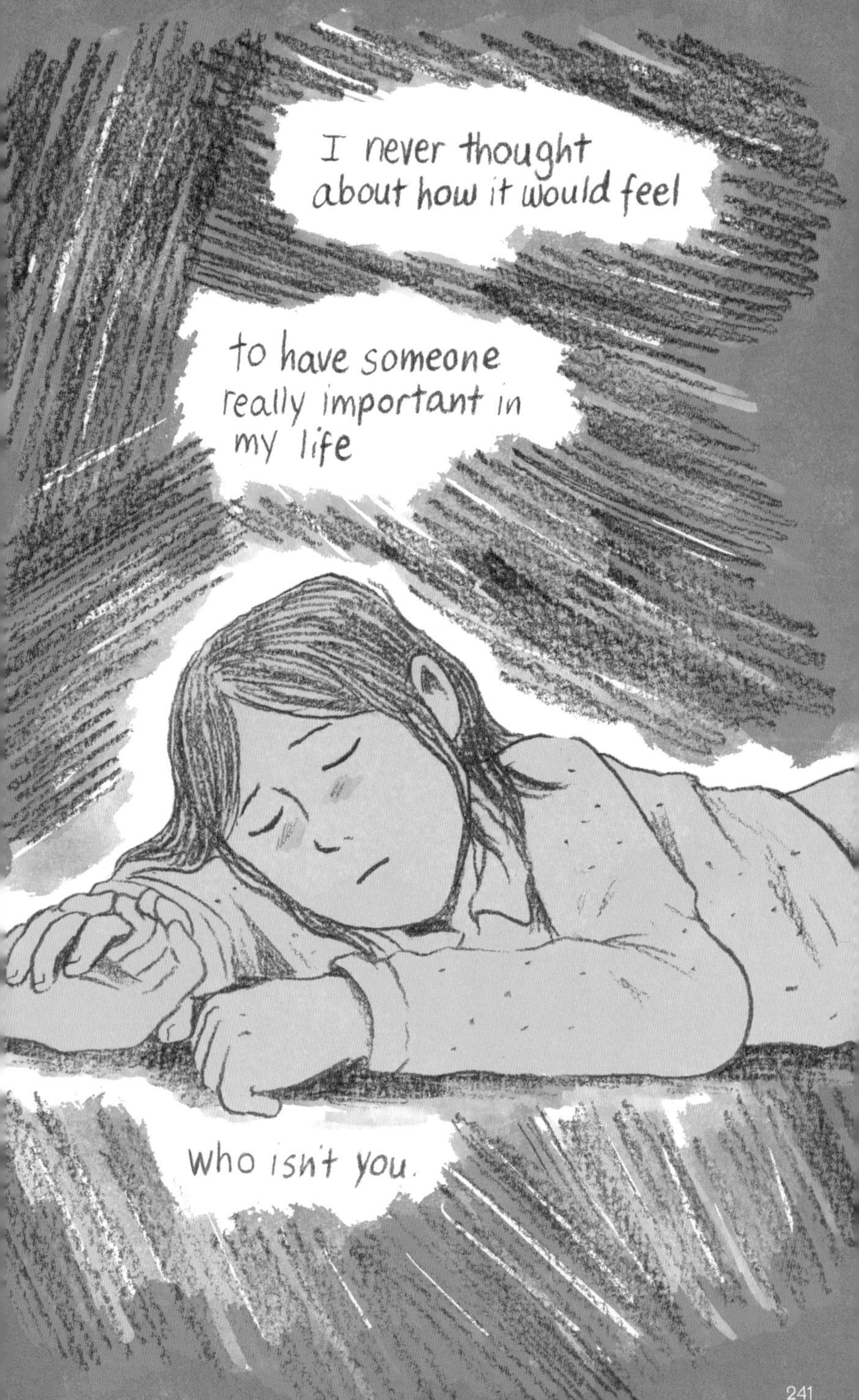
I never thought about how it would feel
to have someone really important in my life
who isn't you.

CHAPTER 14
SKATERS

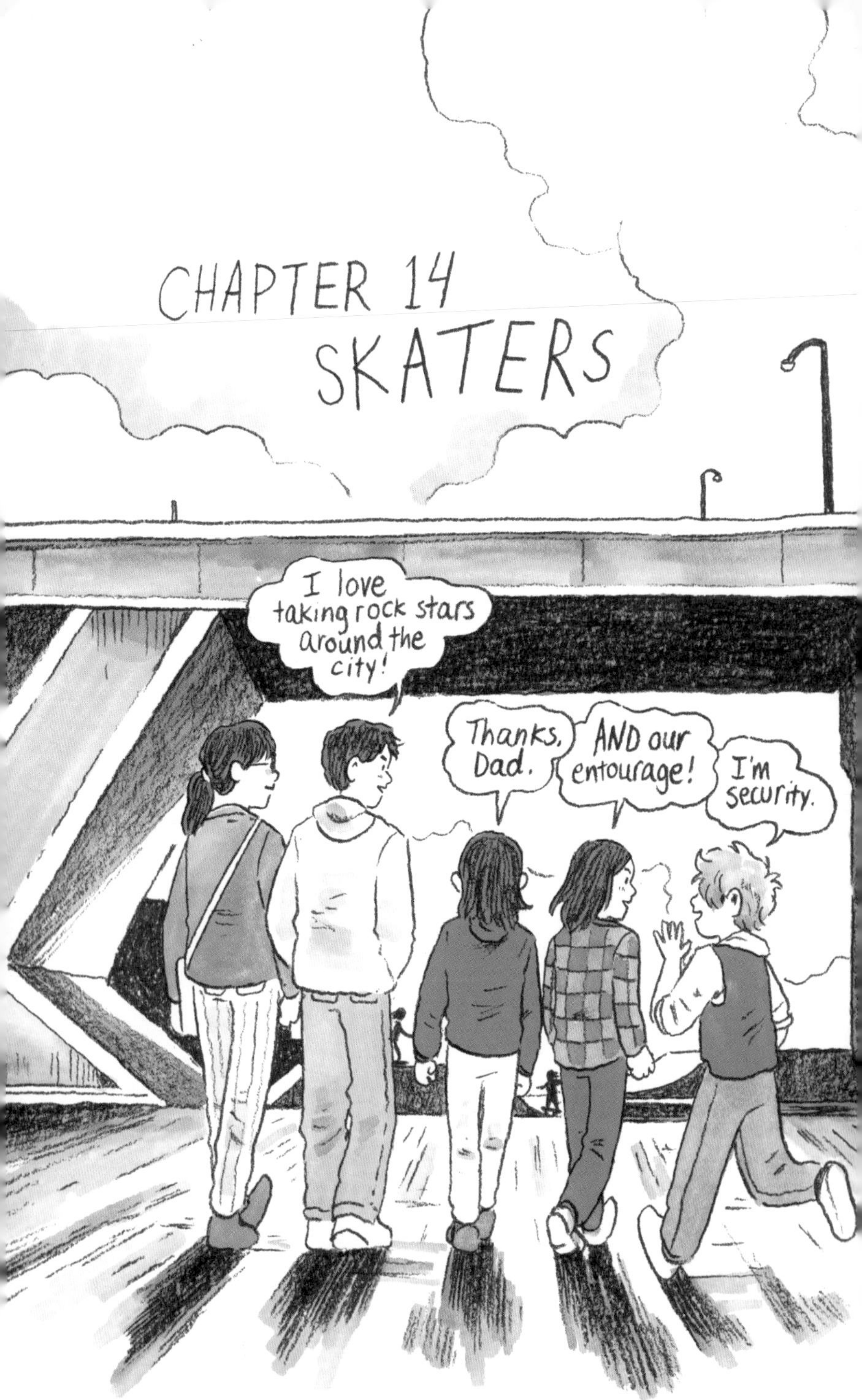
I love taking rock stars around the city!
Thanks, Dad.
AND our entourage!
I'm security.

OK, I'm doing it.

I can't watch. I'm closing my eyes.

The video is UPLOADED.

How many views does it have??

Um, none. Yet.

Oh.

Let's go see Faiza, don't worry about it.

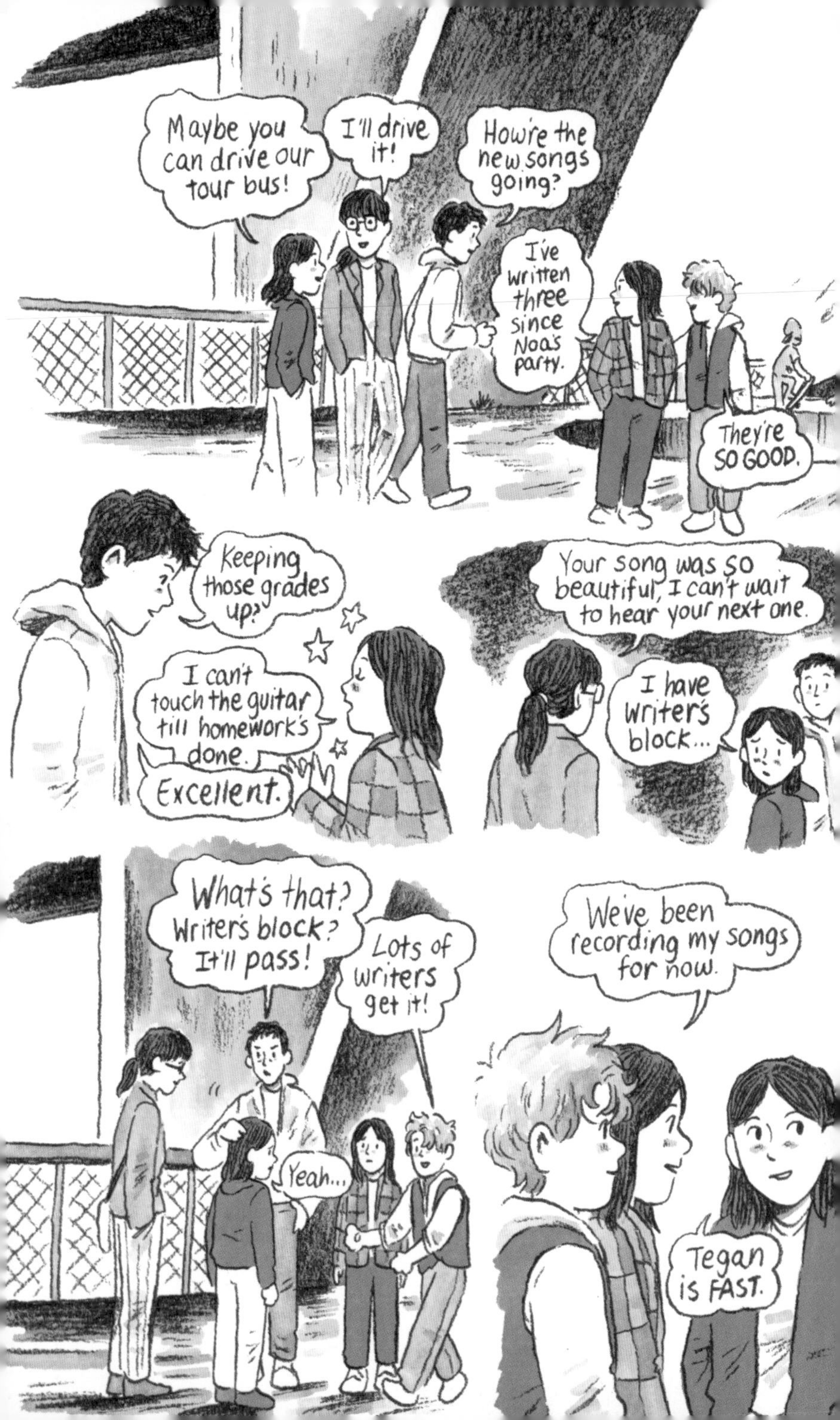
Maybe you can drive our tour bus!
I'll drive it!
How're the new songs going?
I've written three since Noa's party.
They're SO GOOD.
Keeping those grades up?
I can't touch the guitar till homework's done.
Excellent.
Your song was so beautiful, I can't wait to hear your next one.
I have writer's block...
What's that? Writer's block? It'll pass!
Lots of writers get it!
Yeah...
We've been recording my songs for now.
Tegan is FAST.

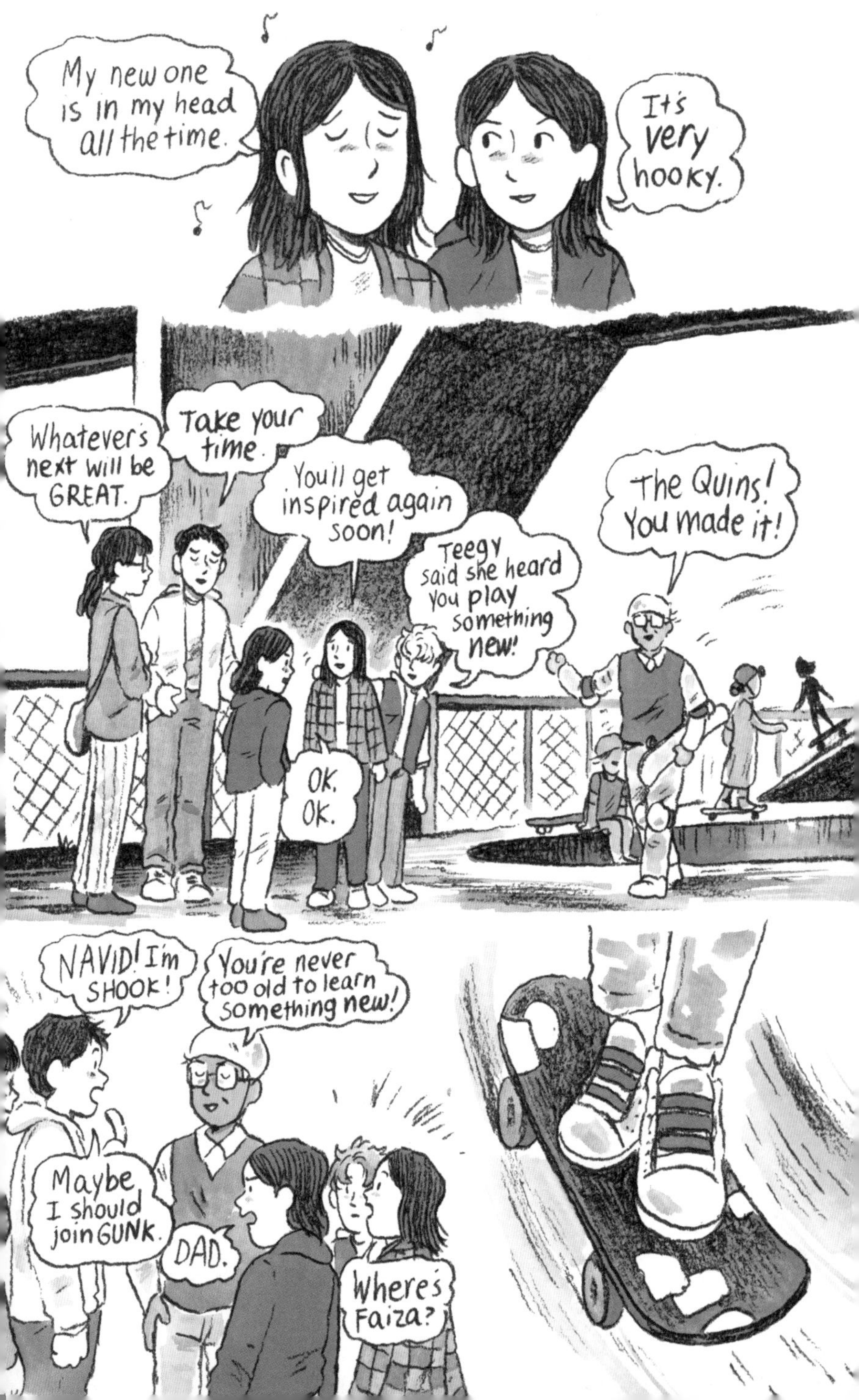
My new one is in my head all the time.
It's very hooky.
Whatever's next will be GREAT.
Take your time.
You'll get inspired again soon!
Teegy said she heard you play something new!
The Quins! You made it!
OK. OK.
NAVID! I'm SHOOK!
You're never too old to learn something new!
Maybe I should join GUNK.
DAD.
Where's Faiza?

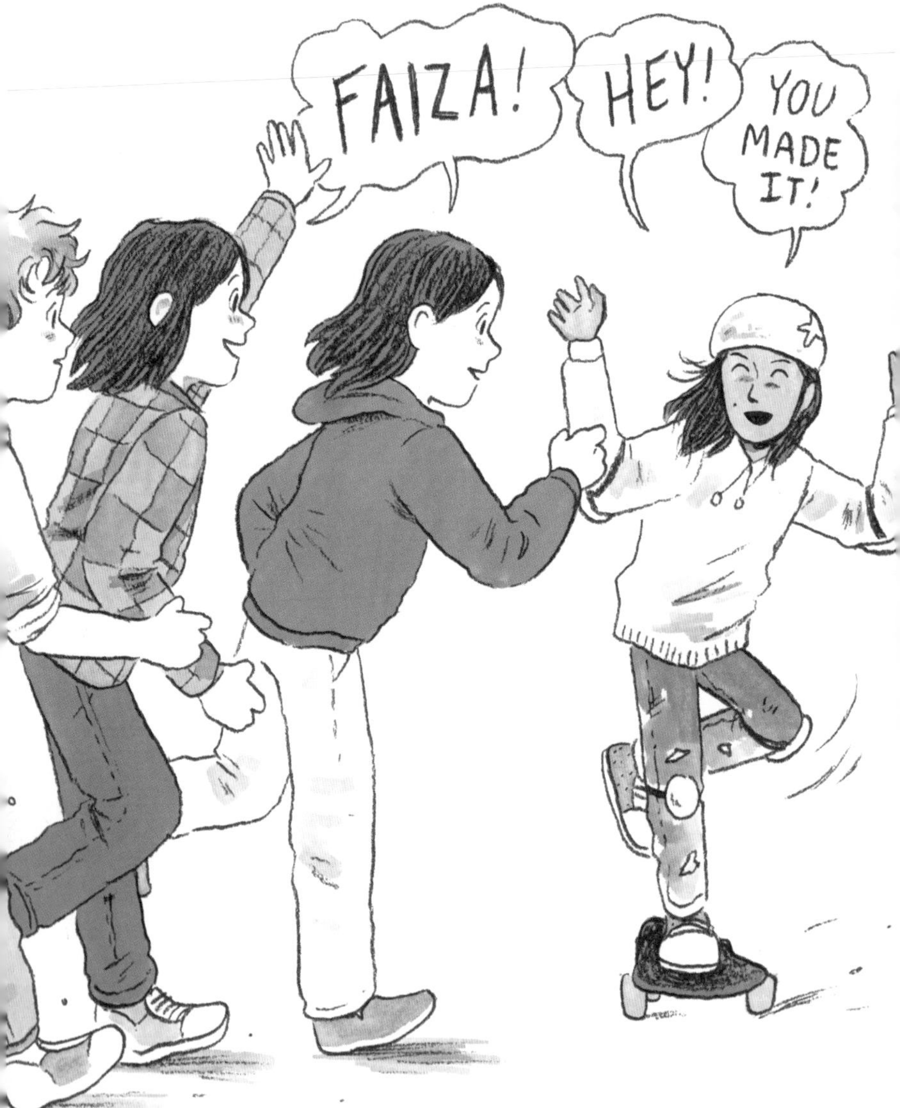
FAIZA!
HEY!
YOU MADE IT!

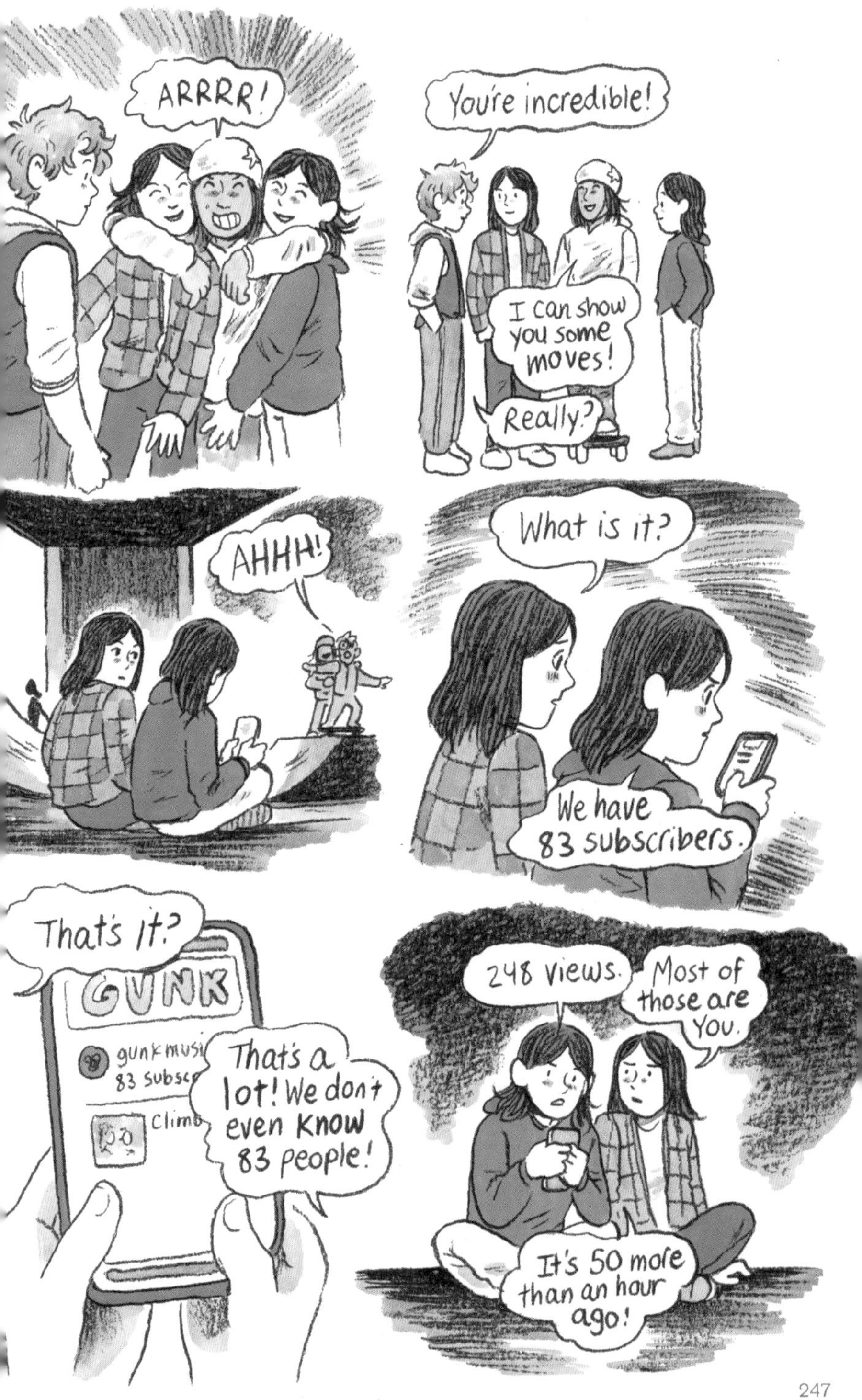

ARRRR!
You're incredible!
I can show you some moves!
Really?
AHHH!
What is it?
We have 83 subscribers.
That's it?
GUNK
gunkmusi
83 subsc
Climb
That's a lot! We don't even know 83 people!
248 views.
Most of those are you.
It's 50 more than an hour ago!

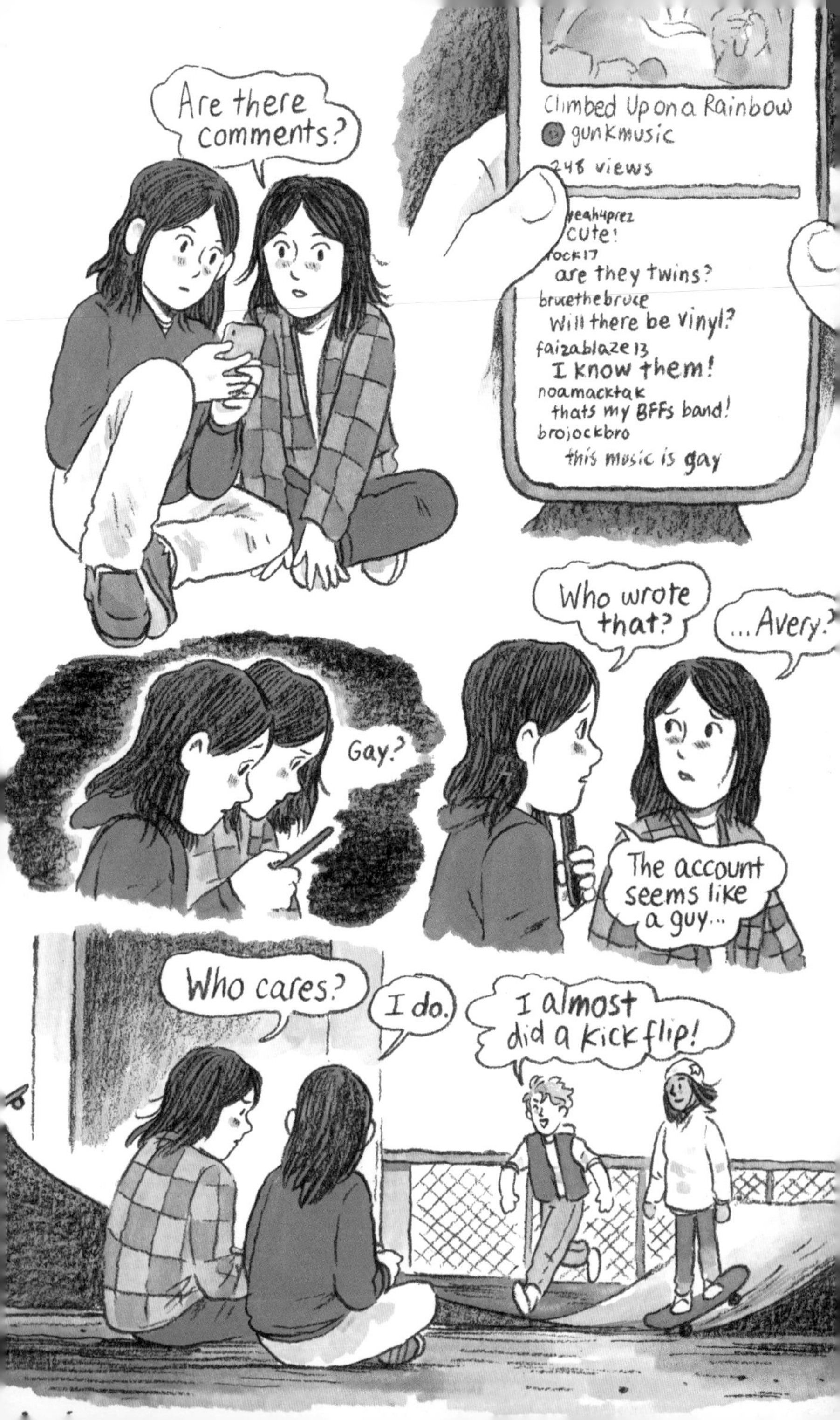
Are there comments?
Climbed Up on a Rainbow
gunkmusic
248 views
yeahuprez
cute!
are they twins?
brucethebruce
Will there be vinyl?
faizablaze13
I know them!
noamacktak
thats my BFFs band!
brojockbro
this music is gay
Gay?
Who wrote that?
...Avery?
The account seems like a guy...
Who cares?
I do.
I almost did a kick flip!

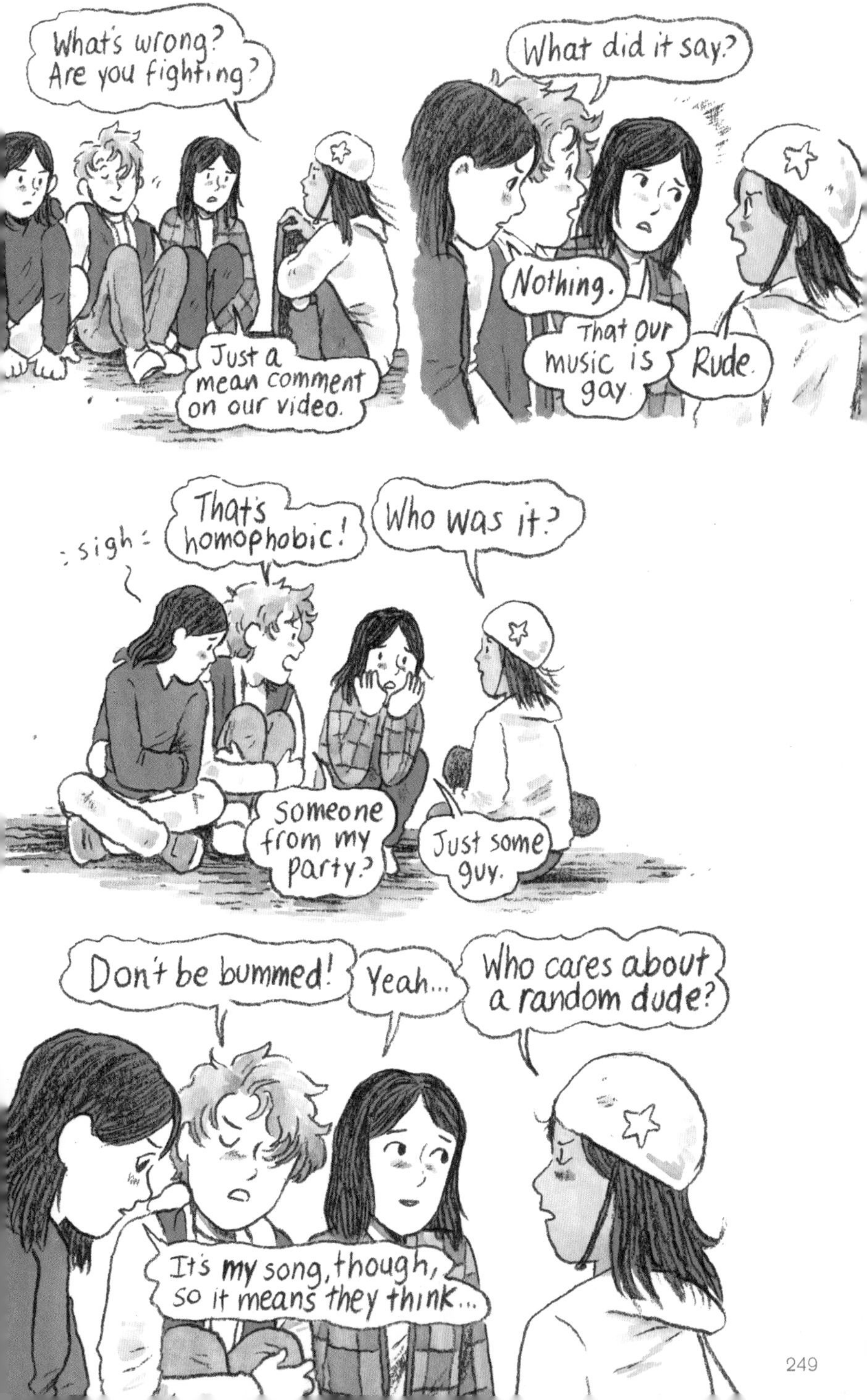
What's wrong? Are you fighting?
Just a mean comment on our video.
What did it say?
Nothing.
That our music is gay.
Rude.
:sigh:
That's homophobic!
Who was it?
Someone from my party?
Just some guy.
Don't be bummed!
Yeah...
Who cares about a random dude?
It's my song, though, so it means they think...

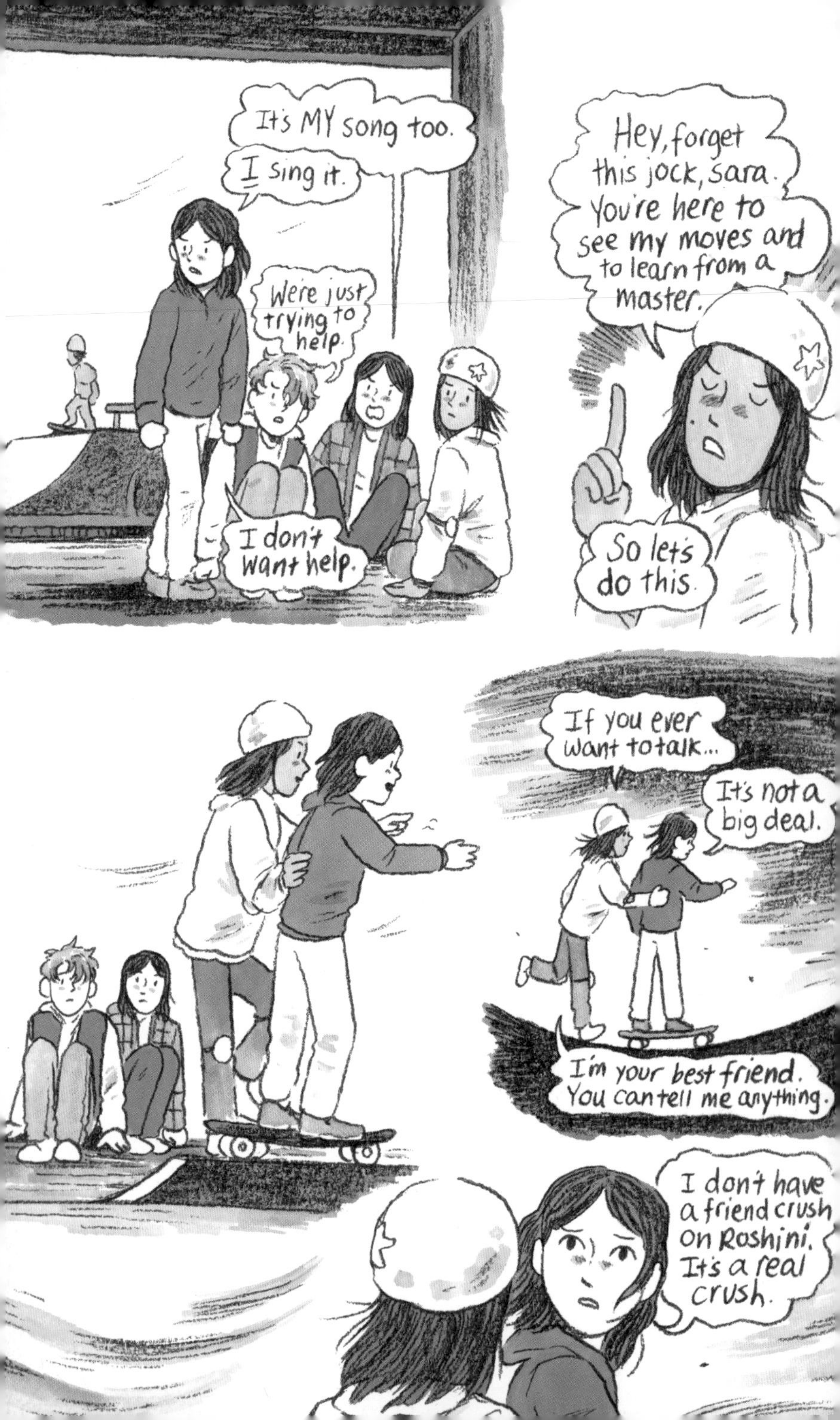
It's MY song too.
I sing it.
We're just trying to help.
I don't want help.
Hey, forget this jock, Sara. You're here to see my moves and to learn from a master.
So let's do this.
If you ever want to talk...
It's not a big deal.
I'm your best friend. You can tell me anything.
I don't have a friend crush on Roshini. It's a real crush.

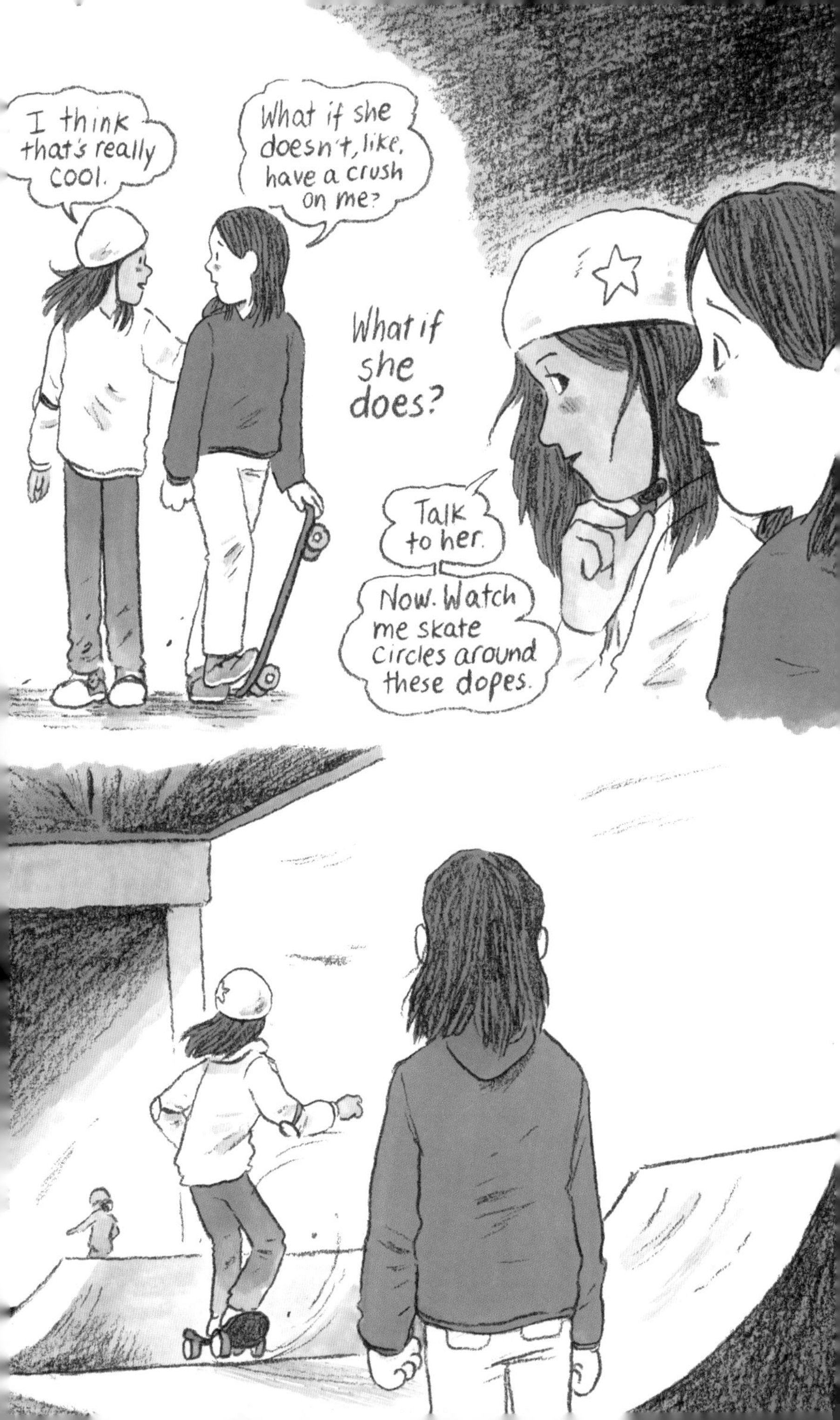
I think that's really cool.
What if she doesn't, like, have a crush on me?
What if she does?
Talk to her.
Now. Watch me skate circles around these dopes.

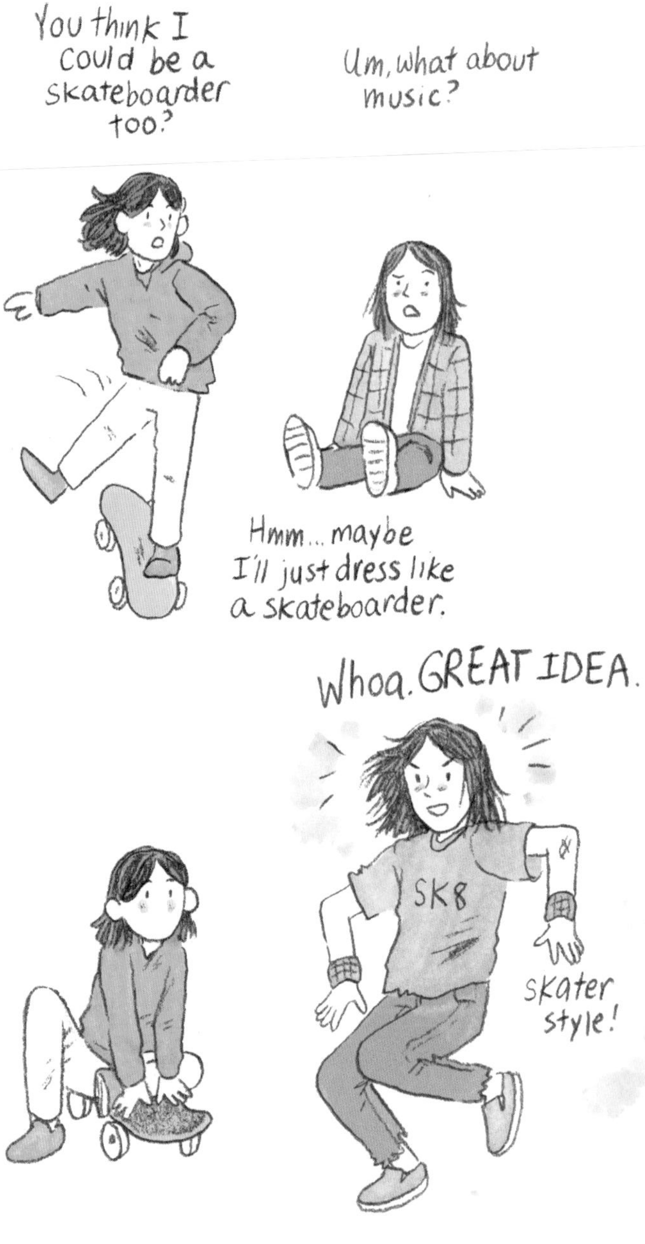
You think I could be a skateboarder too?
Um, what about music?
Hmm... maybe I'll just dress like a skateboarder.
Whoa. GREAT IDEA.
SK8
skater style!

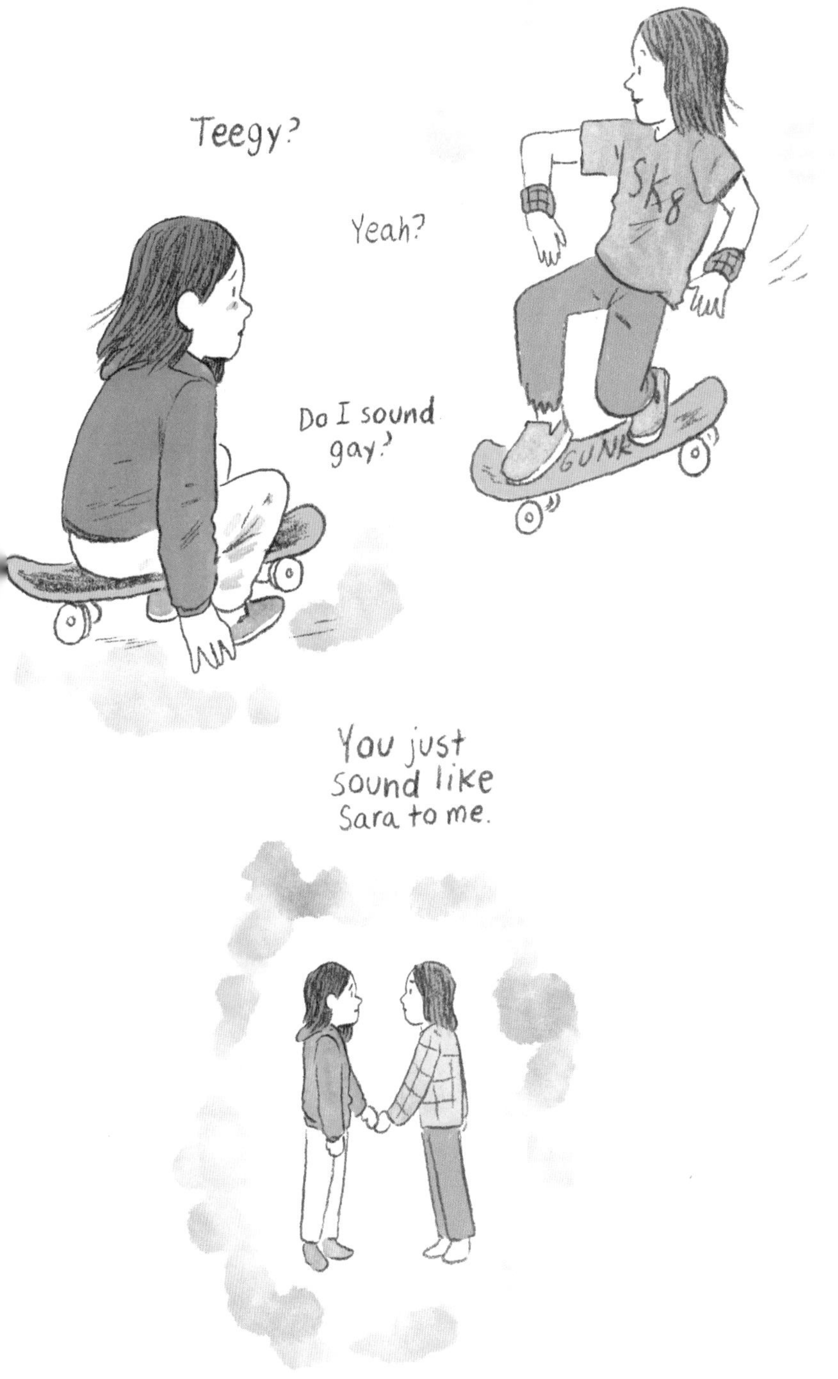
Teegy?
Yeah?
SK8
Do I sound gay?
GUNK
You just sound like Sara to me.

CHAPTER 15
Same

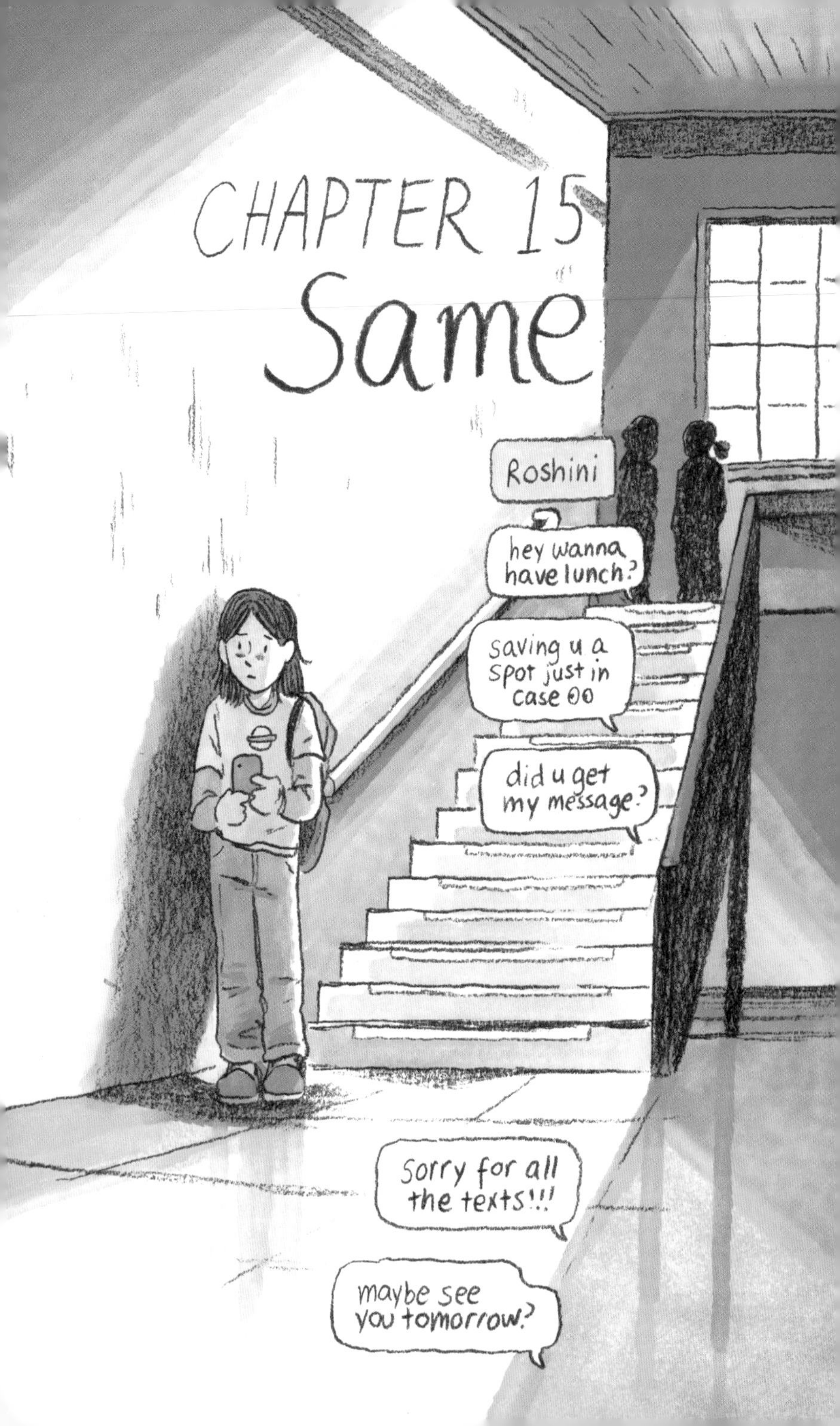
Roshini
hey wanna have lunch?
saving u a spot just in case ⊙⊙
did u get my message?
Sorry for all the texts!!!
maybe see you tomorrow?

Everyone around me
seems to know who
they are.

I still get overwhelmed
ordering at restaurants
or picking out outfits.

Why would Roshini like
someone like me?

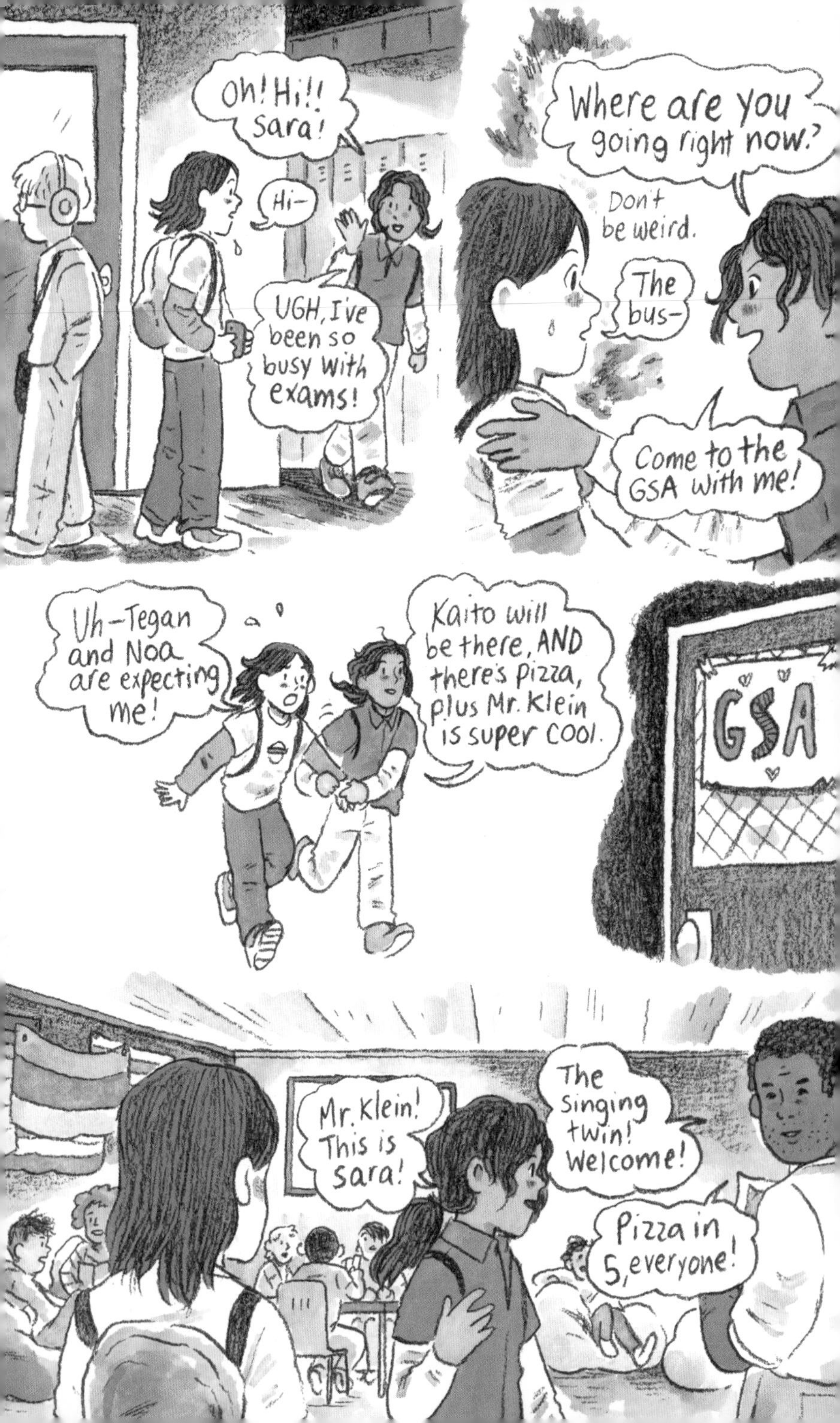
Oh! Hi!! Sara!
Hi-
UGH, I've been so busy with exams!
Where are you going right now?
Don't be weird.
The bus-
Come to the GSA with me!
Uh-Tegan and Noa are expecting me!
Kaito will be there, AND there's pizza, plus Mr. Klein is super cool.
GSA
Mr. Klein! This is Sara!
The singing twin! Welcome!
Pizza in 5, everyone!

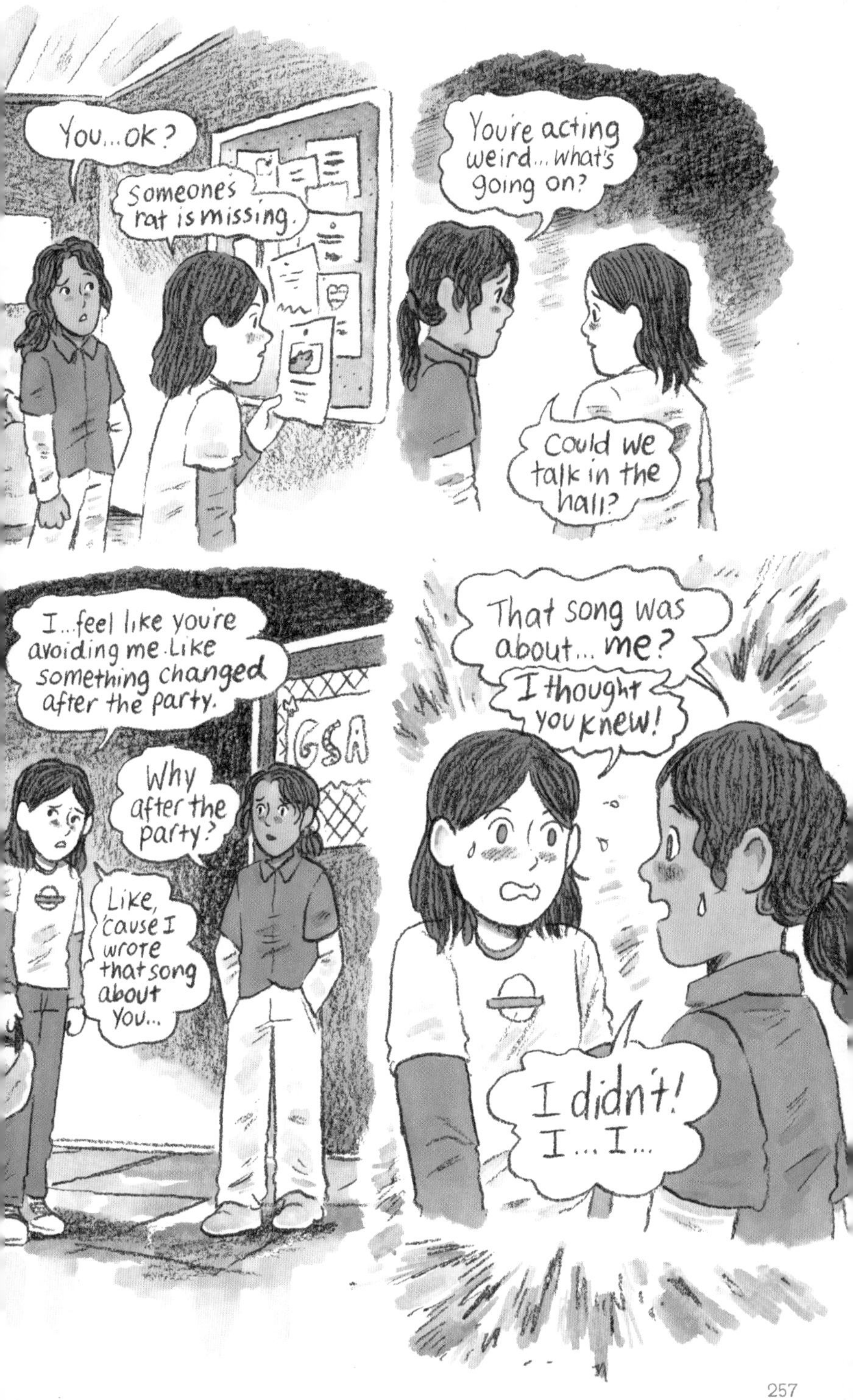
You...ok?
Someone's rat is missing.
You're acting weird... what's going on?
Could we talk in the hall?
I...feel like you're avoiding me. Like something changed after the party.
GSA
Why after the party?
Like, 'cause I wrote that song about you...
That song was about... me?
I thought you knew!
I didn't! I... I...

That just makes me love it even more!
I... I don't want you to think I'm weird for feeling that way about you.

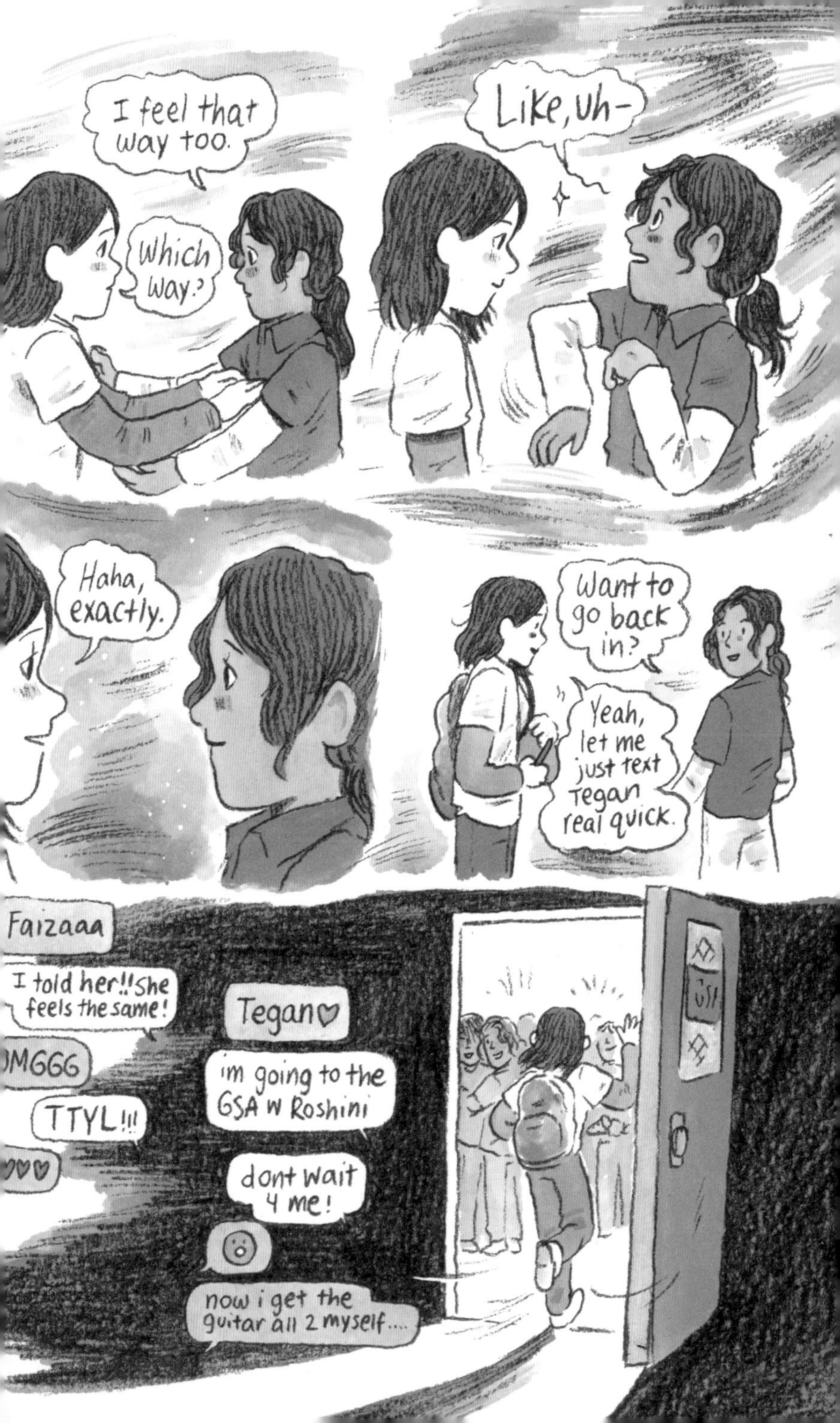
I feel that way too.
Which way?
Like, uh-
Haha, exactly.
Want to go back in?
Yeah, let me just text Tegan real quick.
Faizaaa
I told her!! She feels the same!
OMGGG
TTYL!!!
Tegan♡
im going to the GSA w Roshini
dont wait 4 me!
now i get the guitar all 2 myself....

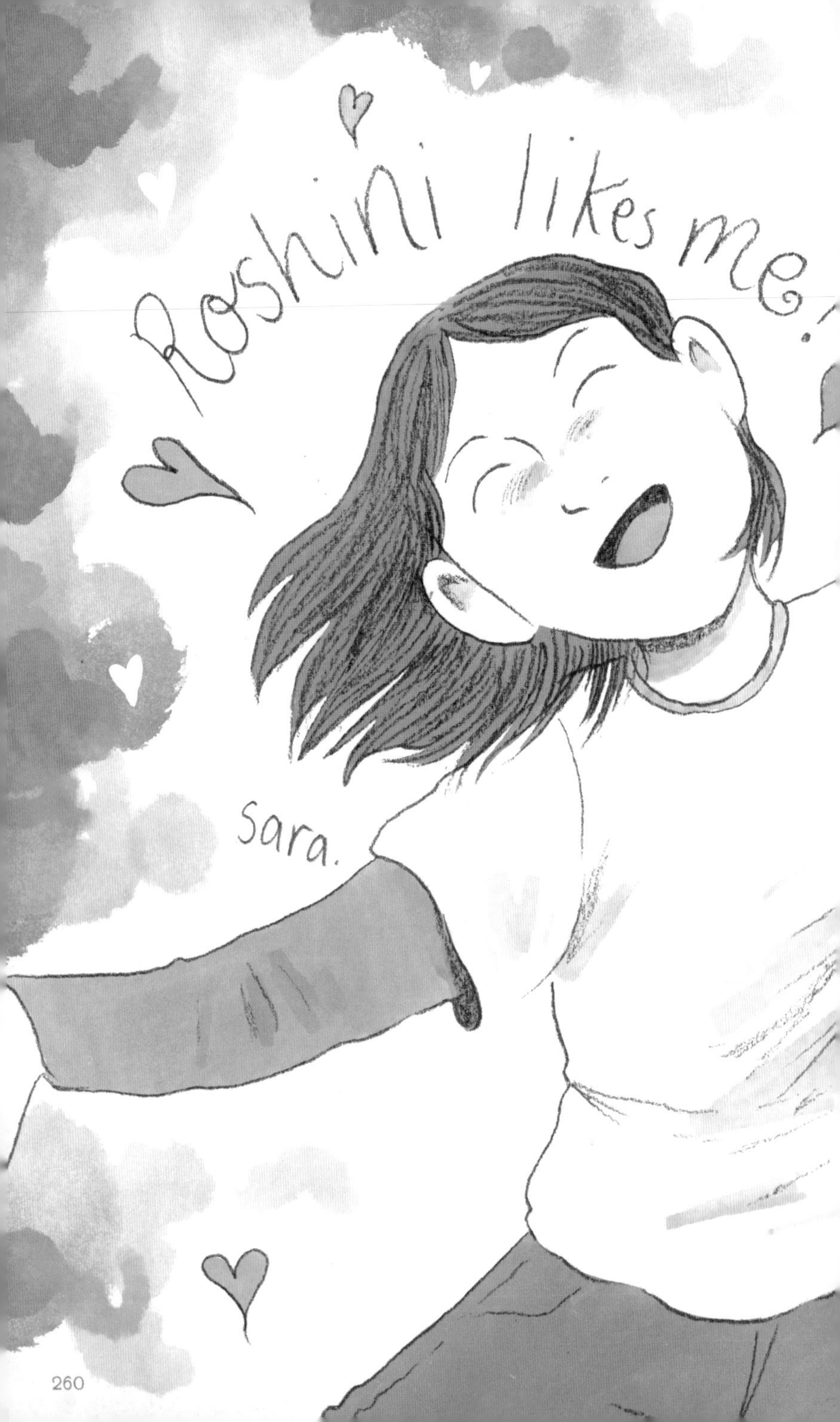
Roshini likes me.!
Sara.

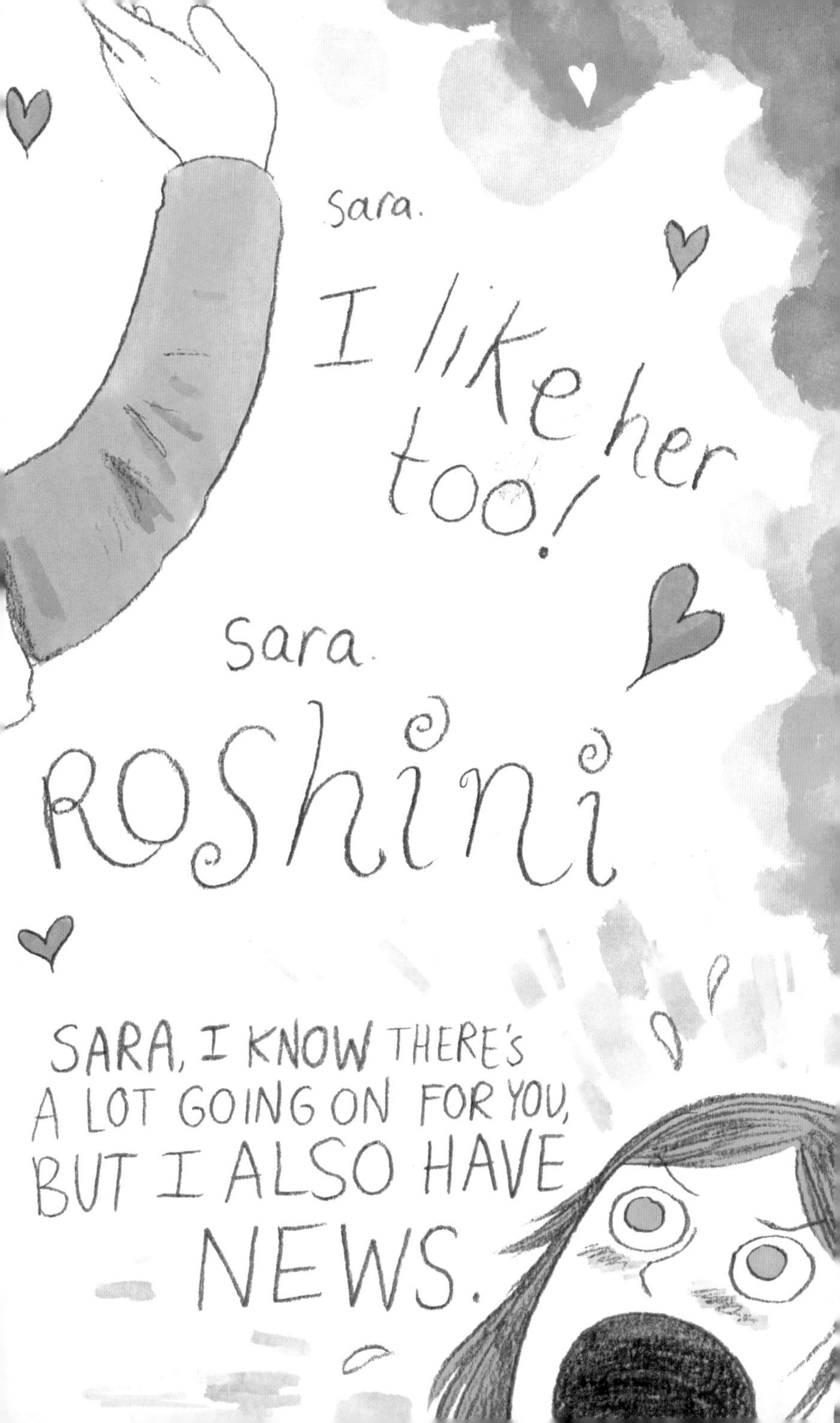

Sara.
I like her too!
Sara.
ROSHINI
SARA, I KNOW THERE'S A LOT GOING ON FOR YOU, BUT I ALSO HAVE NEWS.

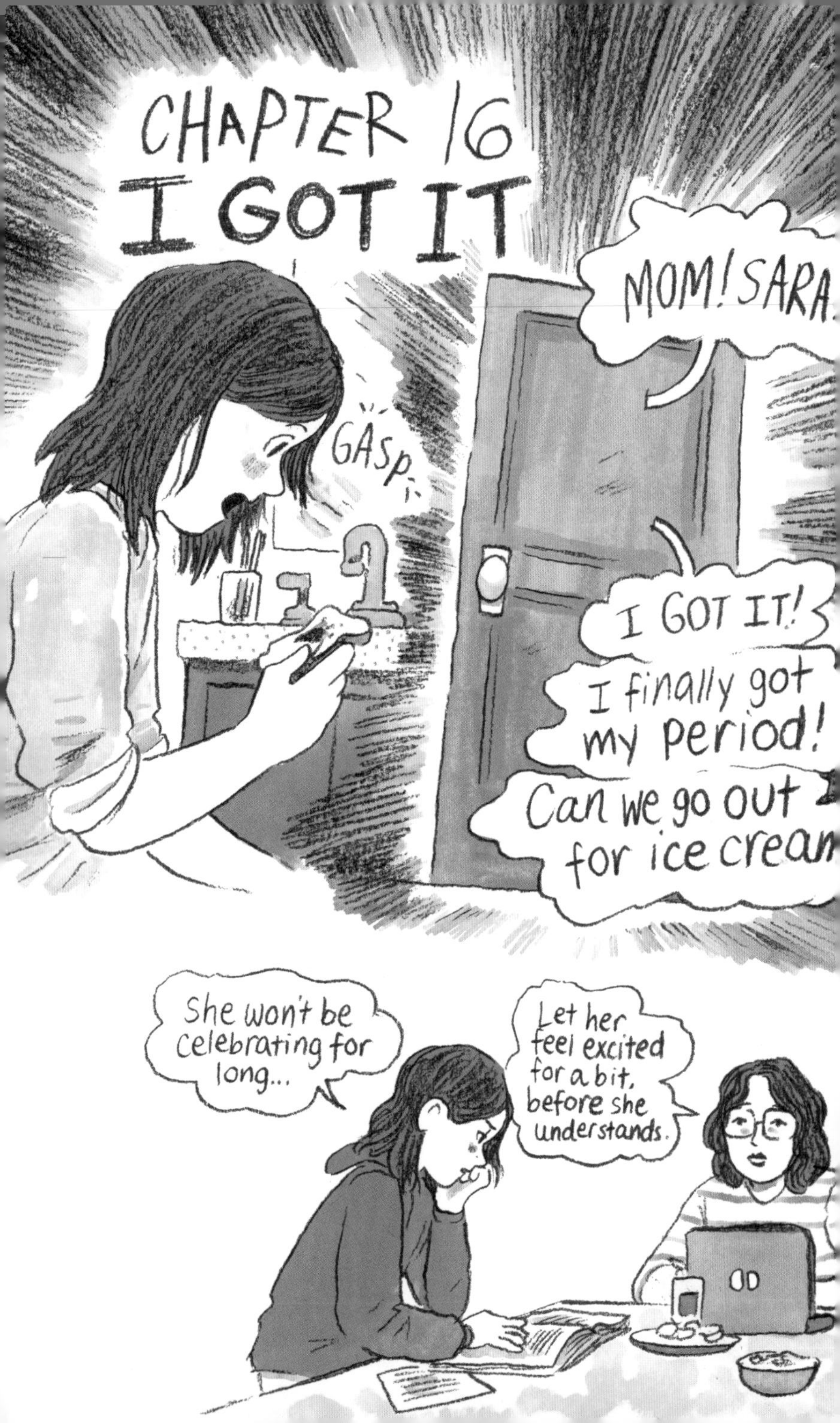
CHAPTER 16
I GOT IT
GASP
MOM! SARA
I GOT IT!
I finally got my period!
Can we go out for ice crean
She won't be celebrating for long...
Let her feel excited for a bit, before she understands.

I GOT IT!
FINALLY!

I felt so behind and
YOUNG.

Why does it have to happen
at different times for everyone?

If it was up to me, we'd
all get it together and take
the day off from school
and get ice cream for FREE
because we deserve it.

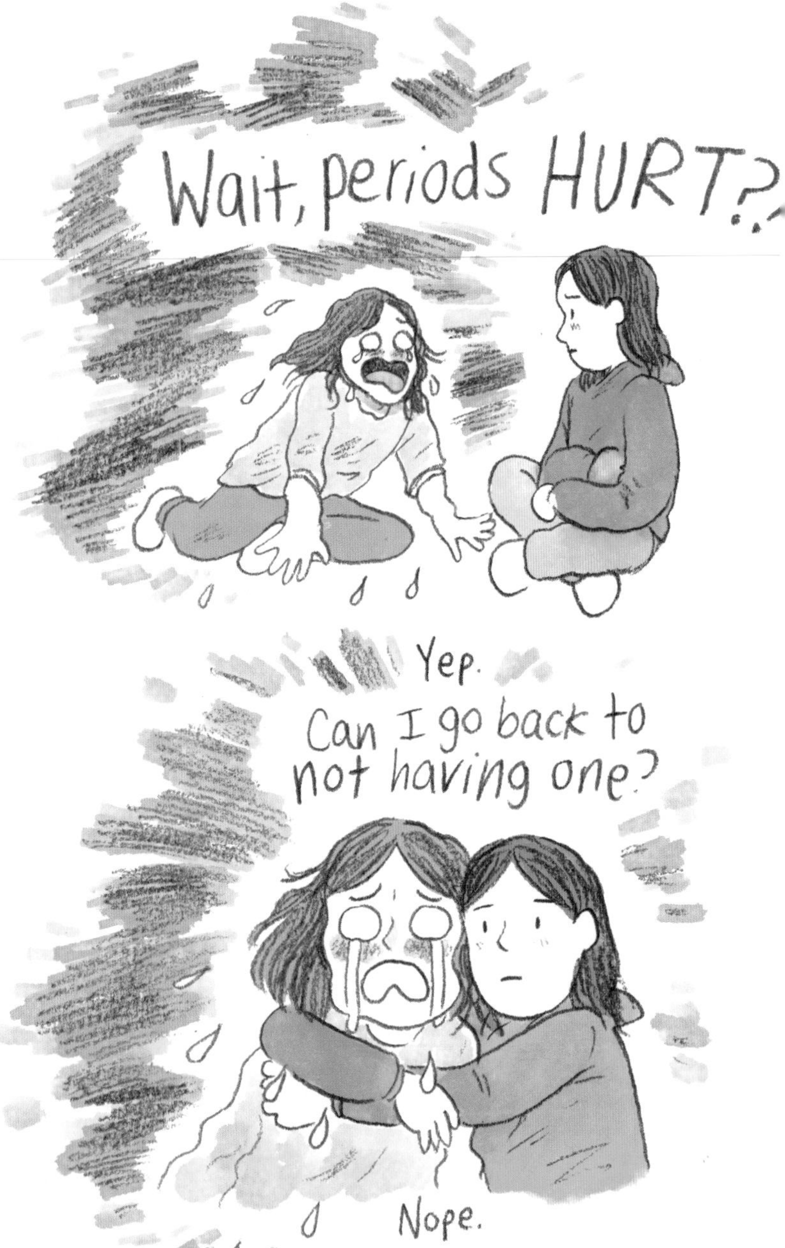

Wait, periods HURT?!
Yep.
Can I go back to not having one?
Nope.

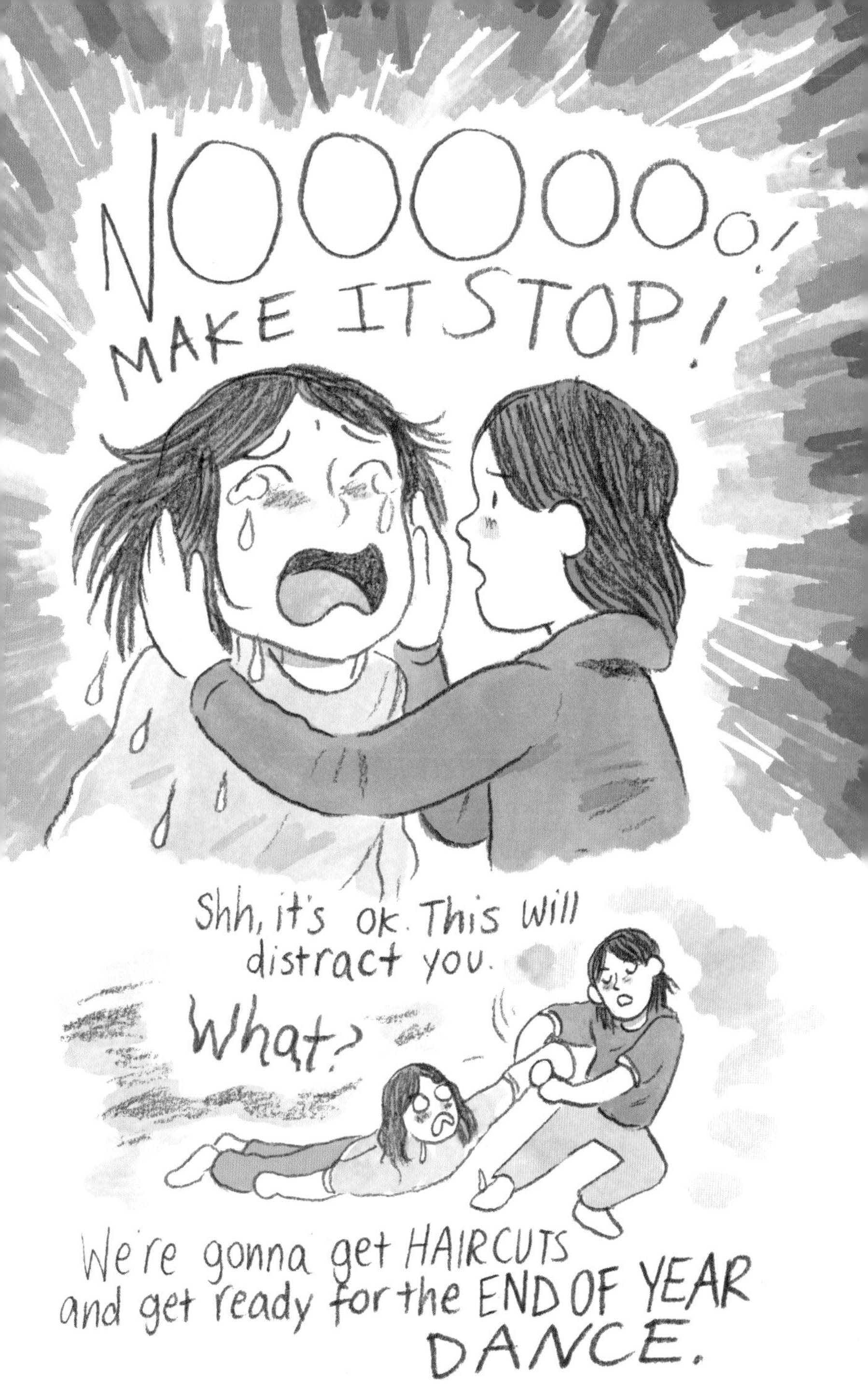
NOOOOOoo!
MAKE IT STOP!
Shh, it's ok. This will distract you.
What?
We're gonna get HAIRCUTS and get ready for the END OF YEAR DANCE.

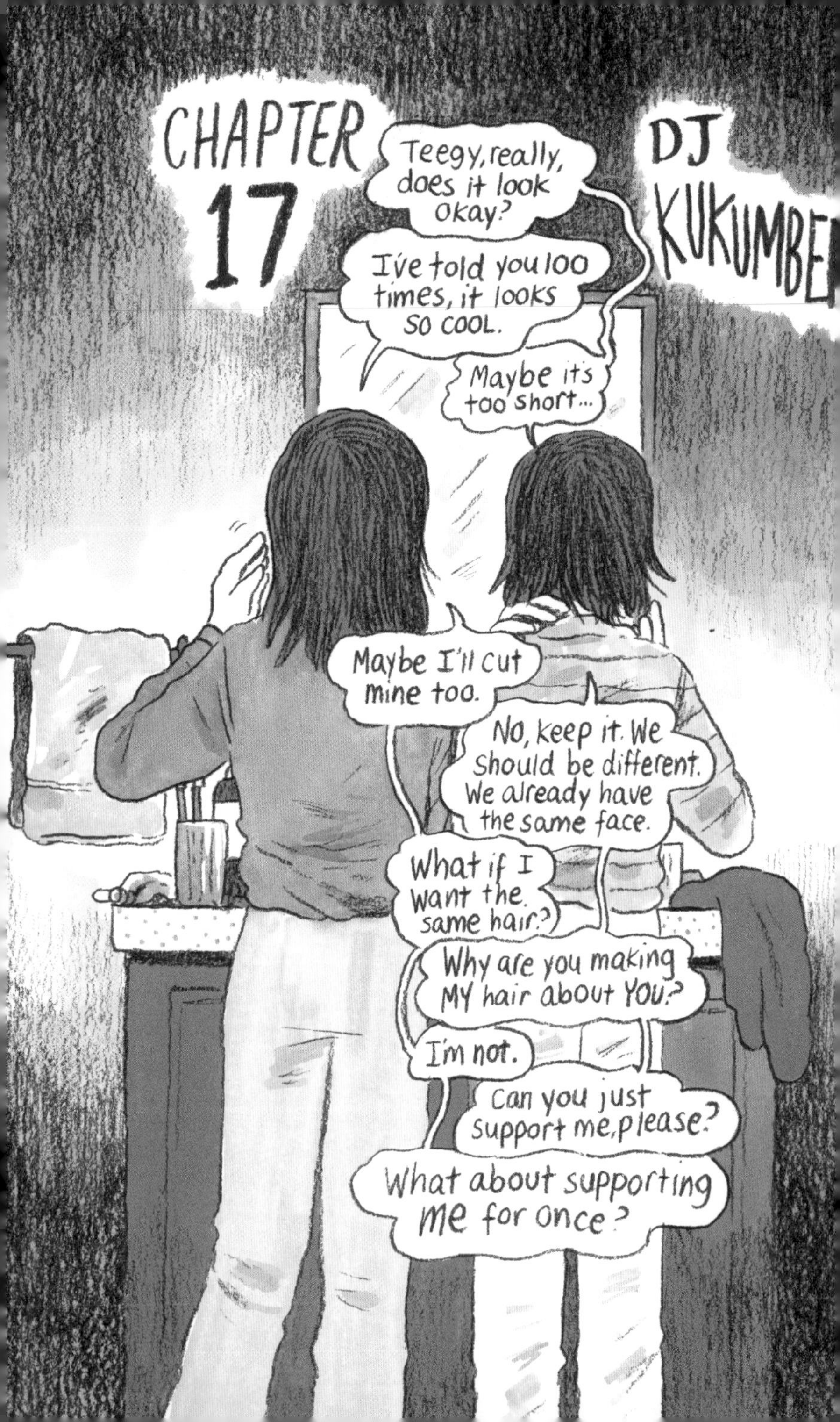
CHAPTER 17
DJ KUKUMBE
Teegy, really, does it look okay?
I've told you 100 times, it looks so cool.
Maybe it's too short...
Maybe I'll cut mine too.
No, keep it. We should be different. We already have the same face.
What if I want the same hair?
Why are you making MY hair about YOU?
I'm not.
Can you just support me, please?
What about supporting me for once?

I AM SHORT HAIR SARA!

Yes, yes, we know.

Tonight will be fun, right?

Yeah... I don't know.

I'm kind of nervous. Everyone
will be there, it almost feels like...

What?

Like the first day of
school all over again.

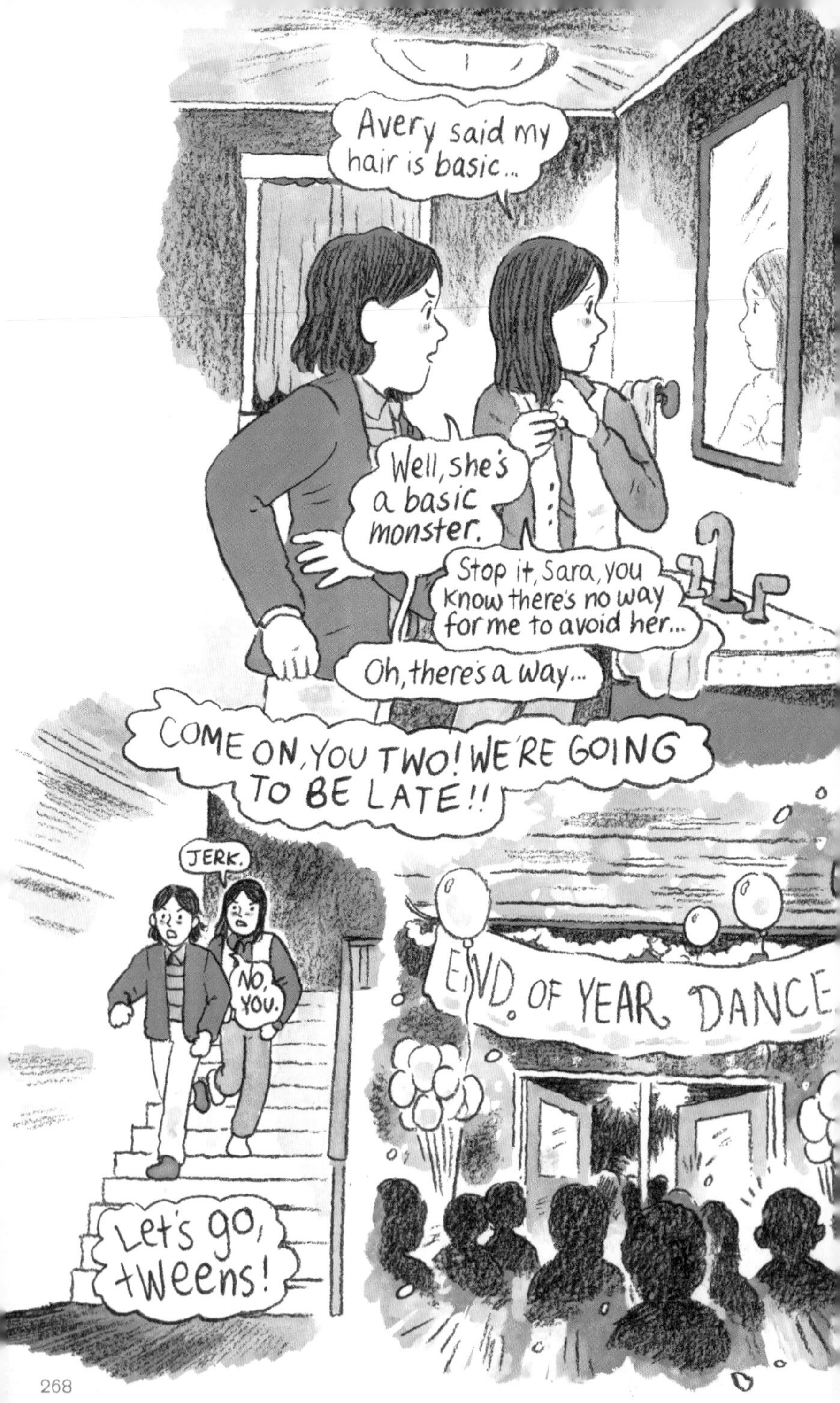
Avery said my hair is basic...
Well, she's a basic monster.
Stop it, Sara, you know there's no way for me to avoid her...
Oh, there's a way...
COME ON, YOU TWO! WE'RE GOING TO BE LATE!!
JERK.
NO, YOU.
Let's go, tweens!
END OF YEAR DANCE

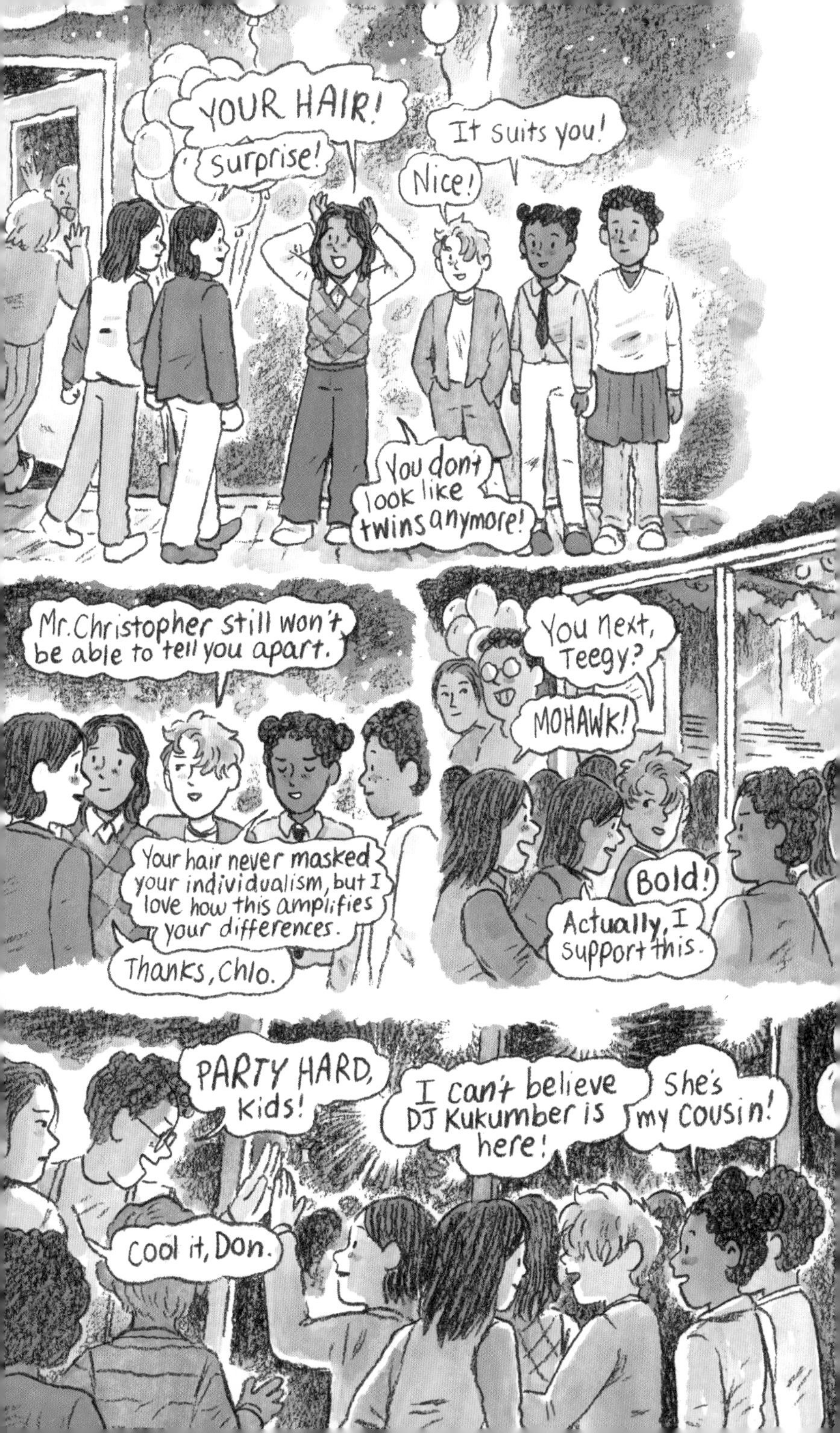
YOUR HAIR!
Surprise!
It suits you!
Nice!
You don't look like twins anymore!
Mr. Christopher still won't be able to tell you apart.
Your hair never masked your individualism, but I love how this amplifies your differences.
Thanks, Chlo.
You next, Teegy?
MOHAWK!
Bold!
Actually, I support this.
PARTY HARD, Kids!
I can't believe DJ Kukumber is here!
She's my cousin!
Cool it, Don.

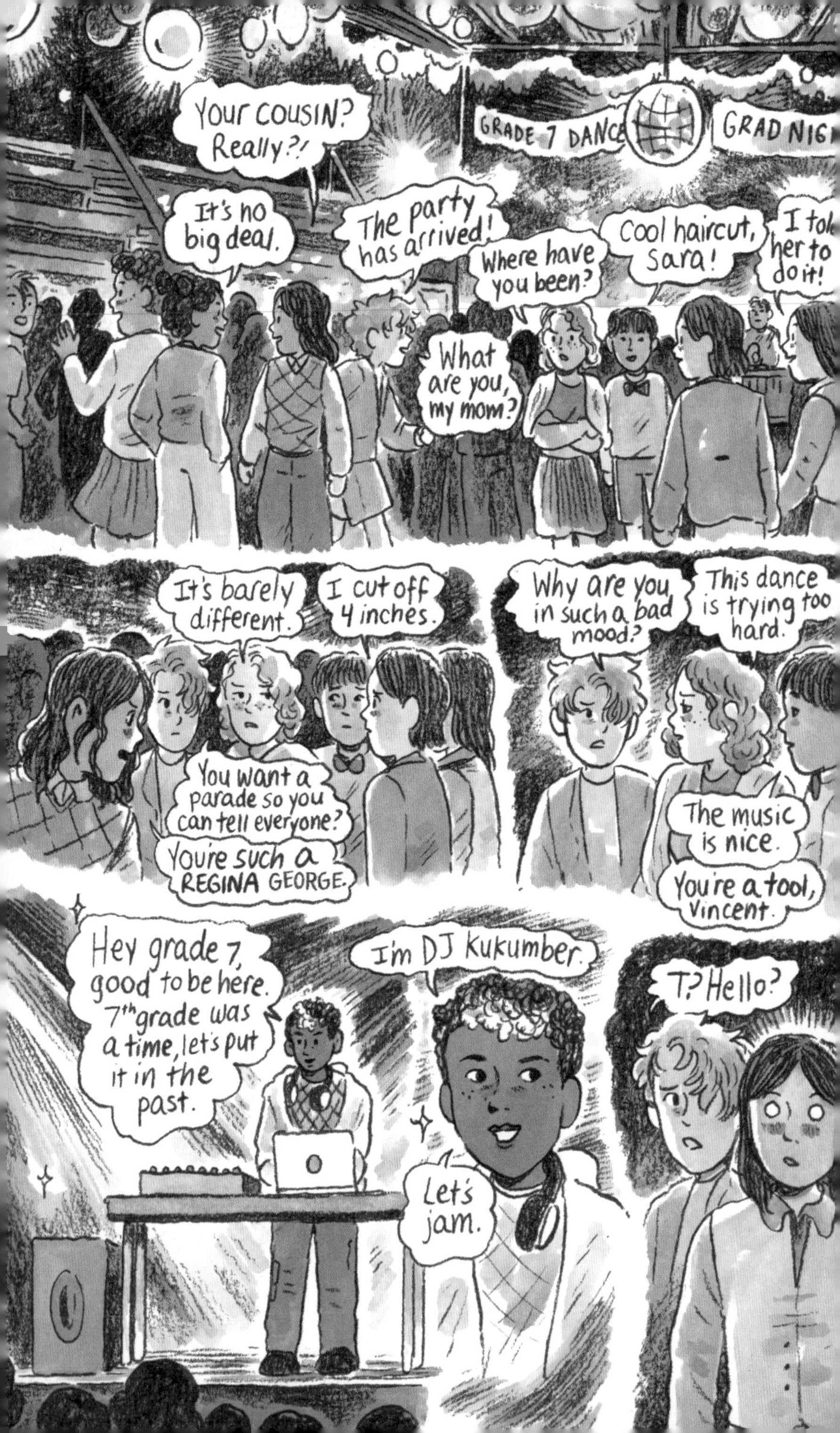
GRADE 7 DANCE
GRAD NIG
Your COUSIN? Really?!
It's no big deal.
The party has arrived!
Where have you been?
What are you, my mom?
Cool haircut, Sara!
I tol her to do it!
It's barely different.
I cut off 4 inches.
You want a parade so you can tell everyone?
You're such a REGINA GEORGE.
Why are you in such a bad mood?
This dance is trying too hard.
The music is nice.
You're a tool, Vincent.
Hey grade 7, good to be here. 7th grade was a time, let's put it in the past.
I'm DJ Kukumber.
Let's jam.
T? Hello?

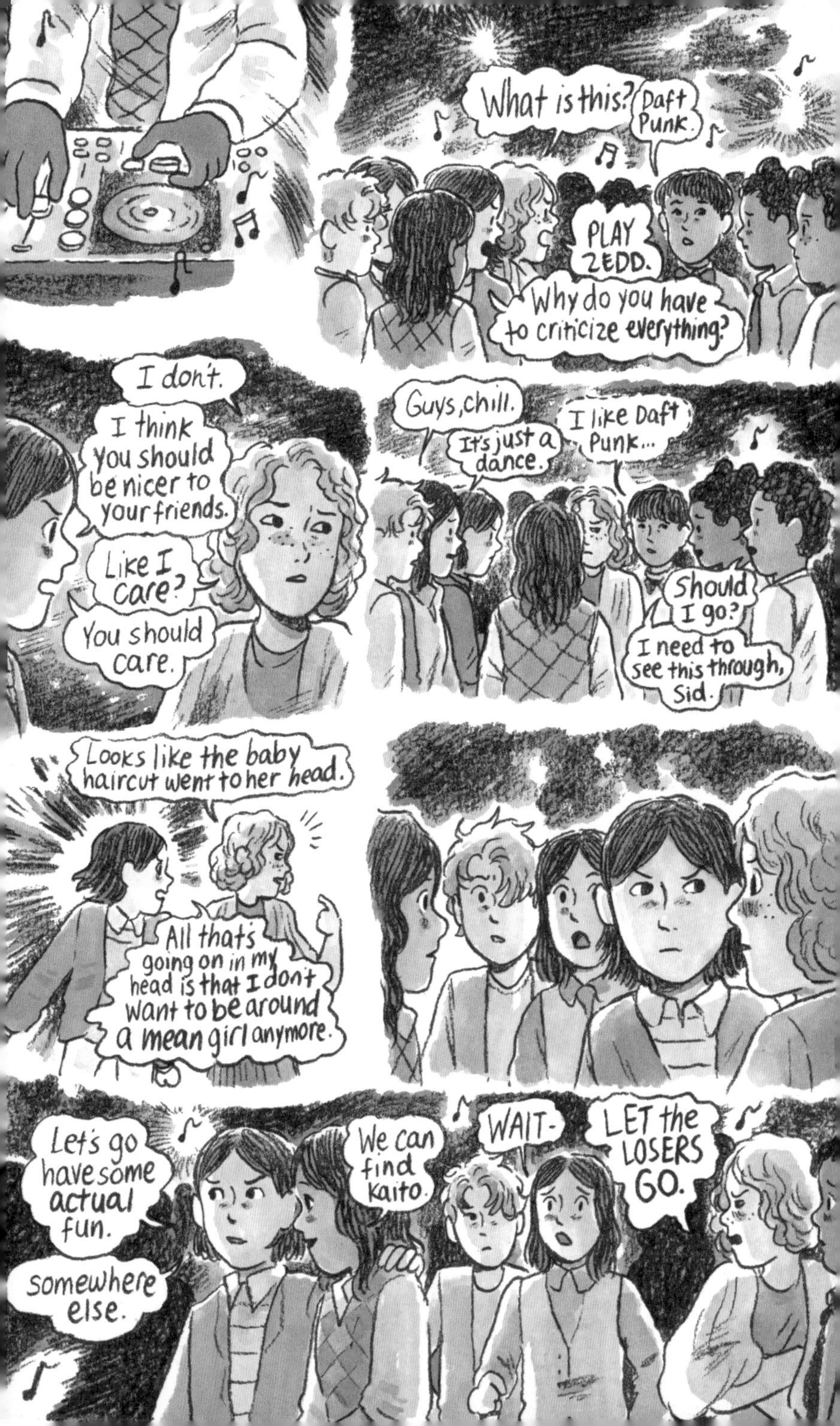
What is this?
Daft Punk.
PLAY ZEDD.
Why do you have to criticize everything?
I don't.
I think you should be nicer to your friends.
Like I care?
You should care.
Guys, chill.
It's just a dance.
I like Daft Punk...
Should I go?
I need to see this through, Sid.
Looks like the baby haircut went to her head.
All that's going on in my head is that I don't want to be around a mean girl anymore.
Let's go have some actual fun.
Somewhere else.
We can find Kaito.
WAIT-
LET the LOSERS GO.

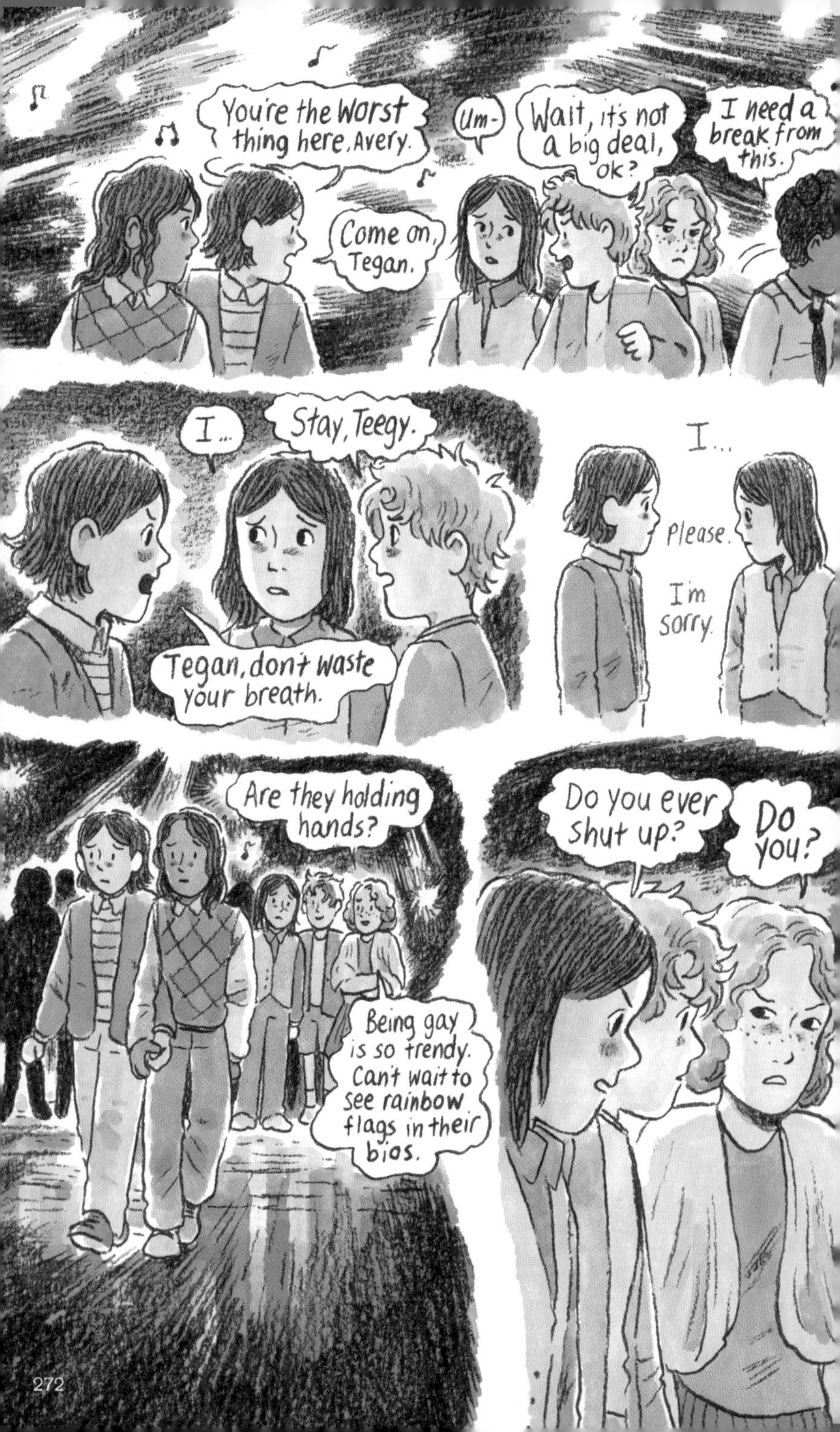
You're the Worst thing here, Avery.
Um-
Wait, it's not a big deal, ok?
I need a break from this.
Come on, Tegan.
I...
Stay, Teegy.
Tegan, don't waste your breath.
I...
Please.
I'm sorry.
Are they holding hands?
Being gay is so trendy. Can't wait to see rainbow flags in their bios.
Do you ever shut up?
Do you?

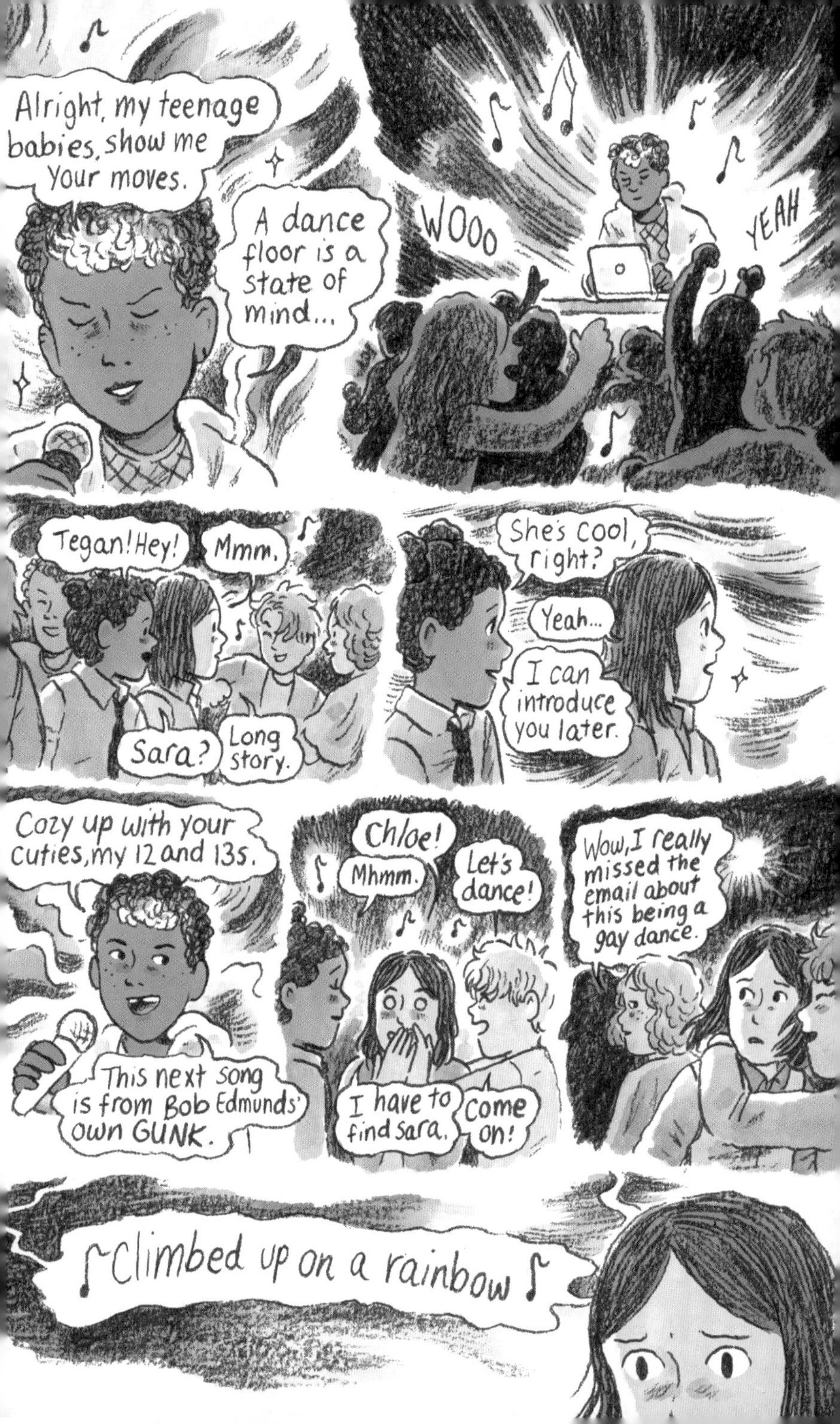
Alright, my teenage babies, show me your moves.
A dance floor is a state of mind...
WOOo
YEAH
Tegan! Hey!
Mmm.
Sara?
Long story.
She's cool, right?
Yeah...
I can introduce you later.
Cozy up with your cuties, my 12 and 13s.
This next song is from Bob Edmunds' own GUNK.
Chloe!
Mhmm.
Let's dance!
I have to find Sara.
Come on!
Wow, I really missed the email about this being a gay dance.
Climbed up on a rainbow

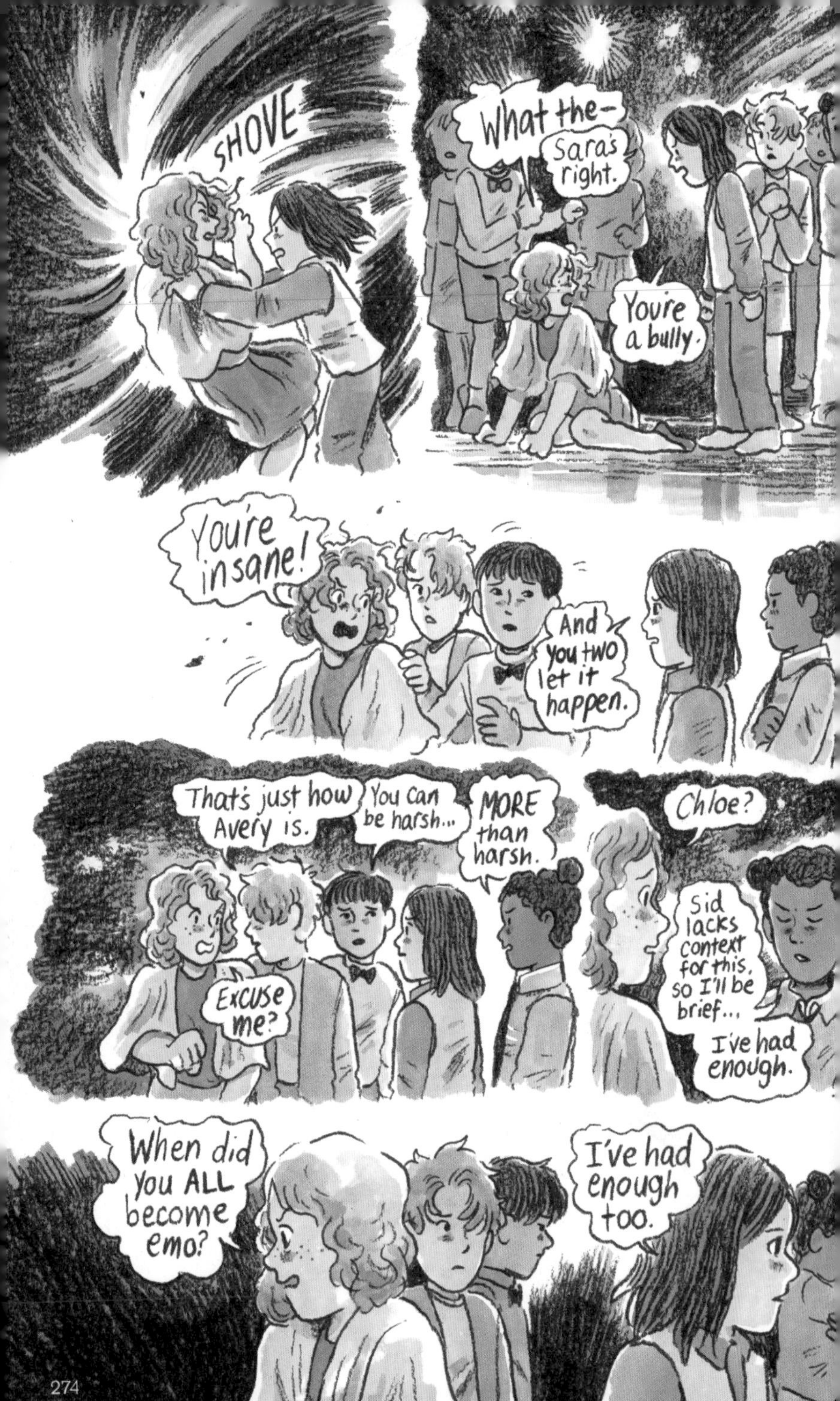
SHOVE
What the-
Sara's right.
You're a bully.
You're insane!
And you two let it happen.
That's just how Avery is.
You can be harsh...
MORE than harsh.
Chloe?
Excuse me?
Sid lacks context for this, so I'll be brief...
I've had enough.
When did you ALL become emo?
I've had enough too.

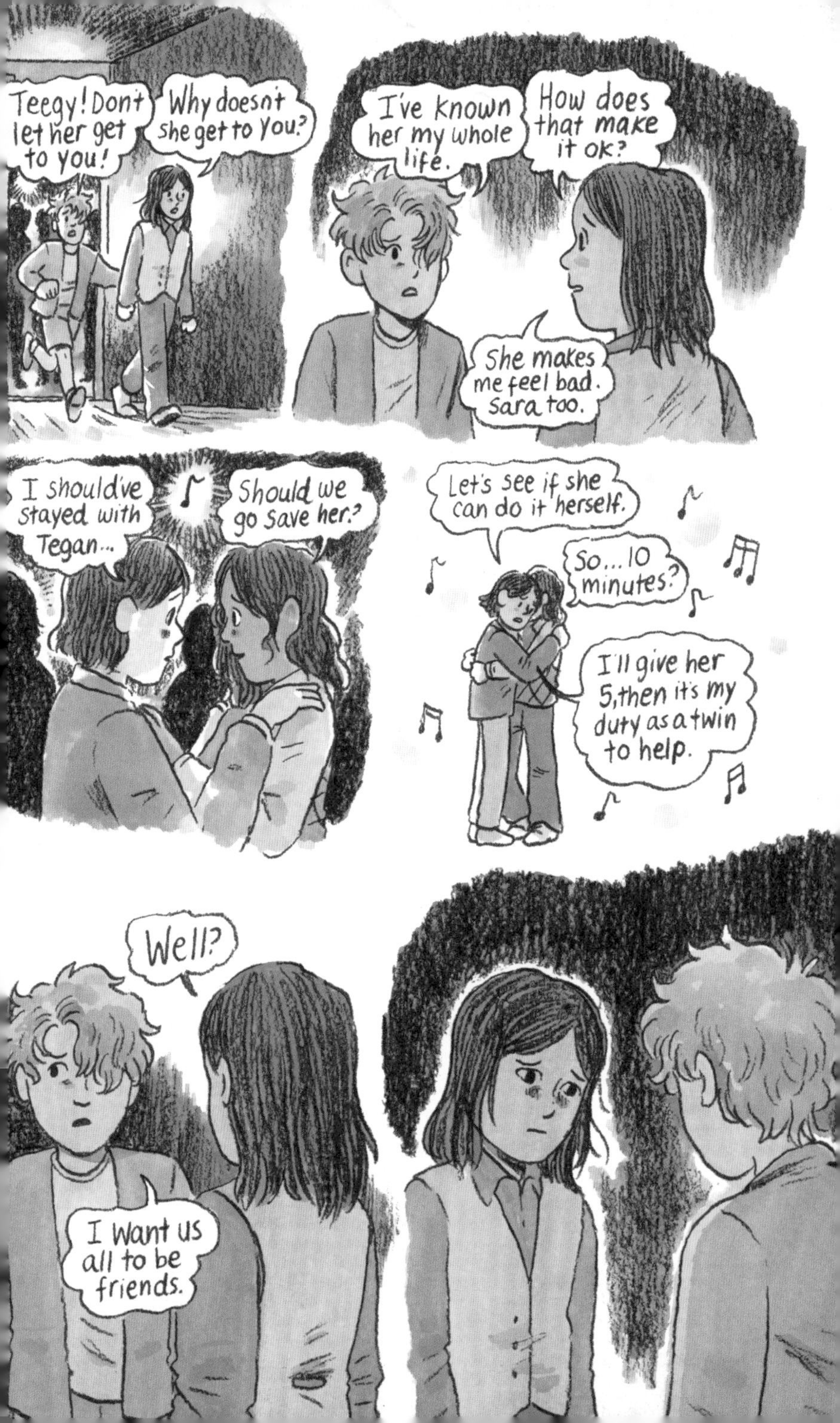
Teegy! Don't let her get to you!
Why doesn't she get to you?
I've known her my whole life.
How does that make it ok?
She makes me feel bad. Sara too.
I should've stayed with Tegan...
Should we go save her?
Let's see if she can do it herself.
So... 10 minutes?
I'll give her 5, then it's my duty as a twin to help.
Well?
I want us all to be friends.

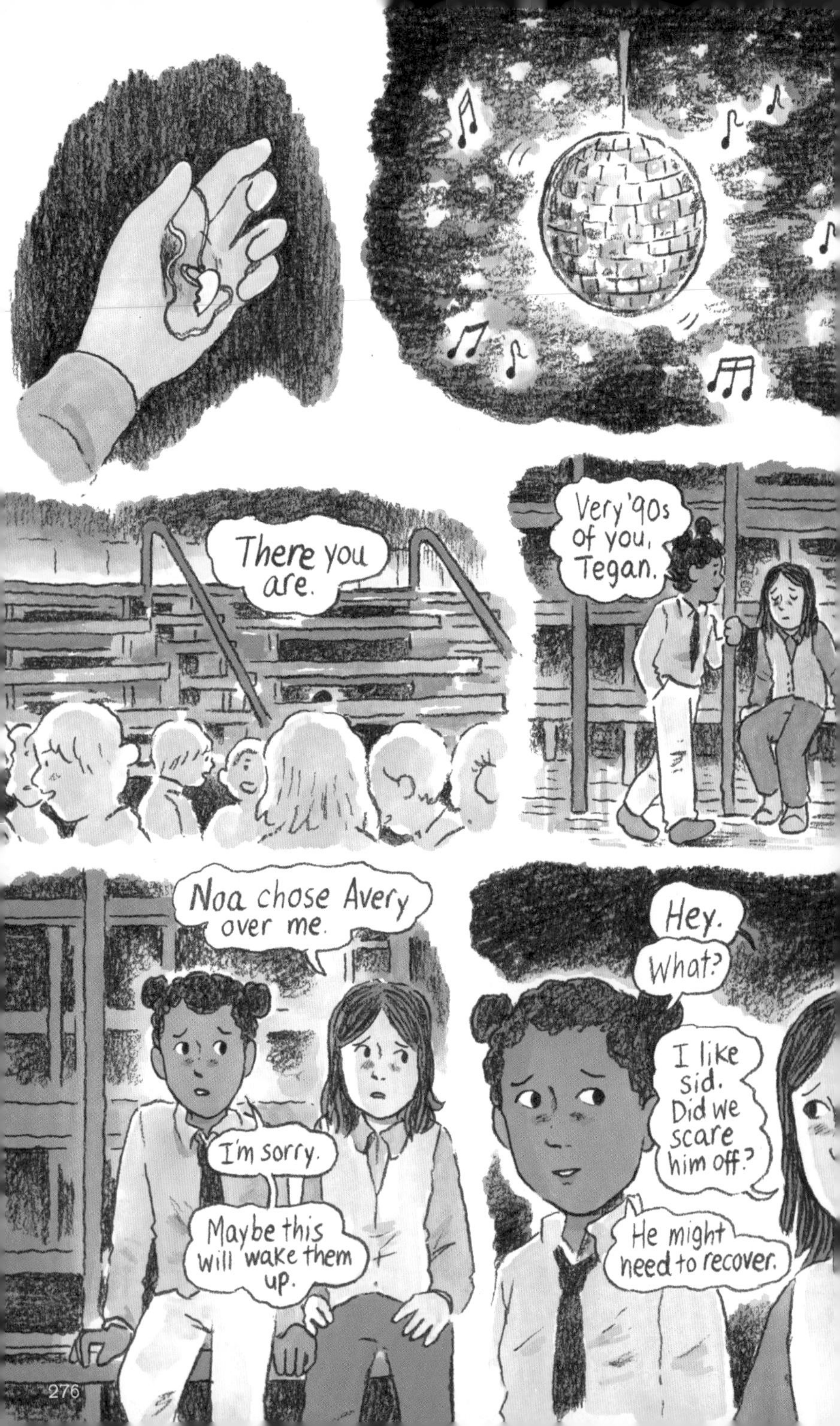
There you are.
Very '90s of you, Tegan.
Noa chose Avery over me.
I'm sorry.
Maybe this will wake them up.
Hey.
What?
I like Sid. Did we scare him off?
He might need to recover.

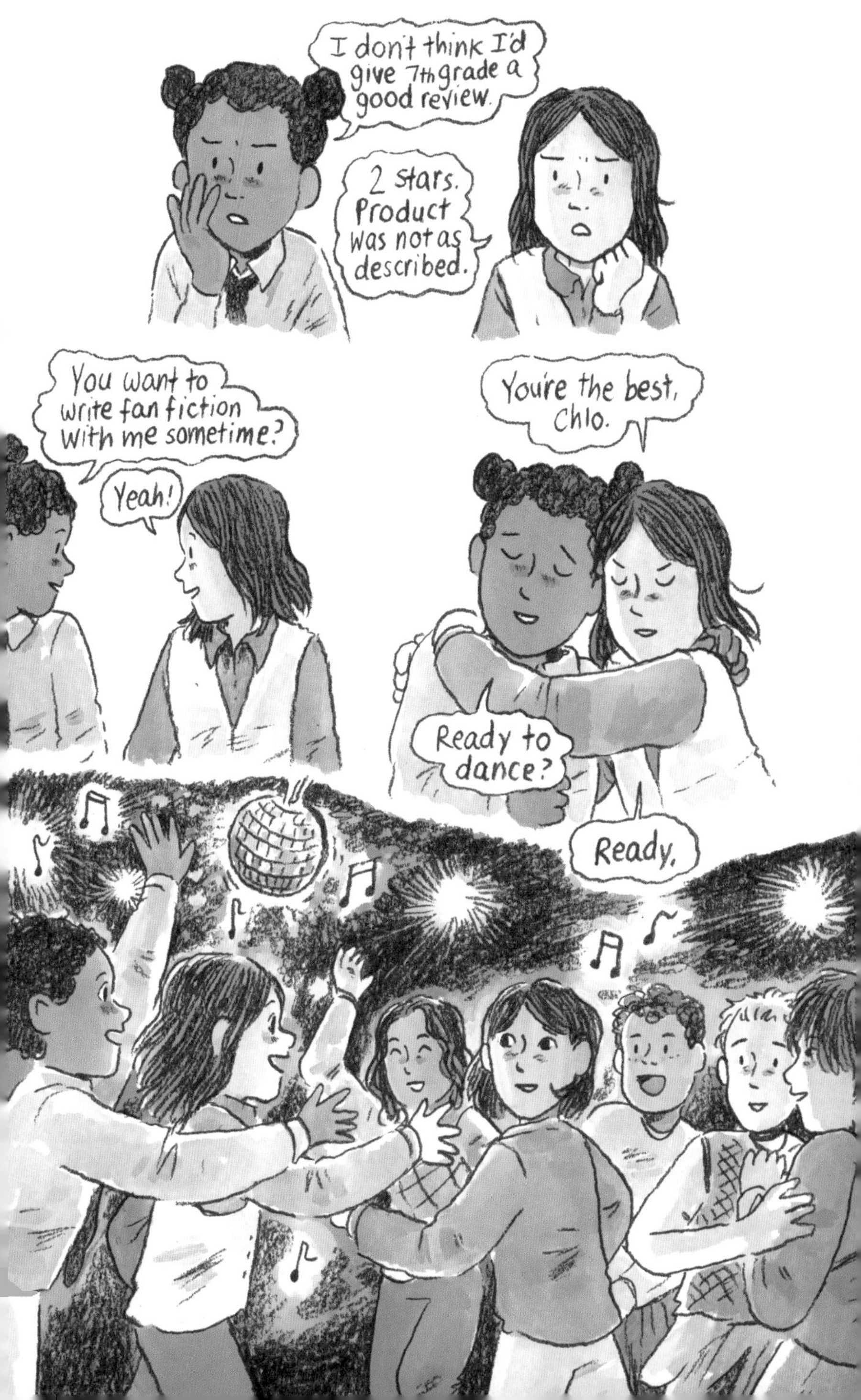
I don't think I'd give 7th grade a good review.
2 stars. Product was not as described.
You want to write fan fiction with me sometime?
Yeah!
You're the best, Chlo.
Ready to dance?
Ready.

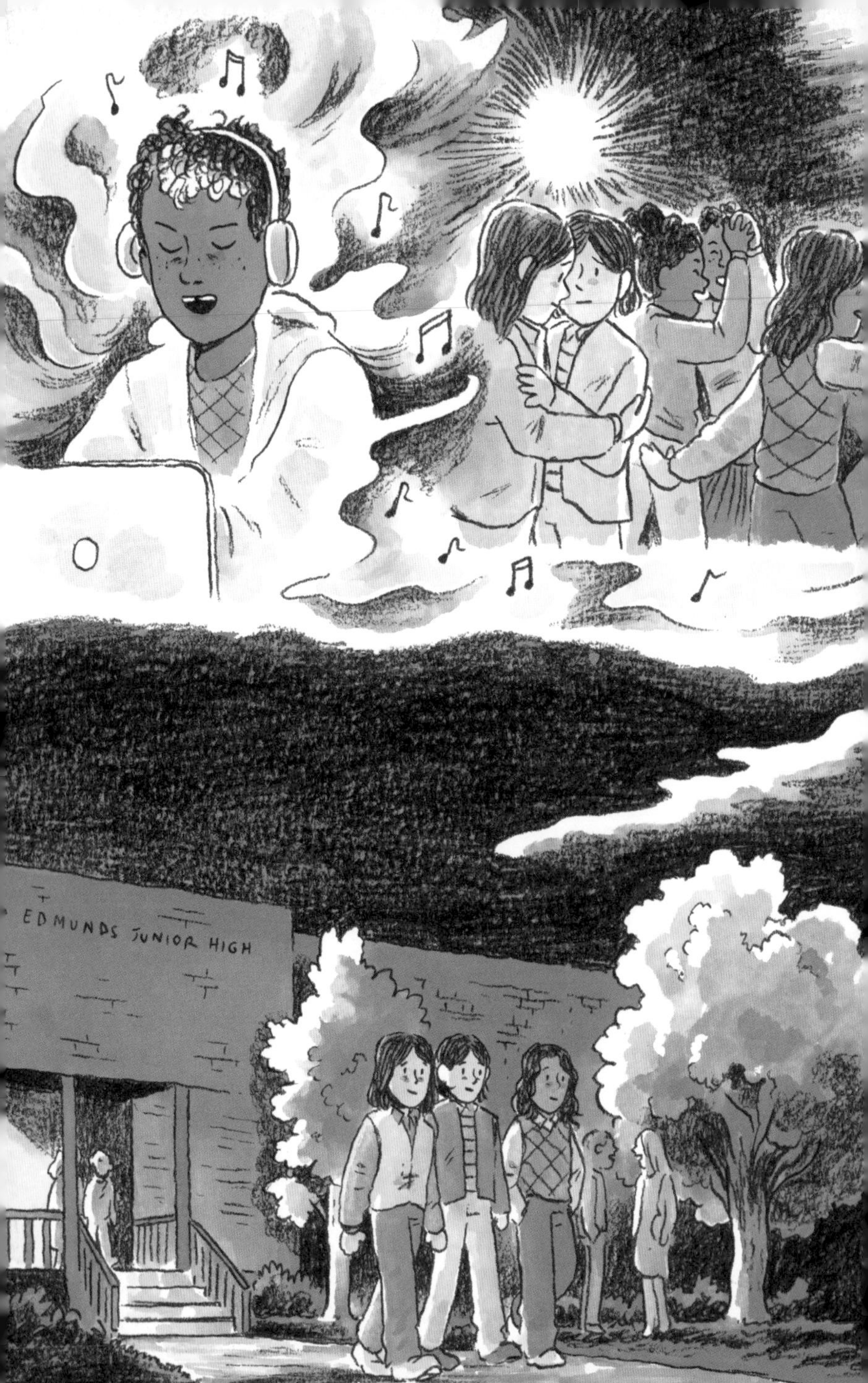
EDMUNDS JUNIOR HIGH

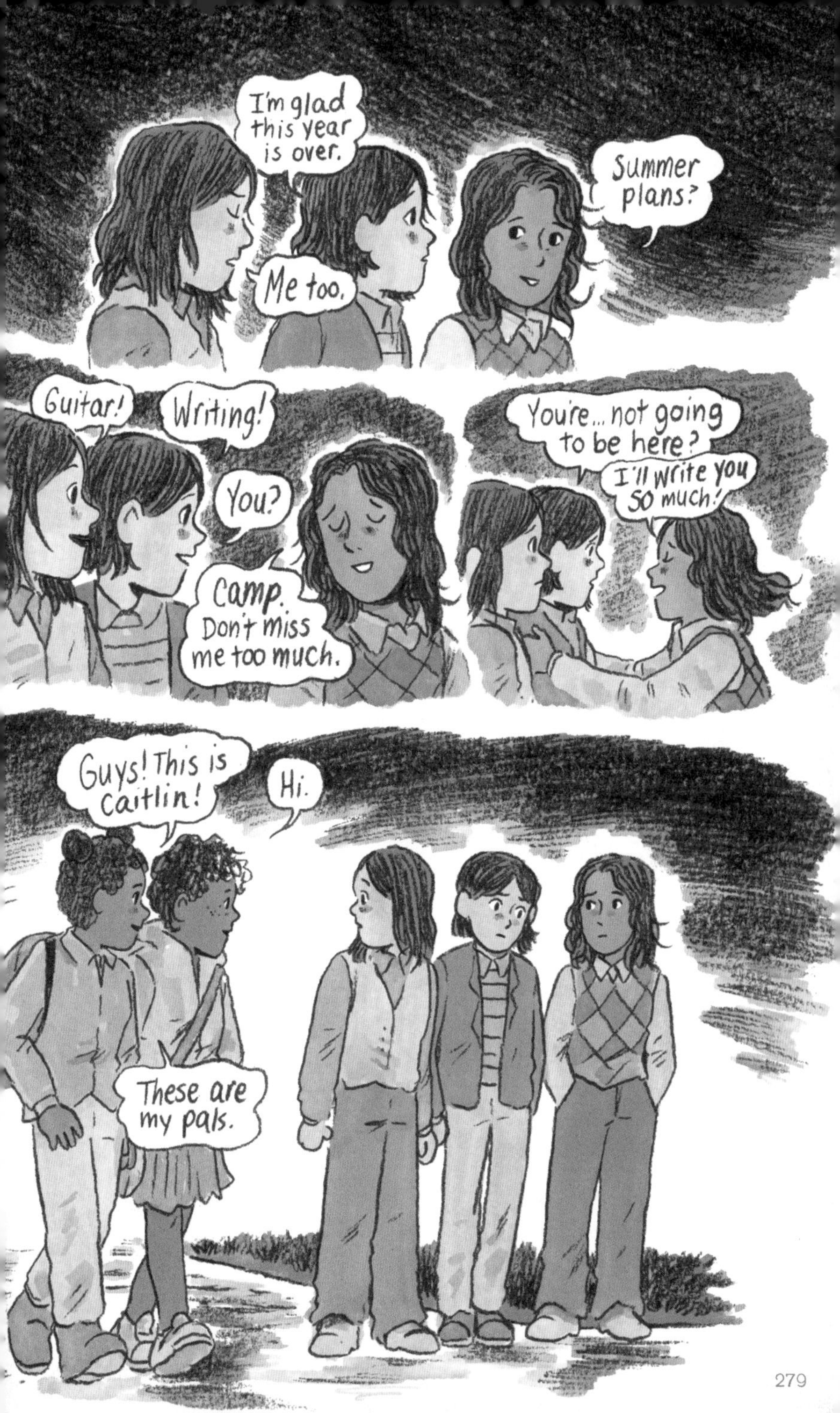
I'm glad this year is over.
Me too.
Summer plans?
Guitar!
Writing!
You?
Camp. Don't miss me too much.
You're... not going to be here?
I'll write you SO much!
Guys! This is Caitlin!
Hi.
These are my pals.

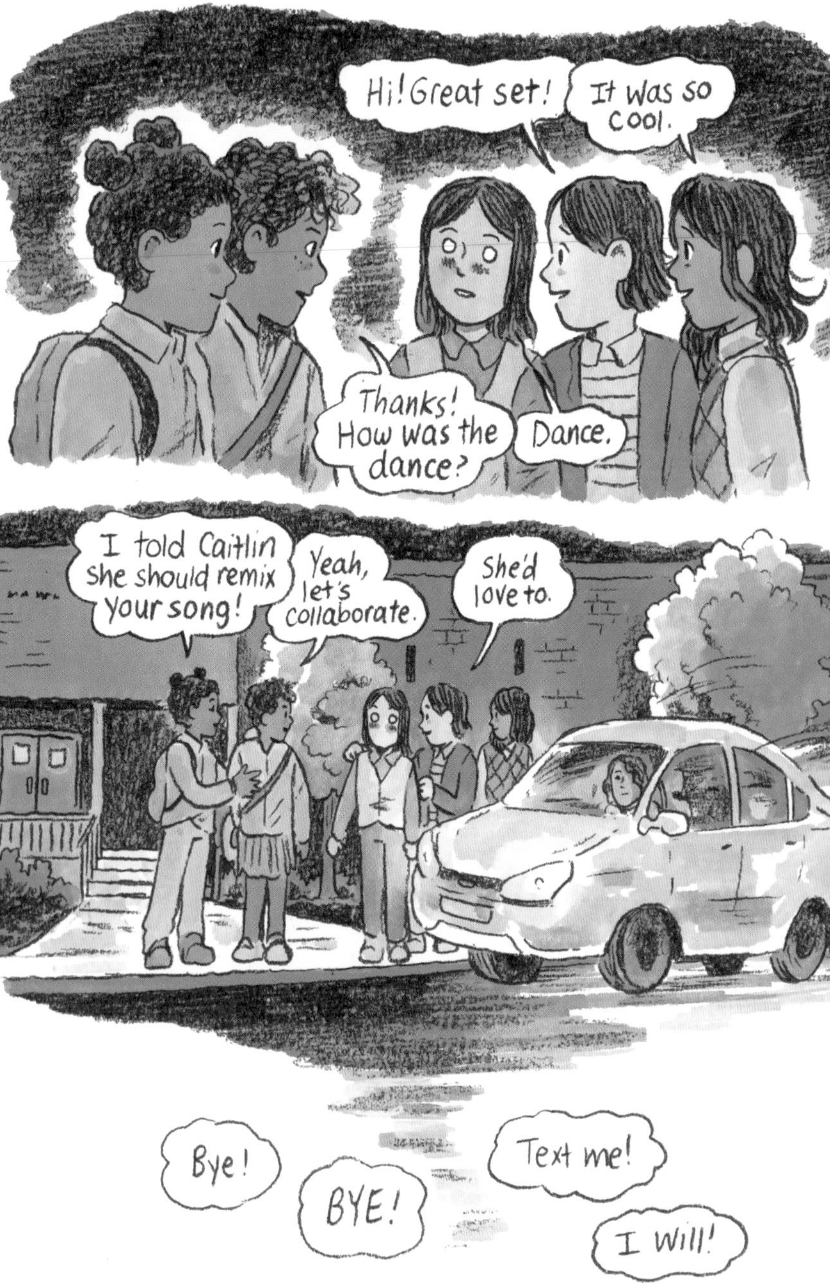
Hi! Great set!
It was so cool.
Thanks! How was the dance?
Dance.
I told Caitlin she should remix your song!
Yeah, let's collaborate.
She'd love to.
Bye!
BYE!
Text me!
I will!

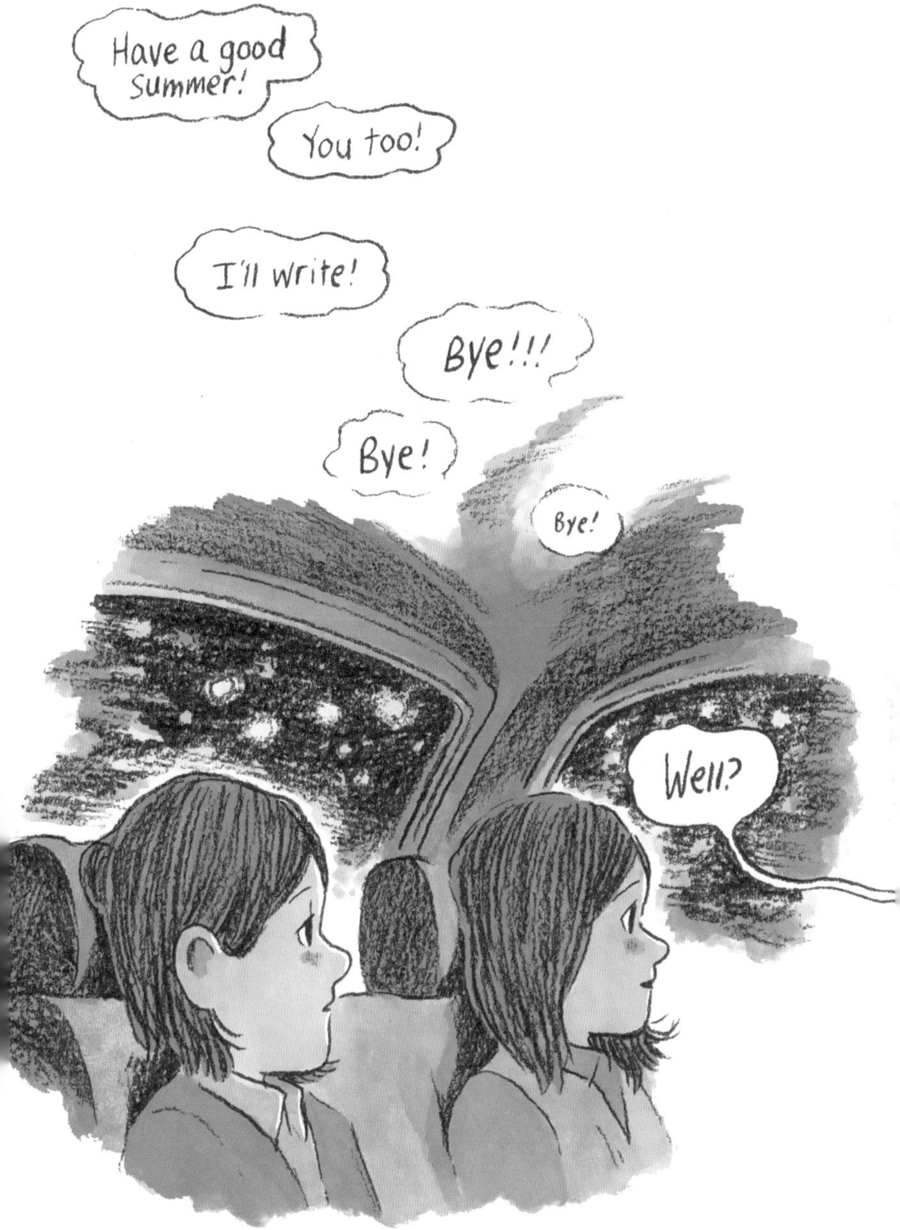
Have a good summer!
You too!
I'll write!
Bye!!!
Bye!
Bye!
Well?

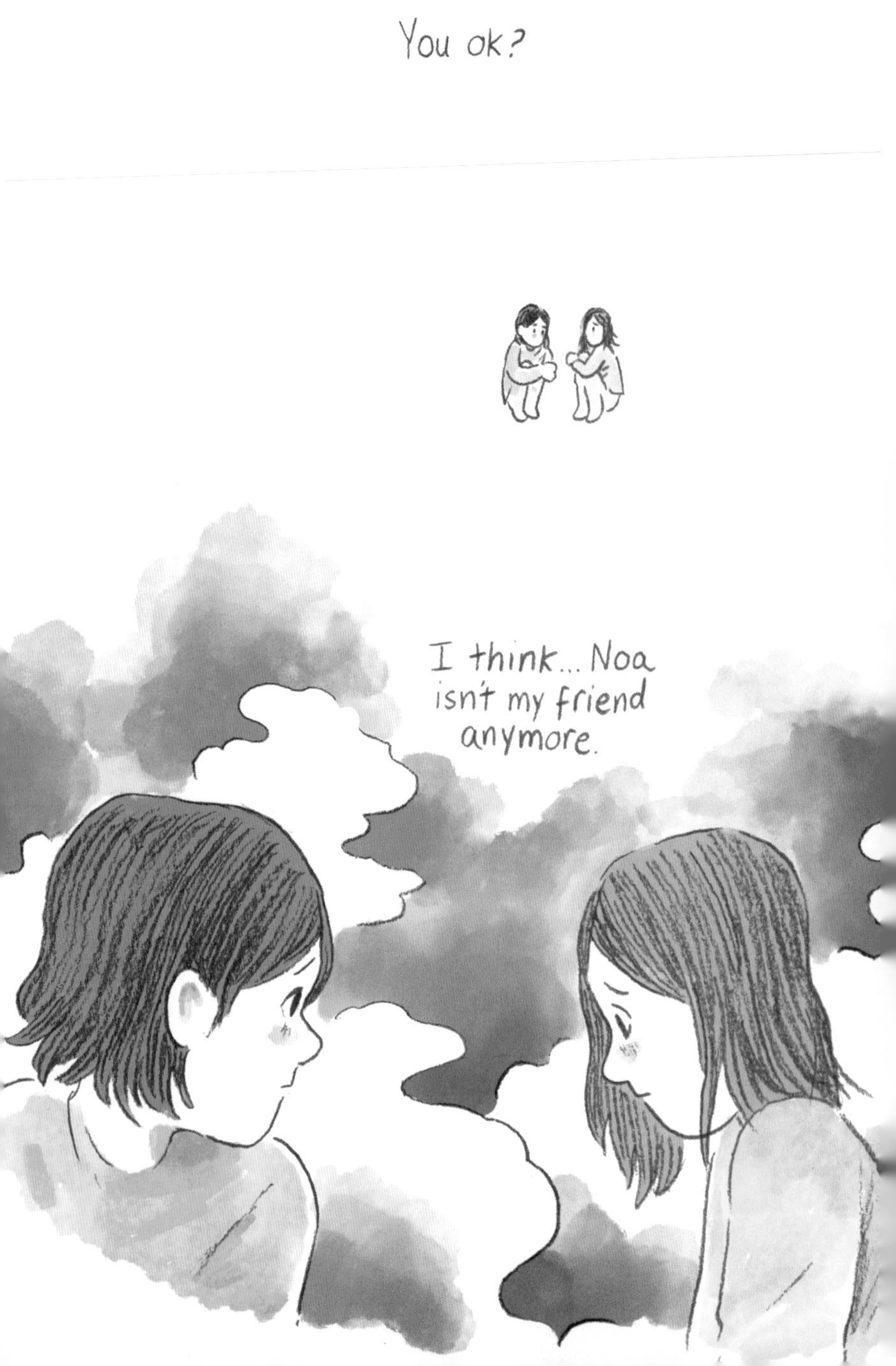
You ok?
I think... Noa isn't my friend anymore.

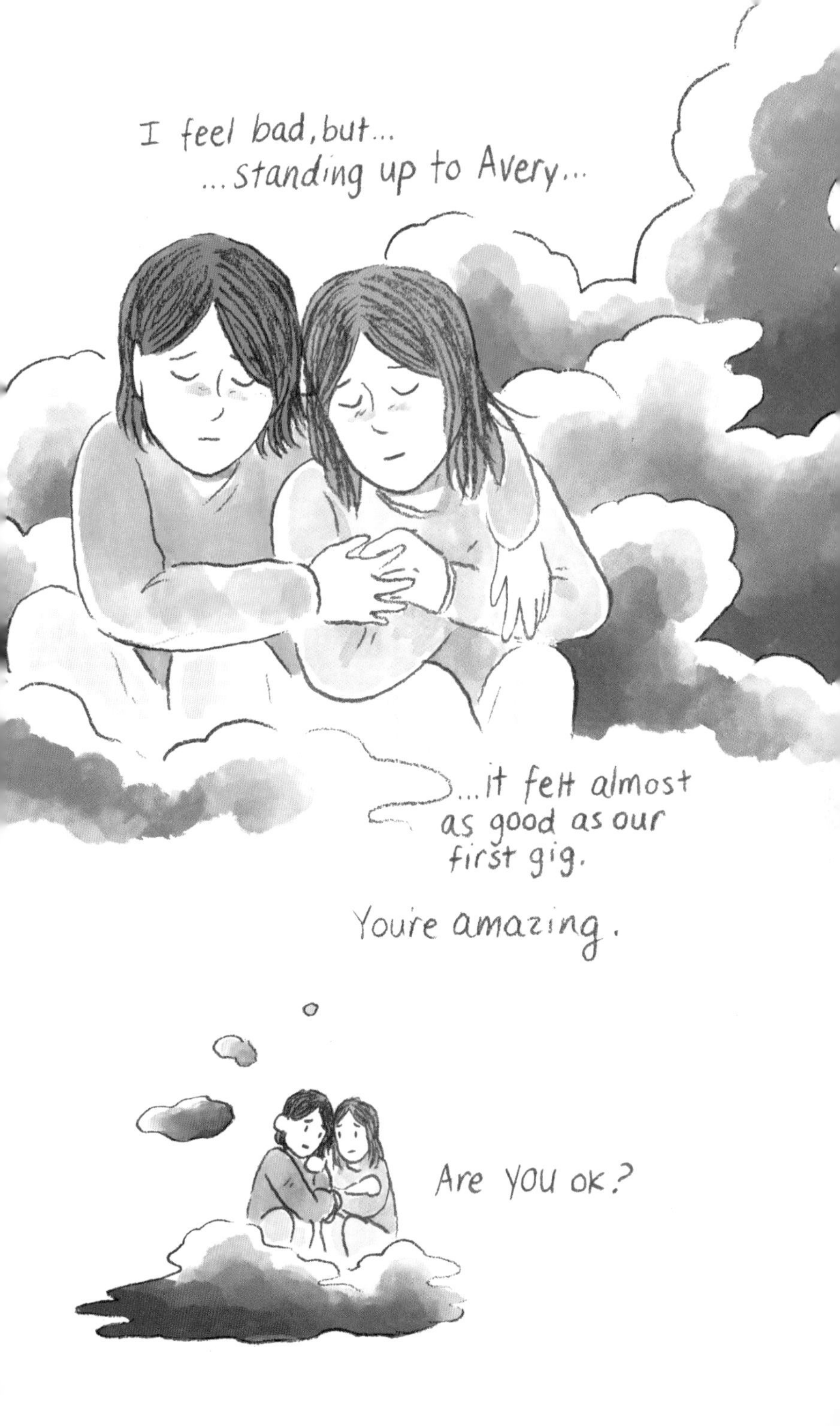
I feel bad, but...
...standing up to Avery...
...it felt almost as good as our first gig.
You're amazing.
Are you ok?

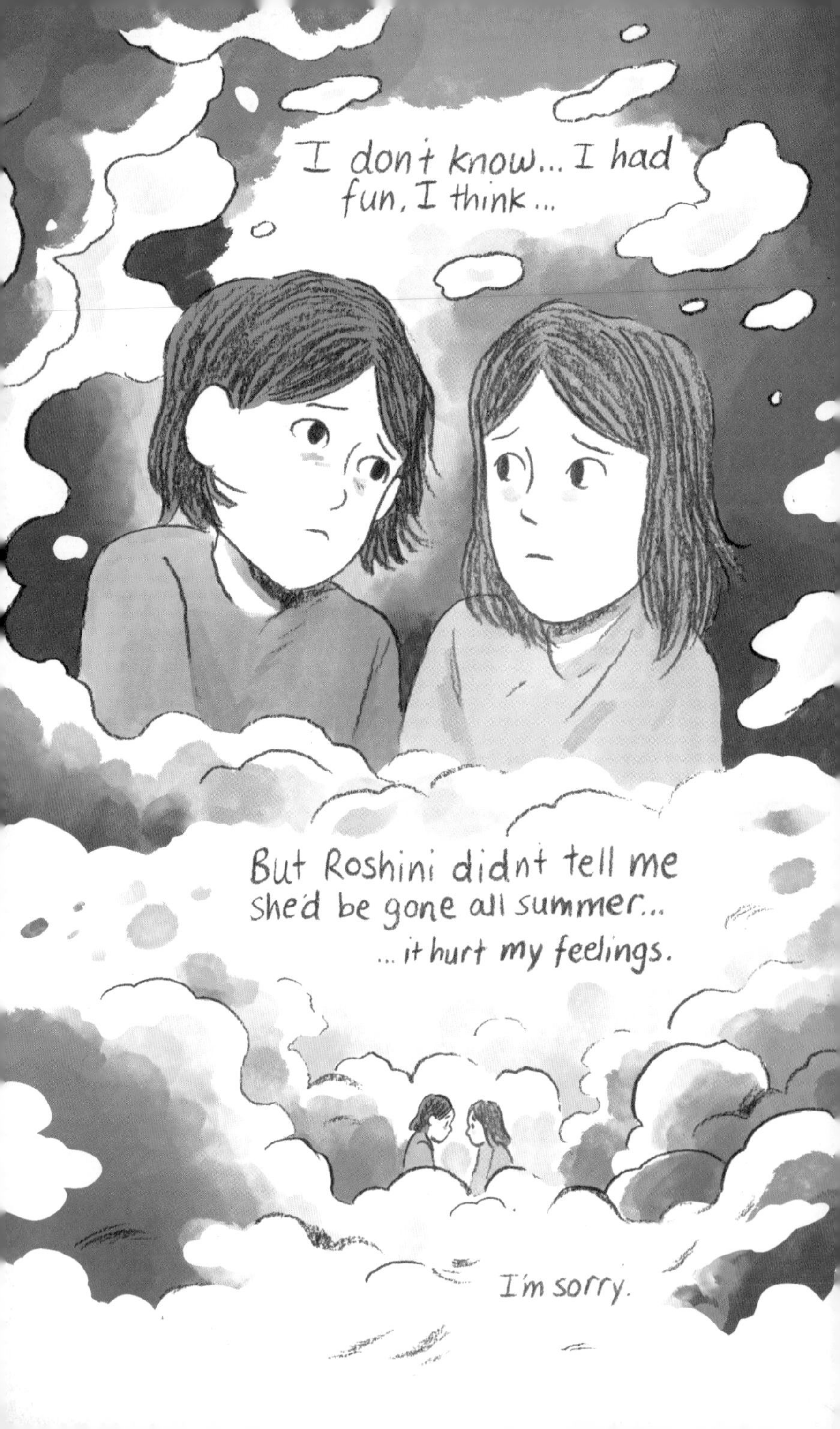
I don't know... I had fun, I think...
But Roshini didn't tell me she'd be gone all summer...
...it hurt my feelings.
I'm sorry.

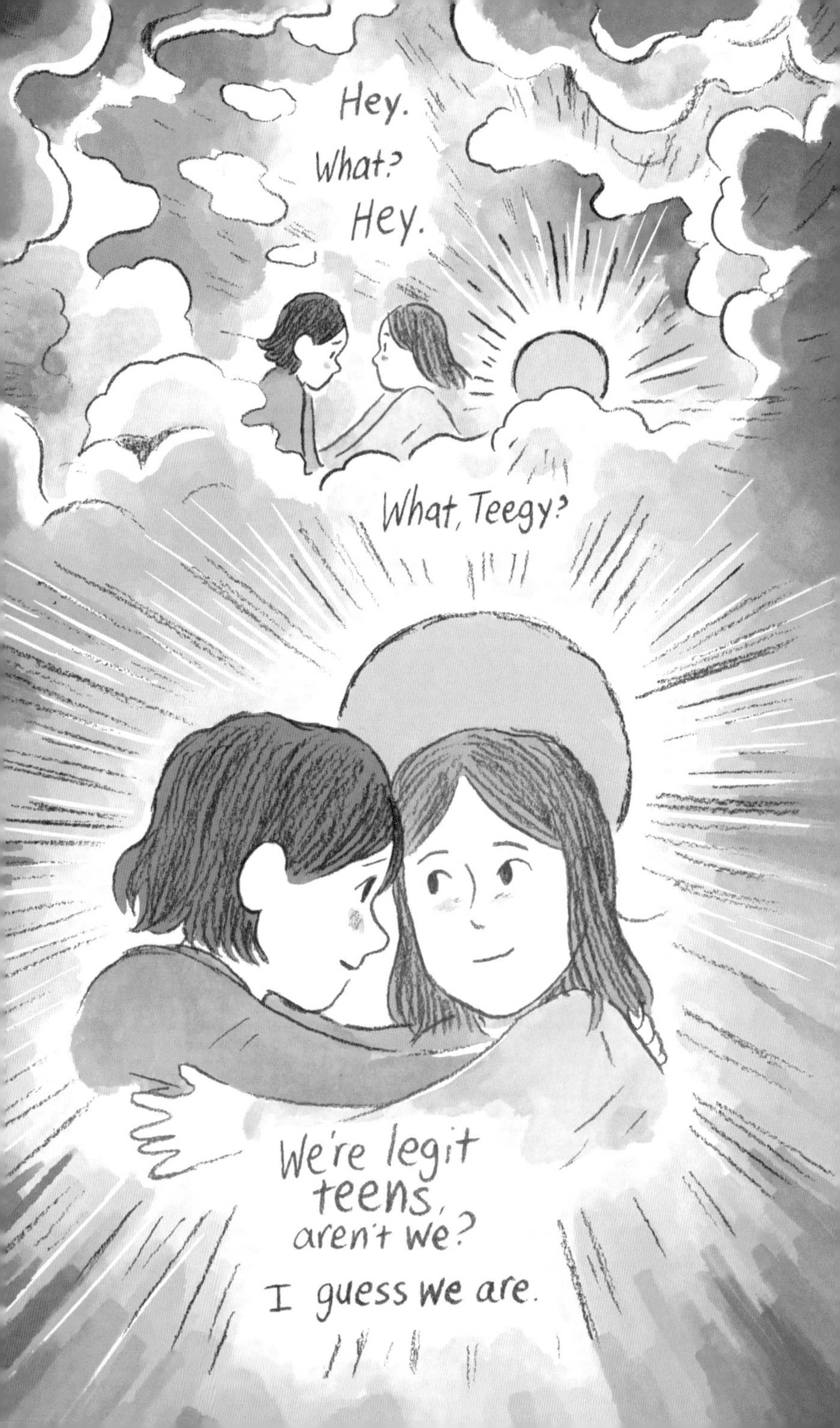
Hey.
What?
Hey.
What, Teegy?
We're legit teens, aren't we?
I guess we are.

CHAPTER 18

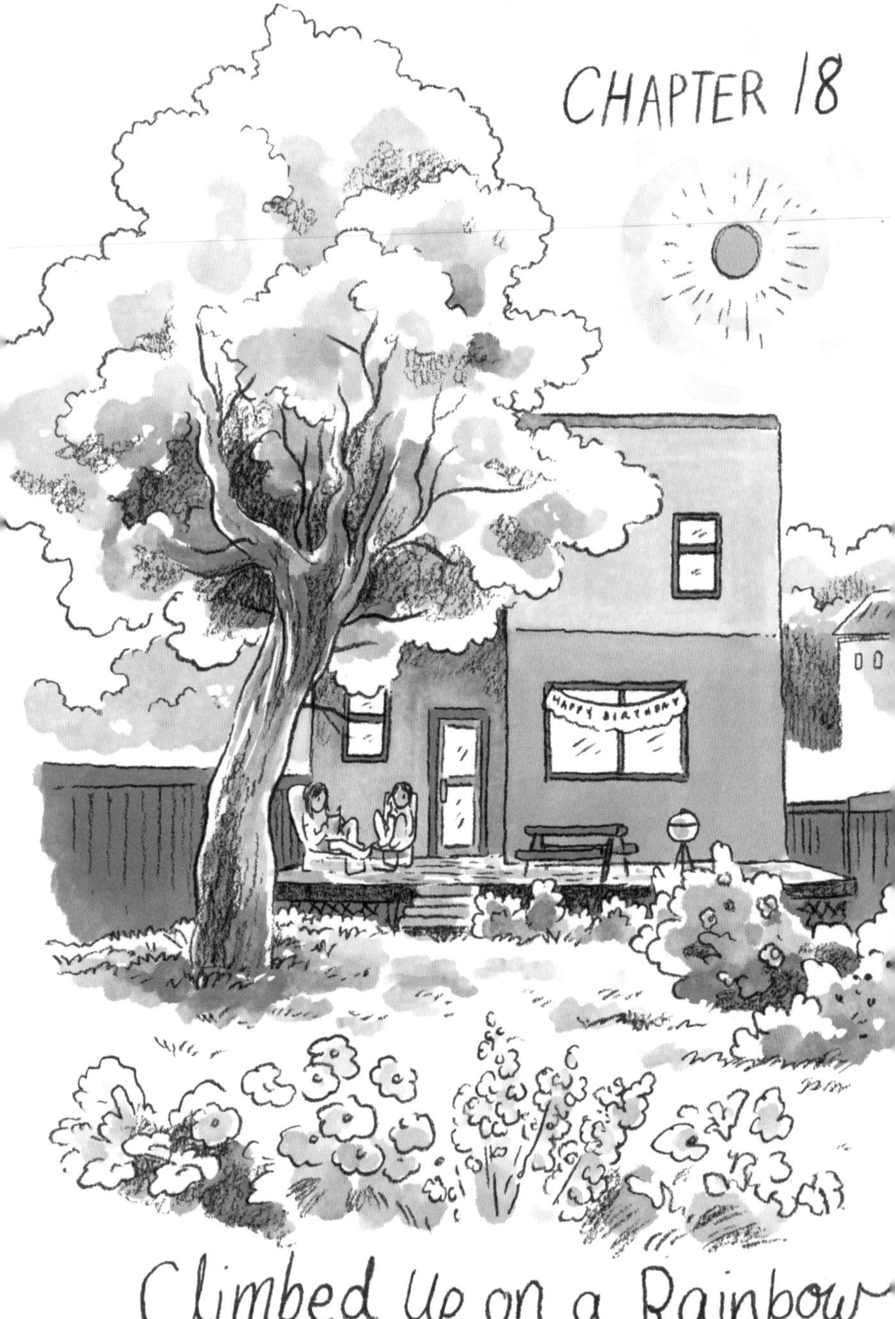
HAPPY BIRTHDAY

Climbed Up on a Rainbow

You know, I think we've
got a lot of material now
for songs...

Enough for a whole
ALBUM.

Gunk presents:
JUNIOR HIGH.

And it'll win 6 Grammys.

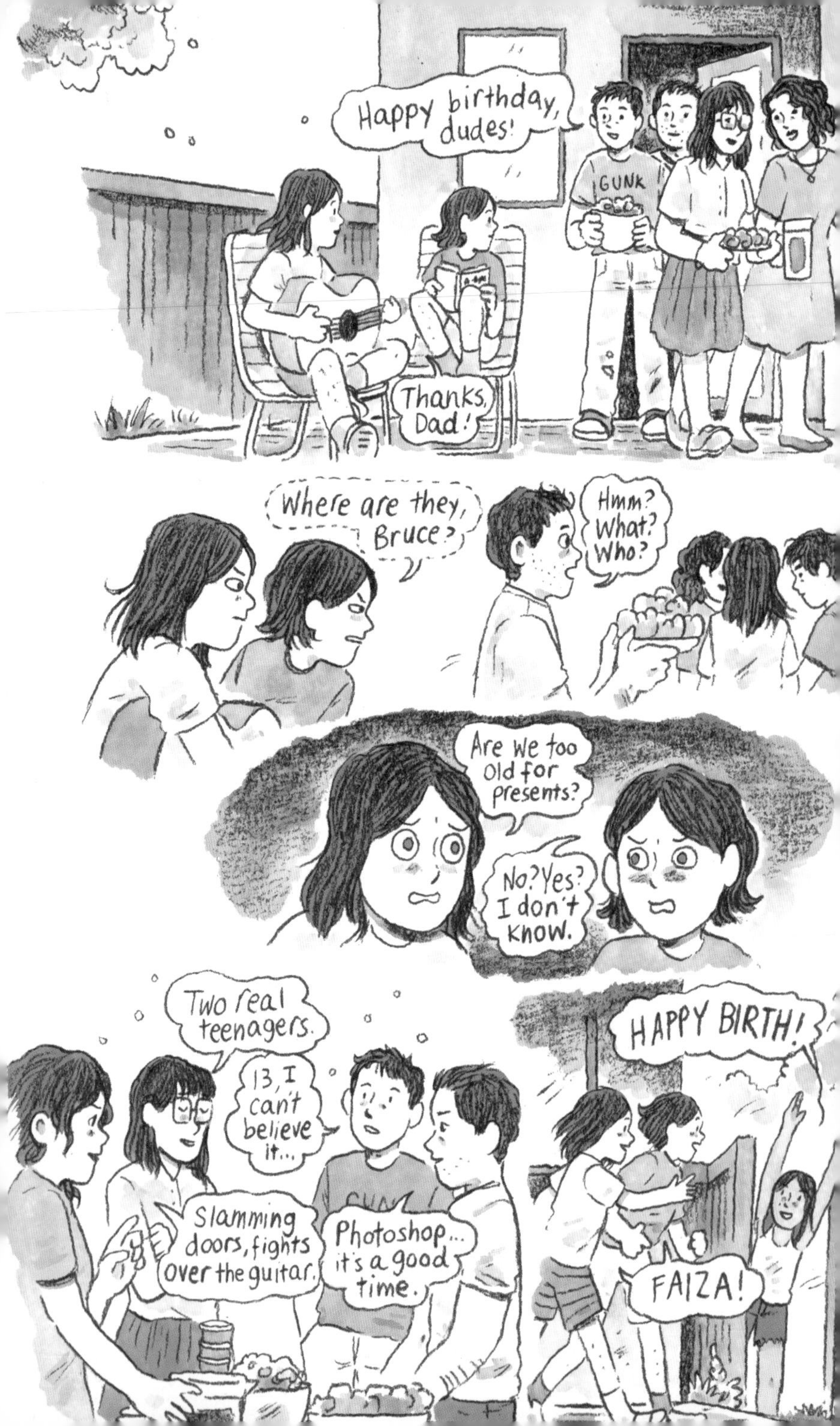
Happy birthday, dudes!
Thanks, Dad!
Where are they, Bruce?
Hmm? What? Who?
Are we too old for presents?
No? Yes? I don't know.
Two real teenagers.
13, I can't believe it...
Slamming doors, fights over the guitar.
Photoshop... it's a good time.
HAPPY BIRTH!
FAIZA!

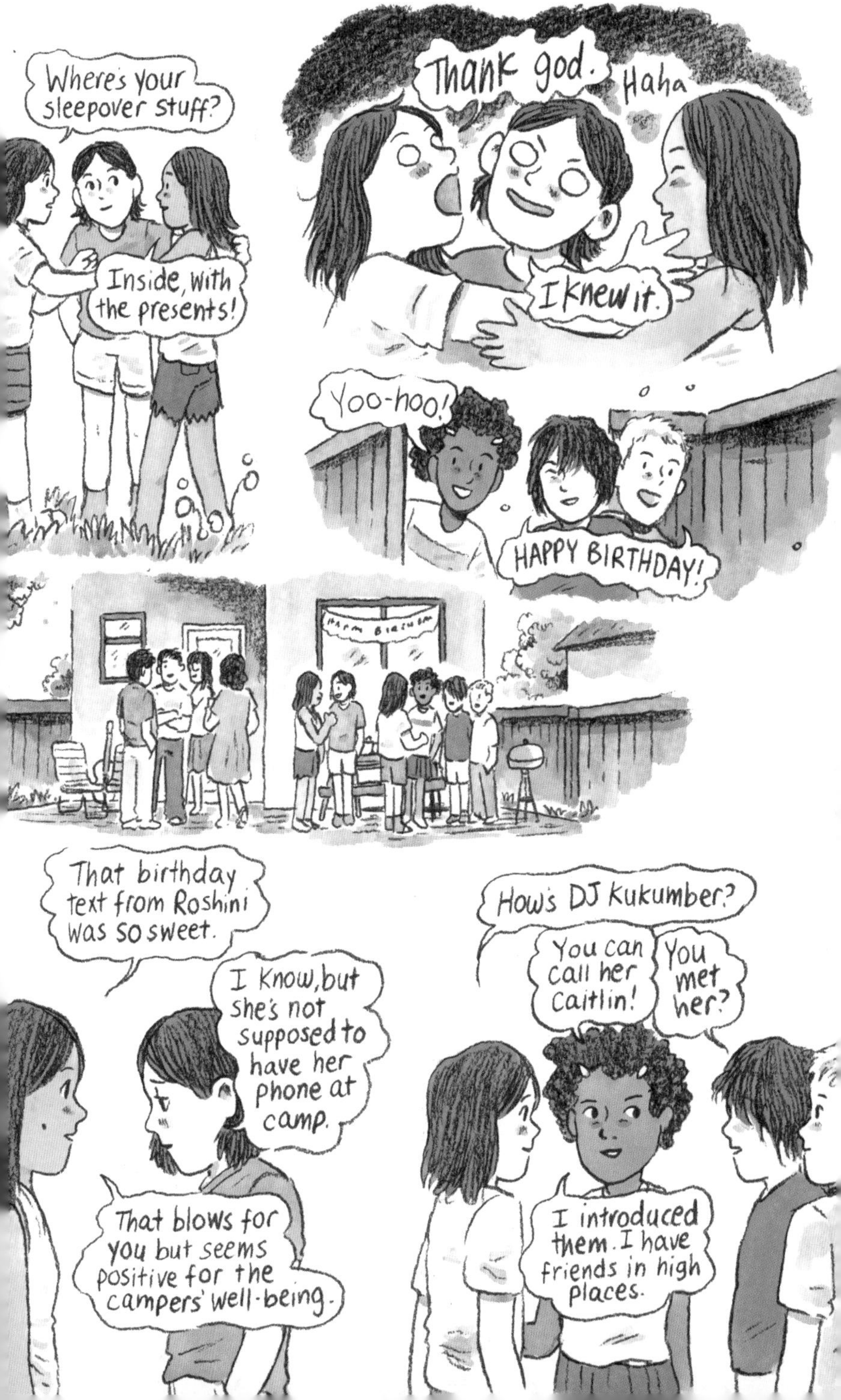
Where's your sleepover stuff?
Inside, with the presents!
Thank god.
Haha
I knew it.
Yoo-hoo!
HAPPY BIRTHDAY!
That birthday text from Roshini was so sweet.
I know, but she's not supposed to have her phone at camp.
That blows for you but seems positive for the campers' well-being.
How's DJ Kukumber?
You can call her Caitlin!
You met her?
I introduced them. I have friends in high places.

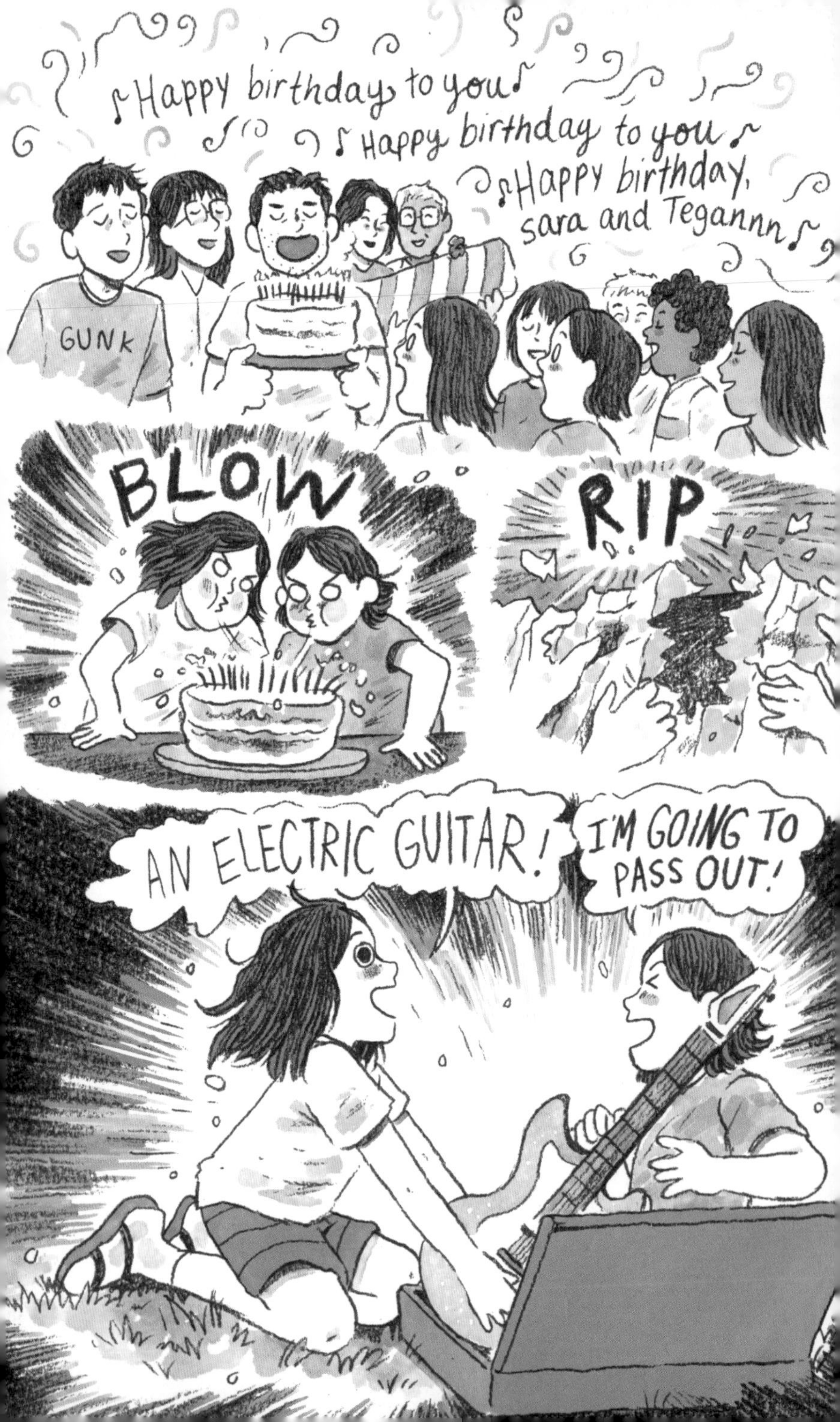
Happy birthday to you
Happy birthday to you
Happy birthday, sara and Tegannn
GUNK
BLOW
RIP
AN ELECTRIC GUITAR!
I'M GOING TO PASS OUT!

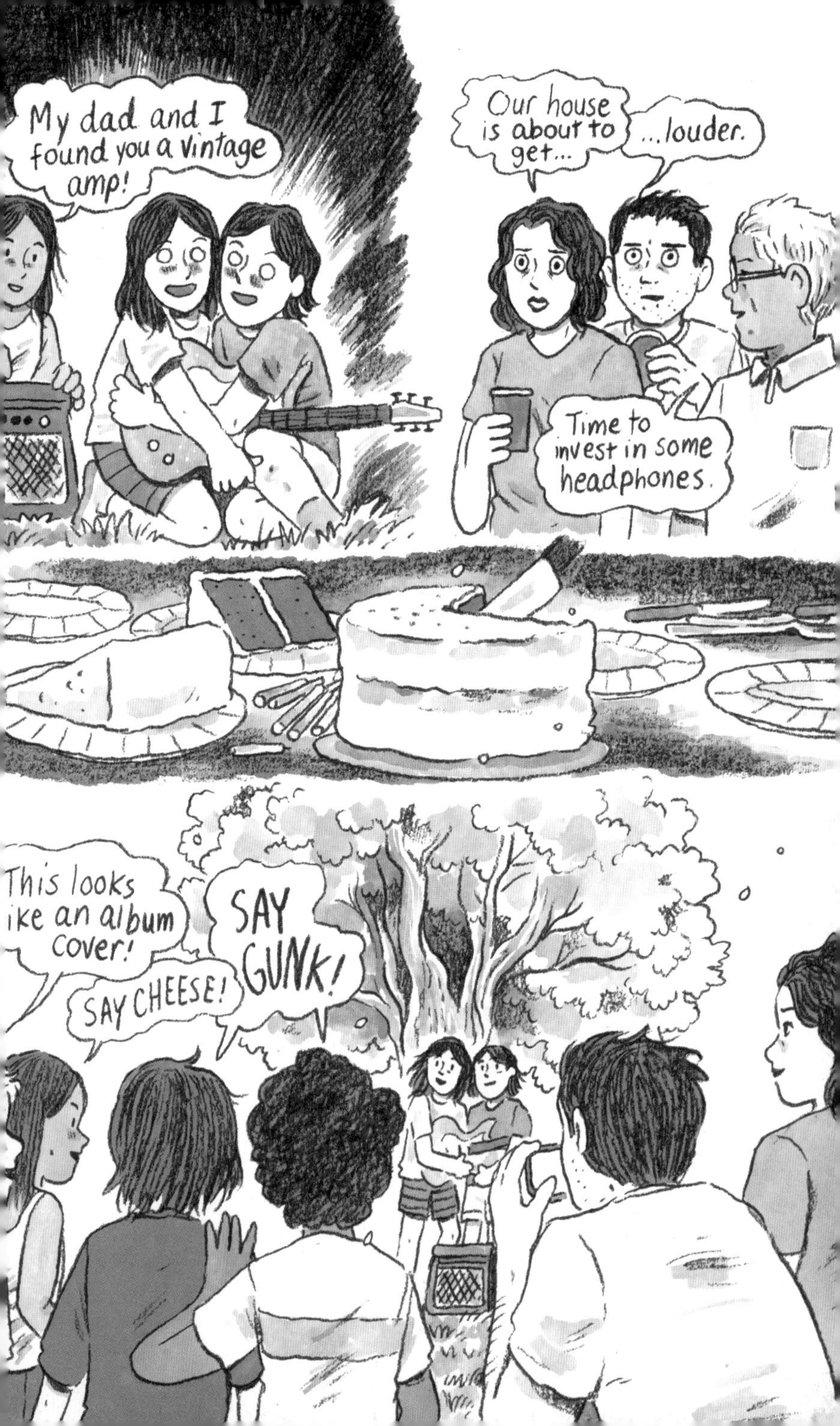
My dad and I found you a vintage amp!
Our house is about to get...
...louder.
Time to invest in some headphones.
This looks ike an album cover!
SAY CHEESE!
SAY GUNK!

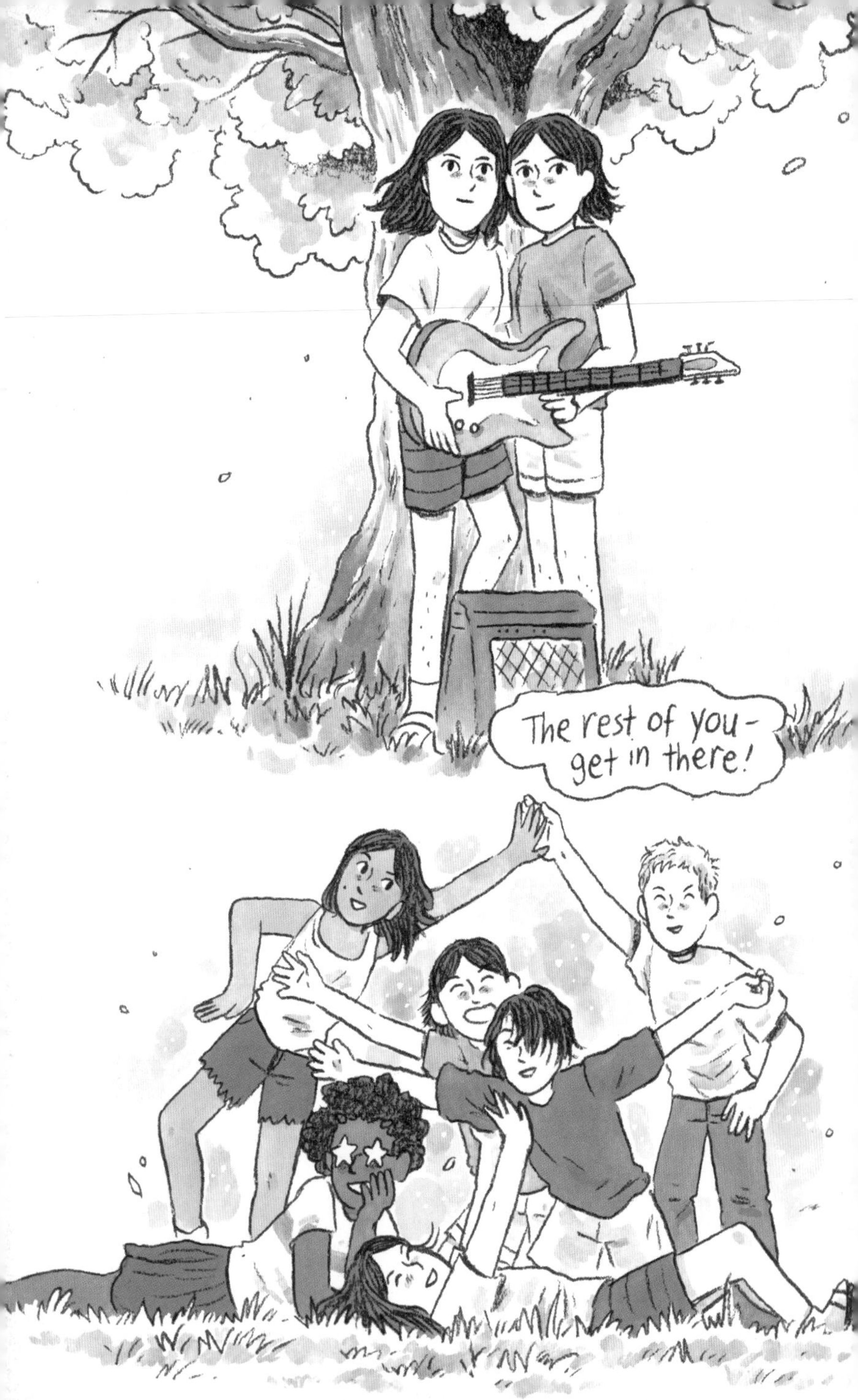
The rest of you-
get in there!

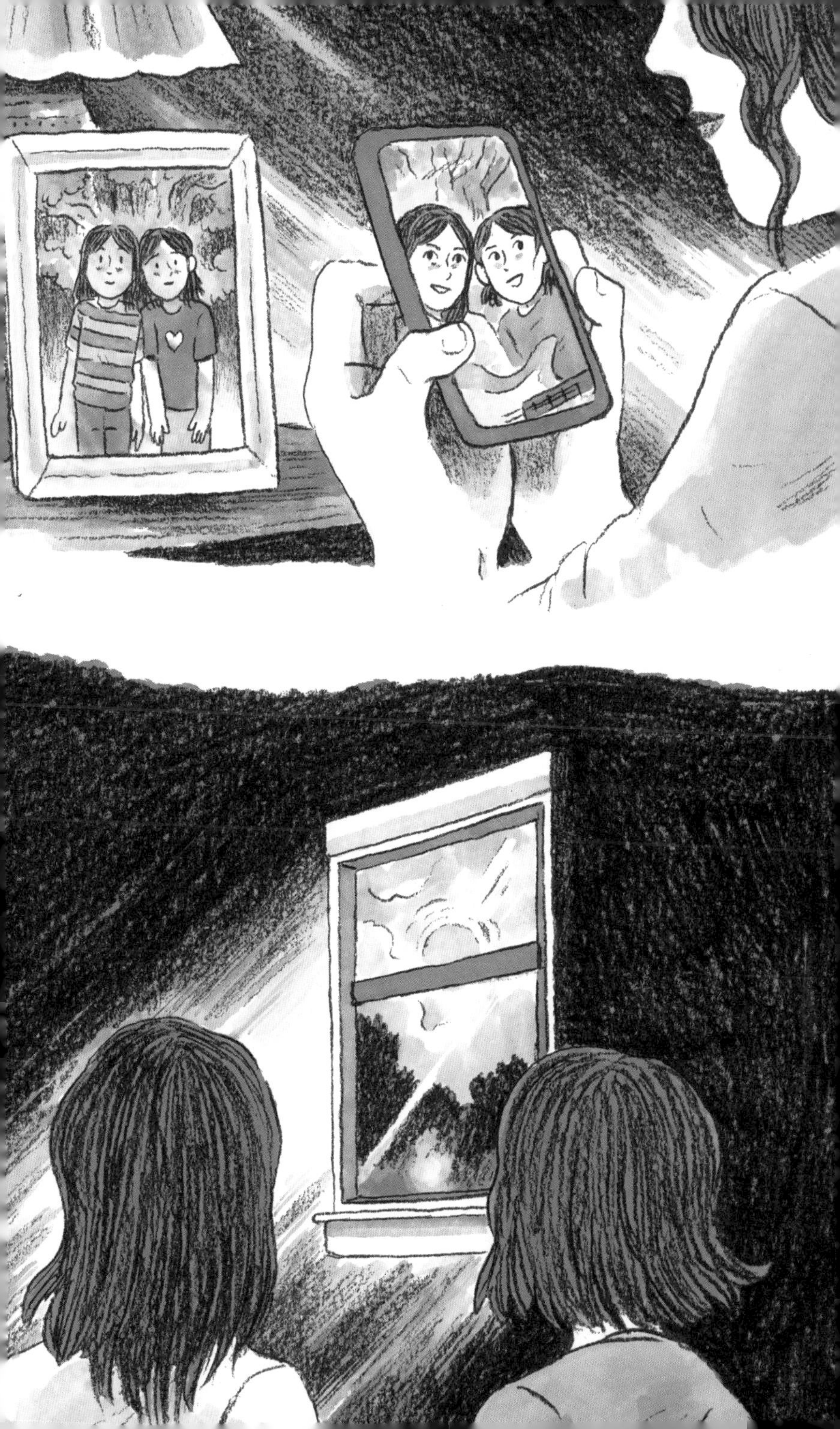

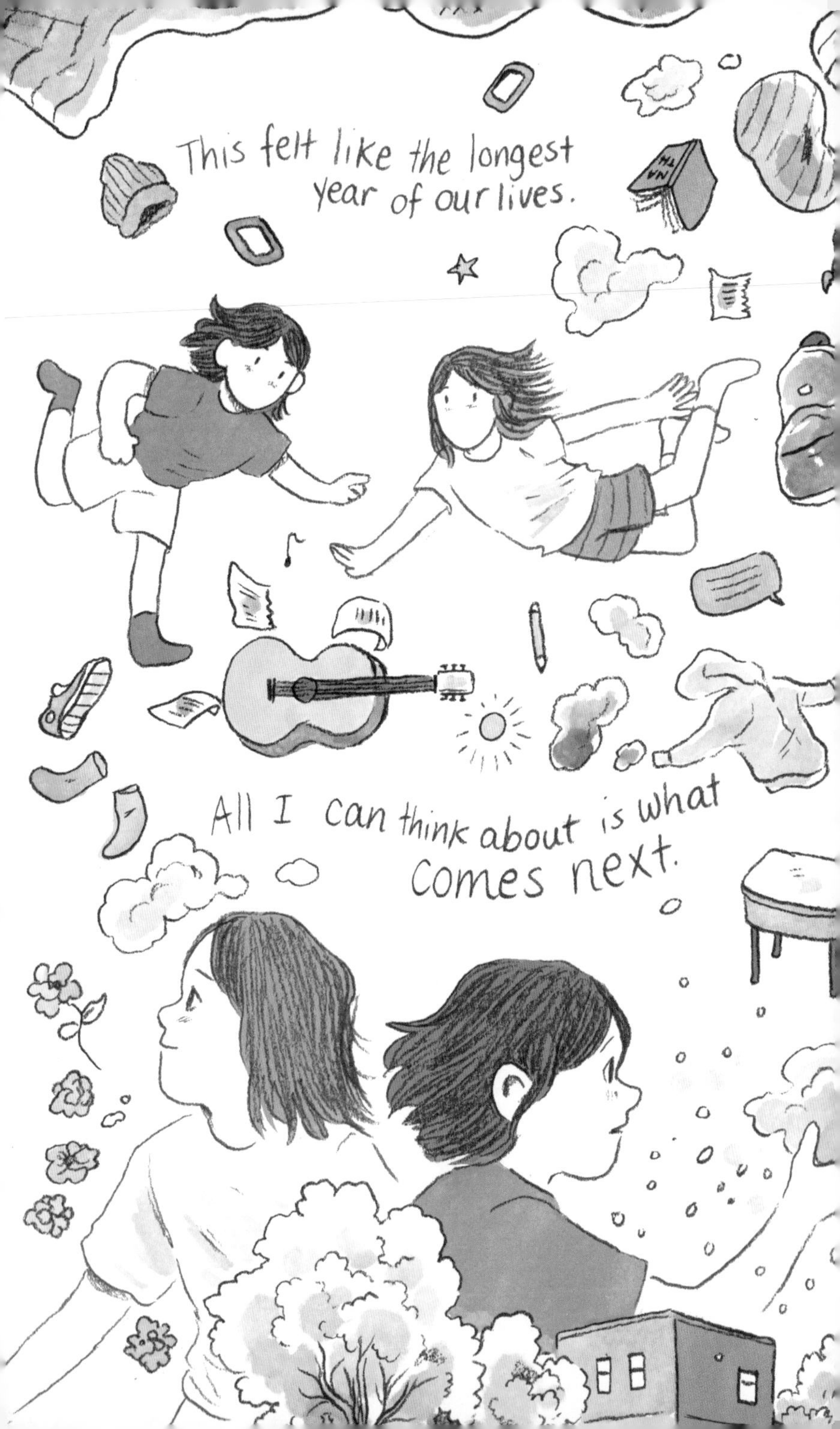
This felt like the longest year of our lives.
All I can think about is what comes next.

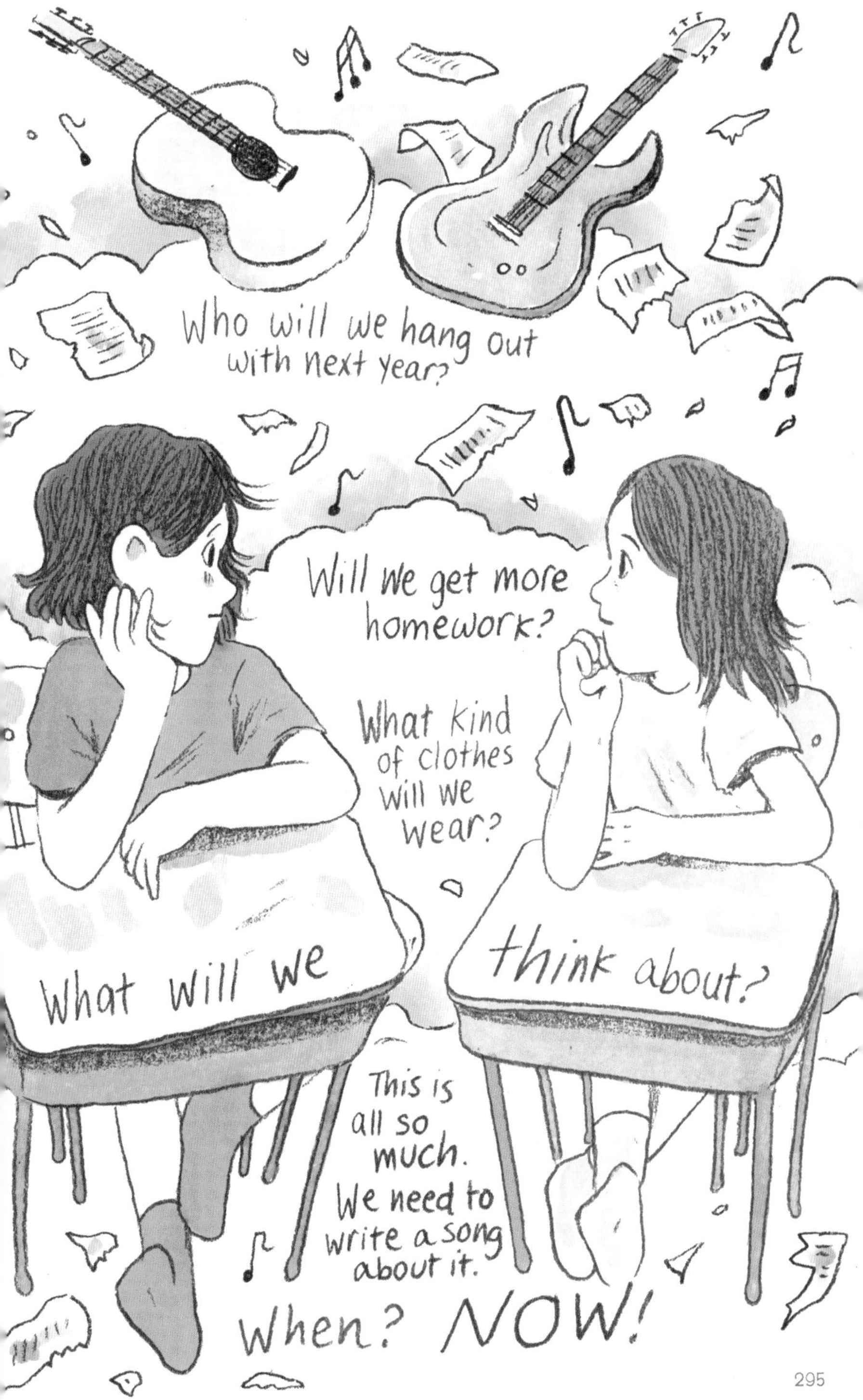

Who will we hang out with next year?
Will we get more homework?
What kind of clothes will we wear?
What will we think about?
This is all so much. We need to write a song about it.
When? NOW!

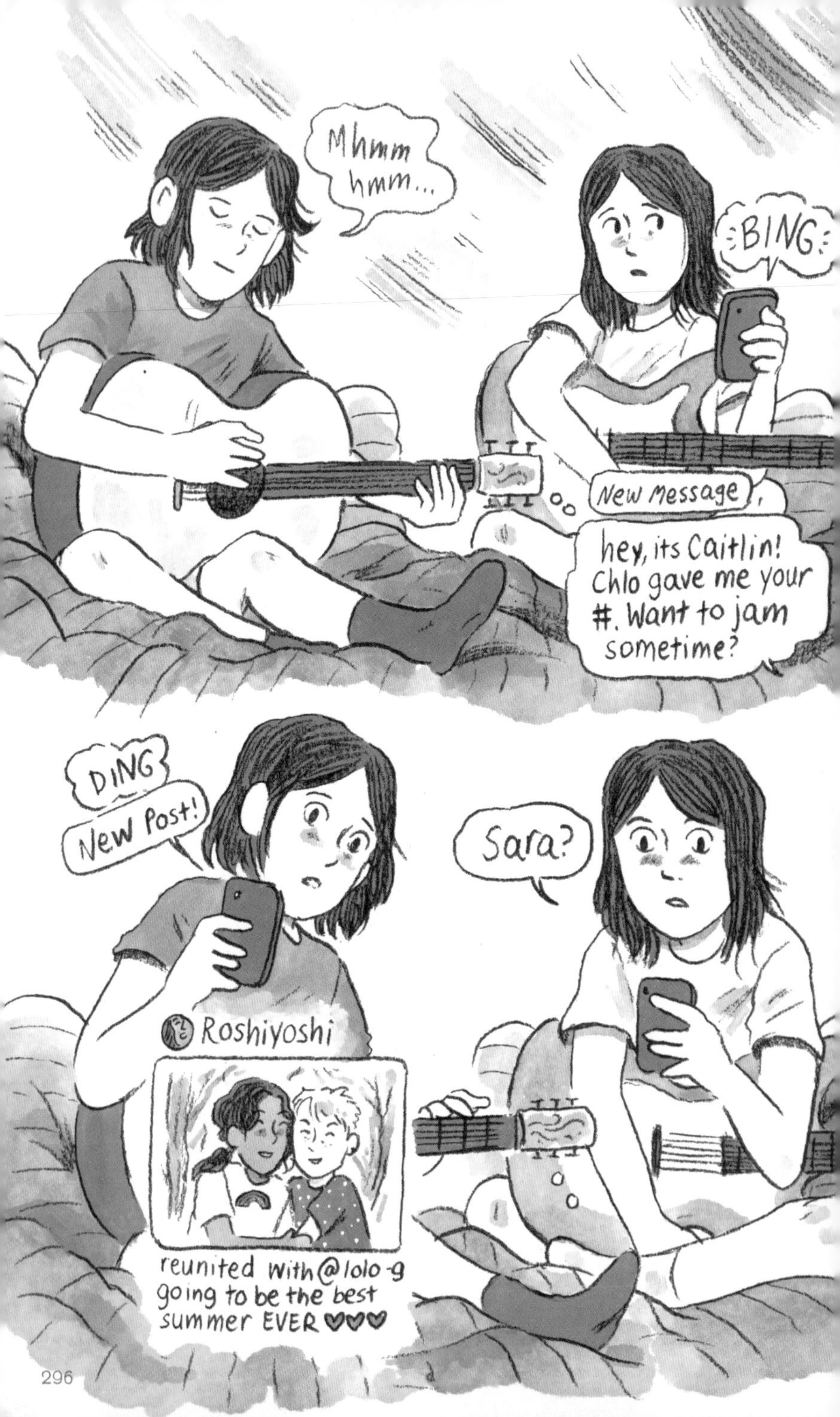
Mhmm hmm...
BING
New message
hey, its Caitlin! Chlo gave me your #. Want to jam sometime?
DING
New Post!
Sara?
Roshiyoshi
reunited with @lolo-g going to be the best summer EVER ♥♥♥

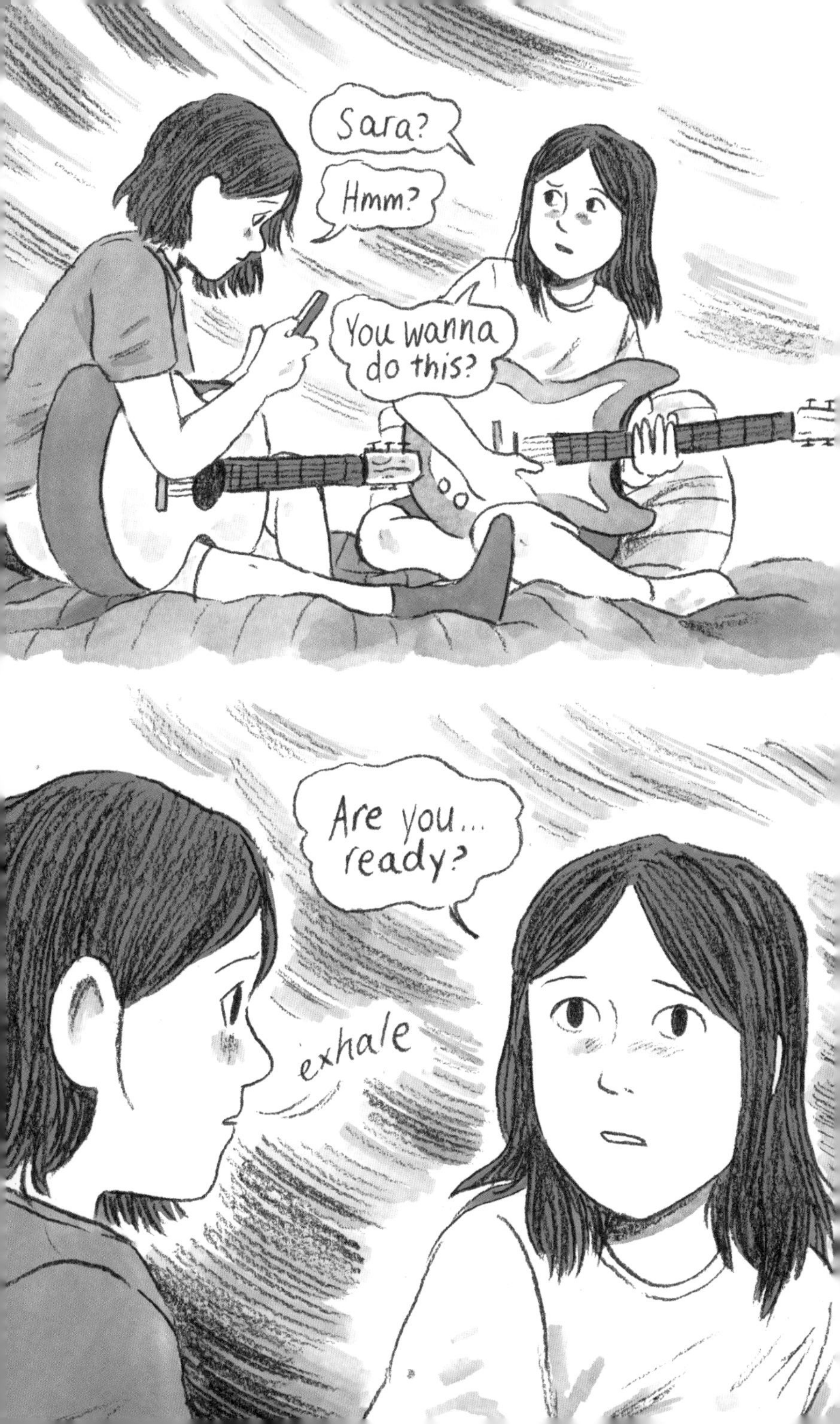
Sara?
Hmm?
You wanna do this?
Are you... ready?
exhale

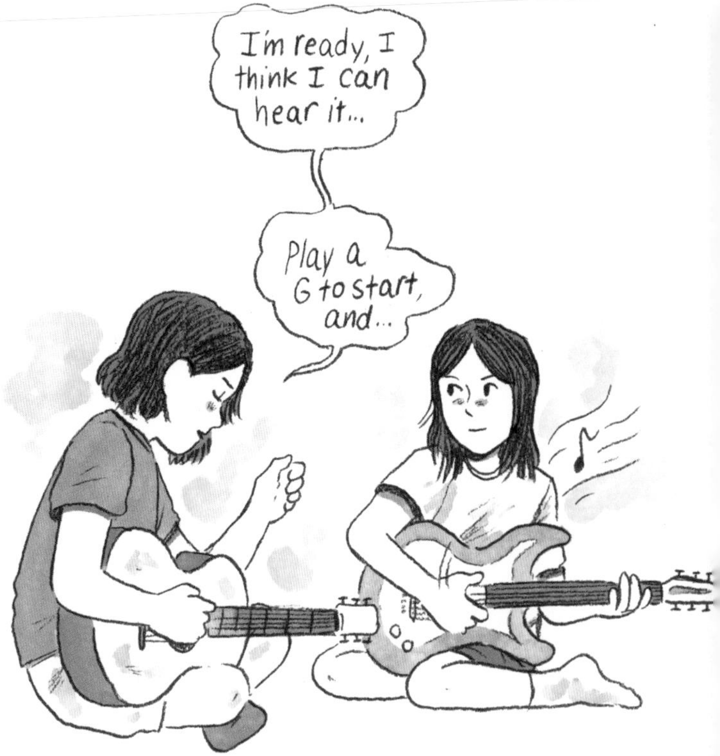
I'm ready, I think I can hear it...
Play a G to start, and...

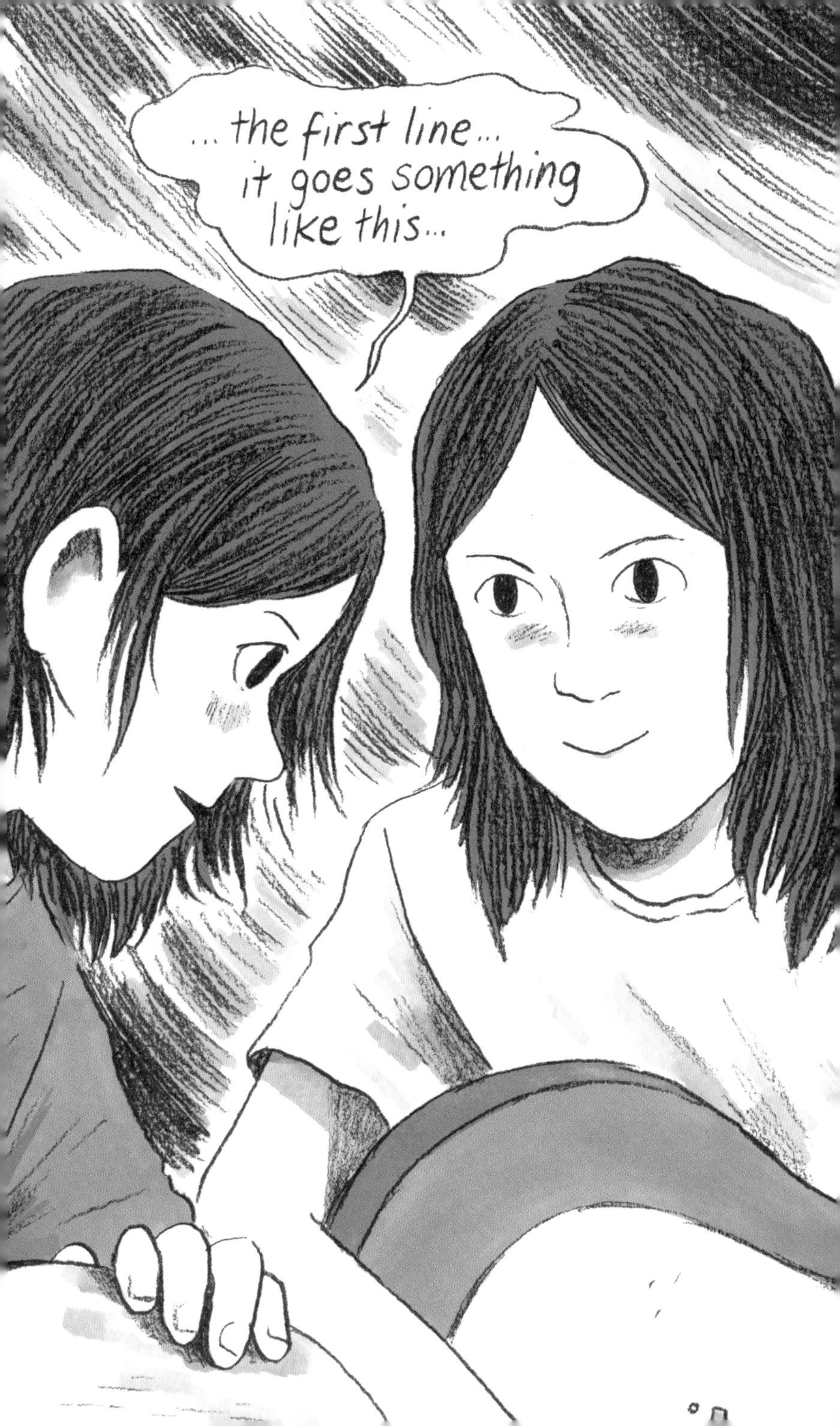
... the first line... it goes something like this...

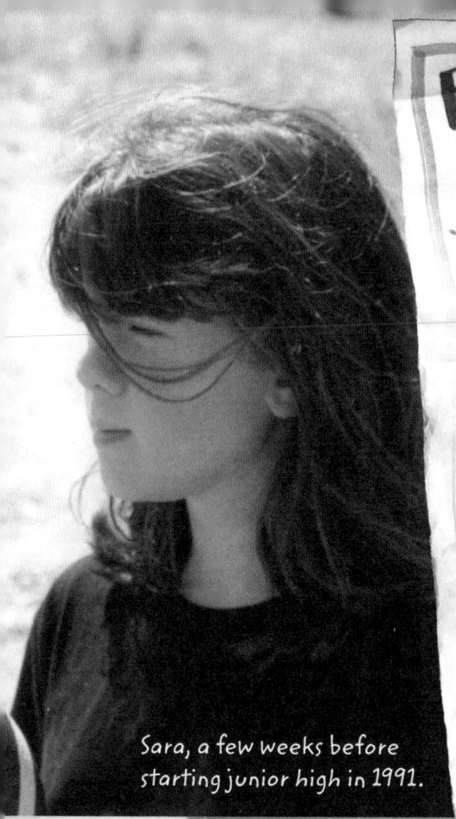

Sara, a few weeks before starting junior high in 1991.

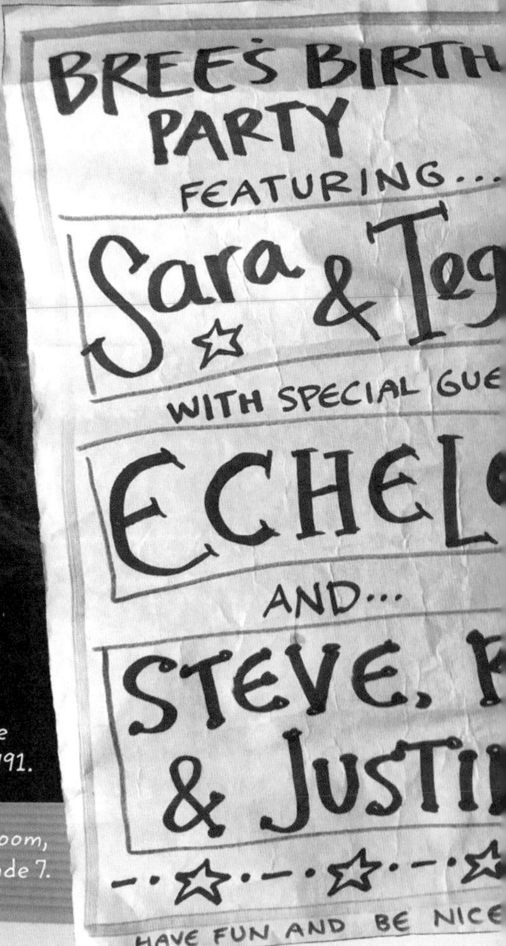
BREE'S BIRTH
PARTY
FEATURING...
Sara & Teg
WITH SPECIAL GUE
ECHEL
AND...
STEVE,
& JUSTI
HAVE FUN AND BE NICE

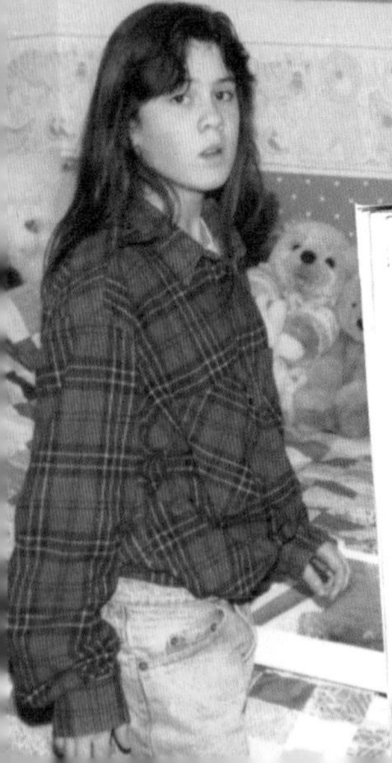

Tegan in her bedroom, 12 years old in Grade 7.

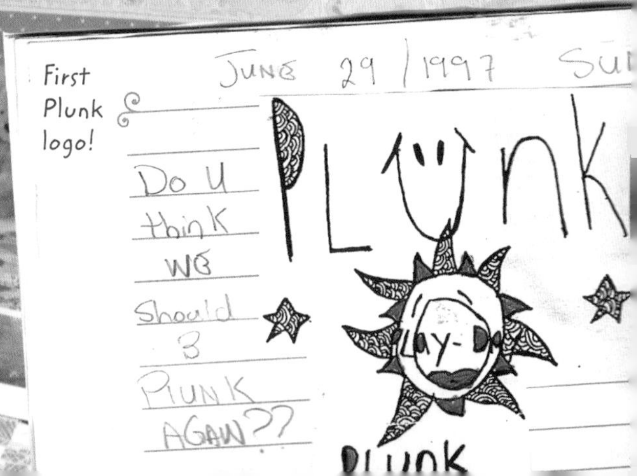
JUNE 29 / 1997 SU
PLUNK
Do U think WE Should 3 PLUNK AGAN??

First Plunk logo!

Hello, Reader!

Just like the sisters in this book, we are identical twins who grew up in Calgary, Canada. The big difference between us and the fictional Tegan and Sara is that when we started junior high it was 1991. You probably weren't even born yet!

In seventh grade, even though we looked similar on the outside, a lot of really big changes were starting to happen to us on the inside. You can probably relate. What we didn't know then was that everyone was feeling that way.

Like our fictional counterparts, we moved a lot growing up, and that meant changing schools and making new friends. Our parents were divorced, and our stepdad, Bruce, lived with us and our mom. Having three parents made us feel extra loved, even though it meant that our life looked different from the lives of the kids we were growing up with. We spent time with our dad on the weekends, and with Mom and Bruce on the weekdays. Although we had two different houses, being with each other always made us feel at home.

In seventh grade, we both started to feel self-conscious about the ways our bodies were changing and nervous about the feelings we were having about girls. Except in 1991 there was no internet for us to investigate any of what we were feeling, and we wouldn't have known what words to search for even if there was. We started to keep secrets from each other, and sometimes that made us fight for reasons we didn't completely understand. It was very complicated to be close to each other but feel so far apart.

In this story, Tegan and Sara find their first guitar in junior high, but in real life we found our guitar when we were fifteen years old. Learning to play, write songs, and start our band (it was called PLUNK, not GUNK) was how we found our way back to being best friends. It was also a way for us to talk about the confusing things we were feeling on the inside, and a less embarrassing way to share those feelings on the outside with each other and our friends. If you're interested in hearing those songs, you can listen to our album *Hey, I'm Just Like You*. We recorded this album in 2019 at the same time we began writing this book, after rediscovering a bunch of cassette tapes of over

forty demo songs we recorded in high school. We decided to reinterpret and rerecord a dozen of these songs for the album. And we have nine other albums with songs we've written about all the confusing, exciting, and complicated feelings we have about life. Check them out!

The biggest lesson we learned growing up is that there's no rush to become YOU, because you're always going to be changing a little bit. That's what makes life fun and exciting! So, no matter where you are on your journey as a person, how you identify, what your favorite band is, or how long or short your hair is, we think you're perfect.

Somebody else we think is perfect is illustrator Tillie Walden. She brought this story to life with her art, and each panel carefully and beautifully captures everything we didn't have words for. Tillie's other books should be on your reading list!

We can't wait to share the next book in Tegan and Sara's junior high adventures. It's called *Tegan and Sara: Crush* and it's all about, well, crushes, crushing it, and getting crushed by life in junior high.

Love,

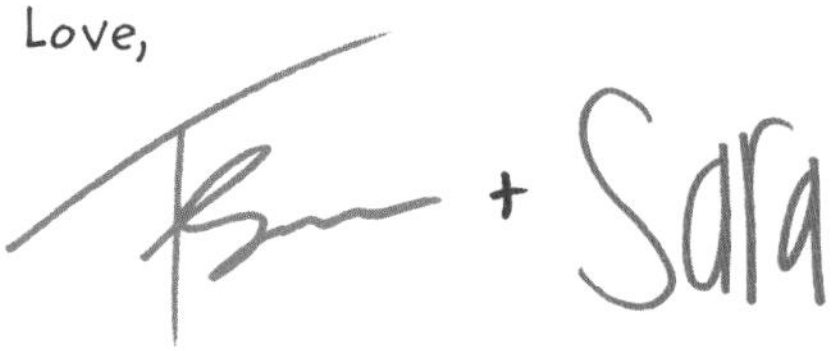
+ Sara

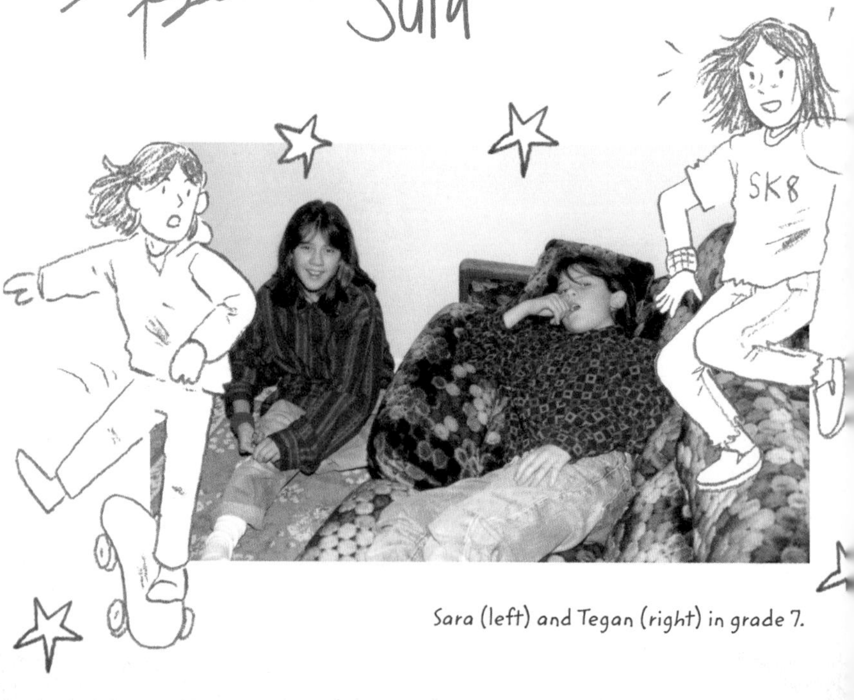
SK8

Sara (left) and Tegan (right) in grade 7.

climed up on a rainbow
to see if i'd fall off
I'm frosted lemom coward
I don't know How to hold you
without shaking
I wish you close encounters
I wish you chochalate memories
I wish you windy fate
I wish you lost anger
I hope you realize
I hope you find you

climed up on a rainbow
to see if i'd fall off
i'm a frosted lemon coward
I'm a whisper in a world of
loud voices
i'm trying so hard to
be loud
...etimes I can't hear my
...

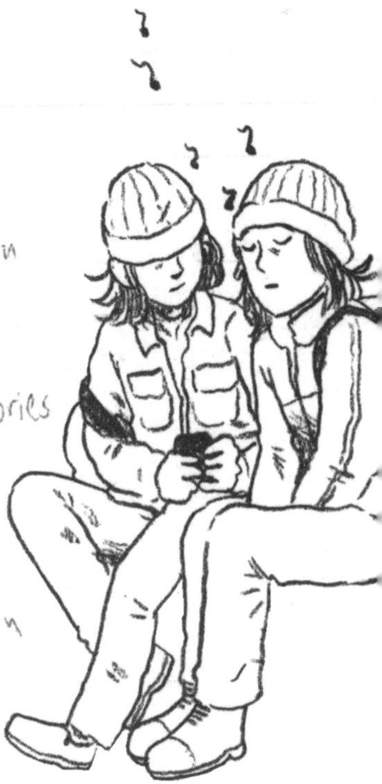

Original journal entry: "Climbed up on a rainbow" from 1997.

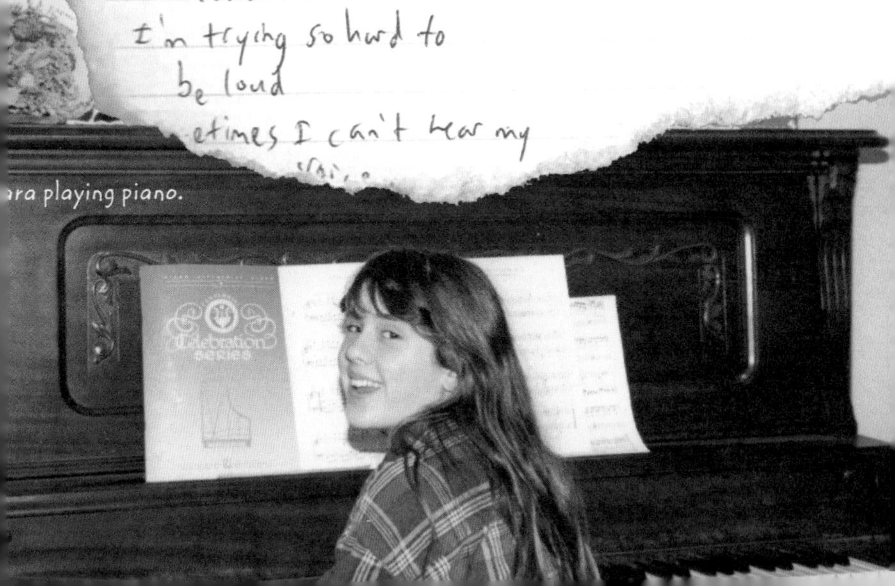
Celebration Series

...ara playing piano.

Junior high was the worst until we found a group of clever, kind, and funny girls who wore alternative clothes, had wild hairdos, and spoke French. They were mischievous, bighearted troublemakers unlike anyone else we'd ever met. They're still our best friends thirty years later. 1994 forever!

Marc Gerald, Wesley Adams, Melissa Warten, and Hannah Miller, thank you for giving us the opportunity to expand our world. And to our parents, thank you for always encouraging us to be ourselves and making us feel cool even when we weren't.

XO Tegan and Sara

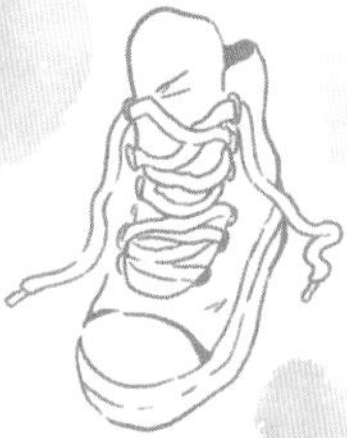

For my twin, and all the music we made together

Tillie

Farrar Straus Giroux Books for Young Readers
An imprint of Macmillan Publishing Group, LLC
120 Broadway, New York, NY 10271 · mackids.com

Our books may be purchased in bulk for promotional, educational, or business use. Please contact your local bookseller or the Macmillan Corporate and Premium Sales Department at (800) 221-7945 ext. 5442 or by email at MacmillanSpecialMarkets@macmillan.com.

Library of Congress Cataloging-in-Publication Data is available.

First edition, 2023
Edited by Wesley Adams, Melissa Warten, and Hannah Miller
Book design by Molly Johanson and Casper Manning
Production editing by Kat Kopit

Drawn on Canson watercolor paper with Blackwing pencils for the line art.
Colored digitally in Procreate using the Quoll brush.

Printed in China by Toppan Leefung Printing Ltd., Dongguan City, Guangdong Province

ISBN 978-0-374-31302-9 (paperback)
10 9 8 7 6 5 4 3 2 1

ISBN 978-0-374-31301-2 (hardcover)
10 9 8 7 6 5 4 3 2 1

ISBN 978-0-374-39161-4 (special edition)
10 9 8 7 6 5 4 3 2 1